ENCYCLOPEDIA OF ASIAN THEATRE

ENCYCLOPEDIA OF ASIAN THEATRE

Volume I: A–N

Edited by
SAMUEL L. LEITER

GREENWOOD PRESS
Westport, Connecticut • London

Library of Congress Cataloging-in-Publication Data

Encyclopedia of Asian theatre / edited by Samuel L. Leiter.
   p. cm.
  Includes bibliographical references and index.
   ISBN 0-313-33529-X (set : alk. paper)—ISBN 0-313-33530-3 (vol 1 : alk. paper)—
ISBN 0-313-33531-1 (vol 2 : alk. paper) 1. Theater—Asia—Encyclopedias. 2. Performing arts—
Asia—Encyclopedias. 3. Oriental drama—Encyclopedias. I. Leiter, Samuel L.
PN2860.E53 2007
792.095—dc22   2006031211

British Library Cataloguing in Publication Data is available.

Library of Congress Catalog Card Number: 2006031211
ISBN: 0-313-33529-X (set)
    0-313-33530-3 (vol. 1)
    0-313-33531-1 (vol. 2)

First published in 2007

Greenwood Press, 88 Post Road West, Westport, CT 06881
An imprint of Greenwood Publishing Group, Inc.
www.greenwood.com

Printed in the United States of America

The paper used in this book complies with the
Permanent Paper Standard issued by the National
Information Standards Organization (Z39.48–1984).

10 9 8 7 6 5 4 3 2 1

The index for these volumes was compiled at the publisher's discretion.

To the artists and scholars of the Association for Asian Performance, for their friendship and encouragement, and for their continuing efforts on behalf of teaching, performing, and researching Asian theatre

CONTENTS

PREFACE

Asian theatre: two words that conjure up infinite and often contrasting images of dramatic expression. A handful of examples shows that Asian theatre ranges from:

simplicity to grandiosity

natural faces to garish makeup and startling masks

elaborate bodily adornments to near nudity

earthy secularism to trance-inducing rituals

performances lasting from fifteen minutes to a month

gender-appropriate to gender-impersonating actors

open-air village spaces to urban architectural tours de force

classical theorists to postmodern ones

dance-acting to dance-less acting

puppets to living players

musical speech to colloquial prose

symbolic scenography to site-specific locales

improvisational ingenuity to literary masterpieces

storytelling narrators to choral reciters

traditional codes to cutting-edge experiments

entertainment to healing goals

apolitical themes to political subversion

single-language to multiple-language performance

free admission to high-priced tickets

Even from this partial listing, it is clear that the entire range of theatrical possibilities is contained within the rainbow suggested by "Asian theatre," especially when viewed in its totality, from its ancient roots to its contemporary manifestations, much of the latter influenced by Western theatre.

Asian theatre covers an immense geographical area comprising many countries. In fact, deciding just which ones could be accommodated in these pages was one of the project's first problems. To be truly comprehensive, it would be necessary to encompass not only nations clearly belonging to South, Southeast, and Far East Asia, but to roam across the Indian and Pakistani borders into Afghanistan, and thereby into much of the Middle East (including Iraq and Iran), and to travel northward, where nations liberated from the Soviet bloc have their own theatrical traditions. But to have included all such places and given each its proper due would have required more pages and contributors than this already large project could afford. So the focus remains on South, Southeast, and Far East Asia, which, it must be said, possess in aggregate a far more significant assortment of theatrical forms and achievements than those of the Middle East. There, theatre, although not absent or insignificant, has been largely stifled in its development by religious restrictions against theatrical performance. It is therefore of deep interest that Muslims are among the most active and creative theatre artists in several cultures east of the Middle East.

Despite the riches of Asia's theatre, the twenty-first century began with only two significant reference books specifically dedicated to the subject. One is *The Cambridge Guide to Asian Theatre* (1993), edited by James R. Brandon, an excellent book organized by country (South, Southeast, and Far East), including Oceania. It is not an encyclopedia, however; despite the semi-encyclopedia format of each chapter, only those persons and forms given special attention are listed in the two-page index of artists and genres. So finding many important figures, like Kan'ami Kiyotsugu, requires searching through the essay on Japan to find a reference to them. Brandon's 253–page book was a start to which the present work, four times its size, is greatly indebted.

The other important contribution, part of a multivolume series, is *The World Encyclopedia of Contemporary Theatre, Volume 5, Asia/Pacific* (1998), edited by Don Rubin. This 524–page volume is also organized by country, although its entries include Afghanistan, Australia, Iran, Kazakhstan, Kyrgyzstan, New Zealand, Papua New Guinea, South Pacific, Tajikistan, Turkmenistan, and Uzbekistan, in addition to the countries of South, Southeast, and Far East Asia represented in the present work. On the other hand, although it necessarily contains some information on traditional theatres, the focus—as its title reveals—is contemporary activity.

The *Encyclopedia of Asian Theatre*, on the other hand, attempts to include both modern and traditional theatre in its purview, although in some cases, where the traditional blends into the modern as it takes on new influences, the distinction can be blurry. Because the editorial responsibilities for most areas were split between one person covering traditional and one modern theatre, the editors sometimes had to make decisions as to which area a form or individual belonged.

Unlike the works previously cited, this book provides an A-to-Z format for all entries (see below: Using the Encyclopedia). It also offers a comprehensive index, which will be invaluable when searching for numerous topics not given their own entries. The book covers the most ancient theatres for each country as well as the most contemporary and avant-garde.

After I created the original taxonomy, the editors made suggestions for improvement, thus leading to the present arrangement. They also were responsible for selecting—within an agreed-on number of words—all the headwords for their area. This continued to develop as they or I would occasionally add or subtract something from the list, as gaps appeared, when further research made earlier choices less appropriate, or when writers assigned to the project offered their own ideas. Despite the encyclopedia's vast coverage, however, it had to be selective and exclude a small number of genres and, of course, a far greater number of artists some might feel deserve inclusion. Moreover, despite entries on a very small number of genres that might be described as more dance than theatre oriented, such as *butô* and *bharata natyam*, the focus has been on theatre work, that is, performances reliant on narrative structures, characters, and—apart from forms that might be described as pantomimic—language, even though many such forms employ dance extensively.

The basic taxonomy is comprised of four general subject types: country/region, biography (the largest number of entries), theatrical genres/forms, and general topics—from Actors and Acting to Women in Asian Theatre. By and large, the shortest essays have around 250 words, thus eliminating topics that might have been explained in fifty to one hundred words, such as in a reference dictionary. The relative length of essays was left to the individual editors to determine, although cutting or supplementing was often later requested. Dancers, except for a tiny number, and musicians are not given biographies, which are mainly for actors, directors, playwrights, and, in a few cases, designers.

The project began with advisory editors selecting the writers working under their leadership. Eventually, various reasons led to my becoming more directly involved in the process. A small number of writers dropped out midway and were replaced by other writers. Partly this was because much of Asia suffered considerable turmoil while this book was being assembled. Natural disasters, political upheavals, economic chaos, civil strife, and other tragic occurrences often made it difficult for writers working from their home countries to supply material in a timely fashion. Still, in the end, over ninety writers, resident in Asia, Australia, England, Canada, and the United States, contributed, some with a single essay, some with many more. I am proud to have worked with so many fine scholars and artists, and thank them for their excellent contributions. I apologize for sometimes having had to play the strict schoolmaster in order to get material in on time.

USING THE ENCYCLOPEDIA

Organization: Finding Entries/Information

The Encyclopedia of Asian Theatre is organized from A to Z. Most headwords in the taxonomy are listed in this way, making them easy to locate. However, many headwords are for general topics, such as Actors and Acting, Directors and Directing, Religion in Theatre, Theatres, and so forth. These general topics are organized by country. Thus readers seeking information on Chinese actors will go to Actors and Acting and then find the subheading, Acting: China.

Not every country is listed under every general topic. Some general topic headwords include almost all Asian nations, some only a handful. Often the kind of information, if not as highly detailed, that such an entry would have contained will be found in other essays for that nation, such as its overview essay.

Cross-References

The encyclopedia makes abundant use of cross-references. These are of two types: words printed in bold and "see" references. The first is used when a word appears in an entry that is directly related to a specific headword, even when the words in question are not precisely the same. For example, the entry on Actors and Acting will be cross-referenced by words such as "actor," "actress," and "acting." Similarly, Politics in Theatre will be referenced not only by "politics" but by "politically" or something similar. "Critic" or even "criticized" should be enough to lead the reader to Criticism, while "folk" should be enough to reference Folk Theatre, "music" or "musicians" should get the reader to Music and Musical Instruments, "puppets," "puppeteers," and "puppetry" to Puppet Theatre, "Western" to Western Influence, "women" to Women in Asian Theatre, and so forth. The word "theatre," however, is only used as a cross-reference to Theatres when the context makes clear that the reference is to theatre venues and not to theatre art itself. Countries are similarly referenced, and may be given in forms such as "Chinese," "Japanese," and so on.

Because many cross-referenced words in bold often appear next to others, the possibility exists of the reader becoming confused regarding how to separate one reference from another. To obviate this problem, the encyclopedia places a raised bold dot between references, thereby separating them. Thus **Indonesian • actor** will refer the reader to Indonesia and Actors and Acting.

"See" (and "see also") references are used more sparingly than bolded ones, both in the text of entries and where alternative headwords are provided for readers who may go to them instead of to a topic given under a different headword.

Index

Many users will want to find information on people, terms, plays, institutions, and so on that is not the subject of entries. A comprehensive index provides access to all such mentions in the text. This is especially important for items that, while not given their own entries, are discussed in some detail elsewhere.

Names: People and Places

Different countries covered follow different practices in the way personal names are given. Japan, Burma (Myanmar), Cambodia, China, Korea, and Vietnam, for example, list the family name first, the given name(s) second. Thus we have Mei Lanfang and Ichikawa Danjûrô, where Mei and Ichikawa are family names. In other countries, the familiar Western practice of given name first, family name second is used. In alphabetizing the names of those people with entries, native practices have been followed. However, in some places, such as Malaysia, name order is not always clear. Thus Malaysian playwright Krishen Jit is typically referred to in his home country as Krishen, and one may find his name alphabetized in different sources as Krishen Jit or Jit, Krishen. In all such problematic cases of name order, I have deferred to the judgment of the writers of the entries in question. Thus certain Malaysian names are alphabetized as Mustapha Kamil Yassin, Shaharom Husain, Syed Alwi, Usman Awang, not Yassin, Mustapha Kamil, and so on. In addition, while numerous people with entries were born with names other than those by which they are most widely known, their birth names are not given in their entries.

Then there are the names of cities and countries, a number of which have changed over the years. The changes from Ceylon to Sri Lanka and Siam to Thailand, for example, are now familiar, so they present no problem. However, the change of Burma's name to Myanmar, while fiercely defended by that country's people, is not officially recognized by all other nations, including the United States. Thus Burma is generally referred to in the encyclopedia as Burma (Myanmar). More common are cities whose names have changed, some only very recently. The chief (but not exclusive) examples are in India, where Calcutta is now Kolkata, Bombay is Mumbai, Benares is Varanasi, and Madras is Chennai, among other examples. Rather than ignore these changes, the encyclopedia refers to these cities by the names they held at the time referred to in entries that mention them, but adds their later (or earlier) name in parentheses. Therefore, an entry's first reference to something occurring in Bombay prior to its becoming Mumbai will say Bombay (Mumbai), but a reference to something occurring after the name change will say Mumbai (Bombay). In Japan, the famous example of Edo, which became Tokyo in the early Meiji period (1868–1912), will say Edo (Tokyo) when the older name is first given, but will not say Tokyo (Edo) for when Tokyo is given unless warranted by the context.

Dates

Every effort has been made to supply birth and death years for all significant Asians mentioned in the text, even nontheatrical ones. (This has not been done for Western figures, though.) There are nevertheless many persons for whom it proved impossible to track down one or both of their dates. When dates are questionable, question marks or ca. (*circa*) have been used. Similarly, the encyclopedia generally supplies dates of productions (and, in some cases, publication) for most plays mentioned, but it has not been possible to do so in every case.

Diacritics

Diacritics, the tiny symbols accompanying letters indicating their proper pronunciation, are used in the encyclopedia only for Korean and Japanese words.

Spelling

Variations in the way many names and terms are spelled in Western languages are rampant. Often, different writers for the same country used different spellings. The best the encyclopedia can hope to do is spell all such words consistently; in a number of cases where genres are concerned, variant spellings have been offered in the text.

Further Reading

A selected number of entries—mainly those under the categories of Countries/ Regions, Theatrical Genres and Forms, and General Topics—conclude with one or more "further reading" suggestions. The citations are simplified, giving just names of authors and title, often shortened. Readers can easily find complete citations for these works in the general bibliography, which is organized according to country. There are also Further Readings for biographical essays when significant works about the subjects are available. Only books, dissertations, or chapters in English-language books are listed; journal or newspaper articles are not. Books in English either partly or entirely about many subjects discussed here do not exist; limited information about a number of such topics may be found in *The World Encyclopedia of Contemporary Theatre*, Vol. 5, *Asia/South Pacific*, edited by Don Rubin.

Translations

Obviously, a work like this contains many Asian-language items, from terms to titles to institutional names. The encyclopedia follows the practice of giving the item first in English, followed by its indigenous version in parentheses. For some, seeing familiar Asian expressions or names in English will seem odd; however, the aim of the encyclopedia is to make the material it presents as accessible as possible, and this seemed a workable compromise. In a few cases, where I deemed that the item is best known to the world at large by its indigenous name, I have given the English, followed by the original, but have reverted to the original, not the English, in subsequent usages within the same entry. An example is the ancient Sanskrit theatre manual, the *Natyashastra*, introduced in various entries as *The Treatise on Drama* (Natyashastra), but afterward referred to only as the *Natyashastra*. On the other hand, English versions are not given for ubiquitously mentioned works like the *Ramayana* and *Mahabharata*. And a small number of indigenous newspaper and journal titles remain untranslated as well.

The encyclopedia seeks to provide translations of all titles mentioned; however, when nothing in parentheses follows a play's title it should be understood that the title given is a proper noun, being the name of a person or place, and therefore not requiring a translation.

Finally, many institutions are mentioned, both in an English version and, in parentheses, the original name. This practice is limited to theatre companies and selected theatre institutions, but in numerous other cases, whether it be educational institutions or political organizations, only the English name is given.

Additional Style Notes

Play titles: Titles of full-length plays are given in italics; one-acts are given in quotation marks.

Terminology: All Asian terms mentioned in the text are given in italicized lowercase letters, including when part of the term is otherwise a proper noun.

ACKNOWLEDGMENTS

This list of acknowledgments must begin with a grateful nod toward George Butler of Greenwood, who asked me to undertake this important project. I also wish to thank the ninety-five contributors to this work for their entries and their advice. Those who gathered photos for the book served an invaluable function in helping to illustrate their own and others' entries. Those who provided their own photos, often free of charge, deserve a special acknowledgment of gratitude; their names are credited in the captions. Also deserving a special thanks are those who obtained both photos and permissions from institutions and individuals. Of particular assistance in such matters were Lorelle Browning, Alexander Huang, Debjani Ray Moulik, Ruru Li, Laurence R. Kominz, Richard Nichols, Joi Barrios, Mari Boyd, John K. Gillespie, M. Cody Poulton, Margaret Coldiron, Pornrat Damrhung, Yukihiro Goto, Nancy Nanney, Claire Pamment, and William Peterson. Additional scholars occasionally provided information to entry writers on certain arcane topics, and their names are recorded in parentheses following the main author's bylines. I extend my thanks to all such persons. Often, it was necessary to check the accuracy of an entry with one of the book's other writers. To all who helped in such matters, I am deeply grateful. And to Marcia, my wife, I once again offer my deepest gratitude for letting me work on yet another huge project when I'm sure she would have preferred to have me pitch in more around the house.

I apologize in advance for any errors that readers may find, and would be happy to learn of them in case it ever becomes possible to fix them for a future edition.

Samuel L. Leiter

ALPHABETICAL LIST OF ENTRIES

TOPICAL GUIDE
TO ENTRIES

The *Encyclopedia of Asian Theatre* includes three principal types of headwords: (1) countries/regions, (2) biographies, (3) theatrical genres and forms. A small number of entries, all of them based on literary sources important in South and Southeast Asia, form a fourth, miscellaneous, category. All headwords are listed below, alphabetically, under these categories. Biographical and genre/form entries include the countries or political states associated with them.

Countries/Regions

Bangladesh
Bhutan
Brunei
Burma (Myanmar)
Cambodia
China
Hong Kong
India
Indonesia
Japan
Korea (South Korea; see also
    North Korea)
Laos
Macao
Malaysia
Mongolia
Myanmar (see Burma)
Nepal
North Korea
Pakistan
Philippines
Singapore
Sri Lanka
Taiwan
Thailand
Tibet
Vietnam

Biographies

Abe Kôbô (Japan)
Abyor Dayagung (Indonesia)
Akimoto Matsuyo (Japan)
Akita Ujaku (Japan)
Alkazi, Ebrahim (India)
Ang Duong (Cambodia)
Armijn Pané (Indonesia)
Asakura Setsu (Japan)
Asari Keita (Japan)
Asep Sunandar Sunarya (Indonesia)
Asmara, Andjar (Indonesia)
Bajaj, Ram Gopal (India)
Bal Gandharva (India)
Bandô Mitsugorô (Japan)
Bandô Tamasaburô (Japan)
Betsuyaku Minoru (Japan)
Bhadhuri, Sisir Kumar (India)
Bharati, Dharmavir (India)
Bhasa (India)
Bhattacharya, Bijon (India)
Bhavabhuti (India)
Binodini Dasi (India)
Cao Yu (China)
Cervantes, Behn (Philippines)
Chang Hsiao-feng (Taiwan)
Chang Yanqiu (China)
Chea Samy (Cambodia)

Yoshida Bungorô (Japan)
Yoshida Bunzaburô (Japan)
Yoshida Tamazô (Japan)
Yoshizawa Ayame (Japan)
Yu Ch'i-jin (Korea)
Yu Sansheng (China)
Yu Shangyuan (China)
Yu Shizhi (China)
Yu Shuyan (China)
Yu Zhenfei (China)
Zeami Motokiyo (Japan)
Zhang Erkui (China)
Zhou Xinfang (China)

Theatrical Genres and Forms

(Note: These are the terms under which the genres are given in the encyclopedia. Variant terms may appear there as well with "see" references. Forms described within other entries, like *huaju*, are not listed here. A selected number of important puppet theatre forms are given with "see Puppet Theatre" references.)

abdul muluk (Indonesia)
ache lhamo (Tibet)
alkap (Bangladesh)
angura (Japan)
ankiya nat (India)
anyein pwe (Burma/Myanmar)
arja (Indonesia)
awaji ningyô jôruri (Japan: see Puppet Theatre)
baltal (India: see Puppet Theatre)
bangsawan (Indonesia, Malaysia, Singapore)
bangzi qiang (China)
barong (Indonesia)
bayalata (India)
bhaand pather (India)
bhagat (India)
bhagavata mela (India)
bharata natyam (India)
bhavai (India)
bidesia (India)
bobadil (Philippines)
bommalatta (India: see Puppet Theatre)
boria (Malaysia)

budai xi (Taiwan; see Puppet Theatre)
bugaku (Japan)
bunraku (Japan; see Puppet Theatre)
burrakatha (India)
butô (Japan)
cai luong (Vietnam)
canjun xi (China)
cavittu natakam (India)
chaiti ghoda nacha (India)
chamadyache bahulya (India: see Puppet Theatre)
ch'angguk (Korea)
cheo (Vietnam)
chhau (India)
chuanju (China)
chuanqi (China)
dagelan (Indonesia)
danda nata (India)
dasarata (India)
dasavatar (India)
dengaku (Japan)
doddata (India)
drama (Philippines)
drama gong (Indonesia)
gambhira (India)
gambuh (Indonesia)
geju (China)
gigaku (Japan)
gombeyata (India: see Puppet Theatre)
hahoe pyŏlshin-gut (Korea)
huaji xi (China)
hun (Thailand; see Puppet Theatre)
jangger (Indonesia)
jatra (India)
jauk (Indonesia)
jikey (Malaysia)
jingju (China)
kabuki (Japan)
kagura (Japan)
kahani ka rangamanch (India)
kalapam (India)
kalarippayattu (India)
kalsutri bahulya (India: see Puppet Theatre)
karyala (India)
kathakali (India)
kathputli (India: see Puppet Theatre)
kecak (Indonesia)

kethoprak (Indonesia)
khon (Thailand)
khyal (India)
kich noi (Vietnam)
kkoktu kakshi (Korea; see Puppet Theatre)
ko-jôruri (Japan; see Puppet Theatre)
kolam (Sri Lanka)
komedi stambul (Indonesia)
komedya (Philippines)
kôwakamai (Japan)
krishnattam (India)
kuchipudi (India)
kumi odori (Japan)
kunqu (China)
kuravanci (India)
kutiyattam (India)
kyôgen (Japan)
lakhon bassac (Cambodia)
lakhon khol (Cambodia)
lakhon niyeay (Cambodia)
lakhon sbaek (Cambodia; see Puppet Theatre)
lakon chatri (Thailand)
lakon dukdamban (Thailand)
lakon nai (Thailand)
lakon nok (Thailand)
lakon phan thang (Thailand)
lakon phut samai mhai (Thailand)
lakon ram (Thailand)
lakon rong (Thailand)
legong (Indonesia)
lenong (Indonesia)
liké (Thailand)
maanch (India)
madangnori (Korea)
mak yong (Malaysia)
manohra (Malaysia, Thailand)
mansŏkjung-nori (Korea; see Puppet Theatre)
mawlam (Laos)
mibu kyôgen (Japan)
mua roi nuoc (Vietnam; see Puppet Theatre)
nacha (India)
nadagam (Sri Lanka)
nang (Thailand: see Puppet Theatre)
nang pramo thai (Thailand: see Puppet Theatre)

nang talung (Thailand; see Puppet Theatre)
nang yai (Thailand; see Puppet Theatre)
nanxi (China)
naqal (India)
nautanki (India)
nibhatkin (Burma/Myanmar)
nô (Japan)
nurti (Sri Lanka)
ogwandae (Korea)
opera batak (Indonesia)
otome bunraku (Japan: see Puppet Theatre)
pandav lila (India)
p'ansori (Korea)
Parsi theatre (India)
pasku (Sri Lanka)
putul nach (India: see Puppet Theatre)
pyŏlsandae (Korea)
ramlila (India)
randai (Indonesia)
raslila (India)
ravanacchaya (India; see Puppet Theatre)
reog (Indonesia)
robam kbach boran (Cambodia)
sakhi kundhai nata (India: see Puppet Theatre)
sandiwara (Brunei, Indonesia, Malaysia)
sangeet natak (India)
sannata (India)
Sanskrit theatre (India)
sarsuwela (Philippines)
sendratari (Indonesia)
shingeki (Japan)
shingŭk (Korea)
shin kabuki (Japan)
shinkokugeki (Japan)
shinpa (Japan)
shinp'agŭk (Korea)
shôgekijô (Japan)
shumang lila (India)
sinakulo (Philippines)
sokari (Sri Lanka)
speshal natakam (India)
supaa kabuki (Japan)
swang (India)
Takarazuka (Japan)

talamaddale (India)
t'alch'um (Korea)
tamasha (India)
tarling (Indonesia)
terukkuttu (India)
teyyam (India)
thang-ta (India)
thol pavaikkuthu (India: see Puppet
    Theatre)
thol pavakuthu (India: see Puppet Theatre)
tholu bommalatta (India: see Puppet
    Theatre)
togalu gombeyata (India: see Puppet
    Theatre)
tonil (Indonesia)
topeng (Indonesia)
trot (Cambodia; See Folk Theatre)
tuong (Vietnam)
wayang (Indonesia; see Puppet
    Theatre)
wayang beber (Indonesia: see Puppet
    Theatre)
wayang golek (Indonesia; see Puppet
    Theatre)
wayang gung (Indonesia: see Puppet
    Theatre)
wayang krucil (Indonesia: see Puppet
    Theatre)
wayang kulit (Indonesia; see Puppet
    Theatre)
wayang wong (Indonesia)
wuju (China)
xinbian lishi ju (China)
xiqu (China)
yakshagana (India)
yangban xi (China)
yaryu (Korea)
yiké (Cambodia)
yokthe pwe (Burma/Myanmar)
yŏsŏng kukkŏk (Korea)
yueju (China)
zaju (China)
zat pwe (Burma/Myanmar)

General Topics

Actors and Acting
    Bangladesh

Cambodia
China
India
Indonesia
Japan
Korea
Malaysia
Nepal
Pakistan
Singapore
Sri Lanka
Thailand
Vietnam
Censorship
    Cambodia
    China
    India
    Indonesia
    Japan
    Korea
    Malaysia
    Pakistan
    Philippines
    Singapore
    Sri Lanka
    Taiwan
    Thailand
    Vietnam
Costumes
    China
    India
    Japan
Criticism
    China
    India
    Indonesia
    Japan
    Korea
    Malaysia
    Philippines
    Singapore
    Thailand
Curtains
    India
    Japan
Dance in Theatre
    Burma/Myanmar
    Cambodia

China
Hong Kong
India
Indonesia
Japan
Korea
Malaysia
Nepal
Pakistan
Philippines
Singapore
Sri Lanka
Taiwan
Thailand
Vietnam
Properties
China
Japan
Puppet Theatre
Burma/Myanmar
Cambodia
China
India
Indonesia
Japan
Korea
Sri Lanka
Taiwan
Thailand
Vietnam
Religion in Theatre
Burma/Myanmar
Cambodia
China
India
Indonesia
Japan
Korea
Malaysia
Philippines
Sri Lanka
Vietnam
Role Types
China
India
Japan
Korea
Scenography

China
India
Indonesia
Japan
Korea
Malaysia
Philippines
Singapore
Thailand
Stages
Cambodia
China
India
Indonesia
Japan
Korea
Malaysia
Singapore
Thailand
Storytelling
China
India
Japan
Theatre Companies
Bangladesh
Cambodia
China
Hong Kong
India
Indonesia
Japan
Korea
Malaysia
Nepal
Pakistan
Philippines
Singapore
Taiwan
Thailand
Vietnam
Theatres
Bangladesh
Cambodia
China
India
Japan
Korea
Malaysia

ABDUL MULUK. Indonesian Malay-language historical drama, a.k.a. *dolmuluk*, *dermuluk*, and *dulmuluk*, practiced in Sumatra and formerly in Borneo and western Java. *Abdul muluk*'s name comes from its principal item, based on the narrative *Poem of Abdul Muluk* (Syair Abdul Muluk), attributed to Riau author Saleha and first published in 1847. The *Poem* relates the trials and tribulations of Siti Rafiah, the secondary wife of Abdul Muluk, sultan of Barbari. After Barbari is defeated in battle and Barbari's sultan is imprisoned, Siti Rafiah disguises herself as a man and enlists the king of Barham to help free her husband and restore him to power.

Abdul muluk appears to have begun in Borneo in the 1870s as an all-male, Malay-language dramatic form based on **Chinese** traditional theatre. **Theatre companies** traveled to Sumatra and western Java, and imitation troupes, called *wayang abdul muluk* or *komedi abdul muluk*, were established in Batavia (Jakarta) and western Sumatra, some combining features of **Parsi theatre** and *bangsawan*. Female fans' licentious behavior prompted a ban in Batavia and environs in 1882, but this was not rigidly enforced. *Dermuluk* continued in Batavia until the 1930s, gradually transforming into a low-key version of *bangsawan* distinguished principally by its syncretic **musical** ensemble of harmonium, Chinese moon guitar (*sampyan*), two violins, Sundanese drum (*gendang*), and tambourine.

Dulmuluk has been performed in the Palembang area of southern Sumatra since at least 1908. Plays are drawn nearly exclusively from the *Poem of Abdul Muluk* and the closely related *Poem of Siti Zubaidah*. Dialogue is poetic, with minimal improvisation, and is spoken and sung to the accompaniment of Malay melodies played on violin, gong, drum (*gendang*), and bass drum (*jidor*). All roles are taken by men, **scenographic** elements are a few chairs and a backdrop, and **properties** like horses and ships are roughly constructed from rattan and cloth. **Acting** is broad and **costumes** richly embroidered. *Dulmuluk* is broadcast on television and radio and promoted by the government as a form of local culture, but is rapidly losing popularity.

FURTHER READING

Yousof, Ghulam Sarwar. *Dictionary of Traditional South-East Asian Theatre*.

Matthew Isaac Cohen

ABE KÔBÔ (1924–1993). Japanese • *shingeki* • playwright, **director**, novelist, and teacher, prominent in the postwar period. Abe's works explore Japan's social divisions and widespread alienation. Through a combination of traditional *shingeki* dramaturgy and absurdist techniques—he shares with Beckett and Pinter a nonlinear ambiguity—he challenged preconceived notions of dramatic content and societal norms.

While Abe gained fame with the film adaptation of his novel *Woman in the Dunes* (Suna no Onna, 1962), his plays are equally noteworthy. They include *Slave Hunting* (Dorei-gari, 1955), *The Ghost Is Here* (Yûrei wa koko ni iru, 1958), winning the **Kishida [Kunio]** Prize, *You, Too, Are Guilty* (Omae nimo tsumi ga aru, 1965), and *The Man Who Turned into a Stick* (Bô ni natta otoko, 1969). Perhaps his best-known play, *Friends* (Tomodachi, 1967), features a family of strangers invading a man's apartment, bent on helping him overcome his social isolation and complacency. Twisting expectations, they eventually imprison and kill him. The absurdity of their actions and the man's plight is evident in Abe's characteristic dialogue of unfinished, suppressed utterances; the strained silences, limned by sound and lighting, are more telling than spoken words.

In 1973, Abe created the Abe Studio with his wife, Yamada Machiko (1926–1993), to **train • actors** in his avant-garde histrionics and to develop collaborative stagings. After *The Little Elephant Is Dead* (Kozô wa shinda, 1979), he returned to fiction, but his plays remain popular, blending humor and pathos, suspense and outrage, in their dissections of the postwar world.

FURTHER READING

Shields, Nancy. *Fake Fish: The Theatre of Kôbô Abe.*

David Jortner

ABYOR DAYAGUNG (1914–1969). Indonesian *wayang kulit* (see Puppet Theatre) master (*dhalang*) from the Cirebon area of West Java, son of a celebrated puppeteer, Cita Janapriya (?–1945), and famous for introducing Islamic mysticism to *wayang*. Abyor received only a rudimentary secular and **religious** education, but read widely. He created his own unconventional plays, often centering on the subaltern clown-servants, who voice grievances of the common people. *Gareng Becomes God* (Gareng dadi pengeran) explores the mystical idea of the presence of God in man in a play that elevates one of the clown-servants to the divine plane. In *Semar Makes the Hajj* (Semar lunga kaji), the poor clown-servant Semar goes on the hajj despite the resistance of his authoritarian older brother, Bathara Guru (Shiva, to South Asians), demonstrating the true meaning of pilgrimage. Abyor bravely exposed corruption and lambasted misuses of authority.

In the 1960s, novelist and folklorist Ajip Rosidi (1938–) championed Abyor nationally, "novelizing" Abyor's *Rikmadenda Quests for God* (Rikmadenda nggolati pengeran, 1962; revised 1991), introducing Abyor to puppeteers and intellectuals in Bandung and elsewhere, and opening doors to radio. Abyor was made an honorary professor by LEKRA, the arts wing of the Indonesian Communist Party (PKI). Following the destruction of PKI in 1965–1966, Abyor was imprisoned; when released he was banned from performing (see Censorship; Politics in Theatre). He died a broken man, but his plays and performance style live on.

Matthew Isaac Cohen

ACHE LHAMO. Tibetan traditional **musical** drama. The term literally means "sister goddesses." Its possible origin was in 1430, when, to fund a bridge, a senior Tibetan Buddhist lama got seven sisters to sing and **dance** a play he had himself created. Audience reaction was rapturous, equating the sisters with goddesses. In later centuries, *ache lhamo* underwent strong influence from both **India** and **China**. However, indigenous song and dance remained crucially important.

The Fifth Dalai Lama (1617–1682) instituted a summer drama **festival**. By the eighteenth century, it was focused on the Dalai Lama's Summer Palace, with performances taking place also in great monasteries, like the Drepung outside the Tibetan capital, Lhasa. The festival's effect was to make this originally entirely **religious** ritual art partly secular.

Over the centuries many items emerged, about a dozen still being performed. They deal with Tibetan history, heroes, kings, princes, and beautiful **women**, the introduction of Buddhism into Tibet, and mythological themes. Several are set in India, and almost all are anonymous. All are infused with Buddhist imagery and motifs, and virtually all have happy endings, since *ache lhamo* admits no tragedy; a typical conclusion sees an appropriate leading character ascending a throne.

There are three sections to a Tibetan drama: the blessing and introduction, the drama itself, and the valedictory epilogue, expressed through song and dance. One major function of the epilogue was to request money from the audience.

Singing is high-pitched and melismatic, individual characters usually singing one melody only and choral accompaniment being very common. **Musical instruments** consist of a drum and a pair of cymbals.

A special feature is the **masks**, representing gods or demons. Humans wear colorcoded **makeup**, red symbolizing a warrior, yellow a king, and black soot a nomad or villain. **Costumes** are elaborate and colorful, but the **stage** area is entirely or largely bare.

The traditional venues include any open space or a temporarily erected tent. Apart from a narrow gangway for the **actors** to enter and exit, the audience sits around the acting space, which is raised slightly or not at all. Lhasa's Drepung Monastery and Potala Palace have specially erected permanent stages; in the past, the Dalai Lama could view the performance from his room above, while the rest of the audience sat or stood below or opposite the stage. Performances still take place at the Drepung Monastery.

Formerly, the actors' social status was very low, despite the favor granted their art by the Dalai Lama and his court. The main troupes that performed for the Dalai Lama had only men or boys, though in less well-known companies, women could take the less important parts. *See also* Nepal.

Ache lhamo performance showing blessing and introduction (prologue) in which goddesses dance in a circle, having descended to the mortal world. It often takes place under a special canopy, with the audience on four sides. This performance was at the Dalai Lama's former summer palace, August 1990. (Photo: Colin Mackerras)

FURTHER READING

Pearlman, Ellen. *Tibetan Sacred Dance, A Journey into the Religious and Folk Traditions.*

Colin Mackerras

ACTORS AND ACTING

Actors and Acting: Bangladesh

Bangladesh's theatre is organized according to a "group theatre" or "theatre group" concept, which relies on ensemble-based acting. Yet the system often sees the **director** emerging as the principal actor and taking on star status. The pattern may be described as one in which a group of unpaid semiprofessional actors gather around a director (often the principal actor) and other founding members, who **train** them in the plays and requirements of their roles. Acting styles are often determined by that of the director and his choice of plays.

The two major Bangladeshi directors, Ali Zaker (1944–) and Nasiruddin Yusuf (1950–), are renowned actors who always take the lead in the productions of their respective **theatre companies**, Citizen (Nagarik) and Dhaka Theatre. By becoming the star performers of their groups, they sometimes inhibit the individual creativity of the young actors. Important actors identified with particular groups are Abul Hayat (1944–) and Liaquat ali Lucky (1957–).

The repertoire, dominated by translations and adaptations of **Western** classic and modern plays, requires strong realistic acting, often developed through instinctive understanding and experience. Themes in native dramas taken from rural Bangladesh allow so-called realistic actors to innovate with a passionate raw authenticity and use of dialects. Such plays also demand frequently breaking into **folk** songs, suggesting a rather limited concept of realism.

Among the extremely powerful **women** dominating Bangladeshi's leading groups are actresses Firdausi Rehman (1943–), Sara Zaker (1954–), and Simul Yusuf (1957–). Their talents have given the repertoire a new dimension. They occasionally foray into directing and take a major role in company administration.

The troupes retain a kind of organizational continuity at a semiprofessional level. Performers keep leaving for television and cinema, but the companies always manage to gain suitable replacements. In recent times, a number of actors have received training in **Indian** theatre schools and institutions.

Bishnupriya Dutt

Actors and Acting: Cambodia

Throughout the twentieth century, a handful of actors rose to prominence in **Cambodia** as performers in specific genres. Even in the early twenty-first century, people still refer to Sang Saron (1922–1973) as the ultimate *lakhon bassac* practitioner, outshone by no one. Chek Maech (?–2002) became an important *lakhon bassac* actress in the mid-twentieth century. Because she survived the genocide of the 1970s, she was central in rebuilding that art in later years. Another actress of the same generation, May Moeun, was proficient in several types of theatre, including *promotey* (a kind of modern **musical** theatre). In the 1980s and early 1990s, she starred in Cambodian movies, often playing the role of the nasty older relative.

Indeed, the late-twentieth-century movie industry (actually videotape because of lack of money, resources, and skilled technicians) produced a number of actors honored in Cambodia and in foreign Cambodian communities; most beloved was Piseth Pilika (1966–1999), also a star of *robam kbach boran* until her murder. Noted *lakhon niyeay* actors Peau Yuleng (1917–1981), **Hang Tun Hak**, **Chheng Phon**, and **Pich Tum Kravel** each went on to prominent careers as arts administrators.

While acting students receive professional **training** at the Royal University of Fine Arts, provincial *lakhon bassac* and *yiké* actors may learn as apprentices rather than through formal studies. Most actors, though, in every genre, are typecast, specializing in one kind of **role type** within that form.

Toni Shapiro-Phim

Actors and Acting: China

Social Attitudes. Although acting and theatre have always been important in **Chinese** society, actors have generally held a very low social status. Confucius (551–479 BC) despised them and even declared of one court group: "commoners who beguile their lord through performing deserve to die."

Some dynasties were more tolerant than others, but by the early fourteenth century, we find a series of anti-actor edicts. In 1313, along with criminals and the severely disabled, actors were forbidden to sit for the imperial examinations whose graduates were selected for the official bureaucracy. Anti-actor edicts became more numerous in later centuries; for example, a 1770 imperial decree not only banned actors from sitting for the examinations, but their sons and grandsons as well.

The strolling player is a prominent feature of Chinese theatre history. Some had a fixed address for part of the year, but at other times traveled around, performing at temple fairs and **festivals**. Such actors were blamed for peasant idleness and corrupting morals.

Another reason for actors' low social status was their association with sexual immorality and the sex industry. Although there is evidence from the Yuan dynasty (1280–1368) that acting, of both males and females, was to some extent a family business, members of all-female troupes were commonly prostitutes or courtesans. There are many surviving sexually centered paeans of praise to actresses. Men and **women** readily performed characters of the opposite sex. The puritanical poet and minister Lu Rong (1436–1494) typified those who were shocked at how realistically female impersonators copied women's mannerisms; he called on decent people to reject them for the sake of their family lives.

From the Ming dynasty (1368–1644) on, **theatre companies** were increasingly of a single gender only; all-male troupes predominated. The association with sex, including prostitution, became stronger, with love affairs frequent between well-off men and either male or female actors. By early in the eighteenth century, it was fashionable to include attractive young actors as banquet entertainers. A nineteenth-century law banning officials from visiting female prostitutes resulted in their replacement by young male actors.

Meanwhile, late in the eighteenth century, all women, including actresses, were banned from public **theatres**. Cross-dressing men (*nandan*) had existed for centuries, but the ban simply strengthened their predominance in major *xiqu* forms. One result was **Wei Changsheng**'s creation of the "false feet" (*caiqiao*), by which men could resemble women walking with bound feet.

Wealthy men also ran private troupes, especially from Ming onward. They would either recruit actors or teach house staff members to perform. A famous example was Ruan Dacheng (ca. 1587–1646), a corrupt politician and **playwright,** who **trained** his troupe to perform his own plays, both inside his mansion and elsewhere. These house-slave actors held low social status, but at least had a connection with the gentry, which put them above ordinary actors.

At the top of the actors' social scale were court eunuchs. In 1390, the first Ming emperor had a eunuch agency set up to provide court entertainment. About 1740, the Qianlong emperor (r. 1736–1796) set up a special organization to recruit eunuch actors for the imperial theatre. In 1860, city actors were briefly invited to perform at court, and again in 1884 the custom was revived, this time lasting until the fall of the Qing dynasty (1644–1911). The Empress Dowager Cixi (1835–1908) had a particular fondness for *jingju* actor **Tan Xinpei**, even conferring a title on him.

The nineteenth century featured many stars—especially **Cheng Changgeng**, **Yu Sansheng**, and **Zhang Erkui**—and the organization of actor guilds. Together with the court invitations, the result was a slight rise in social status, especially in Beijing. A change in the training system in the early twentieth century contributed further, especially because stars like **Mei Lanfang** became famous not only in China but internationally. However, actors' social status was still low and the 1930s Chinese sociologist Pan Guangdan reckoned that to have an actor son was hardly better than having no son at all.

In 1923, an all-female Shaoxing *yueju* troupe performed in Shanghai, the first to do so. It was not welcomed, but established a practice that soon became the Shaoxing standard.

The Chinese Communist Party (CCP) brought about greater change after 1949. It worked hard to attract actors to its cause and to treat them well, listing them as "brain workers" in the same category as scientists and other artists. Training further improved. Cross-gender performance training ceased, greatly weakening the practice. Several distinguished actors not only joined the CCP but the **political** process, among them *jingju* actors Mei Lanfang and **Zhou Xinfang**. Although not so well off materially relative to the rest of the population, actors' livelihoods improved enormously compared to pre-communist years. Actors received salaries, with their troupe looking after their various needs.

During the Cultural Revolution (1966–1976), former stars were attacked and replaced by others according to their support for the leadership, especially CCP Chairman Mao Zedong (1893–1976) and his wife, Jiang Qing (1913–1991). The new stars were then suppressed with Mao's death and Jiang's fall in 1976. The period since has seen the number of *xiqu* actors decrease, and their status determined more by money and artistry than by politics. The training of cross-gender actors has reemerged, to a small degree, based on **role type** requirements, but so few boys are learning female roles that the future for *nandan* art is bleak. Some old prejudices against actors survive but are decreasing.

Amateurs. Amateur actors were hardly new to the twentieth century, but gained prominence then. **Folk** troupes were organized in considerable numbers as part of the propaganda resistance against **Japan** during the Second Sino-Japanese War (1937–1945). After 1949, amateur troupes proliferated, both for traditional and modern theatre, Mao Zedong enthusiastically using amateur drama as propaganda. In the post-Mao years, amateur folk troupes have been the mainstay of traditional forms in the countryside. In the cities, amateur singers of traditional styles, especially *jingju*, often gather to sing their favorite items.

Vocal and Physical Performance. For *xiqu* actors in many forms, including **kunqu** and *jingju*, performance is comprised of four major skills: song (*chang*), speech (*nian*), **dance**-acting (*zuo*; literally, "doing," encompassing dance, dance-like movement and gesture, facial expression, and all other physical aspects of acting), and combat (*da*; literally, "hitting"). Each skill is essentially a complete conventional language, founded in its own set of basic skills (*jiben gong*) learned during training and having an extensive vocabulary of conventions. Some conventions belong to specific role types; others differ in their stylization patterns among types.

To varying but substantial extents, the actor's song skill in most forms of *xiqu* features **musical** composition. The musical conventions of the particular form in essence comprise a musical "language" capable of rich and nuanced expression; actors apply these conventions to expressively join language and music in the interpretation of characters, and lead more often than follow the orchestra.

Musicality is also a crucial quality of *xiqu* speech skill. *Kunqu* speech, for example, is considered more difficult for the actor to perform well than song, since no song manual or flute accompaniment guides the performer, and pronunciation is as strictly prescribed as for singing. Rhymed speech (poetry or parallel prose) sets scenes, and knowing which words to speak in high voice and which to speak lightly and low is crucial to achieving expressivity (*yuqixing*). The same holds for dialogue, whose articulation may be either "hot" or "cold" depending on the mood of the exchange. Both song and speech in *xiqu* are articulated in standardized **stage** language ("Rhymes of the Central Plain" [*Zhongzhou yun*]), somewhat modified to reflect distinctive features of local dialect (for example, "Suzhou zhongzhou yun" for *kunqu*). More colloquial speech patterns are employed by actors of certain role types, however.

In *kunqu*, both "painted face" (*jing*) and "comic male" (*chou*) actors use stage speech based on regional dialect, with that of Suzhou and Beijing most common. In *jingju*, actors for many *chou* and vivacious young "flower female" (*huadan*) roles use speech based on Beijing dialect; the former may employ exaggerated tones and rhythms from other regional dialects as well.

Xiqu actors employ an extraordinary number of named, conventional movements, most of which are originally learned as basic skills. One partial source for *jingju* lists fifty-four hand movements for different circumstances and expressive uses, and eight additional arm movements; seventy-four foot and twelve additional leg movements; thirty-nine for manipulating beards of male characters; twelve for manipulating the long headdress feathers (*lingzi*) worn by some martial characters; and 107 for manipulating "water sleeves" (*shuixiu*), lengths of white silk attached to the wrists of **costumes**. Actors join various movements together in conventional sequences called "body passages/postures" (*shenduan*) that, sometimes in conjunction with the use of **properties**, define time or locale, or show activity such as going through a door, rowing a boat, mounting and dismounting a horse, or traveling from place to place, which is indicated by movement in a circle. On the essentially bare traditional stage, "scenery is in the actors' bodies," often made more effective by traditional costumes. The *liangxiang* is a short dance-like movement sequence culminating in a dynamic pose revealing character and attitude. Longer dance-like sequences establish character and activity, such as a general preparing for battle (*qiba*), horseback travel (*tangma*), or rapid, stealthy movement at night (*zoubian*).

Jingju and *kunqu* combat is derived from traditional martial arts, to which dance-like stylization has been added. It encompasses two major conventional movement types: "handle skill" (*bazi gong*) and "carpet skill" (*tanzi gong*). *Bazi gong* involves entrances, exits, and fighting forms for a wide array of weapons, from sabers to cudgels. Sequences can be performed between opponents or as solos. *Tanzi gong* includes many different, named varieties of difficult acrobatic movements, both on the ground and in the air.

The actor synthesizes these skills, interpreting song, speech, and combat through dance-acting and working closely with the orchestra leader. Actors require a balance between emotional truth and constant technical evaluation.

Acting Schools and Representative Actors. After Liang Chenyu founded the Liang school (*liupai*) in the mid-sixteenth century, schools of *kunqu* acting and singing proliferated. These are exemplified by the Dong school (*dong pai*) of Dong Meichen (fl. 1760), carried from Yangzhou to Suzhou by Zhang Weishang and from Suzhou to Beijing by Chen Jinque (1791–1877), whose grandsons taught Mei Lanfang. By the time purely *kunqu* schools associated with actors dwindled in the nineteenth century, regional styles (*zhipai*) had emerged in Suzhou (*sukun*), Zhejiang (*zhekun*), Jiangxi (*gankun*), Hunan (*xiangkun*), Sichuan (*chuankun*), and Beijing (*beikun*). Excepting Suzhou and its hinterland, these styles reflect various accommodations between *kunqu* and local styles of *xiqu*. Concurrently, as *kunqu* actors were moving to mixed troupes (*heban*), amateurs began to perform with professionals, and "pure singing" accordingly influenced acting styles. Today's predominant *kunqu* style is the "Yu school."

Outstanding nineteenth– and early twentieth–century *jingju* actors who established their own styles and received students wishing to learn them were recognized as having founded a *liupai*. Gaining such recognition today is difficult, and traditional *liupai* are taught as models.

Two leading *jingju* actors of the late nineteenth and early twentieth centuries were "martial male" (*wusheng*) actor **Yang Xiaolou** and "older male" (*laosheng*) actor **Tan Xinpei**. They were succeeded by the "four great bearded *sheng* ['male role']," each of whom established a *liupai*. **Ma Lianliang** is probably best known today. Other important *liupai* include those of Yang Baosen (1909–1958), Xi Xiaobo (1910–1977), and Zhou Xinfang.

Li Duokui (1898–1974) was the leading twentieth-century *jingju* "older female" (*laodan*) actor. He originally studied the *laosheng* type but switched in the 1920s, working with **Chang Yanqiu** and later Qiu Shengrong (1915–1971), one of the finest "painted face" (*hualian*) actors. Qiu was famous for his Judge Bao plays, and established his own *liupai*; he also created one of the leading roles in the model revolutionary (**yangban xi**) *jingju* play *Azalea Mountain* (Dujuan shan).

The "four great *dan* ['female roles']"—Mei Lanfang, Chang Yanqiu, **Xun Huisheng**, and **Shang Xiaoyun**—dominated their speciality in the twentieth century. They also helped bring **women** like **Li Yuru** (1923–) into the *dan* profession.

FURTHER READING

Mackerras, Colin. *The Rise of the Peking Opera, Social Aspects of the Theatre in Manchu China*; Scott, A. C. *Actors Are Madmen: Notebook of a Theatregoer in China*; Shen, Grant Guangren. *Elite Theatre in Ming China, 1368–1644*; Wichmann, Elizabeth. *Listening to Theatre: The Aural Dimension of Beijing Opera*.

Colin Mackerras, Elizabeth Wichmann-Walczak, and Catherine Swatek

Early Modern Actors. The earliest modern Chinese actors were involved in the "civilized drama" (*wenming xi*) genre (see Playwrights and Playwriting). The best emerged either from student dramatic activities in Shanghai, among them Wang Youyou (1888–1937), or, as exemplified by Ren Tianzhi, **Ouyang Yuqian**, and Lu Jingruo (1885–1915), were influenced by **Japan**'s *shinpa*. Although modern, *wenming xi* maintained elements of traditional *xiqu*, including female impersonation, role types, and improvisation using scenarios (*mubiao*).

In the 1920s and 1930s, the rise of the **director**, formalization of rehearsals, and emergence of professional theatre companies prepared some outstanding actors, including Tang Ruoqing (1918–1983), **Shu Xiuwen**, Zhao Dan (1915–1980), Lan Ma (1915–1976), **Shi Hui**, and Jin Shan (1911–1982). Starting in the late 1930s, the Stanislavski system gradually exerted its influence; after 1949, it became the official production and training method under the communists. Since the mid-1950s, most actors have graduated from the two drama academies in Beijing and Shanghai, established with the help of USSR experts. Some theatres trained actors themselves.

Many of the best-known actors since the 1950s have come from the Beijing People's Art Theatre (Beijing Renmin Yishu Juyuan); they include **Yu Shizhi**, Zhu Lin (1923–), Ying Ruocheng (1929–2003), and Lin Liankun (1931–). First achieving national recognition through **Jiao Juyin**'s productions in the 1950s, they later starred in such post-Mao productions as **Lao She**'s *The Teahouse* (Chaguan, 1979), *Death of a Salesman* (1983), *The Gin Game* (1985), and *Uncle Doggie's Nirvana* (Gouer Ye niepan, 1986). Recent productions, like *Hamlet* (1989) and *The Orphan of Zhao* (Zhaoshi guer, 2003), have created a younger generation of stars represented by Pu Cunxin (1951–).

Among Shanghai actors, Jiao Huang (1936–) is famous for roles in *The Younger Generation* (Nianqing de yidai, 1962), *Antony and Cleopatra* (1984), and *Under the Red Banner* (Zhenghongqi xia, 2000). Xi Meijuan (1955–) is known for her versatile performances in *China Dream* (Zhongguo meng, 1987) and *The Woman Who Is Left Behind* (Liushou nüshi, 1991).

Some excellent actors are from regional theatres. Li Moran (1927–), of Liaoning, became president of the All-China Dramatists Association in 1998; Cao Jingyang (1933–2001), from Xi'an, was known for portraying General Zhang Xueliang in *Xi'an Incident* (Xi'an shibian, 1979); Hu Qingshu (1933–2002), from Wuhan, was equally at home as the eunuch Li Lianying in *Story of the Manchu Court* (Qinggong wai shi, 1980), Falstaff in *Merry Wives of Windsor* (1986), and *King Lear* (1994).

Compared to **Western** actors, the models for "spoken drama" (*huaju*) acting, Chinese actors are less naturalistic but more expressive. One important reason is the large size of Chinese theatres, which usually contain over a thousand seats. Theatrical exaggeration has been considerably modified since the late 1980s, when intimate black box theatres were introduced; also, more actors are now involved in television and film.

Actors are well respected, and some have become national idols, though usually as a result of their film and television roles, their major source of income. Except for a few stars, they are employed by theatre companies, which collect a sum or fee if they work outside. As more and more actors freelance, some have called for establishing unions for better professional regulation and protection.

FURTHER READING

Riley, Jo. *Chinese Theatre and the Actor in Performance*; Scott, A. C. *Actors Are Madmen: Notebook of a Theatregoer in China*; Wichmann, Elizabeth. *Listening to Theatre: The Aural Dimension of Beijing Opera*.

Siyuan Liu

Actors and Acting: India

French **director** Ariane Mnouchkine has said, Asians "don't have Chekhov, but they have actors. They invented actors. They discovered the art of acting." *Natya* is **Sanskrit** for acting (or drama), the actor is *nata* (actresses are *nati*), and drama is *nataka*. Each word stems from the same etymological root, *nat*, meaning acting, clearly suggesting **Indian** theatre's actor-centeredness.

The **Natyashastra** *on Acting.* Though Indian theatre's origins are obscure, we know that Bharata Muni's *Treatise on Drama* (Natyashastra; see Theory), the ancient theatre manual, suggests a very early period for theatre's inception and a long process of polishing until a highly codified structure was developed. *Rig Veda* hymns (ca. 3000 BC) mentioning actors are generally regarded as the earliest Indian references to performers. Panini, the fifth century BC grammarian, speaks about *Natasutra*, an acting manual, and the *Ramayana* mentions an actress. However, the oldest surviving form, claiming to date back two thousand years, is **kutiyattam**, whose repertory consists of Sanskrit dramas.

Despite later acting manuals, the *Natyashastra* remains the springboard of any serious discussion of classical acting, particularly because of its emphasis on the aesthetic experience called *rasa* (literally, "flavor"). Thirty chapters describe how *rasa* can be attained though the synchronization of all production elements, from acting to architecture. Bharata identifies eight basic *rasa* (in the sense of "sentiments") that an actor should employ; a ninth was added by Abhinavagupta (ca. 975–1025).

Needless to say, however, there are no living models to help us understand the *Natyashastra*'s explanations; the closest thing available is *kutiyattam*. *Kutiyattam* acting stands out because of the importance given to eye expression. Master teachers say that effective acting requires "breathing through the eyes," though no methodology is known today to make this happen. *Kutiyattam* **training** is strenuous and requires many years. Ammannoor Madhava Chakyar (1917–), known for his elaborate death scenes, is the most senior *kutiyattam* actor still actively teaching.

Abhinaya is the Sanskrit term for acting, meaning, "to lead along," suggesting the importance the Indian theatre brings to the actor and physical action. The *Natyashastra* maintains that acting consists of four elements: *angika,* physical actions; *vachika,* verbal expression; *aharya,* **properties**, **costumes**, and **makeup**; and *satvika,* emotional expression. There are also two types of stylistic representation: *lokadharmi,* widely interpreted as realistic, and *natya*, thought to suggest theatrical, though Bharata's meanings remain uncertain. The distinction between realism and stylization (as understood today) cannot readily be identified in the *Natyashastra*.

There are nine (eight in the *Natyashastra* and a ninth added later) basic emotions (*bhava*) widely practiced by traditional actors and dancers, though the intensity of their expressions differs from one form to another. Acting is described in great detail, including movements of the eyes, eyebrows, eyeballs, eyelids, and so on. Actors still follow these with necessary variations and regional adaptations. Training is meticulous and time-consuming.

Acting is communicated largely through gestural language (*mudra*) employing the hands and fingers, although *mudra* vary according to the forms using them. *Kutiyattam*'s gesture language, for example, is highly codified and follows strictly every aspect of the rules; even **kathakali** does not follow so high a degree of codification. This emphasis on gesture is not common to all traditional forms, being minimal, for instance, in **tamasha** and **nautanki**.

Gender Transformation. It is difficult to distance **dance** and **music** from traditional theatre (though *kutiyattam* does not contain dance in a conventional sense); **yakshagana** and **kuchipudi**, South India's two other major classical forms, are no exceptions. Unlike *kutiyattam*, both *yakshagana* and *kuchipudi* did not traditionally employ **women**; today, *kuchipudi* is performed by both sexes. This gender restriction is also true for most traditional theatres, such as *kathakali*, **ramlila**, **ankiya nat**, **chhau**, and *nautanki*. *Tamasha*, however, does employ actresses. Female impersonation is often on a very high level of artistry, although sometimes exploited for humorous or even vulgar effect. **Bal Gandharva** and **Sundari** were famous female impersonators.

Many forms depict the attractiveness of the female body and a woman's actions in beautifying herself, probably because actors in female costume have to identify themselves with the womanhood they represent by detailed physical behavior. Interestingly, a reversal of this otherness is found in *kutiyattam* actresses' attempts to present male characters through the "play of multiple transcendences" (*pakarnnattam*), a technique designed to impersonate maleness.

Dance in Acting. Traditional theatre is further enriched by dance forms such as **bharata natyam**, *odissi*, *kathak*, and *manipuri*, and ritual or **folk theatre**, such as **teyyam**, as well as street forms such as **terukkuttu**. Though most of these forms give importance to *nritta* ("pure dance") and *nritya* ("expressive dance"), every repertoire has a special piece that focuses on *natya* ("acting"). Dancers of the popular forms begin their training very young, becoming part of the traditional chain of "teacher-student relationships" (*guru-sishya-parampara*). Today, this tradition has been institutionalized mainly to preserve the quality of training.

Kathakali actors like Kalamandalam Gopi (1937–), *teyyam* performers like Kannan Peruvannan, *bharata natyam* dancers like Padma Subrahmanyam, and *kuchipudi* master teacher Vempatti Chinnasatyam, and so on, are considered celebrities.

FURTHER READING

Ambrose, Kay. *Classical Dances and Costumes of India*; Richmond, Farley, Darius L. Swann, and Phillip B. Zarrilli, eds. *Indian Theatre: Traditions of Performance*.

Arya Madhavan

The Modern Actor's Profession. Acting has a similarly equivocal status in India as elsewhere; like other South Asian models, its intensely physical practice has been the envy of many twentieth-century **Western** directors and actor-trainers, from Artaud to Mnouchkine. But as a profession it scarcely exists in terms of theatre. To the general public, the word "actor" refers mainly to film or television actors. There are only a handful of training establishments; dedication is demanded but remuneration is scant; and—apart from some popular touring forms (*jatra*, *yakshagana*, *tamasha*)—there are virtually no professional acting troupes. Except in commercial theatre, actors have no formal contract system, nor do they have the opportunity to play many different roles on a continuing basis, thereby establishing a reputation.

Respectable middle-class, upwardly mobile parents discourage their sons, let alone their daughters, from acting unless they are lucky enough to get into New Delhi's National School of Drama, from whence they can expect to have a chance of making it to Bollywood. Very few theatre actors are known widely unless they have appeared in movies, like Naseeruddin Shah (1950–), who regularly returns to the theatre. On the other hand, movie stars receive immense publicity and even sometimes, like "MGR" (M. G. Ramachandran [1917?–]) or Jayaram Jayalalitha (1948–), adapt their iconic status to the **political** stage, where they have achieved high public office. The number of outstanding actors known and respected nationally is very small: it includes Bengal's **Shombhu Mitra**, **Tripti Mitra**, and **Utpal Dutt**; Maharashtra's Mohan Agashe (1947–), Bhakthi Barve-Inamdar (1945–2001), **P. L. Deshpande**, **Vijaya Mehta**, **Shreeram Lagoo**, and Sulabha Deshpande (1937–); Hindi actors **Prithviraj Kapoor**, Naseeruddin Shah, Manohar Singh (1942–2002), and **Usha Ganguli**; and Kannada actor B. Jayamma (1915–1988), among others.

Lord Shiva, the icon of transformation, is frequently represented as Nataraj, lord of the dance. The elephant-headed deity Ganesh, the materialization of hybridity, is the patron of performers. Acting is thus accredited, at least in the divine scheme, as an articulation of important psycho-physiological capacities, relevant not least in the face of the demands of a postcolonial, postmodern, pluralized society. The history and scope of Indian acting demonstrate the symbolic and pragmatic senses in which it marks a still otherwise undervalued resource.

Eclectic Approaches to Modern Acting. As previously noted, Indian acting's roots lie in the *Natyashastra*, to which all acting teachers and many directors still refer. To an extent, it formalizes and crystallizes practices found in much folk performance, as, for example, **Habib Tanvir**'s New (Naya) Theatre. Both folk forms and more "realistic" work also show the influence of the ubiquitous film industry, especially a tendency to the gestural and melodramatic; but the demands of the wide variety of theatre writing lead in the best cases to a subtle and flexible eclecticism, ranging from the inventive physicality, ingenious verbal improvisation, and dynamic sense of rhythm of much folk work, to the close character work of contemporary urban/bourgeois theatre.

Stylized acting requiring attention to musical verse, dance, and percussive movement became prominent in the work of directors like **Kavalam Narayana Panikkar** and **B. V. Karanth**, who insisted that their actors have a music-based training. In Manipur, directors **Ratan Thiyam** and **Heisnam Kanhailal** demanded that their actors receive physical training based on local martial arts and performative traditions, while Habib Tanvir worked with Chhattisgarh folk performers to extract their traditions for use in a new performance idiom.

The Actress in Indian Theatre. Women were not allowed to act in most forms of traditional theatre, although this was not universal. Many, though not all, folk forms use only males, which in many cases means that women are represented in heavily stereotyped fashion. This has impeded the ability of women to perform on stage. Still, some notable actresses have appeared, often performing solo; they include Gul Bardhan (1928–), B. Jayashree (1950–), Usha Ganguli, and Mallika Sarabhai (1951–). Women's presence and influence are increasing, including as **playwrights** and directors, albeit still fairly slowly. The longstanding existence of the *hijira*, a subcaste of transvestite ("eunuch") performers—acknowledged but largely marginalized—to some extent underlines the ambiguous status and function of acting in terms of gender as well as social roles; plays by writers like **Mahesh Dattani** currently offer more scope for overt encounters with varieties of sexuality.

Theatre and Anthropology. Indian acting has been analyzed regarding the link between theatre and anthropology by such Western writers as Richard Schechner and Eugenio Barba, who focus on the frequently unknown and untrained status of performers in communal or ritual events (especially the Varanasi *ramlila*), and explore aspects of the transformative process they undergo and incarnate. Barba (who takes Orissi dance, rather than theatre, as his main example) especially is interested in the scenic "bios" or dynamic presence they engender. Thus Western investigation has largely ignored actors' verbal or textual ability, although it has helped to explore some important aspects of the ability of performance to transform bodies and engage with the multiplicity of potential "selves" that may be put in play. This somewhat "exoticist" view masks to some extent the fact that India possesses actors with a wide range of skills, some of them now familiar to global audiences because of their TV or film work.

Ralph Yarrow (with B. Ananthakrishnan)

Actors and Acting: Indonesia

Komedi stambul and various related subsequent genres of "Malay opera" (see *Bangsawan*) created a new acting profession in urban **Indonesia** at the beginning of the twentieth century. These professional performers, like their counterparts in **Western** music hall and vaudeville, used eclectic performance skills, from a variety of **dance** styles to singing to acting in short skits.

Professional theatre declined from the 1930s to the early 1950s, harassed by **censors** suspicious of its lack of scripts and ultimately deprived of its market by film and television. Nationalist theatre, in contrast, was an amateur literary movement that held itself aloof from the commercial theatre, and apparently did little to promote acting prior to the 1940s. Plays were most likely "declaimed" in the 1920s and 1930s in the style of poetry performance. Under the **Japanese** occupation in the 1940s, the first nationalist theatre troupes were formed (often in connection with student "study groups"), and acting began to emerge as an element of the genre. One of the most significant troupes was the Illusionist's Theater (Sandiwara Penggemar Maya, 1944.) Among its founders were Usmar Ismail (1921–1971) and Djadoeg Djajakusuma (1918–1987), who, along with Asrul Sani (1927–2004), would found Indonesia's National Academy of Theatre (ATNI) in 1955.

The old "star system" was not an attractive model for Indonesian actors in the 1950s. Just as the literary drama of nineteenth-century Europe inspired Stanislavski's analytic approach to acting, so did Indonesia's literary nationalist theatre inspire the development of a modern acting pedagogy. Asrul Sani, who had studied theatre in Amsterdam and the United States, provided a theoretical framework for the postcolonial theatre by translating the classic texts of realistic (and later "Method") acting by Boleslavsky and Stanislavski and a wide selection of plays from the Western canon. Many leading Indonesian actors attended ATNI, including Wahyu Sihombing (1940–1989), Soekarno M. Noor (1931–), and Steve Lim (1937–2001), who, as Teguh Karya, would become one of Indonesia's leading **directors** and advocates of realism. Meanwhile, "study groups" and troupes, such as Bandung Theatre Study Club (Studiklub Teater Bandung) and the literature faculty of Gajah Mada University in Yogyakarta, began offering acting courses inspired by ATNI's model. Most of Indonesia's leading actors were affiliated with such groups in the 1950s and 1960s. In 1968, ATNI was replaced by the new Jakarta Arts Institute (IKJ).

Since 1968, acting has been taught in academic institutions such as IKJ and the Indonesian Institute of the Arts in Bandung. However, most training has taken place within the troupes and in the compounds of leading artists such as **Rendra**, **Putu Wijaya**, **Arifin C. Noer**, Teguh Karya, and Suyatna Anirun (1936–2002). Rendra, Wijaya, and others have influenced acting styles by introducing improvisational ensemble techniques and incorporating performance elements from Indonesian and other global traditions. Acting teachers have moved beyond the Method, and now employ approaches drawn from the work of Grotowski, Brecht, and such contemporary vocabularies as corporeal mime and *butô*.

Evan Winet

Actors and Acting: Japan

Actor-Centered Theatre. **Japanese** theatre has always been actor-centered; even the theatre's ancient foundational myth, described in the *Records of Ancient Matters* (Kojiki, 712), tells how goddess Ame no Uzume performed an erotic dance on an overturned tub to lure the sun goddess, Amaterasu, out of the cave in which she was hiding. She succeeded when the attending gods laughed so loud Amaterasu could not resist coming out to see what was going on.

Japanese traditional actors have long been specialists in song (or chant) and, especially, **dance**. *Nô*, *kyôgen*, and *kabuki* actors express character through a series of codified movements, gestures, and **stage** business (*kata*). In each form, acting is performed by men belonging to acting families, many of which are hundreds of years old, some dating to the fourteenth century. In each, it is very difficult for actors not born or adopted into an acting family to become successful.

Female Performers. Although **women** made contributions to traditional theatre, most significantly to early *kabuki*, through most of history women were banned from the stage, at least in public performances. They began to reappear in the late nineteenth century, when a small number of *kabuki* actresses performed, but—despite several later attempts (notably the Ichikawa Girls' Kabuki [Ichikawa Shôjô Kabuki] of the

1940s and 1950s)—the idea never caught on. Since World War II, women have performed *nô* and *kyôgen* as well, both as amateurs and professionals, but these forms continue to be dominated and defined by men.

Nô *Actors*. *Nô*'s forerunners emerged in the tenth century, but its flowering happened in the fourteenth, when it was called "monkey music" (*sarugaku*). **Kan'ami Kiyotsugu** combined a popular song of the time (*kuse*) with dance (*mai*) and incorporated this combination into a Buddhist-tinged theatrical narrative that became *nô*. Kan'ami is credited with incorporating imitation and portrayal of character (*monomane*; see Theory) into *nô*. His son, **Zeami Motokiyo**, advanced the form by writing *nô* plays and treatises with advice for actors. Zeami described the actor's art through the metaphor of a flower (*hana*) and, in terms both practical and metaphysical, discussed the path to artistic accomplishment. He advised the actor to "move seven if the heart feels ten," a way of showing restraint and quality of expression in acting. Mysterious beauty (*yûgen*) experienced by the actor and the audience was a trait strived for in performance.

Three different types of actors perform in *nô*. The protagonist (*shite*; see Role Types) often wears a **mask**. The *shite* frequently plays a character whose true identity (typically a spirit of some sort) is not revealed until the play's second half; this revelation usually includes a change of **costume** and mask. The supporting character's (*waki*) primary job is generally to draw out the *shite* by asking questions (*mondo*) that elicit the *shite*'s true identity and purpose. The *ai-kyôgen* is an actor from the *kyôgen* genre who often appears during a pause in the action to recapitulate the story in plain language. Children's roles (*kokata*) are played by future *shite*, and companion (*tsure*) roles are acted by either *shite* or *waki*. A chorus (*jiutai*) of six to eight *shite* actors sits in two rows at stage left, chanting verse describing the action and expressing the *shite*'s thoughts.

Shite actors speak in prose and also chant verse in either strong chant (*tsuyogin*) or melodic song (*yowagin*). The *waki* does not chant, but speaks in heightened prose (*kotoba*). Actors use a basic walking movement (*hakobi*) involving gliding on the heels and gently releasing the toes in a slight upward movement after each step. The actor's torso remains firmly aligned with the abdomen, much of the movement coming from the rhythmic stepping as well as from arm and hand movements during dance sections. When no mask is worn, the actor's face is mask-like, forcing the audience to experience meaning through movement, **music**, and words. Because acting is a family art, movement and voice are normally taught by father (or another important relative) to son.

There are five schools (*ryû*) of *shite* acting: Kanze, Hôshô, Konparu, Kongô, and Kita. There also are schools of *waki*, just as there are for each musical instrument. Interestingly, all performers, including the musicians, are considered "actors" (*yakusha*), although those who play characters are also known as "dance persons" (*maikata*), or by the nature of the role (*shite* or *waki*) they specialize in. (*Nô* actors never cross the lines from their *shite* or *waki* specialties; a *shite* plays only *shite* and a *waki* only *waki* roles. The same goes for any crossover between *nô* and *kyôgen* acting.) Actors in other traditional genres also are called *yakusha*, although the term *haiyû* came into fashion for *kabuki* actors in the late nineteenth century because it had a cachet of greater respectability.

Performers of early *nô* were itinerant, although belonging to **theatre companies** affiliated with important temples and shrines. In the seventeenth century, *nô* actors were given the formal patronage of the shogunate and important lords, and their art came to be considered the "ceremonial music" (*shikigaku*) of the samurai class. The actors were not actually promoted to samurai status but were granted many privileges, including comfortable stipends. After the Meiji Restoration (1868) and the abolition of the shogunate and its attendant feudalism, these privileges vanished. With their chief patrons gone and an anti-shogunate atmosphere with which to contend, many turned to other professions to survive. By about 1870, however, **Umewaka Minoru** and **Hôshô Kurô** began holding public performances and charging admission. They and **Sakurama Banma** became the three leading stars of the Meiji period (1868–1912). Soon, encouraged by events such as ex–United States president Ulysses S. Grant praising a performance he witnessed in 1878, *nô* experienced a resurgence.

During the twentieth century, many *nô* actors gained fame for their artistry. Perhaps the greatest postwar actor was **Kanze Hisao**, who represented the new breed, many of whom studied abroad and expanded their artistry by appearing not only in **experimental** *nô* productions but in **Western** classics as well.

Kyôgen *Actors*. *Kyôgen*, like *nô*, had earlier antecedents but took form in the fourteenth century. Traditionally, it is performed with *nô* on the same programs, although nowadays it is just as likely to be seen on all-*kyôgen* programs. Actors concentrate on breathing, pacing, and delivery of the dialogue (*serifu*) and singing (*kouta*); while examples are limited, dance is also part of the actor's arsenal. Although masks are sometimes worn, facial expression—within convention-bound limits—is important, as are flexibility and agility. As in *nô*, actors perform with minimal **properties** and with costumes that easily identify types, such as the difference between servants and masters. Roles are classified as *shite*, *ado*, and *koado*, in descending hierarchical order, but the distinctions are far looser than between *shite* and *waki* in most *nô*, and the *shite* is just as likely to be a secondary as a principal character. *Kyôgen* actors do not specialize in specific types, as casting is decided on the actor's skill level.

Unlike *nô*, which was tied to a strong textual tradition, actors improvised until the seventeenth century when **Ôkura Tora'akira** compiled a collection of 203 texts. He also wrote *Young Leaves* (Waranbe gusa, 1660), a valuable treatise on *kyôgen* acting.

Kyôgen plays are classed according to their level of difficulty; the most difficult are performed as a rite of passage. Children begin by playing small roles (*konarai*), such as a monkey. As an actor grows in accomplishment he demonstrates his skills in more challenging performances. There are now two main schools of *kyôgen* acting, that of the Nomura family, which belongs to the **Izumi school**, and that of the Shigeyama family, belonging to the **Ôkura school**.

Kabuki *Acting*. Unlike *nô* and *kyôgen*, which only on special occasions were seen by the general public, *kabuki* arose as a diversion for the commoner/townsman class. *Kabuki*'s first performances were created by a woman, **Izumo no Okuni**, who began a tradition of cross-dressing, playing a swaggering samurai visiting the brothel quarters. Soon, groups of women were imitating Okuni, adding dances accompanied by the three-stringed, banjo-like *shamisen*, birthing a tradition of "prostitutes'" (*yûjo*) *kabuki*. Early *kabuki* was preoccupied with showing off the performers' attractiveness, not their artistry. This led to social disorder, causing actresses to be banned in 1629; for the same reasons, the homosexual boys who succeeded them were banned in 1652.

Thereafter, *kabuki* survived by offering performances featuring older actors who shaved off their forelocks (a sign of sex appeal) and developing a more sensually restrained and artistically sophisticated approach under government regulations. Plots became more complex, important acting methods developed, and a detailed system of types evolved.

Kabuki had begun with women playing men. Over the years, both sexes performed in cross-dressed roles, but the focus was mainly on physical appeal. With the new stress on intensifying the dramatic quality of both writing and performance, the art of playing women deepened, and roles for women became increasingly three-dimensional. The actors, forced by law to register as players of either male (*tachiyaku*) or female roles (*onnagata*), began to specialize at one or the other, leading to what became one of the world's most sophisticated forms of female impersonation.

Genroku-period (1688–1704) star **Yoshizawa Ayame** I was perhaps the greatest early *onnagata*. His classic statements on acting were recorded in the "Words of Ayame" (*Ayame gusa*), where he called for the *onnagata* to live as a woman offstage. Although married and a father, he followed his own dictates, refusing to eat foods he considered unfeminine or to speak unfeminine words, and using the women's facilities in public baths.

By Genroku, *kabuki* had created two important regional acting styles. In the samurai-dominated young city of Edo (Tokyo), audiences were drawn to the bombastic "rough style" (*aragoto*) approach developed by **Ichikawa Danjûrô** I (1660–) and his son, Danjûrô II (1689–1758), and probably inspired by statues of powerful Buddhist gods, such as Fudô, with his cross-eyed stare. Highly formalized *aragoto* conventions, such as dramatic, rhythmically timed poses (*mie*) and bounding, theatrical exits (*roppô*) were established for early versions of still popular plays, such as *Narukami* (1684) and *Wait a Moment!* (Shibaraku, 1696). Actors playing arrogant young *aragoto* samurai (both heroes and villains, although the style began with heroes) used exaggerated gestures and movements, dynamic vocal inflections, flamboyant costumes and wigs, and a variety of bold **makeup** styles called *kumadori* in which the face's musculature was highlighted in various colors, usually against a white background. *Kabuki* is the only one of the three traditional acting arts to use makeup.

Mie and *roppô* became highlights and developed numerous variations. For example, during the "around the pillar pose" (*hashira maki no mie*), the actor throws one leg around a pillar, poses with one arm in the air and the other around the pillar, rotates his head before bringing it to a stop, and crosses one eye (*nirami*). In the "stone throwing pose" (*ishinage no mie*), the actor poses with one knee on the ground and a hand raised as if in the act of throwing something. In *Wait a Moment!*, the fantastical hero, Gongorô, wearing one of world theatre's most overstated costumes, extends his left hand and holds a huge sword in his right as he sashays down the runway (*hanamichi*) in a "one-handed bounding exit" (*katate roppô*). At the end of *Yoshitsune and the Thousand Cherry Trees* (Yoshitsune senbon zakura, 1748), the fox character exits using the "fox bounding exit" (*kitsune roppô*), holding his hands like paws and moving in a manner suggesting a fox.

The chief *aragoto* family remains the Ichikawa Danjûrô line. It began the "family art" (*ie no gei*) practice of actors creating methods associated with their line and usually associated with specific plays in which such specialties are highlighted. The play collection epitomizing Danjûrô *aragoto* is "Kabuki's Eighteen Favorites" (*kabuki jûhachiban*).

In the Kamigata (Kyoto/Osaka) region of western Japan, where business and traditional culture dominated, audiences enjoyed "domestic dramas" (*sewa mono*) in which the plot often depicts a merchant's young son who spends his family's (or business's) money in pursuit of his prostitute mistress. **Sakata Tôjûrô** I and Yamashita Hanzaemon I (ca. 1650–1717) specialized in leading male roles acted in what came to be called the "gentle style" (*wagoto*), in contrast to Edo's *aragoto*. Tôjûrô I's *wagoto* depicted a petulant, scorned young lover, whose behavior was almost feminine in its delicacy, but which, in contrast to *aragoto*, was considered realistic.

Wagoto characters may be former samurai who are forced by circumstances to abandon the samurai world and take on the persona of a young townsman as a ploy to help them recover some precious heirloom. This is called "disguise" (*yatsushi*). Actors of handsome young lovers, not always acted as *wagoto* characters, are *nimaime* (literally, "second flat thing") because their names were printed on the second advertising billboard (*kanban*) out front. Fans flocked to see their "lovemaking scenes" (*nureba*).

During the mid-eighteenth century, as plays from the **puppet theatre** (*ningyô jôruri* or *bunraku*) were adapted by *kabuki*, new puppet-based techniques appeared. Among them were "riding the strings" (*ito ni nori*), that is, performing one's lines in rhythm with the *shamisen*'s accompaniment, and "puppet acting" (*ningyô buri*), by which the star's movements appeared to be under the control of actors dressed like black-clad (and hooded) puppeteers.

Acting techniques requiring special effects or acrobatics (*keren*) include flying through the air (*chûnori*) and quick costume changes (*hayagawari*), which became especially popular in the nineteenth century, both in "ghost plays" (*kaidan mono*) and "transformation pieces" (*henge mono*), dances in which an actor played multiple roles. Although many such techniques gradually vanished, in the late twentieth century **Ichikawa Ennosuke** III revived them, returning them to popularity.

Kabuki actors also are expert at choreographed combat (*tachimawari*), in which the hero fights off any number of attackers, using a wide assortment of codified techniques, and in which various acrobatics are performed, most notably somersaults (*tonbo*) of one sort or the other. Musical accompaniment and wooden clappers (*tsuke*) punctuate the movements.

In the Meiji era (1868–1912), attempts to reform *kabuki* included Danjûrô IX's productions of "living history plays" (*katsureki geki*), which placed an emphasis on psychologically realistic "gut acting" (*haragei*), while eliminating traditions like the *mie*. Archaeological accuracy was more important than theatrical effect. Danjûrô's rival, **Onoe Kikugorô** V, aimed to create a genre more in tune with the contemporary world. These "cropped hair plays" (*zangiri mono*) featured things like Western haircuts, bicycles, pocket watches, and hot air balloons. Although these new techniques were attempts to keep up with the times, both actors eventually returned to their traditional styles.

During Genroku, a major difference between the styles of Edo and Kamigata was that, in the former, actors were expected to learn and repeat *kata* as they learned them from their fathers; in Kamigata, actors were supposed to develop their own styles. By Meiji, when *kabuki*'s future was in question, *kata* began to be formalized as a preservative measure, and one was judged in both Edo and Kamigata by whether he could duplicate his father's style. An actor, then, is expected to perform his family's art, and once he has mastered it, will seek to prove himself by adding his own interpretative touches, but always within the framework of tradition.

Actors are judged by their voice, movement, and dance skills, so **training** begins early. They debut in a role specifically designed for children between two and six.

Young actors will take singing lessons in *kabuki*'s musical styles, such as *nagauta* and *takemoto*, although *kabuki* actors rarely actually sing during a performance. Most take dance lessons throughout their careers and receive a professional dance name.

Beginning in Genroku, actors were ranked according to a highly organized system, and annual **critical** appraisals (*yakusha hyôbanki*) were published in Edo, Kyoto, and Osaka. Audiences were never loath to hide their opinions, and would often shout during highlight moments laudatory comments such as "Exactly like your father" or "I've been waiting for this," as well as insults such as "radish" (*daikon*).

Early actors were dubbed "riverbed beggars" (*kawara kojiki*) and had a social status as low as prostitutes, yet their popularity among the townsmen elevated them to celebrities. Top stars earned the equivalent of millions of dollars, often bankrupting their managements and living lives of luxury, despite sumptuary laws designed to restrain such expenditures (occasionally actors were jailed or even banished from their hometowns). Social disdain for actors began to change after *kabuki* gave its first command performance for the emperor's family, in 1887.

Nô, *kyôgen*, and *kabuki* actors all are likely to change their names during their career to mark their development. *Kabuki* makes the most of such name changes, presenting ritualized, public name-taking ceremonies (*shûmei hiro*) on stage during regular programs. The announcement of the new name—usually that of one's father or significant relative—has two basic methods. It may occur as a separate, formal ceremony, with the actor and his company in traditional clothes and wigs, or the action of a play may be stopped so that the cast can introduce the name-changing or new actor (as in a child's debut) before returning to the dramatic action. These ceremonies, especially when the name is a venerable one, are excellent public relations stunts considered landmark events by fans.

Today, top *kabuki* actors are widely recognized and star on television, stage, and screen. Ichikawa Danjûrô XII, **Kataoka Nizaemon** XV**,** and **Nakamura Kanzaburô** XVIII are among the top male-role actors of the day, while **Bandô Tamasaburô** V and Nakamura Shikan VII (1928–) are among the leading *onnagata*. Some, like Sakata Tôjûrô IV and Ichikawa Ennosuke III, are famous for their versatility in playing both males and females, old and young, heroes and villains.

In recent years, a generation of young actors in *nô*, *kyôgen*, and *kabuki* has attracted a new, more youthful audience. For example, there is Toppa!, a group of Shigeyama *kyôgen* actors performing classic and new *kyôgen* plays to sold-out houses. Young Stars' Kabuki (Hanagata Kabuki) is a special January *kabuki* performance in Asakusa, Tokyo, that showcases rising young stars in difficult classic roles.

FURTHER READING

Kominz, Laurence R. *The Stars Who Created Kabuki: Their Lives, Loves and Legacy;* Komparu, Kunio. *The Noh Theatre: Principles and Perspectives;* Leiter, Samuel L. *New Kabuki Encyclopedia: A Revised Adaptation of Kubuki Jiten.*

Holly A. Blumner

Modern Acting and Westernization. Modern styles are strongly influenced by company training and reflect shifting **political**, artistic, and social climates. Despite increasing emphasis on **playwriting** and **directing**, actor-driven theatre dominated through the late 1960s. Compared to **Western** psychological realism, emotion is relatively externalized. Meiji-era desires to "equal" the major powers tied Western-style acting (despite little first-hand knowledge) to new artistic and/or national agendas. *Kabuki* was considered vulgar, *nô* feudal. The former began to face the question of allowing women in its ranks.

As noted, Danjûrô IX and the Theatre Reform Society promulgated "living history plays" to modernize *kabuki,* advocating quieter, psychological acting, historically accurate properties and costumes, and decreased music, dance, and "vulgarity." In contrast, **Tsubouchi Shôyô**'s Literary Arts Society (Bungei Kyôkai) featured male and female amateurs attempting to grasp Western ways by studying Shakespeare, Ibsen, and Chekhov. Performances by talented professional actresses like **Matsui Sumako** fueled debates about females on stage. The all-female **Takarazuka**, founded in 1913, emphasized another approach: acting, dancing, and singing lessons would create "good wives, wise mothers" to reinforce Confucian-influenced notions of femininity.

In 1917, actor **Sawada Shôjirô**, regarding *shingeki* acting as ignoring popular taste, founded *shinkokugeki,* emphasizing *kabuki*-like, historical scripts featuring realistic (not stylized) swordfights. After Sawada's death, Shimada Shôgo (1905–2004), with elegant, calm, emotional acting, and Tatsumi Ryûtarô (1905–1989), with a bold, masculine style, took over, maintaining Sawada's versatility.

Shinpa *and* Shingeki. Acting styles in these genres sometimes converge. **Kawakami Otojirô** and his wife, **Kawakami Sadayakko**'s, new *shinpa* genre—born in the 1890s—encouraged colonialist/imperialistic notions domestically, and Orientalist fantasies abroad. Although Japanese intellectuals derided the form, European critics praised Sadayakko's emotionally charged death scenes, comparing her to Sarah Bernhardt. Sadayakko founded the Imperial Actress School in 1908, emphasizing *kabuki*-style "actress plays" (*joyû geki*) filled with song, dance, and spectacle. Tokyo's new Imperial Theatre (Teikoku Gekijô, 1911) featured comedienne Mori Ritsuko (1890–1961), tragedienne Hatsuse Namiko (1888–1951), farceuse Satô Chiyako (1897–1968), and the versatile Murata Kakuko (1893–1969). These actresses, though ridiculed as glorified geisha, were considered "national exemplars" by association with the Imperial Theatre.

Shinpa often emphasized sentiment, with actresses and "female impersonators" (*onnagata*) performing together. Hanayagi Shôtarô (1894–1965), *shinpa*'s last great *onnagata,* also played male roles. Praised for passionate psychological realism, he was named a Living National Treasure (1960). Famed as Otsuta in **Izumi Kyôka**'s *A Woman's Pedigree* (Onna keizu, 1908), he trained **Mizutani Yaeko**, his frequent costar. A *shingeki* child star, Mizutani, whose acting resembled an *onnagata*'s, eventually played Nora in *A Doll's House.* Her professional itinerary (*shingeki* to *shinpa*) troubles the concept of linear progression (*kabuki-shinpa-shingeki*). After World War II, *shinpa-shingeki* and *shinpa-kabuki* collaborations gained popularity. Izumi's *The Castle Tower* (Tenshu monogatari, 1951), codirected by *shingeki* star **Senda Koreya** and his brother Itô Michio (1893–1961), with sets by another brother, Itô Kisaku (1899–1967), starred Hanayagi as the male lead and Mizutani as the female. *Kabuki onnagata* Bandô Tamasaburô V often performs *shinpa.* Since the 1990s, **experimental** theatre companies, including Ku Na'uka and Hanagumi Shibai, have interpreted *shinpa,* especially plays by Izumi.

Nevertheless, *shingeki* dominated prewar and postwar theatre. In the 1920s, actors at **Osanai Kaoru**'s Tsukiji Little Theatre (Tsukiji Shôgekijô) analyzed character and situation using Stanislavskian realism and Piscatorian expressionism, often highlighting leftist social commentary. **Yamamoto Yasue**, praised for beautiful declamation, left the Imperial Actress School in 1924 for the Tsukiji; in 1929, she followed **Hijikata Yoshi** to the New Tsukiji Troupe (Shin Tsukiji Gekidan). After the war, she established the Grape Society (Budô no Kai) with **Kinoshita Junji**; acting exclusively in Kinoshita's plays, she performed her signature role, Tsu in Kinoshita's *Twilight Crane* (Yûzuru), 1,037 times.

Tomoda Kyôsuke (1899–1937) developed his realistic, detailed acting style at the Tsukiji. After Osanai's death, he and his wife, Tamura Akiko (1905–1983), established the Tsukiji Theatre (Tsukiji-za). The Tsukiji Theatre advocated pure art, opposing leftist ideology. Tamura had trained with Senda Koreya, Yamamoto Yasue, and Maruyama Sadao (1901–1945) at the Tsukiji Little Theatre. Known for intelligent portrayals, especially of mothers, Tamura helped found the Literary Theatre (Bungaku-za), winning many awards, including one for *Hedda Gabler* (1950).

Sugimura Haruko followed Tomoda and Tamura from the Tsukiji Little Theatre to the Tsukiji Theatre. In 1937, she replaced Tamura (who left when her husband died) as the Literary Theatre's leading actress. A fine teacher, her acting was realistic, and emotional; she also portrayed cold, calculating roles. In 1945, with the nation nearing defeat, **Morimoto Kaoru** wrote Nunobiki Kei in *A Woman's Life* (Onna no isshô) for Sugimura; she performed it over eight hundred times. Typical of wartime drama, the role glorified personal sacrifice, imperial loyalty, and national pride. Although Morimoto revised the play after the war, softening its propagandistic elements, Sugimura at eighty-seven reprised her role in the wartime version. Her roles ranged from Blanche in *A Streetcar Named Desire* to Lady Kageyama Asako in Mishima Yukio's *The Deer Cry Pavilion* (Rokumeikan, 1956).

Takizawa Osamu, called *shingeki*'s finest actor, excelled in minute character analysis and fine elocution, often in proletarian plays. For the New Cooperative Troupe's (Shinkyô Gekidan) initial production, *Before the Dawn* (Yoake mae, 1934), foreshadowing the coming of Meiji, he portrayed Hanzô, conflicted over his family duty to tax peasants and his desire to see the new Japan emerge. With **Kubo Sakae** and **Murayama Tomoyoshi**, Takizawa defined prewar *shingeki*'s "golden age." A founder of the leftist People's Art Theatre (Mingei-za), he starred in *The Seagull*, *Death of a Salesman*, and **Miyoshi Jûrô**'s *The Ardent Soul* (Honô no hito, 1951), about Van Gogh. Unô Jûkichi (1914–1988), another People's Art Theatre founder, exuded wit, pathos, and compassion for ordinary people in plays ranging from *Waiting for Godot* to *Twilight Crane;* his face and acting were compared to simple "warm potatoes."

Other *shingeki* stars included Nakamura Nobuo (1908–1991), known for sophisticated, man-about-town roles and intelligent, cynical characters. He performed in **Betsuyaku Minoru**'s plays and, for ten years, in Ionesco's *The Lesson*. Kishida Kyôko (1930–), Kishida Kunio's daughter, was known for erotic characterizations of Salomé, Lady Macbeth, and Blanche DuBois; she also has performed experimental works by Betsuyaku, **Shimizu Kunio**, and **Ôta Shôgo**. Actress Watanabe Misako (1932–) trained at the Actor's Theatre (Haiyû-za), gained notice freelancing in Brecht, Albee, and **Tanaka Chikao**, and internationally with **Inoue Hisashi**'s one-person *Makeup* (Keshô).

Post-**Shingeki** *Acting.* Younger postwar actors rejected psychological realism, preferring physical or confrontational acting, as in the experimental troupes of **Terayama Shûji**, **Suzuki Tadashi**, and others. In turn, the next generation rejected the "underground" (*angura*) theatre of the 1960s and 1970s, training with masters of mime/dance/silence, like Ôta; of hyper-parody, speed, and comic athleticism, like **Noda Hideki**; of "quiet theatre" (*shizuka na engeki*), like **Hirata Oriza**; and of other post-*shingeki* styles.

Shiraishi Kayoko trained with Suzuki, whose productions showcased her deep voice, charismatic intensity, and physical prowess. Key roles include Hecuba/Cassandra/Madwoman in *The Trojan Women* (Toroia no onna) and Dionysus/Agave in *The Bacchae.*

Kara Jûrô's "theory of privileged bodies" insists that physical moments energize acting. He has trained many, including his former wife, Ri Reisen (1942–), and *butô* performer Maro Akaji (1943–).

Otake Shinobu (1957–) began in film and television, depicting ordinary women hiding sadness beneath a cheerful veneer. Since the 1990s, she has performed stage plays, including Noda's *Midsummer Night's Dream* and **Ninagawa Yukio**'s *Electra* (2003) and *Medea* (2005)—Ninagawa's only female Medea.

In the new century, old divisions have broken down as acting has matured. For example, Oida Yoshi (1933–) and Nomura Mansai (1966–), both trained in *kyôgen,* are talented comedians who often perform intense, serious roles. Oida has performed multiple cross-cultural experiments since 1968 with Peter Brook, while Mansai performs in *shingeki,* film, and television; he portrayed Hamlet in London and runs the Setagaya Public Theatre.

FURTHER READING

Kano, Ayako. *Acting Like a Woman in Modern Japan: Theater, Gender, and Nationalism;* Powell, Brian. *Japan's Modern Theatre: A Century of Continuity and Change.*

Carol Fisher Sorgenfrei with Peter Eckersall

Actors and Acting: Korea

Social Status. **Korean** • **folk theatre** actors were anonymous itinerant social outcasts whose nomadic existence often was excluded from written documents, their history being handed down orally. Information about actors was scarce, but mid-nineteenth-century historical documents and the famous "Song of Actors" (Kwangdaeka) by Shin Chae-hyo (1812–1884) provide rare glimpses of *p'ansori*'s singer-actors. Around the same time, eight outstanding singer-actors (*myŏngch'ang*) gained recognition and, toward the end of the century, some even received official government posts.

P'ansori *Training.* As in all folk theatres, *p'ansori* performers began their **training** at an early age. Once their talent was recognized, the young performers received years of intense education based on imitation, memorization, and repetition. Although improvisation and spontaneity were key performance elements, creativity was not necessarily considered a virtue and therefore not encouraged during training. Only accomplished singer-actors earned the privilege to create new segments or scenes to add to an existing text, a convention called "adding" (*dŏnŭm*).

Today, *p'ansori* and its training have adjusted to modern realities, and popular singer-actors like An Suk-sŏn (1949–), Important Intangible Cultural Asset No. 23, cross genres from authentic *p'ansori* to *ch'anggŭk* to even postmodern **experimental theatre**.

Realistic Modern Acting. In the twentieth century, **shingŭk** actors sought what they perceived as realistic acting of European origin. Lee Hae-rang (1916–1989), the most celebrated actor, devoted his life to the establishment of **Western** realism. However, early actors were mostly amateurs without any formal theatre background and with little or no direct knowledge of Western theatre. Moreover, *shinp'agŭk*'s audience-pleasing melodramatic style was a detriment to the advancement of realistic acting. Although *shinp'agŭk*'s popularity waned by the 1930s, its influence lingered, not only on the *shingŭk* stage but also in radio, film, and, later, television up into the 1950s. This pseudo-realistic acting long was accepted as the standard for modern Korean theatre, effective especially for translated Western dramas.

Search for a Korean Acting Method. Over a couple of decades after the Korean War (1950–1953), various approaches to realistic acting developed (Stanislavski's influence, for example, continues), but an acute realization that *shingŭk* and Western-based realism failed to capture Korean reality prompted a search for a "Korean" acting among post-*shingŭk* experimenters in the 1970s. Initial experiments involved uses of traditional **music** and **dance** as well as gestures, movements, and expressions peculiar to Koreans. Recently, however, more experiments have focused on aspects of the actor's physical instrument, such as voice, energy, balance, rhythm, and breathing, in search of a universal language beyond the binary opposition of Eastern and Western techniques.

Today, systematic training encompassing Western and native Korean traditions is offered at theatre arts institutions and professional **theatre companies**. As in much of the rest of the world, the majority of professional actors struggle economically, unless they move on to more lucrative film and television venues. But, in contemporary Korean society, actors no longer occupy the bottom rung of the social hierarchy— *shingŭk* pioneer Lee Hae-rang served as a member of the National Assembly, and leading actress Son Suk (1944–) is a former minister of the Department of Environment.

Ah-Jeong Kim

Actors and Acting: Malaysia

Development of a Modern Malay Acting Style. In modern Malay-language drama prior to the 1980s, actors developed a performance style that was influenced by traditional theatre forms as well as the melodramatic style of the popular **bangsawan** theatre. The actors' **stage** delivery, and their emotional and declamatory presentation mode, indicates that less attention was given to the use of blocking and gestures. However, since the mid-1980s, the **Malaysian** acting style has grown increasingly similar to that encountered in modern English- and **Chinese**-language plays.

Once enthusiasm for the **experimental theatre** of the 1970s began to wane, Malay **playwrights** resumed a more realistic style, for the most part abandoning the traditional forms that had been incorporated into the previous experimental works. These newer plays invited a more precise acting style. Although, on occasion, traditional forms, such as *mak yong* and *menohra*, were still staged with customary vocal and movement patterns, these stylized elements did not seem as appropriate for post-1970s plays as they were for earlier experimental productions. In addition, by the 1980s, many performers had received **training** in modern methods that cut across cultures, some having studied abroad. In addition, comprehensive training has increasingly been provided by experienced local practitioners.

Major Actors. The Malaysian theatre encourages the development of new talent. At the same time, accomplished veterans contribute to continuity, their names being familiar to theatregoers. The acting career of Faridah Merican (1939–), often called the "first lady" of Malaysian theatre, dates back to 1957, and Rahim Razali (1949–) took to the stage in 1967. Merican and Razali, along with a number of other actors, work in both Malay and English-language theatre. At times actors perform in multilingual productions. Additionally, there are plays staged by **Indian** and **Chinese** groups that utilize the language (e.g., Tamil, Malayalam, Bengali, Mandarin, Cantonese, and so on) of their respective communities.

Kee Thuan Chye in a scene from the monodrama "The Coffin Is Too Big for the Hole" by the late Singaporean playwright Kuo Pao Kun. (Photo: Courtesy of Kee Thuan Chye)

Some actors are known for performing in plays by international as well as local playwrights. Anne James (1955–) played major roles in *Romeo and Juliet,* Anouilh's *Antigone,* and **Kôbô Abe's** *Friends* (Tomodachi), as well as in local experimental works such as K. S. Maniam's (1942–) *Skin Trilogy* (1995) and *Family* (1998), based on a play by Leow Puay Tin (1957–). Kee Thuan Chye (1954–) played the lead in Australian Robert Hewett's *Gulls* and Miller's *Death of a Salesman*; he also starred in Singaporean **Kuo Pao Kun's** monodrama "The Coffin Is Too Big for the Hole" (1996) and performed notable roles in **Noordin Hassan's** Malay-language drama, *Children of This Land (Anak tanjung,* 1989) and Maniam's *The Cord* (1994). The versatile Mano Maniam (1945–) has held leads in musicals, Shakespeare, Indian classics, O'Neill, Brecht, and Pinter, as well as *Caught in the Middle,* the **theatre company** Kamikasih's comic series about Malaysian life. The cofounders of the Instant Café Theatre (ICT)—Jo Kukathas, Andrew Leci, Jit Murad, and Zahim Albakri—all have acted in ICT productions as well as major works produced by other companies. Murad also performs in stagings of his own scripts, including assuming multiple roles in his highly successful *Gold Rain and Hailstones* (1992).

Some actors have performed in Malaysian plays abroad. In 2002, Kukathas gave a solo rendition of Shahimah Idris's *From Table Mountain to Teluk Intan* at the New York International Fringe Festival. In 2003, Mano Maniam costarred in Kannan Menon's (1952–) *At a Plank Bridge* at New York's Theatre for a New City. Zahim Albakri performed in Tokyo in *Pulau Antara: The Island in Between* (2001), a **Japanese**-Malaysian collaboration.

Many actors perform in television dramas and film as well as live theatre. Actors may also be recognized as playwrights, **directors**, **dancers**, producers, and drama educators. Although theatre cannot provide actors a major livelihood, Malaysia is host to an impressive number of ardent, talented performers who approach their craft with dedication and professionalism.

Nancy Nanney

Actors and Acting: Nepal

Monks, priests, or laymen perform in theatrical rituals (see Religion in Theatre), but **Nepal**'s early professional actors were beautiful girls kept by royalty to perform for them. **Women** of the Badi caste were professional performers but today are prostitutes. King Mahendra (r. 1955–1972) sponsored a stable of respected actors at the Royal Nepal Academy. In the 1990s, international aid organizations began hiring actors to carry their messages to a nonliterate populace, inflating acting wages and making it difficult for domestic organizations to compete. Most actors earn meager wages and supplement income with television, film, and other work. Traditionally, actors learn on the job or from family members, but in 2003 **Sunil Pokharel** founded Nepal's first theatre school, Practical Training Collective (Gurukul), offering a full-time two-year acting **training** program.

Leading Actors. An account of Nepal's most important actors might begin with pre-eminent actor-**director-playwright** Balakrisna Sama (1902–1982), who changed his name from Rana, the nomenclature of the hereditary prime ministers, to Sama, meaning "equal." Nepal's first relatively realistic actor, Sama played with ex-patriot amateurs from Great Britain and men in women's roles. Harihar Sharma (1950–) and his wife, Sakuntala Sharma (1955–), were principal members of the Royal Nepal Academy cadre, performing modern Nepali and **Indian** dramas for the pleasure of kings. Nisha Sharma (1965–) and Anju Shakya (1972–) began with street theatre and went on to participate in international exchanges. The lead actress of the **theatre company** To Climb (Aarohan), Sharma has played more leading roles in European plays than any other Nepali actress, while Nepali playwrights, such as Abhi Subedi (1945–), write roles especially for her. In To Climb's 2004 tour to Denmark and Russia, Sharma played Nora in *A Doll's House* and Bhiksuni Purnima in Subedi's *Fire in the Monastery* (Agniko katha, 2002).

Anju Shakya, lead actress of Representing Everyone (Sarwarnam) from 1990–1996, performs plays aimed at changing society, including the title role in *Witch* (Boksi, asesh malla, 1993), about a woman accused of witchcraft. In 1994, Shakya was the only Nepali actress to participate in *Big Wind*, a production initiated by the San Francisco Mime Troupe, written and acted by artists from nine countries, and toured internationally. In 1996, she became the lead actress and field director of Nepal Health Project

Nepal Health Project's *Our Health Is in Our Hands*, 1996, featuring Anju Shakya and Rupkeshwori Shakya. (Photo: Carol Davis)

Theatre Troupe. For seven years she walked thousands of miles throughout the Himalayan foothills taking theatre to villagers in Nepal's most remote areas, performing the group-developed *Our Health Is in Our Hands* (Hamro swasta hamro haatma cha, 1996) for over half a million people.

Carol Davis

Actors and Acting: Pakistan

Pakistani acting finds its oldest inspiration in oral traditions, manifested in performers of the *lok* **folk theatre**, skilled at improvisation as typified in the wandering *mirasis* (literally, "performers/inheritors of traditions"), "clowns" (*bhaand*s), "**storytellers**" (*dastaan go*), and actors (*saangi*s). Popular folk stories and legends, such as "Heer and Ranjha" (Heer-Ranjha), "Sohni and Mahinwal" (Sohni-Mahinwal), and "Puran Bhagat," are told through **dance**-like epic gestures, **music**, and recitation. The style is loud and declamatory, with impromptu song-dance items and direct audience interactions. After Partition (1947), *lok* thrived through popular performers Inayat Hussain Bhatti (1934–1999), Alam Lohar (?–1979), Bali Jatti (1938–), and Tufail Niazi (?–1990).

While *lok* has almost reached extinction, the urban commercial theatre has absorbed much of its style in a comedy of declamatory gestures, physical caricature, dance, and vulgar jokes. As in *lok*, the performers follow a loose script with frequent bursts into dance unrelated to the narrative, mostly improvising to the whims of the audience. Actors outwit each other by verbal punning in the mode of *bhaand*s. Popular comedian Aman Ullah (1967–) perhaps ironically states that the actor's skill relies on "He who speaks loudest." Significant performers include Sohail Ahmed (1963–), Babu Barral (1959–), Omer Sharif (1958–), and Nargis.

Rafi Peerzada in rehearsal (1939). (Photo: Courtesy of Rafi Peer Theatre Workshop)

Conversely, the court tradition of poetry recitation is exemplified in the art of elocution. Nawab Wajid Ali Shah (1822–1887), at his court in Awadh (Oudh), staged his first "theatrical gathering" (*rahas ka jalsah*) in 1851, epic-scale enactments of his Urdu verse-narratives synthesizing dance, **costume**, music, and poetry. Emphasis on strict elocution continued in post-Partition theatre by writer-**directors** from radio backgrounds, including Safdar Mir (1922–1997), Imtiaz Ali Taj (1900–1970), and Rafi Peerzada (1898–1974). Promoting a methodology of mannered speech they inspired a host of younger actors, such as Zia Mohyuddin, or Moyeddin, (1933–), Khalid Saeed Butt (1934–), Kurshid Shahid (1934–), Yasmin Tahir, Kamal Ahmed Rizvi (1930–), Izhaq Kazmi, and Naeem Tahir (1937–).

With growing national consciousness in the early twentieth century, theatre became a platform for social reform. Exposure to writers like Ibsen, and the movement of the Marxist-leaning Indian People's Theatre Association, founded in 1942–1943, began to inspire social realism, with a repertoire of themes that shifted from the epic to the social and psychological. Actors Sania Saeed (1972–), Sheema Kermani (1951–), and Khalid Ahmed, like their predecessors of the 1940s, have been inspired by realism in the interests of reform.

In Pakistan's formative years, college theatres' English-language drawing-room comedies encouraged realistic acting by artists such as Promilla Thomas, Perin Cooper (1942–), Shoaib Hashmi (1938–), and Navid Shehzhad (1945–); the style, however, was inevitably underpinned by the histrionic epic gestures that had long dominated technique. Later exposure to realism through television and film furthered realistic performances by Rahat Kazmi (1946–) and Talat Hussein (1945–).

Like the **Parsi theatre** actors who fused British, *rahas*, and *lok* techniques, a few actors are known for combining styles and working in multiple genres, from comedy to tragedy, and from pathos to farce, mostly in Arts Council productions. Notable for mixing *lok*'s declamatory style with oratory refinement are Jamil Bismil (?–2005), Muhammed Qavi Khan (1942–), Babbu Younis Bhai Subbani, Khalid Abbas Dhar, and Mahmood Ali.

Claire Pamment

Actors and Acting: Singapore

Prior to the 1990s, few **Singaporeans** considered careers in acting, in large measure because the push toward economic development favored industries such as finance, shipping, and high-tech manufacturing while discouraging active arts participation. **Training** was largely the province of a few small, independent programs, supplemented by seminars and workshops by overseas "experts"; apart from roles in several fledgling sitcoms and television dramas, few opportunities existed to earn a living. This situation began to change during the 1990s as the government invested in an arts infrastructure, while theatre programs were created at academic institutions and the number of training programs expanded considerably.

Today, **stage** acting is largely a youthful enterprise, with only a handful of actors over forty managing to carve out careers. Many established actors, such as Lim Kay Tong, Lim Kay Siu, and actress Tan Kheng Hua, continue with film and television careers. Increased opportunities for paid work and the loosening of restrictions on theatre have no doubt encouraged some actors who have met with success overseas, such as Glen Goei (1962–) and Ivan Heng, to return home. Among those over fifty, Margaret Chan (1949–) stands out for creating Singapore's best-known dramatic personage,

Margaret Chan as Emily, the proud Peranakan matriarch, in Stella Kon's *Emily of Emerald Hill*, 1985, an important milestone in Singaporean theatre. (Photo: Courtesy of Margaret Chan)

that of Emily, the proud matriarch in Stella Kon's (1944–) *Emily of Emerald Hill.* Others who have made contributions to theatre include singer Jacintha Abisheganaden, film actor Jack Neo, and drag artist Kumar.

William Peterson

Actors and Acting: Sri Lanka

Sri Lankan theatre is performed in Sinhalese, Tamil, or English. Acting in Sinhalese theatre can be regarded as semiprofessional, while in the English and Tamil theatres it is amateur. In traditional theatre, actors were largely drawn from village communities, and performed the "village hall" (*gammaduva*) or other folk rituals. The **folk theatre** acting troupes involved in the *nadagam*, *kolam*, and *sokari* genres are engaged in other occupations, and periodically come together to perform their pieces.

Until the advent of *nurti*—adapted from **India**'s **Parsi theatre**, which visited in the late nineteenth century—only male actors appeared. *Nurti* was the first example of mixed gender casts, although this meant that it lacked complete respectability for the educated classes.

In the contemporary theatre, many Sinhalese actors come from the universities, or are employed in other professions, and freelance as actors. They rehearse after work or on weekends. A small group of established actors often takes the lead roles in the larger, best-known productions. Depending on the play—that is, the degree of its popularity or the length of its run—the actors may receive a fee per performance.

Traditionally, **stage** acting is more respected than television or film acting. However, since television's advent in 1979, there has been a decrease in commercial theatre sponsorship and audiences, and it has been difficult to draw more talented young actors to the stage. Though a segment of the population still respects serious theatre, the numbers have dwindled in the face of mass media popularity. Most actors involved solely in theatre earn very little, and those who work in it do so out of dedication to the art. Many actors supplement their income via television soap operas (*tele-drama*s) or in movies.

Actors often progress to **directing** or **playwriting**. Unemployed young actors also get involved in technical aspects of film or television production. Television and movie actors who sometimes act on stage attract larger audiences. They like stage acting, even in cameo roles, because of its cachet of respectability, even though such activity is commercially problematic.

The most famous Sri Lanka theatre artist was singer-actress **Rukmani Devi** (a.k.a. Daisy Daniels, 1923–1978), Sri Lanka's first film idol. Of Tamil background, she was one of the first **women** to gain wide respect as a professional performer, since theatre was considered disreputable.

Important Sinhalese actors include Jemini Kanta, Somalatha Subasinghe (1936–), Henry Jayasena (1931–), Manel Jayasena (1935–2004), Trilicia Gunawardene (1934–1999), Kaushalya Fernando (1963–), Dharmasiri Bandaranayake (1949–), Jayalath Manoratne (1948–), and Mahendra Perera (1956–). A number have become directors or playwrights.

Tamil actors are mainly amateurs and rarely receive financial remuneration. Many come from university drama groups. Theatre is not a "respected" profession in the

Tamil community, and there is little opportunity to gain popularity in it. Film and television work also is limited.

English-language theatre, which has high status, attracts young, middle-class actors. Though serious theatre is not very popular, acting in either serious theatre or comedies can help one to become well-known. In the post-independence (1948) era, acting emerged from university groups who produced mainly serious theatre. Beginning in the 1970s, a number of prominent English-speaking actors appeared, including Iranganie Serasinghe (1927–), Winston Serasinghe (1909–1999), Shelagh Goonewardene (1935–), Karen Breckenridge (1936–1982), Rohan Ponniah (1953–), Richard de Zoysa (1958–1990), Feroze Kamardeen (1972–), Ruwanthi de Chickera (1975–), and Jehan Aloysius (1977–).

Apart from the experience gained in actual practice, or when important foreign artists visit to provide workshops, Sri Lanka's actors have few serious **training** opportunities at home.

Neluka Silva

Actors and Acting: Thailand

All **Thai** college theatre departments offer comprehensive **training** in Stanislavski-based, realistic acting. However, many graduates do not perform professionally, but work as either coaches or casting **directors** for film, advertising, and television. Most **stage** actors learn their craft on the job. They frequently perform in popular media to supplement their stage earnings.

Saranyoo Wongkrachang (1960–) started in university theatre (as an architecture major), became a television and movie star, occasionally returns to the stage, and is acclaimed equally for his screen and stage work. He gave memorable performances in **Sodsai Pantoomkomol**'s translation of *Ondine* (1982), Theatre 28's *Man of La Mancha* (1987) and *Hamlet* (1995), and DASS Entertainment's *Old Maids* (1992).

Many actors cross over between traditional and modern disciplines, which supports the rise of *lakon khanob niyom mhai,* a modern dance-drama genre with some speaking. Pradit Prasartthong (1960–) joined both Thammasat University's **khon** troupe and drama club. After graduation, he practiced *liké* with three troupes. Manop Meejamrat (1967–) studied acting and directing with **Patravadi Mejudhon,** and then was trained in *khon* as the "demon" (*yak*) character by National Artist Rakhop Bhothiveth. Both Prasartthong and Meejamrat won the Ministry of Culture's Silpathorn Awards (national recognition for outstanding mid-career contemporary artists) in 2004 and 2005, respectively. In reverse order, Pichet Klunchuen (1971–) was originally trained as a *yak* by Chaiyot Khummanee, and learned **Western**-style acting in Janaprakal Chandruang's productions.

Other notable stage actors are Crescent Moon Theatre's (Prachan Siew Karn Lakon) Soontorn Meesri, Grassroots Micromedia Project's (Klum Lakon Makhampom), Duangjai Hiransri, B-Floor Theatre's Sumontha Suanpholrat, and Flower of Entertainment's (Dokmai Karn Bunterng) Wannasak Sirilar.

Pawit Mahasarinand

Actors and Acting: Vietnam

Stylized movement, singing, and improvisation are core elements in **Vietnam**'s *cheo, tuong,* and *cai luong. Tuong* is believed to have begun in 1285 when **Chinese** actor Ly Nguyen Cat taught local performers. Actor Dao Duy Tu (1572–1634) introduced **music** from the southern kingdom of Champa, localizing *tuong.* Around 1800, Chinese teachers re-infused Cantonese opera styles, but music and repertoire remained Vietnamese. In 1959, *tuong* **training** was established at the Vietnam School of **Stage** Arts.

Cheo evolved from song, **dance**, and skits of rural amateurs, contrasting with *tuong*'s professionals patronized by aristocrats. *Cheo* training was informal until support came from Ho Chi Minh's (1890–1969) government after World War II. *Cheo* is taught currently at the National Film and Theatre Academy. Major performers include Nguyen Thi Hong Ngat (1958–) and Hong To Mai (1972–).

Cai luong melds **Western** and traditional Vietnamese influences. Song is emphasized. In the 1930s, actress Nam Phi introduced Folies Bergere-style dance, and actor Mui Buu incorporated Hong Kong martial arts. Pham Thi Thanh (1941–) is a current actress of both *cai luong* and "spoken drama" (***kich noi***).

French acting ideas and literature were introduced with *kich noi* from the 1920s. French approaches were superseded by Russian and Eastern European training, which became available from the 1950s to the 1970s. Stanislavskian, socialist realism, and Brechtian ideas gained currency in North Vietnam and spread to the South after 1975, with **experimental** techniques growing from the teaching of Russian-educated Nguyen Tuong Tran. Representative contemporary actors are Ai Nhu (1963–) and Thanh Loc.

Kathy Foley and Lorelle Browning

AKIMOTO MATSUYO (1911–2001). Japanese • *shingeki* • playwright.

Youngest of seven siblings raised in poverty, Akimoto ended her formal education with elementary school. In 1946, she joined **Miyoshi Jûrô**'s Drama Research Group (Gikyoku Kenkyûkai). Miyoshi praised her first play, *Light Dust* (Keijin, 1946), about a single woman in destitute postwar Tokyo. On Miyoshi's recommendation, she wrote her first radio drama, *Transition* (Utsuroi, 1947), and became prominent in the 1950s golden age of Japanese radio drama.

Akimoto's first **stage** success was *Formal Dress* (Reifuku, 1949), a play caricaturing the Japanese postwar family, staged by **Senda Koreya**'s Actor's Theatre (Haiyû-za). In 1960, her play *The Story of Muraoka Iheiji* (Muraoka Iheiji den) and radio drama *Kaison the Priest of Hitachi* (Hitachibô Kaison) received Art Festival Encouragement Prizes. *Kaison,* revised in 1964, and *A Study of Syphilitic Shikibu* (Kasabuta Shikibu kô, 1969), both inspired by folklorist Yanagita Kunio's (1875–1962) study of Japanese legends, concern, respectively, a war orphan and his savior, the monk-soldier Kaison, and a coal miner poisoned by carbon monoxide and his savior, the amorous poet Izumi Shikibu. By evoking indigenous Japanese beliefs, Akimoto would reconnect them to— and revivify—the lives of modern Japanese.

After writing her last *shingeki* play, the folkloric *Seven Dead Spirits* (Shichinin misaki, 1975), about the depopulation of Shikoku, Akimoto moved into commercial theatre, collaborating successfully with **director** • **Ninagawa Yukio** on *The Story of*

Chikamatsu's Double Suicide (Chikamatsu shinjû monogatari, 1979) and her last play, *Nanboku's Love Stories* (Nanboku koi-monogatari, 1982).

Yoshiko Fukushima

AKITA UJAKU (1883–1962). Japanese • *shingeki* • **playwright**, novelist, and writer of children's books, best known as a leader of the prewar leftwing **political** theatre. His first plays, however, were romantic in tone, coming soon after he graduated from Waseda University in 1907; by the early 1910s, he was an established dramatist. He supported **Osanai Kaoru**'s Free Theatre (Jiyû Gekijô), and then became involved with practical theatre by managing **Shimamura Hôgetsu**'s Art Theatre (Geijutsu-za). His subsequent work evinces a strong humanist thread, as in *An Evening at the Frontier* (1920), a nightmarish study of the dehumanizing egoism of a Hokkaidô frontiersman.

In 1922, Akita founded one of the earliest leftwing **theatre companies**, the Pioneer Troupe (Senku-za). In 1924, he published perhaps Japan's finest expressionist play, *Dance of Skeletons* (Gaikotsu no buchô). Set in the aftermath of 1923's Great Kantô Earthquake, it utilizes a full range of expressionist technique to ridicule representatives of authority, who are turned into skeletons and made to dance.

Akita was the leading figure in many leftist theatrical enterprises, notably the theatre journal *Teatoro,* still publishing today, and the New Cooperative Company (Shinkyô Gekidan), one of only two substantial 1930s leftwing companies. Briefly imprisoned in 1940 for his association with the company, Akita in the postwar period became a literary and theatrical *doyen.*

Brian Powell

ALKAP. *See* Bangladesh.

ALKAZI, EBRAHIM (1925–). **Indian** Hindi- and English-language **director, scenographer**, art collector and connoisseur, and educator, born in Pune, Maharashtra, to a wealthy Saudi Arabian father and Kuwaiti mother. He was educated in Arabic, English, Marathi, and Gujurati. While still a student in Bombay (Mumbai), he joined Sultan "Bobby" Padamsee's English-language **theatre company**, Theatre Group. In 1947, he traveled to England to study, enrolling at the Royal Academy of Dramatic Arts. Although honored by the British Drama League and the British Broadcasting Corporation, he turned down career opportunities in London to return home and rejoin Theatre Group, which he ran from 1950–1954. Soon after, he set up the independent Theatre Unit (1954).

To maintain consistency in his group's performances, he established a 150-seat, open-air **theatre** on the terrace of his apartment building. Though most of the plays he staged were from the West—including *Oedipus Rex* (1954), *Murder in the Cathedral* (1955), *Antigone* (1957), and *Medea* (1960)—and were performed in English, Alkazi made them expressive of Indian viewpoints.

In addition to directing, he founded the monthly *Theatre Unit Bulletin* (1953), which reported on theatre events within and outside the country. He established one of the first acting schools, the School of Dramatic Arts, and also served as principal of Bombay's Natya Academy. In 1962, Alkazi became director of the National School of Drama (NSD), New Delhi, for which he had created the original blueprint, and which he ran until 1977. He also founded the school's Repertory Company in 1964, and directed many of its major productions until his departure. This was a major period both for him and for modern drama, especially because he committed himself to theatre in Hindi, India's majority language. He produced **Western** as well as Indian classics in Hindi translation, among them **Kalidasa**'s *The Recognition of Shakuntala* (Abhijnana Shakuntalam, 1964), which inspired the revival of many other **Sanskrit** plays. Original Hindi dramas he directed included **Mohan Rakesh**'s *A Day in Early Autumn* (Ashadh ka ek din, 1962).

A strict disciplinarian, even a martinet, he demanded diligent research and preparation before a play was put into production. Not only acting and directing, but **scenographic** design made important advances under his guidance at the NSD. The standards he set were influential; many of his students command high places in India's theatre annals.

Alkazi, winner of some of India's most prestigious awards, inculcated an awareness of theatre's contemporary sensibility and successfully brought together the best of traditional and modern expression. He staged more than fifty plays, using not only proscenium **stages** but unusual open-air venues that often contributed greatly to their success. For example, the space behind the NSD campus served well for *A Day in Early Autumn*, while **Dharmavir Bharati**'s *Blind Age* (Andha yug, 1963) was staged in ancient ruins, with a gigantic broken wheel set against a wall, to capture the archetypal nature and tragic destiny of the characters. His designs were acclaimed for their visual beauty, particularly when spectacular effects were in order. Even when designing the same play multiple times, he did so with an original approach for each production.

Shashikant Barhanpurkar

ANG DUONG (1796–1869). King (r. 1841–1860; not crowned until 1848) of **Cambodia**, credited with having restored *robam kbach boran* and *lakhon khol*. These forms, traditionally linked to the reigning monarch, had been all but obliterated—in part because there had been no reigning king to host a **dance** troupe between the death of Ang Chan in 1835 and the crowning of Ang Duong in 1848. He also is credited with substantially transforming **costumes** and choreography. Details of Ang Duong's contributions were passed down orally for a century among dance mistresses and royals and were written down in the mid-twentieth century by a French advisor to King Norodom Sihanouk (1921–), Charles Meyer.

With Cambodia a vassal state, pulled between its **Thai** and **Vietnamese** neighbors, Ang Duong's authority was largely limited to ceremonial duties. In renovating the royal dance, with its **religious** dimensions as well as its legendary ties to Cambodia's glorious past, Ang Duong helped to make it an important emblem of Cambodian royalty, Cambodia's Angkorean heritage, and Cambodia itself.

Ang Duong's changes to costumes and choreography no doubt reflected his having been raised in Thailand. But, in fact, Thai dance strongly reflected traditional Khmer dance—having been shaped by dancers taken from the Angkor empire in the fifteenth century. In any case, at the beginning of his reign, Khmer female costumes resembled those of bas-reliefs on the Angkor temples—bare-breasted with a light, flowing *sampot* (a cloth wrapped into a kind of skirt). Ang Duong replaced those with costumes he personally designed, made of heavy brocade *sampot*s plus tight-fitting, ornamented bodices, and high crowns—all similar to Thai costumes.

Ang Duong also specified choreography changes, having dancers curl their hands back at the wrist and stand on one bent leg, with the other bent sharply behind. This body architecture, combining stances in Angkor reliefs with Thai dance postures, has become central to *robam kbach boran* and *lakhon khol*. Ang Duong also excised certain gestures that some scholars believe had incorporated Vietnamese-style movement.

Besides renovating the dance, Ang Duong separated Cambodian performers into all-female and all-male troupes (both palace-trained). By the reign of his son, King Norodom (1834–1904, r. 1864–1904), the female troupe had become the king's sequestered harem.

Eileen Blumenthal

ANGURA. **Japanese** • **experimental**, anti-establishment theatre movement, whose name derives from "underground." It emerged in the turbulent socio-**political** cultural environment of 1960s Japan and figured centrally in that decade's international vanguard. Spawned from dissatisfaction with Japan's traditional theatre, *angura* performances were antirealist, eclectic, darkly expressive, and postmodern; they eschewed the literary dramaturgical conservatism of **shingeki.** *Angura* **theatre companies** staged street performances and played to student audiences in small shop fronts and tents. A theatre of self-discovery and rebellion, *angura* debated cultural politics through ideas of human transformation, complex mythic narratives, and radical **scenography**.

Led by young **playwright**-**directors**, each *angura* group had its own artistic vision. For example, **Terayama Shûji**'s Peanut Gallery (Tenjô Sajiki) was a carnival of avant-garde playfulness. **Suzuki Tadashi** nurtured his influential **acting** style and innovative adaptations of classic texts at the Waseda Little Theatre (Waseda Shôgekijô) and the Suzuki Company of Toga (SCOT). **Kara Jûrô**'s Situation Theatre (Jokyô Gekijô) and Kara Company (Karagumi) drew inspiration from premodern *kabuki* and toured the countryside in a red tent. At the Free Theatre (Jiyû Gekijô) and the Black Tent (Kokoshoku Tento), **Satoh Makoto** explored Japanese cultural politics and imperialism. Others associated with *angura* include *butô* performer **Hijikata Tatsumi**, film director Oshima Nagisa (1932–), graphic designer Yokoo Tadanori (1936–), playwright **Betsuyaku Minoru**, and actress **Shiraishi Kayoko**. By mingling sources of tradition with the modern world, and inventing uniquely hybrid Japanese aesthetic forms, *angura* transformed Japanese theatre.

FURTHER READING

Eckersall, Peter. *Theorizing the Angura Space: Avant-garde Performance and Politics in Japan, 1960–2000;* Powell, Brian. *Japan's Modern Theatre: A Century of Continuity and Change.*

Peter Eckersall

ANKIYA NAT. **Indian** • **dance**-drama of Assam, which integrates many different components into a single, devotional performance. *Bhaona* is often used interchangeably with *ankiya nat* (also spelled *ankia nat*), though *bhaona* may specifically refer to the spoken drama portions of this form.

Various styles of **music** and dance, and specific **religious** rituals combine in *ankiya nat* with spoken drama, recited verse, and improvisation. There also are significant classical influences, and its literary history goes back several centuries. Performances take place in ritual spaces and are framed by ritual activity.

Ankiya nat's character is Vaishnavist, a function of devotion to the god Vishnu. Its principle subjects are Krishna and Ram (Rama), Vishnu's most important incarnations; it is one of several important Krishna dramas (see *Krishnattam*; *Raslila*). Most stories come from the *Ancient Stories of the Lord* (Bhagavata Purana), a sacred compendium of Krishna-related tales. It also relies on the ***Ramayana*** and other versions of the Rama story. Performances draw crowds of devotees who approach plays as spiritual events. Audiences are composed of all castes, as well as all economic and social stations. Because performances are generally paid for by wealthy individuals and organizations, admission is free.

All **actors** are men—amateurs—as in other Vaishnavist performance traditions, such as ***raslila*** and ***ramlila***. However, *ankiya nat* actors are not necessarily Brahmans. In recent years, **women** have begun to perform *ankiya nat* dance as traditional art. **Costumes** are elaborate and uniquely Assamese. Supporting characters wear colorful garments, ornamented with glass and mirror work. Principals dress similarly, but in appropriate colors. Krishna, for instance, always wears yellow. Men playing women are dressed to satisfy a certain degree of illusion, with artificial breasts and hair, jewelry, bracelets, and heavy **makeup**. Musicians also wear white. Some supernatural figures, such as Brahma or the demon Ravanna, wear **masks**, as does the clown (*behuwa*). The masks are often made by monks out of wood, clay, and cloth.

Particularly striking in a completely white costume, including a full-sleeved tunic and tall cap, is the *sutradhara*, the **director** and commentator. He supervises the action and dialogue, and explains and interprets the play for the audience.

Performances take place in a monastery's prayer hall (*namaghara*), or in a *rabha*, a specially built, open structure. Both **stage** spaces are similarly rectangular, with space designated for musicians to sit at one narrow end facing a shrine opposite them at the other. The performance takes place between the musicians and the shrine, and spectators sitting on the ground fill the remaining space. Performances are preceded by ritual preliminaries, including the musicians' entry processions. Rites are divided from each other, as well as from scenes and dances, with a **curtain**. As in other Indian traditions, it is handheld and used to dramatically reveal actors and musicians in tableau; unlike other curtains, *ankiya nat*'s is white. Performances, typically at night, are illuminated by mustard oil lamps. Torches are also used to dramatic effect.

Percussion is central to the music, including a variety of drums, such as the *khol* or *mrdangam*, as well as cymbals. The musical style, popularly attributed to the genre's founder, exhibits characteristics of both Hindustani and Assamese traditions.

Sankaradeva (ca. 1449–1568), a Vaishnavist saint who greatly influenced Assamese religion and culture, is credited with *ankiya nat*'s origin. Like his contemporaries, Caitanya (1486–1534) and Vallabhacarya (1479–1587), Sankaradeva encouraged activities that bring congregations together, such as group singing and theatre. Sankaradeva himself wrote several plays, including *Subduing Kaliya* (Kaliya damana) and *Taking the Parijata* (Parijata harana). All but one of his plays, *Lord Rama Triumphant* (Sri Rama vijaya), are based on stories from the *Ancient Stories of the Lord*. Structurally, his plays are heavily influenced by medieval **Sanskrit theatre**. They combine Sanskrit verse with Brajaboli, the language of devotional poetry, and vernacular dialogue. Special emphasis is given to song and dance. Partly because of this clear influence of Sanskrit theatre, some have argued that *ankiya nat* should be credited alongside *kutiyattam* with preserving Sanskrit drama's form.

Sankaradeva encouraged monastic living, and required monastery leaders to compose at least one devotional play. This not only contributed to the spread of Vaishnavism in Assam, but also built a healthy literary tradition into *ankiya nat*'s history. Sankaradeva himself did not use the term *ankiya nat*, but his followers created it by adapting the term *anka*, a type of one-act Sanskrit play. Sankaradeva's disciple Madhavadeva (ca. 1489–1596) is given almost equal regard for his contributions to devotional theatre in Assam.

FURTHER READING

Mukhopadyay, Durgadas. *Lesser Known Forms of Performing Arts in India*; Varadpande, M. L. *History of Indian Theatre: Loka Ranga; Panorama of Indian Folk Theatre*; Vatsyayan, Kapila. *Traditional Indian Theatre: Multiple Streams.*

David V. Mason

ANYEIN PWE. Traditional form of theatre in **Burma** (Myanmar) featuring female dancers, four clowns (*lubyet*, also spelled *lupyet*), a classical orchestra (*saing waing*), and lively choreography. Once a slow, female, palace **dance** accompanied by harp and xylophone **music**, it became—after Britain's 1886 annexation of Burma—popular entertainment in the form known today. Often seen at **festivals**, sometimes alone and sometimes with other genres, it begins around 7 p.m. and ends about 1 a.m. The youngest member dances first, followed by two or three others. The leader, after whom the troupe is named, enters last and performs the longest. Both large and small troupes exist.

Anyein, which means "gently," was once a slow dance performed by palace **women** to harp and xylophone music. After the British exiled the last Burmese king in 1885, court dancers had to find work among the public. Among them was singer-comic U Chit Hpwe (1873–1944) who, with his dancer wife, Ma Sein Thone (1885–1939), formed the first *anyein* troupe around 1900, incorporating comics, with music provided by a *saing waing* orchestra.

The songs for *anyein* dancers are written with their names as part of the lyrics. It is a tradition for the attractive dancers to flirt with the audience and for the clowns to satirize social and **political** issues. However, like all forms of Burmese performance, it is subject to **censorship**; clowns have been jailed for overstepping their bounds. The dancing and singing are performed in alternation with the clowning. Larger troupes may also perform dramatic scenes. By the 1910s, the choreography became livelier, but even when it uses vigorous leaps, *anyein* retains its gentleness. *Anyein* is more popular with male audiences while women prefer *zat pwe*.

Three of the most famous dancers of the colonial period were Mya Chaychin Ma Ngwe Myaing (1895–1959), Laybarti ("Liberty") Ma Mya Yin (1904–1946), and Awbar Thaung (1898–1971). In 1967, Awbar Thaung catalogued the 125 basic steps, including some that she once learned by copying a marionette's movements.

FURTHER READING

Singer, Noel F. *Burmese Dance and Theatre.*

Ma Thanegi

ARJA. Balinese (see Indonesia) genre combining song, *gamelan* **music**, comedy, **dance**, and drama, believed to have originated in 1825 from an innovative collaboration between two *gambuh* troupes to mark the cremation ceremony of the prince of Klungkung, East Bali. These troupes sang the dialogue, emphasizing vocal expression and plot over *gambuh*'s predilection for dance and drama. Lengthy, nonmusical passages became common. The narratives also moved beyond the *Mahabharata* and classical Javanese romances of the *gambuh* repertoire to include **Chinese** and Balinese vernacular love stories. Because of this emphasis on song, and its intense sentimentality, this all-night form is now commonly known as "Balinese opera."

Although originally all male, by the 1920s, **women** replaced men in the principal, refined (*alus*) **role types**. Their voices were considered more appropriate for the songs, many of which were, at the same time, changed from archaic Kawi to vernacular Balinese. One of the key features of *arja* is humor. Eight clowns (*penasar*), who improvise in the vernacular, are standard. The genre grew increasingly popular during the twentieth century, and mixed-gender companies became usual. Since the 1960s, *arja* has undergone a structural consolidation, with the development of "all-star" (*arja bon*) groups, whose performances are broadcast regularly on Balinese radio. In a peculiar turn-around, an all-male troupe from Printing Mas, Denpasar, has become immensely popular with its comic performances.

This all-night form includes well-defined role types, including a masculine woman (*limbur*), typically a mother-in-law, usually played by a man. A **curtain** is manipulated to create anticipation of entrances, somewhat as in *topeng*.

FURTHER READING

Dibia, I Wayan, and Rucina Ballinger. *Balinese Dance, Drama and Music: A Guide to the Performing Arts of Bali.*

Laura Noszlopy

ARMIJN PANÉ (1908–1970). Indonesian • *sandiwara* • **playwright**, cultural **critic**, poet, and editor. Armijn's plays were models for many playwrights through the 1960s, and his forward-looking cultural nationalism is an important compass point for debates on modernity and tradition. Born in Tapanuli, western Sumatra, he studied language and literature in Solo, Java, and went to medical school in Batavia (Jakarta). After achieving recognition as a poet in the early 1930s, he cofounded *Pujangga Baru* (1933), a major literary journal.

The seven plays in Armijn's collection *Acting Shy but Actually Liking Him* (Jinak-jinak merpati, 1953) explore a variety of themes and styles. (Additional radio and stage plays are lost.) *Princess Lenggang Kencana* (Nyai Lenggang Kencana, 1938), set in the semilegendary Sundanese kingdom of Pajajaran, probes psychological conflict between love and duty to one's nation. One can see the influence of **Rabindranath Tagore** and

Shakespeare on its dramaturgy. Other works are Ibsenian problem plays dealing with contemporary social and **political** issues; not coincidentally, Armijn translated *A Doll's House*, retitled *Ratna* (1943). Armijn headed up the Javanese Sandiwara Union during the Japanese occupation (1942–1945), and his plays and cultural policies helped define the *sandiwara* genre. While his earlier dramas had been performed by amateurs, his wartime plays were premiered by large-scale **theatre companies** for mass audiences. Armijn adapted his play *Between Earth and Heaven* (Antara bumi dan langit, 1947), concerning alliances of mixed-race Eurasians with the Dutch during the revolution, as the screenplay for a controversial film, *Frieda* (1951). Depression prevented him from writing after 1955. His brother, Sanoesi Pané (1903–1968), was also a playwright and poet.

Matthew Isaac Cohen

ASAKURA SETSU (1922–). **Japanese** • **scenographer**, painter, and illustrator. The daughter of sculptor Asakura Fumio (1883–1964), she initially studied Japanese-style painting under Itô Shinsui (1898–1972) but gradually shifted to theatre work. By the 1960s, she was designing sets for **experimental** • *shôgekijô* spaces as well as opera and large-scale commercial spectacles. Her designs for **Suzuki Tadashi**'s Waseda Little **Theatre** (Waseda Shôgekijô) productions and **Noda Hideki**'s plays with his former **theatre company**, Dream Wanderers (Yume no Yûminsha), were integral to the very process of creating the plays.

Asakura's dynamic, symbolic sets often invigorated **director** • **Ninagawa Yukio**'s elegant but gloomy world. Giant stairs, for example, inspired by Eisenstein's film *The Battleship Potemkin* (1925), partly defined Ninagawa's *Romeo and Juliet* (1974), *Oedipus Rex* (1976), and *Hamlet* (1978); bloody red flowers of cluster-amaryllis bloomed ominously on the brothel's roof in *The Story of Chikamatsu's Double Suicide* (Chikamatsu shinjû monogatari, 1979). In 1983, Asakura traveled with Ninagawa to Greece and Italy, where her set for his all-male *Medea* was modeled after Hôryû-ji Temple's Hall of Dreams (Yumedono).

Foreign audiences have found deeply appealing Asakura's elaborate use of Japanese traditional motifs, often inspired by *nô* and *kabuki,* as with her sets and **costume**s in Miki Minoru's productions of *Jôruri* (1985) and *The Tale of Genji* (2000) for the St. Louis Opera Theatre. In 1995, Asakura became the first female set designer for *kabuki,* working on **Ichikawa Ennosuke** III's "super" (*supaa*) *kabuki Yamato Takeru.* In 2004, she was appointed artistic director at Tokyo's Theatre 1010.

Yoshiko Fukushima

ASARI KEITA (1933–). **Japanese director**. Founder of the Four Seasons Theatre (Gekidan Shiki) in 1953 and still its leader, Asari is known for producing **Western**-style **musicals** and transforming Japanese commercial theatre. Shiki now owns five **theatres** in Japan, producing about two thousand performances annually.

Asari's initial offerings were spoken dramas, including the first Japanese productions of works by French **playwrights** Giraudoux and Anouilh. Using orthodox *shingeki* style, he also has staged Shakespeare and Molière, Peter Shaffer's *Equus,* and Bernard Pomerance's *The Elephant Man.* Asari's venture into musicals, inspired by *West Side*

Story in 1964, began that year with the original Japanese musical *The Emperor's New Clothes* (Hadaka no ôsama). The 1970s saw a series of Christmas charity musicals for the Automobile Workers Union, including *Dream Within a Dream* (Yume kara sameta yume), from Akagawa Jirô's (1948–) novel. These efforts led to his first mega-musical hit, taken directly from Broadway, *Applause* (1972), followed by *Jesus Christ Superstar* (1973); its 1994 revival in **Korea** made it the first Japanese-language musical produced there. *Cats* (1983) cemented his reputation as the premier producer of Japanese versions of Western musicals. Recent productions include *The Lion King* (1998), which broke long-run records in Japan. *Ri Kôran* (1991) was Asari's first fully original, commercial, Japanese musical; it concerned the colorful life of actress-singer Li Xianglan (Japanese pronunciation Ri Kôran), born Yamaguchi Yoshiko in Manchuria, who became active in **Chinese** films, was acquitted by the Chinese of having spied for the Japanese, had a successful postwar show business career, and, as Otaka Yoshiko, became a television journalist and a member of the Diet. This long-run show toured to China and **Singapore**.

Asari produced the 1998 Winter Olympics opening ceremony, featuring ice-skater Itô Midori (1969–). He enhanced his international reputation with productions of Puccini's *Madama Butterfly* at La Scala in 1986 and in Beijing in 2002.

John D. Swain

ASEP SUNANDAR SUNARYA (1955–). **Puppet** master (*dalang*) of *wayang golek* of the Sundanese region of West Java, **Indonesia**, who creates innovations in puppetry, comedy, and cultural critique through live performance, media presentations, and international tours. Asep's grandfather, Johari (fl. 1920–1940), and father, Abah Sunarya (fl. 1950–1980), combined puppetry and indigenous shamanism (*dukun*) (see Religion in Theatre). Asep emerged in 1968 and by 1980 was a style setter, leading his **theatre company**, Mountain of Good Fortune (Giri Harja III), in Jelekong, near Bandung. His innovations, including slow-motion fights inspired by kung-fu films and ogres that vomit spaghetti, became the norm. He popularized a new style *gamelan* ensemble, which can play in different **musical** modes, and imported tunes from other regions. His life-like manipulation, raucous comedy, and masterful vocal technique are constants.

His content follows popular taste. Early work gently questioned **political** corruption, but by the 1990s his plays attacked ogre kings (metaphorically urging President Suharto's [1921–] ouster) and urged Islamic observance. Asep's work is a barometer of public opinion. His technical prowess, creativity, and skillful use of media (commercial recordings, Web sites, radio, and television appearances) have made him the most influential contemporary performer of *wayang golek* and Sundanese art.

Kathy Foley

ASMARA, ANDJAR (1902–1961). Indonesian • **director**, producer, **playwright**, editor, translator, and **critic**, active in both theatre and film. He was born in western Sumatra and attended school in Batavia (Jakarta). His editing of the Indonesian edition of *Filmland* led to his first contact with the *tonil* • **theatre company**, Dardanella, which he joined as publicist in 1930.

Asmara turned playwright and director with *Dr. Samsi* (1930), a psychological drama inspired by the Hollywood movie *Madame X* (1929). This tale of babies switched in a hospital, blackmail, and murder provided the first major adult role for **Devi Dja**. It was performed more than a thousand times by Dardanella and others, and was filmed in 1936 and in 1952. Asmara and his wife, actress Ratna Asmara, left Dardanella in 1937 and founded their own company, the **politically** engaged Bolero, with Bachtiar Effendi. Asmara also wrote and directed films based on his plays, and novelized films and plays. He returned to full-time theatre work during the **Japanese** occupation (1942–1945), directing the youth theatre Light of the East (Tjahaja Timoer). After Indonesia's independence, he worked primarily in films and journalism and contributed to various national cultural projects, coining the term *sendratari* for the outdoor *Ramayana* ballet at Prambanan.

Matthew Isaac Cohen

AWAJI NINGYÔ JORURI. *See* Puppet Theatre: Japan.

B

BAJAJ, RAM GOPAL (1940–). Indian Hindi-language **actor**, **director**, **critic**, educator, and translator, born in Darbangha, Bihar. After graduating from Bihar University, he studied acting at the National School of Drama (NSD), New Delhi, graduating in 1965 and acting in its repertory company before founding the Dishantar **theatre company** (1967). He also spent several years teaching theatre to children and producing children's plays. Bajaj's academic career included teaching drama in high schools and universities before being appointed as an acting professor at the NSD, which he headed from 1996–2001. There, he founded Hindi and English theatre (*Theatre India*) journals. Afterward, he joined the faculty of S.N. School, University of Hyderabad.

A deep believer in theatre's power to oppose society's ills, and to bind diverse communities together, Bajaj advocates for theatre in education, at all levels. He organized a nationwide children's theatre **festival**, Jashn-e-Bachpan, in 1999. Bajaj—also renowned as a poetry reciter—acted in over three dozen plays (and a dozen films), directing many more; most of his work has been with Indian plays. He also translated eighteen Indian and foreign plays into Indian languages, including works by **Girish Karnad**, **Badal Sircar**, and Heiner Müller. Films, television, and radio benefited from his artistry.

Among his major **stage** roles were Yuyutsu in **Dharmavir Bharati**'s *Blind Age* (Andha yug, 1963), Devadatta in **Girish Karnad**'s *Horse-Head* (Hayavadana, 1972), and the title role in **Vijay Tendulkar**'s *Ghashiram the Policeman* (Ghashiram Kotwal), as well as Nana in the 1993 revival. His directorial record includes numerous challenging productions, including the above-mentioned *Blind Age*, **Mohan Rakesh**'s *A Day in Early Autumn* (Ashad ka ek din, 1970), Surendra Verma's (1941–) *From the Sun's Last Ray to the Sun's First Ray* (Surya ki antim kiran se surya ki pahli kiran tak, 1974), and Verma's *Imprisonment for Life* (Qaid-e-hayat, 1989).

For *Blind Age*, staged outdoors on the NSD campus, he built a large, pond-shaped structure with steps, with the audience surrounding them. The actors manipulated their robes in a way that instantly turned them into a group of **storytellers** when needed. His numerous awards include the National Academy of Music, Dance, and Drama (Sangeet Natak Akademi) award (1998).

Shashikant Barhanpurkar

BAL GANDHARVA (1888–1967). Indian Marathi-language **actor**-singer, renowned for his artistry as a great female impersonator in Maharashtra's once popular *sangeet natak*. Born in Pune, Maharashtra, to a middle-class Brahman family, he was gifted with a divine voice and an equally beautiful, feminine face, attaining celebrity status as a child. The name Bal Gandharva (literally, "young celestial singer") was bestowed on him when he was ten by the nationalist leader Bal Gangadhar Tilak (1856–1920), the "Lion of India." At seventeen, he joined the then fading Kirloskar Drama Company (Kirloskar Natak Mandali), and single-handedly restored it to glory.

His **costuming**, **makeup**, elaborate hairstyles, and body language, reflecting his deep understanding of the female psyche, made him enormously popular with the middle-class **women** of his day. They bought soaps and perfumes under his brand name, and took pride in imitating him, just as happened with the female impersonators (*onnagata*) of **Japan**'s *kabuki*. Audiences were particularly delighted with his execution of the "thrice-bent" pose (*thribangi*), consisting of a gentle bend of the head, with the body's weight slightly shifted to one leg, and the torso thrown forward.

Bal Gandharva, a student of classical singing, employed a blend of various forms of Hindustani and Carnatic **music** so successfully that such music became popular in the households of the masses. His recordings sold numerous copies and are still treasured.

In 1913, he set up the Gandharva Drama Company (Gandharva Natak Mandali) in Bombay (Mumbai), with actors Covindrao Tembe (1881–1955) and Ganesh Bodas (1880–1965) and **playwrights** Krishnaji Prabhakar Khadilkar (1872–1948) and Govind Ballal Deval (1855–1916). He played major roles in plays of all sorts, both period and modern, and was as comfortable in domestic dramas as in classical ones. Among the thirty-five characters he immortalized were Shakuntala in **Annasaheb Kirloskar**'s *Musical of Shakuntala* (Sangeet Shakuntal, 1905), Subhadra in *Musical of Saubhadra* (Sangeet Saubhadra, 1905), Bhamini in Khadilkar's *Musical of Honor and Dishonor* (Sangeet Manapaman, 1911), and his most famous role, Sindhu, the self-sacrificing wife of a drunk, in Ram Ganesh Gadkari's (1885–1919) *Just One More Glass* (Ekach pyala, 1919).

Bal Gandharva spent lavishly on expensive **scenography** (including the perfuming of the **stage**), costumes, and jewelry; he insisted on authentic jewels that often cost a fortune. This extravagance took its toll when he lost his company to moneylenders in 1921 (he retrieved it in 1928). Although he married singer-actress Goharbai in 1955, he spent the post-1952 years paralyzed and poverty-stricken. His last role was in 1955.

His accomplishments included bringing many talented artists, both actors and musi-cians, to the Marathi stage. He also appeared in two films, most notably *Soul of Dharma* (Dharmatma, 1935), in which he played a male saint, but his fans preferred him live. He returned to the theatre but too late to recapture his stage appeal. He was given the National Academy of Music, Dance, and Drama (Sangeet Natak Akademi) award (1955) and the Padma Bhushan (1964).

FURTHER READING

Nadkarni, Mohan. *Bal Gandharva: The Nonpareil Thespian*; Nadkarni, Dnyaneshwar. *Balgand-harva and the Marathi Theatre*.

Shashikant Barhanpurkar

BALTAL. *See* Puppet Theatre: India.

BANDI PETHIR. *See Bhaand Pather.*

BANDÔ MITSUGORÔ. Line of ten **Japanese** • *kabuki* • **actors**, most of them "male **role type**" (*tachiyaku*) specialists. Their "house name" (*yagô*) is Yamatoya. The most significant in the line were Mitsugorô III, IV, V, VII, VIII, and IX.

Mitsugorô III (1773–1881)—earlier names: Bandô Mitahachi I, Bandô Minosuke I, and Morita Kanjirô—took the name in 1799 after rising to fame in Edo (Tokyo) playing major roles in famous "history plays" (*jidai mono*), such as Kanpei in *The Treasury of Loyal Retainers* (Kanadehon Chûshingura). He enjoyed a great rivalry with Osaka's **Nakamura Utaemon** III, and fans loudly debated their relative talents in "transformation pieces" (*henge mono*), **dances** in which they played multiple characters. Tall and good-looking, he excelled in both history and "domestic plays" (*sewa mono*) as well as dance, and played female roles (*onnagata*) as well as male. He founded the important Bandô school (*ryû*) of dance.

Mitsugorô IV (1800–1863), adopted son of Mitsugorô III, took the name in 1832. He was a handsome leading man, excelling in heroic, romantic, and villainous roles, the latter including a brilliant Moronao in *The Treasury of Loyal Retainers*. He continued the family's dance excellence, but also specialized in the "raw domestic play" (*kizewa mono*) genre then gaining prominence. His rival was Nakamura Shikan II (later Nakamura Utaemon IV). He became **Morita Kanya** XI in 1850 and served as manager of the financially unsteady Morita **Theatre** (Morita-za).

Mitsugorô V (1812–1855), adopted son of Mitsugorô III, was a popular *onnagata*, earlier known as Bandô Tamanosuke, **Bandô Tamasaburô** I, and Bandô Shûka. He was named Mitsugorô V posthumously.

Mitsugorô VII (1882–1961), eldest son of Morita Kanya XII, held the name Bandô Yasosuke II before becoming Mitsugorô in 1906. He became actor-manager of the Ichimura Theatre (Ichimura-za) in 1908, costarring with the great **Onoe Kikugorô** VI and **Nakamura Kichiemon** I. He was one of the greatest dancers of his time, recognizable by his small size and high voice. His accomplishments included the creation of several dance plays closely based on *kyôgen*, such as *Tied to a Pole* (Bôshibari) and *The Zen Substitute* (Migawari zazen). Oft honored, he wrote several books on his art.

Mitsugorô VIII (1906–1975), adopted son of Mitsugorô VII, was a *kabuki* scholar who wrote a number of books, and was also a great actor-dancer. His earlier names were Bandô Yasosuke III and Bandô Minosuke VI; he became Mitsugorô in 1962. A progressive actor, he left the Shôchiku Company (see Theatre Companies) from 1935–1939 to join the rival Tôhô troupe, but returned to Shôchiku in 1940 and became active in Osaka *kabuki*, working in the **experimental** *kabuki* of **Takechi Tetsuji** in the postwar period. His specialties were old men and villains.

Mitsugorô IX (1929–1999), son of Bandô Shûchô III (1880–1935) and adopted son of Mitsugorô VIII, was Bandô Mitsunobu, Bandô Yasosuke IV, and Bandô Minosuke VII before becoming Mitsugorô in 1987. He was a stalwart supporting player, excellent in old men's roles, but also excelling in dance. His son, Yasosuke V (1956–), became Mitsugorô X in 2003, the first Mitsugorô in seventy-four years to achieve the name by direct descent and not by adoption. He is a popular actor-dancer, with advanced ideas for *kabuki*'s future.

Samuel L. Leiter

BANDÔ TAMASABURÔ. Line of **Japanese** • *kabuki* actors, the most renowned being female **role type** (*onnagata*) specialist Tamasaburô V (1950–). Adopted into the Bandô line by **Morita Kanya** XIV, and using the actor's "house name" (*yagô*) Yamatoya, he debuted in 1964. Tamasaburô is today's most highly regarded *onnagata*, known for his height and angular body, which contribute greatly to his graceful movement style. His artistic range and foreign tours have contributed to his international reputation.

His pairings—first with Ichikawa Ebizô X (see Ichikawa Danjûrô XII), as Lady Taema in *Narukami* and Agemaki in *Sukeroku: Flower of Edo* (Sukeroku Yukari Edo no Zakura); then with the actor later known as **Kataoka Nizaemon** XV as Princess Sakura in *The Scarlet Princess of Edo* (Sakura-hime azuma bunshô) and Yûgiri in *Love Letters from the Licensed Quarter* (Kuruwa bunshô)—were acclaimed. His famous **dance** roles include *The Heron Maiden* (Sagi musume) and *Maiden at Dôjô-ji Temple* (Musume Dôjô-ji), available on DVD with English narration. In addition to traditional *kabuki* roles, Tamasaburô V is well known for performing *shin kabuki*, *shinpa*, and **experimental** pieces using ballet and traditional **Chinese** movement. He also is renowned for playing Shakespeare's Desdemona and Lady Macbeth, as well as Queen Elizabeth I, among famous **Western** characters.

Holly A. Blumner

BANGLADESH. Bangladesh, population approximately 147 million (2006), was established following the departure from **India** of British colonial occupation in 1947, when the Muslim state of **Pakistan** was formed. Originally called East Pakistan, the region eventually gained independence from Pakistan in 1971 after a bloody civil war over the need for greater **political** and cultural autonomy. Despite these painful partitions, this Muslim nation is still connected to the language and customs of Bengali-speaking India, and its theatrical traditions, including *jatra*, were born out of that common heritage.

Jatra, Gambhira, Alkap, *and* **Kavigan.** *Jatra*'s long history in the region originated in Hindu **religious** ritual processions. *Jatra* became a voice of the social and cultural resistance under the British and played an important role in the 1969 pro-democracy movement. Bangladeshi *jatra* performers have not fared as well as their Indian counterparts. Unlike some traditional forms, *jatra* has not received government support; from 1986 to 1991, its performances were outlawed for being too vulgar. *Jatra* is also one of India's principal forms.

Another venerable form is *gambhira*, also still found in Bengal. It developed from Hindu rituals and came to be connected with the worship of Shiva. Related to *gambhira* is the rural theatre called *alkap*, an improvised theatre composed of skits and songs that seems to have taken shape sometime in the middle of the nineteenth century. *Alkap* long ago shed its religious content and adopted a style similar to *jatra*, but without the fancy **scenographic** elements and **costumes**.

The Bengali-speaking areas also are home to a number of narrative **folk** song traditions including *panchali* and *kavigan*. Prior to the eighteenth century, *panchali* included a **puppet** • **dance** and, according to some, the name is derived from that ancient tradition. Today, instead of a puppet, a lead singer dances holding a flywhisk and cymbals, singing or reciting rhymes and songs and occasionally enacting the part of a character from the **Ramayana**, **Mahabharata**, *Mangalkavya*, or other local legends. Dasharathi Roy (1806–1857) was one of the most renowned *panchali* composers and singers.

Kavigan, formerly known as *kaviyal*, is a choral competition between two groups of singers that emerged in the eighteenth century and became popular with the emerging middle-class audiences of Calcutta (Kolkata). The groups of singers improvise verses in Bangla based on a theme. Traditionally these were devotional songs to Krishna, but they evolved in the modern era to debate pertinent issues concerning contemporary society.

Robert Petersen

Modern Bangladeshi Theatre. The emergence of modern, **Western**-influenced Bangladeshi theatre is integrated with the history of the modern Indian theatre, particularly Bengali theatre. During the Bengal presidency there developed a suburban model of the Calcutta theatre, conceived in terms of a theatre born, politically and culturally, in a colonial environment. As the colonial theatre emerged in the mid-nineteenth century, the popular traditional urban forms succumbed to the evolution of an institution of **actor**-managers, each with his own theatre and **theatre company**, and modeled after visiting British companies and the amateur theatricals of English naval officers. Farces and Shakespeare were staged in proscenium theatres built for this purpose.

The general trend was toward Victorian-style **Parsi theatre,** with a large infusion of songs and spectacle and a loose narrative structure emphasizing themes of mythology and saint lore. Modern theatre starts with **Dinbandhu Mitra**'s iconic *The Indigo Mirror* (Nildarpan, publ. 1860), about dire living conditions among indigo farmers, produced in 1872 by the anti-British National Theatre Company of Calcutta, which soon became two groups, the Hindi National Company and the Bengali National Company. The nationalistic sentiments of such groups eventually led to British crackdowns.

Dhaka built its first professional theatre in 1872. Local Bengali **women** first performed in Dhaka in 1880 with the widely popular Urdu play *The Court of Lord Indra* (Indar sabha, 1855) by Amanat Lakhnawi (1815–1859).

Reform. British fear of subversive themes culminated in the establishment of a powerful **censorship** instrument, the Dramatic Performances Control Act of 1876, which created a magnified impression of the tussle between theatre and the colonial state. In practice, nationalism and protest surfaced through carefully veiled allusions, as in the 1882 operatic play *Mother India* (Bharat-mata), by Ramchandra Chakravarty and Kedarnath Ghosh.

Although 1947's Partition led to eastern Bengal becoming part of Pakistan, it never became, culturally or linguistically, part of Urdu-speaking western Pakistan. It was necessary for a new and distinct Bengali cultural identity to be created. **Playwrights** like Ibrahim Khan (1894–1978) and Ibrahim Khalil (1916–) wrote plays appealing to an Islamic nationalism, like *Kamal Pasha*, *Anwar Pasha*, and *Musa, the Victor of Spain* (Spain bijoyi Musa). The realistic genre was developed by playwrights like Shawkat Osman in plays such as the anti-capitalist *The Bureaucrat's Trial* (Amlar mamla, 1949); Nurul Momen's (1906–1989) one-act "Nemesis" (1984), about a 1940s Bengali famine; and Ascar Ibn Shaikh's (1925–) dramas about rural life, such as *Opposition* (Birodh).

By 1952, Bengali theatre became a contested space in the reaction to the arbitrary imposition of Urdu as the national language. The theatre went from one political contestation to another: from the conspiracy and military rule of 1954 to the student movement of 1962, to the communal riots of 1964 and 1969, to the mass insurgency of 1969, to the freedom movement leading to independence from Pakistan in 1971. The atrocities inflicted by Pakistani soldiers and the active participation in the fronts provided inspiration for playwrights such as **Munier Chowdhury**, whose expressionist *Graves* (Kabor, 1953), written while he was in prison, became a classic. Important plays included *Everyday One Day* (Pratidin ekdin, 1978) by Saeed Ahmed (1931–), *Executioner's Court* (Jallader durbar, 1972) by Kalyan Mitra (1939–), *Once More My People* (He janata arekbar, 1974) by Al Mansoor (1925–), and *Ferry Arrives* (Feri ashche) by Ranesh Dasgupta (1919–1999).

National Theatre Movement. The post-independence period saw the emergence of a national theatrical agenda aiming to bring the rural, urban, traditional, and folk theatres together. It was hoped that the success of the freedom struggle would culminate in a "national theatre." Returned from the battlefront, cultural enthusiasts formed theatre groups to dramatize the new national sentiments. One of the first such groups was Wilderness (Aryanak). University campuses became active sites when students returning from war took up serious theatre activities. Citizen (Nagarik), the second major group, opened its first production in 1973. By the 1990s, there were over fifty groups, none commercial. Wilderness and Citizen started performing at the Engineer's Institute and the British Council in 1973. While Wilderness responded to political and social issues through a new repertoire, Citizen specialized in translations and adaptations and created a new aesthetic of performance. Soon the Mahila Samiti auditorium, despite its limitations of space and facilities, emerged as the new **experimental** venue.

Theatres. Bangladesh has very few well-equipped, sizable performance venues, most seating no more than 350. Most groups possess a definite image or identity, a certain stylistic orientation, and, above everything else, a **directorial** presence. An important development is the "theatre of roots" movement, which attempts to incorporate native forms with Western styles, a major exemplar being playwright Selim Al-Deen (1948–). A parallel shift to capture a theatre space on television has sustained the actors and actresses of these companies.

FURTHER READING

Ahmed, Syed Jamil Ahmed. *Acin Pakhi Infinity: Indigenous Theatre of Bangladesh.*

Bishnupriya Dutt

BANGSAWAN. "Malay opera" of **Malaysia, Singapore**, and **Indonesia** featuring **music**, **dance**, song, and **scenographic** spectacle. This popular form originated ca. 1875 in Penang, Johore, and Singapore as a Malay-language imitation of **India**-based Parsi **theatre companies** that toured the Malay peninsula in the 1870s. *Bangsawan* was, in fact, originally called *wayang parsi* (**Parsi theatre**) or *wayang parsi tiruan* ("imitation Parsi theatre"), and its melodramatic **acting**, **costumes**, painted canvas backdrops and wings, and musical accompaniment of drums (*dhol* and *tabla*) and harmonium were directly modeled after its Indian prototype.

Plays were initially largely based on Hindustani, Persian, and Arabic sources, but it was not long before Malay chronicles and legends were added to the mix. Unlike Parsi theatre, which depended on written scripts, *bangsawan* dialogue was improvised. The name *bangsawan* itself appears to have been derived from a troupe named Indra Bangsawan, founded in 1885 by a Parsi entrepreneur from Penang named Mamat Pushi. Mamat Pushi's troupe took its name from the *Hikayat Indra Bangsawan*, a well-known Malay tale and central repertoire item.

Performance Conditions. Although receiving occasional support and honors from the traditional rulers of Malaysia, *bangsawan* was from its start a secular entertainment for the masses performed primarily in public **theatres**. Performances typically began at 8 p.m. and were over by midnight, and thus, unlike all-night traditional theatres, could be easily fitted into the working week of urbanites. Audiences were bowled over by the spectacle of flying nymphs, richly embroidered costumes, catchy tunes, highly choreographed dances, and magic. **Actors** and actresses were romanced by members of the public. By the 1880s, Malayan troupes were regularly touring to Sumatra and other islands of Indonesia, resulting in the establishment of local variants. *Bangsawan*'s influence can also be seen on the *liké* theatre of **Thailand** initiated by Thai-speaking Muslim Malays.

Diversification of Repertoire. Tours of Malayan *bangsawan* troupes to Java starting in 1893 contributed to the diversification of the genre. Performers from ***komedi stambul***, including **Auguste Mahieu**, were recruited in such numbers that by 1910 the two genres were essentially indistinguishable. With the recruits came a mixed repertoire of true crime stories, **Chinese** romances, and European fairy tales and operas. *Hamlet* was a *bangsawan* standard by 1899. The Indian musical accompaniment was supplemented, and eventually displaced, by the violin, trumpet, piano, and other **Western** instruments used in *komedi stambul*. This allowed the incorporation of a diverse repertoire of waltzes, marches, ragtime, foxtrots, Tin Pan Alley songs, and jazz, along with arrangements of Malay, Arabic, Indian, and Javanese music.

Extra turns were introduced in 1902 by Indra Zanibar, a Singaporean troupe owned by Bai Kassim. The first recorded extra turns were *keroncong* ballads and a high wire trapeze act, inserted between acts of plays. Later came sailor dances, cakewalks, circus clowns, Chinese jugglers, chorus lines, magic acts, vaudeville turns, and even boxing matches.

Heyday and Decline. *Bangsawan*'s heyday was roughly 1905–1935. Big itinerant troupes, such as Dean's Opera and Nooran's Opera of Malacca, toured Southeast Asia on steamship and rail performing shows lasting three or four hours with casts of fifty or more, heterogeneous repertoires, and stocks of Malay, Javanese, Arabian, Chinese, and European costumes and décor. *Bangsawan* has been compared to *commedia dell'arte* in its reliance on formulaic language, conventional dramaturgy, and **role types**, such as despotic kings, rapacious genies, refined princesses, wise old men, and comic maidservants. However, it was viewed in its heyday as a flexible and adaptable medium. Novelty was placed at a premium and an image of modernity courted.

Bangsawan's popularity declined due to competition from sound film and **tonil**. Malaya's first feature film, *Laila and Majnu* (Laila-Majnu, 1933), was essentially a recording of a *bangsawan* play about star-crossed lovers, which in turn was drawn from Parsi theatre. Film continued to draw actors, writers, and designers away from the **stage** after World War II, and the more naturalistic **sandiwara** had greater appeal among the increasingly educated Malay public. A 1960s camped-up version of *bangsawan* called "comic *bangsawan*" (*jenaka bangsawan*) and a 1967 radio show called "Bangsawan on the Air" (Bangsawan di Udara) met with little success. Since the 1970s, *bangsawan* has been revived under the patronage of the Malaysian state, taught in universities, and performed on television and on national stages, such as the Palace of Culture (Istana Budaya). This revival has stripped *bangsawan* of non-Malay elements, and replaced the old improvised stories with scripts. It has failed to attract large audiences.

A continual tradition of *bangsawan* exists in North Sumatra and Riau, Indonesia, however, in which three-hour versions of plays with High Malay dialogue set in Southeast Asian, Hindustani, Persian, Arabic, and European kingdoms are performed by a singing and dancing cast accompanied by violin, guitar, drum kit, tambourine, and flute. Extra numbers of traditional and modern songs and dances are inserted between scenes.

FURTHER READING

Tan Sooi Beng. *Bangsawan: A Social and Stylistic History of Popular Malay Opera.*

Matthew Isaac Cohen

BANGZI QIANG. **Chinese** genre of **xiqu**, often translated as "clapper opera," that takes its name from a hard wooden clapper (*bangzi*) that beats out the rhythm. It follows the **musical** structure called *banqiang ti*, its lyrics mainly being in seven- and ten-character couplets. Among surviving *xiqu* genres, *bangzi qiang* is the first to originate in north China and follow *banqiang ti* structure.

The system probably developed from **folk** songs and music in Shaanxi and Gansu Provinces in the sixteenth century, spreading east and south. Early texts call it *xiqin qiang* (literally, "western Shaanxi tunes"). The earliest and most influential styles are *tongzhou bangzi* (from its origin in Tongzhou, now Dali, in eastern Shaanxi Province) and *puzhou bangzi*, from southwestern Shanxi's Puzhou, or *puju*. A **kunqu** dated 1620 lists a song-name showing it had spread south by that time. Liu Xianting (1648–1695) refers to the "new sounds of Shaanxi's **actor**s" in the southern central provinces of Hunan and Hubei in his time.

Scholar Yan Changming (1731–1787) refers to thirty-six famous *bangzi qiang* companies in the Shaanxi capital Xi'an in the 1770s, a larger number even than in Beijing then, the best reputed being the Shuangsai. Especially famous historically is Sichuanese female **role type** (*dan*) actor Wei Changsheng (1744–1802), who in 1779 took Beijing by storm by introducing *bangzi qiang* there.

Themes of *bangzi qiang* items are similar to other systems, many based on popular novels. A famous eighteenth-century item was *Selling Cosmetics* (Mai yanzhi), about a scholar and cosmetics seller falling in love at first sight.

The system is now found over most of China, with specific *bangzi qiang* styles especially prevalent in northern provinces like Shaanxi, Shanxi, Shandong, and Hebei.

Scene from *Selling Water*, a *bangzi qiang* from Puzhou, Shanxi Province, 1980. The water-seller (right, played by a woman) is in love with the girl (left), but her father opposes the marriage because of his low status. Her maid (center) explains the real situation to him. (Photo: Colin Mackerras)

FURTHER READING

Mackerras, Colin, ed. *Chinese Theatre from Its Origins to the Present Day*; Wang-Ngai, Siu, and Peter Lovrick. *Chinese Opera: Images and Stories*.

Colin Mackerras

BARONG. Traditional **dance** and dance-drama form of Java and Bali, **Indonesia**, in which performers in full body **costumes** impersonate animals and mythological beasts to *gamelan* **musical** accompaniment. There is a huge variety of *barong* figures, including birds, boars, bulls, cows, dragons, elephants, giant ogres, goats, horses, lions, pigs, tigers, and various chimeras. *Barong* can frighten children, but are simultaneously endearingly comic. Some require two performers, one in front and one in back, like a panto horse or Chinese dragon. Possibly the connection to **China** is genetic; Chinese lion dancing, called *barong sai*, is common in Indonesia. Performances sometimes involve trance and usually have healing properties. **Masks** are considered sacred and receive regular offerings.

Most performances are non-narrative, but in the *Calon Arang* dance drama of Bali, a two-man *barong ketet* (lion-like *barong* with a long beard and clacking jaw) takes a dramatic role, fighting the forces of the masked witch Rangda and turning her destructive powers to good. Both the *barong ketet* and Rangda are usually danced by men. *Calon Arang* was once a **religious** drama performed to avert plague. Masks were made from potent *pule* wood and stored in temples. In the twentieth century, it became a tourist genre. Rangda's bulging eyes, outstretched tongue, protruding fangs, wild hair, pendulous breasts, and long quivering fingernails make for a distinctive profile, and her image is often used to promote Bali. In Hindu cosmology, Rangda is an incarnation of the female creative-destructive power of "divine power" (*sakti*), but Rangda's iconography corresponds to **Western** conceptions of the demonic; consequently, Rangda masks often find their way into Western horror films.

Calon Arang is linked in many tourist productions to the so-called "dagger" (*keris*) dance in which followers of the *barong* are forced by Rangda's magic to turn their daggers upon themselves. Trance and convulsions are mimed by Rangda's victims; in past generations, performers experienced out-of-body experiences.

FURTHER READING

Hobart, Angela. *Healing Performances of Bali: Between Darkness and Light.*

Matthew Isaac Cohen

BAYALATA. Kannada-language term referring to various outdoor theatre forms of Karnataka, **India**. *Bayal* means "outdoor space, field, or plain" and *ata* means "play" (as in drama, **acting** or **dancing**, or as in games). *Bayalata* was originally used by local people to refer only to their particular local outdoor theatre form. It still may be used in that context, but nowadays, with so many different forms, it is commonly used for outdoor theatre in general.

Regional theatre forms initially referred to generally as *bayalata* now have more specific names. A form of Karnataka's coastal South Kanara district, which was initially called and still remains *bayalata*, has changed its name a few times. It became *dashavatara*, meaning plays about the ten incarnations of the god Vishnu. (Similarly named forms [see *Dasavatar*], which also concern Vishnu's incarnations, exist in Goa and in the Konkan area of Maharashtra, but they are not the same as the forms of the Kanara coast.) Later, the Kanara coastal form was called **yakshagana**. In time, another *yakshagana bayalata* style developed in the region. To distinguish these two, they became known as the northern and southern styles. North Kanara's *yakshagana bayalata* types were distinguished by the names of the families that established them, the Hegdes and Hasyagars.

A similar situation occurred in the northern/northeastern areas of Karnataka. The *bayalata* there added the designation "eastern style" (*mudalapaya*) to distinguish it from the *bayalata* of the coastal region. After another *bayalata* form developed, *mudalapaya* also came to be known as **doddata** and a newer form as **sannata**.

FURTHER READING

Naikar, Basavaraj S. *The Folk-Theatre of North-Karnataka.*

Martha Ashton-Sikora

BEIGUAN. *See* Taiwan.

BETSUYAKU MINORU (1937–). Japanese • **playwright, director**, scenarist, and writer of children's fiction. Born in Manchuria, Betsuyaku returned to Japan with his widowed mother after the war, but linguistically felt like an outsider, which probably influenced his playwriting. He briefly studied at Waseda University, where he met

actor Ono Seki and director **Suzuki Tadashi**, with whom he established the Free **Stage** Company (Jiyû Butai) in 1961, forerunner of the **experimental** Waseda Little **Theatre** (Waseda Shôgekijô). This partnership dissolved in 1969, with Betsuyaku, who advocated the primacy of text, unhappy over Suzuki's overwhelming emphasis on acting and movement.

Betsuyaku was among the first major figures of Japanese absurdist theatre. Beckett and Ionesco's influence is evident in the stark simplicity of his **scenography**, almost devoid of **properties**, often featuring a single telephone pole, bench, or hospital bed, and in his dialogue, with characters talking past each other, failing to communicate. Betsuyaku's first significant work was *Elephant* (Zô, 1962), about Hiroshima survivors, often considered the ***angura*** play that launched the "little theatre movement" (*shôgekijo undô*). The play also emblematized *angura* attempts to articulate the post-1960 generation's vision, particularly its inability to grasp Japan's postwar realities and construct its identity. Betsuyaku's fame grew with *The Little Match Girl* (Machi-uri no shôjo, 1966), a searing indictment of postwar deprivations; it won the **Kishida [Kunio]** Prize, the first for an *angura* playwright.

By the mid-1960s, Betsuyaku was writing for several **theatre companies**, unusual for playwrights of his generation. The first production for the Hands Company (Te no Kai), which Betsuyaku helped organize, was *The Move* (Idô, 1973), a play marking a style change; retaining absurdist techniques, he abandoned Beckett's bleak worldview, favoring lighter comedy that was more commercial and less **political**.

A physiological awareness pervades his works in the 1980s and 1990s, as in his "corpse" (*shitai*) plays, such as *A Corpse with Feet* (Ashi no aru shitai, 1982)—a woman places her dead boyfriend's body into a futon bag, his feet sticking out, and waits by a railroad crossing. She cannot cross, because the gate is down and doesn't rise, even after trains pass. Instead, she blithely exchanges small talk with a bystander. The looming presence of the corpse grounds the action in the physical reality of being human, while simultaneously juxtaposing the absurdity of the human condition on an intellectual and social level.

Betsuyaku is an iconoclast whose work remains influential. His plays are less theatrical than quiescent, filled with silences and awkward exchanges, replete with his engaging language—the source of his genius. He has published over one hundred plays, writing for many companies, even while serving as the primary dramatist for the Snail Society (Katatsumuri no Kai), a company cofounded in 1978 by his wife, Kusunoki Yûko (1933–). He is also a founding member of the Japan Playwrights Association.

Kevin J. Wetmore, Jr.

BHAAND JASHNA. *See Bhaand pather.*

BHAAND PATHER. **Indian • folk theatre**, also spelled *bandi pethir*, that tours to villages throughout the mountainous region of Kashmir, and is believed to have been born two thousand years ago. Also known as *bhaand jashna* (literally, "clown **festival**"), it is performed outdoors in natural environments, such as hillsides and village squares, with no clear separation of audience and **acting** space. Anything present can be used by the actors, even roofs and trees. The performers—all male—are traditional comedians (*bhaands*), skilled at improvisational acting, acrobatics, **music**, and **dance**, who speak a combination of the local Kashmiri dialect mixed—for comical effect— with various modern tongues, including Gujarti, Punjabi, Urdu, Persian, Dogri, and English. Their leader is the *magun*, suggesting someone versatile. Other chief actors are the clown (*vidushak* or *maskhari*), commentator (*sutardhar*), and "lasher" (*kurivol* or *pariparsok*).

Although their art is secular, the *bhaand*s, who are Muslims, and who often perform at Muslim and Sufi sites, annually perform a solemn **religious** ritual dance called *chhok* at a Hindu temple devoted to Shiva Bhagvati. The *bhaands* themselves were once Hindu, and some believe that their continued respect for Hindu traditions—even to their turbans—betrays their forced conversion. Most earn their living weaving baskets, blankets, and carpets. Performances provide some money along with rice and clothes.

The art of the strolling *bhaands*, which has changed much over the years, blends elements from ancient **Sanskrit theatre** as well as other folk theatres. The *bhaands* perform scriptless plays called *pather* ("character"). *Bhaand pather* is a socially oriented farce mingling myth and contemporary satire inspired by the difficulties faced by Kashmiris in a society that has been subject for a thousand years to constant oppression under foreign cultural, religious, and socio-**political** systems. The *bhaands* early on developed a code whereby they conveyed to the people their underlying attacks on wicked sultans and despotic governments. Even officials observing the play and conversant with the language could not detect the subversive messages.

Plays, based on familiar old stories, poke fun at moneylenders, landlords, arrogant rulers, and the dowry system. In one piece, alien soldiers who beat Kashmiris for not understanding Persian are ridiculed. When necessary, the oppressive forces are depicted with oversize **puppets** and **masks**. The locals—including sweepers, barbers, peasants, and monks—always win. Some works depict popular folk heroes. Commoners, like filthy scavengers and hypocritical hermits, are mocked. Performances are held during the day or as all-nighters that begin at dusk with the *chhok* and end with another ritual, performed by the *magun*, during which he prays on behalf of the people, with his prayer repeated by the audience.

The principal **properties** include a whip with a gunshot-like crack symbolizing oppression. Equally important is the *ban*, a "slapstick" used for humorous effect by the outspoken clowns, whose pantomime skewers corrupt authority figures and who serve as political messengers. As in **kathakali** and **yakshagana**, certain characters enter from behind a half-**curtain** that also serves as a king's canopy. Simultaneity of action is a unique feature, as in *The Sweepers' Play* (Watel pather), about Kashmiri sweepers, in which the crowd follows a wedding procession to where another episode is already underway.

Music is provided by a standing ensemble playing an oboe-like instrument (*swarnai*), a small stick-drum (*nagari*), a large drum (*dhol*), and a metal cymbal (*thalij*). Folk songs are sung as well.

The form nearly died out during the famine of 1877 but witnessed an upsurge following Partition (1947) when it proved an attractive means of educating the masses on various social issues. A key player in this revival, **playwright-director**-actor Mohammed Subhan Bhagat (1927–1993), provided new masks, **costumes**, and properties, composed new songs, and brought much freshness to *bhaand pather*. State support for folk theatre was instituted, but today this once very popular form is again endangered because of Kashmir's political turmoil. A major exemplar is the National Bhaand Theatre, acclaimed when it appeared at the first National Theatre **Festival** of the National Academy of Music, Dance, and Drama (Sangeet Natak Akademi) in 1984.

Samuel L. Leiter

BHADHURI, SISIR KUMAR (1889–1959). **Indian** Bengali-language **actor** and **director**, born at Ramrajatala, Howrah District, West Bengal. After graduating with an arts degree from Scottish Church College in 1910, Bhadhuri took an MA in English literature in 1913 and was active in school theatricals. He started his acting career in 1921 with Calcutta's (Kolkata) Madan **Theatre** immediately after resigning two college teaching jobs. During the 1920s and 1930s, he brought new energy into Bengali theatre through his major roles and also inspired the emergence of several Calcutta theatres.

A disagreement with Madan's management led him to briefly work in films as an actor-director, but he returned to the **stage** in 1923, performing under the auspices of his **theatre company**, Natyamandir, which he founded at the Manmohan Theatre, after greatly renovating it. The following year, he produced Dwijendra Lal Roy's (1863–1913) *Sita*, playing the central character of Rama. In 1930, he joined the rival Star Theatre. He became popular for his roles of Chanakya in *Chandragupta* (1922), Raghupati and Jaysingh in *The Relinquishment* (Bisarjan, 1926), Yogesh in *Prafulla* (1927), Jibananda in *The Teenage Girl* (Sodashi, 1927), Nadir Shah in *The World Conqueror* (Digbijayi, 1928), Nimchand in *The Widow's Fasting* (Sadhabar ekadashi, 1928), and Chandrababu in *Celibates' Club* (Chirakumar sabha, 1929).

The top Bengali actor of his day, he is believed to have been the first Indian director in the modern sense. His stagings, considered very advanced in their exploration of perspective **scenography** and contemporary lighting, were much favored by the intellectual elite.

Bhaduri visited the United States in 1930 with his company, performing *Sita* in New York. The critics were not kind, however. He returned to India to perform in less than stellar plays for a variety of companies, including his own Srirangam (1941–1956). The **Japanese** invasion and their military preparations in Calcutta, the Quit India movement in 1942, and the Bengal famine in 1943 all produced disastrous effects nationwide; thus most Calcutta playhouses were closed because of financial stringencies during 1944–1945.

Although he staged some memorable productions in the mid-1950s, Bhaduri retired in 1956 and spent his final days lonely and disillusioned.

Sreenath K. Nair

BHAGAT. **Indian** operatic **folk theatre** of Uttar Pradesh, found in cities such as Agra, Vrindaban, and Mathura. *Bhagat* ("devotee"), which is closely related to *nautanki*, also is associated with *raslila* and *swang* from which it differs mainly in its originally very **religious** orientation, its noncommercial organization, its use of fewer languages (only Hindi, Braj, and Urdu), its all-male composition, its generally serious tone, and the sophistication of its song and **dance**, which employ frequent changes of meter. Admission is free, and the troupe (*akhada*; literally, "gymnasium") depends on patrons for its subsistence.

Bhagat originated in the late sixteenth or early seventeenth century as a form of Vaishnavist expression and developed into a folk form when a play called *Roop Basant*, about brothers maltreated by their stepmother, was produced in Agra by Johari Rai in 1827. In the mid-nineteenth century, *bhagat* practitioners were paid by the colonial government to perform titillating pieces designed to divert attention from potentially subversive anti-British activities. A decrease in their religiosity followed.

Bhagat still offers ritual ceremonies during rehearsals, to honor the construction of the **stage**, and to begin and end the performance. Performances are generally given on a high platform set up in the marketplace and adorned with flowers and cloths with religious designs; the audience sits on two sides. The elephant-headed god Ganesha (a.k.a. Ganapati) appears, dances, and is worshiped by the troupe manager (*khalifa*). A sung prayer to a goddess—Sarawaswati, Lakshmi, or Shakti—follows, after which the "**director**" (*ranga*) explains the essence of the story, characters, and theme. After the play concludes, a prayer ceremony in the dressing room thanks the presiding deities.

FURTHER READING

Richmond, Farley, Darius L. Swann, and Phillip B. Zarrilli, eds. *Indian Theatre: Traditions of Performance.*

Samuel L. Leiter

BHAGAVATA MELA. Southeast **Indian •** **dance**-drama of Tamilnadu, dating back to the eighteenth century. It was rescued from extinction in the 1930s. Both *bhagavata mela* (literally, "worshippers' ensemble") and **kuchipudi** share the same origin story traceable to the devotional (*bhakti*) **religious** movement/cult that flourished from the twelfth through sixteenth centuries.

Venkatarama Sastri (1759–1847), son of the so-called "father" of *kuchipudi*, is credited with having created *bhagavata mela* through twelve plays he wrote for Brahman boys; six of the plays were discovered only in the 1930s. The genre is thought to have originated in Achyutapuram village, now Melattur, from whence it spread to nearby villages, although only Melattur still gives regular performances. Because this theatre was associated with Hinduism from its inception, it was performed only in those temples—one in each village—devoted to Vaishnavist belief. The plays are staged once a year, during the annual temple **festival**.

Prahlada's Story (Prahlada charitam), written in honor of the temple deity Narasimha (an avatar of Vishnu), is Sastri's most important play. *The Wedding of Usha* (Usha parinayam), *Harishchandra,* and *Markandeya* are among his other popular plays. All are written in Telugu, signifying the genre's affinity to *kuchipudi*.

Bhagavata mela at Melattur starts with the May or June Narasimha Jayanthi celebrations, lasting ten days. Performances, which usually start at 10 p.m. and last until early morning, are given on a raised **stage** before the deity. The performers are all men, mostly amateurs. All **actors** and **musicians**—followers of Narasimha—normally observe certain austerities in their personal and social lives during this period.

The performance starts with the entry of the clown (*konnagi*), who dances about before the appearance of the "conductor" (*nattuvanar*), who sings the invocatory song (*todiya-mangalam*) along with other musicians. A boy disguised as the god Ganesha (wearing an elephant **mask**) enters, and the musicians sing in his honor as he performs a few hand gestures and foot movements. The play and its characters are introduced in song and dance by the stage manager-singer (*bhagavata*), and then the play is performed.

As in *kuchipudi*, each principal character is introduced in special songs (*daru*) performed in a slow rhythm by singers—who enter through half-**curtains**—as the actors mime the words. Dance, using ***bharata natyam***–like gestures, is a major constituent. Also important is the worship of the mask of the half-lion and half-man Narasimha, who seeks to kill the demon Hiranyakashipu. The mask is removed from the temple of Varadaraja Perumal and worn by the chief actor—who must purify himself first—when *Prahlada's Story* is performed. The climax occurs when he falls into a trance. Devotees take him to the temple where the mask is ceremoniously removed and restored to its resting place.

Music is in the classical Carnatic style. Males wear pajama-like **costumes** and knee-length coats (*dhotis*) and jackets; some also wear turbans. **Women** characters mostly wear saris similar to those of *bharata natyam*. **Makeup** is realistic.

FURTHER READING

Gargi, Balwant. *Folk Theater of India*; Vatsyayan, Kapila. *Traditional Indian Theatre: Multiple Streams*.

Arya Madhavan

BHAONA. *See Ankiya nat.*

BHARATA NATYAM. South **Indian** • **dance** form, once known as *sadir natch* and *dasi attam*. Widely thought of as a temple dance, *bharata natyam* emerged and developed in Tamilnadu. Its inception can be traced back to the *devadasi* system, which prevailed for centuries until abolished by the twentieth-century British colonial government. *Devadasi*s, literally "servants of God," are **women** dedicated and attached to Hindu temples at a young age to perform for the deity by dancing and singing in rituals and **religious** celebrations.

Historical Background. References to *bharata natyam* can be found in *The Story of the Anklet* (Silappadikaram) and *The Story of the Golden Belt* (Manimekhalai), the twin epics of Tamil literature; both concern dancing girls. They also articulate dancing techniques and presentation that do not correlate with the **Sanskrit** *Treatise on Drama* (Natyashastra; see Theory). Though *bharata natyam* became more refined during the Pallava dynasty (fourth to ninth centuries), it flourished during the Chola dynasty (ninth to twelfth centuries). Temples were provided with dancers and **musicians**. During Chola, however, the *devadasi* became "servants of the king" (*rajadasi*), and the form became associated with prostitution.

Dance Divisions. Dance (*kuttu* in Tamil) has two main divisions: the refined *santi kuttu* and the more public *vinoda kuttu*. *Santi kuttu* later was known as *bharatam*, which could be the source of the term *bharata natyam*. Its ultimate perfection owed much to the contribution in the nineteenth century of four brothers of the Thanjavur family, who systematized the technique. In the early twentieth century, Rukmini Devi Arundale (1904–1997), founder of Kalakshetra, a major dance school, devised a successful **training** system.

Nrita *and* Nritya. *Bharata natyam*'s long years of association with temples provided two cardinal elements, devotion and erotic love. It encompasses all three aspects of Indian performance: "pure dance" (*nrita*), "expressive dance" (*nritya*), and "drama" (*natya*); the main emphasis is on *nrita* and *nritya*. The basis of *nrita* is *adavu*, a systematic pattern with an opening posture followed by a specific coupling of steps and movement, designated by rhythmic syllables (*jati*). There are about twelve families of *adavu*, starting with *tattadavu*, nine basic foot stampings that gradually progress to more complex movements.

The rhythmic syllables of *nrita* are largely created by the main percussion instrument, a wooden barrel drum (*mridangam*). *Nritya*, on the other hand, is the interpretation of expressive, thematically inspired songs; equal importance is given to both body and facial movements. Communicative hand gestures (*mudra*) consist of symbolic independent gestures and combined gestures. Each use of the hands denotes a particular meaning.

Performance Techniques. The basic posture consists of an erect upper body with the legs bent at the knees, which are spread out, with the feet forming a "half-open fan" and the heels close to each other. Common steps include stamping with the sole, placing the heel forward or to the side, leaps and jumps of the toes, or stretching the limbs in different directions. Hand positions usually frame the body in symmetrical lines and include positions stretched above the head, around the body, and downward, contributing to the form's geometric exactitude.

A conventional performance starts with an invocatory dance without verse (*alarippu*), followed by a pure dance set to musical notes (*jatiswaram*). Next comes *shabdam*, an expressive dance, followed by *varnam*, a combination of *nrita* and *nritya*; it is the longest and most trying dance. Then follows the predominantly erotic *padam* and *javali*, which emphasize *natya*. The *tillana*, an energetic pure dance, ensues, demanding considerable skill. Performances normally conclude with a Sanskrit verse (*slokam*), although there might also be invocatory dances, verses from the *Gita Govindam* elaborating on the love of deities Krishna and Radha, and a special combination of interpretative verse and pure dance passages.

Music and rhythm are based on South India's Carnatic system. The performance is directed by a dance conductor (*nattuvanar*) who sings and keeps the rhythm with a pair of cymbals. Instrumental accompanists are the barrel drummer, a violinist, a *veena* player, and a flautist. **Makeup** is simple though the eyes are painted dark. The hair is plaited and decorated with flowers and jewels. The **costume** is a colorful Kancheepuram sari, a blouse, and pajamas accompanied by gold-coated necklaces, bangles, and waistbands.

FURTHER READING

Khokar, Mohan. *Traditions of Indian Classical Dance*; Samson, Leela. *Rhythm in Joy: Classical Indian Dance Traditions*; Sathyanarayana, R. *Bharatanatya: A Critical Study.*

Arya Madhavan

BHARATI, DHARMAVIR (1926–1997). **Indian** Hindi-language **playwright**, journalist, poet, and novelist, born in Allahabad, Uttar Pradesh. As a student, he participated in the struggle for independence. In 1947, he received his doctorate in literature. From 1960–1989, he edited *Dharmayug*, a widely circulated Hindi magazine.

Although he wrote five one-acts, collected as *The River Was Thirsty* (Nadi yasi thi, 1954), his sole full-length play was the five-act, free verse *Blind Age* (Andha yugha, publ. 1954; first prod. 1962), based on the concluding part of the **Mahabharata**. This landmark tragedy uses a **storyteller** to depict how human values die with human life; set on the final day of the epic's great war, *Blind Age* offers Bharati's thoughts on global conflict (and the danger of nuclear disaster) and such national issues as Partition and Indian identity, toward which Bharati takes a strongly **critical** stance. Specially written for the radio, it was first brought to the **stage** in Bombay (Mumbai). **Ebrahim Alkazi**'s 1963 production for the National School of Drama assured the play's immortality; since then every generation of **directors** has experimented with it, each time bringing out undiscovered strengths. Some tried to express its themes by producing it in **folk** style, others found musical narration more relevant, while yet others adapted it in the manner of **Western** tragedy.

Shashikant Barhanpurkar

BHASA. Ancient **Indian** • **playwright** of **Sanskrit theatre**. **Kalidasa** named him a renowned playwright famous for the quality of his work, and later literary **critics** quoted approvingly some verses attributed to him. Nonetheless, we do not possess any dramas that can be credited to Bhasa without doubt.

At the beginning of the twentieth century in Trivandrum (Thiruvananthapuram), Kerala, scholar T. Ganapati Shastri came across a set of thirteen handwritten manuscripts used by *kutiyattam* performers. In it he saw two features associated with Bhasa's reputation—namely, a drama entitled *The Vision of Vasavadatta* (Svapna-Vasavadatta) and one featuring a wooden elephant as a **property**. He published the entire set as Bhasa's dramas. Subsequently, others have disputed this claim, pointing to the fact that verses attributed to Bhasa by literary critics are not found within these dramas, and that the plays vary in quality considerably. Moreover, the manuscripts do not name Bhasa as their author. Also, the **actors** who had been performing these dramas and transmitting copies of them for centuries did not attribute them to Bhasa, though some now do.

We know nothing of Bhasa's personal life, nor do we know the time or place he lived. He was at least an older contemporary of Kalidasa, but he might also have lived long before Kalidasa.

Of the thirteen dramas attributed to Bhasa, six are based on **Mahabharata** episodes, including the famous *The Broken Thighs* (Urubhanga), in which Duryodhana is depicted dying nobly. Two are based on the **Ramayana**: *The Statue* (Pratima) and *The Coronation* (Abhisheka). One (*Charudatta*) is incomplete, its plot unresolved after four acts, and must be the basis for Shudraka's brilliant *Little Clay Cart* (Mricchakatika), which closely follows it.

Bruce M. Sullivan

BHATTACHARYA, BIJON (1915–1978). Indian Bengali-language **play-wright** and **actor,** born in rural Faridpur District. Bhattacharya's **political** involvement during college led to his abandoning his studies. In 1931, he worked as a journalist writing on political, social, artistic, and literary topics. In 1943, he joined India's Communist Party and was a founder of the leftwing Indian People's Theatre Association. Active in the Quit India Movement, Bijan was arrested several times.

A force in the New Drama Movement (Nabyanatya Andolan), Bhattacharya became prominent in the 1940s. His plays, colored but not distorted by his Marxist beliefs, depict society's struggles and sorrows amid political unrest. Bhattacharya dramatized the life of poor peasants and the working classes, whom he had come to know in East Bengal and whose language and behavior he captured with documentary accuracy. *New Harvest* (Nabanna, 1944) depicts the tragedy of Bengal's farmers within the context of the devastating famine of 1943; codirected in Calcutta (Kolkata) with **Sombhu Mitra**, it became one of India's most popular political plays, renowned for its realistic style. *The Disgrace* (Kalanka, 1946) was about tribal Baul singers. *The Blockade* (Abarodh, 1947) concerns the exploitation of mill workers by their greedy bosses, and *Change of Lineage* (Gotrantar, 1959) depicts the travails of East Bengal's refugees after 1947's Partition.

Bhattacharya founded the Calcutta **Theatre** in 1948 and was its creative force into the 1960s. In 1970, he founded a theatre institute called Kabachkundal. Bhattacharya, who was married to famed Bengali writer Mahashweta Devi (1926–), also acted in and wrote for Bollywood films in the late 1940s.

Sreenath K. Nair

BHAVABHUTI (FL. SEVENTH–EIGHTH CENTURIES). Indian • **play-wright** of ancient **Sanskrit theatre**, born into the Brahman caste. His three extant plays demonstrate an extraordinary range and depth of learning concerning Vedic lore and yoga philosophy. While not much is known of him and his artistic development, two of his plays—*Exploits of the Great Hero* (Mahaviracharita) and *The Latter Story of Rama* (Uttararamacharita)—concern the **Ramayana**; the other is a ten-act play in the *prakarana* style (an invented story based on the minor nobility) called *Malati and Madhava* (Malati-Madhava).

Bhavabuti's plays emphasize verbal art; in his earlier plays, literary artistry sometimes gets in the way of dramatic development. *The Latter Story of Rama* is based on the twelve years following the recovery of Rama's wife, Sita, from her abductor. It explores Sita's banishment by Rama, the birth of their two children in exile, and the family's eventual reconciliation and reunion. More contemplative than Bhavabhuti's other works, it uses the notion of memory and reflection to convey a psychological depth and to develop a sense of tragic irony. Rather than merely retelling the epic, Bhavabhuti inserts several new scenes that allow him to develop the characters and action. An important example is when Rama, Sita, and Lakshmana view a gallery of paintings depicting their previous adventures. By allowing the audience to see them reacting to events depicted in art works, Bhavabhuti creates a layering of events and reveals some of the emotional turmoil that forms the background to this drama. He is a master at using physical conditions to convey emotional feelings, and his plays are credited for providing a deeper, more philosophical, basis for the aesthetic **theory** of *rasa*.

Robert Petersen

BHAVAI. Indian • **folk theatre** of Gujarat and southern parts of Rajasthan, performed in honor of the mother goddess, Amba-ma, usually on ritually appropriate **religious** holidays, especially Navaratri (**festival** of the mother goddess), in rural areas. The term may derive from the word *bhav* ("world") or be a derivation of the Sanskrit for emotion, *bhava* (see Theory).

A typical performance occurs before an improvised shrine to Amba consisting of a large earthen lamp, which provides the primary lighting, and a drawing on the ground of a trident (a symbol for the goddess). Performances last all night long as male **actors** come forward carrying torches for their own illumination and portray scenes about legendary heroes and ordinary folk characters from every imaginable caste, faith, and walk of life. Though a *bhavai* performance is an act of devotion to the goddess, the scenes are fundamentally secular, spectacular, and humorous.

Legends claim that *bhavai* was largely created by a fourteenth-century Brahman, Asait Thakar, who offended his caste when he rescued a lower-caste girl by pretending she too was a Brahman. His generosity cost him his own clan's caste identity, but it also earned him the enduring gratitude of the girl's clan. In exile, Asait used his skills as a narrator of Puranic stories and, joined by his three sons, formed a troupe of wandering performers.

Though professional players predominantly come from the Brahman Targalas caste, today *bhavai* is performed by many different castes and they pass their knowledge on from teacher (*guru*) to disciple (*shishya*), largely from memory. *Bhavai* still uses men as female impersonators. The largely male audiences enjoy the raunchy humor and carnivalesque play that they expertly provide.

Thakar is credited with having written some 360 scenes (*vesha*); however, only sixty remain in the active repertory. *Vesha* literally means "**costume**"; each *vesha* is usually centered on a single colorful character, vividly represented in cultural and gender-specific dress and manners. Many different versions of the *vesha* exist, and actors only loosely follow the scripted material, preferring to partially improvise in response to the audience's mood. The actual plots are rather straightforward, focusing on the vivid, satiric personalities shown by actors who **dance** and sing in character. A single *vesha* will include an introductory song (*avnu*), which introduces the main character, followed by a series of actions and narration interspersed with song and dance that can last from a few minutes to several hours.

At the beginning, *vesha* will either represent Amba-ma or the elephant-headed god Ganesha. Thereafter, most common *vesha* represent village characters, such as the farmer, the shepherd, and the cutler. Many others represent various castes and ethnic groups, such as Brahmans and Vaniyas. Each is presented with the appropriate mannerisms, costumes, and dialect. Male costumes vary tremendously from character to character, but from the waist down often include a *dhoti*, a simple rectangular cloth that may be worn in as many as sixty different ways. Female characters wear a basic costume of a highly flared skirt, advantageous for the swirling dances, which is then accessorized with ornaments and shawls to convey different castes and cultures.

Some *vesha* reflect Muslim culture from the Mughal dynasty. Partially spoken in Urdu, the *vesha* of the Muslim soldier Jhandho tells of how a Muslim governor fell in love with a Hindu woman. The intermingling of characters of different religions harkens back in time to a more diverse and tolerant society.

A **theatre company** has twelve to fourteen members, including a leader (*naik*), performers (*bhavaayas*), including a clown, and a few **musicians**. The performance commences around 10 p.m., when the *naik* demarcates the **stage** by drawing a ten- to twenty-foot-wide circle on the ground with the tip of a sword. Only the performers are allowed to enter the circle. The *naik* also introduces each *vesha* and provides humorous commentary as the action unfolds. The clown, called either Juthana or Ranglo, interjects satirical commentary on the actions of the characters, like the *vidushaka* in **Sanskrit theatre**. Musicians sit to one side and commonly play shoulder and hip drums, the bowed, three-string *sarangi*, cymbals, and a couple of long copper horns (*bhungal*), which provide a flourish for dramatic entrances and exits.

Modern **Western**-style scripted theatre stole away most of the urban audience early in the twentieth century. Rising middle-class **playwrights**, such as Ranchhod-ray Udayram (1837–1923), rejected *bhavai* and instead looked to the more literary Sanskrit theatre for inspiration. It was not until 1953 that Jaishankar Bhojak "**Sundari**," a veteran actor, **director**, and renowned female impersonator, was able to revive interest in *bhavai* with *Mena of Gujarat* (Mena Gujari, 1953) by Rasiklal Parikh (1897–1982). *Bhavai* also occasionally has been used in a limited way as a vehicle for government propaganda as actors have sought state sponsorship in order to achieve greater economic stability. Modern directors, like **Shanta Ghandhi**, have continued to **experiment** with *bhavai*, while Darpan Academy in Gujarat has been active in researching and preserving this vanishing form.

FURTHER READING

Desai, Sudha R. *Bhavai: A Medieval Form of Ancient Indian Dramatic Art* (*Natya*) *Prevalent in Gujarat*; Baradi, Hasmukh. *History of Gujurati Theatre*.

Robert Petersen

BHUTAN. The small mountainous kingdom of Bhutan (Drukyul), bordering **China** to the north and **India** to the south, is about the size of Switzerland, with a little more than 1 million inhabitants. Despite Bhutan's relative isolation in the Himalayas, its relative proximity to China, India, **Tibet**, and **Nepal** has had a significant influence on its cultural history. Bhutan grew out of the state of Lhomon in the seventh century. Shortly thereafter, Mahayana ("Greater Vehicle") Buddhism was adopted as the state **religion**, and a dual religious and secular government was established. Since 1907, Bhutan, whose capital is Thimphu, has been ruled by an absolute monarch known as the "dragon king" (*druk gyalpo*). There is no native modern theatre, radio is primarily used to convey service announcements, and television became legal only in 1999.

Festival Performances at Monasteries. Several important **festivals** are celebrated with **masked** and unmasked **dances**, songs, and archery competitions. The most important are the annual *tsechu* (a.k.a. *domcchoe*) festivals, given throughout the year (except for monsoon season), which last three to five days and are celebrated in various fortified monasteries dotting the countryside. Two of the most famous are held at Paro in the spring and at Thimphu in the autumn. Each consists primarily of a series of colorful masked dances (*chham*) performed by monks and laymen. Focused on spiritual rather than aesthetic goals, they invoke morals, as in *The Dance of the Prince and Princess* (Phole mole) and *The Dance of the Judgment of the Dead* (Raksha maksham); bless the audience, as in *The Dance of the Stags* (Shacham) and *The Dance of the Black Hats* (Zhana ngacham); or celebrate the glory of Buddhism, as in *The Dance of the Heroes* (Pacham). The *Dance of the Prince and Princess* is considered the most play-like, with one version telling of two princes who return from battle to find that their beautiful princesses have been misbehaving and punish them by slicing off their noses. Ultimately, they reconcile and a doctor sews the noses back on.

Performance. The dances—which may induce trance-like states in the predominantly male performers—reveal a strong Tibetan influence and are accompanied by long trumpets, oboes, double-sided drums, and cymbals. The dances honor the Buddhist saint Padmasambhava (also "Guru Rinpoche"), credited with having brought Lamaistic Mahayana Buddhism to Bhutan in the eighth century. The heavy dance masks represent animals, angry gods, skulls, and human beings, as well as Guru Rinpoche. The dancer sees through the mouth. While the performances are serious religious affairs, there is an important clown (*atsara*) who interjects comedy, often rather bawdy. He also serves as a stage assistant, even prompting when necessary.

Stages are open areas in temple courtyards backed by large, painted, silk scrolls, sewn together with gold thread, which serve as scenic backgrounds. The audience sits on the ground to watch.

Royal **music** and dance have been supported at court since the beginning of the twentieth century. Since 1954, the Royal Academy of Performing Arts has worked to maintain these traditions. Secular performances for royal audiences were a common feature of public gatherings. These performances by amateurs offered up humorous dances and skits that dramatized local issues. With the advent of a modern education system in Bhutan these secular plays have since been replaced by student productions.

Nationalism and Tourism. With a growing influx of Nepalese minorities in the 1980s, the government began a program—"national customs and etiquette" (*driglam namzha*)—to bolster Bhutan cultural identity and nationalism. It mandated national dress at formal occasions and the use of the official language, Dzongkha, in schools. In 1989, this program was further expanded by a decree forbidding the teaching of Nepali in public schools. Such anti-Nepali laws have strained relations among various ethnic communities.

Tourism is Bhutan's chief industry outside of agriculture and is closely controlled by the state-run tourism agency. Because the government wishes to protect the culture from external, that is, **Western**, corruption, only a limited number of tourists are annually allowed to attend Bhutan's traditional performances, but they must belong to a state-licensed tour group. Despite the government's protective measures restraining Western development, secular theatre is on the rise. Commercial productions of traditional dances that include raised platform stages and modern technology are becoming common, and secular theatre along with amateur film is beginning to attract larger audiences.

Robert Petersen

BIDESIA. Indian • **folk theatre** of western Bihar, also spelled *bidesiya*, which came to prominence in the late nineteenth century when it was developed by Bhikhari Thakur (1887–1971), a strolling **actor**-poet-**dancer**-singer who came from the low-caste of barbers and wrote, composed **music** for, and **directed** his Bhikhari **Theatre**. *Bidesia* ("immigrant") is a musical form in Bhojpur, a Hindi dialect, produced out of doors wherever a village audience can be gathered. Production elements are simple, casts are limited to three or four long-haired, male actor-dancers who play multiple roles of both genders, and subject matter is sentimental and didactic.

The form—which bears similarities to *nautanki* and also borrows from other folk genres, such as *rasalila* and *ramlila*—is typified by Thakur's play, *Bidesia* (1917), about a husband who leaves his yearning wife behind in their village to earn money in Calcutta (Kolkata). Her loneliness through the passing seasons is depicted until her husband is forced to return after meeting with crushing disappointment. This situation mirrored that of many rural laborers and their downtrodden wives, and was the basis for other plays; it also inspired the genre's name.

Thakur's later plays deal with socially progressive subjects, such as the sale of young girls to older men as brides, the dangers to the family of drink and whoremongering, the problem of old parents dependent on their married children, the opprobrium borne by widows, and so on. The plays remain relevant and, with their sympathy for the lower castes and their satire, continue to be popular.

These works are performed with a harmonium and drums playing local folk and popular tunes exploiting the wit of the Bhojpuri dialect. The characters' **makeup** and **costumes** (mainly the *dhoti*), depicting mainly commoner types, are realistic, and acting mingles realism with song and dance and melodramatic excess.

Samuel L. Leiter

BINODINI DASI (CA. 1862–1941). **Indian** Bengali-language **actress**, born to an impoverished and disreputable family in Calcutta (Kolkata), whose artistic persona dominated the nineteenth-century theatre. **Trained** as a singer by a courtesan, Binodini Dasi was recruited as an actress from a prostitute's quarters at eleven.

Her acting career commenced when she was twelve in *The Destruction of Enemies* (Shatrusamhar, 1874) at Calcutta's Great National Theatre. Binodini soon became a leading actress for prestigious **theatre companies** and worked under the guidance of **playwright-director** • **Girish Chandra Ghosh**.

Despite the brevity of her career, Binodini appeared in eighty roles. In Ghosh's *Killing of Meghnad* (Meghnadbadh, 1881), she displayed remarkable versatility in performing six sharply differentiated roles; she handled three in Ghosh's *Chieftain's Daughter* (Durgeshnandini, 1876).

Despite her achievements, Binodini met with betrayal and misfortune. A famous example is when, in order to secure funds to build a new **theatre**, she became a wealthy man's mistress only for the theatre—which she had been promised would be named for her—to be called the Star Theatre instead.

Binodini's accomplishments included developing **makeup** techniques—a blend of **Western** and native styles—for the modern **stage**. As an actress she was highly imaginative and had a natural quality of intense trancelike transformation.

In 1884, the famous ascetic Sri Ramakrishnan Paramahamsa (1836–1886) saw Binodini act and visited her after the performance. She became an ardent devotee of Paramahamsa, retiring at the peak of her career. Her final appearance was in *Bazaar of the Impudent* (Bellik bajar, 1887). She lived a lonely life, stimulated by writing and occasional theatregoing. Binodini published *My Story* (Amar katha) in 1913, which reveals not only the historical graph of the development of Bengal's nineteenth-century public theatres but also the condition of **women** in theatre at the time.

Sreenath K. Nair

BODABIL. **Philippine** popular entertainment form, first known as *vod-a-vil*, that was derived from American vaudeville and consisted of comedy skits, **musical** numbers, and magic and novelty acts, usually ending with a "musical **dance** choreography."

Introduced in Manila in the early 1900s by traveling troupes featuring such foreign performers as the Rosebud Sisters, Willie Green, and Eva Roland, *bodabil* became a part of the Manila scene in the 1920s through a **theatre company** set up by Lou Borromeo. First performed between short plays, *sarsuwela* acts, or film screenings, it gained such popularity that some **theatres**, such as the Savoy (later, the Clover) and the Sirena, were devoted solely to *bodabil*.

Although most of the song numbers consisted of American jazz, blues, and ballads, and Filipino performers such as tap dancer Bayani Casimiro (1928–1989), comedian Canuplin (1872–1941), and singer Katy de la Cruz (1907–) imitated American icons such as Fred Astaire, Charlie Chaplin, and Sophie Tucker respectively, entertainers also indigenized vaudeville by inserting traditional song numbers (*kundiman*). Later, during the **Japanese** occupation (1942–1945), film **actors** performed translations or original Filipino plays, such as Wilfrido Ma' Guerrero's (1917–1995) *Forever* (1941). With this new development, *bodabil* came to be called the "**stage** show," and actors used their skits to mock the Japanese. The song "You Will Return" (Babalik ka rin) refers to General MacArthur's promise to return to the Philippines.

After the war, *bodabil* slowly degenerated because of film's popularity. Acts were performed only in run-down theatres, attracting audiences through scantily dressed performers. During the martial law years (1972–1981), however, a street theatre group, U.P. Vaudeville Troupe (later, Peryante), used the form in several plays critical of the government. Today, *bodabil* continues to inform shows performed during small town celebrations (*fiestas*), as well as variety shows on television.

Joi Barrios

BOMMALATTA(M). *See* Puppet Theatre: India.

BORIA. **Malaysian** song and response choral theatre performed mainly on the island of Penang; it includes comic sketches, **music**, and **dance**. *Boria* was first introduced on the island in the nineteenth century by Shiite Muslims from **India**, who traditionally paraded before wealthy residents, often of the merchant class, singing songs of Shiite martyrdom, an allusion to the deaths of Hassan and Hussain, sons of the fourth Muslim caliph, Ali, killed by **political** opponents on the battlefield of Kerbala (located in present-day Iraq). *Boria* is still generally performed during the Islamic lunar month of Muharram, which for Shiites marks the time of the martyred sons' deaths. However, the Sunni Malays changed the original **religious**ly motivated performance into a nonreligious form.

In adopting the form, Malays made it a choral presentation with a lead singer (*tukang karang*) and comic skits. They gave less attention to the daytime parade and focused on the staging of a nighttime drama. By the 1930s, *boria* was performed purely for entertainment and had become highly popular. Also, rich Malay businessmen and local leaders would invite groups to perform in their houses. However, during the **Japanese** occupation (1941–1945), the theatre declined due to the hardships of war; also, the occupiers used *boria* as a propaganda vehicle. At the same time, however, troupes managed to inject a nationalist spirit into their performances, especially the song lyrics. This spirit continued into the 1950s, when there was a growing desire for independence from the British, who had resumed control after World War II. The Malay political party also sought to gain influence through using *boria* during that era.

After independence, during the 1960s and 1970s, *boria* groups concentrated on humor and political satire. In the 1980s, *boria* became a conduit for conveying socially instructive messages, with group appearances at annual **festivals** and for holidays and official occasions. It was also in the 1980s that troupes began to incorporate more modern cultural elements, such as a large modern band accompanying the dancing and singing. Contemporary groups may also combine **Western**, Indian, and traditional Malay instruments. Musicians may play the guitar, ukulele, flute, violin, bongos, tabla, and accordion instead of traditional Malay instruments, such as the *rebana*, gong, and *gambus*.

There are no scripts; the lead singer improvises the lyrics. His songs reflect tunes drawn from Western, Malay, and Indian popular music, while the dance steps of the chorus may resemble Western styles, like the cha-cha or tango, or local dance styles, such as the *zapin, inang,* or *joget*.

Typically, troupes represented a specific village or district and competed annually. Originally a male performance genre, *boria* eventually incorporated **women**. However, the tradition of female impersonators is retained as a convention and increases the comedy. Groups include about a dozen chorus members (men, women, or both), a lead singer, and several **actors** to create the skits. Once the earlier processional *boria* was no longer performed, a platform or proscenium **stage** was used; there is not much open-air staging. However, performances can also be held in halls and hotels.

The lead singer always wears an elaborate **costume** while chorus members typically wear white pants and a shirt with a sash. Women usually wear a Malay outfit (the *sarung kebaya*): a long-sleeved blouse and a skirt that wraps around the waist. In the past, performers dressed in a more varied fashion, that is, in a Western, Middle Eastern, **Chinese**, and Indian, as well as Malay style.

Boria is now mainly a choral performance headed by the lead vocalist. Choreography and gestures are not elaborate. The performance begins with a comic sketch, music is played, and the singing begins. Current issues are cleverly introduced. While there used to be many plots, complete tales are no longer told. In addition to themes dealing with social issues, stories were drawn from local folktales, legends, and history. Western, Indian, and Chinese literature provided further sources, an influence of **bangsawan**. *Boria* also drew upon Arab tales from *The Thousand and One Nights*; however, the original Shiite tribute to Hassan and Hussain might only occasionally contribute to content.

Overall, *boria* affords entertainment and social critique. Although, for the most part, *boria* remains in Penang, it has received wider coverage through the **experimental theatre** of **playwright ⦁ Noordin Hassan**. Originally from Penang, Hassan was intrigued by *boria* since his father was an active performer. In his landmark music drama, *'Tis Not the Tall Grass Blown by the Wind* (Bukan lalang ditiup angin, 1970), Hassan projects important social messages through a *boria*-style sequence.

FURTHER READING

Nur Nina Zuhra (Nancy Nanney). *An Analysis of Modern Malay Drama*; Rahmah Bujang. *Boria: A Form of Malay Theatre*.

Nancy Nanney

BRUNEI. Also known as Negara Brunei Darussalam ("Abode of Peace"), the oil-rich sultanate of Brunei is a tiny nation of 2,200 square miles, plus thirty-three small islands, situated on the northwest coast of Borneo. Bandar Seri Begawan is the capital. Malay is the official language, but both **Chinese** and English are spoken as well. Brunei's 372,000 people are approximately 67 percent Muslim, 13 percent Buddhist, and 10 percent Christian; the remainder belong to various indigenous **religions**. Ethnic Malays constitute over 60 percent of the population, around 20 percent are Chinese, and the rest are from different minorities. Brunei's golden age was in the fifteenth and sixteenth centuries. It became a British protectorate in 1888 and did not become free of British dependency until 1984.

Although **dancing**, **folk** singing, poetry reading (often to **musical** accompaniment), and **storytelling** are practiced as traditional performing arts, Brunei does not have a tradition of narrative-driven or dance theatre. Traditional dances are concerned with exorcistic practices on behalf of the community, or are connected with the harvest season.

Historical Background. In 1922, a group of traditional performers traveled to Singapore in the company of Sultan Muhammad Jamallul Alam II to participate in the Malaya and Borneo Cultural **Festival**, in honor of a visit by England's Prince of Wales, resulting in their coming under **Western** artistic influences. In the 1930s, following a visit from the Seri Indera Zanzibar Bangsawan troupe, visits from a series of commercial Indonesian and Malaysian *bangsawan* (a.k.a. Malay opera; see also *Komedi stambul*) became popular; a local troupe was formed, although foreign companies continued to visit into the 1940s. *Bangsawan* (*wayang bangsawan* in Brunei) introduced the proscenium **theatre** to Brunei, along with many other elements of popular theatre, including largely improvised performance.

During World War II, the **Japanese** occupiers used the form to spread anti-British propaganda, although performances were severely limited because of wartime conditions and the need for constant Japanese scrutiny. A significant occurrence was the production of a pro-Japanese play by H. M. Salleh, *The Emperor's Reign* (Kimigayo), inspired by the eponymous Japanese national anthem. Salleh, who had been in prison, was released so he could produce more such propaganda. By the time he began to turn such methods against the occupiers, the war had ended.

After the war, *wayang bangsawan* regained its earlier popularity in Brunei, once more under British rule. Local and foreign **actors** combined in a single troupe, creating a new approach, including stories taken from Malay legend and folklore. This musical genre, produced on a proscenium **stage** against a **scenographic** backdrop, presented romantic or comic tales with happy endings; an orchestra and singer entertained during intermissions.

In the 1950s, *bangsawan* declined in favor of Indonesian and Malaysian **sandiwara**, recognized as the true start of modern theatre in Brunei. *Sandiwara* was considered more progressive than *bangsawan*, whose excesses it sought to eliminate, including its reliance on improvisation. *Sandiwara* **playwrights** used the stage as a means for examining important local social issues, including those promoting nationalist concerns, and a modern-style **director** served to bring polish to the acting and production elements. The two chief play types, both of which were scripted and available for reading, were "history plays" (*drama sejarah*) and "old-style plays" (*purbawara*). Among important examples is *Seven Cavemen* (Tujuh penghuni gua, 1957), by Shukri Zain, a noted religious intellectual.

In 1962, the Brunei writers' association, Angkatan Sasterawan dan Sasterawani Brunei, was formed. Its promising young playwrights included Haji Ahmad Hussain, Ghafar Jumat, Ahmad Arsad, and A. Rahman Yusof. However, conditions created by the **political** rebellion of December 1962 brought theatrical activity to a halt; under the State of Emergency Laws, playwriting came under suspicion of subversion, leading to severe **censorship**. Most playwrights of the time had studied in Malaya, where they learned to introduce social criticism into their work. They often adapted *sandiwara* plays to reflect the Bruneian context. But the 1960s gave them no opportunity to voice their concerns. When *sandiwara* activity began to re-emerge at the end of the decade and in the 1970s, the focus shifted to plays preoccupied by Islamic ideology, since the writers, such as Shukri Zain, Adi Rumi, and Saman Kahar, were largely associated with Islamic religious colleges, especially those in Cairo. Their work formed a new genre of one-acts called *drama sebabak*.

The first period of Brunei's "modern drama" (*drama moden*) is considered to have begun in 1969 and ended in 1979, when Brunei signed a new, pre-independence treaty with Great Britain. Most plays of the 1970s were history dramas, such as Shukri Zain's *Seri Begawan Abdul Kahar* (1970), produced to celebrate the change of the capital city's name from Brunei Town to Bandar Seri Begawan, and dealing with the sixteenth-century nationalists who prevented the spread of Christianity by Spaniards. Among further signs of progress was a drama competition held in 1973.

The advent of local television in 1975 drew many artists away from live performance, leading to a serious decline in production reminiscent of the theatre's silence in the 1960s.

A resurgence of modern drama occurred between 1980 and 1983, when the post-independence nationalist spirit led to plays and productions honoring Brunei's history. In 1982, the governmental Language and Literature Bureau sponsored **playwriting** competitions that led important writers to dramatize important issues, with their work eventually being shown on television. In 1983, the National **Stage** Drama Competition was inaugurated. Twenty groups totaling a thousand performers participated, and the ten top plays were anthologized. The principal **theatre company** that emerged was Rusila (Rumpun Seni Lakon Negara Association, 1982), which presented an eclectic repertory over the years. Rusila branched out to produce social activist theatre in 1990, dealing with subjects like drug abuse and police-community relationships. It was one of three groups—the others being its offshoots, the **experimentally** inclined Young Artists' Group (Kumpulan Putera Semi, 1980) and the more absurdist-oriented Kastea (Kumpulan Artis Teater Nasional, 1984)—that dominated Brunei's theatre in recent decades. All are amateur-based, providing free admission, and performing in makeshift venues, there being no purpose-built theatres available.

In 1984, Brunei achieved independence, thereby launching a modest new phase in its modern drama development. That year, a spectacular historical drama, *Blood Is Thicker than Water* (Biduk Lalu Kiambang Bertaut), staged and written by A. Rahman Yusof, was produced on a large, open field using four stages and recounting the nation's history.

Theatre still lags behind other arts in Brunei, and suffers from a lack of venues, audience interest, and decent plays. Performances are few and far between, and a significant number of people have anti-theatre prejudices. All plays must receive official endorsement before being produced or published, and the threat of interrogation and prosecution is ever-present. Plays dealing with people's private lives are forbidden, thereby hampering freedom of expression and dissuading young people from venturing into theatrical expression, either in writing or performance. Local audiences are reluctant to experience plays that use nonrealistic methods. Reviews or serious discussion of plays are limited or nonexistent.

The one institution offering theatre studies for undergraduates is the University of Brunei Darussalam. The many secondary school students interested in theatre have only their end-of-the-year school performances honoring His Majesty's birthday in which to gain experience. Without subsequent support, these students gradually lose interest in theatre. Opportunities are continually disappearing, making the future look bleak for the country's theatre.

Samuel L. Leiter (additional information provided by Ena Herni Wasli)

BUDAI XI. *See* Puppet Theatre: Taiwan.

BUGAKU. **Japanese** classical **dance** form that is part of *gagaku*, the general term for a body of ancient **music** and dances. Traditionally performed by the Music Department of the Imperial Palace, as well as by ensembles associated with certain Shinto shrines and Buddhist temples (see Religion in Theatre), *gagaku/bugaku*, with its origins in **China** and **Korea**, had its first pieces brought to Japan in the sixth century. This importation increased with Japan's large-scale adoption of the **political** and social apparatus of Tang dynasty (618–907) China.

Historical Development. *Bugaku*'s heyday was during the Heian period (782–1184), when it was a major part of imperial court ceremonies. During the Kamakura period (1185–1333), when the military government transferred from Kyoto to Kamakura, there was a reduction in the scale of court ceremonies. Later, during the civil wars of the fifteenth century, the form was near extinction. With the establishment of peace during the Edo period (1603–1868), movements emerged to reinstate *bugaku* at court and reconstruct lost elements of the tradition.

This continued after the Meiji Restoration (1868), when the emperor was once again given head-of-state powers. Performers from Kyoto, Nara, and Osaka were brought to Tokyo (Edo), the new capital, to standardize the traditions. In the late nineteenth century, the concept of tradition unchanged from ancient times was promoted in order to strengthen imperial prestige. That image of *gagaku/bugaku* still largely exists today despite scholarship demonstrating how the art has undergone considerable reconstruction throughout its long history.

Left and Right Dances. Although *gagaku* dances include those of indigenous origin employed in imperial and Shinto ceremonies, *bugaku* refers to dances derived from the Asian mainland. These are divided into two styles: dances of the left (*sahô*), which are accompanied by "Chinese music" (*tôgaku*), and which were imported mainly from Tang dynasty China; and dances of the right (*uhô*), which are accompanied by "Korean music" (*komagaku*), deriving from the Korean kingdoms of Silla, Paekche, and Koguryo, and which most likely predate dances of the left. The terms left and right grew out of *bugaku*'s role at the Heian court with its Chinese-influenced ministries and militia of the left and right. Even today, dancers of left pieces enter along the left bridge leading to the **stage**, and dancers of right pieces enter along the right.

Representative pieces include the left dance *King Ranryô* (Ranryô-ô), featuring a lone dancer in a strong dragon **mask** and said to originate when a Chinese king wore such a mask to encourage his army to victory; the left dance *Music of 10,000 Years* (Manzairaku), featuring the formation dance of four phoenixes; and the right dance *Nasori*, thought to be a Koguryo dynasty place name, featuring the paired dance of two dragons.

The stage, seen at various larger shrines and temples throughout Japan as well as at the imperial palace, is square with a set of stairs leading to the stage at the center back. A low railing surrounds the stage. Musicians sit behind the stage to accompany the dancers, although in orchestral (*kangen*) pieces they sit directly on the stage.

Costumes, Masks, and Movements. The two dance styles contain twenty or so pieces each; there are clear differences between the two in **costumes**, masks, and movements. Traditionally, dancers specialize in one or the other and do not perform both styles. There are one-person, two-person, and four-person (sometimes increased to six) dances.

Bugaku's elaborate costumes feature a wide variety of embroidered patterns and designs including symmetrical, interlocking, and repeating patterns, and many flora and fauna. The use of silk shoes is a major distinguishing element from the split-toed *tabi* socks employed by **nô** and **kabuki**, which developed centuries later. The costumes of left dances are primarily red, while those of right dances are primarily green, blue, and yellow. Approximately half of the dances employ masks specific to the dance. Some have moving parts such as suspended jaws, moving noses, dangling chins, and rolling eyes.

Movement tends to be slow, controlled, and elegant, particularly in "ordinary dances" (*hiramai*) performed in formation by two or more dancers. "Running dances" (*hashirimai*) usually feature a lone dancer who moves energetically about. In general, pieces consist of four parts: an instrumental prelude, the entrance of the dancer or dancers, the main dance, and the exit of the dancer or dancers. The main part generally features a rhythmic structure beginning with a slower introductory section (*jo*), a buildup in tempo (*ha*), and an ending with a fast tempo (*kyû*).

FURTHER READING

Garfias, Robert. *Gagaku: The Music and Dances of the Imperial Household*; Ortolani, Benito. *Bugaku: The Traditional Dance of the Japanese Imperial Court*; Togi, Masataru. *Gagaku: Court Music and Dance.*

Richard Emmert

BUNKÔDÔ. *See* Matsuda Bunkôdô.

BUNRAKU. *See* Puppet Theatre: Japan.

BURMA (MYANMAR). Burma's name was changed to Myanmar in 1989, although the name has not been accepted universally. It is situated on the Bay of Bengal and has nearly 54 million people. The dominant **religion** is Theravada (Hinayana) Buddhism (a.k.a. "Lesser Vehicle" Buddhism), but the people also believe in the spirits called *nat* of which thirty-seven are especially prevalent. They pay a significant role in native theatre practices, and are central to Burmese spirit **festivals** (*nat pwe*) carried out by male and female "mediums" (*nat kadaw*), who employ song and dance in their rites.

Historical Background. Although the Burmese arrived in the region in the ninth century, the earlier Mon and Pyu peoples (second through ninth centuries) already had developed forms of **dance** and **music**; **Chinese** records tell of a troupe of Pyu musicians and dancers paying tribute to the Tang emperor in 802. The Pagan dynasty (1044–1287) produced major cultural achievements. *Jataka*, familiar from the *hawsa* **storytelling** tradition, were the principal subject of early dramas, which first appeared during the fourteenth century in the pageant-like Buddhist "mystery play" genre (*nibhatkin*), now rare, with tableaux of Buddha's life shown on carts that rolled through village streets, accompanied by a recitation. The clown (*lubyet*) was a vital element and has remained significant because of his satirical commentary. *Nibhatkin* was a major step in the development of the classical theatre, *zat pwe*.

Puppet Theatre. Among Burma's performing arts is the traditional, but now infrequently seen, **puppet theatre**, *yokthe pwe*, in which *nat* play an important part alongside *zat* (from *jataka*) tales. This form, which arose in the eighteenth century, and whose origins are believed to be indigenous, mingles dialogue, song, music, and clowning. It offers both hour-long and all-night performances, and is believed to have inspired Burma's classical traditions with live **actors**.

Asian Influences. **India**—and to a degree, China and **Sri Lanka**—has influenced Burma's performing arts, but so has **Thailand**, especially after Burma's conquest of the Siamese capital Ayutthaya in 1767, which led to the "Age of Triumph." The enormously influential ***Ramayana*** (through Thailand's *Ramakien* version) and **Panji** Cycle (Thailand's *Inao*) entered Burma from Thailand, and had a great cultural impact. The Burmese conceived of the Hindu hero Rama as an incarnation of Buddha. Ornately **costumed** dance-drama performances of works modeled on these foreign sources were extremely popular at court. Also, Thailand's **masked** court dance, *khon*, inspired Burma's *zat gyi*, popular in Ava (a premodern Burmese capital) in the eighteenth and nineteenth centuries but still extant. This masked "*Ramayana* play," rare today, depicts stories from the *Ramayana* with dancers enacting a story sung by narrators and a chorus.

Secular Drama. The first secular drama, *Manikhet*, was written by a court poet in the early eighteenth century, but the classical peak came in the nineteenth, with plays written by kings and other nobles. **Playwrights • U Ponnya** and **U Kyin U** flourished in this culture, which even had a minister of performing arts (*thabin*). One of his functions was to control the nation's many theatrical outlets from becoming dangerously **political**, and to show proper deference to the monarchy and religion. Politics nevertheless intruded, as evidenced by U Ponnya's *Wi-za-ya zat* (ca. 1865), which may have led to the playwright's murder. Plays—even those based on *jataka*—became more psychologically honest and were shortened to a single evening's presentation. By the early 1880s, Burma's palace **theatre** was using **stages** and special effects.

Myay waing *and* **Zat pwe.** Meanwhile, the masses viewed the all-night *myay waing* (literally, "earth-circling performance") presented on the mat-covered earth lit by torches, surrounded by the audience, and using a full orchestra. *Myay waing*'s **properties** were minimal: a trunk with the king seated on it symbolized a palace; a branch stuck in the ground meant a jungle. All performances began with ritual devotions. There were two leads, a "prince" (*mintha*) and a "princess" (*minthamee*), whose safety was threatened during the action; in their climactic duet, the *mintha* stood still, arms folded, and sang while the *minthamee* danced. They wore beautiful silken costumes even as poor characters. Each might perform a highlight "weeping song" (*ngo-chin*) to express their distress, although more lighthearted songs might also be sung. Clowns also took part. Masks were used for certain roles.

Myay waing evolved into the all-night *zat pwe*, one of Burma's best-known traditional forms, its stories based on *jataka*, and its *saing waing* orchestra supporting the acting of *mintha* and *minthamee*, clowns, and villains.

Modern Stars. The early twentieth century saw the rise of popular stars, most notably **U Po Sein**. He and his rivals, who headed their own large troupes, added many innovations, one star even including tiny electric lightbulbs on his costumes. Many **Western**-influenced ideas also invaded the traditional Burmese stage. In the 1920s and 1930s, plays were recorded by famous *zat* dancers, and play books with all the songs were published cheaply so that amateurs could practice privately. The books were a great help to lone traveling entertainers, who verbally performed all the roles.

While *zat pwe* long remained the principal form of popular theatre, it was overtaken by modern plays called *pya zat* (see below).

FURTHER READING

Aung, Maung Htin. *Burmese Drama: A Study, with Translations, of Burmese Plays*; Brandon, James R. *Theatre in Southeast Asia*. Ma Thanegi. *The Illusion of Life: Burmese Marionettes*; Sein, Kenneth (Maung Khe), and Joseph A. Withey. *The Great Po Sein*; Singer, Noel. F. *Burmese Dance and Theatre*.

Ma Thanegi

Contemporary Burmese/Myanmar Theatres. There are two kinds of theatres today: those under government administration and privately run theatrical troupes.

Government-run venues are the National Theatres of Yangon and Mandalay and the Padonmar Theatre of Yangon, used most often for foreign cultural exchange programs and national and cultural celebrations. These two theatres were constructed as Western-style venues but plays performed there are mostly based on traditional aesthetics, such as those related to Buddhist philosophy or traditional plays reflecting the national culture and spirit. The annual Myanmar Traditional Cultural Performing Arts Competitions are also held at these venues.

Private **theatre companies** travel and set up performances in bamboo and mat halls with mats for seats at the front and easy chairs at the back. There are numerous private troupes in Mandalay and Yangon. Some possess over one hundred artists, headed by an actor-manager. Among them, the most popular ones during their heyday from the 1970s to 1980s were the Shwe Man Thabin, Myo Daw Thein Aung, Sein Maha Thabin, Thein Zaw Mandaly Zat Pwe, Moe Win Zat Thabin, and Nan Win Zat Thabin. Their evening programs are short musicals called *aw-pai-ya*, modern plays based on social issues, song and dance numbers called *thit-sar-hta*, with one male lead and four to five female dancer-singers, concluding with a classical *zat pwe*. Performances last the entire night, ending at dawn.

Traditional Theatre Declines. Formerly, touring was an important source of income, but, for a time, political uncertainties greatly hampered such activities. However, after the 1990s cease-fire agreements, it became safer to travel throughout the country, but tastes had changed with the popularity of video. As a result, few remained interested in traditional performances.

Many traditional performers retired, including Thein Zaw, who opened a successful art gallery and produces his *zat* songs on CDs and VCDs; those still performing, like dancer Nan Win, are struggling. Doing better is the Shwe Man Thabin troupe run by Shwe Man Tin Maung's sons, who feel they must uphold the family tradition to honor the memory of their father, still fondly remembered. The youngest son, Hsan Win, became leader when his older brother, Win Bo, suffered a stroke and could no longer dance. The middle brother, Chan Thar, lives in the United States and teaches Burmese dancing. The eldest son, Nyunt Win, in his late sixties, is a multiple award-winning movie **actor**. The grandchildren of the great Po Sein were unable to continue with his Sein Maha Thabin troupe, perhaps because memories of Po Sein have largely faded.

Anyein pwe. *Anyein pwe*, being relatively short (performances run from about 7 p.m. to midnight), has fared better, but only government-sponsored troupes, such as Myawaddy, are allowed to perform in the cities, as the clowns' jokes may contain political innuendos. Direct political jokes would not be tolerated, especially since the arrest of the Moustache Brothers following a NLD Headquarters for the 1996 Independence Day celebration (see Censorship).

Many *anyein* dancers and comedians are making VCDs of their shows. These are shot in a studio, but, to attract a broad audience, producers are using movie actresses with limited dancing skills instead of trained *anyein* dancers. Dancers who won medals at the annual performing arts competitions either join the few remaining troupes or perform for tourists.

Puppetry. Puppetry is taught at the Universities of Culture, but very few puppet troupes in the traditional sense still exist; although they travel about to give performances, they take part every year in the annual national contest. Many perform for the tourist market at small halls or at hotels and restaurants for "dinner shows."

Playwrights and Directors. Playwrights vary according to their artistic philosophy. Some focus on the nation's unique culture and traditional and moral values. Dagon Saya Tin invented "human cinema" (*lu bai sa kote*: *bai sa kote* is from Bioscope and *lu* means human), which were performed at the now defunct Win Win Theatre in Yangon, once the nation's most famous playhouse.

During the pre–World War II period, Thakin Kodaw Hming (1875–1964), known for his nationalist politics, was a prolific and widely read dramatist and satirist, and was called the Burmese George Bernard Shaw. Nandaw Shay Saya Tin was a famous composer, and his son, Shwe Nan Tin, produced "spoken theatre" or straight plays (*pya zat*), which came into their own after 1948, reflecting different aspects of contemporary life. Before, plays were sung and danced. *Pya zat* were modern plays, both serious and comic, and used contemporary costumes and music. Dealing with social issues as they did, they represented—until the 1980s, when videos took over—the nation's most popular type of theatre.

Internationally, the best-known Burmese playwright was U Nu (1907–1995), a renowned politician who became prime minister after independence in 1948, until General Ne Win seized power in 1962. He wrote books and plays on social problems and religious issues. His *The People Win Through* (Pyi thu aung than, 1951), a critique of communism's inadequacies, was produced at the Pasadena Playhouse in 1957.

Thu Kha (1910–2005) was a prolific writer and dramatist whose plays, performed before World War II, were later made into films; the best were the satires *Pride* (Gon), *Oh, Woman* (Aw meinma), and *Oh, Life* (Aw law ka). In the 1950s, he began directing movies on social issues, many winning the nation's top film award. In later years, his work became deeply religious.

Lu Nge Kyi Khine (a.k.a. "Youth" Kyi Khine) also presented *pya zat*, his plays reflecting social and political issues during the socialist era (1962–1988). Another *pya zat* writer, B. Ed Aung Thaike, one of the few theatre professionals with a university education, adapted **Indian** and British plays and satirized socioeconomic issues during that era. Myo Daw Maung Yin Aung, of the Myo Daw Thein Aung Troupe, made use of **Western** techniques to attract audiences. He also incorporated cinematic methods. His plays were mostly about the class struggles of the poor and artistic against the Westernized lifestyles of the arrogant wealthy.

Most **directors** are also leading playwrights, including those mentioned, as well as Nyein Min (1951–), **Chit Oo Nyo** (1948–), and Bogalay Tint Aung. Bogalay Tint Aung presented many operas and plays at annual national celebrations, such as Union Day and Independence Day.

Under the period of socialism (1962–1988), theatre thrived. However, in the post-socialist era, theatre lost its popularity due to changing audience tastes. Most theatre artists now make their living in film.

Training. Formal **training** is offered only at the State Schools of Fine Arts in Yangon and Mandalay and, since the 1990s, the Yangon and Mandalay Universities of Culture. Informal training also occurs as artists learn from senior artists during performance, and senior artists teach novices in theatre companies. Private lessons are also given by famous *anyein* dancers. Schoolgirls doing classical dances are often featured as "fillers" on state television, and many girls learn to dance for this purpose, to take part in school concerts, and to enter the annual Myanmar Traditional Cultural Performing Arts Competitions.

Theatre's Struggle to Survive. Theatre survives in Myanmar, although its popularity pales in comparison to films and videos. Still, practitioners remain interested in contemporary Western theatre techniques and technology although the tradition of producing Western plays is practically nonexistent. To advance the nation's theatre, they are eager to incorporate innovations in spite of cultural, political, social, and economic limitations; however, the few plays still written continue to be overly dramatic.

Maung Maung Thein and Ma Thanegi

BURRAKATHA. **Indian • folk theatre** of Andhra Pradesh, a Telugu-language narrative **musical** form or ballad. It is performed out of doors with three singer-**actor**-musicians, a leader (*kathakudu*), and two assistants. It is known in Telangana as *tamburakatha* or *sradakatha*, while in Rayalaseema, it is *tandanakatha* or *suddulu*. There are a number of differences among these different versions; only the Andhra version is discussed here. *Burra* comes from *tambura*, a four-string instrument worn across the right shoulder by the leader; *katha* is a "tale."

The *kathakudu* plays the *tambura*, leads the singing, keeps the beat by clicking a brass ring with interior balls on his thumb against a similar ring in his palm, and uses his face and body to express his feelings; ankle bells accentuate his rhythmic forward and backward **dance** movements. The assistants accompany him on small, one-sided horizontal drums (*gummeta*s) hung from their necks. They also engage the *kathakudu* in a question and answer routine. The assistant on the *kathakudu*'s right is the straight man-like *rajkiya*, who frequently interrupts the story to make a pertinent analogy to some contemporary social, **political**, or economic issue. The other assistant, the *hasyam*, is the clown. All wear colorful garments with turbans. All are now male, but at one time three **women** and one male made up the troupe, with two women doing the narration. At some point, women were excluded.

Performances are at night, beginning with devotional songs, and last two to three hours; longer pieces are given over several nights. The leader introduces the time, place, and background, and the action commences, with performers taking whatever role is necessary as the story proceeds.

The form was developed in 1942 from earlier folk ballad forms, such as the *jangam katha* (literally, "roving minstrel stories") in which a husband and wife performed Hindu **religious** stories concerning Lord Shiva for several days for a village audience. The new form was crafted by a leftist theatre association, the Praja Natya Mandali. Its literary sources included patriotic historical biographies, especially about heroic martyrs and Hindu myths. The repertoire includes *The Battle of Bobbili* (Bobbili yuddham), concerning Queen Mallama, who immolates herself to protect her chastity in the face of an attack by French enemies. Stories about ancient heroes and heroines were also used to comment on current topics like the elimination of caste barriers, the dangers of gambling, and so on.

Burrakatha also presents a twelfth-century sung version of the ***Ramayana*** in Telugu known as the *Dwipada Ramayana* from its use of the *dwipad* metrical system of couplets. Among major differences from the classic Valmiki version of the epic, it includes Rama's request, upon his banishment, for two wishes: fourteen years of sleep for his wife, and fourteen years of being awake for himself.

The communists used *burrakatha* to project stories about their own heroic figures. They introduced innovations, such as having the singers stand and dance, rather than sit; revolutionized the meter to make it more dramatic; established the three-member ensemble; introduced the question and answer format, and so on.

Before Partition (1947), popular nationalist pieces, like *Gandhi's Greatness* (Gandhi mahatwam), were **censored** by the British. After Partition, political propagandizing proved less popular, and had to compete with more traditional subjects or with educational uses. There are over two hundred *burrakatha* **theatre companies** in Andhra Pradesh; the form is also popular on television and radio.

FURTHER READING

Gargi, Balwant. *Folk Theater of India*; Richmond, Farley, Darius L. Swann, and Phillip B. Zarrilli, eds. *Indian Theatre: Traditions of Performance*; Varadpande, M. L. *History of Indian Theatre: Loka Ranga; Panorama of Indian Folk Theatre.*

Samuel L. Leiter

BUTÔ. **Japanese** form of modern **dance,** also spelled *butoh.* The term, meaning "dance" (*bu*) and "stomp" (*tô*), emerged in the Meiji era (1868–1912) to mean **Western**-style dance, but now refers to the style developed by **Hijikata Tatsumi** and **Ôno Kazuo.** Originally called "dance of utter darkness" (*ankoku butô*), *butô* took shape during the late 1950s, reacting against Western influence on modern dance, and blossomed in the 1960s counterculture ferment. Hijikata and Ôno, inspired by French avant-garde revolutionaries Genet and Artaud and **trained** in German Neue Tanz style, sought an approach better suited to the Japanese body and capable of dredging up memories and gestures deeply buried in Japan's cultural heritage. Their radical style has revolutionized notions of what dance can and should be.

While sharing its roots with traditional forms of Japanese expression, *butô* is nothing like *nô* or *kabuki.* Undefined by one specific style, a *butô* performance can be regarded as an intense way of existing, rather than a means of expressing ideas. Most practitioners, though lacking a fixed style, share certain characteristics, including grotesque, erotic imagery, contorted gestures and movements, bowlegged stances, and white-painted, nearly naked bodies.

Butô gained international recognition in the 1980s, when artists like Ashikawa Yôko (1947–), Tanaka Min (1945–), Kasai Akira (1943–), and Tamano Kôichi (1946–), and groups like the Mountain-Ocean School (Sankaijuku), the Great Camel Battleship (Dairakudakan), and the White Tiger Brigade (Byakkosha) began performing internationally. While *butô* has spawned multifarious styles abroad, in Japan it has become rather esoteric.

FURTHER READING

Fraleigh, Sondra Horton. *Dancing into Darkness: Butoh, Zen, and Japan*; Fraleigh, Sondra Horton. *Hijikata Tatsumi and Ohno Kazuo;* Klein, Susan Blakely. *Ankoku Butô: The Premodern and Postmodern Influences on the Dance of Utter Darkness.*

Yukihiro Goto

CAI LUONG. **Vietnamese** theatre that originated in the country's south during the early twentieth century; it was created in response to society's modernization under **Western** (French) influences. Designed to provide entertainment for newly emerged middle-class audiences, *cai luong* (literally, "reformed" or "renovated theatre") is a fusion of southern amateur **music** (*nhac tai tu*), elements of Western realistic drama, and popular theatre from neighboring Asian countries. *Nhac tai tu* evolved from ceremonial music by adding lyrics and staging performances of songs (*ca ra bo*). These were later combined into longer programs, the earliest forms of *cai luong*.

A *cai luong* performance integrates music, singing, **dance**, and dialogue employing less stylized and more realistic **acting** and language. During the 1920s, many **theatre companies** were set up; from the 1930s, *cai luong* spread from its southern cradle to the rest of Vietnam although it never attained such popularity as in its native region. The 1950s and 1960s were the genre's most prolific decades.

Cai luong plays have an expansive thematic range. The earliest plays were **Chinese**-inspired, but as *cai luong* evolved it adapted historical and **religious** themes, legends, and myths, as well as themes from Western plays. A significant part of the repertoire, often didactic, tackles contemporary topics and social issues, for example, the collapse of morals, disintegration of traditional family ties, corruptive power of money, alcoholism, gambling, opium addiction, and so on.

Leading **playwrights** include Nguyen Thanh Chau (1906–1978), Tran Huu Trang (1906–1966), and Le Hoai No (1908–2000). Outstanding plays are Nguyen Thanh Chau's *The Stage at Midnight* (San khau ve khuya), *The Wine Yeast and the Taste of Love* (Men ruoi huong tinh), and *The Princess Si Van* (Si Van cong chua), an adaptation of *Tristan and Isolde*; Tran Huu Trang's *Miss Luu's Life* (Doi co Luu); and Le Hoai No's *The Horse Chaser* (Vo ngua truy phong), *Brother and Sister Beggar* (Anh chi an may), *The Woman Cook's Heart* (Noi long chi bep), and *"Husband-Loving" Association* (Hoi yeu chong).

Although the traditional orchestra consisted of string instruments with the occasional addition of drums, most contemporary orchestras combine Vietnamese and Western instruments. *Cai luong* retains its popularity by updating its repertoire and embracing elements of contemporary culture.

FURTHER READING

Brandon, James R. *Theatre in Southeast Asia*; Quang, Dinh et al. *Vietnamese Theater*.

Dana Healy

CAMBODIA. Cambodia (Kampuchea) is a mainly agricultural Southeast Asian country of nearly 14 million people, mostly ethnic Khmer. The dominant **religion**, Theravada Buddhism, incorporates Hindu and local elements, including ritual **dance**-dramas.

From the ninth through the early fifteenth centuries, the Khmer controlled almost all of Southeast Asia. Their kings built monumental temple complexes, including Angkor Wat, adorned with thousands of bas-reliefs, many depicting dancers. Religious life included sacred dance, and kings and temples supported performers. Modern Khmer trace their culture, particularly the dance forms *robam kbach boran* and *lakhon khol*, back to the Angkor empire.

Khmer influence plummeted after the fifteenth century. In 1863, following a period of vassalage to the neighboring Thais and Vietnamese, Cambodia became a French protectorate. It finally achieved independence in 1953. Notwithstanding these changes, sacred dance remained part of royal ceremonial life.

Cambodia's performing arts enjoy a special hybrid vigor nurtured by geography. Its theatre is most akin to that of **Thailand**, Java (see Indonesia), **Malaysia**, and **India**, cultures to its south and west. *Robam kbach boran*, for example, uses a South/Southeast Asian type of body architecture including sharply angled elbows, wrists, knees, and ankles, bare feet, and expressive hand gestures. (Similarities with Thai forms are particularly close. Khmer performers abducted after the fall of the Angkor empire helped to shape Thai dance, which then was reimported to Cambodia by nineteenth-century Khmer kings raised in Thailand.)

There also are significant artistic affinities with **Chinese**-influenced traditions, coming via Cambodia's eastern neighbor, **Vietnam**. For example, *lakhon bassac* shows a strong kinship with Vietnamese *cai luong*. Performance forms with distinctive local roots also have interacted and melded with these two major phyla of Asian performance.

The result is a unique mix. Battle episodes in the basically Southeast Asian–style *robam kbach boran* use poles as stylized weapons, much as *cai luong* and Chinese *xiqu* do. **Women**'s *lakhon bassac* **costumes** resemble those of *robam kbach boran*, but male ogres have boldly painted faces à la Chinese *jingju*. *Yiké* • **folk** opera features the *skor yiké* drum, traditionally used by the Cham, Muslims with centuries-old roots in Cambodia—but *yiké* also has similarities with Malaysian *bangsawan*, and its **scenography** recalls *jingju*'s emblematic use of objects.

Cambodia's most widely known theatre form is *robam kbach boran*. Sumptuously costumed dancers, traditionally only women, perform tales from the *Reamker* (the Khmer version of the *Ramayana*) and lives of the Buddha using a legato choreography of expressive gestures. Cambodian legends credit this dance with the founding of the Khmer people: The churning of the primordial sea of milk produced a flock of celestial dancers (*apsaras*), one of whom consorted with the hermit Kampu to produce the first Kampucheans. Even in modern times *robam kbach boran* has been part of most major religious and civil ceremonies. When Norodom Sihanouk (1921–) returned as king in 1990 after a twenty-year exile, his airport greeting ceremony was a performance of *robam kbach boran*. *Apsaras* are such a pervasive emblem of Khmer identity that they appear on everything from school notebook covers to toothpaste.

Robam kbach boran's all-male **masked** counterpart, **lakhon khol**, uses a similar repertory of gestures and stories, and, like the all-female form, is associated with religious ceremonies and other public occasions. The same basic family of "ancient gestures" also forms the basis of *yiké*, though its staging is more eclectic.

Cambodia's most popular form is *lakhon bassac*. This eclectic form has been particularly amenable to change. Adapted for contemporary, modern-dress stories, it has incorporated much from Bollywood melodramas.

In another popular genre, *ayay chlong chlay*, male and female singers improvise using traditional poetic forms, usually incorporating comic, often topical, banter. The performers may use snippets of dance movement, but *ayay* is closer to a vaudeville stand-up routine than to a staged play.

The influence of non-Khmer minorities is evident in a variety of folk performances. Dances often are stylized enactments of everyday activities, such as hunting or fishing, usually with chanted and instrumental accompaniment. Since the mid-twentieth century, some of these—along with several examples from neighboring countries—have been formalized into a "folk dance" (*robam prapeyney*) repertory.

Cambodia has several forms of shadow **puppet theatre**. *Lakhon sbaek* uses large, unarticulated scene-illustration panels to perform a repertory mainly drawn from the *Reamker*. *Lakhon sbaek touch* uses smaller, articulated, individual-character puppets and often includes topical satire. Until the mid-twentieth century, the latter was Cambodia's only spoken (rather than sung) theatre form. "Spoken drama" (***lakhon niyeay***), using **actors**, arrived with returning Khmer who had studied in France in the 1950s, particularly **Hang Tun Hak**.

Few cultures have undergone cultural devastation such as Cambodia suffered in the late twentieth century. Shortly after independence, Cambodia became caught up as a tragic "sideshow" to the Vietnam War, ultimately falling in 1975 to the fanatical Khmer Rouge. Determined to rebuild Cambodia from "year zero," the Khmer Rouge set about obliterating all cultural and social institutions. The country was ravaged, and the great majority of actors, dancers, and **musicians**—as well as other artists, teachers, doctors, engineers, lawyers, and judges—perished.

Since the Khmer Rouge's ouster in 1979, surviving artists have played a significant role in the attempt to heal the country. Within months they set up a Fine Arts School in Phnom Penh. The school, which began offering a bachelor's degree in 1999, has concentrated on dance and *lakhon sbaek*, but also has revived *lakhon sbaek touch, lakhon bassac, yiké,* and *lakhon niyeay*. Besides school- and government-sponsored shows, private troupes now play *lakhon bassac* and other genres commercially in the cities, and dance companies perform classical and folk dance in the tourist areas around the ancient Angkor temples. Having endured a dozen years of post–Khmer Rouge **political** instability and then a fifteen-year-long tidal wave of development replete with corruption, displacements, and an influx of lowest common denominator "entertainments," Cambodian performers continue to struggle.

FURTHER READING

Brandon, James R. *Theatre in Southeast Asia*; Kravel, Pech Tum. *Sbek Thom: Khmer Shadow Theater*; Phim, Toni Samantha, and Ashley Thompson. *Dance in Cambodia*.

Eileen Blumenthal

CANJUN XI. **Chinese** "adjutant plays," named for a featured character, were impromptu skits first performed at the imperial court, which subsequently became widely popular. An official (the "adjutant") was made to endure ridicule from court players while dressed in a smock (white, yellow, or green) and holding a bamboo tablet of office. Late Tang (618–907) and Song (960–1279) sources name specific corrupt officials who had been made to play the adjutant in this fashion, but sometime during the period of *canjun xi*'s popularity (eighth to twelfth centuries), the *canjun* evolved from a corrupt official to a general **role type**, the comic butt. "Teasing the adjutant" (*nong canjun*) thus exhibited two features found in early Chinese dramas: comic repartee and the role type.

In its heyday, *canjun xi* featured two **actors**, one playing the adjutant—the more important character—and the other the "grey hawk" (*canggu*), **costumed** in feathers or tufted hemp, his hair loose, and armed with a leather-cushioned cudgel. Originally, the *canggu* attacked the *canjun* verbally and even physically, but he subsequently became the straight man as well as knave by feeding jokes to the *canjun*. **Women** also performed *canjun xi*. Tang sources mention a Liu Caichun, who performed with her husband and another man and was "good at teasing Adjutant Lu"; the sources also describe "false official plays" performed by women at the court of Suzong (r. 756–762), which clearly were *canjun xi*. While some have doubted that dialogue was used, the current view is that performers both sang and spoke and probably also used **makeup** and costumes, but no scripts.

Canjun xi's signal contributions were the *canjun* and *canggu* roles, which evolved into the comic duo of clown (*jing*) and second male lead (*fumo*) in Song dynasty (960–1279) farces (*yuanben*, literally, "scripts from the entertainer's quarters") and, subsequently, into clownish roles common to many genres (for example, *jing* and *mo* of **nanxi** and *jing* and *chou* of **kunqu**).

FURTHER READING

Dolby, William. *A History of Chinese Drama*; Mackerras, Colin. *Chinese Theatre from its Origins to the Present Day*.

Catherine Swatek

CAO YU (1910–1996). Chinese "spoken drama" (*huaju*) **playwright**, the so-called "Shakespeare of China." He is credited with aiding the non-indigenous type of drama to reach a degree of maturity in both form and reception in the mid-1930s. His early plays gained canonical status largely due to their artistry and skillful fusion of **political** themes.

Born in Tianjin, Cao Yu grew up in an upper-class household with a large collection of Chinese and **Western** literature. His father had once served as secretary to Li Yuanhong (1864–1928), president of China. His stepmother, an aficionado of China's operatic and **storytelling** traditions, initiated Cao Yu into the theatre. While enrolled at Tianjin's Nankai Middle School, Cao Yu gained experience as an **actor**, often playing female roles, in its well-known amateur troupe.

In 1930, he entered Qinghua University's Department of Western Languages and Literatures in Beijing. He completed his first work, the four-act *huaju Thunderstorm* (Leiyu) at twenty-three. Performed in **Japanese** by Chinese students in Tokyo in 1935 before premiering in China later the same year, *Thunderstorm* became one of China's most important plays and established *huaju*'s position in the 1930s.

Thunderstorm has a realistic plot imbued with political themes reflecting the iconoclasm of the May Fourth political movement in the 1920s and 1930s; it advocates the

The Wilderness by Cao Yu, directed by Wang Yansong for the Tianjin People's Art Theatre, 2005. (Photo: Courtesy of Wang Yansong)

liberation of the individual from patriarchal society and the emancipation of workers from capitalist exploitation. *Thunderstorm*'s tragic ending, inspired in part by Greek tragedy, is also a meditation upon fate, or what Cao Yu called "cosmic cruelty," and the Chinese concept of "retribution."

While teaching at Tianjin's Hebei Women's Normal College, Cao Yu wrote *Sunrise* (Richu, 1936), which tragically reveals the disparity between classes during the 1930s, the moral dissolution of the powerful, and the inequities faced by the downtrodden. In *The Wilderness* (Yuanye, 1937), set in rural China, he fused realism with expressionism to present the hardships of peasants and their fight for enlightenment and justice.

During the war with Japan, Cao Yu moved to Sichuan Province. In 1940, he finished *Metamorphosis* (Tuibian) and *Peking Man* (Beijing ren), the latter a Chekhovian tragicomedy about the downfall of an aristocratic family's outdated values. In 1942, he adapted *Family* (Jia) from Ba Jin's (1904–2005) novel. Invited by the U.S. State Department, Cao Yu, along with playwright **Lao She**, lectured in the United States in 1946.

Cao Yu's post-1949 plays, such as *Bright Skies* (Minglang de tian, 1954) and *Consort of Peace* (Wang zhaojun, 1978), were largely written to serve state politics. He held numerous official positions, including president of the Beijing People's Art Theatre (Beijing Renmin Yishu Juyuan), chairman of the All-China Dramatic Workers' Association, deputy of the National People's Congress, and so on.

FURTHER READING

Hu, John Y. H. *Ts'ao Yu*; Lau, Joseph S. M. *Ts'ao Yu: The Reluctant Disciple of Chekhov and O'Neill: A Study in Literary Influence.*

Jonathan Noble

CAVITTU NATAKAM. South **Indian ⁕ folk theatre** of Kerala, distinctive because its episodes and narratives are drawn from the Christian tradition. Kerala has the highest percentage of Christians in India. *Cavittu natakam*, which dates from the latter half of the sixteenth century, originated in the activities of Christian missionaries. It attempted to introduce a Christian theatre that would provide a **religious** entertainment alternative to Hindu-based forms, such as *kathakali* and *kutiyattam*. While these latter dramatize and celebrate episodes focusing on the Hindu epics' kings, royalty, and deities, *cavittu natakam* does likewise for royal and sacred figures of Christiandom. The Jesuits, very influential in establishing educational institutions throughout India, used drama in their educational and proselytizing missions; *cavittu natakam* appears to be an outgrowth of this. It resembles in many ways the worldwide use of drama to inculcate Christianity.

Cavittu means "stamping" or "stomping," and *natakam* means "drama," the composite title referring to the stamping steps that predominate and bring power and rhythm to the **dance** movements. While it is unclear how much and how direct an influence *kathakali* and other Kerala forms have had on its movements, *kalarippayattu*, the martial arts system, has had an important influence.

The "master" (*asan*) of a performance is, like the classical *sutradhara*, a visible **stage** manager, **directing** everything and interpreting the words. The language is Tamil, although that of the **actors** and audience is Malayalam, a Tamil sister language. **Musical** accompaniment is provided by a harmonium, clarinet, cymbals, and drums (*mridangam* and *centa*).

Cavittu natakam reenacts the narratives of Charlemagne, Saint George and the dragon, the lives of the saints, and so on. These are presented on Catholic feast days, weddings, and during other celebrations. Performances are usually presented on wooden stages in the precincts of a church or cathedral.

FURTHER READING

Richmond, Farley, Darius L. Swann, and Phillip B. Zarrilli, eds. *Indian Theatre: Traditions of Performance.*

Richard A. Frasca

CENSORSHIP

Censorship: Cambodia

Cambodia was a kingdom for centuries until a coup d'état in 1970. Under the monarch, official arts—those of the court or other royal institutions—often praised or strengthened the symbolic power of the king and the kingdom. It was rare, in all genres, to find stories openly critical of the powers-that-be. By the mid-twentieth century, some "spoken dramas" (*lakhon niyeay*) began taking on controversial societal issues. In one famous incident, only the intercession of Queen **Sisowath Kossamak** saved **actors** from imprisonment for criticizing the government.

Following the coup d'état and the establishment of a republic, certain arts remained tools for official messages, including *robam kbach boran* and **folk • dances** taught at the University of Fine Arts. Though the dances remained the same, lyrics were changed to eliminate royal references. Under the communist Khmer Rouge (1975–1979), all dance and theatre, as Cambodians had known them, were forbidden. Only performances supportive of the revolution were permitted, mainly new creations. From 1979–1991, Cambodia was ruled by another communist regime, which encouraged the revival of many performance arts not practiced under the Khmer Rouge, while promoting anti–Khmer Rouge and anti-capitalist/anti-**West • political** messages.

Cambodia became a kingdom again in 1993. Many new *lakhon niyeay* and *robam kbach boran* dramas, such as *Samritechak* (1999–2000), *Seasons of Migration* (2004–2005), and *Pamina Devi* (2005–2006), all choreographed by Sophiline Cheam Shapiro (1967–), address contemporary issues and are reviewed by a panel of arts administrators (including, sometimes, the minister of culture) before being given permission for public presentation.

FURTHER READING

Brandon, James R. *Theatre in Southeast Asia.*

Toni Shapiro-Phim

Censorship: China

Xiqu *Censorship.* There is a long tradition of censorship in **China**'s *xiqu*, which persists to the present day. Emperors of virtually all periods kept alert for theatrical items inimical to their rule. Those of the Ming (1368–1644) and especially the Qing (1644–1911) dynasties were keen to keep the theatre free of subversive **political** and moral values. During Ming and Qing many edicts were directed against the novel *Water Margin* (Shuihu zhuan), which paints rebels against the government in a positive light, as well as against dramas based on it. Laws of 1373 and ca. 1412 banned showing emperors, princes, or sages on **stage**, but favored "righteous men and chaste women, filial sons and obedient grandsons." In 1777, the Qianlong emperor (r. 1736–1796) set up a special commission to revise dramas to conform to his rigid Confucian moral and political standards, which included filial piety, loyalty to the state, and **women**'s chastity. The censors carefully examined over one thousand items, not completing their job until 1782.

Theatre censorship remains prominent. In the first half of the twentieth century, any *xiqu* item that could be construed as pornographic or lewd or advocated rebellion was likely to be censored, whether the relevant authorities were controlled by a warlord, the Nationalist Party, or the **Japanese**. However, censorship was actually much worse for modern "spoken drama" (*huaju*; see Playwrights and Playwriting) than for *xiqu* because even though *xiqu* writers and **actors** were interested in reform, the most seriously subversive items were much more likely to be in modern than *xiqu* forms.

The People's Republic of China has seen continuing, and sometimes much worse, censorship. In line with the Communist Party's *xiqu* reform policies the Ministry of Culture banned items it believed unpatriotic, lewd, insulting to women or minority nationalities, or in other ways "unhealthy." During political campaigns of the sort that Mao Zedong (1893–1976) occasionally orchestrated, items not in accordance with the party line were either forbidden or simply ignored by actors, who feared government retribution.

The Cultural Revolution (1966–1976) probably saw the worst censorship in Chinese theatre history. Authorities went beyond a list of dramas *forbidden* performance to a very small number *allowed*. Virtually none were permitted except for those designated "model plays" (*yangban xi*).

Colin Mackerras

Modern Censorship. Although differing in degree, theatre censorship has been pervasive in modern China. Adopted at both central and local government levels, censorship usually is based on moral, ideological, and political grounds, and has proved harmful to both *xiqu* and *huaju*.

The first modern censorship law was the 1914 Publication Law during the "warlord period." Under the Nationalist government (1912–1949), the growing popularity of *huaju*, the ideological and political clashes between the Communist and Nationalist Parties, and the Second Sino-Japanese War (1937–1945) contributed to increasingly strict censorship through registration of practitioners, mandated script approval, and, eventually, inspections during rehearsal and production. The 1942 establishment of Rules for the Supervision of Script Publication and Performance Inspection marked the height of such censorship; 114 *huaju* plays were banned within the eighteen months following April 1942. Censorship in Japanese-controlled areas was equally rampant.

Although outright bans of plays were common, censorship in pre-1949 communist-controlled regions and in the People's Republic thereafter was more pervasive and devastating through political campaigns primarily targeted at intellectuals and artists, eventually driving them to self-censorship. As a result, most proven **playwrights** failed to write plays comparable to their pre-1949 works. As noted above, the height of censorship was the Cultural Revolution, when the model plays were mainly in *jingju* style, excluding both *huaju* and other regional theatres.

The post-Mao era has been generally more tolerant, but still marked by episodes of censorship, most noticeably the banning in the 1980s of plays openly critical of contemporary social injustice. The aftermath of 1989's Tiananmen Square student uprising led to especially strict crackdowns. Later censorship largely shifted from post-production to before and during the creative process, resulting in less outright bans but more effective government control.

Siyuan Liu

Censorship: India

Dramatic Performances Control Act of 1876. Official **Indian** theatre censorship starts with the Dramatic Performances Control Act of 1876 (DPCA), implemented by the British authorities. Its intent was to suppress the nationalist wrath being expressed in **theatres** during the nation's freedom struggle. In 1872, **Dinabandhu Mitra**'s

Bengali 1860 play *The Indigo Mirror* (Nildarpan; prod. 1872), about British oppression of indigo planters, caused colonial authorities to become suspicious of dangerous themes. Among a number of other anti-British works that ran into trouble was Bengali **playwright** Dakshina Charan Chattopadhyay's *The Mirror of Tea* (Chakar darpan), whose depiction of working conditions on tea plantations angered the governor general of India, Lord Northbrook, after he read an English translation in 1875. Spurred by Lieutenant Governor Richard Temple, steps were taken to prevent its performance and prosecute the author and **actors**. The lack of a law to prevent such performances led to an ordinance designed to prohibit the "ill-feeling against the British name and nation, against the tendency of British civilization and institutions, and against the result of British rule" manifested in performance. Proclaimed on February 29, 1876, enacted on March 18, 1876, and overseen by the lieutenant governor, it prohibited "dramatic performances which are scandalous, defamatory, seditious, and obscene, or otherwise prejudicial to the public interest." Even spectators could be arrested.

In 1876, the police cracked down hard when Calcutta's (Kolkata) Great National Theatre produced Amritalal Basu's *Gajadananda and Crown Prince* (Gajadananda o jubaraj), about an Indian lawyer whose toadying to the Prince of Wales by inviting him into his household's female quarters was a breach of Bengali etiquette. The theatre then produced a double bill of Upendranath Das's (1848/9–1895) *Surendra and Binodini* (Surendra-Binodini, 1875), about a British magistrate shown as a would-be rapist, and Das's *The Police of Pigs and Sheep*, a snipe at two Calcutta officials named Hogg and Lamb; charges of obscenity were brought. The high court rejected the charges, leading the British, on December 16, 1876, to pass the DPCA. It empowered the police to enter a venue, seize performance-related material, and insist that the **theatre company** seek prior permission for performances in "specified localities" after submitting the script for official approval. Theatres thereafter often elected to make **political** statements by disguising them in stories from history and myth, although plays of this nature, like Prabhakar Khadilkar's (1872–1948) *Killing of Kichaka* (Kichaka vadh, 1910) and **Girish Chandra Ghosh**'s *Sirajuddaula* (1911), were also sometimes banned.

Post-Independence Censorship. The DPCA continued even after independence (1947). But it shifted to leftwing activity, especially that stemming from the leftist Indian People's Theatre Association (IPTA), founded in 1942–1943, which was more subject to suppression under this act by the Indian government than were theatre people under the British. Many states revised the DPCA to fortify their own interventions in dramatic expression. In 1950, Bombay's (Mumbai) police powers were strengthened; in 1955, the Rajasthan government introduced the Rajasthan Dramatic Performances Act and Entertainment Rules, and so forth. In 1953, the West Bengal government asked the Bengal chapter of IPTA to submit all scripts ever performed by the organization, even *The Indigo Mirror*. Also in 1953, Travancore–Cochin (Kerala) banned Thoppil Bhasi's (1925–1992) highly popular *You Made Me a Communist* (Ningalenne cammunistakki, 1952)—which used **music** and comedy to discuss issues of social inequality; later, the court rescinded the ban. In Tamilnadu during the 1950s and 1960s, the government invoked the same act to prohibit plays by the then emerging Dravidian Political Movement. For its part, this party, on taking power in 1967, took the same attitude toward plays with opposing viewpoints. But, by the 1970s, many states, like Karnataka, Andhra Pradesh, and West Bengal, gave blanket exemption from DPCA formalities to registered theatre companies. Despite West Bengal's having repealed the DPCA in 1962, **Utpal Dutt** was charged with sedition for his *Nightmare City* (Dushwapner nagari, 1974). During the state of emergency in India from 1975–1977, there was considerable use of the DPCA, and many theatre people ended up in jail or saw their groups outlawed.

The numerous political transformations and changing power relations in various parts of the country forced differing applications of the DPCA. With the Communist Party accepted under Indian democracy, the DPCA's target became radical Marxists, like Dutt, who continued to advocate for class war and revolution. In 1987, Kerala banned P. J. Antony's (1923–1979) *The Sixth Wound of Christ* (based on Kazantzakis's *The Last Temptation of Christ*) because of its allegedly disturbing **religious** sentiments; the ban was upheld by the Supreme Court.

It must be emphasized that, although the DPCA was created by the British as a way of suppressing the nationalist upsurge of the 1870s, even after independence governmental censorship of theatre continues under different power structures and under either the DPCA or alternative constitutional remedies. It was only in 2001 that **Bangladesh** repealed the DPCA.

FURTHER READING

Das, Pulin. *Persecution of Drama and Stage: Chronicles and Documents.*

B. Ananthakrishnan

Censorship: Indonesia

Arts censorship in **Indonesia** relies upon legal frameworks established under the Dutch. Under these and subsequent laws, Indonesian censors oversee any art that "could disturb public order." Theatrical productions must submit scripts to censor boards, and refrain from "embellishing" them in performance. Furthermore, any government level can become involved, from the attorney general to local police. Artists can never be entirely confident that their work is safe.

Post-independence Indonesian theatre reflected a diverse spectrum of **political** and **religious** perspectives until late in the 1950s, when Marxist institutions such as the People's Cultural Association (Lekra) allied with President Sukarno (1901–1970) to blacklist artists of differing views. President Suharto's (1921–) New Order (1966–1998) initially seemed to promise greater freedoms and independence. However, the limits of the regime's tolerance became clear with the rise of the student movement in the 1970s. **Playwright-director-actor • Rendra** was harassed by police and banned altogether from performing in 1978. Subsequently, most artists practiced self-censorship, avoiding controversial topics and cultivating "safe" aesthetics.

In August 1990, Suharto responded to Russian president Gorbachev's *glasnost* by announcing a new Indonesian "openness" (*keterbukaan*) toward free speech. However, in October of that year, authorities banned a Comma Theatre (Teater Koma) production of *Succession* (Sukseski) directed and written by **Nano Riantiarno** and dealing with the controversial issue of presidential succession. **Ratna Sarumpaet**, who produced several plays that invoked a raped and murdered labor activist named Marsinah to denounce New Order corruption, was persecuted and imprisoned throughout the decade. These incidents fueled dissatisfaction with free speech restrictions, leading to Suharto's resignation in 1998. Although new artistic and press freedoms subsequently emerged, Indonesians are wary against losing such freedoms as the spirit of reform subsides.

FURTHER READING

Brandon, James R. *Theatre in Southeast Asia.*

Evan Winet

Censorship: Japan

Edo-Period Practices. During the Edo period (1603–1868), censorship affected all forms of **Japanese** entertainment. It was not just an urban phenomenon: numerous edicts aimed at restricting rural entertainments were also promulgated. Censorship was motivated by fear of **political** instability and by the related desire to maintain moral order. Thus there were prohibitions, for example, on *bunraku* (see Puppet Theatre) and *kabuki* dramatizations of events involving the government and on the presentation of samurai-class characters bearing the same name as actual individuals of the day. Sexually suggestive scenes were also a target of those who wanted to circumscribe onstage representations of encounters between courtesans and their customers. Even place names had to be changed so as not to suggest too close a depiction of actual locales.

Dynamic, unruly, and hugely popular, *kabuki* was a particular challenge for officials. From its earliest days, *kabuki* was subject to strict controls. **Women** (many of them prostitutes) were banned in 1629, ending "prostitutes'" (*yûjo*) *kabuki*. In 1652, "boys" (*wakashu*) *kabuki*, with its male prostitutes, was banned as well. *Kabuki* was allowed to survive as "men's" (*yarô*) *kabuki* in 1653, but only because the **actors** were forced to shave off their sexy forelocks and concentrate on making *kabuki* less sensual and more dramatic. Although the history of Edo-period *kabuki* shows a constant struggle between government censors on the one hand and **theatre** owners, **playwrights**, and actors on the other, the very samurai who ruled Japan and feared expressions of subversion and moral turpitude were among those who thronged the theatres. Censorship decrees were not always strictly enforced. Moreover, *kabuki*, *bunraku*, and other forms of entertainment proved themselves highly adaptable, if not ready to flaunt the rules, often to good theatrical effect.

The Treasury of Loyal Retainers (Kanadehon chûshingura, 1748) is the classic example of a work that fooled no one in its depiction of a notorious early-eighteenth-century incident of samurai loyalty and revenge presented in the guise of a story from the distant past. The dramatists sidestepped censorship by using a fourteenth-century setting and by changing the names of the characters—some only slightly, such as chief retainer Ôishi Kuranosuke, who became Ôboshi Yuranosuke. A century later, the period's first and only overtly political play, *The Tale of the Martyr of Sakura* (Sakura Giminden, 1851), used a fifteenth-century world to contain a seventeenth-century story. It concerns Sakura Sôgo (Asakura Tôgo in the original, but now Sakura Sôgo), a rural mayor executed—along with his family—for daring to petition the shogun on behalf of his fellow villagers being starved under the burdens of taxation. That this play was produced, even in its somewhat veiled form, points to the breakdown of late-Tokugawa shogunate authority and censorship restrictions.

Barbara E. Thornbury

Modern Censorship. Theatre censorship in the Meiji period (1868–1912) extended the Edo-period practice of government censors reviewing scripts and banning productions construed as rewarding vice and punishing virtue or presenting morality opposed to Japanese values.

During the 1920s and 1930s, plays also came under scrutiny for their **political** ideas. Unlike *bunraku* and *kabuki,* where political issues were veiled in historical context, *shinpa* and *shingeki* often used the stage for direct political comment. As the militarist government veered toward war, it prohibited plays from advocating communism and criticizing the war effort or emperor system. Recalcitrant figures like **Kubo Sakae** and **Senda Koreya** were arrested for "thought crimes." Some, like Senda, renounced their views to remain free, but others spent the war in prison. The only *shingeki* **theatre company** allowed to operate throughout the war was **Kishida Kunio**'s Literary Theatre (Bungaku-za), which avoided politics, even canceling a questionable production. In 1944, the government enacted the Regulations for the Control of Theatrical Production, recalling Tokugawa censorship.

The Occupation exercised its own censorship on plays celebrating imperial or feudal values (like revenge plays), war and militarism, and plays portraying the subjugation of women. Much of *kabuki*'s traditional repertoire, therefore, was banned. *Nô,* deemed safe, went uncensored, and *bunraku* was shackled only for a year and a half. The Occupation promoted *shingeki* companies and artists, especially those who had been imprisoned. Many *kabuki* and *shingeki* troupes voluntarily withheld texts from the censors, fearing they would not pass. By 1949, with lobbying by companies and the work of Occupation censors Earle Ernst and Faubion Bowers—their respective responsibility for helping to lift censorship is still debated—most restrictions on *kabuki* were lifted.

By 1950, Occupation censorship had shifted to concerns about communism. *Shingeki* plays were closely monitored for leftist content, though few productions were actually shut down. With the Occupation's end in April 1952, all censorship restrictions were lifted.

FURTHER READING

Okamoto, Shiro. *The Man Who Saved Kabuki: Faubion Bowers and Theatre Censorship in Occupied Japan.*

David Jortner

Censorship: Korea

Korean theatre was censored even in premodern society, but official censorship was first enforced during **Japanese** colonialism (1910–1945), a practice altered little until pre-performance manuscript reviews ended around 1989. Colonial authorities looked askance at theatre because they feared its subversive influence and its potential power to mobilize the masses. Legislated control of public performances was deemed necessary to maintain Japanese hegemony.

Censorship during the colonial period was practiced largely in two forms. First, **theatre companies** were required to submit manuscripts to the police for a license subject to arbitrary decisions. Second, police monitors viewed performances, empowered to stop any that deviated from the approved manuscript and arrest the **actors**, if necessary. Initially, censorship aimed to repress and obliterate Korea's national spirit and heritage, but in the 1920s colonial government interest shifted from cultural to ideological control as a socialist theatre movement emerged.

After the country's liberation (1945), the division of the nation (1948), and the Korean War (1950–1953), ideological confrontations increased in number and severity under South Korean military regimes, leading to passage of the powerful National Security Law (1948) and the Anti-Communism Law (1961). As an anti-communist mentality became a pseudo public morality, the Anti-Communism Law transformed into a superior means of cultural and **political** control. Accordingly, a public performance law was legislated in 1961, claiming to protect national security as well as public morals and social ethics. This law, nearly identical to its Japanese predecessor, strictly mandated registration of performers, pre-performance script review, on-site inspection, the licensing system of new performance facilities, and so on, to curb content seen as sexually provocative or ideologically subversive. The 1975–1976 revision of the Performance Law resulted in the establishment of the Korean Public Performance Ethics Committee, a government-sponsored civil agency charged with pre-censoring all public performances. It was not until 1989—after the controversy over Oh T'ae-yŏng's *Prostitution* (Maech'un, 1988) and in a more tolerant atmosphere following the 1988 Seoul Olympics—that regulation eased.

Since the 1960s, aside from fostering politically safe, but artistically limited governmentally sponsored plays, censorship had three notable effects. First, audiences and artists were denied performances of foreign works the government deemed suspect, such as those by German **playwright** Brecht. Second, it eventually suffocated some South Korean playwrights' literary passion and creativity. Third, South Korean playwrights such as **Lee Kang-baek** and **Kim Kwang-lim** had to couch their socio-political criticisms in an allegorical style. For example, Kim's *A Changed Underworld* (Tallajin chŏsŭng, 1987) satirizes censorship's abusive power through an imaginary underworld setting, intending to avoid a confrontation with the government. But confrontation was sometimes unavoidable and playwrights such as Pak Jo-yŏl (1930–), who expressed nostalgia for his hometown in North Korea, suffered under arbitrary censorship. Five decades after the end of the war, years of censorship still resonate in South Korean theatre.

Hyung-jin Lee

Censorship: Malaysia

When officials, sponsors, or vocal members of **Malaysia**'s public deem that a production raises issues too sensitive for public exposure, their decisions or views may critically affect performance events. Artists may find themselves positioned ambiguously between their desire for free expression and the practicality of compliance. Even traditional forms with pre-Islamic roots, such as *mak yong* and *wayang kulit* (see Puppet Theatre), may be restricted, especially in states where the Islamic **political** party holds sway. There one may find special performances for tourists, but local audiences are not encouraged to attend them.

Theatre companies generally need to apply for a police permit before staging a performance. Groups must submit a script and a list of participants. They must wait about a month for the police to determine whether anything is inappropriate. Meanwhile, the artists rehearse in anticipation of being licensed.

Some performances have been banned before production. This happened in 1980 to *Refugee: Images*, Chin San Sooi's response to the **Vietnamese** refugee situation, and in 1986 to "The Coffin Is Too Big for the Hole" by **Singapore ● playwright Kuo Pao Kun**. In 1990, Henry Ong's *Madame Mao's Memories*—in which Mao Zedong's widow reviews her past from inside a prison cell—was refused a permit, possibly because it was thought that a play set in communist **China** might raise a security issue.

Such actions have led some writers to self-censor or to find opportunities outside the country. Kee Thuan Chye's (1954–) *The Big Purge* (1988)—a response to the detention of more than a hundred people in 1987 under the Internal Security Act—received a 1988 staging at a British university and a 2005 reading in London.

Groups may also face pressure from sponsors. In 1987, the premiere of *Emptiness* (Kelongsong) by Kemala (Ahmad Kamal Abdullah, 1941–) lost its sponsorship shortly before opening. Because Islam rejects suicide, the fate of the Muslim antagonist, the play was deemed unsuitable. Even with the procurement of a last-minute sponsor, the suicide was changed to marginal repentance. In 1997, *Cheryl Kimberly Says "Just Do It—Lah!,"* designed for a young audience to explore a variety of perspectives on sexual identity, was set to open at the Penang Arts **Festival**. However, its poster's explicitness raised concern, causing the sponsor to withdraw and the show to be cancelled.

Members of the public are a third source of pressure. In 1989, a group of students was ready to present an outdoor performance project they had worked on, with faculty, for six months. A full house, including **critics** and artists, was waiting for this innovative work to begin when a group of Muslim students staged a prayer sit-in to protest the production. Tensions mounted until the performers finally dismantled their set, canceling the show.

Protests may also arise during a show's run as when, in 1996, members of Malaysia's Hindu community objected to a contemporary version of the ***Ramayana*** called *Rama and Sita—The New Generation* (Rama and Sita—generasi baru), in which Rama and Sita meet via the Internet. To this segment of Malaysia's Hindu community, the play was an inappropriate portrayal of their **religion.** The show proceeded, but the incident caused concern to those involved in the production and raised questions about the parameters of innovation.

Public opinion in the press can also influence a production. In 1993, **director** Joe Hasham (1948–) staged a production of *A Streetcar Named Desire* in which Stella and Stanley embraced and kissed provocatively; offended Muslims criticized actress Ramona Rahman for her actions. Rahman, a Muslim, pointed out that she should not be confused with her character. Hasham toned down the scene to accommodate those who accused it of opposing Malaysian (and, especially, Islamic) mores.

Subsequently, Kuala Lumpur's City Hall decided that a review panel had to see a run-through of all plays prior to granting permission. They opined that scripts gave too limited an idea of content and that performance was a more accurate gauge. The panel created a new source of pressure. In 1995, a playwriting workshop culminated in a program called *One by One: Monologues*. Dina Zaman's "The Respected Unemployed Person" (Penggangur Terhormat) concerns a Muslim woman who, because she covers her hair in public, has a hard time getting a job in advertising. She thus voices her frustration to God. Finally, she adjusts to her circumstances and prays conventionally. This ending resulted from the advice of an imam on the panel who felt that the play should close with the young woman's dissatisfaction subsiding into prayer. Some argued that Zaman had buckled to **religious** pressure, but the producer explained that without the change the performance would not have been licensed and that this way Zaman's work could at least be seen.

ArtisProActiv, an arts advocacy group, actively supports freedom of expression. When the satirical group Instant Café Theatre was denied a license in 2003, ArtisProActiv issued a strongly worded statement, with ninety-three signatures, arguing for the public and politicians to consider the effect of censorship on the nation's creative, political, and economic growth and for a license to be granted. In 2004, ArtisProActiv, disturbed by the denial of a permit to Huzir Sulaiman's *Election Day*, requested the panel's elimination. City Hall agreed to license the production but it did not cancel the policy.

Even after a play has closed, controversy can tail it. A 1980 university production of *Hamlet* was successfully staged outdoors at the remnants of a fort on Penang Island. When a television station wanted to air the play, a Muslim student organization objected because the **costumes** were "popish" and the "to be or not to be" speech implied potential suicide. The broadcast was cancelled.

Thus have artists encountered pressure on their freedom of expression. These examples illustrate the ongoing vulnerability, as well as conviction, of artists intent on encouraging a responsive community striving to keep the arts relevant and expressive in a multidimensional society.

FURTHER READING

Brandon, James R. *Theatre in Southeast Asia*; Lo, Jacqueline. *Staging Nation: English Language Theatre in Malaysia and Singapore*.

Nancy Nanney

Censorship: Pakistan

The Dramatic Performances Control Act (DPCA) of 1876 (see Censorship: India) has continued to regulate theatrical activity in post-Partition (1947) **Pakistan**. Producers have had to undergo a cumbersome procedure of applying for "No Objection Certificates" from the police to ensure "good conduct," with the Department of Film and Publications and/or Arts Councils editing scripts for "scandalous, defamatory, seditious or obscene" content. For approved productions, hefty entertainment taxes are deducted from ticket sales. While countless scripts have been withdrawn under the DPCA, many pretexts may prevent a play's being staged.

Consideration of the arts as being un-Islamic has been reinforced by martial regimes, particularly under General Zia-ul-Haq's government (1979–1988) when female **dance** was officially banned. Many **theatre companies** set up in this period, subverting the establishment with provocative **political** content disguised through the use of parables and foreign adaptations. Since official **theatres** were closed to them, they took to the streets, people's houses, and foreign cultural centers. Many such groups are supported by General Pervez Musharraf's (1943–) current government.

The popular commercial theatre, which boomed in the 1980s, often has committees screening dress rehearsals before the play is publicly advertised; in actual performance perceived improprieties are re-incorporated through improvisation. Although **actors** have been arrested, and managers claim to censor vulgarity of sexual jokes and female dress and dance, performers continue to lampoon the official social and moral order. Titillating **Western** adaptations performed by and for the elite are given significantly more freedom.

FURTHER READING

Afzal-Khan, Fawzia. *A Critical Stage: The Role of Secular Alternative Theatre in Pakistan.*

Claire Pamment

Censorship: Philippines

Philippine theatre has had two kinds of censorship: outright, especially during colonization, and intimidation during times of **political** repression. During the American colonial period (ca. 1900–1946), Act 292 (the Sedition Act) was used to arrest artists advocating independence. Three **playwright-directors** were indicted through this act. The plays of Juan Abad (1872–1939) led to his being arrested thrice, while Juan Matapang Cruz, alleged author of *I Am Not Dead* (Hindi aco patay, 1903), was indicted for sedition, fined $2,000, and served two years. **Aurelio Tolentino** (1867–1915) was arrested nine times.

Theatre companies and audiences were also persecuted. In one performance of *I Am Not Dead*, an American soldier hurled a beer bottle at the rising sun symbolizing the revolutionary anti-Spanish organization Katipunan. At another performance, **actors** and spectators were arrested. Plays under surveillance, raided, or closed down included *The Freedom Not Attained* (Ang kalayaang hindi natupad, 1903), Mariano Martinez's *Subjugated Island* (Pulong pinaglahuan, 1904), Gabriel Beato Francisco's *The Katipunan* (Ang Katipunan, 1905), and Pantaleon Lopez's *Bird of Prey* (Ave de rapiña a.k.a. Ibong manlulupig, 1909).

During the **Japanese** occupation, **theatres** had to register with the authorities. Many were shut down. The occupiers' cultural policy was implemented by its Propaganda Corps, which advocated for the use of Tagalog as a national language. Eighteen of the twenty plays presented at the Metropolitan Theatre by Dramatic Philippines were in Tagalog.

The martial law years (1972–1981) were equally dangerous. Even in 1971, a performance by Panday Sining at the Clark Air Base gate resulted in the arrest of its members. Early in the martial law period, the Office of Civil Defense and Relations required that all scripts be submitted for review. Casts and crews of plays like *People's Worship* (Pagsambang bayan, 1977) and *People's Cry* (Sigaw ng bayan, 1980) were harassed by the military. **Director •** Behn Cervantes was jailed four times and playwright Bonifacio Ilagan (1951–) three.

Censorship, however, did inspire creativity. The symbolic characters in turn-of-the-century dramas, the use of historical events to discuss contemporary issues, and the black and red Zorro-like **masks** worn by street actors during martial law all show that repressive conditions did not deter artists from expressing their politics.

FURTHER READING

Brandon, James R. *Theatre in Southeast Asia.*

Joi Barrios

Censorship: Singapore

Prior to 1992, all plays intended for public presentation in **Singapore** had to be submitted for approval to the Public Entertainment Licensing Unit (PELU), essentially a police branch. While plays considered a threat to domestic or **religious** harmony or a challenge to the country's "core moral values" are still prohibited, considerable latitude is given to established **theatre companies** to self-censor. Nevertheless, such companies generally refrain from detailed explorations of controversial subjects, especially because what Singaporeans refer to as the "out of bounds markers" for public expression are never absolutely clear or fixed.

Many practitioners recall that the forms of forum theatre and performance art were banned for a period in the mid-1990s because of their potential for spontaneous and unscripted interventions by **actors** and spectators. Plays with homosexual themes were also routinely suppressed until well into the 1990s, when the more challenging gay-themed works of Singapore-born **playwright** Chay Yew (1967–) were denied permission. Since then, however, rules have relaxed, and it is now acceptable to stage plays in which gay and lesbian relationships appear as normal and healthy, rather than aberrant. Nevertheless, a public forum arising from the production of a gay play is still the province of PELU and would probably be banned, as one was as recently as 2004.

Religion is still touchy given Singapore's multi-ethnic and multi-religious character, as is any perceived criticism of the government: generally speaking, both topics are off-limits.

FURTHER READING

Lo, Jacqueline. *Staging Nation: English Language Theatre in Malaysia and Singapore;* Peterson, William. *Theater and the Politics of Culture in Contemporary Singapore.*

William Peterson

Censorship: Sri Lanka

Sri Lanka endured several decades of **political** turmoil at the end of the twentieth century and into the twenty-first; the issues went from highly unpopular economic policies to the fierce ethnic civil war that erupted from the Tamil separatist movement. Those who spoke out against such things came under increasing pressure to keep their mouths shut. Every aspect of Sri Lankan life was affected by the consequent violence and fear, and repressive "Emergency" laws were passed restricting freedom of expression. Even casual discussions of politics were suspect, and people carefully censored their speech and writing. During the mid-1980s, the mass media were especially hard hit by suppressive measures, and there was a widespread lack of confidence in official news reports.

This took its toll on the people, who had a long tradition of vigorous political and **religious** discussion, but who now had to worry about the repercussions. Creativity among writers suffered a crushing blow and many put down their pens. Yet, as Ranjini Obeyesekere points out, the theatre became a surprisingly "permitted space," where ideas that had no outlet in other media were generally free to be put forth.

This first became evident under the leadership of President J. R. Jayawardene (1906–1996), whose otherwise repressive government showed significant support for the theatre, renovating Colombo's Tower Hall and Elphinstone **Theatres** and expanding the state-sponsored Annual Drama **Festivals**. When widespread outcry against Jayawar-dene's policies was met with hard-fisted reactions, no similar crackdown transpired with regard to theatrical dissent. A significant example was when, in 1987, a number of important theatre people publicly objected to that year's Annual Drama Festival being supported by a powerful multinational corporation; the government simply ignored them. Even between 1988 to 1990, when Sinhalese youth—who were officially encouraged to participate in theatrical activities—were caught up in the government's "elimination" campaigns against young subversives, the theatre remained free to express dissident ideas. Although plays were reviewed by a Censor Board before being permitted production, none were banned, possibly because their writers managed to keep their criticism too subtle to make them liable to censorship. Theatres remained open and, despite virulent censorship of other media, barely any incidents of theatre censorship were reported. The main target of theatrical suppression was "street theatre," produced by political activists, and sometimes broken up by police.

Obeyesekere ponders the reasons for this situation, suggesting that theatre's "populist" image with large audience support may have given it immunity, or that, perhaps, "the government considered theatrical performances of little political significance," and possibly worth encouraging as a form of "cathartic" release. She also notes that, while censors can spot objectionable material in written scripts, effective performance can make even innocuous material subversive.

FURTHER READING

Obeyesekere, Ranjini. *Sri Lankan Theatre in a Time of Terror: Political Satire in a Permitted Space.*

Samuel L. Leiter

Censorship: Taiwan

Until martial law (1949–1987) was lifted, **Taiwan**'s theatre was fashioned by **politics** and censorship in significant ways. Theatre was, in different historical periods, used in various ways—from propagandistic and pedagogical to reformative and sociolinguistic—to harness public opinion and educate the masses. In the Japanization campaign during the **Japanese** colonization period, the Taiwanese Drama Society (Taiwan Yanju Xiehui) censored Taiwanese- and **Chinese**-speaking theatre and replaced it with "Japanization" (*kominka* or *huangminhua*) drama. The colonial cultural policy also encouraged Taiwanese artists to study (in Japan) and emulate *shingeki*.

Tight censorship did not recede with the departure of the Japanese in 1945. The Chinese Nationalist government, which took over Taiwan, perceived an urgent need to counter the Japanese legacy and to promote Mandarin as the national tongue. The Nationalist government censored not only the language but also the content of presentations. With martial law in place after 1949, the first three decades of Nationalist rule witnessed an outpouring of anti-communist and anti-Soviet plays. There were many poorly attended state-sponsored free performances. Since most **theatre companies** were affiliated with government units, the most enthusiastic audiences were found in the armed forces because they constituted the period's main Mandarin-speaking population. However, as censorship guidelines developed, even these audiences lost interest in plays of outright propaganda.

The dynamics started to change in the 1960s, when **directors** and **playwrights** returned from living in the West to revive "spoken drama" (*huaju*) with a sense of refreshed theatricality. Non-propaganda plays dealing with nonsensitive topics began to appear. **Yao I-wei** and **Ma Sen** experimented with plays that challenged the dominant illusionist style, appropriating themes from **Western** dramas. **Chang Hsiao-feng** wrote Christian-themed plays. Others explored their characters' subconscious and revisited the question of representation. In other words, this generation negotiated the complex censorship limitations by first exploring new expressive modes and performing styles, which led to gradual but significant changes in dramatic content. The 1980s saw loosened control and reduced state funding for theatre companies. Commercial and **experimental theatres** emerged from nearly a century of politicization and censorship.

Alexander C. Y. Huang

Censorship: Thailand

The relationship between modern **Thai** theatre and censorship deals with many double standards. This is perhaps not surprising in a country where pornography and prostitution are illegal, and yet its red light districts are world famous.

Of all performing arts, modern theatre is among the least censored, probably because it is not a mainstream culture. While the government censors movies and television for their **political** and sexual content, theatre artists do not have to submit scripts or seek permission before staging a play. During demonstrations, theatre becomes a powerful medium. In quieter times, undercover police are reported to attend theatre. No productions have been shut down because of political reasons, yet theatre artists carefully choose their subject matter.

Homosexuality is also controversial. The Ministry of Culture prevents gays from portraying gays on television, and soap operas employ gay caricatures performed by straight **actors**. This restriction does not apply to **stage** performers. Montienthong **Theatre**'s longest running production was an adaptation of Mart Crowley's *The Boys in the Band* (1986). More recently, performance artist Wannasak Sirilar (1969–) rose to stardom with his solo show *Last Night Keanu Reeves Kissed Me* (Kuen thee Keanu Reeves joob chan, 1996), inspired by David Drake's *The Night Larry Kramer Kissed Me*. Sirilar followed with *Chalai Goes to War* (Chailai pai rob, 2000), *Internal Soul* (Khor khantee, 2001), and *I Wanna Say Thank You* (Chan Yak Klao kam wa kobkhun, 2005), which audiences appreciated for their humor and their straightforward presentation of homosexual issues.

Pawit Mahasarinand

Censorship: Vietnam

Censorship has been widely practiced through **Vietnamese** history by regimes of virtually all **political** persuasions. Censorship was widely practiced under the imperial regimes, especially on the *tuong* plays put on at their own court, but reached a height under the Nguyen dynasty (1802–1945). They aimed to obstruct the performance of plays that directly or indirectly espoused anti-Confucian politics and morality. While French ideas eschewed censorship, the colonialists certainly imposed it in Vietnam, especially against those many nationalists in the theatre who opposed their rule. The **Japanese** occupation (1940–1945) also imposed its own censorship.

The Ngo Dinh Diem (1901–1963) regime, which governed South Vietnam after the country was split under the Geneva Accords of 1954, established a Censorship Board under the Ministry of Information, with a section devoted to theatre. Diem was particularly keen to prevent the performance of plays with pro-communist ideas or those that offended his strict Catholic moral values. Plays required a stamp of approval before performance, and police had the duty of ensuring that there were no deviations from the approved version. The board and its theatre section survived Diem's assassination in 1963, though its precise Catholic direction underwent change.

While proclaiming freedom of thought and speech, the communists practiced censorship against plays that contravened their versions of nationalism and socialism. Although the reform policies of 1986 have much reduced the extent of theatre censorship, the 1992 Constitution (Article 33) still bans all culture detrimental to Vietnamese national interests or "destructive of the personality, morals, and fine lifestyle of the Vietnamese."

FURTHER READING

Brandon, James R. *Theatre in Southeast Asia.*

Colin Mackerras

CERVANTES, BEHN (1940–). Filipino **stage** and film **director, actor, critic,** and teacher, best known for being in the forefront of **political** theatre and developing forms and styles responding to issues of society and performance conditions. After obtaining his BA from the University of the **Philippines** (UP) and his MFA from the University of Hawaii, he taught theatre at the former.

Cervantes founded and mentored two **theatre companies:** Golden Rays (Gintong Silahis), the performing group of the Youth Democratic Organization, during the First Quarter Storm (late 1960s and early 1970s), a period of militant nationalism; and UP Repertory Company, a university-based troupe that has been staging original Filipino plays for more than three decades. Among the plays Cervantes directed are *Barricade* (Barikada, 1971), *The Mountain* (Ang bundok, 1976), *People's Worship* (Pagsambang bayan, 1977), and *People's Cry!* (Sigaw ng bayan, 1978).

As an actor, Cervantes has worked with the UP Dramatic Club, Arena Theatre, the Manila Theatre Guild, Repertory Philippines, the Philippine Educational Theatre Association, and New York's Ma-Yi Theatre Company. Among his memorable performances are the Marquis de Sade in *Marat/Sade* (1984), the diplomat in *M. Butterfly* (1980), and Narrator/Azdak in Ma-Yi's production of *The Caucasian Chalk Circle* at the Vintage Theater, New York (1995).

One of Cervantes's films, *Sakada* (1976), on the plight of the eponymous sugarcane workers, was banned for exhibition. His political activities in theatre and film as well as with several organizations led to his arrest and detention several times between 1972 and 1985 (see Censorship). Cervantes continues to mentor theatre groups from various universities, give workshops to migrant laborers, and direct plays for overseas workers in **Hong Kong**, Israel, and elsewhere.

Joi Barrios

CHAITI GHODA NACHA. Indian • folk • dance-drama of the fishermen of coastal Orissa. This "horse dance in the month of Chaitra" is performed by the Kaibarta caste of fishermen for a month from the full moon in Chaitra to the full moon in Baisakh (that is, March-April to April-May). It is performed at the annual **festival** in honor of the horse-headed Kaibarta goddess, Baseli.

The chief performers are the main singer (*rauta*), his wife (*rautani*, formerly played by a man), and a male horse dancer using a dummy horse representing Baseli. This is a decorative wooden horse-head connected to a brown bamboo trunk adorned with red flowers; it fits over the dancer, who behaves as if riding the horse, which moves rhythmically to a drum's beating and the playing of a flute as he sings, thereby invoking the goddess's presence.

The most familiar story, interpreted by the *rauta*, comes from the "Fisherman's Song" (Kaibarta gita). This **religious** text tells how Baseli, sleeping on a banyan tree leaf tossed about on the waves, uses the dirt in his ear to create someone to man a rudder to keep the leaf steady. The rudder-man, however, is swallowed by a fish, which makes the leaf bob again so that the god captures the fish and releases the rudder-man. He becomes the descendant of a caste of fishermen, while part of the leaf becomes a horse. The man and the horse become the tutelary deities of the fisherfolk. When the horse dies, the man's grief is calmed when he learns that the horse was Baseli, whose worship will save his soul. During the enactment, humorous interpolations by the *rauta* and his wife are presented. Additional stories based on myths are now also performed.

Samuel L. Leiter

'CHAM. *See* Tibet.

CHAMADYACHE BAHULYA. *See* Puppet Theatre: India.

CH'ANGGŬK. Korean • **musical** theatre developed since the early twentieth century on the basis of traditional *p'ansori* narrative singing. *Ch'anggŭk* (literally, "singing drama") retains the distinctive, husky style of *p'ansori*, and the most popular *ch'anggŭk* operas are dramatizations of *p'ansori* stories, although new works based on other sources are also composed. Instead of *p'ansori*'s single singer-**storyteller**, who performs all roles and provides narrative as well, *ch'anggŭk* uses a whole cast of *p'ansori* singers to impersonate the various characters, often with a third-person narrator as well. The *p'ansori* barrel drum (*puk*) is supplemented by an orchestra of traditional Korean instruments, melodic as well as rhythmic, and the visual presentation uses realistic **costuming** and **scenography**, often on a lavish scale. In response to the perceived lack of an indigenous, professional, indoor **theatre** tradition in Korea to compare with those of other Asian countries, *ch'anggŭk* is increasingly put forward as "traditional Korean opera."

Korea had no indoor commercial theatres before the twentieth century, and it was the introduction of such venues around 1900 that permitted the transformation of *p'ansori* into *ch'anggŭk*. This took place on the model of Japanese **shinpa** plays, themselves inspired by **Western** melodrama, and at first *ch'anggŭk* was promoted as a new and modern art form under the name of *shinyŏn-gŭk* (literally, "new drama"). The performers soon found, however, that they could not compete for novelty value with actual "new school" plays (*shinp'agŭk*), let alone imported silent films, and turned instead to tradition as a basis of audience appeal, quickly renaming the genre *kugŭk* (literally, "old drama") or *kup'a* ("old school"). Yet it was clearly not as traditional as *p'ansori*, and throughout its history, *p'ansori*-based opera has negotiated an ambivalent relationship between tradition and modernity.

After a brief spell of popularity in Seoul in the 1910s, *ch'anggŭk* was mainly performed in the more conservative rural areas, but was dwindling there too by the 1930s. A revival in Seoul was initiated in 1934 by the Korean Vocal Music Association, an organization of *p'ansori* singers and other traditional musicians concerned about the future of their art. This revival introduced the name *ch'anggŭk* along with many features that remain to this day, including the performance of complete dramas rather than episodes, the collaboration of a **playwright** and **director**, the use of accompanying instruments other than the *puk*, and the elaboration of scenery and costumes. This form continued through the 1940s, but after 1950 it was eclipsed by a new all-female variant, *yŏsŏng kukkŭk*.

Ch'anggŭk with mixed casts was once more revived in 1962 with the foundation of the National Ch'anggŭk Company (Kungnip Ch'anggŭkdan), which remains its leading exponent and has greatly expanded its repertory and resources, performing as a program of the Korean National Theatre (Kungnip Kŭkchang).

FURTHER READING

Korean International Theatre Institute, ed. *Korean Performing Arts: Drama, Dance and Music Theatre.*

Andrew Killick

CHANG HSIAO-FENG [ZHANG XIAOFENG] (1941–). Taiwanese •
playwright, and professor of **Chinese**, National Yang-Ming University (Taipei). She is a well-known Christian author of lyrical essays and **religious** dramas. After studying drama with **Lee Man-kuei**, Chang started writing plays, most of them at the center of heated debates about art and religion. Between 1968, when she completed *A Painting* (Hua), and 1978, she wrote nine plays, all of them successfully staged by Christian fellowship troupes.

Chang's plays uniquely combine **experimental theatre** methods with themes selected from medieval morality drama. Her abundance of Christian-themed scenes earned Chang a reputation as one whose plays make the audience feel as if the **theatre** had been turned into a church. These works include the appearance of a prophet preaching directly to the audience in *The Fifth Wall* (Diwu qiang, 1971), the protagonist's decision in *A Man from Wuling* (Wuling ren, 1972) to stay in the mundane world to defend humanity rather than escaping to a readily accessible utopia, and the presence of a missionary-like character in *Jade of the He* (Heshibi, 1974).

A significant number of Chang's plays adapt Chinese folklore and pseudo-history. Chang draws inspiration from traditional Chinese stories and the Bible. She claims that if one analyzes her plays, he shall find only "China and Christianity" as their ingredients. Chang uses grotesque yet poetic language, minimalist **scenography**, and Christian themes to resist the anti-communist ideologies of the 1970s that permeated the arts and theatre.

Alexander C. Y. Huang

CHANG YANQIU (1904–1958). Chinese • actor of the female **role type** (*dan*), one of "the four great *dan*" of the first half of the twentieth century (the others being **Mei Lanfang**, **Shang Xiaoyun**, and **Xun Huisheng**). Born in humble circumstances in Beijing, he began **training** for *jingju* at six, along the way studying under masters like Mei, and learning *qingyi* (literally, "blue garments") and "sword and horse" (*daoma*) *dan* roles. By eleven he was performing such works as *The Pavilion of the Imperial Tablet* (Yubei ting), establishing a reputation for versatility. He performed in Shanghai in 1922, rapidly becoming famous.

Chang had a graceful singing style and was adept in tragedies. Despite his strong physique, he could play gentle, fragile **women**. After the establishment of his own **theatre company**, he was celebrated for his performance as *qingyi* and *daoma dan*, especially in *The Rainbow Pass* (Hongni guan) and *The Story of Su Pan* (Su San qi jie). From the 1920s, he wrote and played in many new works, notably *The Blue Frost Sword* (Qingxue dao), *The Emerald Hairpin* (Biyu zan), and *The Bride's Dream* (Chungui meng).

He founded his own "Chang school" (*cheng pai*), famous in *jingju* history. He was noted for his soft, pleasant singing, and for his ability to portray the emotions of his characters and produce an emotional response in his audiences. He was also renowned for his adaptation of the "water sleeves" (*shuixiu*) **costume** technique, and for the way his performance contributed to the development of this art among *dan* performers.

Chang visited several European countries during a research tour in 1932. He had a reputation as an upright and patriotic man and, during the Second Sino-**Japanese** War (1937–1945), lived a reclusive life in a Beijing suburb. In 1984, the Municipal Antiquities Bureau declared his house a special cultural site.

Before 1949, Chang became the head of the Beijing branch of the Nanjing **Xiqu** Music College and of the Chinese Xiqu Specialist School. In 1953, he was appointed vice-principal of the Chinese Xiqu Research Institute and in 1949 attended the first full session of the Chinese People's Political Consultative Conference. He joined the Communist Party in 1957.

Chang, who published several theatre books, was honored with various commemorations in 2004, the centenary of his birth. The culture bureaus of Beijing, Tianjin, and Shanghai highlighted his work, and famous performers presented Chang's signature pieces.

Trevor Hay

CHEA SAMY (1919?–1994). Cambodian • *robam kbach boran* dancer and **dance**-mistress. A star during the reign of King Monivong (1875–1941; r. 1927–1941), Chea Samy became a key figure in restoring the dance after 1979, in the wake of the Khmer Rouge genocide. Born to peasants in Kompong Cham Province, she was brought to Phnom Penh at five to enter the royal harem of dancers. Specializing in female (*neang*) roles, she became the most admired dancer of her generation and a favorite of King Monivong, who gave her the (low-level) royal title *neak neang*.

After French colonial authorities razed the harem when Monivong died, Chea Samy continued to dance and teach, living outside the palace. In 1955, she married Loth Suong, a cousin of Monivong's chief concubine, Look Khun Meak. The couple helped

Chea Samy training a young Cambodian dancer. (Photo: Eileen Blumenthal)

to raise Loth Suong's brothers, one of whom, Saloth Sar, eventually became Khmer Rouge leader Pol Pot (1925–1998).

Chea Samy and Loth Suong remained in Phnom Penh through the turbulent 1960s. Lacking resources to leave, she continued to teach even after the 1970 overthrow of the monarchy, living amid the worsening guerilla war.

When the Khmer Rouge took control in 1975, the family was evacuated along with the entire city into rural conditions of slave labor. Unaware that their relative (using a nom de guerre) was the new leader, they survived the period largely by lying about their royal connections.

After the Vietnamese ousted the Khmer Rouge in 1979, Chea Samy was the most accomplished royal dance artist left alive. Working with other surviving teachers and former students, she began within months to train a new generation of dancers—working against time to transmit the art before she died.

Eileen Blumenthal

CHENG CHANGGENG (1811–1880). Chinese • *jingju* • actor, the greatest player of the "older male" (*laosheng*) **role type** of the nineteenth century. Cheng is sometimes called "the father of *jingju*" for his integration of the style's arts and for his development of the *laosheng* roles that have become so crucial to *jingju*.

Cheng came from Anqing, Anhui Province, but in his youth went to Beijing, where his uncle encouraged him to go on the **stage**. He studied with eminent *laosheng* Mi Xizi (1780–1832), but undertook his first public appearance prematurely and was ridiculed. After practicing for three years he was given another opportunity at a banquet performance attended by royal princes and other eminent persons, and was greeted with thunderous acclaim. Throughout his career he performed many times before aristocratic audiences, as well as in **theatres** frequented by lower-class audiences.

From about 1845 until his death Cheng was the leader of the Three Celebrations Company (Sanqing), one of the "four great famous companies" responsible for the rise of *jingju*. Under Emperor Xianfeng (r. 1851–1862) he became the leader of the Actors' Guild, giving him significant authority. The guild head was a government appointee and all actors and **theatre companies** had to register with it. In 1860, when for a few months actors from the city were invited to perform at the imperial court, Cheng attended, winning an official title from Xianfeng himself, then an extremely unusual honor for an actor.

Although Cheng is said to have smoked opium, in all other respects, sources portray him as morally upright, Confucian in nature, hard-working, principled and trustworthy, disciplined, demanding discipline of others, unafraid of high-ranking persons, generous to company members, and patriotic. He had no sons, but adopted two of a relation's sons. He was an inspiring teacher, his students including not only *laosheng* but other types as well. Among his students were eminent actors like **Tan Xinpei**.

Cheng founded the "Cheng school" (*cheng pai*) of *jingju*, which emphasized Anhui **music**. He had a resounding voice, with clear diction, and his acting showed nobility and eminence. Although he was versatile artistically and had a wide repertoire, he was most renowned as loyal ministers and righteous men, especially heroes in dramas from the civil wars of the Three Kingdoms period (220–265). One example was Guan Yu (160–219) in *Battle for Changsha* (Zhan Changsha), in which Guan Yu (the "God of War"), having attacked Changsha in Hunan Province, refuses to thrust to victory when his enemy's horse stumbles because that would be mean-spirited.

Colin Mackerras

CHEO. **Vietnamese • folk theatre** rooted in rural villages and revealing of simple country life and its values. *Cheo* can also be traced back to its tenth-century precursor, *tro nhai* (literally, "mimicry"), but is most often linked to village folk **music** and **dance** of the Red River Delta. Unlike the **Chinese**-influenced *tuong*, *cheo*—originally performed in gratitude for a good harvest—is thoroughly Vietnamese in origin, style, and themes. *Cheo* reflected desires for peaceful, harmonious lives amidst the oppressive feudal system.

Pure *cheo* consists of folk songs, spoken dialogue, poetry, and dance, accompanied by pantomime and instrumental music. Plays consist of interpretive sketches from legends, poetry, history, or daily life, and are replete with nonrealistic conventions. *Cheo* is typically performed in close proximity to the audience, which is summoned by a complex drumbeat.

The close proximity of **actors**, musicians (seated on both sides of the performance mat), and audience allows for participatory interaction. The musicians welcome the actors, provide exposition, exchange repartee with actors, and comment about the characters' motives.

Dance is intricate yet seems effortless when performed by the graceful actresses, who sing and use fans to convey emotions while performing alluring arm, wrist, and hand gestures. Female characters tend to dominate and be more individuated than the male **role types**: the foolish mandarin and his servants, the clown, the lecherous village leader, and the village "witch" or fortune-teller, who dupes villagers

Scene from the *cheo* play, *Thi Kinh the Goddess of Mercy*, in which a young woman (right), forced to disguise herself as a man, becomes the romantic object of another woman. (Photo: Lorelle Browning)

of their money. Clowns, as elsewhere, ridicule authority figures or expose the hypocrisy of abusive or compassionless persons.

Morality tends to reflect Buddhist benevolence and Confucian virtues, especially in maintaining harmonious social relationships. Most plays are comical, lyrical, and end hopefully. Yet they also portray human foibles, as well as the hardships of feudal society.

FURTHER READING

Quang, Dinh et al. *Vietnamese Theater.*

Lorelle Browning

CHHAU. Indian • folk • dance-drama that developed in Bihar, West Bengal, and Orissa. Like other Indian dance-dramas, *chhau*, which has over a dozen varieties, is accompanied by traditional **music**, relies on **religious** and literary characters, and is associated with **festivals**. Its name's meaning is disputed, but it may mean "mask," "shadow," or "disguise." Unique characteristics include its generally consisting of solo or paired performances, its dances' brevity, and movement more angular and energetic than other Indian dance forms. Additionally, two of *chhau*'s three major forms—*seraikella* (Bihar) and *purulia* (West Bengal)—are among the few in India to use **masks**. *Mayurbhanj chhau*, the third major form, which developed in Orissa, does not use masks, but faces evince little expression. *Chhau* is an art of the body, not the face.

Masks are smaller and simpler than their counterparts in South India. *Seraikella chhau* masks tend to be more graceful and less elaborate than those of *purulia chhau*, which are often grotesque. *Seraikella chhau*'s masks are notable for their smooth, oval-faced beauty, their delicate noses, and their almond-shaped, half-closed, dreamily exotic eyes.

Performance. The dancers, all male, do not speak or sing, and vocal accompaniment is limited. The accompanying music is based on drums, especially the large *dhamsa* and the smaller *dholak*, although there is also a double-reed woodwind (*shehnai*). The musicians themselves perform dramatically by wandering the space and physically interacting with dancers. With few exceptions dancers do not perform professionally, but keep jobs as farmers, shopkeepers, drivers, and so forth. In recent history, the maharajas of Seraikella invested significant money in support of performers; this support has evolved into government patronage in Bihar.

Festivals. *Seraikella chhau* is especially associated with the springtime Chaitra Parva festival, and is performed on four of the final five nights. During the first three, a variety of dances is performed in conjunction with other ritual activities. Especially notable is the visit of a patron dressed as Krishna, who watches the dances and then visits area households as an embodiment of divinity. The fourth night is dedicated to the deity Kali, and only the payment of a ritual fee allows for dancing. No dances occur on the final night, partly owing to the solemnity of the occasion.

Besides dramatizing traditional subjects such as gods and heroes, *seraikella chhau* offers highly allegorical dances, involving animals, forces of nature, and anthropomorphized concepts. Both *purulia chhau* and *mayurbhanj chhau* are less allegorical. Instead, they rely almost exclusively on subjects from epic and religious literature.

Training. **Training** is based on sword-and-shield exercises (*parikhanda*), and fundamental positions resemble postures required by these weapons. *Mayurbhanj chhau* also predicates fundamental movements on the activities of household life, including sweeping, grinding spices, washing clothes, and so on.

Although nothing identifies *chhau*'s origin definitively, it seems to have arisen from martial training, vitally important in dance education. Circumstantial evidence construed from sculpture and scroll painting suggests the tradition goes back several centuries, and it is possible to identify strictly classical elements of movement and style. Certainly, the vigorous choreography links it to the region's martial arts, and its form cannot be exclusively attributed to folk traditions.

Patronage. Local maharajas were especially important to the form's practice in the early twentieth century, giving official recognition to the most accomplished troupes. In the early 1930s, Maharaja Aditya Pratap Singh Deo gave official support to the mask-makers of Mahapatra. In the late 1930s, a Seraikella troupe toured Europe—perhaps the first time *chhau* was seen outside of India. A *purulia chhau* troupe first toured the United States in the 1970s.

FURTHER READING

Bhattacharyya, Asutosh. *Chhau Dance of Purulia*; Gargi, Balwant. *Folk Theater of India*; Richmond, Farley, Darius L. Swann, and Phillip B. Zarrilli, eds. *Indian Theatre: Traditions of Performance*.

David V. Mason

CHHENG PHON (1930–). Cambodian • **actor, playwright**, teacher, scholar, and culture minister, who has had a far-reaching impact on a range of Khmer performing arts. Chheng Phon has influenced a range of performing arts, including social and **political** satire, **folk** performance, and classical **dance**.

Born in Prey Veng Province and raised in poverty, Phon attended the free-tuition École Normale, the teacher-**training** college in Phnom Penh, where he began to study and perform theatre. Upon graduation in 1956, he joined **Hang Tun Hak**'s "spoken drama" (**lakhon niyeay**) troupe and became one of its stars, renowned for comedy. After a year, that troupe was dispersed—barely escaping imprisonment—for criticizing the government. But Queen **Sisowath Kossamak** was a fan, and Phon became a member of the royal *robam kbach boran* troupe, playing comic old men. There, he also studied the other **role types**—female, male, ogre, and monkey. He was the first man to work alongside young girls in that way. He studied dance in **China** from 1961 to 1964.

Returning in 1964, he began the first serious study of Cambodia's folk performance, including that of ethnic minorities, and in 1966 became head of the Folk Dance Division of Cambodia's new Royal University of Fine Arts. Over the next four years, he also became the director of the National Conservatory, the country's professional performing group, and president of the Artists' Union of Cambodia. He retained all three posts until the Khmer Rouge takeover of April 1975. Meanwhile, he opened an "art farm," where he housed and taught more than one hundred arts students displaced by the escalating war.

Of Cambodia's three major arts figures of the latter twentieth century—Queen Sisowath Kossamak, Hang Tun Hak, and Chheng Phon—Phon was the only one still alive when the Khmer Rouge was routed in 1979. He became the key figure in restoring the traditional arts, which the Khmer Rouge had left in shambles. He gathered teachers and students, and he taught dance and arts philosophy, successfully navigating the complex politics of an occupied country. He became minister of information and culture in 1981 and oversaw the founding of a new Fine Arts School in 1981 and a Fine Arts University in 1989.

After his retirement from his official duties, around 1989, he founded the Vipassana Center, a center of Buddhist meditation. He has remained involved in the arts as a teacher and guide to artists.

Eileen Blumenthal

CHIKAMATSU HANJI (1725–1783). Japanese *bunraku* (see Puppet Theatre) **playwright**, one of the last of his breed. Like his father, Confucian scholar Hozumi Ikan (1692–1769), Hanji was an enthusiastic admirer of **Chikamatsu Monzaemon**—to the point of adopting the master's name. Hanji joined the Takemoto Theatre (Takemoto-za) in his mid-twenties. Serving a long apprenticeship under **Takeda Izumo** II and others, he eventually became the **theatre**'s chief playwright and the author (or coauthor) of more than fifty works. His forte was "history plays" (*jidai mono*), such as *Japan's Twenty-four Paragons of Filial Piety* (Honchô nijûshikô, 1766) and *Mount Imo and Mount Se: An Exemplary Tale of Womanly Virtue* (Imoseyama onna teikin, 1771). He was also successful at "domestic dramas" (*sewa mono*), including *The Balladeer's New Tale* (Shinpan utazaimon, 1780) and *Through Iga Pass with the Tôkaidô Board Game* (Igagoe dôchû sugoroku, 1783), his last play.

Hanji faced many challenges. In 1759 the Takemoto Theatre burned down. It was rebuilt, but never recovered stable financial footing. Hanji used every means possible—stunning plot devices and performance styles borrowed from *kabuki*—to attract audiences and keep the puppet theatre afloat. His skill was such that his plays continue to be admired and performed today in both *bunraku* and *kabuki*.

Barbara E. Thornbury

CHIKAMATSU MONZAEMON (1653–1725). Japanese *bunraku* (see Puppet Theatre) and *kabuki* • **playwright**, widely considered the greatest of the Edo period (1603–1868). He wrote over ninety works for *bunraku*, with which he is most closely associated, and some thirty for *kabuki*.

Chikamatsu was born and raised in what is now Fukui Prefecture, the son of Sugimori Nobuyoshi (1621–1687), a samurai. By Chikamatsu's early- to mid-teens, his father had resigned his samurai position and moved the family to Kyoto. Life there brought educational and employment opportunities. He began his literary career at eighteen under the poet Yamaoka Genrin (1631–1672). He also took positions in several aristocratic households, among them that of Ôgimachi Kimmochi (1653–1733), a noble interested in writing. Ôgimachi appreciated the puppet theatre and is known to have written plays for *ko-jôruri* narrator (*tayû*) Uji Kaga no jô (1635–1711).

The Soga Heir (Yotsugi Soga, 1683), written for Uji, was Chikamatsu's first major success. Based on the *Tale of the Soga Brothers* (Soga monogatari), an often-dramatized thirteenth-century epic, the play displayed Chikamatsu's ability to bring a fresh interpretation to a well-known story in an audience-pleasing way. Chikamatsu proved particularly adept at writing the crucial "travel" scenes (*michiyuki*), which use highly poetic language to capture emotional content. The play's many clever allusions attest to Chikamatsu's familiarity with the range of Japanese literary history.

Chikamatsu eventually began writing for Uji's rival, the brilliant **Takemoto Gidayû**. Gidayû, who in 1684 opened his Takemoto Theatre (Takemoto-za) in Osaka, had formerly studied under and worked for Uji. Together, Chikamatsu and Gidayû brought *bunraku* to a new level of popularity and brilliance, so much so that earlier *bunraku* (then called *jôruri*) became known as "old" *jôruri* (*ko-jôruri*). *Kagekiyo Victorious* (Shusse Kagekiyo, 1686), a vividly dramatic work in which the bodhisattva Kannon intervenes to save the hero, is considered to have closed the book on *ko-jôruri*.

Despite his success with Gidayû, Chikamatsu did not limit himself to the puppets. He crafted *The Seventh Anniversary of Yûgiri's Death* (Yûgiri shichinen ki, 1684) for Osaka *kabuki* **actor • Sakata Tôjûrô** I. From 1693 until 1702, Chikamatsu wrote most of his plays for Tôjûrô. During his *kabuki* period, Chikamatsu created characters to suit Tôjûrô's "gentle style" (*wagoto*) specialty in roles depicting prosperous young men who wind up in unfortunate situations. Rarely seen today, the works include plays such as *The Courtesan on the Buddha Plain* (Keisei Hotoke no Hara, 1699).

Returning to *bunraku* after Tôjûrô retired in 1702, Chikamatsu began once more writing for Gidayû. In 1703, Chikamatsu scored an overwhelming success with *The Love Suicides at Sonezaki* (Sonezaki shinjû). It not only secured the financial footing of Gidayû's theatre, but it also set off a demand for Chikamatsu to write more "love suicide plays" (*shinjû mono*). Chikamatsu continued to write them until nearly the end of his career, including *Love Suicides at Amijima* (Shinjû Ten no Amijima, 1721), widely considered his masterpiece, and *Love Suicides on the Eve of the Kôshin Festival* (Shinjû yoi Gôshin, 1722). Their immense popularity can be attributed to the realistic portrayals of contemporary people trapped by circumstances outside of their control, and finding themselves torn between duty (*giri*) to family and society and emotion (*ninjô*). Fearing that such works might inspire frustrated lovers to take their own lives, the authorities banned them in 1722 (see Censorship).

Having held the position of staff playwright for Tôjûrô at Kyoto's Miyako Theatre (Miyako-za), Chikamatsu was hired in 1705 by **Takeda Izumo** I, who succeeded Gidayû that year as manager of the Takemoto. Encouraged by Izumo and Gidayû's support, Chikamatsu used his *kabuki* experience to produce plays richer in dramatic detail and **scenographic** effects than ever seen before. The popularity of their very first joint effort, *Emperor Yômei and the Mirror of Craftsmen* (Yômei tennô no shokunin kagami, 1705), encouraged Chikamatsu to produce increasingly spectacular and multi-faceted plays.

The Battles of Coxinga (Kokusenya kassen, 1715) cemented the playwright's significance. Produced a year after Gidayû's death, it brought a highly imaginative view of **Chinese** and Japanese history to life with its epic battle scenes and a veritable pageant of ministers, courtiers, princesses, and even a tiger. The hero is Watônai, who overcomes the tiger, and is eventually renamed Coxinga in the course of his ultimately successful struggle to restore the Ming dynasty to power. The play broke long-run records.

During his last decade, Chikamatsu continued writing for narrators such as Takemoto Gidayû II, for whom he wrote *Love Suicides at Amijima* and *Woman Killer and the Hell of Oil* (Onna goroshi abura jigoku, 1721). Chikamatsu was equally skilled at writing "domestic plays" (*sewa mono*) and "history plays" (*jidai mono*). A recent scholar says that Chikamatsu's late historical plays should be read as commentaries on his government and society.

FURTHER READING

Gerstle, Andrew C., ed. and trans. *Chikamatsu: 5 Late Plays*; Keene, Donald. trans. *Major Plays of Chikamatsu*.

Barbara E. Thornbury

CHINA. China is in the far east of the Eurasian continent. Its population is 1.266 billion (2000 census), and its principal **religions** are Confucianism and Buddhism. The present Chinese state identifies fifty-six ethnic groups, the most populous being the Han, with about 91.59 percent (2000). The other 8.41 percent are fifty-five "minority nationalities," their habitat being about two-thirds of China's area, mainly border regions and the country's western half. Many minorities have their own **folk** religions. The main universalist religion is Islam, but Buddhism has a major following, the **Tibetans** and **Mongolians** practicing an esoteric tantric form (Tibetan Buddhism).

Early Historical Background. The combination of song, **dance**, **costume**, gesture, and representation by one person of another, or of a spirit or animal, goes back to very ancient shamanistic ceremonies, possibly as early as the third millennium BC. Records and archaeological remains concerning proto-theatrical performances abound. Communal dancing for **festival** celebrations or other purposes, including the use of costumes and impersonation of animals, dates back to the prehistoric period. Archaeological evidence suggests that, at the first appearance of an aristocratic class as early as the second millennium BC, nobles had dancing performances at their banquets and may even have owned dancing troupes of slaves.

Historian Sima Qian (145–86 BC) cites Confucius (551–479 BC) in two major theatrical connections. One is Confucius's description of *The Great Warrior* (Dawu) dance about the establishment of the Zhou dynasty in the eleventh century BC. It has a variety of theatrical phenomena, including dance, impersonation, and the beginnings of a story. Another is Confucius's demand that dancers be killed because of their evil influence on the nobility, showing that **actors** held a very low status from early times.

Yet many of the most ancient dynasties, from the Zhou on, had court offices overseeing performances connected to official ceremonies. Tang dynasty (618–907) Emperor Xuanzong (a.k.a. Minghuang, r. 712–756) set up a **music** school in the Pear Garden (Liyuan) in his capital Chang'an. Actors continued to be called "children of the Pear Garden" (see Training). Court jesters giving advice or warning through impersonation of **political** figures date from the pre-BC era, and probably so does **puppetry**.

Canjun xi, Yuanben, *and* Zaju. The Tang dynasty saw the development of skits called *canjun xi*, distinctive for the **role types** of "adjutant" and "grey hawk." These were actually the basis for many later comic types. During the Song dynasty (960–1279) and Jin dynasty (1115–1234) of northern China, which expelled the Song to the south in 1126 but was itself overcome by the Mongols in 1234, *canjun xi* developed into a farce called *yuanben*, the term a contraction of *hangyuan zhi ben* (literally, "scripts from the performers' quarters"). Sometimes also called ***zaju***, it flourished at all levels, from popular to court.

Yuanben had several role types. Rather than just single items, there were music, dance, comic sketches, acrobatics, and slapstick. Central was a short comic play with a simple but identifiable story, and themes including love affairs, ghosts, gods, or demons. Costumes and **properties** were more complex than before, as were **masks** and **makeup**. A range of wind instruments and drums, as well as a plucked lute (*pipa*), provided music.

Nanxi. In the twelfth century, southern China enjoyed ***nanxi***, a popular form based on folk song and with percussion only. In contrast to *yuanben*, these were stand-alone theatrical pieces. Because *nanxi* clearly included complex storylines showing a number of sophisticated theatrical conventions, some scholars regard it as China's earliest drama form, the beginnings of ***xiqu***. Although it declined when the Mongols took over southern China in 1280, it is the basis of many later southern forms, including ***chuanqi*** and ***kunqu***.

Nowadays many regard the Yuan dynasty (1280–1368) as the "great age of Chinese drama." Certainly, *zaju* was the most developed theatre yet produced. Although the music has not survived, the instrumentation suggests musical adaptation into later styles.

Ming through Qing Dynasties. Beginning in the north, *zaju* spread all over China. The late Yuan and early Ming (1368–1644) dynasties saw the revival of southern styles like *chuanqi* and from the sixteenth century the rise of *kunqu* and other regional styles. During the Qing dynasty (1644–1911), these styles developed greatly, climaxing in ***jingju***, which began late in the eighteenth century and flowered in the nineteenth. It is perhaps the acme of Chinese theatrical art in all its facets, including acrobatic battle scenes. Although initially centered on Beijing, *jingju* spread throughout the country, being the closest to a Chinese "national theatre."

Several Ming theatre features endured to the early twentieth century. One is the stronger differentiation into popular and aristocratic theatre, with *kunqu* the "elegant" drama of the educated classes and aristocracy while other regional styles are mass theatre. The higher classes owned private troupes, seen at banquets and special occasions. For the popular styles, venues were mainly temple **stages**, temporary stages in marketplaces, or any open space; performance occasions included fairs and festivals. The nineteenth century also saw the rise of **theatres**, especially in Beijing.

Actors' low social status was legally confirmed through edicts. Discrimination against **women** was greatly strengthened, with male-only **theatre companies** becoming the norm, and most actresses being prostitutes. At court, the Ming set up a eunuch entertainment agency in 1390, which came to include drama, and from about 1740 the Qing trained eunuchs at court with the special duty of performing plays. Initially this meant *kunqu*, but from 1884 Empress Dowager Cixi (1835–1908) invited *jingju* actors from the city to perform for her.

Twentieth Century through 1949. The twentieth century's first half saw several major developments in *xiqu*, including:

- Efforts toward various reforms in the direction of modernization.
- The heyday of *jingju* and several major regional forms. Important *jingju* actors emerged, most notably female role (*dan*) actor **Mei Lanfang**, but

also *dan* **Chang Yanqiu**, and "older male" (*laosheng*) **Yu Shuyan** and **Zhou Xinfang**.

- Internationalization, with Mei becoming China's first major world theatre star.
- The use of *xiqu* (and other forms) as anti-**Japanese** propaganda during the Second Sino-Japanese War (1937–1945).
- The postwar decline of many of the small-scale regional folk styles, and even major styles, some to the point of extinction.

With the establishment of the People's Republic of China (PRC) in 1949, the Chinese Communist Party (CCP) immediately set about *xiqu*'s revival through state sponsorship. *Xiqu* was viewed as a traditional art in which to take pride. However, in line with propaganda purposes, the CCP also carried out intensive reform in all *xiqu* styles.

Almost all the main actors remained in China in 1949. Several became national icons, showing the profession's rise in status. They were also pushed into administrative tasks less suitable to their talents than theatre.

FURTHER READING

Dolby, William. *A History of Chinese Drama*; Hsu, Tao-ching. *The Chinese Conception of the Theatre*; Mackerras, Colin. *Chinese Theatre from its Origins to the Present Day*; Mackerras, Colin. *Chinese Drama, A Historical Survey*.

Colin Mackerras

Post-1949 Reform. *Xiqu* reform began at the turn of the twentieth century and was affected by the upheavals of the time, from the Boxer Uprising of 1900 on. Unlike the later PRC period, reform initiatives early in the century came mainly from **playwrights** and actors themselves, often being resisted by governments.

Until 1949, the main styles affected by reform included *jingju*, especially the Shanghai style, *chuanju*, and Cantonese ***yueju***. Reform features were:

- New content that portrayed contemporary problems and social issues, frequently trying to incite patriotism in the face of imperialist attacks, or historical content that presented characterization emphasizing patriotism or opposition to oppressive feudal practices.
- Contemporary costumes and realistic acting to suit contemporary themes.
- A new **training** system.
- New, **Western**-style theatres.
- A rise in actors' social status.

Chuanju dramatist Huang Ji'an (1836–1924) wrote some eighty items from 1901 onward. Although his plays are set in the past, character choice and characterization bring out patriotism or condemn women's oppression.

Shanghai *jingju* actor Pan Yueqiao (1869–1929) not only acted in "new plays with contemporary costumes" but helped build China's first modern-style theatre

(Shanghai, 1908). After a 1913 visit to Shanghai, Mei Lanfang was for a time active in social dramas. In 1914, he acted in a drama on prostitution, *Waves of the Sea of Sin* (Niehai bolan), with realistic acting, contemporary costumes, and a clear social message.

Cantonese *yueju* was much affected by Western patterns, especially because of its proximity to Britain's colony, **Hong Kong**. Some foreign novels and films, as well as modern "spoken drama" (*huaju*) with political and social content, were adapted to *yueju* music. Meanwhile, several Western instruments were introduced.

The May Fourth Movement (1919) exercised far more influence on *huaju* reform than on *xiqu*, though earlier *xiqu* reforms persisted. The war with Japan provoked all of China's theatre workers to use their art for patriotic purposes, with dramas having contemporary themes, costumes, and actions. Meanwhile, in May 1942, in Yan'an, CCP Chairman Mao Zedong (1893–1976) specifically advocated using the arts for propaganda purposes. Also, the CCP undertook its reform of *jingju* and other *xiqu* forms that focused on extolling past rebels against feudal oppression.

On coming to power in 1949, the CCP quickly took action toward *xiqu* reform. The government established professional *xiqu* companies and in 1956 took over the main pre-existing ones. In 1950, the Ministry of Culture set up the Xiqu Reform Committee, which immediately held a national conference to decide on an appropriate methodology. In line with party ideology, the conference promoted old and newly created items in favor of patriotism, women's and minority rights, and love of labor, but opposed pornographic items and those promoting superstition and cruelty, while showing arranged marriages positively. Items were formally categorized as "traditional plays" (*chuantong xi*), **xinbian lishi ju**, and "contemporary (modern dress) plays" (*xiandai xi*); companies were called upon to create more of the latter two types. After the conference, a few items were banned while others disappeared. Late in 1952, a government-sponsored festival of twenty-three *xiqu* styles took place, showing those types the government favored.

In 1954, *xiqu* actor **Ouyang Yuqian** chaired a conference attended by many luminaries to consider reform. The conclusion was to preserve most aspects of traditional stagecraft, from music to painted faces. However, some particularly "feudal" skills were abolished, such as the "false feet" (*caiqiao*), which **Wei Changsheng** had introduced to imitate the gait of a woman's bound feet.

In an effort to modernize *xiqu* creative processes, artists with Western-style training and background were assigned to companies throughout the 1950s, and actor training, especially in *jingju*, was augmented with realistic techniques taught by USSR experts. Playwrights, **directors**, and **scenographers** with realist sensibilities have held prominent positions ever since, resulting in fundamental changes in creative process and authority.

Cultural Revolution. Though a 1958 call on *xiqu* artists to create new contemporary plays resulted in very few, Mao's wife, Jiang Qing (1913–1991), a former actress, continued to champion their cause, demanding that socialist theatre not only be *for* the proletariat, but also *about* them. In 1964, Jiang and Mao convened a five-day National Festival of Contemporary Jingju at which twenty-nine troupes presented thirty-five new contemporary plays. The following year, criticism of the new historical *jingju Hai Rui Dismissed from Office* (Hai Rui baguan) ignited the Cultural Revolution (see below), and from 1966 to 1976, all but contemporary plays disappeared. In 1966, eight "model plays" (**yangban xi**) were identified, including five contemporary *jingju*, a number that was doubled by 1976.

Creation of each "model" took about a year, followed by major revisions, with large companies working full-time with virtually unlimited funds. This was the largest **experimental theatrical** movement of the century. One of the most important theoretical principles guiding the process was the "three prominences" (*san tuchu*): of all characters, give prominence to the positive; among the positive, to the heroic; and among the heroic, to the principle heroic character(s). There was extensive musical experimentation, and the expansion of traditional practices. Ironically, many highly successful approaches were then **censored**, along with the specific items themselves, from 1976 until 1990.

Postcultural Revolution Reforms. Immediately after the Cultural Revolution, traditional and newly written historical plays returned. The Cultural Revolution was formally discredited in 1981. But shrinking audiences and decreasing funding led to new reforms. Modernization and the hope of attracting new audiences spawned the use of elaborate scenography involving extensive sets and special effects, especially for new historical plays. Other reforms have been financial and organizational, with troupes being disbanded, reduced in size, or merged. Leading artists have been encouraged to take responsibility for the livelihood of a troupe's members. Companies have instituted incentive-based salary structures, and most have sought additional funding through "extra income enterprises" and corporate sponsorship.

Many reforms aimed at increasing audiences have involved training, either of professional artists to raise their level of performance, or of potential new audience members through artists-in-the-schools' teaching and performance efforts. Some companies, such as the Shanghai Drama Society (Shanghai Xiju Xieshe), have undertaken long-term research to identify and appeal to target audiences.

Despite reforms, interest flagged during the 1990s, especially among young people, and the modernization thrust has not been good for *xiqu*. The government has worked on *xiqu*'s behalf in several ways, including:

- Setting up new theatres in largely traditional style, especially for *xiqu*. Representative is the Pear Garden Theatre (Liyuan) in a tourist hotel in the south of Beijing.
- Making *jingju* and other major *xiqu* styles tourist attractions.
- Organizing *xiqu* festivals, such as the First Festival of Jingju Arts, held in Tianjin in November 1995.
- Allocating one channel of China Central Television entirely to traditional theatre.

FURTHER READING

Chen, Xiaomei. *Acting the Right Part: Political Theater and Popular Drama in Contemporary China*; Cheung, Martha, and Jane Lai, eds. *An Oxford Anthology of Contemporary Chinese Drama*; Yu, Shiao-ling, ed. *Chinese Drama after the Cultural Revolution, 1979–1989: An Anthology.*

Colin Mackerras and Elizabeth Wichmann-Walczak

Ethnic Minority Theatres. Among the fifty-five ethnic minorities, most have their own traditions of song and dance, with styles, language, and, sometimes, group-specific stories. The most distinguished of minority drama styles is Tibetan drama. Several ethnic minorities, notably the Hui or Chinese Muslims (2000 population: 9,816,805), found over most of China, and Manchus (2000 population: 10,682,262) of the northeast, have contributed to Han *xiqu* forms, especially *jingju*. Among the main ethnic groups with their own traditional drama styles are the Manchus of the northeast, Yunnan Province's Bai (2000 population: 1,858,063) and Dai (2000 population: 1,158,989), and Guangxi's Zhuang (2000 population: 16,178,811), the most populous minorities. All have been strongly influenced by Han *xiqu*. There are also **Korean** and Mongolian populations in China (2000 population, respectively: 1,923,842 and 5,813,947).

Traditional Manchu drama consisted of ballad stories performed through song and dance. Small-scale items had only two performers, the larger categorizing the characters in ways similar to *xiqu*. What was distinctive were Manchu language and stories, which concerned Manchu religion and personalities. However, the Manchu language declined sharply while the Manchus controlled China through the Qing dynasty; Manchu drama itself died out before 1949.

One general form found among several ethnic groups of southern provinces like Guizhou, Guangxi, and Hunan is *nuo*. Originating as early as the Song dynasty, this is a ritual theatre deriving from exorcistic dances found among the ethnic groups, including several of the minorities. The most striking shared feature of the *nuo* forms is the use of masks. These masks vary according to which ethnic group is being portrayed, making characters immediately recognizable. Despite the religious origin and social context, many *nuo* stories are secular, dealing with things like the civil wars of the Three Kingdoms period (220–265).

Bai drama may date from the early Ming, but is actually a *xiqu* derivative and followed the Chinese conquest of Yunnan in the fourteenth century. Some of the stories concern the Bai, but most are actually based on Chinese novels and dramas. The dramas use lyrics in Bai style, structure, and language, and include more dance than most *xiqu* styles.

The Dai of southern Yunnan are similar culturally to the **Thais** and **Burma**'s (Myanmar) Shan people. Although their balladry and song-and-dance traditions are very old, Dai drama does not go back beyond the nineteenth century. Dialogue, courtship songs, and dances were adapted to the main local *xiqu* form, *dianju*, to form a small-scale Dai folk theatre, with many Dai dance movements and stories retained. The first Dai professional troupe dates from about 1910; its repertoire was mainly based on Chinese stories translated into Dai.

There are several Zhuang styles. The one most conspicuously showing Zhuang features is the "shaman drama." Based on the religious dances of professional masked shamans, it treated religious topics such as appeals for good harvests, but from the nineteenth century it dramatized secular narrative poems. In the Republican period (1912–1949), the influence of Han Chinese styles, especially Cantonese *yueju*, seriously diluted the Zhuang features. Long shamanistic robes and dances gave way to Han-style costumes and makeup, and the original single drum to a combination of wind and string instruments, gongs, and drums.

Almost all minority drama forms were popular theatre. They functioned within society for such purposes as petitioning or giving thanks to gods for good harvests, as companions to festivals or temple gatherings, or as part of personal or family events like weddings or funerals. Among the southwestern ethnic minorities, which were generally much more relaxed in relations between young men and women than Confucian or Islamic groups, performances were occasions for courtship.

Most minority companies were amateur or semiprofessional, though the princely houses of some minorities maintained their own troupes. Performers were often also monks and shamans, depending on the ethnic group, and except among a few ethnic groups were mostly male. On the whole, however, the social status of performers was low.

Under the PRC the main trends in traditional minority theatres include:

- The establishment of schools and companies to revive and reform various ethnic styles, as well as the sponsorship of new items in traditional ethnic styles and even the creation of new ethnic styles.
- The revival in the 1980s of ethnic traditional styles that had all but died out during the Cultural Revolution, including several *nuo* styles. *Xinbian lishi ju* were composed in some of the traditional styles, in an attempt to preserve ethnic characteristics.
- The decline of folk traditions since the 1990s under the pressures of modernization; some ethnic troupes now perform mostly for tourists.

Regional Theatre. There are some 330 styles of regional theatre (*difang xi*), ranging from simple folk styles to highly sophisticated and widely spread forms like *jingju*. From the mid-Ming to the late Qing, regional styles proliferated. Many began in the rural villages, performed during festivals or markets or to celebrate harvests or special occasions, and later spread into the cities, the trade routes along the Yangzi River, and elsewhere in the south assisting the process. With a few exceptions, regional actors held low social status.

Regional styles differ in several major ways. Their instruments vary, their languages/dialects are locally based, and their melodies have local qualities. Variations of one degree or another are found in gestures, movements, costumes, makeup, and other aspects. Role type categorization is similar or identical among most styles, and stories are similar or identical.

There are four main regional systems. The earliest is *yiyang qiang*, which originated in Yiyang, Jiangxi Province. It spread to many parts of the country, especially in the south, based on village dialects. Loved by the masses, literati condemned it as coarse. The main shared features are the insertion of parenthetical sung or spoken passages in colloquial language designed to explain the action to the audience, and a small chorus that takes up tunes sung by the main characters.

A second system is *kunqu*. In sharp contrast to most regional styles, *kunqu* was favored by the literate classes, not the masses, and was often called "elegant troupes" (*yabu*).

Bangzi qiang, a third system, was a popular theatre that developed in the north. The fourth system is *pihuang*. Found all over China, *pihuang* combines two musical styles, *xipi* and *erhuang*, the former initially a *bangzi qiang* style, the latter of southern origin. From the eighteenth century the two are always found together.

Pihuang developed into numerous major styles. The best known is *jingju*. Among the many others are Cantonese *yueju*, *dianju*, Yunnan Province's *xiangju*, Hunan

Province's *hanju* (the main Hubei provincial style), and part of the *chuanju* repertoire. Two important shared *pihuang* features are musical accompaniment by the two-string bowed fiddle (*huqin*), and the marking of accentuated beats by a clapper (*ban*).

Quite a few village styles developed into major ones, especially if they were introduced into cities. A major example is Shaoxing *yueju*.

FURTHER READING

Dolby, William. *A History of Chinese Drama*; Hsu, Tao-ching. *The Chinese Conception of the Theatre*; Mackerras, Colin. *Chinese Drama, A Historical Survey;* Mackerras, Colin, ed. *Chinese Theater from Its Origins to the Present Day.*

Colin Mackerras

Modern Theatre. The development of modern theatre since the start of the twentieth century closely followed major historical events, including the end of China's imperial dynastic rule in 1911, the May Fourth New Culture Movement, war against Japan in the 1930s and 1940s, the establishment of the PRC in 1949, and China's post-Mao reforms since the late 1970s. These events demarcate periods during which modern theatre's interaction with political and socio-cultural factors shaped its particular cultural expressions, social functions, and institutional practices.

General modern theatre trends since the start of the twentieth century include:

- Adoption of *huaju* from the West, initially via Japan, and the subsequent **Western influence** in all areas, including **directing**, acting, scenographic techniques, and music, as well as playwriting.
- Reform and modernization of *xiqu*.
- Appropriation of various theatrical forms by politics.
- Synthesis of aesthetic elements from *xiqu* with Western stage forms, resulting in the creation of new forms, such as *geju* and *wuju*.
- Development of dramatic **theory** and exploration of theatrical modes, especially as embodied by experimental theatre.
- Commercialization and internationalization, especially since the 1980s.

Birth of a New Stage Form (1907–1919). Calls by reform intellectuals Chen Duxiu (1880–1942) and Liu Yazi (1887–1958) in 1904 for drama to serve a political and educational function to strengthen the state portended the search for and creation of a modern theatre that would be inextricably linked to the fate of the nation. One year later in Tokyo, Sun Yat-sen (1866–1925), the revolutionary leader, called for a new republican government. Western theatre had been performed in missionary schools, as well as by amateur foreign drama clubs. But Japan was the place where students first adopted the new form, originally called "new drama" (*xinju*) to differentiate it from the traditional, often referred as "old drama" (*jiuju*). It was also called "civilized drama" (*wenming xi*) because of its promotion of social reforms associated with the Revolution of 1911 and the end of China's dynastic rule.

Influenced by Japan's ***shinpa***, Zeng Xiaogu (1873–1936) and Li Shutong (1880– 1942) organized the all-male, amateur, Spring Willow Society (Chunliu She) in Tokyo

Scene from *wenming xi* adaptation of Japanese *shinpa* play *Foster Sisters*, staged in Shanghai's Xiaowutai Theatre, 1916. (Photo: Courtesy of Waseda University Theatre Museum)

in 1906; its performances included one act from Dumas fils' *Camille* and *The Black Slave's Cry to Heaven* (Heinu yu tian lu, an adaptation of *Uncle Tom's Cabin*), both in 1907, and *Hot Tears* (Re lei), based on Sardou's *La Tosca*, in 1909. **Ouyang Yuqian**, who joined the society in 1907, considered the performance of *The Black Slave's Cry to Heaven* at Shanghai's Lyceum Theatre by the Spring Sun Society (Chunyang She) as the beginning of China's modern theatre.

By 1918, other amateur groups, such as the Nankai New Drama Company (Nankai Xin Jutuan), and professional troupes had been established to perform *xinju* in Shanghai, Tianjin, Beijing, Nanjing, and Wuhan. Lacking formal scripts but featuring impromptu addresses to the audience about current affairs, these performances remained undeveloped in writing and performance. The desire to promote social reform also motivated a *xiqu* reform movement, described above. Ouyang, who moved between *huaju* and *xiqu*, and *jingju* star Mei Lanfang, demonstrated a common mission to develop a modern theatre. In contrast to *xiqu*, however, *xinju* or *wenming xi* used the vernacular and emphasized verisimilitude in dramatic action and characterization. *New Drama* (Xinju zazhi), the first professional journal on *huaju*, was published in 1914, and promoted discussion on the new genre.

Impact of the May Fourth Movement (1918–1929). On May 4, 1919, students protested the government's acquiescence to the humiliating terms of the Versailles Treaty. The May Fourth Movement broadly refers to a radical, iconoclastic cultural movement that attacked tradition, promoted a sense of nationalism, and looked toward the West for science, democracy, and culture. The May Fourth movement energized the second phase of the modern theatre's development as intellectuals and artists adopted different theatrical forms, and in particular *huaju*, in their mission to strengthen China through social reform and their pursuit of Western-inspired innovation. In a special issue of *New Youth* (Xin qingnian), the movement's leading forum, whose June 1918 issue was devoted to Ibsen, Hu Shi (1891–1962) promoted *A Doll's House* as a model of the "social problem play" that could support the movement's call for enlightenment. His one-act "The Greatest Event in Life" (Zhongshen dashi, publ. 1919), inspired by Ibsen's play, was a step in this direction.

The People's Drama Society (Minzhong Xiju She), founded in 1921 in Shanghai by Chen Dabei (1887–1944), Ouyang Yuqian, **Xiong Foxi**, and others, advanced "amateur drama" (*aimeide ju*) to promote social change and artistic achievement, oppose *wenming xi*'s commercialization, and encourage the ideal of French writer Romain Rolland's "people's theatre." The society organized student troupes to perform on academic campuses in Beijing and Shanghai and published a monthly journal, *Drama* (Xiju), which printed original and translated scripts and encouraged **criticism**. Playwriting advanced, especially one-acts, including Ding Xilin's (1893–1974) "Wasp" (Yizhi mafeng, 1923), "Flushed Wine" (Jiuhou, 1925), and "Oppression" (Yapo, 1926), and Ouyang's "Shrew" (Pofu, 1922) and "After Returning Home" (Huijia yihou, 1924). Inspired by Ibsen and Shaw, these well-made plays use clever dialogue and sardonic wit to convey social criticism, including women's issues.

Western experimental movements, such as expressionism, were eagerly adopted to explore a larger range of theatrical styles. Wilde's plays contributed to an art-for-art's-sake movement, inspiring, for example, Xiang Peiliang's (1905–1961) *Amnon* (Annen, 1926), based on the Old Testament, and **Yu Shangyuan**'s *Statue* (Suxiang, 1928). Influential women dramatists, including Bai Wei (1894–1987) and Yuan Changying (1895–1973), experimented with combining modernist expression with themes of women's romantic and marital plights.

The exploration of modernist expression developed along with an increased attention to stage presentation. **Hong Shen**'s *Yama Chao* (Zhao Yanwang, 1922) was not only inspired by the expressionism of O'Neill's *The Emperor Jones*, but also significantly employed more comprehensive stagecraft to represent the psychological complexity of someone fraught with inner fear. Hong focused on the development of playwriting in conjunction with directing and scenography, and advocated mixed-gender acting. When he joined **Tian Han**'s Southern China Society (Nanguo She) in 1928, he coined *huaju* as a translation of the English "drama" to represent a more complete and integrated form.

Rise of Drama Schools. Drama schools also encouraged increased training and professionalism. In 1925, Yu Shangyuan and Xiong Foxi established the drama department of the Beijing National School for the Arts, renamed Beiping National University College of the Arts in 1926, and Tian Han founded the Southern China Arts Academy in 1928. The Beiping Private Advanced Xiqu School, established in 1930, facilitated increased professionalism in *xiqu* while adopting the modern practice of training both sexes.

Leftist Influence and* Huaju's *Maturity (1929–1937). The establishment of the CCP in 1921 and the integration of leftist thought into dramatic production influenced the third phase of modern theatre's development. In 1929, Xia Yan organized the Shanghai Art Drama Company (Shanghai Yishu Jushe) to perform "proletariat drama." In 1930, China's League of Leftwing Drama Companies (changed to China's League of

Leftwing Dramatists in 1931) was established with more than fifty branches to perform leftist plays that opposed imperialism and capitalism. Tian Han's "The Alarm Bell" (Luan zhong, 1932), a call to resist the Japanese invasion, was performed in Shanghai after the Japanese occupied Shenyang in 1931. To expand their audience, in 1935 the association organized the Shanghai Amateur Dramatist Association (Shanghai Yeyu Juren Xiehui) with director Zhang Min (1906–1975) and actors Jin Shan (1911–1982) and Zhao Dan (1915–1980). They performed Western plays such as *A Doll's House* and *The Inspector General*. Actors, such as **Shu Xiuwen**, in addition to directors and playwrights, skillfully moved between films and theatre.

Huaju reached relative maturity toward the end of this period due to successful new plays, the development of stage design promoted by the establishment of professional companies, and the development of dramatic theory and scholarship, including the introduction of the Stanislavski System. A number of China's most influential and commercially successful modern dramas were written between 1933 and 1937, including **Cao Yu**'s *Thunderstorm* (Leiyu, 1933) and *Sunrise* (Richu, 1936), and Xia Yan's *Under Shanghai Eaves* (Shanghai wuyan xia, 1937).

The War of Resistance against Japan and Civil War (1937–1949). The fourth phase in the development of the modern theatre coincided with China's war against Japan's invasion, which began on July 7, 1937. The newly established Chinese Dramatist Association wrote *Defending Marco Polo Bridge* (Baowei Lugouqiao), whose introduction declared that modern plays should "expose the enemy's plot to invade and enlighten fellow countrymen." Thirteen "Performance Teams to Rescue China" were sent to different areas to "fight the enemies and save the country." In December 1937, the China National Association of Drama Circles to Resist Japan was established in Wuhan and sent acting teams to the warfront in ten provinces.

"Street theatre" (*jietou ju*), seemingly impromptu plays performed in public spaces or teahouses, was performed throughout China to educate people about Japan's aggression. A popular example was *Put Down Your Whip* (Fangxia ni de bianzi, publ. 1936), which actively aroused anger toward the Japanese. Whereas *huaju* in theatres was aimed primarily at the urban educated, street theatre targeted audiences in smaller cities and in the countryside, calling upon them to become directly involved in the "dramas" to punish traitors and resist the enemy. The Dingxian Peasant Theatre Experiment (Dingxian nongmin xiju shiyan), led by Xiong Foxi between 1932 and 1937, used *huaju* to educate and unite rural communities, such as warning them against superstitious beliefs and high interest loans, while also organizing peasants to join troupes. Like street theatre, performances often blurred the boundaries between actors and audience.

During the war of resistance to Japan (1937–1945), modern theatre developed differently in three regions: the Nationalist-controlled area in the southwest, Shanghai and areas occupied by Japan, and the communist-held Yan'an region in the northwest. After the fall of Wuhan in 1938, many dramatists moved to Nationalist-controlled areas in southwestern China. The success of the Chongqing Fog Season Public Performances, a festival held between 1941 and 1945 during the foggy season, demonstrated that China was part of "civilized" world culture even during a period of national crisis. The China Art Drama Troupe (Zhongguo Yishu Jushe) toured the area from 1942 to 1946, increasing the genre's audience while bolstering the resistance. This period saw an increase in historical dramas (*lishiju*) because of preoccupations with the question of China's historical fate and the playwrights' use of history to evade censorship and even criticize the Nationalists. An important example was Guo Moruo's (1892–1978) *Qu Yuan* (1942), which, by adulating a celebrated ancient poet as a patriotic hero, was received as an oblique attack on the Nationalists. A number of *lishiju*, such as Wu Zuguang's (1917–2003) *Return on a Snowy Night* (Fengxueye guiren, 1942), blurred the line between *huaju* and *xiqu* by featuring *jingju* stars in contemporary settings. Political satires also flourished, including Chen Baichen's (1908–1994) *Wedding March* (Jiehun jinxing qu, 1942) and *Seeking Political Promotion* (Shengguan tu, 1945).

After the Japanese occupied Shanghai in November 1937, the foreign concessions became severed from the rest of China. Although dramatists had to cooperate with the authorities of the concessions until they were occupied by the Japanese in December 1941, and then were subjected to Japanese censorship until August 1945, modern theatre managed to flourish. The Shanghai Drama Art Troupe (Shanghai Juyi She), actively led by Yu Ling (1907–1997) between 1938 and 1941, performed *lishiju*, such as Ah Ying's (1900–1977) *Jade Blood Flower* (Ming mo yi hen), popular for its indirect criticism of the occupation. Adaptations of non-Chinese plays, including *Behind the Stage Beauty* (Wutai yan hou), adapted from Ostrovsky, and *The Hero of the Turmoil* (Luanshi yingxiong, 1945), adapted from *Macbeth*, were performed by the Bitter Toilers Company (Kugan Jutuan), led by **Huang Zuolin** from 1942 until 1946. Although *huaju* performances dwindled in Beijing between 1938 and 1941, traveling troupes helped revitalize *huaju* in Japanese-occupied Beijing from 1942 to 1944.

Modern theatre in Yan'an and other communist-controlled areas primarily promoted the communist war effort; after Mao's "Talks at the Yan'an Forums on Literature and Art" in 1942, modern theatre began to adhere more rigorously to the party's cultural policy, such as serving the workers, peasants, and soldiers while opposing the capitalist class. New forms, such as *yangge* drama (*yangge ju*)—which fuses the rural folk dance style (*yangge*) of the Yan'an region with revolutionary drama—were developed to represent the new communist spirit. *The White-Haired Girl* (Baimao nü), a "new opera" (*xin geju*), promotes communist ideology by staging the rescue of a woman raped by a cruel landlord. Hundreds of rural troupes were formed in the Yan'an region to support the mission of liberating the Chinese from the shackles of the old society, building communist spirit, and fighting the enemies. During the civil war between the communists and the Nationalists (1946–1949), student activists in the CCP commonly performed "living newspaper drama" (*huobao ju*), a fusion of drama and propaganda.

Under the Communist Cultural Ideology (1949–1966). In 1949, the communists defeated the Nationalists and the PRC was established. From 1949 to 1966, modern theatre developed under the leadership of the PRC. The Soviet Union provided particular influence, from Stanislavski's theories to socialist realism. The China Drama Workers Association was established immediately (called China Dramatists Association, 1953) to oversee the role of *huaju* and *xiqu*, in addition to other performance arts, such as **puppet theatre**, in the construction of a socialist society. In accordance with the Ministry of Culture's 1952 directive, theatres, companies, festivals, and academies were established at the national, provincial, and municipal levels.

Bolstering the didactic function first assigned to it decades earlier, *huaju* introduced political initiatives, such as banning prostitution and arranged marriages, dispatching "volunteers" to fight with the North Koreans, and re-educating intellectuals who had made political "mistakes," while also promoting the Maoist tenets of class struggle and communist victory. Chen Qitong's (1916–?) *The Long March* (Wanshui qianshan, 1954) praises the government's victory and extols the soldiers as heroes for their service and sacrifice by staging the hardships endured by the army during the Long March. Other plays extolled the party while inserting a more personal narrative, such as Yue Ye's *Through Thick and Thin* (Tonggan gongku, 1956) and Shen Ximeng et al.'s *Sentries under the Neon Lights* (Nihong deng xia de shaobing, 1962).

Lao She perfected the "slice of life drama" in *Dragon Beard Ditch* (Longxugou, 1950) and *The Teahouse* (Chaguan, 1957). Both have become cornerstones in the Beijing People's Art Theatre's (Beijing Renmin Yishu Juyuan) repertoire, and exemplify the possibility of great artistic achievement despite ideological demands.

Staging Western plays offered alternatives from the orthodox propaganda themes, albeit they were subject to justification and scrutiny. Huang Zuolin introduced Brecht to China with his 1959 production of *Mother Courage*. Shakespeare has been China's most popular Western playwright since Yevgenia Konstantinovna Lipkovskaya and other Soviets staged several of his works in the 1950s. In the late 1950s and 1960s, *lishiju*, including Tian Han's *Guan Hanqing* (1958), Guo Moruo's (1892–1978) *Cai Wenji* (1959) and *Wu Zetian* (1962), and Ding Xilin's *Meng Lijun* (1961), reappeared as a dominant subgenre, partly because of its ability to provide a veiled critique and partly because of its opportunities for experimentation, especially in design.

Hai Rui Dismissed from Office (Hai Rui baguan), a *jingju* about a Ming dynasty official imprisoned for criticizing the emperor, was interpreted by Mao as an attack upon his leadership. Official censure of *lishiju* was used to attack party opponents and resulted in the launching of the Cultural Revolution. The revolutionary *yangban xi* genre was mainly in *jingju* form but also included *wuju*, such as the ballet-influenced *The Red Detachment of Women* (Hongse niangzijun, 1964). They espoused the Gang of Four's radical ideology of continual class struggle and revolution and entirely dominated the stage during this decade.

Diversification of Stage Expression (1978–). Immediately following the Cultural Revolution, *huaju*, such as Zong Fuxian's (1947–) *In a Land of Silence* (Yu wusheng chu, 1978), Cui Dezhi's *Flowers Announcing Spring* (Bao chun hua, 1979), and Xing Yixun's *Power Versus Law* (Quan yu fa, 1979), blamed the Gang of Four for the catastrophe while cautiously pointing to party hypocrisy. Sha Yexin's (1939–) *If I Were Real* (Jiaru wo shi zhende, 1979), inspired by Gogol, was banned for its open criticism of the party officials.

Since the early 1980s, party doctrine has remained influential, especially by endorsing national unity, as in Liang Bingkun's (1936–) anticorruption social realist play *Who's the Strongest of Us All?* (Shei shi qiangzhe, 1981). Yang Limin's (1947–) *Black Stones* (Heise de shitou, 1986), and Zhang Mingyuan's (1954–) *Wild Grass* (Yecao, 1989) realistically portray the hardships of petroleum workers and poor peasants, respectively, while Tian Xinxin's (1969–) adaptation of Xiao Hong's novel about a northeast Chinese peasant uprising against Japanese aggression, *The Field of Life and Death* (Shengsi chang, 1999), was produced in conjunction with the PRC's fiftieth anniversary. *North Street, South Yard* (Beijie nanyuan, 2002) celebrates Beijing's victory over the SARS virus.

A major theme of the 1980s was reflection upon China's twentieth-century history. "Slice of life plays," inspired by Lao She, include Li Longyun's (1948–) *Small Well*

Alley (Xiaojing hutong, 1981), which portrays four decades of historical turmoil for a Beijing community, and He Jiping's (1951–) *The World's Top Restaurant* (Tianxia diyi lou, 1988), a nostalgic portrayal of the gradual rise and sudden fall of a duck restaurant during the turbulent 1917–1928 years. Guo Shixing's (1952–) *Birdmen* (Niao ren, 1993) offers a confrontation between local Beijing traditions and encroaching post-Mao Western influence.

Dramatists also boldly explored a range of theatrical styles to examine historical and cultural identity, as in Liu Jinyun's (1938–) Brechtian *Uncle Doggie's Nirvana* (Gouer Ye niepan, 1986), which portrays the relationship between peasants and their land from pre-1949 to the land reforms and collectivization of the 1950s and economic reforms of the 1980s. Experimenting with Greek theatre, *Sangshuping Chronicles* (Sangshuping jishi, 1988) presents rural China's struggle to change and develop. The expressionist-influenced *WM* (1985), by Wang Peigong (1943–), challenges China's post-1978 economic reforms by juxtaposing the lives of its "re-educated youth" during and after the Cultural Revolution.

Experimental theatre developed during the 1980s, especially under the guidance of directors **Gao Xingjian**, Lin Zhaohua, Zhang Xian (1955–), Mou Sen (1963–), Meng Jinghui (1965–), and Li Liuyi (1961–), as a reaction to the control exerted by the party and as an exploration of styles facilitated by newly formed private companies.

Huaju, which initially distinguished itself from *xiqu* by emphasizing the "spoken word," has—especially since the 1990s—become more focused on providing a total performance event. Due to a similar transformation in Taiwan, *huaju* was there renamed "stage drama" (*wutai ju*) in the 1980s, yet it remains a generic term for drama in China, **Macao**, **Hong Kong**, and **Singapore**. Scenography, in addition to sound effects and choreography, helps create commercially oriented, spectacle-like performances in a variety of forms, including the children's theatre (*ertongju*) *Labyrinth* (Migong, 2004), the *wuju* dance-drama *Raise the Red Lanterns* (Dahong denglong gaogao gua, 2001), and spectacular outdoors mega-performances, such as *Third Sister Liu* (Liu sanjie, 2004). A number of these spectacles have reached international audiences by touring and attracting foreign tourists. Spectacles that mix "traditional" forms with Western styles are slated to play an important role in the pageantry of the 2008 Beijing Olympics.

Huaju, usually performed in Mandarin, is also performed in local dialects. **Huaji xi**, comic theatre in the Southern Yangtze River area, is usually performed in the various dialects of that region. Theatre academies have also organized special training courses on ethnic minority *huaju*. Works include Shakespeare plays and those by local playwrights, such as *The History of Potala Palace* (Budalagong fengyun, 1994), performed by the Tibetan Autonomous Region Drama Company (Xizang Zizhiqu Huaju Tuan), *Woman Village Head* (Nü cunzhang), performed by the Ningxia Hui Minority Autonomous Region Drama Company (Ningxia Huizu Zizhiqu Huaju Tuan), and *Hairless Dog* (Mei mao de gou, published 1992), performed by the Jilin Province Yanbian Drama Company (Jilin Sheng Yanbian Huaju Tuan).

FURTHER READING

Chen, Xiaomei. *Acting the Right Part: Political Theater and Popular Drama in Contemporary China*; Cheung, Martha, and Jane Lai, eds. *An Oxford Anthology of Contemporary Chinese Drama*; Gunn, Edward, ed. *Twentieth-Century Chinese Drama*; Yu, Shiao-ling, ed. *Chinese Drama after the Cultural Revolution, 1979–1989*.

Jonathan Noble

CHIT OO NYO (1948–). Burmese (Myanmar) **playwright**, **director**, novelist, short story writer, poet, and philosopher, born in Mandalay, son of well-known classical male **dancer** and teacher Shwe Daung Nyo. After graduating in philosophy from the University of Yangon (1968), he worked as a tutor, then, in the late 1970s, as a playwright and director at Mandalay's Sandar Oo Dance Theatre Group. He wrote novels and short stories based on the Bagan era (ninth to twelfth centuries), during which time dress and use of Burmese words were different, making that period highly romantic and attractive.

His best-selling first novel, *Linkar Dipa Lover* (Linkar Dipa chit-thu, 1977), also performed as a play (like many of his other writings), is the **Ramayana** story with a twist: it portrays the villainous ogre king Ravana sympathetically as a heartbroken, love-sick man. His later fiction was based on the Bagan period, which immediately caught the interest of the masses and started a Bagan-**costumed** choreography based on wall paintings and old records, although no one could be sure if the dance moves and **music** were accurate. This cultivation of a still-popular interest in Bagan culture for the masses was his greatest theatre contribution. His themes are romantic, dramatic, and often tragic; many have undertones of class struggle.

From 1983 to 1988, he edited *Theatre Magazine* (Thabin magazine). From 2001 to 2002, he edited the *Shwe Pyi Tan Journal*. Since 1998, he has served as chair of the Central Judging Committee for the annual Myanmar Traditional Cultural Performing Arts Competitions and as an external examiner and adviser for the Drama Department of the Cultural University of Yangon.

Maung Maung Thein and Ma Thanegi

CHO KWANG-HWA (1965–). Korean • **playwright** and **director** whose professional career began with his 1992 prize-winning play, *Rainy Season* (Changma). In 1997 he wrote and directed *The Male Urge* (Namja ch'ungdong), a hit play that swept major awards, including the Seoul Theatre **Festival** Award and the Baek Sang Arts Award. He is highly respected among the younger generation of theatre artists.

Arguably his best play, *The Male Urge* is a caricature of a modern character, Chang-jung, who obsessively admires a gangster boss and attempts to be like him. Through Chang-jung's behavior and ultimate downfall, Cho indicts patriarchal values and violence. Most of his plays focus on the rediscovery of the human values that he claims have been obliterated by superficial, contrived images of modernity. *Crazy Kiss* (Mich'in k'isŭ, 1998) portrays futile love among alienated and fragmented modern people. *Ironclad Buddha* (Ch'ŏlan Putta, 1999) is a rare Korean science-fiction play, warning of the danger in human cloning. Other plays include *Chongno Cat* (Chongno koyangi, 1995) and *At the Serpent's Seduction* (Kkotbaemi nadŏrŏ tari rŭl kamaboja hayŏ, 1995), a monodrama for a **woman**, utilizing traditional theatre elements. Cho also has directed several **musicals**, such as *Rock Hamlet* (Rak Haemlit, 1995), *Picture of a Yellow Dog* (Hwang gu do, 1999), *The Sorrows of Young Werther* (Chŏlmŭn Berŭterŭ ŭi sŭlpŭm, 2000), and *Dalgona Candy* (Dalgona, 2004).

Hyung-jin Lee

CH'OE YŎN-HO (1926–1996). Korean • **scenographer** who left a legacy of some one thousand works, 863 of which have been catalogued. Born in Pyongyang, Ch'oe was sent to South Korea after the outbreak of the Korean War, beginning a life-long separation from his family. Discharged from the army in 1954, he developed his skills designing theatre and film posters, billboards, and leaflets.

Self-taught, Ch'oe joined the design department at the Korean Broadcasting System in 1961, becoming a pioneer in design for television historical sagas, but his vision also was instrumental in the development of South Korean theatre in general, transforming design from a craft into an art. He designed settings for realistic Korean and **Western** dramas, *ch'angguk*, opera, Western musicals, and large-scale public events, such as the pre-opening ceremonies for the 1986 Seoul Asian Games and the 1988 Seoul Olympics.

His output was extraordinary and influential. In 1975, for example, Ch'oe designed twenty-two productions, among them Ch'a Bŏm-sŏk's *Mountain Fires* (San-bul) and the premier of **Yu Ch'i-jin**'s *The Han River Flows* (Hangang eun Hŭrŭnda). In 1988, Ch'oe designed Pak Jo-yŏl's *General Oh's Toenail* (Oh Changgun ui palt'op) for **Sohn Jin-Chaek** and his Beauty and Ugliness Company (Kŭkdan Michoo). In 1995, Ch'oe created some forty-two designs for television, celebrations, **dance**, and theatre.

Ch'oe's ability to reproduce the traditional Korean house on **stage** was unparalleled, but his influence extended beyond realism. Sohn Jin-Chaek, for instance, acknowledges that Ch'oe's designs for large events were instrumental in Sohn's developing concept of *madangori*.

Richard Nichols

CHONG WISHIN (1957–). Korean-Japanese • **playwright**, known for his work with Tokyo's Shinjuku Ryôzanpaku (literally, "Shinjuku Go-Getters' Club")—the **theatre company** founded in 1987 by "Special Permanent Resident Koreans." Chong's plays address Korean marginalization in Japan. In contrast to 1980s Japanese comedy, Chong draws on the physicality of **Kara Jûrô**'s Red Tent (Aka Tento) and **Satoh Makoto**'s Black Tent (Kokushoku Tento, a.k.a. Kuro Tento) performances, while seriously regarding human existence and social issues.

Chong's *A Legend of Mermaids* (Ningyô densetsu, 1989), the company's signature piece, portrays a family "turned away by every town," but with the desire to find a home without losing its identity as nomads. This paradox epitomizes Chong's work and his identity as a Korean in Japan. The play leverages the potential of tent-theatre; pitched at the water's edge, the tent allows the family to enter and exit by watercraft.

For Chong, crossing water is a metaphor for crossing from Korea to Japan. In *One Thousand Years of Solitude* (Sennen no kodoku, 1988), a young woman named Ageha, or "swallowtail butterfly," keeps a live *ageha* in a glass case. Like a swallowtail variety that migrates across the sea between Japan and Korea, Ageha longs to cross the river to home but is trapped like her butterfly. Named for the cardinal compass points, the four Medeas in *Beloved Medea* (Itoshi no Medea, 1986) represent diaspora. Ever nomadic, they return to the sea in self-sacrifice as the play ends.

John D. Swain

CHOWDHRY, NEELAM MANSINGH (1950?–). Indian Punjabi- and Hindi-language **director** and **actress**. Born into a wealthy Sikh family, Chowdhry received a degree in art history at Chandigarh's Punjab University before attending New Delhi's National School of Drama (NSD), where she studied under **Ebrahim Alkazi** and **B. V. Karanth**. Moving to Bombay (Mumbai), she cofounded the Hindi **theatre company** Majma with fellow NSD graduates, but her relocation to Bhopal, Madhya Pradesh, in 1979 led to Hindi productions of Molière's *The Miser*, Sartre's *The Respectable Prostitute,* Jaywant Dalvi's *Barrister*, and Ratnakar Matkari's (1938–) *Folktale* (*Lok-katha*), all at the Bharat Bhavan Cultural Center (Bharat Bhavan Rangmandal) between 1980 and 1982. In 1983, Chowdhry returned to Chandigarh, and the following year she founded The Company, which established Punjabi as a major dramatic language and reduced the serious gap between serious and popular theatre.

Like many contemporary directors, Chowdhry has employed a uniform linguistic medium, in her case, Punjabi, to present a range of Indian as well as **Western** plays. While **Girish Karnad**'s *Play with a Cobra* (Naga-mandala, 1989) is her most important Indian production, Punjabi productions of Lorca's *Yerma* (1991), Giraudoux's *The Madwoman of Chaillot* (1995), and Racine's *Phaedra* (1997) are among her most successful foreign works. She develops her adaptations in collaboration with the Sikh poet Surjit Patar (1944–); the duo also have drawn upon an eclectic range of fictional works to create pieces such as *Kitchen Tale* (Kitchen katha, 1999), *A Packet of Seeds* (2003), and *Sibbo in Supermarket* (2003). Chowdhry is one of the most visible Indian directors abroad, with appearances at major international **festivals**.

Aparna Dharwadker

CHOWDHURY, MUNIER (1925–1971). Bangladeshi • **playwright**, educator, and literary **critic**. After completing his postgraduate studies in linguistics at Harvard, he taught at Dhaka University (1950–1971) and was associated with leftist **politics** and progressive cultural movements. In 1948, he attended the Communist Party conference in Calcutta (Kolkata). Subsequently, he became secretary of the Progressive Writer's and Artist's Association. In 1952, he was arrested for protesting police repression and a massacre of students. In detention he wrote his landmark play "The Grave" (Kabar, 1953), a long one-act, which was first staged in jail by the inmates. Chowdhury actively participated in the liberation movement. His plays depict the political turmoil and his commitment to a free and independent Bangladesh. His one-acts include "Dandakaranya" (1966) and "The Barracks of Plassey and Others" (Palashi barrock o anyanya, 1969). His spirit of commitment continues in his other plays, such as *The Blood Fields* (Raktakta prantar, 1959), set against the backdrop of the Third Battle of Panipat, and *Letter* (Chithi, 1966), an exposé of the selfishness and autocratic attitude of leaders who aim to head popular movements. His plays combine serious themes with lively dialogue and an absurd sense of humor.

Chowdhury translated a number of plays from the international repertoire into Bengali. He also **acted** and **directed** for theatre, radio, television, and film. Two days before liberation he was kidnapped and executed.

Bishnupriya Dutt

CHUANJU. Chinese traditional theatre popular in Sichuan Province and in some regions of neighboring Yunnan and Guizhou Provinces. Stylistically, *chuanju* is a unique hybrid of five different **musical** systems, with four systems introduced from other regions and with one native to Sichuan.

Local **theatre companies** performing the "lantern theatre" (*dengxi*), the song and dance • **folk theatre** native to rural Sichuan, existed as early as the Ming dynasty (1368–1644). *Dengxi*'s name is derived from the many lanterns that were a prerequisite for performing the dramas. The large population flow into Sichuan in the seventeenth century, due to decades of war and plagues, brought many kinds of musical systems to the region, including *yiyang qiang* from Jiangxi, **bangzi qiang** from Shaanxi, *pihuang* from Hunan and Hubei, and **kunqu**. These musical systems were quickly adapted to Sichuan dialect, **folk** customs, and local entertainments, and thus developed into the Sichuan *gaoqiang*, *tanqiang*, *huqin qiang*, and *kunqiang* styles, respectively. Troupes throughout Sichuan and the neighboring provinces usually specialized in one of the systems.

In 1912, **actors** Kang Zilin (1870–1930) and Yang Sulan (1877–1926) founded the Three Celebrations Company (Sanqing) in Chengdu. Both strongly supported the "new society" propagated at that time: they called for reform in traditional *xiqu* in respect to content, troupe organizational structures, and actors' social status and education. Under Three Celebrations' influence, ten troupes merged, and the company's artists began to fuse *dengxi*, *gaoqiang*, *tanqiang*, *huqin qiang*, and *kunqiang* into the unique system of acting, singing, and music called *chuanju*.

A *chuanju* drama can include elements from as many as three of the five systems, but one system always remains dominant. The two thousand–plus works in the repertoire are categorized according to the dominant style. The *gaoqiang* operas, with their wooden clapper accompaniment and "helping chorus" (*bangqiang*), are the largest contingent and most frequently performed.

Popular traditional dramas include *The White Snake* (Bai she zhuan), *Red Lotus on Blue Water* (Bi bo hong lian), *Rolling the Lantern* (Gun deng), *Fifteen Strings of Cash* (Shiwu guan), *The Story of the Lute* (Pipa ji), and *The Monkey King Creating Havoc in Heaven* (Wuxing zhu). Dramas are known for their fantasy and magic realism. The lyrics are simple and lively, combined with a type of humor special to Sichuan's people.

Role types follow the common division of "male role" (*sheng*), "female role" (*dan*), "painted face" (*jing*), and "clown" (*chou*), but show their own characteristics in subcategories as well as in the use of particular **costume** components, **masks** (including beards), and headdresses.

In performance and stagecraft *chuanju* is, in general, similar to other traditional styles, including **jingju**. However, *chuanju* is famous for its stunts, including sword swallowing, walking on stilts, fire breathing, and the sudden appearance of a "third eye" on the forehead. But the most closely guarded secret and signature feature is the "face changing" (*bianlian*) through the use of painted, full-face, silk masks. Face changing can consist of up to fourteen masks being pulled down in front of the performer's head in magically quick succession.

With the foundation of the People's Republic of China in 1949, *chuanju* experienced a new prosperity with the emergence of many "newly written historical dramas" (**xinbian lishi ju**), such as the *The Scholar from Bashan* (Bashan xiucai) and *Fourth Sister* (Si guniang), and the "contemporary dramas" (*xiandai xi*) that became the most influential propaganda medium. But with the beginning of the Cultural Revolution in 1966, *chuanju* was banned, and its troupes disbanded. In 1976, *chuanju* was one of the first regional styles to be revived after the fall of the Gang of Four. Nevertheless, the decade-long hiatus and the rapid modernization process that followed after 1989 made *chuanju* performers face a challenging future.

Alarmingly shrinking audiences, a lack of highly skilled artists, and a diminished interest by young people in learning *chuanju* incited a reform movement in 1982. It focused on saving, inheriting, reforming, and developing *chuanju*. Given a certain freedom in creativity, Sichuan theatre workers began to experiment with **Western** techniques, creating innovative work such as **Wei Minglun**'s *Pan Jinlian* and Wu Xiaofei's *The Good Person of Sichuan* [Setzuan] (Sichuan hao ren), an adaptation of Brecht. By incorporating elements of modern drama and producing socially relevant plays, artists hope to attract modern-day audiences.

Since the mid-1980s, troupes have toured Europe, **Japan**, **Singapore**, **Hong Kong**, **Macao**, and **Taiwan** to acclaim. Companies like the Sichuan Provincial Theatre Troupe (Sichuan Sheng Chuanju Tuan) have won numerous **festival** awards. But despite *chuanju*'s national and international achievements, Sichuan's artists continue to face dwindling audiences and interest in **training**.

Only a small number of professional troupes still perform, mainly for festivals and tourists. A handful of semiprofessional and amateur groups perform irregularly in city and countryside parks and teahouses.

FURTHER READING

Dauth, Ursula. "Strategies of Reform in Sichuan Opera Since 1982: Confronting the Challenge of Rejuvenating a Regional Opera Style."

Ursula Dauth

CHUANQI. **Chinese** southern drama, in contrast to northern **zaju**. The term, meaning "transmission of the marvelous," was used for short fiction in the Tang (618–907) and for drama in the late Yuan (1280–1368) dynasties. Only in the early Qing (1644–1911) did it come to denote southern drama. After southern drama re-emerged with the resurgence of South China about 1330, a gradual evolution took place from **nanxi** to *chuanqi*. The "Four Great Southern Dramas" that emerged at the Yuan-Ming transition—*Thorn Hairpin* (Jingchai ji), *Moon Gazing Pavilion* (Baiyue ting), *The White Rabbit* (Baitu ji), and *Killing the Dog* (Shagou ji)—resemble earlier *nanxi*. Three depict the tribulations of ambitious men and the **women** who love them, and two revolve around a man's passing the examinations and becoming top graduate—a common *nanxi* plot that remained popular in *chuanqi*. These plays use plain, even crude, language that lacks the allusiveness, elaborate imagery, and interplay between earthy and elegant linguistic registers that came to typify *chuanqi* librettos.

Such embellishments first appear in *The Lute* (Pipa ji), about a filial son caught between desire to care for aging parents and duty to serve his ruler. It was written by advanced graduate scholar Gao Ming (1305–1370), who had served the Mongols. Like *nanxi* **playwright**s, Gao did not demarcate scene divisions, but his arrangement of song sequences exploits contrasts—between settings of opulence in the capital and poverty in the countryside and between lush and allusive arias and plain and direct ones—to generate tension and create tragic atmosphere. Imagery orchestrated around motifs and disciplined use of song sequences made *The Lute* a foundational *chuanqi*, but it was not until the mid-fifteenth century that other literati began writing plays. When they did, they used language far more ornate and allusive than Gao's, making *chuanqi* drama henceforth largely by and for the literati.

In the 1500s, regional **musical** styles such as *haiyan qiang* and *yiyang qiang* supplanted the official stringed music used to perform *The Lute*. *Chuanqi*'s regional diversity marked another difference from *nanxi*, and culminated in the emergence of **kunqu**, which became the style of choice for southern drama with the enormous popularity of *Washing Silk* (Huansha ji) by Liang Chenyu (1520–ca. 1593). By the 1620s, *chuanqi* were increasingly performed as *kunqu*, whether or not their librettos had originally been composed to its song repertoire.

Other features that distinguish *chuanqi* from *nanxi* are: a well-defined prologue (*jiamen*) that incorporates the four-line topic used in *nanxi* prologues, scene divisions marked by scene titles, elaborate entrance conventions for lead characters, use of quatrains to conclude scenes, and play titles that name an object of symbolic import (for example, *Thorn Hairpin* and *The Lute*). The **role-type** system inherited from *nanxi* became more elaborate, especially after *kunqu* became the hegemonic style and performances of "highlights" transferred creative agency from playwrights to **actors** in the Qing.

Laosheng actor with white beard and hat in "Entrusting the Son" from the *kunqu* version of *Washing Silk*. (Photo: Yuan Shuo; Courtesy of Jiangsu Provincial Kunju Troupe)

FURTHER READING

Mackerras, Colin. *Chinese Theatre from its Origins to the Present Day*; Wang-Ngai, Siu, and Peter Lovrick. *Chinese Opera: Images and Stories*.

Catherine Swatek

COSTUMES

Costumes: China

Costumes were probably worn in **China**'s Zhou dynasty (770–256 BC) shamanic and court performance, and certainly featured in Tang (618–907) *canjun xi*, Song (960–1279) *zaju* and **nanxi**, and Yuan (1280–1368) *zaju*. The rise of **kunqu** in the Ming (1368–1644) led to great elaboration in costume and related conventions. Further elaboration continued in the Qing (1644–1911), including in *jingju* and other regional forms, but most costumes reached their current forms by mid-Qing and are based on those of late Ming. By late Qing, however, reforms were being introduced by individual **actors** and more recently by designers employed by **theatre companies**.

Today's traditional costumes, historically known as "traveling things" (*xingtou*), constitute a comprehensive system for indicating characters' **role type**, age, social status, temperament, and general circumstances. Costumes do not show season or indicate historical period; based on Tang through Qing styles often simultaneously employed, most have been exaggerated to better serve as vehicles for movement and **dance**.

Color and Motif Symbolism. Color is an important signifying aspect. Of colors considered "pure," red is worn by upper-class characters in formal circumstances, and by all characters for celebration. Green indicates virtue, and yellow the imperial family. For men, black is worn by commoners, and by upper-class characters of fierce virtue; for **women**, it signifies virtue in distress. Decorated white garments indicate youth or old age, and plain ones signify mourning. "Secondary" colors include pink and turquoise for youth, blue for high rank, dark crimson for high-ranking non-Chinese, and purple for older "painted-face roles" (*jing*). Other colors include olive green for "older women" (*laodan*) and bronze for high-ranking elderly characters. Secondary colors are now more widely used, especially for more realistic "males" (*sheng*) and younger "females" (*dan*)—a **yueju** influence; *yueju* broke with *jingju*'s color-coding in the early twentieth century.

Decorative designs also have significance. In general, civil officials are indicated by bird motifs, such as cranes (connoting longevity), and military officials by animal designs, including tigers (suggesting fighting prowess). Other common designs include dragons for imperial power, flowers such as plum blossoms for wisdom, and peonies for feminine beauty, while *yin yang* and "eight diagrams" (*bagua*) patterns represent metaphysical powers. Round designs often signify middle age, while designs for youthful characters are frequently scattered or in borders. Fur trim indicates non-Chinese ethnicity.

Garment Types. Garment style is the most extensive conventional system. *Jingju* and many other forms of *xiqu* use over seventy named pieces, broadly categorized as: "robes" (*pao*), primarily for civil activities; "armor" (*kai*), for martial activities; and "short clothes" (*duan yi*), for various circumstances. Most robes are loose-fitting and worn with "water sleeves" (*shuixiu*), each a long piece of white silk attached to the bottom edge of a long, wide sleeve, and manipulated by the actor. Most also have ankle-length male and knee-length female versions, the latter worn over a long pleated skirt, often white.

The *mang* ("python") is the most formal robe, worn by imperial and aristocratic characters in ceremonial settings. It has a high round neck and closes at the right shoulder and side; dragon and cloud designs adorn the upper portion, and a stylized wave pattern borders the hem. The "official's garment" (*guanyi*) is worn by civil officials and their spouses in formal circumstances. Constructed like the *mang*, it is plainer, with one square ornamental pattern on the chest and another on the back. The "jade belt" (*yudai*), a large, flat hoop suspended at the waist, is worn with both garments. The "reformed *mang*" (*gailiang mang*) lacks groundwork embroidery covering the whole robe and fits the body more closely, while the "reformed *guanyi*" uses circular patterns rather than square ones and adds embroidery at the hem and sides.

The "cloak" (*pi*) is informal wear for aristocrats and high officials, normal wear for gentry, and formal wear for young people. It fastens symmetrically at center front with a V-shaped neckline, usually has embroidered decorations, and is worn over a *xuezi* ("pleat/crease"), which is normal wear for commoners. In the male version, the left side crosses over to fasten under the right arm, creating an angular, asymmetrical neckline. The female version closes symmetrically at center front and has a high mandarin collar. Both male and female *xuezi* may be plain or embroidered. "Reformed" versions use a more varied palette, confine embroidery to corners and edges, and forego lustrous satin for a softer crepe more suited to the highly lit modern **stage**. The *jianyi* ("arrow garment") is martial male dress for horse riding and combat with weapons. The top is constructed like a form-fitting *mang* with narrow sleeves, but the lower portion is split into four panels. The "palace dress" (*gongzhuang*) is informal wear for princesses and concubines; the top is constructed like the *mang*, but the lower portion is replaced by up to sixty-four narrow panels.

The most important armor representation is the *kao* ("lean/rely on"), an elaborate garment composed of stiff, ankle-length front and back panels with a solid, padded stomach section, tightly cuffed sleeves, two separate panels covering the sides of the legs, and four triangular flags tied to the back and rising up behind the head. The lower portion of the female *kao* may be replaced with many narrow panels like the *gongzhuang*'s. The "reformed *kao*" is a soft, form-fitting version for dance and acrobatic combat.

"Short clothes" include a wide variety of "jackets" (*ao*), "pants" (*ku*), and "skirts" (*qun*). Lower-class women and maidservants wear soft jackets with narrow sleeves, mandarin collars, and right-side closures over soft pants or pleated skirts, all decorated with embroidery. The "hero's garment" (*yingxiong yi*), worn by chivalrous male outlaws, has a hip-length jacket constructed like the *xuezi* but extended to knee-length by two layers of skirt-like fabric, and matching soft pants. Worn with two separate panels covering the sides of the legs, the costume becomes the "fighting garment and fighting pants" (*dayi daku*); the form-fitting female jacket has a mandarin collar, center closure, and no fabric extension at the hem. The *kuaiyi* ("fast/sharp garment"), a tight-fitting, black jacket with a round collar and center front frog closures, is worn with soft black pants by nonmilitary male fighters.

Garments are worn over inner clothes, some padded, and with a variety of belts and sashes. Additionally, many named and categorized accessories contribute to *xiqu* conventions.

Footwear. Numerous types of footwear suit different circumstances and roles. The most widely used include "thick sole boots" (*houdixue*), tall black cloth boots with hard white soles two to three inches thick, worn by *sheng* and *jing* characters for formal and semiformal dress; "thin sole boots" (*bodi xue*), ankle-high black or colored cloth boots with thin soles, worn for many "martial males" (*wusheng*), "martial clowns" (*wuchou*), and "martial women" (*wudan*) roles; and "colorful shoes" (*caixie*), soft, colored, cloth shoes with thin soles, worn by *dan*.

Hair and Beards. Hair is represented conventionally through separate pieces tied or affixed to the head. Most characters wear "nets" (*wangzi*), caps wrapped with a long piece of damp gauze. Males may add swatches of hair or the "swinging hair" (*shuaifa*), a ponytail, and *laodan* add a small bun. Most other *dan* styles are constructed from a number of pieces including "locks" (*pianzi*), flat curls soaked in adhesive solution; "string hair" (*xianyizi*), a fall of black silk cord that hangs down the back; a large bun; and at least some items of *toumian* ("head surface"), sets of jewels, with silver indicating poverty, shiny glass for most characters, and kingfisher feathers for wealthy aristocrats.

All "older males" (*laosheng*), most *jing*, and many *chou* also wear *rankou* ("beard edges"), wire frames hung on the ears from which hair is suspended. The "three part beard" (*sanran*) has separate lengths of hair at the sideburns and chin, suggesting elegance and refinement, and is primarily worn by *laosheng*. The "full beard" (*manran*), for strong, robust characters, is worn by both *laosheng* and *jing*. Many other varieties indicate particular circumstances and character traits for *laosheng*, *jing*, and *chou*.

Headwear. There are over three hundred types of headwear in four categories. "Crowns" (*guan*) identify the emperor and imperial family members; decorations include white glass "pearls," pompoms, and long silk tassels. "Helmets" (*kui*) indicate relative rank of martial characters; more elaborate and imposing than *guan*, many support two long feathers (*lingzi*) manipulated by the actor. *Jin* ("cloth") are soft caps for males in informal circumstances; various styles indicate age, temperament, and occupation. "Hats" (*mao*) for males include a wide variety. "Black gauze hats" (*shamao*), officials' hats with "wings" (*chi*) extending from the back to the sides, can indicate relative honesty and competence through wing size and shape.

Actors of traditional plays stress the importance of proper costumes with the axiom, "Wear a worn out, but not a wrong one." For **xinbian lishi ju** and contemporary plays, however, costumes are newly designed and built, with artists drawing on historical, topical, and imaginative material in addition to principles of traditional costuming.

FURTHER READING

Scott, A. C. *Chinese Costume in Transition*; Zhao Shaohua, ed. *Costumes of Peking Opera.*

Elizabeth Wichmann-Walczak and Catherine Swatek

Costumes: India

There are as many modes of costume in **India** as there are theatrical genres. In some cases the costumes used by traditional theatre are variations of accepted local modes of dress. In other cases, costumes bear only a slight resemblance to everyday clothing. In ritual dramas and other sacred theatre, costumes often have a significant **religious** function, while costumes in more secular traditions are strictly artistic and practical.

In northern India, **nautanki**, which dramatizes secular legends and tales for the sake of popular entertainment, uses simple stylizations of common, traditional dress. The main male characters, kings, government ministers, and the like, wear **stage** variations of *dhoti*s and *kurta*s, while their female counterparts (often played by men) typically appear in saris. Aside from their colors possibly being more intense or their ornamentation more ostentatious—in order to identify characters with an idealized, mythical history—these costumes are not especially different from what many spectators wear to performances. In a typical fashion, clowns may adopt modern elements, such as sunglasses and hats (including pith helmets).

Ankiya nat, in East India, similarly adapts conventional clothing as costumes, although in this case performances are distinctly religious in character. The onstage **director**-commentator (*sutradhara*) wears an all-white variation of traditional clothing, which makes him distinct from other performers.

Raslila and *ramlila* are traditional forms in which costumes are styled to evoke a mythical, but familiar, past, and also include elements with special religious meaning. Most important to both traditions is the "crown" (*mukut*) worn by the young leading **actors**; it identifies them as *svarups*, physical manifestations of divinity. Often the actor dons the *mukut* ceremonially, to the chanting of **Sanskrit** verses. Once the ritual is complete and the *mukut* on his head, patrons defer to him as the incarnation of his character. These actors also may be adorned by elements such as bead necklaces, earrings, and flowers tied into their hair, around their arms, and garlanded around their necks, further identifying them as objects of devotion. Actors of both traditions are exclusively male, and boys playing girls wear long braids of faux hair, tied to their own. In *raslila*, adult men who play **women** generally wear simple, though brightly colored, saris, draping the end over their heads to obscure their faces.

South Indian theatre tends toward more extravagant stylization. The headgear employed in the ritualistic *teyyam*, for example, can be more than twenty feet high, and acts as crown and set piece at once. This crown possesses a spiritual power and is handled with deference. Costumes are constructed anew for each performance from leaves, bamboo, and tree bark layered with cloth and paper.

Kathakali and *kutiyattam*, forms related to *teyyam*, also crown their principal males. Their less overwhelming headpieces are designed for specific **role types**. These conical coronets with wide, vertical haloes are made of light wooden frames covered with a variety of multicolored and reflective materials, including paper, foil, glass and plastic beads, and mirrors. Among the other distinctive elements of both *kathakali* and *kutiyattam* is the broadly flared skirt worn by male characters. An outer skirt is buoyed by many layers of heavily starched pieces of material tied in succession around an actor's waist, to the effect that the skirt extends horizontally around him to the reach of his arms. Actors are accommodated to female roles through hip padding and breast pieces made from wood or papier-maché.

Although one finds little continuity in the look of costumes across India, traditional theatre commonly regards costumes and the costuming process as spiritually significant, and the transformation of the actor that they effect is more than superficial.

FURTHER READING

Ambrose, Kay. *Classical Dances and Costumes of India*; Ghurye, G. S. *Indian Costume*.

David V. Mason

Costumes: Japan

The basic garment for both male and female characters commonly used in the four major traditional genres of **nô**, **kyôgen**, **kabuki**, and *bunraku* (see Puppet Theatre) is the *kitsuke*, a slightly wider version of the contemporary kimono. This full-length, long-sleeved robe folds left over right on the front of the wearer and is fastened with a "sash" (*obi*), usually tied in back. A second important garment, worn mainly by male but some female characters, is divided skirt-like pants (*hakama*), pleated in front and worn over the kimono. All four traditional forms feature a limited number of possible pieces, with the character's nature—gender, age, status, profession, and even state of mind and season—being visually displayed by the combination of pieces, fabric, pattern, color, length, and drape of garments. The fabric, width, and manner in which *obi* are tied are also indicative of both genre and character status and age.

Developments in textile techniques and production beginning in the Tenshô era (1573–1593) made it possible to produce domestically sumptuous brocades, silk satin damask, and other fabrics formerly only available as imports from **China** and Europe. These advances resulted in more sumptuous *nô* costumes from the early seventeenth century. These same fabrics used by *kabuki* commoners invited periodic sumptuary laws issued by the Tokugawa shogunate during the Edo period (1603–1868) in an attempt to limit the use of luxurious costumes.

Nô *and* Kyôgen. Both *nô* and *kyôgen* call costumes *shôzoku* to differentiate them from *ishô*, the term used by other genres. Costumes are generally owned and maintained by individual **actors** or acting families, and may be used for generations. Costumes developed from samurai dress of the fifteenth to seventeenth centuries, reflecting the custom of performers wearing clothing items presented to them by patrons as a reward for good performance.

Nô employs four basic garment types, defined according to cut and function, and subdivided by weaving technique or type of material. Inner kimono (*kitsuke*) types include plaid or plain silks (*noshime*), silk satin embedded with embroidery and silver and gold appliqué (*nuihaku*), plain colored silk embossed with gold or silver (*surihaku*), heavy silk with designs woven into the woof (*atsuita*), and white glossed silk (*shironeri*). Any of these, together with the kind of thick silk kimono with embroidered designs that stand out in relief (*karaori*), can also be worn as an outer kimono (*kosode*). Outer robes, such as a wide-sleeved travel cloak (*mizugoromo*), dancing cloak (*chôken*), hunting cloak (*karaginu*), generals' waist-length jacket representing armor (*happi*), or sleeveless, open-sided, waist-length garment (*sobatsugi*), may be worn over the outer kimono. Some characters may wear ankle-length *hakama*, either the stiff-backed and plain-colored type (*ôguchi*), used for men and **women**, or the satin weave with gold and silver patterning type (*hangire*), used for males and nonhumans. There also are the "long" *hakama* (*nagabakama*) that trail on the ground behind the foot. Females' costumes are divided into those for younger women, which use red, and those for middle-aged and older women, which do not.

Kyôgen costumes are similar in cut though generally much simpler in texture and design than *nô*. The *kitsuke*, made of silk, forms the basis of the costume, varying in pattern depending on character: wide stripes for lords; plaids (*noshime*) for lower class characters such as servants, farmers, and mountain priests; and small uniform patterns (*nuihaku*) for females. Over this on the upper body, servants, masters, and other male commoners wear a vest-like jacket with pointed shoulders (*kataginu*). Lords wear wide-sleeved short jackets (*suô*), while priests don the *mizugoromo*. On the lower body, servants, farmers, and other commoners wear *hangire*, usually bearing designs in circular motifs. Lords generally wear *nagabakama*. *Kataginu* for commoners typically sport bold whimsical designs such as a plant, animal, or utensil that graphically depicts some theme from the character's daily life. Masters wear matching *nagabakama* and *kataginu*, while those of servants and other commoners do not match.

Both *nô* and *kyôgen* actors wear waist-length padded cotton undergarments (*dôgi*) to give volume and size. *Nô* uses silk *obi*, while *kyôgen obi* are of plain white cotton for all males, and embroidered silk for females. All *kyôgen* females wear a white linen cloth (*binan*) that wraps around the head and hangs down on either side of the face. This is worn in lieu of a wig, although *nô* females do wear wigs.

Both *nô* and *kyôgen* characters wear bifurcated socks (*tabi*), white in *nô* and, for the most part, yellow in *kyôgen*. There is also a wide variety of headgear worn by *nô* and *kyôgen* characters, ranging from broad-brimmed straw hats (*kasa*) to priests' cloth turbans (*zukin*) to courtiers' hats with side pieces (*eboshi*), and so on.

Kabuki *and* Bunraku. *Kabuki* and *bunraku* costumes are termed *ishô*. *Kabuki* costumes are constructed and maintained by professional companies, the most important being Shôchiku Costume Company. Osaka's National Bunraku Theatre (Kokuritsu Bunraku Gekijô) owns and maintains *bunraku* costumes. Costumes have a fixed style (*kata*) for each classical role, though pattern and color variations, as in *nô*, are both a responsibility and a creative act left to the actor or **puppeteer**. Costumes are newly fashioned for major characters for each production, with slight variances depending on performer preference; lesser characters are pulled from stock. Given the large casts of characters in both genres, whose respective repertories share many plays, it is not uncommon for full-length plays to require two hundred to three hundred costumes.

Costumes can generally be divided into those used for "history plays" (*jidai mono*), which have wide-ranging styles and pieces, and "domestic plays" (*sewa mono*), which more closely resemble clothing used in daily life during the Edo period. Overall the range reflects *kabuki*'s eclecticism. This includes imaginary, purely made-for-the-**stage** costumes, such as the *yoten*, a wide-sleeved kimono slit on both sides at the hem, hiked up to the calves and worn with tights; highly theatricalized versions of actual dress, such as the giant sleeves and outrageously long *nagabakama* of the hero in *Wait a Moment!* (Shibaraku); the complex battle armor (*yoroi*) worn by samurai in history plays; the elaborate brocade kimono worn by courtesans, with their fantastical *obi* tied in front and descending in a cascade of images and color; and the plain and simple garments of everyday life among the lower classes in "raw domestic plays" (*kizewa mono*).

Kabuki uses a number of "quick-change" (*hayagawari*) techniques, such as "pulling out" (*hikinuki*), in which a kimono is completely pulled away within seconds, revealing another one underneath, and "sudden change" (*bukkaeri*), in which the top half of the kimono comes down and its interior fabric held up to view by stagehands as part of a commanding pose (*mie*).

Bunraku costumes are similar to *kabuki*, with modifications made to suit the medium of the puppet. An approximately seven-inch horizontal opening in the back of the kimono, just below the *obi*, allows the main puppeteer to insert his hand to hold the puppet's head grip. Slits in the kimono underarms allow the puppeteer's hand to be inserted to control arms, while the bottom of the left sleeve is often left open to facilitate manipulation of the left arm control rod. Costume proportions are also adjusted to match the puppet, whose body is on average ten times the length of its head. Costume changes in *bunraku* are done by inserting the puppet head into a second dressed puppet body.

Bunraku and *kabuki* costumes would not be complete without a very wide assortment of undergarments, headgear, footgear, and multiple accessories. Interestingly, the *nuigurumi* costumes worn by the actors who play large animals in *kabuki*, including dogs, horses, oversized rats, and toads, are the responsibility of the **property** master, not the wardrobe staff.

FURTHER READING

Kirihata, Ken. *Kyôgen Costumes: Suô (Jackets) and Kataginu (Shoulder-Wings)*; Kirihata, Ken. *Kabuki Costumes*; Kongô, Iwao. *Nô Costumes;* Shaver, Ruth M. *Kabuki Costume.*

Julie A. Iezzi

CRITICISM

Criticism: China

Pre-Fourteenth Century. Full-scale drama appeared in **China** with the emergence of *qu*, the last and freest form of sung verse, in the late twelfth century. While the earliest preserved play texts are for a southern form of *qu* (*nanxi*), the earliest critical texts concern northern *zaju*. These works include *Treatise on Singing* (Changlun, ca. 1340) by Yan'an Zhi'an (fl. 1340); *Rhymes of the Central Plain* (Zhongyuan yinyun, 1324), by Zhou Deqing (ca. 1270–1324), a treatise on phonology and techniques of composition; and *A Register of Ghosts* (Lugui bu, 1330) by Zhong Sicheng (ca. 1279–1360), which consists of short biographies that fashion an image of Yuan **playwrights** as frustrated geniuses. The Ming ruling family was keenly interested in drama; one of its members, Zhu Quan (1378–1448), published a treatise in 1398 that synthesized the Yuan critical literature while further enhancing the image of *zaju* playwrights, describing them as men of leisure who wrote for romantic diversion. Some two centuries later, Zang Maoxun (1550–1620) published an anthology of one hundred Yuan plays that developed this romanticized ethos of *zaju* even further.

Post-Fourteenth Century. Critical writings by literati reappear after 1500, especially in a period from 1550 to 1680, when a mature form of southern *chuanqi* was popular. After **Xu Wei**'s pioneering treatise on *nanxi* appeared in 1557, criticism became more comprehensive and systematic. *Rules for Songs* (Qulü, ca. 1620) by Wang Jide (?–1623), Xu's disciple, reflects the Ming literati's interest in theatre. Its forty sections reveal broad knowledge of dramatic traditions (northern and southern) and discuss topics such as composition, **dramatic structure**, diction (the proper balance of elegant and common language), prosody, dialogue, and comedy. *Qulü* anticipates the criticism of **Li Yu** (see Theory) in its breadth and originality. The writings of Pan Zhiheng (1556–1620), Wang's contemporary, articulated the literati's ideal performance technique and aesthetics in highly allusive language, while **Tang Xianzu** discussed performance artistry in straightforward language in his letters to **actors**.

For Feng Menglong (1574–1646) and Jin Shengtan (1608–1681), criticism was bound up with reproducing existing plays in editions furnished with supplementary materials. Feng's revisions, guidelines, and comments address the practical side of production, while Jin's more extensive revisions and commentary convey his literary appreciation of one play—*The Story of the Western Wing* (Xixiang ji)—in reader-oriented criticism that addresses moral and aesthetic textual aspects. Later Qing criticism separately addressed the concerns of theatre performers and pure singers.

Mind-Illumining Mirror (Mingxin jian, ca. 1830), written by and for actors, for the first time discusses movement and gesture as well as singing and dialogue, while **musically** annotated texts (*gongche pu*) for pure singing first appear in 1791.

More recently, the edition-based criticism of Wu Mei (1884–1939) has paved the way for scholarly and critical work focused on texts as artifacts ("text systems") that conceal various readers and multiple audiences within their pages.

Post-1949. Under the People's Republic of China (founded 1949), criticism of contemporary *xiqu* has generally been similar in approach to that for modern forms (see below). However, most *yangban xi* were in the *jingju* form. During the Cultural Revolution (1966–1976), criticism of these items followed laudatory lines based on Mao Zedong's (1893–1976) extreme class struggle theories, which were repudiated very soon after Mao died.

FURTHER READING

Fei, Faye Chunfang, ed. and trans. *Chinese Theories of Theater and Performance from Confucius to the Present*; Leung, K. C. *Hsü Wei as Drama Critic: An Annotated Translation of the Nan-tz'u hsü-lü.*

Catherine Swatek

Modern Theatre: Early Twentieth Century. Modern Chinese theatrical criticism had origins similar to those that inspired the young radicals who created "spoken drama" (*huaju*) as a form to convey people's increasing awareness of social, **political**, and cultural issues. Thus it focused on the question of theatre's essential function. In September 1904, the first theatrical journal appeared in Beijing, *Big Stage in the Twentieth Century* (Ershi shiji da wutai). It emphasized theatre's "powerful capability for persuasion" and advocated that theatrical work "should represent China's fight against foreign imperialism, and other nations' revolutionary history." It was quickly banned by the Manchu court.

Alongside the argument on theatre's function, criticism started paying more attention to theatrical art. Journals appeared that discussed plays and playwrights, translated foreign theories, and reviewed productions. Important periodicals included *Nanguo Monthly* (Nanguo yuekan, edited by **Tian Han**), *Drama Studies Monthly* (Juxue yuekan, edited by Jin Zhongsun et al.), and *The Drama Journal* (*Ju kan*, edited by **Yu Shangyuan** et al.).

Post-1949. After the Communist Party established the People's Republic of China in 1949, criticism became predominantly influenced by propagandist themes, which lasted until the early 1980s. Mao's declaration that "revolutionary culture is a powerful revolutionary weapon for the broad masses of the people" was the ruling doctrine. Soviet social-realist theatre and realism as advocated by Marx and Engels were the only criteria by which to understand or review plays. Many political campaigns started by attacking theatrical works, and criticism was often used to mobilize such campaigns.

Critics have enjoyed much more freedom since the implementation of the "open-door policy" in the 1980s. Unprecedented numbers of works have been published covering a wide range of history, acting, **directing**, playwriting, and **scenography**; some tackle controversial issues.

Major newspapers, including the *People's Daily*, regarded as the Communist Party's "throat and tongue," publish criticism on important works. Criticism that launched ideological attacks would always appear first in these media.

The Drama Publishing House (Xiju Chubanshe) has contributed tremendously to academic publications. Important periodicals include *The Drama Bulletin* (Xiju bao), provincial theatre magazines, and the academic journals edited by the two prestigious drama academies, *Dramatic Art* (Xiju yishu) and *Drama* (Xiju). *Foreign Theatre* (Waiguo xiju), which had helped broaden people's horizons concerning the outside world after the Cultural Revolution, closed down in the early 1990s because of a severe cutback of government subsidies.

FURTHER READING

Fei, Faye Chunfang, ed. and trans. *Chinese Theories of Theater and Performance.*

Ruru Li

Criticism: India

Criticism Categories. Generally speaking, **Indian** theatre criticism is spread across a landscape of categories. These include writings on traditions and scholarship related to the ancient *Treatise on Drama* (Natyashastra; see Theory), on **Sanskrit theatre**, on India's many **folk theatres**, on the numerous regional-language theatres, on different **playwrights**, on **Western** dramatic theory, and on renowned **directors** and productions. It appears in regional-language publications, English-language publications, and in reviews and articles appearing in newspapers and periodicals. Despite the occasional appearance of purposefully critical writing in the above-mentioned work, criticism, in the strict definition of the term, has not been extensive for modern Indian theatre.

Foreign Scholarship. India's linguistic and cultural diversity means that work published in English serves a crucial function in fostering a national theatre discourse of criticism and scholarship, including research. Although major books on Indian theatre by foreign scholars, such as those by Frasca, Richmond, Zarrilli, Hanson, Blackburn, Byrski, de Bruin, Yarrow, and so on, attracted serious critiques from many Indian academics, they have definitely made a major contribution to the enhancement of Indian theatre scholarship and discourse. Among the many indigenous writers whose English-language books have contributed to international knowledge of Indian theatre, including classical, folk, and modern, are Iyer, Vatsyayan, Gargi, Awasthi, Varadpande, Bhat, Bharucha, Lal, Dharwadker, and so on, as listed in the bibliography.

Nationalist Movement. A number of serious writings appeared during the period of the nationalist movement, under the banner of the Indian People's Theatre Association (founded 1942–1943) in the form of manifestoes. Western intervention in Indian cultural expression, especially in theatre, was sharply critiqued, the argument being that India, because of its strong, native traditions, should employ expressive methods rooted in its own traditions to express local issues. This discourse, referred to as "theatre of roots" (*tanatu natakavedi*), appeared as a result of the growing awareness of indigenous theatre's value. It was repeatedly argued, pro and con, in national and international publications.

Writers such as Suresh Awasthi and Nemi Chandra Jain supported "theatre of roots," while others, including **Safdar Hashmi** and Rustom Bharucha, opposed it on the grounds of **political** ideology, alleging that it represented a trend toward cultural revivalism. Some leading playwrights, like **Girish Karnad**, **Habib Tanvir**, **Chandrasekhar Kambar**, **K. V. Panikkar**, and **Ratan Thiyam**, are deeply invested in "theatre of roots," while others, like **G. P. Deshpande**, **Vijay Tendulkar**, **Mahesh Elkunchwar**, and **Mahesh Dattani**, feel that realism is a more significant means by which to express Indian themes on stage. The highly esteemed Bharucha wrote extensively on different Indian theatres while questioning Western attitudes toward the subject, especially in the context of the intercultural activities of directors and theorists like Barba and Brook. His sharp arguments attracted global theatre scholars and generated a new direction in intercultural debate.

Publications. The most prominent English-language theatre journals are *Theatre India*, *Seagull Theatre Quarterly*, and *Sangeet Natak*, the latter published by the National Academy of Music, Dance, and Drama (Sangeet Natak Akademi). *Seagull* and *Theatre India* address cardinal issues related to contemporary practice, while also introducing new international trends. Both journals discuss India's regional-language theatres on both an artistic and an intellectual level. However, they provide mainly documentary information about theatre happenings, and their introduction of new concepts is often aimed at a popular rather than academic readership.

Rangvarta is a newsletter providing current information on theatrical activities; it publishes short articles on theatre activists. Research-based theatre criticism is uncommon in theatre journals. Two once-prominent English-language journals, *Theatre Unity* and *Enact*, were important from the 1960s through the 1980s, but are now defunct.

Among theatre-oriented periodicals published in Indian languages are *Veli* (Tamil), *Keli* (Malayalam), *Natrang*, *Rang Prasang*, *Bharat Ranga* (Hindi), and so on.

FURTHER READING

Paulose, K. G., ed. *Natankusa: A Critique on Dramaturgy.*

B. Ananthakrishnan

Criticism: Indonesia

The Cultural Polemic. The prevailing framework for criticism of modern arts in **Indonesia** derives from the "cultural polemic" (*polemik kebudayaan*) debated in the 1930s literary journal *Modern Poet* (Poedjangga baroe). Sutan Takdir Alisjahbana (1908–1994) argued that Indonesian art requires a "fresh wind" of **Western influence**, against which Sanoesi Pané (1905–1968) countered that only native traditions can inspire local modernity. Subsequent criticism has vacillated between these positions, alternately privileging Western drama and **theory** and bemoaning those influences in favor of Indonesianization (*meng-Indonesian-kan*).

From the late 1940s to 1965, Alisjahbana's view found expression through figures such as Usmar Ismail (1921–1972), Asrul Sani (1927–2004), and Teguh Karya (1937–2001). By the late 1960s, however, the prevailing trends favored Pané's camp, with figures like **Rendra**, **Arifin C. Noer**, **Putu Wijaya**, and Suyatna Anirun (1936–2002) adapting native traditions and organizational structures to make the modern theatre a "new tradition" (*tradisi baru*). Throughout, critics have grappled with the relevance to local conditions of Western intellectual movements, from existentialism to postmodernism.

Publications. Most Indonesian criticism appears first in newspapers (such as *Kompas* and *Republika*), news magazines (such as *Tempo* and *Gatra*), or cultural journals (such as *Basis* and *Horizon*). Bakdi Sumanto, for example, has established himself as an eminent critic for *Kompas*. Individual theorists (such as Sani and Rendra) have published collections of their own articles, and institutions (such as the Jakarta Arts Institute and the Bandung Theatre Study Club [Studiklub Teater Bandung]) have published collections of statements by associated artists and institutional retrospectives. Boen S. Oemarjati and Jakob Sumardjo (1939–) have published seminal histories of modern Indonesian theatre, and a handful of scholars, such as Radha Panca Dahana (1965–) and **Saini K. M.**, have written criticism from academic perspectives.

Evan Winet

Criticism: Japan

Actor Critiques. In medieval **Japan**, writing about drama was intended solely for transmitting artistic traditions from masters to disciples. In the Edo period (1603–1868), while such "secret treatises" (*hidensho;* see Theory) continued to be written, many publications, particularly about *kabuki*, appeared for a readership of interested theatregoers. These included books explaining methods of production, books recording the wisdom and experiences of famous **actors** (*geidan*), and, most important, the "actor critique" (*yakusha hyôbanki*) booklets. From the late seventeenth century to the late nineteenth, annual volumes—one for each of the three major cities of Edo (Tokyo), Kyoto, and Osaka—were published containing rankings, illustrations, and critical evaluations of actors' artistic skill.

Modern* Kabuki *Criticism. Unlike the *yakusha hyôbanki*, modern *kabuki* criticism has addressed plays and productions, along with acting skill. In the early Meiji period (1868–1912), the advent of magazine and newspaper criticism marked the demise of the *yakusha hyôbanki*, and the term for "theatre criticism" (*engeki hihyô* or *gekihyô*) was coined. The earliest critics came from the Six-Two Group (Rokuniren), a group of connoisseurs that published the periodical *Actor Critiques* (Haiyû hyôbanki). Lasting from 1878 to 1887, this periodical printed synopses and articles on productions at various **theatres**. Group members also contributed to *Kabuki News* (Kabuki shinpô), a magazine publishing criticism, synopses, and articles on productions for most of 1879–1897.

Meiji critics generally made their careers as writers of fiction or plays, or in other capacities, with dramatic criticism as a sideline. As critics, their work was often connected to efforts at reforming theatre practices. Among the most famous pioneering modern critics were **playwright** and Shakespeare scholar **Tsubouchi Shôyô**, dramatist and scholar Matsui Shôyô (1870–1933), playwright and scholar Ihara Seiseien (1870–1941), playwright and novelist **Okamoto Kidô**, and dramatist and novelist **Osanai Kaoru**.

Newspaper criticism has remained important throughout the modern period, and most post-Meiji magazines devoted to *kabuki* have continued a mix of criticism and illustrated feature articles focusing on actors and plays. Others have had more scholarly offerings, as, for example, *Kabuki Studies* (Kabuki kenkyû), published from 1926 to 1928 by Tokyo's Kabuki **Theatre** (Kabuki-za) or the current *Kabuki: Research and Criticism* (Kabuki: kenkyû to hihyô).

FURTHER READING

Leiter, Samuel. *New Kabuki Encyclopedia: A Revised Adaptation of Kabuki Jiten.*

Katherine Saltzman-Li

Modern Criticism. Modern criticism originates in three contesting formulations of modernity—liberal academic, leftwing **political**, and rightwing literary—taking shape in the Tsukiji Little Theatre (Tsukiji Shôgekijô, 1924). The Tsukiji initially staged only translated **Western** plays—forty-five in its first two years. Tsukiji's driving force, **Osanai Kaoru**, had concluded that a truly modern Japanese theatre, *shingeki*, could emerge only after first mastering Western models; only then could *shingeki* engage traditional theatre on equal footing. Osanai advocated a democratic, pluralistic, performance-centered, didactic theatre, and specialized in **directing** plays by Western realists. His Tsukiji cofounder Hijikata Yoshi was influenced by the USSR's Meyerhold, while Aoyama Sugisaku (1889–1956), third member of the leadership triumvirate, directed works by Pirandello and Maeterlinck.

In contrast to this performance-oriented approach, the playwrights initially excluded from the Tsukiji advocated a literary, text-centered "theatre for the soul." They congregated around the journal *New Trends in Drama* (Engeki shinchô), wrote biting criticism of the Tsukiji's choices, the quality of its translations, and its increasingly leftist posture. **Kishida Kunio**, who had studied with Copeau in Paris, became leader of this faction. He founded *Playwriting* (Gekisaku, 1932) magazine, published *Treatise on Contemporary Drama* (Gendai engekiron, 1936), and founded the Literary Theatre (Bungaku-za, 1937).

Osanai's sudden death in 1928 split his troupe into three factions: proletarian, literary, and academic. Competition among these factions continued through the 1930s but abruptly ended in August 1940, when the government arrested more than one hundred leftists and ordered their troupes disbanded.

During World War II, critical discourse, in chauvinist journals like *National People's Theatre* (Kokumin engeki), centered on how theatre could best serve the state. The proletarian movement was decimated, but Kishida's Literary Theatre, ostensibly apolitical, continued to perform. In 1944, **Senda Koreya**, a leftist recently released from prison, organized the Actor's Theatre (Haiyû-za), extending the Tsukiji's academic legacy into the postwar period.

At war's end, prewar factions immediately reconstituted themselves. The left-leaning magazine *Teatro* resumed publication in October 1946, edited by Hijikata and **Murayama Tomoyoshi**. A conservative counterpart, *Tragedy/Comedy* (Higeki/Kigeki), was established in 1947, continuing the legacy of *Playwriting*. *New Theatre* (Shingeki), edited by **Tanaka Chikao** and fourteen contributing editors spanning the ideological spectrum, began as a centrist, liberal journal in 1954.

Among individual critics, the conservative **Fukuda Tsuneari**, influenced by Kishida and T. S. Eliot, commented prolifically on literary and theatrical issues. The left-leaning **Kinoshita Junji** developed a quasi-Hegelian theory of modern tragedy, arguing that drama should reflect history's dialectical process. Tanaka taught drama theory at the Actor's Theatre's acting school and Tôhô Academy, and was the leading postwar academic critic. His *Logique du Récit* (Mono-iu jutsu, 1949; title borrowed from a work by critic Claude Bremond) and the two-volume *Introduction to the Theory of Dramatic Style* (Gekiteki buntairon josetsu, 1977–1978) are classics.

After 1960's mass demonstrations against renewing the U.S.-Japan Mutual Security Treaty (Anpo), temporarily uniting *shingeki*'s various branches, a new generation of playwrights and critics emerged. They saw that, despite some vestigial ideological differences, *shingeki* had arrived at a powerful consensus about the nature of theatrical modernity, privileging realism to the virtual exclusion of all **experimentation**. Alternative movements, *shôgekijô* and *angura*, developed from the work of playwrights like **Fukuda Yoshiyuki**, **Betsuyaku Minoru**, **Kara Jûrô**, **Satoh Makoto**, **Ôta Shôgo**, and **Terayama Shûji**. Following the unorthodox Marxist critic Hanada Kiyoteru (1909–1974), literary scholar Hirosue Tamotsu (1919–1993), and playwright **Akimoto Matsuyo**—and in an ironic way fulfilling Osanai's original vision—*angura* sought to reclaim theatre's popular, premodern roots. Foreign writers such as Lautréamont, Artaud, Sartre, Beckett, Brecht, and Benjamin, some of whom had themselves been influenced by Asia's premodern theatre, aided them in this enterprise, which also referenced foreign films and Off-Broadway **musicals**.

Three quarterly journals, all begun in 1969, chronicled the movement: the avant-gardist *Underground Theatre* (Chika engeki) published by Terayama Shûji's Peanut Gallery (Tenjô Sajiki) troupe, and the more politically oriented *Contemporary Theatre* (Dôjidai engeki) and *Concerned Theatre Japan* (in English). Tsuno Kaitarô's (1938–) *Critique of Tragedy* (Higeki no hihan, 1970) and **Suzuki Tadashi**'s *Sum of Interior Angles* (Naikaku no wa, 1973) were manifestoes of the new alternative theatre. Leftist critic Kan Takayuki (1939–) played devil's advocate in *Postwar Theatre: Has Shingeki Been Transcended?* (Sengo engeki: shingeki wa norikoerareta ka, 1981), asking whether, despite its intentions, *angura* had not in important ways continued the legacy of orthodox *shingeki*.

The *angura* breakthrough of the 1960s spawned dozens of new troupes. Senda Akihiko (1940–), the liberal *Asahi* newspaper's influential drama critic from the 1960s through the 1990s, parsed the proliferating troupes into succeeding "generations," each with its particular emphasis. By the mid-1980s, modern theatre had become sufficiently historical for scholar and critic Ôzasa Yoshio (1941–) to write a comprehensive eight-volume *History of Contemporary Japanese Theatre* (Nihon gendai engeki-shi, 1985–2001).

FURTHER READING

Powell, Brian. *Japan's Modern Theatre: A Century of Continuity and Change;* Senda, Akihiko. *The Voyage of Contemporary Japanese Theatre.*

David G. Goodman

Criticism: Korea

Challenges to Korean Criticism. Premodern **Korea** never fostered a body of dramatic criticism, and the development of modern drama, theatre, and criticism was hampered by eight decades of repressive **censorship**. Today, though the Korean Theatre Critics Association publishes a scholarly monthly, *The Korean Theatre Journal*

(Yŏngŭk p'yŏng-ron), Korean dramatic criticism generally seems unable to elevate **playwriting** and performance. At least five challenges impede its development.

First, there is no lengthy history of productive tension between insightful, demanding criticism and talented artists. Second, media reviews appear only once a week, and because most productions play for two weeks or less, they often appear after a given production has closed. Third, despite the more than sixty-five members of the Critics Association, there is a lack of professional critics. Most critics support themselves by university teaching; writing criticism is an avocation. Fourth, social harmony is prized in daily life, but the relationships between **theatre companies** and critics can be too cozy. Playwright, **director**, and critic may be colleagues on a university faculty; favoritism or shared artistic agendas blunt objective criticism. Fifth, most critics come from literature departments, leading them to focus on the literary aspect of a given work, neglecting or misunderstanding the theatrical aspects of a production: directorial concept, **scenographic** contributions, quality of **acting**, and so on. As more and more playwrights direct their own plays, perceptive responses from mature, objective critics especially will be needed.

Yun-Cheol Kim and Richard Nichols

Criticism: Malaysia

Emergence of Mature Criticism. Prior to World War II and through the 1950s, commentary about Malay theatre centered mainly on a play's dramatic content and theme. Reviewers were less concerned with how a work was structured or with evaluating performance elements. However, with the introduction of realistic drama in the 1960s, a more detailed criticism emerged; reviews highlighted **scenography** and performance styles as well as message and content. Since then, criticism has continued to be more comprehensive. Critics envision their role as vital to the development of quality theatre; they focus, therefore, on both positive and negative aspects. Scholarly research also has contributed to the development of the performing arts, providing useful surveys of **Malaysian** theatre history and theoretical perspectives. Most critics and scholars are Malaysian, with substantial output in both Malay and English. In addition, there has been significant international attention accorded to Malaysian drama, mainly from the academic community, with notable publications available in books and periodicals.

Publications. Critical interest in modern theatre is apparent in Malay-language periodicals from the 1960s onwards, among the earliest being *Jewel* (Mastika) in 1960. Articles by **Mustapha Kamil Yassin** in 1963 in *Social Forum* (Dewan masyarakat) were instrumental in developing a **theory** of realistic drama and promoting what was at that time a new style. Articles about modern theatre have appeared regularly in the Malay journals *Language Forum* (Dewan bahasa, 1959–), *Literary Forum* (Dewan sastera, 1971–present), and *Cultural Forum* (Dewan budaya, 1979–). These periodicals provide a forum for the discussion of **playwrights**, plays, productions, and current theatre issues; in so doing, they encourage the development of criticism and scholarship. In addition, *Cultural Forum* features essays on the traditional performing arts; these have provided a resource for modern artists **experimenting** with traditional elements in their work. *Literary Forum* and *Cultural Forum* also feature color photos that provide a record of production styles over time. English-language articles about Malay theatre appear regularly in *Malay Literature*.

The National Publishing Agency. The Modern Literature Department and Library at Dewan Bahasa dan Pustaka (the national publishing agency) maintains resource materials on dramatists, productions, and reviews. The agency also publishes theatre books, plays, and most of the literary magazines and journals mentioned above, which contain essays, reviews, and scripts. The agency also arranges seminars and conferences that promote criticism and research. English-language articles about Malaysian theatre have appeared in publications with wide areas of interest, such as *Southeast* (Tenggara), featuring Southeast Asian literature and drama, and the American *Asian Theatre Journal*, which covers the continent as a whole. In addition, an active arts Web site serves as a critical resource for the performing arts: <http:www.kakiseni.com>.

Theatre articles and reviews can be found in several Malaysian newspapers, including the special weekend editions: *Malay Messenger* (Utusan Melayu) and *Era's Messenger* (Utusan zaman), *Daily News* (Berita harian) and *Week's News* (Berita minggu), *Malaysia Messenger* (Utusan Malaysia) and *Malaysian Weekly* (Mingguan Malaysia), and the *New Straits Times* and the *New Sunday Times*. From 1972 to 1994, **Krishen Jit** wrote a weekly column in the latter. Written from a historical perspective, it featured insightful commentary about playwrights and their work as well as productions and practitioners. For about a year, beginning in early 1974, Dinsman (1949–) wrote a weekly column in *Malaysian Weekly* using the pen name "Jebat." Being then one of the new breed of experimental dramatists, Dinsman provided insider commentary on experimental theatre work.

Other Critics and Scholars. Other critics and scholars who have helped shape the discourse about modern theatre include Johan Jaaffar (1953–), Mana Sikana, Hatta Azad Khan (1952–), Ismail Dahaman, Zakaria Ariffin (1952–), Mohammed Ghouse Nasuruddin (1953–), Ghulam Sarwar Yousof (1939–), Solehah Ishak (1951–), Rahmah Bujang (1947–), and Kee Thuan Chye (1954–).

In addition to writing about the theatre, most critics and scholars are active as playwrights, producers, **directors**, educators, and/or **actors**. Their commentary may reflect their own approach to theatre. Universities are also major centers for research by faculty as well as graduate students. Book-length critical studies of the traditional, popular, and modern theatre are available in both Malay and English. While, for the most part, critics and scholars have viewed theatre in terms of language groupings (speaking of Malay, English, **Chinese**, and **Indian** theatre separately), some tend to view Malaysian theatre as a whole, attempting to encourage an inclusive theatre arts.

FURTHER READING

Nina Zuhra (Nancy Nanney). *An Analysis of Modern Malay Drama.*

Nancy Nanney

Criticism: Philippines

The first critical essays on **Philippines** theatre were written during the nineteenth century, and dealt not only with the ***komedya*** *Lady Ines with the Swan Neck and Prince Nicanor* (Doña Ines Cuello de Garza y el Principe Nicanor), but with colonial rule and the **politics** of race. In 1889, Vicente Barrantes, a Spaniard, wrote *Tagalog Theatre* (El teatro Tagalog) which included a critique of contemporary plays, including *komedya*. In response, Jose Rizal (1861–1896) wrote the essay "His Excellency, Mr. Vicente Barrantes" (1889) published in the newspaper *Solidarity* (La Solidaridad). Rizal countered that Barrantes had no knowledge of Philippine or Asian theatre history, and that the article was written to insult the Filipino people.

Two manuscripts contained criticism of the plays performed during the early years of American colonial rule (1900–1946). Wenceslao Retana's *Theatre in the Philippines* (El teatro en Filipinas, 1910) commented on plays he had viewed or read, while newspaper editor Arthur S. Riggs's *The Filipino Drama* (1905) included a negative critique of **Aurelio Tolentino**'s "seditious" *Yesterday, Today, and Tomorrow* (Kahapon, ngayon, at bukas, 1903).

Debates on performance continued during the first half of the twentieth century, with **Severino Reyes** attacking the *komedya*, and Isabelo de los Reyes defending it. It was only in the 1930s that criticism was practiced by university-based writers, such as Ignacio Manlapaz and Jean Edades, and later in the 1950s by regular reviewers such as Morli Dharam, Jose Lardizabal, J. Zuleta de Costa, Rosalinda Orosa, and Leonor Orosa-Goquinco.

Commitment to responsible, insightful, and well-written criticism was spearheaded in the 1960s by Rodrigo Perez III and Bienvenido Lumbera. They were joined in the next two decades by Nicanor Tiongson, Doreen Fernandez, Isagani Cruz, Rosalinda Orosa, Mauro Avena, Pio de Castro, Amadis Guerrero, and Preachy Legasto. Nevertheless, the lack of full-time critics led Fernandez to write an essay calling for them, "A Plea for Critics" (1988).

Joi Barrios

Criticism: Singapore

Theatre criticism in **Singapore** in print is largely limited to features and reviews appearing in the daily English-language *Singapore Straits Times,* though reviews of productions also sometimes appear in *The Business Times*, *The New Paper*, and the **Chinese**-language daily, *Lianhe Zaobao*. For many years until the early 1990s, Hannah Pandian set a high standard for local writing by providing *Straits Times* readers with concise descriptions of productions, combined with a clear, well-considered critical response. Following Pandian at the *Straits Times* was Clarissa Oon (1975–), who wrote the first real history of Singaporean theatre with her *Theatre Life! A History of English Language Theatre in Singapore* (2000). Less historical in its orientation is the thematically organized *Theatre and the Politics of Culture in Contemporary Singapore* (2001) by William Peterson.

Singaporean intercultural theatre has received increasing attention by scholars, and many leading international journals now contain articles on these works. Newspaper reviewing in the *Straits Times* has become increasingly uneven in quality since Oon left the arts desk. Perhaps more useful is the large body of reviews dating back to 1997 that appears on the well-established Flying Inkpot Web site. Singapore's short-lived *Arts Magazine* provides a range of articles on theatre from 1997 to 2003 in a glossy format, while the more scholarly *FOCAS (Forum on Contemporary Art and Society)*, issued bi-annually since 2001, casts a wide net on the arts while maintaining a sharp, critical edge.

Oon, Clarissa. *Theatre Life! A History of English Language Theatre in Singapore through the Straits Times, 1958–2000.*

William Peterson

Criticism: Thailand

From 1999 to 2005, a group of **Thai** scholars led by renowned critic Chetana Nagava-jara (1937–) conducted a study entitled "Criticism as an Intellectual Force in Contemporary Society," supported by the Thailand Research Fund and covering criticism of literature, visual arts, theatre, and **music**.

According to the study, theatre criticism has been regarded as a peripheral activity. As a written culture, it gained popularity when university lecturers began staging translated **Western** plays and incorporated modern theatre studies into their curriculum in the 1970s. Simultaneously, criticism of traditional theatre began declining. As in criticism of other arts, Thai theatre practitioners prefer the informal and private form of oral criticism to that of formal, published expression, which is deemed Western. The study also notes that university theatre programs do not provide **training** for criticism careers, although criticism is among the study's core courses.

Currently, reviews are published most regularly by two English-language newspapers, *Bangkok Post* and *The Nation*, as well as a few other entertainment magazines, yet very few are found in academic journals. As the number of productions is low and the space allocated for reviews is relatively limited, Thai critics wear many hats. Examples of theatre critics are Nantakwang Sirasunthorn (1968–) of the *Bangkok BizNews*, who is also a film critic; Alongkorn Parivudhiphongs (1970–) of the *Bangkok Post*, who also critiques **dance** and music; and Pawit Mahasarinand (1972–) of *The Nation* and *Bizweek*, a lecturer and play translator.

Pawit Mahasarinand

CURTAINS

Curtains: China. *See* Scenography: China

Curtains: India

The use of curtains to initiate or introduce characters into the action is found in various forms of South Asian traditional theatre. The curtains used range from **Western**-style proscenium arch arrangements to an unattached rectangular cloth handheld by its four corners across the performing area by performers, the use of which appears to be rooted in ritual.

The handheld curtain is part of entrance conventions in several traditional South **Indian** forms, such as *kathakali*, *terukkuttu*, and *yakshagana*. Such entrances not only initiate an important character into the enactment of the sacred Hindu narratives but also heighten the effect of each entrance by revealing the entering characters only in degrees. For example, when a *terukkuttu* or *kathakali* character enters, he will first perform certain **dance** movements behind the curtain. In the case of *terukkuttu*, the character will also chant and sing devotional passages revealing his identity, all while still concealed by the handheld curtain. The audience hears the rhythmic sounds of ankle bells and the character's songs, but does not see him. The character then manipulates the curtain to selectively reveal certain aspects of his image, such as lifting the curtain's bottom to show glimpses of his ankle bells. Finally, this tantalizing revelation culminates in the curtain being swiftly whisked away, fully revealing the character, fulfilling audience expectations, and completing a dramatically and ritually heightened entrance.

Kathakali actor Nelliyode Vasudevan Namboodiri performs the initial "curtain-look" as the demoness Simhika in *The Killing of Kirmira*. (Photo: Phillip Zarrilli)

In *terukkuttu*, the curtain (*tirai*) is not only a visual marker and entrance intensifier, but also catalyzes the transformation of a narrative figure into a dramatic one. It is here that one detects the powerful ritual origins and aspects of this curtain use. When a heroic or villainous king first comes behind the curtain, the performer will sing a song of praise/worship to his personal deity. Only after this does he sing a chant (*viruttam*) related to the dramatic action. It is significant that this chant is sung in the third person in a narrative mode. The following piece is the actual entering song of the curtain entrance (*tirai varutal*), sung in the first person in a dramatic mode, during which the handheld curtain is pulled away, and the entering character joins the action onstage. The curtain, therefore, is a vital part of a transformative ritual that initiates the character into the action and transforms the sacred narrative of the epics into ritual theatre.

The roots of the curtain as a revelatory visual device in *terukkuttu* are traceable to temple rituals in Tamilnadu. In important and complex rites directed to presiding deities of major temples, a vital experience for devotees is the revelation of the "secret" (*rahasya*) of the shrine, which is the deity's image at the ritual's culminating moment. The revelation is accomplished by whisking aside a curtain held across the front of the deity's image at a vital transition. At the most intense and powerful moment, this curtain is yanked away, and the rite's powerful secret is revealed. The parallels between curtain use in *terukkuttu* and temple ritual are clear.

Numerous other traditional forms use conventions of curtain entrance homologous to the *terukkuttu*. *Kathakali* utilizes a parallel convention called a "curtain look" (*tirai nokku*) as do **kutiyattam** and *yakshagana*.

FURTHER READING

Frasca, Richard A. *The Theater of the Mahabharata: Terukkuttu Performances in South India.*

Richard A. Frasca

Curtains: Japan

Curtains (*maku*) play a vital role in traditional **Japanese** theatre. In *nô* and *kyôgen*, there is only the "lift curtain" (*agemaku*), placed in the doorway leading from "mirror room" (*kagami no ma*) to the "bridgeway" (*hashigakari*). This silk curtain consists of five vertical stripes of white, green, red, yellow, and black, a spectrum said to symbolize the sun's colors in its path through the day. Shortly before the beginning of a *nô* play, the **musicians** enter through it as it is lifted slightly from the lower right hand corner. When **actors** enter, it is lifted from the bottom by bamboo poles drawing it into the greenroom. The curtain is also lifted for the exit of characters.

Both *kabuki* and *bunraku* (see Puppet Theatre) also have *agemaku*. There are two kinds. One is navy-colored, with large crests signifying the **theatre** in which the play is being given, and placed at stage left and right in many sets; a similar curtain is at the back of the theatre at the entrance to the runway (*hanamichi*), although this is infrequently used in *bunraku*. These curtains hang on rings and open laterally, not vertically. The other kind, which does open vertically, is seen in plays adapted from *nô* and *kyôgen* that use a *nô*-like scenic background; it resembles the *nô-kyôgen agemaku* and is placed in the stage right scenic wall, although—since no *hashigakari* is used—it leads directly onto the main acting area.

The above curtains are door-sized cloths through which actors enter or exit one at a time. But both *kabuki* and *bunraku* also use curtains to separate the audience from the **stage** proper, an innovation that first appeared in *kabuki* in 1664, when multi-act plays were first produced, providing a means of separating one act from the other as sets were changed. Both *kabuki* and *bunraku* developed vertically striped traveler curtains (*jôshiki maku*; *hiki maku*), the colors of which varied from theatre to theatre, although today the standard colors are persimmon, green, and black. The curtains open and close by means of a black-robed stage assistant (*kurogo*) who runs the curtain across the stage in time to the beating of wooden clappers (*tsuke*).

There are also scenic curtains on which images are painted, including snow, mountains, and the like, as well; a large, red and white, horizontally striped curtain (*dandara maku*) used to temporarily hide the scenic background in *The Maiden at the Dôjô-ji Temple* (Musume Dôjô-ji); a number of minor, specialized curtains, such as one used to hide dead characters as they exit from the stage; a billowing, pale blue one that hides the upstage scenery until whisked away in a blaze of light when the set is revealed; and so on.

Drop curtains (*donchô*) also were used in *kabuki*, but were restricted to the minor theatres (*koshibai* and *miyaji shibai*), since the traveler curtains had become status symbols for the better-class playhouses. After 1878, beautifully designed drop curtains were introduced into the major theatres as well, and were used for commercial advertisements, as they still are today.

Curtains have long been presented as gifts to actors by fan clubs and even today one sometimes sees productions that begin with such a gift curtain (*okuri maku*) on which the name of the star is boldly painted within a striking traditional design.

FURTHER READING

Leiter, Samuel. *New Kabuki Encyclopedia: A Revised Adaptation of Kabuki Jiten.*

Samuel L. Leiter

DAGELAN. Comic sketch theatre performed in Javanese and **Indonesian**. "Comedy" (*dagelan*, also spelled *dhagelan*) scenes are enacted by clowns in **kethoprak** and **ludrug** theatre. These emphasize physical humor, scatological wordplay, and humorous songs. The Yogyakarta *kethoprak* company Krida Muda (1929) initiated the practice of preceding plays with an "extra number *dagelan*" (*dagelan ekstra*), a comic sketch with a simple plot. Yogyakarta's Mataram Radio Association station aired these **curtain**-raisers as stand-alone programs under the title *Dagelan Mataram* starting in 1939. Among the stars was the great comic actor Basiyo. These broadcasts were imitated by live *dagelan* troupes featuring four or five clowns accompanied by *gamelan* **music**. The plays find humor in the problems the "little man" of rural Java has in coping with modernity. Troupes were compelled during the **Japanese** occupation (1942–1945) to perform semi-scripted comic propaganda plays (*lelucon*) in Indonesian and Javanese. Post-independence *dagelan* continued to be used for **political** propaganda.

Gema Malam Srimulat (or just Srimulat) was founded in 1950 by singer-actor Srimulat (1908–1968) and her husband, musician Teguh (1926–). It departed from *dagelan mataram* practice with its pop band and ninety-minute extemporized plays that centralized urban issues like drugs and prostitution and parodied pop culture. Much of Srimulat's comedy comes out of nonsequiturs and the bizarre, like the vampire "Dracula." In the 1980s, Srimulat had its own television show and three troupes in permanent **theatres** in Solo, Surabaya, and Jakarta. The company disbanded in 1989, but former members dominate television comedy, and live "reunions" are staged occasionally. Student groups performing *dagelan* in Indonesian and regional languages have flourished at colleges since the 1970s.

FURTHER READING

Yousof, Ghulam Sarwar. *Dictionary of Traditional South-East Asian Theatre.*

Matthew Isaac Cohen

DANCE IN THEATRE

Dance in Theatre: Burma (Myanmar)

The aesthetics, movement repertoire, and musical accompaniment for **Burmese** dance and dance-drama have been shaped by four streams of influence: indigenous Pyu and Mon **folk** dances, dance traditions of **India**, **Thai/Cambodian** court dances, and indigenous marionette **puppetry**. Court dance-dramas in their full-fledged form reached their apex in the early nineteenth century, after Burma conquered the Thai capital of Ayutthaya (1767) and localized the highly refined Thai court traditions. The marionette influence is prominently visible in dances with exaggerated jerkiness of arm and head movements, unblinking eyes, a very low crouch, high angular elbow position, and the characteristic fall into a frozen pose as if the strings have been dropped. Pure court dance-dramas are rare today, but contemporary *pwe* variety shows feature extended dance sections alongside songs and dramatic skits.

Although the most highly developed dances were to be found in the court dance-dramas, other dramatic genres feature dance as well. One of the folk forms of Burmese performance, *nat pwe*, is based in animistic spirit (*nat*) worship. In it a shaman dances while entering and sustaining a trance, employing a mixture of court and folk dance styles common in Burma, combined with dramatic enactment of the spirit character. During trance the movement is more ecstatic, yet retains clearly recognizable features of Burmese dance. *See also* Dance in Theatre: Southeast Asia.

FURTHER READING

Brandon, James R. *Theatre in Southeast Asia*; Miettenen, Jukka O. *Classical Dance and Theatre in South-East Asia*; Singer, Noel F. *Burmese Dance and Theatre*.

Kirstin Pauka

Dance in Theatre: Cambodia and Thailand

Classical dance-drama traditions in **Cambodia** and **Thailand** have been closely linked throughout their history and are among the most dance-centered genres of Southeast Asian dramatic arts. They share common roots in the court cultures of the Hinduized kingdoms in mainland Southeast Asia. The Khmer culture of Angkor is considered the cradle of the classical dance style that has shaped Thai, **Laotian**, and **Burmese** dance and dance-drama. After the capture of Angkor by the Thai empire (1431)—which included the kidnapping of most court artists and especially the dancers—the further development of dance-drama took place in the Thai capital Ayutthaya, where it underwent aesthetic changes to conform with Thai tastes. A reversal influence in the nineteenth century brought Thai court dance troupes to Cambodia, peacefully this time.

A defining characteristic now prevalent in classical dance-dramas such as Thai *khon* or Cambodian *lakhon* is the division of movement styles following four basic **role types**: refined females, refined males, demons, and monkeys. During **training**, prospective dancers are selected for these specific role types based on their physique. Refined male and female styles are very similar, with the male using a slightly wider stance. Both move with delicate slowness and elegance, with faces remaining almost expressionless, arms curving in space, and hands flowing through a series of intricate gestures. Elbows are often overextended to emphasize the curve, and fingers are bent far back. Conventional gestures can be directly symbolic or purely ornamental. Refined males frequently dance with weapons, mainly light spears or bow and arrow, for battle scenes. Demon and monkey roles require a high level of stamina as well as athletic and martial arts skills to execute the energetic acrobatics and vigorous movements, with the added challenge of performing while wearing a full **mask**. Both are based in a very low, open stance. Demons often dance with a club or spear, and display their power in difficult balancing poses. Monkey roles integrate stylized animal movements like twitching and scratching. Generally, the dancers' movements illustrate offstage narration and songs delivered by a chorus. Group choreography prominently uses line, row, and pair configurations, with movement sequences frequently interspersed with dramatic poses. Large-cast combat scenes often peak in expressive multifigure tableaux, the signature image of classical Thai and Cambodian dance-drama.

FURTHER READING

Brandon, James R. *Theatre in Southeast Asia*; Phim, Toni Samantha, and Ashley Thompson. *Dance in Cambodia*; Rutnin, Mattani Mojdara. *Dance, Drama, and Theatre in Thailand: The Process of Development and Modernization.*

Kirstin Pauka

Dance in Theatre: India

In **Indian** and South Asian traditional theatre, theatre is dance and dance is theatre. The divisions and bifurcations found in **Western** terminology in the terms "theatre," "dance," and "drama" are not found in long-standing Indian terminology; if they occur in contemporary dialogue in Indian languages it is probably in imitation of English usages.

The inherent and integral role that dance has in traditional theatre has been recognized and conceptualized from the earliest recorded periods. One of the most important early crystallizations of these ideas is in the ancient **Sanskrit** *Treatise on Drama* (Natyashastra; see Theory), which posits the concept of *natya*, a coalescence of **acting** and dance. Two vital elements of *natya* are types of dance. First is *nrtta*, decorative or abstract dance, frequently referred to as "pure dance." Second is *nrtya*, **storytelling** dance in which mime or gesture comes together with dance movement to interpret and animate a narrative. Both performatively and lexically these two elements combine with acting to create *natya*.

The conceptualizations according to which dance pervades and animates theatre and theatre pervades and animates dance are manifested and reflected in many important traditional forms, including *terukkuttu, bharata natyam, kathakali, kutiyattam, yakshagana, raslila, ramlila*, and others. As evidenced in the terminology of *terukkuttu, yakshagana,* and *kutiyattam,* theatre is "danced." With *terukkuttu*, the operative Tamil verb is *atta* ("to dance," literally, to perform) while in *yakshagana* the Kannada verbal derivative *atta* ("dance," literally, performance) is used. We find homologous conceptualizations in *kutiyattam* and *krishnattam*, where the Malayalam verbal derivative *attam* ("dance," literally, performance) is central. It is also significant that *bharata natyam*, a form often described as "South Indian classical dance" because of its heavy reliance on dance movement, uses *natya* in its name.

Terukkuttu dance is created out of a repertoire of movements and steps that are conceptually and rhythmically parallel to the dance element in *bharata natyam*. In these forms, the actors/dancers wear ankle bells to add an auditory articulation to the movements. Both genres alternate between interpretive and pure dance, reflecting the concepts of *nrtya* and *nrtta*. Interpretive dance animates and "brings forward" (*abhinaya*) the performance of a narrative while pure dance ornaments and punctuates it.

A close look at dance in a *terukkuttu* **curtain** entrance is instructive. In *The Dicegame and the Disrobing* (Pakatai tuyil), the arch-villain Duhshasana enters the action behind a handheld curtain and sings a number of "chants" (*viruttam*). The first is devotional, intended to bless the actor/character's entrance into the sacred action, while the following chants are dramatic, constituting the actual beginning of Duhshasana's entrance. It is during these entering chants that the element of pure dance comes into play. Even though he is still behind the curtain, Duhshasana executes dance steps at the midpoints and endpoints of the chant to provide **musical**, rhythmic, and kinetic punctuation with his ankle bells and the portions of his legs that can be seen below the curtain's bottom.

Most of Duhshasana's onstage image is still hidden by the curtain; therefore, interpretive dance does not come into play until the curtain is whisked away and he fully joins the action, at which point the audience beholds his entire persona in terms of **makeup**, **costuming**, song, dance, and movement. At this point Duhshasana performs *nrtya*. He executes a series of spinning, leaping, and powerfully rhythmic sequences and steps that convey his violent nature.

Kathakali has an even stronger dance element. The lines are not sung by the actors/dancers as in *terukkuttu*. They are presented by a background ensemble of singers and percussionists. The actors/dancers perform this sung narrative/drama using both *nrtya* and *nrtta* to produce *natya*, that is, theatre, paralleling what we see in *terukkuttu*. What is distinctive is that *kathakali*'s *nrtya* is composed of a very complex, specific, and detailed vocabulary of hand gestures (*mudra*) and facial expressions (*abhinaya*) homologous to the spoken and sung words of the onstage *terukkuttu* actors/dancers. The audience, attuned to and educated in this language, thus comprehends the episode.

Each traditional South Asian theatre form reflects and transforms this underlying melding and blending of the elements of interpretive dance, rhythmic punctuating dance, and acting in a compelling balance that produces a distinctive dance-drama genre.

FURTHER READING

Ambrose, Kay. *Classical Dances and Costumes of India*; Bowers, Faubion. *The Dance of India*; de Zoete, Beryl. *Other Mind: A Study of Dance in South India*.

Richard A. Frasca

Dance in Theatre: Indonesia

A vast variety of dance styles exists within the abundant dramatic traditions of **Indonesia**. The most famous genres are found on Java and Bali; however, most ethnic groups in the archipelago have developed complex dance traditions with dramatic content. Javanese **wayang wong** originated in the courts of Yogyakarta and Surakarta around the middle of the eighteenth century, influenced in its aesthetics and movement repertoire by preceding court dance traditions, and adopting the structure, iconography, **musical** accompaniment, and story material of *wayang kulit* shadow **puppetry**. Dance sequences in *wayang wong* consist of extended entrance and exit numbers, choreographed fighting sequences, and courting scenes. Interspersed between dialogue or narration are shorter movement sections; movement is always stylized.

The defining movement qualities for refined characters (*alus*) are a downcast gaze, bent knees, very slow, graceful, and restrained steps, and small, curving wrist and neck movements. Female steps involve subtly manipulating a long train of cloth with the feet. Females and males manipulate long scarves or sashes with their hands, so that a flick of the fabric visually emphasizes the movements' elegant flow. In poses the dancers often imitate puppet profile positions.

Stronger or less refined (*kasar*) characters dance more energetically and faster, almost jerkily. Flicking their sashes more energetically, they gaze straight out at the audience. The overall body position takes up considerably more space than those of refined characters; the legs are in a wide stance, the arms are frequently raised above shoulder level or thrust out to the sides.

In Bali, **gambuh** can be considered the ur-genre of local dance-drama styles (it is itself derived from Javanese origins). As in Java, the dance styles follow similar differentiation into female and male and *alus* and *kasar* types, with the addition of a strong female **role type**, the *condong*. In general, dance movements are much faster, almost frantic at times, with quick changes of direction, level, and tempo, fluttering fingers, and lively and captivating eye movements. Clowns have less restricted styles, but often imitate or ridicule those of refined characters. Based on *gambuh*, Balinese *wayang wong* developed its own distinct features by incorporating *wayang kulit* elements and using as story material the **Ramayana**. It features a large cast of dancers; all except the refined characters are **masked**. Developed in the courts, it includes complex group dances, with prominent monkey characters. Animal movements are tightly choreographed, despite being seemingly improvised.

Java and Bali both feature smaller cast, masked dance-dramas (**topeng**). In Balinese *topeng pajegan* and in Cirebon's *topeng babakan*, a single **actor** dances with a series of masks portraying various stock characters according to their level of refinement. While refined characters do not speak, their overall personality and state of mind is clearly and intricately defined through a distinct conventionalized movement style for each role and situation. In Balinese *topeng*, the hand gestures are very expressive with individually articulated finger movements. With shoulders raised in typical Balinese fashion, the body position creates a supportive energized tension around the neck area on top of which the mask obtains even more prominence. The narration and commentary is carried by clowns who move in a stylized yet more natural-looking manner.

Folk or popular dance-dramas often emulate classical styles, but mix them with specific regional dances, acting styles, and music. Unique regional elements such as martial arts are sometimes integrated as well. Starting in the early 1960s, both Java and Bali developed modern dance-dramas (**sendratari**) based on styles and aesthetics of older genres, but featuring modern staging methods, new choreography, large casts, and a faster pace. *See also* Dance in Theatre: Southeast Asia.

FURTHER READING

Brakel-Papenhuyzen, Clara. *Classical Javanese Dance*; Coast, John. *Dancing out of Bali*; Dibia, I Wayan, and Rucina Ballinger. *Balinese Dance, Drama and Music: A Guide to the Performing Arts of Bali*; de Zoete, Beryl, and Walter Spies. *Dance and Drama in Bali*; Soedarsono. *Dances in Indonesia*.

Kirstin Pauka

Dance in Theatre: Japan

Buyô. *Buyô*, the generic term for dance used in Japan's traditional theatre, was coined by the dance scholar **Tsubouchi Shôyô**. It combines two earlier words for dance, *mai* and *odori*. *Mai*, the older term, refers to the dance of *nô* and of earlier court and **religious** dances. *Odori* appeared in the seventeenth century with the advent of *kabuki*, and is also associated with rural **festival** dances, such as celebratory dances for the festival of the dead (*bon odori*), religious dances (*nenbutsu odori*) of Pure Land Buddhism accompanying the chanting of the name of Amida Buddha, and the *furyû odori* of parades and spectacles from which *kabuki* dance (*kabuki buyô*) developed. *Mai* has been described as a refined form of dance that emphasizes horizontal and circular movements, while the more rustic *odori* is characterized by jumping. Hand movements predominate in *mai* while rapid foot movements are central to *odori*, although *kabuki* dance originating in Kamigata, the Kyoto-Osaka region, has a strong *mai* orientation and is known as *kamigata mai*. *Nô* is restricted to *mai*, while *kabuki* incorporates *mai*, *odori*, and realistic pantomime (*furi*).

The very beginnings of Japanese theatre are memorialized in a legend about a goddess who danced on an overturned tub to lure another goddess out of a cave in which she had hidden herself. Dance was the core of all early forms of Japanese theatre, such as **gigaku**, **bugaku**, and **dengaku**, prior to the development of dialogue. Most forms of ritual (**kagura**) and **folk theatre** (*minzoku geinô*) continue to be based on dance, the most famous example being the "lion dances" (*shishi mai*) seen in one form or another all over Japan.

Nô *and* Kyôgen *Dance*. In the language of actors, *nô* is "danced" instead of being performed, which indicates that dance is at *nô*'s core. The **actors'** distinct movement and posture are dancelike. Actors lower their center of gravity into their hips in a posture called *kamae*, and they slide their feet across the polished **stage** when walking. This sliding footwork (*suriashi*) allowing them to glide gracefully with white, bifurcated socks (*tabi*) is a *nô* trademark. All movement is choreographed. Finally, the importance of dance is evident in the art's historical development. *Nô* incorporated earlier dance arts—such as *ennen mai* and *kusemai* (the latter enacted in male **costume** by female entertainers called *shirabyôshi*)—performed at banquets and religious institutions. Three-fourths of *nô* plays contain *kusemai* sections marking the principal actor's (*shite*; see Role Types) climactic dance. Although generally sedate, *nô* dances are occasionally punctuated by leaps and stomping, which echo on the wood stage by virtue of strategically placed, large ceramic containers underneath.

For selections from *nô* dances performed outside of a play (*shimai*), actors wearing formal black kimono and broad divided skirts (*hakama*) perform a highlight accompanied by four or five performers singing as a chorus. When an actor performs these excerpts with **musicians** (*hayashi*), it is *maibayashi*.

Kyôgen occasionally incorporates "brief dances" (*komai*) that are usually accompanied by another actor singing a popular song (*kouta*). *Kyôgen*'s dances are predominantly light and humorous. As in *nô*, the most common **property** is a fan, but other objects are occasionally used, depending on the role.

Kata. *Kata*, discrete movement "patterns," are the building blocks of traditional dance. *Kata* are usually combinations of arm and leg movements; all have names that serve as memory aids for performers learning new dances. In the *nô kata* called *sashikomi*, the dancer takes a number of sliding steps forward and raises his right arm to shoulder level in front of him. Some *kata* mime recognizable actions such as the thrust of a sword, while others like *sashikomi* are more abstract. An average *nô* dance is composed of some thirty different *kata*.

Theatre dance in the major genres is based on meaning, often expressed in lyrics sung by a soloist or chorus. The range of movements extends from recognizable actions to those that have been highly abstracted to the point of symbolism, yet they are almost always grounded in meaning and are not purely decorative.

Kabuki *Dance.* As in *nô*, dance forms the basis for *kabuki* movement, and there are also dances within plays called "dance-dramas" (*buyô geki*) as well as "pure dance pieces" (*shosagoto*) that are exclusively dances, although these terms are often used interchangeably. Since *shosagoto* are purely dance, they can feature quick costume changes (*hayagawari*) to indicate character development. In *The Maiden at Dôjô-ji Temple* (Musume Dôjô-ji), several quick changes reveal the character's gradual metamorphosis from a woman into a serpent.

The nineteenth century saw an explosion of "transformation dances" (*henge mono*), in which stars, using quick changes, enacted as many as twelve characters in a single performance. Most remaining examples are of only a single dance from such multiple-dance works. Dances within plays include those associated with particular roles, such as the "footman's dance" (*yakko odori*) performed by a low-ranking samurai heading a procession, and Benkei's drunken dance in *The Subscription List* (Kanjinchô), which concludes with a dramatic "flying" exit (*tobi roppô*) as he bounds in huge strides down the runway (*hanamichi*). So-called "traveling pieces" (*michiyuki mono* a.k.a. *keigoto*), in which characters dance a journey—often to commit double suicide—can also be considered *buyô geki*.

Characteristic of *kabuki* dance is the inclusion of pantomime (*furi*), which can be realistic (*monomane buri*), as when an actor mimes writing a letter with a fan on a piece of cloth, or abstract (*fuzei buri*). In "doll pantomime" (*ningyô buri*) sequences, performers act as if they were *bunraku* **puppets** manipulated by black-garbed stage assistants. (*Bunraku* also includes a number of dances, most of them borrowed from *kabuki*.)

Some dances are based on *nô* and *kyôgen* originals, especially those in plays adapted directly from *nô*: "pine-board pieces" (*matsubame mono*). A number of dances are purely comic, while others are dark, even tragic. Properties are essential to most dances, and include fans, hand towels, weapons, hats, and so on.

Although **women** are not accepted as professional *kabuki* performers, they dominate *kabuki* dance as teachers and students in Japanese dance (*nihon buyô*) schools, which number more than 150.

FURTHER READING

Bethe, Monika, and Karen Brazell. *Dance in the Nô Theater*; Hata, Michio. *Tradition and Creativity in Japanese Dance*; Masakatsu, Gunji. *Buyo: The Classical Dance*.

Eric C. Rath

Dance in Theatre: Korea

Dance is an important aspect of **Korean** culture found in shamanistic, Confucian court, and Buddhist **religious** rituals. Agrarian life is expressed in dance. *T'alch'um* and modern-day *madangnori* feature dance as a key element and as a performance-ending social ritual bringing performers and audience together. As the number of **Western**-style and modern Korean **musical** theatre productions increase, tap, jazz, ballet, and traditional dance gain artistic importance. Even in daily urban life, outbreaks of traditional dance at family gatherings or informal drinking parties are not uncommon. Dance expresses the ideal of harmony in the universe.

There are four general categories of traditional dance: ritual dance, including the Buddhist "cymbal dance" (*parach'um*) and the Confucian "line dance" performed at ancestral rites; **folk** dance, including **masked** dances (*t'alch'um*); dance by professional entertainers (*kyobang muyong*), including the "dance of peace" (*t'aep'yŏngmu*) with its restrained footwork; and court dance (*chŏngjae*), including the "crane dance" (*hangmu*).

Though there are differences in vigor, rhythms, gravity, and other qualities among these categories, Korean dance has general characteristics. There is an emphasis on movements from nature—tortoise and stork dances seen in impromptu farmers' dances (*hŏt'unch'um*), for example. With arms extended to the side, energy is concentrated in the torso, shoulders and arms rising and falling to the tempo of the breath, often suspended to create greater energy, which then flairs outward, releases, and returns to repose in motion.

Ch'angguk choreography may borrow from all four categories, depending upon the classic story being performed. In the modern theatre, dance has been used effectively since the 1960s in the search for theatre forms free of dominating Western influences. **Playwright-director** • **Kim Kwang-lim** combined elements of *t'alch'um* with the Korean martial art *kich'ŏnmun* in *Our Country, Uturi* (Uri nara Uturi, 2002). **Oh T'ae-sŏk** wrote and directed a dance-drama, *Occasional Snow or Rain in the Morning* (Ach'im hanttae nun ina pi, 1993), and **Lee Yun-t'aek**'s *O-Gu* (1997) employs the folk "shoulder dance" (*ŏkkae ch'um*), while shamanistic dances convey character relationships. Even in realistic dramas, traditional dance is used to provide audiences with immediate visual and kinesthetic—rather than linguistic—information about locale, social status, and emotional states.

As contemporary theatre evolves, moving away from realism, dance in its many manifestations likely will become an even more important source of artistic inspiration.

FURTHER READING

Cho, Dong-il. *Korean Mask Dance;* Cultural Properties Administration. *Korean Intangible Cultural Properties: Traditional Music and Dance;* Kim, Malborg. *Korean Dance*; Van Zile, Judy. *Perspectives on Korean Dance.*

Richard Nichols

Dance in Theatre: Southeast Asia

Overview: Dance-Theatre Forms. Most genres of traditional Southeast Asian theatre feature dance as a vital element of performance. Several genres rely so heavily on dance that they are best classified as dance-dramas, such as **Thai** • *lakon nai* and *khon*, **Cambodian** • *robam kbach boran*, Javanese classical *wayang wong*, and Balinese *gambuh* and *topeng* (see Indonesia). In these genres the movements follow tightly choreographed patterns for individual and group dances. The only characters that move more freely are typically clowns or animals. Many genres of **folk theatre**, such as Sumatran *randai*, **Malay** • *mak yong*, and Thai *lakon chatri*, also heavily feature dance and stylized movement. Dance is so deeply rooted within theatrical tradition that even genres of more recent origin, such as **Burmese** • *zat pwe* or Javanese *sandiwara*, prominently feature individual dance numbers interspersed with **acted** scenes and **music**.

Royal Patronage. Large-scale dance-drama reached its apex of development under royal patronage in nineteenth- and early twentieth-century Southeast Asia, manifesting consistently high levels of refinement and artistry. Monarchs throughout the region permanently employed choreographers and dancers. Many royals took a personal interest in the arts, contributing to the creation of new artistic forms and works. In Java and elsewhere in the region, it was common for children and concubines of kings and princes to perform dance-drama in their youth to cultivate moral deportment. Court dance-dramas were not divorced from the arts of the rural hinterlands. Some of the court forms evolved out of folk theatre, and royal dancers often left courts to form their own popular companies or were hired as dancing instructors for nonroyal troupes. Today few courts can afford to maintain their own troupes, but court genres and their derivatives are taught in academies and conservatories.

Dancing Methods. Thai, Cambodian, and Javanese dance-dramas associated with the courts rely on large ensembles as supernumeraries. Soloists portray main characters, as, for instance, Rama and Sita in *Ramayana*-derived dance-dramas. Smaller scale dance-drama forms, such as Balinese *legong*, some forms of Indonesian *topeng*, and Thai *lakon chatri*, commonly emphasize virtuosic solos or duets. Performers typically dance silently to musical accompaniment, but can also dance and speak simultaneously (in *gambuh*) or sing choral parts while dancing (in *randai*). Some traditions classify dance-drama according to the degree of narrative abstraction. For instance, the Cambodian dance-drama repertoire is subdivided into *robam* pieces that are predominantly dance, and *roeung* pieces with a stronger narrative. In genres with a more equal emphasis on dance and acting, such as Javanese **kethoprak**, the major dance sections are typically elaborate entrance and exit dances of main characters, as well as stylized fights.

Styles are defined by their degree of refinement. Most female and many noble male types are restrained in their movement flow and use of space, and slower in tempo, while strong or coarse characters dance faster and more vigorously. Comic types such as clown-servants develop their own idiosyncratic styles, often mimicking their masters. Animals, especially monkeys, have their own stylized movements artistically reflecting their nature.

FURTHER READING

Brandon, James R. *Theatre in Southeast Asia*; Miettenen, Jukka O. *Classical Dance and Theatre in South-East Asia*.

Kirstin Pauka

Dance in Theatre: Thailand. *See* Dance in Theatre: Cambodia and Thailand

DANDA NATA. Indian • dance-drama produced in around twenty rural villages of Orissa during the month of Chaitra (March-April). It is an ancient, nonliterate, Hindu **folk** form devoted to Lord Shiva and his consort Parvati (a.k.a. Gauri and Kali, according to the context), given in a **festival** milieu, and imbued with tantric ritualistic elements. *Danda nata* literally means "pole dance," although *danda* has multiple meanings, including "creation"—Shiva being the god of creation and destruction. It requires thirteen to twenty-one days (depending on the year). During the festival's ritual part, thirteen men, called *bhokta*s, undergo extreme purification through dietary practices, vows of celibacy, pious behavior, and various acts of painful self-punishment.

There are three distinctly **religious** aspects to the ritual, held on the temple grounds during daylight hours and involving acrobatic feats, including somersaults and human pyramids. The rituals concern the elements of earth, water, and fire, including walking over hot coals and other trials by fire. Trance occupies an important part in the proceedings.

In the most theatrical part of the ritual festival, held all night long, the performers are others than those who take part in the ritual practices. This part is performed in an open village space demarcated by four poles and surrounded by hundreds of spectators seated on the ground, with a pathway left open for entrances and exits. The performances involve two rival troupes competing to perform their scenes with the most artistry and, toward the end, the best improvisational responses to sung and rhymed theological questions. The all-male troupes (**women**'s roles are played by men, often with considerable suggestiveness) offer a sequence of short stories enacted in brief scenes on topics familiar to village folk, such as poverty, adultery, family disputes, and religious practices, always with a moral purpose. The dialogue is sung and there is occasional dancing, with the musical accompaniment provided by a drum (*dhol*) and a wind instrument (*mahuri*). Characters, usually shown in pairs, include folk figures such as bird-catchers, hunters, beggars, fakirs, snake charmers, and preachers, each in a piece whose title notes their type. Modern influences have brought contemporary lighting and sound technology, as well as present-day instruments to join traditional ones.

FURTHER READING

Dash, Dhiren. *Danda Nata of Orissa.*

Samuel L. Leiter

DASARATA. Indian form of north and northeast Karnataka, now extinct, performed by the *kabbera* subcaste of the *dasaru*, a singing and **dancing** community. The *dasaru* are thought to be descendants of the *devadasi*s (female servants of god) who danced and sang in temples. *Dasa* has come to mean either servant or slave of man or god, and *ata* means play (as in drama, **acting**, or dancing, or play as in games). *Dasarata* was revolutionary in its time in that **women** played the female roles and influenced some local all-male forms to adopt that practice later.

Dasarata was a simple production by about six performers held at outdoor venues such as **religious** fairs, temples, private homes, or on the veranda of a public hall. Preliminaries began with an invocation to the elephant-headed god, Ganesh, followed by two young girls performing the role of youthful Lord Krishna through song and dance. The latter suggests that *dasarata* initially performed stories about Krishna, especially his amorous relationships with Radha. In time, Radha and Krishna were replaced by a female lead named Chimana, a male lead named Goddibhima, and a male comic named Jawari. The remaining players were the chorus. The story line then became a man and a woman romantically attracted, alternately rejecting each other, and finally becoming lovers. The songs were risqué, the dance lascivious, and the repartee cleverly racy. Finally, *dasarata* became licentious and obscene and degraded into oblivion.

FURTHER READING

Naikar, Basavaraj S. *The Folk-Theatre of North-Karnataka.*

Martha Ashton-Sikora

DASAVATAR. Indian • **folk theatre** of Goa and the Konkan area of Maharashtra, also spelled *dashavatar*, originating in the seventeenth century, and presenting stories of any one of Vishnu's ten avatars. Performed outdoors at night between October and April in open village spaces, it uses an all-male troupe (called *dasavatari* or "players" [*khelye*]) to represent both genders and has a two-part structure of ritual prologue and performance. There is no text, so songs and dialogue are improvised.

The troupe leader (*sutradhara*), also called the "leader" (*naik*) or "devotee" (*hardas*), participates in the preliminaries with an orchestra consisting of drums, cymbals, and harmonium. Actors portray the elephant-headed god Ganesha and the goddess Saraswati, a priest performs a ritual service and engages in humorous repartee with the *sutradhara*, verses and mantras are sung, and the gods **dance** off.

There ensues a comical dance-drama scene showing the slaying of the black-robed demon Sankhasur, whose conical hat has a cloth, **mask**-like piece that falls over the face, with eyes, mouth, and a large tongue attached. The demon has stolen the Vedas, so an amusing battle ensues between him and a fish avatar of Vishnu. Then follows an avatar's story, the most popular being that of the man-lion Narasimha; among other avatars whose stories may be performed are Rama, Krishna, Buddha, or the heavenly horse Kalki. An additional piece agreed upon between the troupe and the village is presented next, followed by a concluding song by the *sutradhara* and various rituals as dawn rises.

Samuel L. Leiter

DATTANI, MAHESH (1958–). Indian English-language **playwright, dancer, actor, director**, and educator, born into a business family of Bangalore, Karnataka. He studied dance while managing his family business, also working as an advertising copywriter. During the early 1980s, he became active in the Bangalore Little **Theatre**, acting, directing, and studying theatre.

Dattani stands apart from his contemporaries in that his work is limited to the English theatre, of which he is considered the foremost dramatist. In 1998, he became the first Indian English-language playwright to win the prestigious Sahitya Akademi award (founded in 1955), in recognition of his play *Final Solutions* (1992–1993).

In 1984, he established Playpen, a Bangalore-based, English-language **theatre company** for which he both acted and directed. Finding English-language Indian plays was not easy. This led him to write *Where There's a Will* (1986), about inheritances, following it with *Dance Like a Man* (1989), about a male dancer. *Tara* (1990), based on the tragic aftermath of conjoined twins being separated, and the possibility that the boy twin's condition was privileged by the family over that of the girl's, was followed by *Final Solutions*, which takes stock of communal confrontations. Its controversial topic led to its being rejected by a Bangalore **festival**, although it was staged in 1993 by Playpen. Other plays—all of them in the realistic, proscenium mode—include the sexually charged family drama *Bravely Fought the Queen* (1991), set in the nineteenth century; the highly controversial *On a Muggy Night in Mumbai* (1998), considered India's first play to openly deal with homosexuality (it remains a rare sympathetic example of the genre); and *Thirty Days in September* (2001), concerned with child sexual abuse. Several of his plays have been produced in London and New York. In 1995, he made playwriting his full-time vocation (also writing for radio and films), and, in 1998, created a small theatre for his productions.

As an actor, he appeared in Indian plays as well as familiar **Western** works ranging from *Five Finger Exercise* (1985) to *Henry IV* (2001). Dattani also has given dance recitals, and has taught workshops and classes in India and at American universities.

Dattani's plays, several of which have been produced in Indian languages such as Hindi and Kannada, strive to explore how past and present socio-cultural values influence human lives, but always with a leavening of humor. He realistically confronts topical issues such as sexual identity, gender equality, **religious** tolerance, and the nature of the Indian family. The **scenography** in his plays is architecturally innovative, displaying an imaginative use of space.

Shashikant Barhanpurkar

DENGAKU. **Japanese** performing art dating from the late Heian period (794–1185). *Dengaku* (literally, "field **music**") once had dramatic elements, but today exists only as a **folk • dance**. *Dengaku*'s origins are uncertain, but by the 1300s professional *dengaku* dancers (*dengaku hôshi*) organized into troupes, usually of thirteen players. The "Main Troupe" (Hon Za) from Kyoto and the "New Troupe" (Shin Za) from Nara were best known. Troupes performed acrobatic dances (*dengaku odori*), sometimes on stilts, and they typically wore gaudy **costumes** and flat straw hats. They also juggled and **experimented** with wearing **masks** and creating skits (*dengaku nô*). *Dengaku* reached its peak in the mid- to late-1300s, when performers such as Itchû and Kiami (fl. ca. 1350) inspired **Kan'ami**, **Zeami**, and other *nô* • **actors**, who revered them as early patriarchs of their own art. Itchû participated in the infamous benefit (*kanjin*) performance in 1349 in Kyoto, where the multitiered stands collapsed, killing many—a tragedy, but also a testimony to the art's popularity. *Dengaku* and *nô* performers competed with each other for popularity and elite patronage, and they occasionally fought one another. *Nô* gradually eclipsed *dengaku* in popularity, and professional *dengaku* died out in the 1500s.

Dengaku dances are performed today at shrines and in fields by members of local communities who conduct processions, field entertainments (*ta'asobi*), and rice-planting dances (*tamai*) accompanied by percussion instruments and chanting (see *Kagura*). In this context, *dengaku* is both an entertainment and a fete for the deities to ensure agricultural productivity. This form might be the origin of the professional *dengaku* described above.

Dengaku music is lively and characterized by the use of flutes, drums, and a long rattle-like instrument (*binzasara*) consisting of bamboo or wooden slats strung together and played in both hands.

FURTHER READING

Ortolani, Benito. *Japanese Theatre: From Shamanistic Ritual to Contemporary Pluralism.*

Eric C. Rath

DESHPANDE, GOVIND PURUSHOTTAM (1938–). Indian Marathi-language **playwright**, **critic**, scholar, and **theorist**, born in Nashik, Maharashtra. He earned his doctorate in **Chinese** studies from Jawaharlal Nehru University (JNU), New Delhi, later becoming a professor there and a well-known sinologist. He is active mainly in New Delhi, Satara, and Pune.

Each of Deshpande's nine plays is based on Marxist-leaning **political** themes, his purpose usually being to demonstrate the demise of so-called progressive values in contemporary society. Most have been translated into English and other Indian languages. Known as a founder of the Indian "play of ideas," his work falls into the category of realistic domestic drama intended for proscenium **theatres**. *The Ruined Sanctuary* (Uddhwasta dharmashala, 1974; transl. as *A Man in Dark Times*) is concerned with the harassment inflicted on an ideologically leftwing professor by a presumably academic committee. It was recognized for successfully capturing the political tenor of its period; despite Deshpande's own Marxism, his play offers criticism of certain leftwing positions.

Deshpande's *Passage to Darkness* (Andhar yatre, 1987) examines issues related to the Naxalite movement and also confronts feminist concerns. In *It's Past One O'Clock* (Ek vajoon gela ahe, 1983), a family gathering to celebrate the seventy-fifth birthday of a leftwing intellectual culminates in the surprise arrival of his politically radical son, who denounces the family for its lack of activism. *Chanakya Vishnugupta* (1988), a historical drama, focuses on the chief councillor of the fourth-century emperor Chandragupta in order to deal with issues of empire and the problem of the individual versus the state. Later plays include *Roads* (Raaste, 1994) and *Last Day* (Shevatcha dees, 1999).

Deshpande privileges dialogue and discussion over visual effects, believing that modern Indian theatre has denied the power of the word. On the other hand, he dismisses the widespread preoccupation of many dramatists of recent years with the "theatre of roots" movement, claiming that their interest in **folk theatre** for inspiration is shallow and sentimental. He also has attacked those directors who employ Brechtian theatre techniques on only the most superficial of levels.

Deshpande's many honors include the Maharashtra State Award (1977), best Indian-language playwright award (1997–1998), and the National Academy of Music, Dance, and Drama (Sangeet Natak Akademi) award (1996).

Shashikant Barhanpurkar

DESHPANDE, PURUSHOTTAM LAXMAN (1919–2000). Indian Marathi-language **playwright**, **stage** and film **actor** and **director**, singer, author, composer, **musician**, and philanthropist, born in Bombay (Mumbai), and popularly known as Pu. La. In the 1940s, he left teaching to act in musical and straight theatre; he also became a prolific writer of novels, short stories, essays, translations and adaptations, comic travelogues (based on his worldwide travels), and scripts for broadcasting (he studied television production in Britain), films, and theatre. Strong influences were the female impersonator **Bal Gandharva**, the playwright **Rabindranath Tagore**, and the British writer P. G. Wodehouse. He always considered himself a performer, even in his guise as a writer.

He wrote fourteen plays, the most famous and commercially successful being *Whatever Is Yours Belongs to You* (Tujhe ae tujapashi, 1957), a satirical piece contrasting a Gandhian ascetic with a pleasure-seeking lover of life. His other plays included *Now Tuka Says* (Tuka mhane ata, 1948), *Wanted, a Leader* (Pudhari pahije, 1951), and *Fortunate* (Bhagyavan, 1953), but most of his work was adaptations of **Western** dramas, ranging from Gogol's *The Inspector General* (1952) to Brecht's *Threepenny Opera* (1978). As an actor, he was renowned for his one-man display of versatility, *Low Cost Housing* (Batatyachi chaal, 1958), in which he presented multiple tenement dwellers.

Beloved for his compassionate humor about the vanishing urban lower-middle class, he was honored when Bombay's P. L. Deshpande Kala Academy was named for him. He received two honorary doctorates, held high cultural positions, and was given many prestigious awards, such as the Padma Bhushan, the Sahitya Akademi award (1965), and a National Academy of Music, **Dance**, and Drama (Sangeet Natak Akademi) fellowship.

Samuel L. Leiter

DEVI, RUKMANI (1923–1978).

Sri Lankan • **stage** and screen singer and **actress**, a.k.a. Daisy Daniels. Considered Sri Lanka's first film idol. Devi (not to be confused with **bharata natyam** • **dancer** Rukmani [or Rukmini] Devi Arundale [1904–1997]), was of Tamil ancestry. She was a pathbreaker, her success coming when Sri Lankan **women** suffered great restrictions in their personal and professional lives.

She began acting as a child. At twelve, she was noticed in Walter Rupasinhe's dramatization of the **Ramayana** (1935), which led to various professional engagements. Later, B. A. W. Jayamanne, head of Negombo's Minerva Dramatic Club (and later a major filmmaker), cast her in a series of his plays, one of which, *Broken Promise* (Kadavunu Poronduwa), became the first Sinhala film (1947), making Devi a star known as the "nightingale of Sri Lanka." It was during her work with Minerva that she met her future husband, popular actor-comedian Eddie Jayamanne (B. A. W. Jayamanne's brother), the "Charlie Chaplin of Ceylon."

Devi's greatest repute came from her singing, which she performed in Tamil, Sinhala, and English. E. R. Sarachchandra writes that she "brought refinement and modulation into her singing by virtue of a western **training**, and was able, at the same time to retain some eastern quality in her voice. [Her] singing was a welcome relief after the high-pitched nasal singing that characterized the Public Hall and Tower Hall stage." Her death in a highway crash was crushing news to her many devoted fans, who commemorated the twenty-fifth anniversary of her passing in 2003.

FURTHER READING

Sarachchandra, E. R. *The Folk Drama of Ceylon.*

Samuel L. Leiter

DIRECTORS AND DIRECTING

Directors and Directing: Bangladesh

Bangladesh's **theatre companies** are called "group theatres," after the popular Kolkata (Calcutta) model implying a definite image or identity associated, for each group, with a certain attitude evident in its choice of plays, a unique stylistic orientation, and, most important, a directorial presence. With most of these groups a single director has led the group for a long enough time to leave his personal artistic mark on it. Important directors who have come to be associated with the leading groups are Ataur Rahman (1941–) and Ali Zaker (1944–) with Citizen (Nagarik), Abdullah al Mamun (1942–) with Theatre, and Nasiruddin Yusuf (1950–) with the Dhaka Theatre. Younger directors, like S. M. Solomain (1954–), and Kamaluddin Nilu (1955–), also work with their own groups, each of them associated with specific directorial approaches.

Directorial work has remained confined to proscenium **theatres** and a limited concept of realism. Innovations are restricted to negotiation with the limitations of the available **stages**, which are scarce and dated. Rahman, who also is a **playwright** and **Rabindranath Tagore** scholar, and who has staged plays by Brecht and Beckett, as well as the works of Tagore and other Bengalis, struggled with the visual limitations of the performance space in his production of *Red Oleanders*, restricted to a couple of inadequate Dhaka auditoriums.

Zaker, best known for directing *The Life of Nuruldin* (Nuruldiner sarajiban, 1982), presented the story of the Rangpur revolt (1783) against British imperialism as a metaphor for a Bangladesh war of liberation. He **experimented** with the proscenium, seeking ways to widen its visual scope to capture the forests and the fields of Rangpur. He used the local dialects of Rangpur to give the work authenticity.

Al-Mamun, Solomain, and Nilu employ an approach conceived in terms of "total theater," a hallmark of which is a fusion of lighting, **music**, and sound. Difficulties of the performance space have often prompted them to look at spaces outside Dhaka.

The real breakthrough in terms of spatial experimentation can be attributed to Yusuf and his activity with Dhaka Theatre and the works of Selim al Din (1948–). Yusuf began working with the Dhaka Theatre in 1973, directing the **political** farce, *News Cartoon* (Sambad cartoon). While working on *Jaundice and the Colorful Balloon* (Jaundice o bibidha balloon, 1976) and the absurdist *Fantasy of Muntasi* (Muntasir fantasy), Yusuf realized the limitations of the space, particularly in the context of the need for a stronger indigenous subject and form. He resorted to agitprop plays, such as *Land Crabs* (Char kakra, 1977), depicting the postflood plight of the common people.

In moving out of theatre buildings, Yusuf and his group have organized fairground spectacles encompassing rural Bangladesh. Dhaka Theatre has also taken up a program known as Gram Theatre, which stages plays enacted by villagers in any available open place. As a director, Yusuf's engagement with rural idioms and the rural way of life is prominent. His direction of *Kirtan Performance* (Kittonkhola, 1980) deals extensively with village life and culture. It weaves a narrative of oppression and revolt into a depiction of daily rural life and performative culture, like poetry contests (*kabigan*), **folk** performances, and village theatre. His productions often take on the dimensions of a carnival, displaying spectacular teamwork and **scenography**, which breaks the proscenium's restrictions.

Bishnupriya Dutt

Directors and Directing: China

The director's role—a major source of **Western** influence on Chinese theatre—as the center of a coherent theatrical art did not exist until the 1920s when "spoken drama" (*huaju*) evolved from its predecessor, "civilized drama" (*wenming xi*). **Hong Shen** is generally credited as introducing the director with his 1924 *Young Mistress's Fan* (Shao nainai de shanzi), produced by the Shanghai Drama Society (Shanghai Xiju Xieshe). Since then, the director has gained authority over the **playwright** and **actor** as the interpreter of the script, enforcer of the rehearsal system, and coordinator of the theatre's multifarious creative intentions.

Early Directors. Early directors were essential in advancing *huaju*'s status to rival that of traditional *xiqu* in a series of landmark 1930s and 1940s productions. Apart from Hong Shen, **Ouyang Yuqian** directed, among others, the premiere of **Cao Yu**'s *Sunrise* (Richu, 1937). Ying Yunwei (1904–1967), an alumnus of the Shanghai Drama Society, was known for his 1933 staging of Tretyakov's Soviet play *Roar! China*, and wartime productions like Guo Moruo's (1892–1979) *Qu Yuan* (1942). Influential director Tang Huaiqiu (1898–1954) staged many plays, including Cao Yu's *Thunderstorm* (Leiyu, 1935), for his China Traveling Company (Zhongguo Lüxing Jutuan), *huaju*'s first professional **theatre company**. As a cotranslator of Stanislavski's *An Actor Prepares* (1939), Zhang Min (1906–1975) was among the first to adopt Stanislavski's System in his productions of *A Doll's House* (1934, 1935), *The Inspector-General* (1936), Ostrotrovsky's *The Thunderstorm* (1936), and *Romeo and Juliet* (1937).

A favorite student of Hong Shen, Zhu Duanjun (1907–1978) directed such landmarks as Hong Shen's *Wukui Bridge* (Wukuiqiao, 1933) and Yu Ling's (1907–1997) *Shanghai at Night* (Ye Shanghai, 1939). After 1949, he became a strong Stanislavski advocate, including his chairmanship of the actor **training** department at the Shanghai Theatre Academy.

Post-1949 Directors. After 1949, several European- and USSR-trained directors helped shape *huaju*'s landscape in the communist era. Among them, Sun Weishi (1921–1968) applied her Soviet training to a series of foreign productions, including *How the Steel Was Tempered* (1950), *The Inspector-General* (1952), *Uncle Vanya* (1954), and *The Servant of Two Masters* (1956). **Jiao Juyin**'s System-based approach earned him national acclaim in **Lao She**'s *Dragon Beard Ditch* (Longxugou, 1951) and *The Teahouse* (Chaguan, 1958), and Cao Yu's *The Bright Sky* (Minglang de tian, 1954). However, his experience as principal of a *jingju* school and his understanding of Stanislavski's **theories** regarding external technique encouraged him to extensively employ *xiqu* elements in subsequent productions, such as *The Tiger Tally* (Hufu, 1957), *Cai Wenji* (1959), and *Wu Zetian* (1962).

Huang Zuolin introduced Brecht's epic theatre in *Mother Courage* (1959) and *Galileo* (1979). Brecht's fascination with classical actor **Mei Lanfang** inspired Huang's **theory** of *xieyi* drama, which combined *xiqu* with *huaju*, as evidenced in his productions of *China Dream* (Zhongguo meng, 1987) and *The Alarm Clock* (Nao zhong, 1991).

Post-Mao Directors. Many new directors appeared and made great contributions to **experimental theatre** in the post–Mao Zedong (1893–1976) period. Among Shanghai directors, Su Leci (1945–), whose *In a Land of Silence* (Yu wu sheng chu, 1978) became the first high-profile post–Cultural Revolution (1966–1976) production, ventured into unprecedented spatial and temporal dimensions in *Hot Currents Outside the House* (Wu wai you reliu, 1980–1981) and *Blood Is Always Hot* (Xie zongshi re de, 1980–1981). After bringing existentialism to a soul-searching nation in Sartre's *Dirty Hands* (1979), Hu Weimin (1932–1989) sought to break the dominance of language by mixing it with **dance** and **music** in *Red Room, White Room, Black Room* (Hong fangjian, bai fangjian, hei fangjian, 1986).

Of major Beijing directors, **Lin Zhaohua** was known for staging **Gao Xingjian**'s early plays and **Xu Xiaozhong** for his 1988 *Sangshuping Chronicles* (Sangshuping jishi). Still, the influence of Stanislavski proved prominent in this generation of academy-trained directors. As an assistant to a USSR expert in the 1950s, Hu Weimin adhered to the System in most of his productions, including his *yueju* adaptation of *Twelfth Night* (1986), in which an orthodox interpretation of Shakespeare superseded the characteristics of the genre. Xu Xiaozhong, trained in the USSR in the 1950s, always insisted on the role of the System in actor training and character creation.

Recent Directors. The most prominent directors of recent decades are arguably such **experimental theatre** artists as Lin Zhaohua, Mou Sen (1963–), Meng Jinghui (1964–), and Li Liuyi (1961–). Often controversial and embraced only by a dedicated audience, their productions have effectively redefined some of the basic tenets of the Ibsenian-Stanislavskian tradition, which includes the supremacy of the script, the predominance of dialogue in plot and character development, the didactic character-audience relationship of the proscenium **stage**, and the division between *huaju* and *xiqu*. Through deconstruction and pastiche, they have challenged such canonical plays as *Hamlet* (1989, directed by Lin Zhaohua) and Cao Yu's *The Wilderness* (Yuanye, 2000, directed by Li Liuyi). Movement, improvisation, and seemingly random wordplay were privileged over structured dialogue in Mou Sen's *The Other Bank—A Chinese Grammatical Discussion* (Bi'an: guanyu bi'an de Hanyu yufa taolun, 1993) and Meng Jinghui's *I Love XXX* (Wo ai chachacha, 1994). Instead of the proscenium, they have relied on the black box and outdoor productions as exemplified in Meng Jinghui's *Lay Down Your Whip, Woyzeck* (Fangxia nide bianzi Woyicaike, 1995). No longer satisfied with merely borrowing *xiqu* elements, some of them have based their works on *xiqu* stories, employing *xiqu* actors and conventions, while superimposing them with modern interpretations and **stage** techniques, as in Li Liuyi's *Of Puppet and Man* (Ou ren ji, 2002) and *Hua Mulan* (2004).

Although most directors are resident with companies, many have directed *huaju* and *xiqu* for other theatres. In recent years, a few star directors have also worked with opera, film, and television, and have been invited to work abroad.

FURTHER READING

Evans, Anne Megan. "The Evolving Role of the Director in *Xiqu* Innovation."

Siyuan Liu

Directors and Directing: India

The director, in the modern sense, is a relatively new idea in **Indian** theatre. Even though India had a strong theatre practice and performance tradition, the concept of a director, who comprehensively conceives a production in all its components and holds equal importance with **playwrights** and **actors**, emerged only toward the middle of the twentieth century. His predecessor was the actor-manager, a nineteenth-century concept borrowed from the British and first made prominent in **Parsi theatre**. Leading Parsi examples were Agha Hashra Kashmiri and Narayan Prasad Betab, who served as directors, acting teachers, **scenographers**, **musical** arrangers, and so on. The most prominent director cum man-of-all-trades in late nineteenth-century Bengali theatre was **Girish Chandra Ghosh**, directing and acting in his own plays, while also serving as manager of two major **theatres**.

The Nationalist Movement. The director first came to attention during the nationalist movement, inspired by the need to modernize and define the Indian **stage**. In many cases, the director reflected a revolt against conventional styles of presentation then current, in keeping with a growing awareness of international theatrical developments.

New **theatre companies** emerging within a **political** ideology influenced by nationalist concerns contributed an objective and meaning to production, hitherto preoccupied essentially with commercial goals. This objective made it necessary for plays to express a particular interpretation. Productions sponsored by the communist-supported Indian People's Theatre Association (IPTA), begun in 1942–1943, adhered to a Marxist and anti-imperialist socio-political philosophy designed to help liberate the nation from colonial rule. ITPA directors sought to express an ideology aiming to make theatre assume a meaningful social function and go beyond being simply a form of entertainment.

Free "street theatre" advocating leftwing positions played an important role, especially in the work of **Shombhu Mitra, Utpal Dutt**, and, later, **Badal Sircar**, **M. K. Raina**, Gursharan Singh (1929–), and **Safdar Hashmi**. These presentations could be highly provocative; Hashmi, for example, was murdered by hoodlums during a performance outside a factory near Delhi. There have been circumstances, such as the 1984 poison gas incident at Bhopal, that led even mainstream directors to stage protest plays in the streets.

Rise of the Director. The Indian people began using the term "director" in theatre only in the 1930s and 1940s. It became widespread in the 1950s as a result of different organizations and groups that began to employ up-to-date production methods. It was further disseminated by ongoing workshops and productions carried out by the National School of Drama (NSD), the National Academy of Music, Dance, and Drama (Sangeet Natak Akademi), state academies, and other academic and **training** institutions. The 1930s had seen efforts to modernize Indian theatre by bringing together all components in order to create meaning in place of conventional declamatory methods. Theatre of a Changing Age (Natyamanwantar Ltd.), founded in Bombay (Mumbai) in 1933, made a revolutionary initiative with its staging of contemporary European intellectual drama, under director K. Narayan Kale. During its two years it was highly influential in abandoning the actor-manager system and demonstrating that actresses deserved a place on the modern stage; it also insisted on doing problem plays using realistic acting and scenography, a bare minimum of songs, the elimination of clowns, and artistic unification of production elements.

Subsequently, many groups and movements appeared in different regions. The NSD workshops of the 1960s created a serious awareness of the director and the production process; participants became theatre leaders throughout the nation. NSD graduates spread the seminal concept of the director through their work. As the 1960s ended, directors and directing became common, and audiences came to appreciate the director as a collaborator who works with other artists yet leaves his own mark. University theatre departments, initiated in the 1960s, also contributed, along with academies and other organizations. On the other hand, directing also had another, more controversial, face. Many directors used their position to cut and even mutilate scripts to conform to their vision, imposing their own idiosyncratic visual images exclusive of the dramatic values they should have been serving. Such directors saw their role as that of a visual artist whose job was to create startling pictures regardless of the impact on a play's integrity. Ultimately, however, such directors disappeared because audiences rejected their excesses and irrelevancies.

Leading Directors. Direction advanced by leaps and bounds in the hands of talented artists trained at home and abroad. The first was **Habib Tanvir**, who studied at London's Royal Academy of Dramatic Arts (RADA); his directing also involved activity with tribal cultures. He was followed by such greats as **Ebrahim Alkazi**, also trained at RADA, who inculcated the idea of a systematic approach to direction during his tenure as head of the NSD, and whose brilliant productions in Bombay and New Delhi of **Western** and **Sanskrit theatre** classics were major contributions that also benefited from his outstanding scenography.

Other prominent and innovative directors of this first generation of the 1950s and 1960s include **Sombhu Mitra**, Utpal Dutt, Shanti Vardhan (?–1954), **Shyamanand Jalan**, **P. L. Deshpande**, **Satyadev Dubey** (1936–), **Adya Rangacharya**, and so on. Although rare, female directors like **Shanta Gandhi** (1917–2002) and **Veejay Mehta** (1934–) also gained renown. Some directors broke with conventional ideas of space by mounting plays in unusual locations; Alkazi—influenced by the environmental theatre of Richard Schechner—preferred historical monuments, for example.

Theatre of Roots. They were followed by many who started to explore their own styles and **theories**. The 1960s also saw the emergence of the "theatre of roots" (*tanatu natakavedi*), which sparked a shift in the nature of directorial explorations. Directors working in its shade started to study and work with traditional performance culture in search of a new vocabulary. Badal Sircar, **B. V. Karanth**, **Kavalam Narayana Panikkar**, **Ratan Thiyam**, Bhanu Bharti (1946–), **Heisnam Kanhailal**, **S. Ramanujam**, Arun Mukherji (1937–), **Chandrashekhar Kambar**, and **Rudraprasad Sengupta** brought their own unique perspective to such work. Many directed classics from both East and West, often making attempts to blend traditional with modern methods. Panikkar, for example, tried to synthesize ancient and contemporary notions in his staging of Sanskrit plays.

University theatre education became relatively common from 1970s onward, generating improved understanding of directorial art and giving birth to many new directors.

Identifying Features. A number of leading directors are associated with a specific geographical place, company, or language, while others move around more, work with different groups, and direct in two or more Indian languages (and, in some cases, English as well). They may also direct plays indigenous to their own backgrounds, or translations from other Indian languages or from foreign sources. The great majority are also renowned playwrights (and/or translators), actors, designers, and/or managers; a good many also write about theatre **theory**, both in self-reflexive and more universal ways. And directors like Panikkar, Karanth, and Thiyam also compose music for their own and others' work, which has greatly advanced music's place and role in stylized productions.

Various kinds of directors are working in many Indian languages; they engage plays in every style, from classical and folk theatre to naturalism or avant-garde and/or politically pointed, and in venues ranging from proscenium playhouses to urban streetcorners, although the proscenium has gradually diminished in importance. Younger directors increasingly choose unconventional venues, allowing the play to shape the space, rather than the other way around. Most directors are identified with a specific approach that they themselves may have theorized about in print. By the end of the twentieth century, the director had been established as an independent artist equal or superior in prestige to the playwright and leading actor. *See also* Prasanna; Jabbar Patel; Usha Ganguli; Bensi Kaul; Anuradha Kapur; Ram Gopal Bajaj; Anamika Haksar; Mohan Maharishi.

FURTHER READING

Dharwadker, Aparna Bhargava. *Theatres of Independence: Drama, Theory, and Urban Performance in India since 1947*; Lal, Ananda. *The Oxford Companion to Indian Theatre*; Dalmia, Vasudha. *Poetics, Plays, and Performances: The Politics of Modern Indian Theatre.*

B. Ananthakrishnan

Directors and Directing: Indonesia

In contrast to **Western** theatre artists who specialize in one discipline, **Indonesian** directors are typically involved in several aspects of production, including **playwriting**, **acting**, and **scenography**. Two prominent artists who influenced the role of the director in contemporary Indonesian theatre are Teguh Karya (1937–2001) and Suyatna Anirun (1936–2002).

Teguh adapted plays by Brecht, Williams, Molière, Lorca, and Strindberg, which he directed for the Popular Theatre (Teater Populer) primarily during the 1970s and 1980s. He was later known for his film directing. Suyatna directed for the Bandung Theatre Study Club (Studiklub Teater Bandung), and was a well-regarded actor. Drawing on Western techniques combined with Indonesian traditional and popular forms, Teguh and Suyatna introduced an intercultural practice that influenced the artists that followed them.

Later artists combined the roles of director and playwright, often acting in their plays as well; most were affiliated with a specific **theatre company**. Indonesia's best-known playwright, **Rendra**, whose influential Workshop Theatre (Bengkel Teater) incorporates a cooperative approach to play development, continues to direct. **Nano Riantiarno,** founding director of Coma Theatre (Teater Koma), directs his own plays or adaptations of Western plays with Indonesian settings, characters, and themes. **Putu Wijaya**, founder of Independent Theatre (Teater Mandiri), is a respected director, actor, and playwright whose works blend movement, sound, and text with often disturbing imagery. Playwright and director **Arifin C. Noer** drew international attention for his work with Little Theatre (Teater Kecil).

Social and political restraints on **women**'s social roles have loosened since the collapse of the Suharto government (1998), leading to an increase in the number and visibility of women artists. Playwright-director **Ratna Sarumpaet** is the first woman to join directing's male-dominated ranks. She is the founding director of One Red **Stage** (Satu Merah Panngung) and often appears in her own work. Shinta Febriany, whose work subverts gender stereotypes, is a playwright, director, and performer with the Makassar-based group Red and White Studio (Sanggar Merah Putih). Lena Siman-juntak, who resides in Germany, formed a women's workers' theatre group in Sumatra in 2002 in order to create a piece from the real-life experiences of the members, thereby drawing attention to the plight of working women.

Several **experimental** directors have gained attention for collaborating with play-wrights on nonrealistic productions leaning heavily on traditional forms. These include Rachman Sabur (1957–) with Black Umbrella Theatre (Teater Payung Hitam, 1982), Yudi Ahmad Tajudin (1972–) with Garage Theatre (Teater Garasi, 1993) in Yogya-karta, and Wisran Hadi (1945–) with Earth Theatre (Teater Bumi, 1978) in Makassar, Sulawesi. Other directors include Asia Ramli Prapanca of Our Theatre (Teater Kita, 1993) also in Makassar, Jujuk Prabowo with Yogyakarta's Lightning Theatre (Teater Gandrik, 1983), Dindon W. S. with Grave Theatre (Teater Kubur, 1983) in West Sumatra, and Azuzan J. G. (1958–), founder of Teater S'Mas (1991) in Jakarta.

James Hesla

Directors and Directing: Japan

As elsewhere, **Japan**'s directors first appeared in the modern period. Most traditional genres, however, continue to resist a single interpretive guide, relying instead on previous performance history supplemented by innovations made by the head of an **acting** school or stars. Even in *shingeki* and **experimental theatre**, freelance directors are rare. Most directors lead their own **theatre companies**, often directing their own plays. Despite dis-tinctive styles, their creative impetus usually derives from their **playwriting** or acting methods. The **Western** "director-as-interpreter" rarely applies. Of those consistently pro-duced abroad, only **Ninagawa Yukio**, known for his lavish stagings of Shakespeare and ancient Greek theatre, fits this definition. He often envisions the plays in specifically Japa-nese terms, though with unaltered text, his style notable for stunning visual effects, including masses of falling cherry blossoms. His *kabuki*-flavored *Macbeth* (1980) featured huge sliding *shôji* doors creating a full-**stage** Buddhist altar/false proscenium, while his Cretan-*kabuki Medea* (1978) featured a male *shingeki* actor as Medea.

Unlike Ninagawa, **Suzuki Tadashi**, also internationally known, emphasizes actors over script or visual elements. Suzuki is more accurately termed an adaptor/director, rather than an interpreter, because he radically transforms, rewrites, or combines exist-ing scripts or well-known tales, including Shakespearean and Greek tragedies. Such creative recycling of well-known material corresponds to a common technique used by traditional and modern playwrights. Even Ninagawa, who seldom modifies text, could not resist rewriting **Terayama Shûji** and **Kishida Rio**'s 1978 *Shintokumaru: Poison Boy* (re-written for Ninagawa in 1995 with Kishida's cooperation).

Directing before **Shingeki.** During the last decades of the nineteenth century, *kabuki* actor **Ichikawa Danjûrô** IX and **theatre** manager **Morita Kanya** XII offered the first attempts at directorial interpretation. To modernize *kabuki*, they advocated historical verisimilitude in **costume**s and **scenography**, greater psychological realism, and eliminating various conventions of staging and **music**. In contrast, directors of translated or adapted Western plays sometimes attempted modernity by copying Western style without either grasping the underlying values of or having seen Western productions.

Both approaches were directorial because they attempted to reject traditional performance, interpreting historical events or pre-existing plays with new eyes. Nevertheless, their focus on perceived authenticity retained the traditional attitudes to time: rather than learning about an actual past or different society, they played with history or cultural difference to evoke an ideological concept of comfortable sameness, thus making their present world seem eternal and universal. This ideology (reflected in *kabuki*'s "worlds" [*sekai*] or *nô*'s constant reinvention of *The Tale of Genji*'s [Genji monogatari] characters) relates to contemporary Western "updaters" who attempt to make classics relevant. In contrast, some later directors, like **Senda Koreya**, influenced by Stanislavski, expressionism, and Brecht, emphasized difference or **politics**. The paucity of original material by post-Meiji-period (1868–1912) playwrights ensured reliance on foreign works. So the development of Japanese directing reflected the complex search for a modern national identity.

Varieties of Modern Directing. **Kawakami Otojirô**, **Tsubouchi Shôyô**, **Osanai Kaoru**, and **Hijikata Yoshi** defined early artistic and ideological differences. Kawakami, seeking to shove Japanese theatre into the twentieth century, established the new *shinpa* style, which drew from *kabuki* as well as Western realism; his sometimes naïve methods were epitomized in a production of *Hamlet* in which the hero rode a bicycle down the traditional runway (*hanamichi*). Tsubouchi, whose work represents another bridge between *kabuki* and the modern world (it led to ***shin kabuki***), venerated Western drama, whereas Osanai and Hijikata, pioneers of *shingeki*, emphasized acting and scenography. *Kabuki*'s anti-literary bent, denigrated by Tsubouchi as regressive, was precisely what Western modernists advocated. Consequently, Osanai and Hijikata's preferences, anchored in traditional Japanese practice and modern Western trends, dominated.

Nevertheless, since the 1960s, most contemporary plays have been either duplications of Western blockbusters (like **Asari Keita**'s productions of Broadway musicals) or new plays idiosyncratically directed by the authors themselves. For example, Terayama's style might be characterized as a nightmarish, sometimes comic fusion recalling Fellini, the Marquis de Sade, *The Cabinet of Dr. Caligari*, ***butô***, and comics (*manga*). Similarly, the directing styles of **Kara Jûrô**, **Ôta Shôgo**, or **Noda Hideki** are intimately tied to their respective playwriting strategies. Kara combines humanistic anger with surreal imagery; Ôta's signature works fused *nô*, modern **dance**, and the absurd; Noda in the 1980s combined commercialized vaudeville, circus, and high-tech theatrics. Matsumoto Yûkichi's (1946–) so-called "Jan-Jan Opera," large-scale outdoor performances using temporary actor-built sets and Osaka dialect chanted to music by Uchihashi Kazuhisa (1959–), has been likened to rap.

Others focus principally on the actors. Kushida Kazuyoshi (1942–), trained in the Actor's Theatre's (Haiyû-za) Stanislavski-inspired, psychological realism, is known for his actors' depicting fully rounded, complex characters. In his popular, jazz-infused staging of *Shanghai 'Vance King* (Shanhai bansu kingu, 1979), by **Saitô Ren**, the actors evoked vivid nostalgia for the prewar period. Later, inspired by Kara's attempt to rediscover early *kabuki*'s frenetic energy, Kushida, the *kabuki* actor now called

Nakamura Kanzaburô XVIII, and *kabuki* actor Nakamura Hashinosuke III (1965–) created Cocoon Kabuki, presenting traditional plays revitalized for contemporary audiences.

Kuriyama Tamiya (1953–) is a rare freelancer. Following an apprenticeship with Kimura Kôichi (1931–), Kuriyama studied in England and now directs Japanese and foreign plays and musicals in many genres. In 2000, he became theatrical art director for Tokyo's New National Theatre (Shinkokuritsu Gekijô). Not a playwright, Kimura directs exclusively for his own company, Earth-Man Group (Chijinkai). He emphasizes Inoue Hisashi's plays and Western translations. His directing style has been called "balanced," allowing plays to speak for themselves while presenting stunning visual effects.

Also noteworthy are "fusion" plays combining traditional and contemporary genres. Examples include *kabuki* actor-director **Ichikawa Ennosuke** III's "super" (*supaa*) *kabuki*, such as *Yamato Takeru* (1986) or *Amaterasu* (2005). *Kabuki* and *shingeki* actors together perform spectacular new works on traditional (often highly nationalistic) themes, elaborately designed, and featuring exciting, advanced technology. On a smaller scale, *kyôgen* master Nomura Mansaku (1931–) and his son, Nomura Mansai (1966–), create *kyôgen*-Shakespeare fusions, such as *The Braggart Samurai* (1991), based on *The Merry Wives of Windsor*. **Miyagi Satoshi** and his company Ku Na'uka often reinterpret Western classics. His *Medea* (1999), a post-colonialist/feminist critique of Japanese imperialism in Korea, derives performance elements from *bunraku*, *kabuki*, **folk** dance, and *shingeki*.

FURTHER READING

Allain, Paul. *The Art of Stillness: The Theater Practice of Tadashi Suzuki;* Jortner, David, Keiko McDonald, and Kevin J. Wetmore, Jr., eds. *Modern Japanese Theatre and Performance;* Sorgenfrei, Carol Fisher. *Unspeakable Acts: The Avant-Garde Theatre of Terayama Shûji and Postwar Japan.*

Carol Fisher Sorgenfrei

Directors and Directing: Korea

Since the 1960s, in accord with a world theatre postmodern trend, directors rather than **playwrights** have taken the leading role in **Korean** theatre. More important, the majority of Korean **theatre companies** have been created and operated by directors, many of them writing and directing their own plays. As many as one-fifth of the plays staged in Seoul in 2005 were written and directed by the same person.

Realism. Largely due to the influence of **Japanese-trained** directors, such as **Yu Chi-jin**, the predominant style has been realism, especially through the Japanese colonial period (1910–1945) on to 1961 and the onset of South Korean military rule. During that tumultuous period of rapid change, theatre was expected to provide education and enlightenment, and realism was considered the best tool for tackling contemporary socio-**political** subjects.

Leading realistic directors include **Lim Young-Woong**, Kwŏn O-il (1932–), Kang Yŏng-gŏl (1943–), Kim Ch'ŏl-lee (1953–), Shim Jae-ch'an (1953–), Yun Kwang-jin (1954–), and Lee Sang-u (1951–). Yun and Lee are known for comedy, while Lim

Young-Woong has been more widely influential. He was the first to popularize absurdist drama with his internationally known production of *Waiting for Godot* (1969), the first to make the themes of feminist plays a social phenomenon (1986), and the first to direct a **musical** in Korea (1966). Today, musical theatre has grown into big business, with productions of translated works from New York, London, or Berlin common. Yun Ho-jin (1948–) is the only successful director of original Korean musicals, attracting audiences with productions such as *The Last Empress* (1995).

Antirealistic Movement. The movement in the 1960s away from realistic staging was shaped by oppressive **censorship**, a growing interest in absurdism, and the emergence of small, communal theatre companies led by young college graduates who showed keen interest in contemporary European theatre. Above all, two American-trained directors—Yu Dŏk-hyŏng (1938–) and An Min-su (1940–)—were shocked and enthralled with productions transcending then-dominant psychological realism. Yu employed Korean martial arts, ritualistic movement, and chanting, even in realistic plays written by his dramatist father, **Yu Ch'i-jin**. An used an Artaudian style in adaptations of *Hamlet* and *King Lear*. Presently, Gi Guk-sŏ (1952–), Ch'ae Sŭng-hun (1955–), and Ch'oe Yong-hun (1963–) direct **experimental**/postmodern productions that continue on the paths set by Yu and An.

"Koreanness" in Modern Theatre. Dissatisfied with Western approaches, however, many directors have sought to establish a "Koreanness" in modern theatre by utilizing aspects of Korean traditional performing arts, such as ***gut***, *kkoktu kakshi* (see Puppet theatre), and ***t'alch'um*** to address contemporary subjects. Among them, **Hŏ Kyu** and **Oh T'ae-sŏk** are pioneers, reinterpreting Korean classical stories. Hŏ Kyu's student, **Sohn Jin-Chaek**, surpassed his mentor in achieving their common aim with an eclectic style and the creation of a uniquely Korean musical form, ***madangnori***. **Lee Yun-t'aek**, though influenced by Oh T'ae-sŏk, has been preoccupied with *gut* in directing his own plays, such as *O-gu* (1990), *The Dummy Bride* (Pabogakshi, 1993), and *A Problematic Man, Yonsan* (Munjejŏk ingan Yŏnsan, 1995).

Interculturalism. It was also in the 1960s that French-educated Kim Jŏng-ok (1932–) began directing intercultural productions, later combining texts such as Lorca's *Blood Wedding* with Korean traditional performance (1985), creating multinational productions using Shakespearean texts, including *King Lear* (1997), and staging a series of collectively created postmodern productions. Multicultural rather than intercultural, Yang Jŏng-ung (1968–) simultaneously employs the aesthetics of several Asian countries, such as Japan, **China**, **India**, and **Singapore**, as in *Macbeth* (2004).

Political Directors/Women Directors. For almost three decades under post-1961 military regimes, theatre became very political under the leadership of directors such as Kim Sŏk-man (1951–), Kim Myŏng-gon (1952–), and Im Jin-t'aek (1950–), in the form of epic, agitprop, and guerrilla theatre, respectively. Among the many other current directors, two independent **women** are most remarkable: **Han T'ae-suk** and Kim A-ra (1956–). Han is well known for her performance-oriented, multidisciplinary staging of *Lady Macbeth* (1998), in which she juxtaposed a woman **dancing** with a huge piece of ice accompanied by a live band of traditional percussion music to reveal Lady Macbeth's psychology. Kim is alone in mounting technology-oriented theatre, such as her *Hamlet Project* (1999), which played at her own rural outdoor **theatre** using, for example, screen images and construction machinery.

FURTHER READING

Kim, Yun-Cheol, and Miy-Ye Kim, eds. *Contemporary Korean Theatre: Playwrights, Directors, Stage-Designers.*

Yun-Cheol Kim

Directors and Directing: Malaysia

Malaysia's theatre community has produced a number of accomplished directors. Malay-language directors, in particular, tend to direct their own works. Malay directors are also often engaged in **playwriting** and performance. Many have pursued their work by means of an institutional affiliation, such as a teacher **training** college, a university, and Dewan Bahasa dan Pustaka, the national publishing agency. In addition, other government bodies have lent support, including the Ministry of Culture, Arts, and Tourism, and state offices of culture. The impressive National Theatre (a.k.a. Palace of Culture or Istana Budaya) has, since its first major production in 2000, provided a venue for talented directors, such as veteran artists Ahmad Yatim, Rahim Razali (1949–), and **Syed Alwi**.

Major Directors. The first individual to receive official recognition for his skill as both director and playwright is **Noordin Hassan**. Hassan is credited with breaking new ground in 1970 when he staged his innovative, antirealistic *'Tis Not the Tall Grass Blown by the Wind* (Bukan lalang ditiup angin). In so doing, he ushered in a new generation of **experimental** practitioners. Since then, Hassan has continued to stage pioneering works that incorporate a variety of techniques. Based on episodic structures, his **music**-dramas are a rich fusion of choral singing, chanting, poetry, **dance**, and proverbs. Traditional theatre, such as *boria*, popular in his state of Penang, and *bangsawan*, is readily apparent in his work. Hassan's settings are often symbolic and at times surrealistic. His works stimulate reflection but are also padded with comic relief. As both playwright and director, he conveys his ideals of a forward-looking society in which **religious** principles can play a positive role in promoting justice and social well-being. In the 1980s, he began to focus on creating an Islamic style of theatre, "theatre of faith" (*teater fitrah*). Through coordinated **scenography**, blocking patterns, chanting, and dialogue, he strives for a spiritual catharsis.

Syed Alwi has experimented with multimedia. Through the use of slides and human shadows projected on a large screen at the back or side of the **stage**, Syed comments on the play's live action. His productions are known for featuring multiethnic casts, and he has, on occasion, placed **women** in male roles.

Inspired by Syed, Hatta Azad Khan (1952–) also has employed multimedia. Drawn earlier in his career to absurdist theatre, Hatta later directed more realistic pieces. Johan Jaaffar (1953–) similarly embraced absurdism in his early work; later, he chose to adapt and direct literary works by well-established Malay writers. Zakaria Ariffin (1953–) directs works by other dramatists as well as his own. Ariffin typically works with a stable ensemble of performers and mounts technically impressive productions.

Mohamed Ghouse Nasuruddin (1943–), a professor of performing arts at Penang's Universiti Sains Malaysia, mainly directs his own plays within the university context, although two notable productions, *Livelihood* (Rezeki, 1992), a realistic play staged in proscenium style, and *Vague* (Kabur, 1995), an experimental piece, were sponsored by the Ministry of Culture, Arts, and Tourism in Kuala Lumpur. While on a Fulbright grant in the United States in 2003, he directed *The Tale of a Malay Princess* (Tengku puteri salasiah), a play he originally wrote and staged in honor of Malaysia's king and queen. The West Virginia at Parkersburg production, featuring a **storyteller** playing the *rebab*, was enacted in a traditional performance structure. Several plays that constitute his *Happening Series* were similarly staged in the round. The actors move in and out of their roles in full view of the audience: they assume their characters when they move into the acting area and leave them when they exit to sit at the periphery of the space. While some productions are shaped within the context of realistic proscenium theatre, in others Nasuruddin combines **Western** stagecraft and acting with elements from traditional Malay theatre, such as *wayang kulit* (see Puppet Theatre) and *mak yong*, to heighten their symbolic quality.

Krishen Jit worked in both Malay and English-language theatre. After co-founding the Five Arts Centre in 1983, he directed plays representing the complexities of life in Malaysia's **Indian** and **Chinese** communities, written by K. S. Maniam (1942–) and Leow Puay Tin (1957–), respectively. He then turned to innovative multiethnic and multilingual productions, such as *Work*, *Us*, *Scorpion Orchid*, *Skin Trilogy*, and *A Chance Encounter* (1999). He engaged in collaborative efforts with **Singaporean** as well as Malaysian theatre artists, sometimes codirecting productions.

Chin San Sooi, also a founding member of the Five Arts Centre, has directed English-language plays since the 1970s. He stages large-scale musical productions, incorporating, when appropriate, Chinese and **Japanese** techniques. He worked extensively with Leow Puay Tin on a popular solo piece, Stella Kon's (1944–) *Emily of Emerald Hill*. Chin San Sooi has also directed his own plays, including *Yap Ah Loy, The Play* (1985), *Lady White* (1989), and *Reunion* (1994).

Joe Hasham (1948–), originally from Australia, directs for the Actor's Studio, which he cofounded with his actress spouse, Faridah Merican (1939–). He has directed American, Australian, British, and Irish drama, and experimented with transposing settings to the Malaysian context.

While many directors are accustomed to staging their own plays, others choose to interpret works by others, including adaptations of Malaysian literature and international dramas, sometimes adapted to a Malaysian milieu. In staging plays by local playwrights, directors seem most eager to handle new material; there is also attention given to revivals of earlier works.

Nancy Nanney

Directors and Directing: Nepal

Nepal's first modern directors were high-ranking noblemen employed to provide **music**, **dance**, and diversions of great spectacle for royalty; today, directors continue to write, produce, and shape Nepal's theatre. Most contemporary directors began as "street theatre" (*saadak naatak*) **actors**, and, while some continue to create agitprop theatre on social and **political** themes, others address such themes in more aesthetic ways and have moved from the street to proscenium theatres.

Dumbar Shamsher Rana (1858–1922) is considered the first "modern" Nepali director. Trained in Calcutta (Kolkata) in 1893, Rana was appointed to the court of King Prithvi Bir bikram Shah Dev (1881–1911) and was the first to make performances available to commoners by moving them out of the royal court and into his own palatial dwellings. His grandson, Balakrisna Sama (1902–1982), born during a performance in his grandfather's home, acted in plays he wrote and directed. His relatively realistic style marked the beginning of Nepal's modern theatre, although he often had to cast men in **women**'s roles for productions outside the court, as his society still frowned on actresses.

The tradition of the director-writer continues today with Ashesh Malla (1950–), known as the "father" of Nepali street theatre, whose Representing Everyone (Sarawanam) **theatre company** rarely produces work by any other writer. Agitprop in style, Malla's early street theatre performances were politically oriented, aiming to bring about democracy. Malla continues to employ agitprop to highlight problems of the innocent victims caught in the crossfire between the royalist government and Maoist insurgents.

Carol Davis

Directors and Directing: Pakistan

The role of the **actor**-manager, as evolved from **Parsi theatre** and **folk theatre**, has perhaps been more significant in **Pakistan** than has the modern notion of the director. The actor-manager may often recruit popular actors and double as the **playwright**, providing a semblance of structure from which the actors improvise.

Three director-mentors came to prominence in Pakistan's early years. Rafi Peer (1898–1974) in his own plays emulated the Urdu poetic tradition, stressing elocution. Imtiaz Ali Taj (1900–1970) diverged from high-sounding rhetoric to explore the **musicality** of the spoken idiom. Safdar Mir (1922–1997), who had worked with the leftist Indian People's Theatre Association (IPTA), reflected the new trends of realism and social-**political** consciousness. The emphasis placed by these three luminaries on the spoken word through mannered speech was mirrored in the style of early directors like Khalid Saeed Butt (1934–), Zia Mohyuddin (or Moyeddin, 1933–), Kamal Ahmed Rizvi (1930–), Moshin Sherazi, Naeem Tahir (1937–), and Farookh Zamir. Translations and adaptations, predominantly of English drawing-room comedies, as directed by Shoaib Hashmi (1938–), C. M. Munir (1938–), and Samina Ahmed (1947–), illustrated a tendency toward realism. All of these directors worked mostly within proscenium **theatres**. Rehearsal periods lasting two to three months in the early post-Partition (1947) decades highlighted the director's emerging role.

Educated in the **Western** tradition and directing a broad range of plays in English are Farookh Nigar Aziz of the Alpha Players and Perin Cooper (1942–) of the Najmuddin Dramatic Society, Kinnaird College. IPTA veteran Ali Ahmed also borrowed from a broad range of European plays, creating politically tinged, radical adaptations.

Jamil Bismil (?–2005) is unusual in his mix of popular physical caricature and drawing-room comedy, as seen in *Full House* (1978). Yasmin Ismail (1950–2002), working on adaptations of plays by Imran Aslam (1951–), also mixed popular humor, song, and

Nadeem and Sajad Hashmi in Sarmad Sehbai's production of *Dark Room*, 1976. (Photo: Mohammed Nadir Shah; Courtesy of Sarmad Sehbai)

physical caricature. Sarmad Sehbai (1945–) furthered a visual **stage** language, often working with abstract **scenography**.

Restraints on the emerging political theatre of the 1980s led to directors like Madeeha Gauhar (1956–), Huma Safdar (1960–), Khalid Ahmed, and Salman Shahid (1952–), who abandoned the proscenium and took to the streets, often with circular formations inspired by folk traditions. Mohammed Waseem (1960–), who works with communities on social issues, has adapted Boal's "forum theatre," and frequently performs in nonproscenium spaces. Gauhar and Safdar have further incorporated folk **dance** and music into their plays, borrowing from a host of techniques for socially oriented ends. Shahid has directed a broad repertory, from street theatre to Urdu and Punjabi plays to English drawing-room comedies.

In recent years, the director's role has been increasingly diminished. Most commercial productions rehearse for less than a week, theatre wings set up by nongovernment agencies are often led by amateurs, and an emerging form (since 2000) in which amateurs perform tableaux against popular movie soundtracks suggests little directorial presence.

FURTHER READING

Afzal-Khan, Fawzia. *A Critical Stage: The Role of Secular Alternative Theatre in Pakistan.*

Claire Pamment

Directors and Directing: Philippines

There are three types of directors in the **Philippines: folk theatre** directors who pass on traditional ways of performing **religious** forms such as *sinakulo*; **playwright**-directors of early professional troupes; and modern directors, who received formal training.

Folk theatre directors are in overall charge of production. They **train** the **actors** in traditional styles, supervise the construction of scenery and **costumes**, coordinate with the community, and sometimes act as prompters. They are fueled by faith, and their work is sustained by the collective effort of the community.

Sarsuwela and *drama* directors stage their own plays and organize troupes. **Severino Reyes** directed *Not Wounded* (Walang Sugat, 1902) and *Philippines for the Filipinos* (Filipinas para los Filipinos, 1905), and organized the Grand Tagalog Sarsuwela Company (Gran Compañia de la Sarsuwela Tagala). Juan Abad (1872–1939) directed his plays *Long Live the Philippines* (Mabuhay ang Pilipinas!, 1900) and *Chains of Gold* (Ang tanikalang ginto, 1902), and later founded East Company (Compañia Silangan). Hermogenes Ilagan (1873–1943) wrote and directed *Country Maiden* (Dalagang bukid, 1917), and also founded both the Ilagan Sarsuwela Company (Compañia Sarsuwela Ilagan) and La Dicha.

Pioneering modern directors of the 1930s through the 1950s were Fr Henry Irwin (1892–1976), Jean Edades (1907–), Severino Montano (1915–1980), Wilfrido Ma Guerrero (1917–), Fr James Reuter (1916–), Lamberto Avellana, Daisy Avellana (1917–), Nick Agudo (1924–), and Sarah Joaquin (1909–). Subsequently, directors made their mark in association with a specific company or theatre type. Examples include Antonio Mabesa (1935–) for UP Theatre (Dulaang UP) and UP Playwrights' Theatre, Zenaida Amador (1933–) for the English plays of Repertory Philippines, Rolando Tinio for the Filipino translations of Filipino Theatre (Teatro Filipino), Cecile Guidote-Alvarez (1943–) for the Philippine Educational Theatre Association, **Behn Cervantes** for the **political** plays of UP Repertory Company, Amelia Lapeña (1930–) for the **puppet** plays of Conscious Theatre (Teatro Mulat), and Leo Rimando (1933–) for regional theatre in Southern Luzon.

Directors of importance from the 1970s through the 1990s include Anton Juan (1950–), Felix Padilla, Jr. (1950–), Ricardo Abad (1946–), Lino Brocka (1939–1991), Joel Lamangan (1954–), Soxy Topacio, Tony Espejo (1948–), Amiel Leonardia (1939–), Chris Millado (1961–), Nestor Horfilla (1955–), Steven Patrick Fernandez (1955–), Jose Estrella (1965–), Alex Cortez (1949–), Bart Guingona (1962–), Lito Casaje (1957–), Paul Morales, Dennis Marasigan (1962–), and Ogie Juliano (1961–).

Joi Barrios

Directors and Directing: Singapore

While the pan-Asian intercultural style of TheatreWorks' artistic director **Ong Keng Sen** is internationally associated with **Singapore**, a number of others have made significant contributions to directing on a more local basis. The untimely deaths of directors **Kuo Pao Kun**, Kuala Lumpur–based **Krishen Jit**, and William Teo (1957–2001) are still deeply felt.

Kuo, whose earliest work involved staging his own class-conscious dramas, directed many of his later plays with his **theatre company** The Theatre Practice. Jit served as mentor to numerous directors who later made a mark, among them Ong Keng Sen and Ivan Heng. Over a fourteen-year period, William Teo and the Asia-in-Theatre Research Center staged an impressive number of haunting and soulful productions, inspired by his encounters with the work of France's Ariane Mnouchkine and his deep and abiding pursuit of the sacred in theatre.

Among the most market-savvy directors are Ekachai Uekrongtham (1962–), whose Action Theatre has staged a number of commercially successful works, and American expatriate Tony Petito, who, along with former London-based director Steven Dexter, guided Singapore Repertory Theatre (SRT) into a prominent position with popular dramas and original **musicals**, such as *Sing to the Dawn* and *Forbidden City*. SRT also provided early directing opportunities for Ivan Heng and Glen Goei (1962–), **actors**

Kit Chan (center) as the Empress Dowager in Singapore Repertory Theatre's *Forbidden City*, a lavish musical forming part of the opening festival of the Esplanade-Theatres on the Bay, 2002. (Photo: Sealey Brandt; Courtesy of Singapore Repertory Theatre)

who met with initial success in London, but who now provide the direction for Wild Rice, a company that produces a mix of new and established works. Other influential directors are Toy Factory's Goh Boon Teck (1971–) and The Necessary **Stage**'s Alvin Tan (1963–).

FURTHER READING

Peterson, William. *Theater and the Politics of Culture in Contemporary Singapore.*

William Peterson

Directors and Directing: Sri Lanka

Sinhalese Theatre. Directing is not a full-time profession in **Sri Lanka**, which offers productions in Sinhalese, Tamil, and English. Although a few Sinhalese directors have concentrated only on theatre work—Somalatha Subasinghe (1936–) and Sugathapala De Silva (1928–2002) among them—most are unable to make a livelihood from directing. Some major directors have also been **playwrights** and/or **actors** and, more recently, have directed television soap operas (*tele-dramas*) and films, as for example, Asoka Handagama (1962–). In terms of styles, the 1970s onward saw **experimentation** with different forms. By the end of that decade, there was a high degree of innovation; the plays of this period influenced the approaches of the 1980s.

From Amateur to Commercial. Although directing has been almost entirely amateur and in the hands of actors whose principal source of income was in another profession, by the mid-1980s theatre in Sri Lanka began to gain commercial status and directing became semiprofessional. Simon Navagathegama's (1940–2005) Sinhalese drama *Subha and Yasa* (Subha saha Yasa, 1974) helped by becoming a box-office success. Sponsorship became available, and directors were able to find some support, even for serious theatre. This trend became more difficult to maintain from the late 1990s onward, however, as *tele-drama*s increasingly dominated the entertainment scene.

Because of theatre's limited opportunities to sustain long-term profits, many directors work with a core group of actors, while others in the cast change from production to production. Directors (like playwrights) tend to focus on one style, and crossover is rare. Despite their inability to make much money, directors enjoy a great deal of social prestige. Most supplement their income by working for television.

Tamil Theatre. Tamil theatre, like English theatre, has had a few directors who have produced and directed plays. Vithianadan (1921–1984) revived the traditional *kuttu* form during the 1960s, and one of his principal actors, Mauneguru, later became a producer and in 2004 revived *Ravaneshan*, originally produced by Vithianadan in 1963.

Kuzanthai M. Shanmugalingam (1931–) was a director-playwright. Most of his plays are written from a feminist point of view. Sumathy Sivamohan generally produces and directs her own plays, although she also has staged works by others.

English-Language Theatre. There have been several English-language directors who have experimented with genres and styles. Cambridge graduate E. F. C. Ludowyk (1906–1985) came to Ceylon in the mid-1930s and remained a professor of English at the University of Colombo and then the University of Ceylon until returning to England in 1956. He began by directing foreign plays adapted to local conditions, making a big splash with the still produced *He Came from Jaffna* (1934), which he adapted from Sidney Grundy's *A Pair of Spectacles*. His work in Sinhalese theatre was also significant, beginning with his successful staging of Gogol's *Marriage* (1933), co-adapted with E. R. Sarachchandra (1914–1996). He directed a vast number of plays—by O'Neill, Shaw, Pirandello, Brecht, Anouilh, and others—as head of the University of Ceylon Dramatic Society (a.k.a. DRAMSOC), where his first production was of the Quintero brothers' Spanish play *Where Women Rule* (1933), and his farewell show was Shaw's *Androcles and the Lion* (1956).

Afterward, only a handful of directors sustained the English theatre, among them Jerome De Silva (1951–), Jith Pieris, Feroze Kamardeen (1972–), Ruwanthi de Chickera (1975–), and Tracy Holsinger (1973–). Many also founded their own groups.

De Silva founded the Workshop Players, and has been instrumental in taking the English-language theatre in a new direction. His stagings of Broadway musicals, such as *Cats* (1981, 1994), *Les Miserables* (1996, 1997), and *The Lion King* (1999, 2000), are the longest running English productions so far. He broke into the Sinhalese theatre in 2003 with an adaptation of Ariel Dorfman's *Widows*, translated as *Not Coming Again* (Aayeth enne naha).

Jith Pieris directed several very popular comedies and satires, such as *Well Mudliya How?* and Ludowyk's *He Came from Jaffna*. Feroze Kamardeen, founder of **Stage**, Light, and Magic, has staged musicals and serious theatre, including *Macbeth* (1996) and *Julius Caesar* (1997), Dorfman's *Widows* (1998), and *R&J* (2004), a musical version of *Romeo and Juliet*.

Ruwanthi de Chickera formed the Stages Theatre Group. Her plays, such as *Middle of Silence* (1997) and *Two Times Two is Two* (1998), have won international awards.

Tracy Holsinger, who formed Mind Adventures in 1999, has also directed several important plays, including Dorfman's *Death and the Maiden* (2000) and *Ubu Rex* (2002).

Neluka Silva (K. Sivathamby assisted with the Tamil material)

Directors and Directing: Thailand

Generally, contemporary **Thai** directors are scholars who receive their graduate **training** overseas, or they are artists who learn from experience, mostly as **actors**, and later form their own **theatre companies**.

On campus, the directing work of *lakon phut samai mhai* ("modern spoken theatre") pioneers **Sodsai Pantoomkomol** and **Mattani Mojdara Rutnin** has paved the way for younger generations. Nopamat Veohong (1950–) has staged her translations of Strindberg's *A Dream Play* (1972) and Sophocles' *Oedipus Rex* (1986). Pannasak Sukhee (1966–) is acclaimed for directing Shaffer's *Equus* (1996) and Kander and Ebb's *Cabaret* (2002), while Dangkamon Na-pombejra (1970–) gained recognition for Wedekind's *Spring's Awakening* (2002) and *Nitra Chakrit* (2003), a musical adaptation of a poetic drama by King Chulalongkorn (Rama V: r. 1868–1910) derived from *1001 Arabian Nights*.

Off campus, Janaprakal Chandruang (1954–), of the New Heritage (Moradok Mhai) troupe, is the most productive. An actor and translator who both adapts **Western** plays into Thai contexts and *lakon nok* and *lakon nai* into Western formats, his **experimental** work includes *Likay [liké]: Faust* (2002), Thailand's sole representative that year in Bangkok's International **Festival** of **Music** and **Dance**. Prolific female directors are Patravadi **Theatre**'s **Patravadi Mejudhon** and Dream Box's Suwandee Jakravoravudh (1961–), who directs most of **Daraka Wongsiri**'s plays and musicals and is noted for her well-paced comedies.

Other noteworthy directors include Crescent Moon Theatre's (Prachan Siew Karn Lakon) Kamron Gunatilaka and Nimit Pipithkul, Theatre 28's **Rassami Paoluengtong** and Euthana Mukdasanit, Grassroots Micromedia Project's (Makhampom) Pradit Prasartthong, Theatre 8×8's Nikorn Tang, B-Floor Theatre's Teerawat Mulvilai, Dream Masks' Ninart Boonpothong and Cherdsak Prathumsreesakhorn, Sao Soong's Nat Nualphang, and Damkerng Thitapiyasak, who has directed for many companies over the past two decades.

Pawit Mahasarinand

Directors and Directing: Vietnam

The concept of a director is not indigenous to **Vietnam** but was introduced with "spoken drama" (*kich noi*) during the late colonial period. **Playwright**-producers like Nguyen The Lu (1907–1989) developed a disciplined style under amateur directors and with trained **actors**. Between 1954 and 1975, directing became professionalized, strengthened by exchanges with the Eastern bloc and **China**. Key artists brought influences, like Stanislavskian acting, socialist realism, and Brecht. Pioneers of "the first golden generation of modern Vietnamese theatre" included Dr. Nguyen Dinh Nghi

(1928–2001) and Prof. Dinh Quang (1928–), who combined *cheo*, French influence, and Marxism in creating new work. Their collective impact between 1945 and 1975 was extraordinary, though limited thematically because the plays were dedicated to issues of achieving independence.

After reunification (1975), similar reforms were extended to traditional genres like *cheo, tuong,* and *cai luong* to unify presentations; still, some critics feel these innovations ultimately weakened those forms. Because theatre colleges catered to actors, not dramatists or directors, innovative scripts and provocative directors were few.

The major directors of post–*doi moi* ("change and newness," that is, economic reform and renovation) Vietnam (a.k.a. "the second golden generation") include *kich noi* directors Pham Thi Thanh (1941–), cofounder of Hanoi's innovative Youth Theatre (Nha Hat Tuoi Tre), and internationally trained Doan Hoang Giang (1936–), director of over three hundred productions of *cheo, cai luong,* and *kich noi*, and author of more than fifty plays. Nguyen Thi Minh Ngoc (1953–), probably the most prolific (and controversial) director-playwright-actor in the south, works closely with director Hoa Ha (1959–); although both **women** work primarily with *kich noi* **theatre companies**, their *cai luong* **training** is evident as well. In traditional theatre, Vu Thuy Ten is the first female artistic director of a *tuong* troupe.

Lorelle Browning and Kathy Foley

DJA, DEVI (1914–1989). Javanese-born *tonil* • **actress**, **dancer**, and choreographer (see Indonesia). She performed East Javanese **folk** dance and song from childhood. When she was about ten, Dja joined a small-scale **komedi stambul** company, performing **Malay**, Dutch, and Javanese songs as interludes between play acts. Dja was discovered in 1927 by A. Piëdro, owner of the **theatre company** Dardanella. Piëdro married her and groomed "Miss Dja" as a star. Dja initially played child and ingénue roles and performed song-and-dance routines between scenes. Her breakthrough was in **Andjar Asmara**'s *Dr. Samsi* (1930), in which she played, in various stages of her life, a woman accused of murder.

As Dardanella toured Southeast Asia, Dja studied ethnic dances with locals and choreographed them for the **stage**. She studied Balinese dance in Bali with dancers returned from the 1931 Exposition Coloniale Internationale and styled herself Devi Dja. While in **India** during a world tour in 1934, Dardanella split: half returned to Indonesia, while Piëdro and Dja refashioned the remainder into Devi Dja's Bali and Java Dancers, and toured Europe. The company fled to the United States before the Nazi onslaught, settled in Chicago, and established a theme nightclub, the Sarong Club.

Piëdro and Dja divorced, and Dja settled in Los Angeles, where she acted in films, toured with her own company, and taught traditional dance at Ruth St. Denis's dance school. A 1959 comeback attempt in Indonesia failed, but Dja played a major role in popularizing Indonesian performance in the United States until her death.

FURTHER READING

Merrin, Leona Mayer. *Devi Dja: Woman of Java.*

Matthew Isaac Cohen

DODDATA. **Indian** form of north and northeast Karnataka, a.k.a. *mudalapaya* and *bayalata*. *Doddata*'s name (literally, "big play") distinguishes it from another regional form, *sannata* ("small play"). *Doddata* generally takes place at night outside at a temple, a home, or near major crossroads. The electrically lighted, raised wooden **stage** is sometimes three-storied.

Scripts are mainly inspired by the **Mahabharata**, **Ramayana**, and *Jaimini Bharata* (a later version of the *Mahabharata*). The **director**, backed by a small chorus, sings all songs in south Indian *raga*s, in south Indian style for male characters and north Indian style for females, accompanied, respectively, by a barrel-shaped drum (*maddale*) and the *tabla-dagga* percussion combination. The singer/director and chorus keep rhythm with small metal cymbals (*tala*). Other **musical** instruments often include harmonium, violin, and reeds (*mukhavine* or *shahanai*). The dialogue is prose and rhyming poetry and combines **Sanskritized** Kannada, old Kannada, modern Kannada, and colloquialisms.

Costumes and **makeup** are mostly specific not to individual characters but to **role types**: noble male, female, comic, and evil. Males wear headdresses, flowing capes, epaulets, and ornaments and carry weapons. Females wear silk saris and jewelry. *Doddata* was an all-male form until the early twentieth century, when **women** began appearing. Basic makeup is light pink. Rama and Krishna wear blue. Comic and demonic characters create their own makeup and costumes.

Dances—male, extremely vigorous; female, graceful—are named for the number of different steps they include, (for example, five-step dance) and are inspired by agricultural harvesting activities. The clown, confidant of the hero and sometimes director, entertains using colloquial and racy language regarding contemporary situations.

FURTHER READING

Gargi, Balwant. *Folk Theater of India*; Naikar, Basavaraj S. *The Folk-Theatre of North-Karnataka*.

Martha Ashton-Sikora

DRAMA. A **Philippines** play with everyday Filipino characters, introduced from Spain in the nineteenth century. Themes generally revolve around love of country, love of family, issues like gambling, adultery, morality, language, colonial mentality, labor, and **politics**. Scripts, containing from one to three acts, are in verse or prose. The dialogue is delivered in a stylized, often sing-song, manner.

Drama has three subtypes: allegory (*drama simboliko*), tragedy (*drama tragico* or *melodrama*), and comedy (*drama comico*). *Drama simboliko* exposes and attacks the American colonization of the islands (ca. 1900–1946). It uses symbol and allegory in order to mask its anti-American messages. An example is **Aurelio V. Tolentino**'s *Yesterday, Today, and Tomorrow* (Kahapon, ngayon, at bukas, 1903).

Drama tragico seeks to elicit sympathy for the tragic fate of its characters. It dominated the Manila **stage**, and elsewhere, from 1910 to 1940, first, because **playwrights** began to shift from anti-American topics to social manners and foibles, and second, because many Filipinos, especially urban dwellers, had begun to accept the American set-up. A good example is Cirio Panganiban's *Veronidia* (1919).

Drama comico tickles the audience with its plot's hilarious twists and turns, often using mistaken identities. Examples include Tomas Remigio's *People as Saints* (Mga santong tao, 1901) and Julian Cruz Balmaseda's *Who Are You?* (Sino ba kayo?, 1940).

Other subtypes are the historical drama and the social drama. The former utilizes scenes from Philippine history as a backdrop for its love story. The social drama comments on current issues in Philippine society.

FURTHER READING

Tiongson, Nicanor G. *Dulaan: An Essay on Philippine Theater.*

Jerry Respeto

DRAMA GONG. Balinese (see Indonesia) **dance**-theatre combining comic banter, didactic monologues, and slapstick comedy to the accompaniment of Javanese *gamelan* **music**. Loosely based around classical comic characters from older genres, including *arja*, its **actors** excel in their exaggerations of appearance and expression, but downplay the characteristic dance movements of their traditional forebears. The acting, bordering on the melodramatic, uses dialogue improvised around a scenario, although plays recently have been transcribed; atmosphere is evoked through singing. Dance is used selectively for scenes involving nymphs, giants, and demons. Company collaboration replaces the need for a **director**. Stories derive from classical and made-up sources. *Drama gong*, presented before a temple, includes ritual preliminaries. Performances run from 9 p.m. to 4 a.m.

Drama gong was created in 1966 by a former student of the Konservatori Karawitan (KOKAR) and named by a KOKAR lecturer to signify a syncretistic fusion of classical Balinese and modern Euro-American art. "*Gong*" is synoptic of the *gamelan* tradition, while "*drama*" connotes **Western**-style realistic plays. One of its main influences—reflected, among other things, in **scenography** using painted backdrops, lighting, and amplification—was the popular *komedi stambul*. While it started off in an academic environment with a traditionalist flavor associated with the ideological values of Suharto's (1921–) New Order (1966–1998), *drama gong* quickly became a profoundly popular grassroots genre. It was performed through the 1980s primarily by village groups in local venues, but subsequently "all-star" groups developed. *Drama gong* is today regularly staged at Denpasar's Bali Arts Centre and broadcast on the private BaliTV station.

FURTHER READING

Yousof, Ghulam Sarwar. *Dictionary of Traditional South-East Asian Theatre.*

Laura Noszlopy

DRAMA MODEN. *See* Brunei; Malaysia; *Sandiwara.*

DRAMA SEBABAK. *See* Brunei.

DRAMATIC STRUCTURE

Dramatic Structure: China

Early **Chinese** dramatic structure is believed to have its roots in shamanic **religious** séances consisting of three parts: a slow invocation wooing the spirits to attend, a central session of communication with them, and a dispersal section in a more rapid tempo urging them to depart. A sophisticated version of this structure developed for the dramatic song and **dance** form *daqu* (literally, "big/great song") of the Sui (581–618) and Tang (618–907) dynasties; it began with a "diverse/unmetered sequence" comprised of unmetered instrumental **music**, followed by a "central sequence" or "beat/metered sequence" featuring ten or more songs and possibly dance as well, and concluded with a final "break/cut" section featuring dance and music at a rapid tempo.

Strongly influenced by *daqu*, the comic *zaju* of the Song (960–1279) and closely related *yuanben* of the Jin (1115–1234) and Yuan (1280–1368) were often performed as the central piece in another version of this three-part structure, the first and last sections consisting of music, dance, and/or a one-person comic act. The *sanyue* (literally, "diverse music/entertainment"), originating in Central Asian drum music, closely resembled Song *zaju* and partially merged with it. These forms may have been among the sources of **Japan**'s *sangaku* and the *jo-ha-kyû* rhythmic structure of *nô*.

During the tenth through thirteenth centuries, with the rise of fully synthesized *xiqu*, two different forms developed, both incorporating the fundamental three-part structure within their basic units. Most Yuan *zaju* consisted of four acts (*zhe*, literally, "break/snap") and a "wedge" (*xiezi*). The latter was often a short introductory scene involving secondary characters, but could also include major characters and/or serve as a transition between acts. Each act was an independent unit, featuring one singer, musical mode, and rhyme scheme, with the wedge generally following the patterns of the ensuing act.

As analyzed by Ming dynasty (1368–1644) scholars, **nanxi** plays comprised multiple scenes (*chu*) and a prologue (*jiamen*). The prologue, usually delivered by the **actor** who would later play the leading male **role type,** did not involve characters in the play but was rather a statement of the **playwright**'s intentions and a plot description designed to arouse audience interest. The scenes functioned as compositional units musically, but could involve multiple singers and changes in rhyme scheme.

Ming **chuanqi** plays, which were so important to **kunqu**, were structurally similar to their ancestor *nanxi*, but generally longer, involving forty to fifty or more scenes and requiring one or more full days to perform completely. As a result, major scenes or groups of scenes portraying a coherent episode and involving compelling song and/or other skills were often excerpted and performed as "[one] act plays" (*zhezi xi*). This was also followed in many regional theatre forms that arose during Ming and Qing (1644–1911), including *jingju*. In these, multiscene structure was generally followed for a full play, with one or more scenes standing alone as *zhezi xi* and transitional scenes connecting them. Earlier structural conventions facilitated the *zhezi xi* practice, most important the delivery of a self-introduction by each major character at first entrance, and one or more recapitulations, usually delivered by supporting characters, in later acts or scenes.

Plays created since the early twentieth century are generally tighter in structure, with fewer, shorter transition scenes; many dispense with most or all of these plot-oriented structural conventions.

FURTHER READING

Wells, H. W. *The Classical Drama in the Orient.*

Elizabeth Wichmann-Walczak

Dramatic Structure: India

In **India**'s **Sanskrit theatre**, the composition of plays was guided by a complex set of rules governing plot and act structure, and the presentation of **role types**. These rules were codified (in the middle of the first millennium AD) in the encyclopedic *Treatise on Drama* (Natyashastra; see Theory), which classifies plays into ten types, ranging from one-act farces to full-fledged (seven- to ten-act) heroic dramas. Each play opens with a prologue in which the **director** (*sutradhara*) and an **actor** or actress discuss the play to be presented, the **playwright**'s skill, and, often, his patron's munificence. Each act of a multiact play likewise has a prologue, usually delivered by one or more minor characters, in which events occurring between the former and current acts are described.

The plot construction rules are noteworthy because they impose a very restricted notion of what constitutes a drama's proper action. Five stages of narrative development are prescribed, beginning with the hero (*nayaka*) undertaking to pursue a specific result (*phala*), and necessarily culminating with the attainment (*prapti*) of this goal; in a well-constructed plot, the hero must ultimately prove successful. It is further prescribed that the action should unfold through a procession of five junctures (*sandhis*) subdivided into sixty-four subjunctures (*sandhi-angas*). Judging from extant dramas, it appears that these elaborate rules were, with rare exceptions, followed faithfully.

In adapting stories drawn from the Sanskrit epics, playwrights typically truncated or altered their source narratives so as to produce a plot in which the hero attains his goal after passing through the prescribed stages. This effectively precluded the portrayal of anything like "tragedy"; it was required that all plays should have a "happy ending."

In addition to these strict limits on plot, further structure restrictions abound. There are detailed instructions for the portrayal of various character types, governing **costume**, gesture, manner of speaking, and even language: all "Sanskrit" dramas are in fact multilingual. While kings and other high status male characters speak Sanskrit, **women** and men of lower status speak one of several regional dialects of the related Prakrit language. Apart from these linguistically coded gradations of social status, heroes are classified on the basis of emotional disposition (playful, noble, fierce, or calm); heroines and secondary characters are similarly divided into subclasses on the basis of physical, social, and emotional characteristics.

FURTHER READING

Wells, Henry W. *The Classical Drama of India: Studies in Its Value for the Literature and Theatre of the World.*

Lawrence McCrea

Dramatic Structure: Indonesia

Traditional **Indonesian** theatres often strive to balance discourse on statesmanship and ethics, humor and clowning, choreographed battles, and extra-narrative displays of **dance**, **music**, and special effects. In many genres, narratives concern noble and virtuous heroes who by chance or design must leave the order and stability of the royal court (or natal village) and venture into the chaos of the wilderness to gain their fortune or right a wrong. They are often accompanied by comic sidekicks, whose pastoral antics counterpoint the principals' high morals. Audiences selectively attend elements of interest, and might slip out for a bite or go to sleep during less appealing parts. Some genres, such as *randai*, are loosely episodic; others, such as classical *wayang* (see Puppet Theatre) in Central Java, are highly uniform in structure. Performances are often preceded by musical overtures and begin and end with ritual incantations addressing local spirits and divine forces (see Religion in Theatre).

Surakarta's *wayang kulit* provides a prime example of dramatic structure, with great conformity in nearly all plays (*lakhon*, *lampahan*). Performances begin at 7:30 p.m. with a musical overture and a preshow battle demonstration by a junior puppeteer. At 9 p.m., the *gamelan* plays music in the mode of *pathet nem* as the main puppeteer ceremoniously removes the spade-shaped "tree of life" (*kayon*) puppet from the screen's center, recites incantations for the performance's success, and sets up puppets for the first scene, usually set in a royal court. A long narration describing the kingdom is followed by an equally long dialogue between the king and his men. After the king retires to his chambers, two comical maidservants provide laughs, song, and dance. The king's army gathers in the courtyard outside the palace and departs in chariots and on horses. The next scene is often set in an overseas kingdom, which decides to invade Java. This invasion is routed in an "inconclusive battle." Around 1 a.m., the music changes to *pathet sanga*. Clown servants (*punakawan*) exchange comic banter and their employer, a refined "knight" (*kesatriya*), dispatches a gang of forest ogres in the "flower battle" (*perang kembang*). In the third part of the play (*pathet manyura*), starting after 3 a.m., the plot unfolds quickly through dialogue and battle. Villains are defeated and unmasked, the status quo restored. The audience dissipates as the play concludes with a victory dance, formulaic wishes for peace, the restoration of the *kayon* to center **stage**, and a final musical piece ending around 5 a.m.

Matthew Isaac Cohen

Dramatic Structure: Japan

Nô *and* Kyôgen. *Nô* plays are usually divided into two scenes (*ba*). In the kind of play called "dream" (*mugen*) *nô*, the principal **actor** (*shite*; see Role Types) appears incognito in the first *ba* and through interchange with the secondary character (*waki*) is led to the point of revealing his or her true identity. In the second *ba*, the *shite* tells and **dances** the story of primary significance in his life, frequently in order to find peace from spiritual torment. Between the two *ba*, an "interlude" (*ai-kyôgen*) serves two functions: it allows the *shite*'s story to be told clearly in colloquial language (as opposed to the poetry in which the *shite*'s lines are delivered), and it gives the *shite* time to change **costume** and **mask** offstage in preparation for the second *ba*.

The structural units of each *ba* are its five sections (*dan*), and within these are the "small *dan*" (*shodan*). *Shodan* are categorized by the way in which text corresponds with rhythmic beats, and are named for their function. For example, the "name announcing" (*nanori*) is the passage in which a character introduces himself, and the "travel section" (*michiyuki*) is when a character describes his journey to the play's locale. *Dan* and *shodan* are the building blocks, offering a formula of ordered units that gave **playwrights** and audiences a recognizable blueprint.

Nô came to be organized in a set program order according to the nature of the *shite*; for example, when the *shite* is a deity, it is a "god" (*kami*) *nô*. A five-play sequence developed as (according to one set of terms) "god" (*kami*), "warrior" (*shura*), "woman" (*onna*), "miscellaneous" (*zatsu*), and "concluding" (*kiri*), arranged according to the pacing principle of *jo-ha-kyû* (literally, "beginning-break-fast," that is, "introduction-development-conclusion"). According to one system, god plays came first for their congratulatory and stately nature and were considered the program's *jo*. Warrior, woman, and miscellaneous *nô* comprised the *ha* part, and demon plays ended the program with their quickened pace as the *kyû* portion. The five *dan* of each *ba* were also arranged according to this principle, as were the smaller units.

Kyôgen are one-scene plays originally improvised according to scenarios and written down only in the Edo period (1603–1868). Structure varies with the kind of play. As one example, during the short beginning of "minor feudal lord plays" (*shômyô kyôgen*) a master gives instructions to his servants before leaving on a journey. Then follows a relatively long section in which the two servants disobey the master, with potentially disastrous consequences. In a final short section, the master returns, and the main servant outwits him and gets away with the trouble he has caused. *Jo-ha-kyû* is clearly significant in structuring these plays.

In conventional practice, *nô* and *kyôgen* alternate on the same program. Premodern programs contained up to five *nô* and four *kyôgen*, all of them preceded by the congratulatory *Okina*. *Nô* and *kyôgen* were combined according to similarity or contrast in theme, mood, or philosophical orientation. A program thus offered variety in content, feeling, and tempo.

Bunraku *and* Kabuki. Structurally—and thematically—there are two kinds of *bunraku* plays (see Puppet Theatre), "history plays" (*jidai mono*) and "domestic plays" (*sewa mono*). The former are concerned with the samurai class and are generally structured into five acts. Many *sewa mono* are one-act, three-scene plays focusing primarily on the merchant class, and were originally performed between two acts of a *jidai mono*. In some cases, mainly in Edo (Tokyo), a connection existed between the characters of the *sewa mono* and the *jidai mono*, and in some cases, principally in Kamigata (Osaka/Kyoto region), the *sewa mono* was completely independent.

Both types progress according to the same *jo-ha-kyû* principle found in *nô*, both in their overall structure and within each act or scene. For example, the first act of the *jidai mono* is the introductory *jo*, the next three acts are the developmental *ha*, and the fifth act is the *kyû* finale. In terms of content, the first act introduces the characters and complications. Conflict and villainy develop over the next three acts. The third act, in particular, is often a highpoint in heart-wrenching events, typically requiring a major sacrifice on the part of important characters in order that an impossible situation might be resolved so that order can be restored by act five.

Aside from *jo-ha-kyû*, particular acts can be expected to offer certain material, for example, a "travel scene" (*michiyuki*) in the fourth act of a *jidai mono* or a *michiyuki* performed by lovers in the third scene of the *sewa mono*, with the action culminating in double suicide (*shinjû*). As with *nô*, variety was important in preparing a program that would usually take the better part of a day.

A large number of **kabuki** plays were borrowed from *bunraku* or were created out of the constant interplay between the two forms. Thus they share the three-scene *sewa mono* and the five-act *jidai mono* structures. A day-long *kabuki* program had a two-part structure, part one (*ichibanme*) consisting of the *jidai mono*, and part two (*nibanme*), the *sewa mono*. From the early eighteenth century in Edo, related play material and one title united the two parts. However, when Osaka playwright **Namiki Gohei** I moved to Edo in 1794, he effected a clear division of the two parts of the day's program, according to the Kamigata custom.

Kabuki also developed a third type, dance-plays (*shosagoto* or *buyô geki*). In *shosagoto*, stories are told primarily through dance; in some, the audience is concerned less with plot and more with the display of dance. Structure is offered through the progression of dance movements. *Jo-ha-kyû* offered its pacing to give these dance-stories their dramatic excitement.

Bimonthly productions, beginning with the season opening "face-showing" (*kaomise*) production in the eleventh month, lasted from a standard forty-two to as many as 150 days, depending on the show's popularity. The most important productions were the *kaomise* (especially in Edo), the New Year's production (especially in Kamigata), and the final ninth-month production. In Edo, the third-month and fifth-month productions also took on special significance once they became associated with particular subject matter.

In both *bunraku* and *kabuki*, a system of "group authorship" (*gassaku*) developed in the eighteenth century. Playwrights were assigned scenes according to rank, with more important sections (for example, scenes from the third act of the *jidai mono*) given to higher-ranked, more skilled writers. The varying writing quality led to differing degrees of attention given by audiences to different parts of a play and to the common occurrence of revivals of favorite individual acts or scenes apart from their complete play. The internalization of stable structure allowed for these practices.

FURTHER READING

Komparu, Kunio. *The Noh Theatre: Principles and Perspectives;* Leiter, Samuel L. *New Kabuki Encyclopedia: A Revised Adaptation of Kabuki Jiten;* Tamba, Akira. *The Musical Structure of Noh*; Yokomichi, Mario. *The Life Structure of Noh.*

Katherine Saltzman-Li

Dramatic Structure: Korea

Korean dramatic structure is discussed within a context of chronology; plays are classified as traditional, new, or contemporary. Traditional refers to forms extant before Korea opened to the outside world in the late nineteenth century; new signifies twentieth-century theatre with **Western** influences (*shingŭk*); and contemporary alludes to the last quarter of the twentieth century.

In general, traditional Korean drama, transmitted orally until the late nineteenth century, did not rely on highly codified, formulaic structures, such as those of **Japanese •** *nô* or **Indian •** *kathakali*, for example. **Masked dance**-dramas such as *t'alch'um* and **puppet theatre** do not employ a linear, cause-effect plot with exposition, complications, climax, and resolution. The plays are episodic; each scene has its own storyline, one often unconnected with others. The structure of masked dance-dramas is similar, but varies with the number of acts. Yangju *pyŏlsandae*, for example, has eight acts with twelve scenes, with dance and **music** prominent elements. Act I is comprised of the Young Monks' dance of exorcism. Act II shows monks attempting to extort valuable items from another monk. Though each act has a complication, conflict, and resolution, no thematic or plot connection exists between the two. Neither time nor place is provided, lending the stories a universal quality. The dramas are unified through lampoons of morally corrupt clergies, derision of aristocratic pedants, and portrayal of comic family disputes.

Kkoktu kakshi puppet theatre usually has eight scenes related thematically but lacking an overriding plot. The main puppet (Pak Ch'ŏmji) appears in each scene, playing the narrator, commenting on the content of subsequent scenes, interacting with other puppets, and, in general, providing continuity in the loosely knit structure.

P'ansori is structured for a single singer-**actor** to perform several characters, as well as narrate. The structure of the five well-known stories performed is elaborate, resembling Western epic poetry, relying essentially on two modes: song and narrative. The plot is straightforward, exposition is provided as needed, and a resolution directly follows the climax. Ad-libs directed to the audience or the sole drum player by the singer-actor are an assumed structural element.

In its infancy, *shingŭk*'s structure was modeled on Western realistic dramas that unfold through cause-and-effect; realism continues as the dominant contemporary form. However, absurdist writers, postmodern **theory**, and traditional forms have influenced the work of many **playwrights**. Contemporary dramas, especially those incorporating elements of traditional theatre, have structures that elude simplistic classifications.

Madangnori, a variety-entertainment form, has a structure resembling a meld of circus, vaudeville, and old riverboat revues. Scenes connected by an overarching theme are structured through comic bits or vignettes, music, song, dance, improvisation, and elements of masked dance-drama. The performance concludes with a grand finale, with the audience invited to dance and sing with the performers.

FURTHER READING

Cho, Oh-Kon, trans. *Traditional Korean Theatre*.

Oh-Kon Cho

DUBEY, SATYADEV (1936–). Indian Hindi-, Marathi-, Gujarati-, and English-language **director, actor**, and screenwriter based in Mumbai (Bombay), and a provocative as well as multifaceted theatre personality. Born in the central Indian town of Bilaspur, Dubey became associated with **Ebrahim Alkazi**'s Theatre Unit in the mid-1950s, taking over its management in 1962. That year he garnered national attention with his pioneering production of **Dharamvir Bharati**'s monumental *Blind Age* (Andha yug, 1954) on a makeshift rooftop **stage**; his successful revivals of it (including a solo recitation in 1990) have established him as one of its principal interpreters.

Like **Rajinder Nath** and **Shyamanand Jalan**, Dubey is a leading metropolitan director mainly of contemporary Indian plays in Hindi and in Hindi translation. His other major productions include **Mohan Rakesh**'s *A Day in Early Autumn* (Ashadh ka ek din, 1964) and *The Unfinished* (Adhe adhure, 1969) from Hindi; **Mahesh Elkunchwar**'s *Flowers of Blood* (Raktapushpa, 1981), *Legacy* (Wada chirebandi, 1985), and *Reflection* (Pratibimb, 1987); and **G. P. Deshpande**'s *Journey in Darkness* (Andhar yatra, 1987), *Chanakya Vishnugupta* (1988), and *Roads* (Raaste, 1995) from Marathi; **Girish Karnad**'s *Yayati* (1967), *Horse-Head* (Hayavadana, 1972), and *Tughlaq* (1966) from Kannada; **Badal Sircar**'s *The Legend of Ballabhpur* (Ballabhpurer roopkatha, 1969), *And Indrajit* (Evam Indrajit, 1970), and *Mad Horse* (Pagla ghoda, 1971) from Bengali; and **Vijay Tendulkar**'s *Sakharam the Book-Binder* (Sakharam Binder, 1973) and *Baby* (1976) from Marathi. Dubey has also directed several of these plays in Marathi (Mumbai's majority language), while Camus's *Cross Purposes* (1962) and Shaw's *Don Juan in Hell* (1983) are among his significant English productions. In addition, he has been an important screenwriter for mainstream but serious Hindi cinema, and an occasional film actor.

Aparna Dharwadker

DUTT, MICHAEL MADHUSUDAN (1824–1873). Indian Bengali-language poet and **playwright**, born to a wealthy family in the village of Sagardari, Jessore, now a district of **Bangladesh**. Dutt's poetic imagination was influenced by his mother's readings of the *Ramayana* and *Mahabharata*.

In 1843, in order to escape an arranged marriage, he converted to Christianity and took the name Michael. Expelled from the Hindu College because of his **religious** conversion, Dutt joined Bishop's College in 1844, studying Greek and Latin. From 1848 to 1856, he lived in Madras, teaching at Madras University High School and writing newspaper essays and English-language poetry. His first wife was British, his second a Continental European.

In 1856, in Calcutta (Kolkata), he turned to playwriting, beginning with an English version of a modern adaptation of Harsha's **Sanskrit** play *Ratnavali* (1858), produced by the amateur Belgachhia Theatre (Belgachhia Natyasala). His first original play, *Sharmishtha (*Sharmistha natak), was written the same year. Based on a *Mahabharata* story, its staging made it one of the earliest modern Bengali plays to be performed. He followed with two comedies in 1860, *Is This Called Civilization?* (Ekei ki bale sabhyata) and *Mane on Old Myna's Neck* (Buro shaliker ghare ron), and introduced blank verse to the Bengali **stage** the same year with *Padmabati* (Padmabati natak). Other plays included *Krishnakumari* (Krishnakumari natak, 1861), *The Girl of Braja* (Brajangana, 1861), *The Brave Woman* (Virangana, 1862), and *Enchanted Bower* (Mayakanan, 1874). His most celebrated blank verse play is *The Poem about the Death of Meghnad* (Meghnadbadhkavya, 1861), based on the *Ramayana*, with the villainous Ravana turned into a hero. It is also regarded as the first Bengali epic poem; Dutt's poetry is believed to have shaped the modern Bengali language.

Dutt not only translated two of his plays into English but also the anti-British *The Indigo Mirror* (Nildarpan, publ. 1860), which he was forced to do anonymously because of its controversial theme (see Censorship). Dutt's early plays were staged by amateurs, but all later received professional productions. His theatrical activity also included advocating for **actresses**, the first example arriving when the Bengal Theatre produced *Sharmishtha* the year he died.

During these years, Dutt seemed mainly interested in Indian literary and theatrical traditions; he criticized young people for elitist attitudes acquired through **Western** education; he also assailed the hypocrisy of conservative Hindu society. Dutt used mythological themes to reflect on contemporary social issues.

In 1862, Dutt went to England to study law; in 1867, he returned to India and became a barrister. Although his law career failed and his reckless spending nearly bankrupted him, he continued to write profusely until he died.

Sreenath K. Nair

DUTT, UTPAL (1929–1993). Indian Bengali-language **director**, **actor**, **theorist**, and **playwright**, born in Shillong, Meghalaya, North Bengal. His theatre work began by doing English plays at college in Calcutta (Kolkata). In 1947, he organized the Amateur Shakespeareans, directing and starring in *Richard III*. He joined Geoffrey Kendal's touring British rep company, Shakespearana, playing supporting roles. An avowed Marxist, he was influenced by **Western** theatre artists like Piscator and Brecht. For several years he belonged to the leftwing Indian People's Theatre Association. In 1950, the Amateur Shakespeareans became the Little Theatre Group (1959). It began with English plays, but later switched to Bengali.

Dutt brought intellectual strength, theatrical imagination, and **political** conviction to Bengali theatre's development. During his long and multifaceted career, he wrote, translated, or adapted numerous Bengali plays, among them traditional *jatra*s and activist, street corner "poster plays" and agitprop. His eclectic tastes included classics by Shakespeare, **Rabindranath Tagore**, **Michael Madhusudan Dutt**, **Girish Chandra Ghosh**, and Gorky. This prolific artist, who also wrote treatises and was a famed film star, sought to reach the "revolutionary masses" by producing his work in an eclectic range of venues, from proscenium **stages** to "street theatre" to large public spaces. His collaborations at Calcutta's Minerva Theatre—which he managed from 1959 to 1970—with **scenographer** Tapas Sen (1924–) attracted audiences with their spectacle.

Plays he wrote and directed include *Coal* (Angar, 1959), based on a coal mine disaster; *Waves* (Kallol, 1965), inspired by the 1946 Royal Indian Navy mutiny; and *Of People's Rights* (Manusher adhikare, 1969), a docudrama—a form new to Bengali theatre—about Alabama's 1931 Scottsboro trial.

In 1969, Dutt renamed his group People's Little Theatre and produced such politically powerful plays as *Tin Sword* (Tiner taloyar, 1971) and *The City of Nightmares* (Duhswapner nagari, 1974). His productions were noted for their mesmerizing spectacle, melodrama, and expert performances.

B. Ananthakrishnan

ELKUNCHWAR, MAHESH (1939–). **Indian** Marathi-language **playwright,** **theorist, actor,** screenwriter, and **critic,** born to a family of landowners in Parwa, a village in Vidarbha, Maharashtra. Elkunchwar took postgraduate degrees in English literature and ancient Indian history, culture, and archaeology. He was an English professor until retiring in 1999.

Elkunchwar's earliest one-acts, "Sultan" (1967) and "Fire Ritual" (Holi, 1969), inspired by **Vijay Tendulkar,** revealed the promise that he later fulfilled. After being published in leading Marathi literary magazines, they were successfully staged by **Vijaya Mehta.** Elkunchwar went on to script eight more one-acts by 1974, attracting critical acclaim for their diverse methods and their effective treatment of themes ranging from creativity to the meaning of choice.

His first full-length plays were heavily symbolic, and included *Angry Rain* (Rudravarsha, 1968), *Flowers of Blood* (Raktaphuspha, 1972), *Garbo* (1973), and *Period of Desire* (Vasnakand, 1974). After *Party* (1976), Elkunchwar acted in a film and created the screenplay adaptations of *Fire Ritual* (1983) and *Party* (1984). Following a long hiatus created by his dissatisfaction with his previous writing, he returned to composing plays with the so-called *Wada* trilogy, consisting of *Old Stone Mansion* (Wada chirebandi, 1985), *Pensive by the Pond* (Magna talya kathi, 1994), and *End of an Age* (Yuganta, 1994). This ambitious project, inspired by the world into which he was born (although he left it at four), examines the sad effects of what happened when urban culture impinged on the feudal world of Brahman rural life in post-independence India. A marathon staging in Bombay (Mumbai) of all three plays in 1994 lasted more than eight hours.

Elkunchwar's other works include *Reflection* (Pratibimb, 1987), *Autobiography* (Atmakatha, 1988), *As Discarded Clothes* (Vasansi jirnani, 2000), *Godson* (Dharmaputra, published 1997), and *Sonata* (2001). His plays, while fundamentally realistic, and performed on proscenium **stages,** employ surrealist, symbolist, expressionist, absurdist, and existentialist modes and philosophies; correspondences with dramatists like Chekhov, Strindberg, O'Neill, Sartre, Lorca, and Albee have been noted. His realistic emphasis contrasts him with the "theatre of roots" (*tanatu natakavedi*) movement, which favors a return to **folk theatre** outside the proscenium environment, and which he calls "artistic kleptomania." His plays have been produced by major **directors** and performed by top actors.

Most of Elkunchwar's plays have been translated into Hindi, Bangala, and English. *Old Stone Mansion* also has been translated into German and French. He has traveled abroad extensively to study and teach theatre, including at several American universities. He has been honored with almost all of the top Indian awards, including the

National Academy of **Music**, **Dance**, and Drama (Sangeet Natak Akademi) award (1989), Sahitya Natak award (2002), and Saraswati Samman award (2003).

Shashikant Barhanpurkar

ENTHUS SUSMONO (1966–). **Indonesian** puppeteer (*dhalang*) known for his unusual **puppets**, departures from traditional dramaturgy, and **stage** antics. Enthus's father performed *wayang golek cepak* and, growing up in Tegal, near the border of West and Central Java, Enthus was exposed to both Cirebonese and Central Javanese *wayang kulit*. Enthus had hoped to pursue tertiary studies in puppetry, but his father died when he was eighteen, and he instead remained in Tegal to fulfill performance engagements. He became involved in Tegal's literary scene, worked in radio, and participated in amateur dramatics. Enthus became known as a spokesperson for the "little man" as a shadow and rod puppeteer, often turning from the screen to talk directly about his own experiences.

In the 1990s, as his reputation and income grew, Enthus turned to puppet collecting and shadow puppet design. He crossed features of many different regional styles and created his own "planetary *wayang*" (*wayang planet*) series: Batman and Superman puppets, a helicopter with moving propeller and flashing light, various aliens, and the clown servants Semar, Gareng, Petruk, and Bagong in Teletubby **costumes**. Enthus treats *wayang* as modern theatre by dressing his **musicians** in costumes and assigning them roles to play, incorporating **dancers** and **actors** into the drama, and making constant metatheatrical references. He also does not shy from preaching Islamic **religious** tenets. Despised by traditionalists, Enthus is at the forefront of a generation of puppeteers recreating *wayang* for the media age.

Matthew Isaac Cohen

EXPERIMENTAL THEATRE

Experimental Theatre: China

China's experimental theatre emerged in the late 1970s as a movement seeking to explore a more diverse range of **stage** expression. It aims to examine the theatrical representation of time and space, a diversity of **acting** styles, the interaction between actors and audience, and the fusion of different performance methods. It looks toward twentieth-century **Western • playwrights** and **directors**, including Meyerhold, Brecht, Artaud, Grotowski, Beckett, Brook, and Schechner, while also seeking inspiration from traditional *xiqu*. In terms of content, it tends to explore the position of the self within society while often addressing **politically** sensitive subjects, such as the Communist Party's past and present role in society.

Post-Mao Developments. Although playwrights and directors such as **Ouyang Yuqian**, **Tian Han**, and **Hong Shen** briefly investigated modernist modes of representation before the communist takeover of 1949, experimental theatre's main objective has come to be the broadening of "spoken drama's" (*huaju*) tradition beyond its domination by illusionist realism and party ideology. Developments since the 1980s coincided with the adoption of black-box **theatres** providing greater flexibility and economy, and productions by private **theatre companies**, whose independence from state-run companies allowed greater autonomy.

Propelled by political reforms in 1978, experimental playwrights began to explore a variety of nonillusionist methods while still working within the sensitive state-run system. Despite following the post–Cultural Revolution (1966–1976) line of condemning the Gang of Four, the expressionist style of Xie Min's (1940–) *Why Did I Die?* (Wo weishenme si le, 1979), performed by the Shanghai Theatre Academy (Shanghai Xiju Xueyuan), boldly challenged the party-endorsed illusionist tradition. Ma Zhongjun et al.'s *Hot Currents outside the House* (Wuwai you reliu, 1980–1981), directed by Su Leci (1945–), while still espousing selfless devotion to the party, combined the aesthetics of Chinese traditional painting and poetry with nonindigenous expressionism.

Playwrights and directors also began to use such formalistic means to encourage audiences to reflect upon the party's construction of historical and cultural identity. Sha Yexin's (1939–) *What If I Were Real?* (Jairu wo shi zhende, 1979), whose expressionist style complements its mockery of party favoritism, was **censored**, as was **Gao Xingjian**'s absurdist-inspired *Bus Stop* (Chezhan, 1983), for casting doubt on the party's credibility.

WM (1985) by Wang Peigong (1943–), directed by Wang Gui (1932–), while receiving inspiration from expressionism and absurdism, interrogates the "success" of China's post-1978 economic reforms. *Sangshuping Chronicles* (Sangshuping jishi, 1988), by Chen Zidu et al. and directed by **Xu Xiaozhong**, features an innovative revolving stage and Greek tragedy–inspired chorus to encourage reflection upon the efficacy of the party's program to "enlighten" China's rural population. Zhang Xian's (1955–) *The Owl inside the House* (Wuli de maotouying, 1987), staged by the Shanghai Youth Spoken Drama Company (Shanghai Qingnian Huaju Tuan), uses Freudian psychoanalysis to explore questions of loneliness, desire, and impotence on a personal level that simultaneously represents social crisis.

Indigenous styles were also mixed with Western ones to explore cultural and gender stereotypes. William Huizhu Sun (1951–) and Faye Chungang Fei's (1957–) *China Dream* (Zhongguo meng, 1987), directed by **Huang Zuolin**, innovatively combines *xiqu* and *gewuju* (literally, "song-dance drama") acting with Brechtian theatrical style to explore the intercultural relationship between an American man and Chinese woman living in the United States. Wei Minglun (1941–) fuses *chuanju* with absurdism to challenge the patriarchal bias of China's literary tradition in *Pan Jinlian* (1986).

Experimental theatre in the late 1980s and 1990s was particularly influenced by greater access to Western modernist drama, the adoption of black-box theatres, and the establishment of private companies. The translation into Chinese of anthologies of Western modernist and absurdist plays inspired performances of Ionesco's *Rhinoceros* (1987) and *Bald Soprano* (1991), O'Neill's *The Great God Brown* (1989), Beckett's *Waiting for Godot* (1991), and Genet's *The Balcony* (1993). The First China Small Theatre **Festival**, held in 1989 in Nanjing, helped to establish the black box as the major experimental stage format.

Rise of Directorial Influence. The director's role grew in importance as theatricality and innovative adaptations superseded written scripts. Mou Sen (1963–) founded the

Frog Experimental Company (Wa Shiyan Jutuan) in 1987, the first private theatre company since 1949, and the Theatre Workshop (Xiju Chejian) in 1992. Mou directed *The Other Bank: A Chinese Grammatical Discussion* (Bi'an: guanyu bi'an de Hanyu yufa taolun, 1993), an adaptation of Gao Xingjian's *The Other Bank*, which adopts Grotowski's concept of "poor theatre" and his training methods. In 1994, Mou directed *File O* (Ling dang'an), a critique of government surveillance, and *Related to AIDS* (Guanyu aizibing), which is comprised of three sections: the act of cooking, a stream of consciousness discussion about sexuality, and cement masons building a wall. Influenced by Artaud and Schechner, Mou's focus on improvisation, physicality, and movement blurs the boundary between performance art and theatre.

The independent Lin Zhaohua Drama Studio (Lin Zhaohua Xiju Gongzuoshi) produced experimental reinterpretations of Western classics, including adaptations of *Hamlet* (1990) and *Richard III* (2001), and a 1988 fusion of Chekhov's *Three Sisters* and Beckett's *Waiting for Godot*. Meng Jinghui's (1964–) *Worldly Pleasures* (Sifan, 1992) interlaces excerpts from Boccaccio's fourteenth-century classic *The Decameron* with an anonymous Ming dynasty (1368–1644) play to explore cultural proscriptions on transgressive desire. Meng wrote and directed *I Love XXX* (Wo ai chachacha, 1994), which explores how language constructs cultural identity while challenging the centrality of dialogue in the *huaju* tradition. Meng also has been active in localizing foreign dramas, including Fo's *Accidental Death of an Anarchist* (1997) and Mayakovsky's *Bedbug* (2000). Meng's combination of satire and romance with popular **music** appealed to China's youth and contributed enormously to the popularization and commercialization of experimental theatre from the late 1990s.

The Story of Puppets, an experimental production employing puppetry, *kunqu*, *huaju*, and Western music. It was adapted and directed by Li Liuyi for the Beijing Arts Creative Centre. (Photo: Courtesy of Li Liuyi)

Playwrights and directors also adopted local culture as a setting for the exploration of existential questions about cultural and historical identity. *Birdmen* (Niaoren, 1991) by Guo Shixing (1952–), directed by Lin Zhaohua, dramatizes the local traditions of bird-raising and amateur *jingju* to challenge modernity and Eurocentrism. Li Liuyi's (1961–) *Extreme Mahjong* (Feichang majiang, 2000), produced in part by the Li Liuyi Workshop (Li Liuyi Gongzuoshi), explores questions of self and truth through the game of mahjong as a theatrical metaphor. Zhang Guangtian (1966–) has promoted innovative forms of theatricality and musicality while playing up a popular brand of "proletarian" values and patriotism, as in *Che Guevara* (Qie Gewala, 2000), *Mr. Lu Xun* (Lu Xun xiansheng, 2001), and *The Sage Confucius* (Shengren Kongzi, 2002).

Although Western **theory** and practice influenced the development of experimental theatre, the movement sought less to imitate than to creatively adapt to the local situation. Some dramatists incorporated a **critical** view of the process of borrowing, while self-consciously engaging in both domestic and global politics.

The privatization of theatre since the 1990s has increased its market orientation, encouraging greater accommodation of popular culture, such as Meng Jinghui's multimedia musical *Amber* (Hupo, 2005), and enhanced appeal to elitist aesthetics, such as Li Liuyi's *Confession* (Kougong, 2005). The Peking University Theatre Research Institute, established in 2004 by Lin Zhaohua, aims to invigorate new directions in production by developing cross-cultural learning and collaborative opportunities.

FURTHER READING

Entell, Bettina S. "Post-Tian'anmen: A New Era in Chinese Theatre—Experimentation during the 1990s at China National Experimental Theatre/CNET"; Zhao, Henry Y. H. *Towards a Modern Zen Theatre: Gao Xingjian and Chinese Theatre Experimentalism.*

Jonathan Noble

Experimental Theatre: Hong Kong

Hong Kong practitioners have never hesitated to explore their theatre's horizons, and experimentation has long been an integral part of the local **stage**. Even the Hong Kong Repertory Theatre (Xianggang Huaju Tuan), the largest mainstream institution in the position of a "national **theatre company**," produced the innovative *The Road* (Dalu, 1981). Subtitled "an experimental theatre event," it was a series of multifocused happenings arranged in an exhibition hall seven hundred meters square, and the audience had to walk around spotting its favorite scenes. It successfully broke up the traditional performer/stage-spectator/auditorium boundary. The Sino-English (Chung Ying) Theatre Company (Zhongying Jutuan), Hong Kong's second largest, produced an environmental play, *The Island that Sings* (Hui gechang de angchuanzhou, 1992). The performance mainly took place on an outlying island, but commenced at the pier, where the audience boarded a ferry, and on the ferry itself during its journey to the island. Thus audiences experienced a performance with mobile **acting** areas.

The most renowned experimental group is Zuni Icosahedron (Jinnian Ershi mian ti), which has staged more than one hundred alternative theatre and multimedia performances. Most, especially the earlier ones, have been essentially nonverbal. This allows them to be accessible to audiences in different countries. Using splendid sound and visual effects and symbolic gestures full of multifold meanings, the company has developed its own aesthetic. Zuni has had considerable influence on others and its effort in building international cultural exchange has been recognized.

The many relatively smaller and younger groups have adopted even bolder and more vibrant styles, and innovative small **theatre** spaces in Hong Kong have played an important role in nurturing them. Their works have also been produced in informal venues, such as bars, factories, streets, parks and piazzas, hospitals, college campuses, and even truck-towed containers. These performances often present a colorful mixture that is ambiguously suggestive. The ultimate objective of these groups is to test the theatre's possibilities and to challenge the audience's habitual patterns of reception and appreciation.

Hong Kong experimental theatre has many sources. In the 1970s, alongside the introduction of **Western** mainstream dramatists, Theatre of the Absurd and Brechtian epic theatre were introduced. Inspired by these movements, both foreign-born artists and young, local dramatists (exposed to theatrical innovation abroad or through self-study) took the lead. Also influential were artists working in **dance**-theatre, film and media arts, and Cantonese *yueju*.

It should also be noted that experimentation has flourished not only in aesthetic innovation, but in the realms of feminist theatre, **political** theatre, and educational theatre.

Ping Kuen Cheung

Experimental Theatre: India

Fundamental changes have taken place in society and culture in post-independence **India**; experimental theatre may be considered part of this vibrant cultural and **political** phase. A new generation of **playwrights**, **directors**, **actors,** and designers emerged with enormous creative energy geared toward finding a **stage** language appropriate for Indian culture and theatrical traditions. This intensive search for a national theatre identity in order to create a contemporary artistic expression contributed toward many experiments in the creation of new plays, unusual performance spaces, and innovative staging methods. A wider social vision, an understanding of **Western** models transcending naturalism, and the imaginative use of traditional resources were the key elements underpinning India's experimental theatre movement.

Theatrical experimentation has had at least five major strands:

- Incorporation of Western styles, including Shakespearian, realistic, absurdist, and Brechtian, in the form of original texts, translations, and adaptations.
- Incorporation of traditional/classical, nonclassical, and indigenous styles into contemporary work.
- Revivals of **Sanskrit** drama.
- Alternative movements like street theatre, feminist theatre, etc.
- Contemporary practices inspired by multimedia and digital images.

Ibsen and other Western figures influenced many playwrights and directors from the 1920s; this interaction helped to provide new ideas that led to abandonment of older practices established by the **Parsi theatre**. In the 1920s and 1930s, artists like **Sisir Kumar Bhaduri**, Naresh Mitra, Ahindra Choudhury (1895–1974), and Durgadas Banerjee in Calcutta (Kolkata); Bhargavram Vittal, **P. L. Deshpande**, and V. K. Atre in Maharashtra; **T. P. Kailasam** and Adya Rengacharya in Karnataka; Raj Mannar and Bellary Raghava (1880–1946) in Andhra Pradesh; **Ram Kumar Varma** and Upendra Nath Ashk (1910–1996) in Hindi worked toward the establishment of this new experimental phase of naturalistic theatre.

Rabindranath Tagore's experiments in creating a synthesis between Western and Eastern traditions founded a new phase that combined traditional expression with contemporary ideas. The Indian People's Theatre Association (IPTA, founded 1942–1943) experimented in the creation of a contemporary stage in the 1940s, bringing together leftwing messages and local performance traditions.

With the decline of IPTA arose a second wave of experimental theatre companies in the 1950s. **Sombhu Mitra** formed Bahurupee (1949), for which he used plays by Tagore and several Western playwrights, including Ibsen, as the basis of his experiments. In 1959, **Utpal Dutt** formed the Little Theatre Group, a milestone in Indian theatre history. Dutt was keen on searching for new possibilities and techniques. His collaborations with lighting designer Tapas Sen (1924–) created memorable theatrical achievements. Returning from the Royal Academy of Dramatic Arts, **Ebrahim Alkazi** also started his efforts in developing a contemporary theatre at this time. In 1957, the National School of Drama was established in New Delhi with the intention of attempting experiments in creating a new theatre idiom by incorporating various regional characteristics.

A new trend established in the 1960s and 1970s had an enormous impact on those seeking to create a contemporary stage language based on the characteristic features of traditional theatre forms. Notable playwrights involved included **Girish Karnad** and **Chandrasekhar Kambar** in Karnataka, **Vijay Tendulkar** and Satish Alekar (1949–) in Marathi, Sarveshwar Dayal Saksena in Hindi, **K. N. Panikkar** and **G. Sankara Pillai** in Malayalam, **Ratan Thiyam** and Lokendra Arambam in Manipuri, and so on. Major directors associated with this trend include Sombhu Mitra, **Habib Tanvir**, **B. V. Karanth**, **Jabbar Patel**, **Vijay Mehta**, Bansi Kaul (1949–), K. N. Panikkar, Ratan Thiyam, **S. Ramanujam**, and **Rajinder Nath**. They have used this new idiom not only to produce Indian playwrights but also Western classics by Shakespeare, Molière, Gogol, Jonson, and Brecht.

Sanskrit play productions examine the aesthetic principles of classical Indian theatre. Bharata's *Treatise on Drama* (Natyashastra; see Theory) and various forms have been reinvestigated in the light of contemporary sensibilities and demands. **Festivals** have been conducted to promote such experiments: the Kalidasa Festival (1957) and the Bhasa Festival (1980), both in Ujaini in Madhya Pradesh. Major directors like **Shanta Gandhi**, K. N. Panikkar, **Maharaj Krishna Raina**, Ratan Thiyam, Habib Tanvir, and others have produced Sanskrit plays in contemporary contexts.

Street theatre, feminist theatre, and children's theatre are other experimental manifestations. The street theatre movement was led by **Badal Sircar** in Calcutta. He developed the politically aware "Third Theatre" (Anganmanch, literally, "open-air theatre") approach, which abandons many expensive mainstream characteristics, like rental of **theatres**, costly publicity, and elaborate lighting, scenic, and sound effects. Sircar's group usually performs every Friday afternoon in Kolkata, wherever it can find a suitable space. This unconventional movement brought radical changes to theatre practice. In the 1970s and 1980s, Sircar's experiments influenced other alternative artists who used his models in their own politically motivated work.

In many ways, modern Indian theatre is extremely diverse and experimental. Some of the world's leading practitioners, like Brook, Barba, and Schechner, are attracted by this broad spectrum of Indian forms; the interaction between global traditions creates new trends and ideologies in India. National and state academies and international agencies like the Ford Foundation financially support experimental theatre, which, in recent years, has promoted interdisciplinary collaborations between tradition and modernity, and art and technology.

FURTHER READING

Dharwadker, Aparna Bhargava. *Theatres of Independence: Drama, Theory, and Urban Performance in India since 1947;* Dalmia, Vasudha. *Poetics, Plays, and Performance: The Politics of Modern Indian Theatre.*

Sreenath K. Nair

Experimental Theatre: Indonesia

Two of **Indonesia**'s best-known **theatre companies** to develop an early experimental aesthetic are Workshop Theatre (Bengkel Teater) and Independent Theatre (Teater Mandiri). Founded in 1968 by **playwright–director • Rendra**, Workshop Theatre has had an important impact on Indonesian theatre's development. Rendra's approach to **acting** and playwriting, as well as his concept for a communal company, has influenced subsequent generations of artists. Workshop Theatre utilizes indigenous forms in an improvisatory rehearsal process emphasizing movement and the minimal use of text over dialogue, plot, character, and conflict. Independent Theatre, founded in 1972 by director-actor-playwright **Putu Wijaya**, is known for a style that similarly shuns **Western** elements and instead produces works of stunning and sometimes disturbing imagery. Another director-playwright, **Arifin C. Noer**, began his career as an actor in Rendra's Workshop Theatre. Noer later moved to Jakarta where he founded the experimental Little Theatre (Teater Kecil, 1967). His work is characterized by a blending of elements from indigenous **folk theatre** with an absurdist approach.

During the 1980s, theatre artists sought to express outrage at the human rights abuses, government corruption, and environmental offenses that brought about the eventual collapse of the Suharto-led government in 1998. By combining traditional **music**, sound effects, lighting, and mood-inducing imagery and movement with sparse text and nonlinear **storytelling**, theatres were able to express their potentially inflammatory **political** and social agendas while avoiding government **censorship**.

The Javanese intellectual centers of Jakarta, Yogyakarta, and Bandung have produced a number of companies characterized by an experimental form. Some well-known Javanese companies include Open Space Theatre (Teater Ruang, 1994), founded in Solo; Black Umbrella Theatre (Teater Payung Hitam, 1982), founded in Bandung by Rachman Sabur (1957–); SAE Theatre (Teater SAE, 1978), founded by Budi S. Otong in Jakarta; the Yogyakarta-based Garage Theatre (Teater Garasi, 1993), led by artistic director Yudi Ahmad Tajudin (1972–); and Lightning Theatre (Teater Gandrik, 1983), founded by Jujuk Prabowo (1954–). Teater Gandrik (*gandrik* being an idiomatic expression of surprise or realization) works in a collaborative process it calls "taking apart the script" (*mbedah naskah*). Members of the company contribute to the final production by building on the dialogue, improvising music and **dance**, and altering their characters.

Indonesia has also witnessed an increase in the number and visibility of experimental groups based outside of Java. Our Theatre (Teater Kita, 1993), established in Makassar, Sulawesi, under the direction of Asia Ramli Prapanca (1960–), combines an experimental approach to dramatic form with a strong sense of tradition and local identity. The political satire *I'm Borrowing a New Shirt* (Aku pinjam baju baru, 2001) featured limited amounts of text along with elements of traditional Makassar-Bugis ritual movement, and a chaotic sound design with trumpets, drums, songs, and laughter, along with the clanging of a huge industrial pulley. Dindon W. S. (1959–) began his career as a performer with other experimental groups, founding Grave Theatre (Teater Kubur, 1983) in Makassar, Sulawesi; it later moved to Jakarta. This company's production of *Dog Circus* (Sirkus anjing, 1990) is emblematic of the imagistic style for which Dindon has become known. Earth Theatre (Teater Bumi, 1978), established by Wisran Hadi (1945–) in Padang, West Sumatra, has established a reputation for politically motivated work.

Such groups have had difficulty gaining recognition from the Jakarta-Yogyakarta-Bandung establishment, which views arts organizations outside of Java as having limited artistic value. Yet many have gained acclaim at major **festivals** in Bali, Java, and abroad. In addition, several experimental theatre festivals in Jakarta have showcased groups from around the archipelago. The Indonesian Festival of Realist Theatre held at the Taman Ismail Marzuki Arts Center in 2004, and the Alternative Theater Festival at Gedung Kesenian Jakarta in 2003, featured works by Popular Theatre (Teater Populer, Jakarta), Bandung Theatre Study Club (Studiklub Teater Bandung, Bandung), and Our Theatre, as well as discussions led by leading artists from Jakarta, Yogyakarta, and Bandung.

There are many small companies with limited life spans. Several notable troupes already have disbanded due to fiscal shortfalls and other external pressures, while others get together for a single production or to participate in an arts festival.

James Hesla

Experimental Theatre: Japan

International Parallels. In its antirealist inventiveness and attention to the expressive qualities of theatrical form, **Japan**'s experimental theatre parallels modern theatre's international evolution. Experimental theatre explores questions about art and **politics**, aiming to transform the perceptions and experiences of viewers and participants. The Russian Revolution and the catastrophe of World War I created the initial wave of experimental theatre in important European centers, especially those of France, Germany, and Russia. Later, the transformative theatre vision of French **theorist** Antonin Artaud and the rise of 1960s countercultures prefigured a second wave, notably in Europe, the United States, and Japan. While the history of Japanese experimental theatre began with artists looking to Europe, Japan's cultural history has influenced its production; moreover, many **Western** artists now look to Japan for inspiration.

Prewar Experimentation. Already in 1906, **Tsubouchi Shôyô's theatre company** Literary Arts Society (Bungei Kyôkai) debated modern theatre. **Director • Osanai Kaoru** studied English director-designer Edward Gordon Craig's visually expressive designs and, as cofounder of the atelier-style Free Theatre (Jiyû Gekijô) in 1909, aimed to transform Japanese theatre through Western-style productions. With modern ideas flourishing in the relatively freethinking Taishô period (1912–1926), Osanai and **Hijikata Yoshi**, who was influenced by Russian director Meyerhold's revolutionary ideas, built Tokyo's Tsukiji Little Theatre (Tsukiji Shôgekijô) in 1924. Although short-lived, it was Japan's most important pre–World War II experimental theatre site.

Murayama Tomoyoshi witnessed expressionist art firsthand in Germany in 1922 and helped found Mavo, a collective of young Japanese artists inspired by the European avant-garde. His famous set for the Tsukiji's 1924 production of Georg Kaiser's *From Morn 'til Midnight* was all jutting edges and contrasting shades, and the **actors'** movements were similarly stylized. It exemplified the influence of European forms on early experimental theatre—a striking reappraisal of expressionism combined with the montage-like abstraction favored by Mavo.

Meanwhile, in 1925, the Japan League for Proletarian Arts and Literature established the agitprop Trunk Theatre (Toranku Gekijô). German director Piscator inspired Murayama's writing on proletarian drama, and socialist-realism popularized leftist causes. However, as the 1930s military government promulgated new laws to limit free expression and social criticism, the situation for experimentalists became increasingly dangerous. By 1940, the military had silenced the cosmopolitan vanguard (see Censorship).

Postwar Developments. After the war, modern theatre's circumstances improved, though realist *shingeki* works dominated the 1950s. By 1960, however, a second experimental wave had emerged. **Hijikata Tatsumi**'s performance of **Mishima Yukio**'s *Forbidden Colors* (Kinjiki, 1959)—the first *butô* performance and a radical transgression of traditional Japanese **dance**—signaled a dramatic new turn. June 1960 saw massive protests against the renewal of the U.S.-Japan Mutual Security Treaty (Anpo); young artists abandoned *shingeki*'s increasingly commercial world for forms more responsive to the current turmoil. Director-**playwrights** of the new "underground" (*angura*) movement, like **Kara Jûrô**, **Terayama Shûji**, **Suzuki Tadashi**, **Ôta Shôgo**, and **Satoh Makoto,** founded revolutionary groups, fusing images of the past with dark, avant-garde sensibilities. A new dramatic synthesis of traditional styles and folktales mixed with 1920s Japanese expressionism, vaudeville, absurdism, and the international flavors of Artaud and existentialism explored Japan's turbulent history, often focusing on the question of personal and national identity.

In the 1960s, responding to the war's lingering physical and psychological wreckage, *angura*'s blasted psyche explored hybrid aesthetics, physicality, and shock tactics. Noisy expressive forms confronted audiences in intimate storefront theatres. Kara took the "little theatre" (*shôgekijô*) approach to the streets in *kabuki*-inspired tent performances, and Suzuki's physical dramaturgy gave new meaning to classical texts. Terayama's group worked in many artistic media; its surreal, visionary performances, films, and art happenings aimed for social revolution through aesthetic experience. Meanwhile, themes of alienation and social conformity infused the absurdist, Kafkaesque works of 1960s playwrights **Abe Kôbô** and **Betsuyaku Minoru**. By 1970, however, the counterculture was already declining. Satoh's *The Dance of Angels Who Burn Their Own Wings* (Tsubasa o moyasu tenshi-tachi no butô, 1970) announced the demise of the dream of revolution; even while *angura* performances waxed in popularity, their political intensity waned.

Another new wave of artists emerged in the 1980s. **Noda Hideki**'s Dream Wanderers (Yume no Yûminsha) became hugely popular with playful, speedy performances transforming *angura*, its hyper-cute idiosyncratic vision reflecting the dizzying spiral of Japan's bubble economy. Meanwhile, **Kawamura Takeshi**'s Third Erotica (Daisan Erochika) cast a darkly satirical, gothic eye on society. **Furuhashi Teiji**'s art collective, dumb type, made hybrid media-performance works, accompanied by Ikeda Ryôji's minimalist electronic soundscapes. Japanese culture turned global; experimental performance was popularized alongside sushi restaurants and comics (*manga*). Japanese companies toured worldwide, and *butô* gathered international disciples. The world's avant-garde came to Suzuki's summer arts festival at remote Toga Village.

Since the 1990s. By contrast, 1990s experimental theatre has become more reflective. **Hirata Oriza** developed "quiet theatre" (*shizuka na engeki*) in which his colloquial dialogue skates across the surface of human experience, hiding a profound sense of unease. **Sakate Yôji**'s sparse political plays, exploring race, the environment, and community, are also more measured and minimal. Social anxiety and political violence are explored in the melancholy *butô*-style performances of Theatre of Deconstruction (Gekidan Kaitaisha), which combine a radical 1960s spirit with a sublime aesthetic sensibility.

Women have been influential in experimental theatre since the 1970s. Playwrights **Kishida Rio** and **Kisaragi Koharu** pioneered feminist theatre in Japan. Brilliant performances by **Shiraishi Kayoko** and *butô* performer Ashikawa Yôko helped define *angura* styles. Moreover, Japan's cultural institutions have expanded, allowing groups opportunity to apply for funding to perform at venues ranging from tiny rooms to the vast New National Theatre (Shin Kokuritsu Gekijô).

From being highly marginal in prewar Japan, and controversial in the 1960s, Japan's experimental theatre scene is now among the world's most vibrant and influential.

FURTHER READING

Eckersall, Peter. *Theorizing the Angura Space Avant-garde Performance and Politics in Japan, 1960–2000;* Jortner, David, Keiko McDonald, and Kevin J. Wetmore, Jr., eds. *Modern Japanese Theatre and Performance;* Rolf, Robert T., and John K. Gillespie, eds. *Alternative Japanese Drama: Ten Plays;* Sorgenfrei, Carol Fisher. *Unspeakable Acts: The Avant-Garde Theatre of Terayama Shûji and Postwar Japan.*

Peter Eckersall

Experimental Theatre: Korea

The 1960 founding of Seoul's Experimental (Shilhŏm) Theatre Group marked the beginning of three decades of fervent experimentation. Though **Western**-style realism remained popular, **Korean** experimentation took many forms, including allegory and metaphor, to criticize the government and skirt **censorship**; the use of history, legends, shamanistic **religious** rituals, and **masked** • **dance**-drama in a search for an essentially Korean theatre; the use of traditional entertainments, such as *madanggŭk* (open-air plays and **folk** entertainment), in pro-democratic, anti-military **political** movements; the borrowing from Asian theatre, including **Chinese** traditional forms or **Suzuki**

Tadashi's techniques; the adaptation of Shakespearean and Greek classics in the search for timeless truths; and implementation of European avant-garde techniques and postmodernist **theories**. Experiments in nonverbal or movement-based performance are among the most recent attempts to eschew realism.

Kim Jŏng-ok (1932–) experimented with adaptations of Western classics in a Korean context in the 1980s and 1990s, as have Kim A-ra (1956–) and **Lee Yun-t'aek.** Recently, Yun Jŭng-sŭp (1950–) experimented with verbally minimal, imagistic movement pieces, and **Kim Kwang-lim**'s writing and directing ingeniously fuse Korean dance, masked-drama, **puppetry**, and martial arts.

However, since the early 1990s, the trend has been away from experimentation. Censorship ended in 1989 and a democratically elected government now is in place. Former avant-garde artists have become the establishment, innovative young talents choose film careers, and socio-political movements are diffused. Finances remain limited, and younger audiences privilege entertainment over intellectual stimulation. Some **critics** contend that South Korean theatre seems directionless, apolitical, and artistically less venturesome than twenty years ago, making today's experimental theatre more often an interesting event, rather than the socio-political artistic necessity it once was.

FURTHER READING

Kim, Ah-jeong, and R. B. Graves, trans. *The Metacultural Theatre of Oh T'ae-sŏk: Five Plays from the Korean Avant-Garde*; Kim, Yun-Cheol, and Miy-Ye Kim, eds. *Contemporary Korean Theatre: Playwrights, Directors, Stage-Designers.*

Richard Nichols

Experimental Theatre: Malaysia

Malay theatre became markedly experimental in the 1970s, when what is called "contemporary theatre" (*teater kontemporari*) became prevalent. It emerged as a reaction against the realism of the preceding decade, which was inspired by the social dramas of writers such as Usmar Ismail (1921–1972) and Utuy T. Sontani (1920–1979), and **Western** realists such as Ibsen. Socially, *teater kontemporari* was a response to the tragedy of May 13, 1969, when ethnic riots in major cities stunned the nation.

The first major theatrical response to the riots was **Noordin Hassan**'s experimental, national award-winning *'Tis Not the Tall Grass Blown by the Wind* (Bukan lalang ditiup angin, 1970). Culturally introspective, the play in part allegorizes May 13th, examining the problems of rural Malay life and seeking ways to resolve them. Its abstract, symbolic nature reflects a post–May 13th concern with discretion in confronting socio-**political** matters. Stylistically, Hassan mixes Malay traditional forms, such as *boria*, with surrealist art and a Western-style Greek chorus to create a uniquely eclectic **music**-drama.

In 1974, **Syed Alwi**, known earlier for his work in English theatre, won the national award for his Malay play *Tok Perak,* a multimedia exploration of an individual caught between the existential demands of his independent, free self, exemplified by his traveling medicine-seller lifestyle, and the desires of his social self, portrayed in his dream of a settled family life. The innovative production featured slides, shadows, music, and poetry recited by an offstage voice.

During the 1970s, universities also encouraged theatrical experimentation, fostering a third generation of Malay **playwrights** who were cutting-edge: Dinsman (1949–), Johan

Jaaffar (1953–), and Hatta Azad Khan (1952–) created signature pieces, such as *It Is Not Suicide* (Bukan bunuh diri, 1974), *The One* (Dia, 1977), and *Corpse* (Mayat, 1978), respectively. Overall, experimental theatre was a pluralistic venture; individual artists developed distinctive production styles, as playwrights tended to **direct** their own works.

Writing in the aftermath of May 13th, Malay dramatists sought to establish a vision that would affirm Malay creativity and cultural identity. For this reason, they often incorporated elements from traditional theatre to help shape a unique contemporary image. Traditions they explored and adapted include *wayang kulit* (see Puppet Theatre), **mak yong**, *main puteri* (a healing ceremony with trance and dramatic aspects), *dikir barat* (poetry sung to music in a call and response format), *boria*, and **storytelling** (*penglipur lara*), in addition to **bangsawan**. Dramatists of the 1970s were also influenced by the absurdism of Indonesian playwrights, such as **Arifin C. Noer**, Iwan Simatupang (1928–1970), and **Putu Wijaya**, and utilized a surrealist aesthetic in creating abstract, symbolic staging.

Overall, the experimentalists emphasized the theatricality and presentational quality of a work, incorporating music, song, choral effects, poetry, **dance**, slides, film, mime, and traditional forms, while also drawing on personal, imaginative images. Thematically, experimental plays deal with the root causes of social problems, the loss of humanistic values, the examination of self and others, and the nature of drama itself. Characters are symbolic, abstract, and extraordinary, including searchers as well as redesigned historical and legendary figures. **Dramatic structures** diverge from standard act, and scene divisions and may be episodic or circular.

Although initially the plays were enthusiastically received, they became increasingly difficult to understand, causing an attendance decline. Mainstream Malay viewers were accustomed to theatre that connected with society; the experimental work, often a commentary on theatre itself, thereby lost its significance for society-at-large. In addition, the presence of Islamic revivalism in Malaysia by the end of the 1970s and the early 1980s further discredited experimentalism, which some identified as problematically "absurd" and nihilistic from a **religious** point of view. There was also competition from film and television. Audiences sought more easily accessible forms of entertainment, and theatre artists themselves began shifting to these media as well as other enterprises.

In the 1980s and 1990s, a revived English-language theatre became the site for experimentation, with innovative plays by K. S. Maniam (1942–), Kee Thuan Chye (1954–), and Leow Puay Tin (1957–). Meanwhile, Soon Chua Mae (1963–), affiliated with the Malaysian Institute of Art and the offshoot company, Dan Dan Theatre, was working experimentally in Mandarin.

FURTHER READING

Nur Nina Zuhra (Nancy Nanney). *An Analysis of Modern Malay Drama.*

Nancy Nanney

Experimental Theatre: Philippines

Experimental theatre in the **Philippines** has become almost synonymous with "expressionist" theatre, defined by one scholar as any kind of nonrealistic theatre. Experimental theatre is influenced not only by absurdism and Brechtian theatre. Productions have been shaped by the desire to reach a larger audience, a nationalism urging artists to uphold indigenous culture, **censorship**, and **political** repression.

Productions considered experimental for their use of traditional and new devices include Anton Juan's (1950–) staging of Paul Dumol's (1951–) *The Trial of Mang Serapio* (Ang paglilitis ni Mang Serapio), which drew from absurdist theatre; **Behn Cervantes**'s (1940–) staging of Bonifacio Ilagan's (1951–) *People's Worship* (Pagsambang bayan, 1977), which followed the structure of the Catholic Mass while drawing from documentary style; Bienvenido Lumbera's use of rock opera in narrating and interrogating the lives of national heroes in plays like *Bayani*; dance-dramas such as Al Santos's (1954–) and choreographer Denisa Reyes's (1952–) *Demons* (Diablos, 1992), which highlights traditional **music** and **dance**, fusing modern ballet and indigenous movement; UP Repertory Company's short poem-plays, such as "The People's Scholar" (Iskolar ng bayan), performed during rallies and demonstrations, thus adapting to alternative spaces; the Peryante troupe's *People's Oratorio* (Oratoryo ng bayan, 1984), which presents street theatre forms, such as improvisational theatre, vaudeville, poetry-movement, mock ballet, and effigy theatre, in a lobby; Aureus Solito's (1969–) integration of Palawan rituals and exploration of indigenous **stages**; and Antonio Mabesa's (1935–) merging of video, music, a speech chorale, and dance in *Gabriela: An Oratorio* (Gabriela: isang oratoryo, 2006), which deconstructs **dramatic structure**.

Joi Barrios

Experimental Theatre: Taiwan

The emergence of **Taiwanese** experimental theatre in the 1960s was a reaction against the government's anti-communist and anti-Soviet cultural policy. It was initiated and

A Taiwanese-Mandarin bilingual, experimental version of *Romeo and Juliet*, directed by Wang Rongyu. It was produced by Golden Bough Theater, a community-based theatre in Tamshui, near Taipei, May 2003. Romeo was played by cross-dressed actress Huang Caiyi. (Photo: Liu Chen-Hsiang; Courtesy of Golden Bough Theater)

advocated by scholars and **directors** who had returned from the West in the 1970s. While the Little Theatre Promotion Committee was founded by **Lee Man-kuei** in 1960, the broader term "experimental theatre" was not widely used until eight "experimental dramas" were staged by students at Chinese Culture University in 1979. **Playwright**-director **Yao I-wei** called the event "the birth of experimental theatre," a broad term for works that seek a refreshed sense of theatricality by breaking out of confining **political** ideologies (such as anti-communism) and illusionist conventions. Under its rubric are "little theatre" (*xiao juchang*), avant-garde theatre, and Taiwanese-language "spoken drama" (*wutai ju*).

Like its **Western** counterpart, Taiwanese experimental theatre is politically subversive and artistically innovative. But unlike the corresponding Western form, it has not been limited to a small audience. It emphasizes improvisation, the contemporaneity of audience and **actors**, nonlinear narrative, gestural and body language, and creative use of the **stage**.

Experimental theatre was developed under the leadership of several generations of directors, including Lee Man-kuei, Yao I-wei, and **Ma Sen**. The first notable and commercially successful example was *Hezhu's New Match* (Hezhu xin pei, 1980), written and directed by Chin Shi-chieh (Jin Shijie, 1951–) and produced by the Lan Ling Theatre Company (Lan Ling Ju Fang) for the first Experimental Theatre **Festival**. The play freely adapts a *jingju* play and its conventions in a satiric fashion, using minimalist decor and "spoken drama"–style dialogue.

Alexander C. Y. Huang

Experimental Theatre: Thailand

Shortly after **Western** realistic drama was introduced on Thai campuses in the 1970s, its nonrealistic counterparts followed. Notable examples are **Sodsai Pantoomkomol**'s productions of Albee's *The American Dream* (1978), Brecht's *The Good Person of Setzuan* (1979), and Giraudoux's *Ondine* (1982), as well as Nopamat Veohong's staging of Strindberg's *A Dream Play* (1983). In addition, Western dramaturgy was also adapted in the process of experimentation. For instance, when Brechtian techniques were first introduced through the Crescent Moon Theatre's (Prachan Siew Karn Lakon) seminal production of *The Exception and the Rule* (1976), semi-improvised scenes developed from contemporary local issues were added to the translation.

Of all the recent experimentations, the most significant is probably *lakon khanob niyom mhai* ("new traditional dance-drama"), a form of modern dance-drama using some speaking. These reinterpretations of traditional drama in modern contexts and experimental styles are drawn from both traditional and modern practices. Three of the most active **directors** are **Patravadi Mejudhon,** Pornrat Damrhung (1955–), and Pichet Klunchuen (1971–). The latter two's collaborations include *Nontook* (1998), *Trial by Fire* (Lui fai, 2000), and *Sita: Sri Rama?* (Sida: Sri Ram?, 2005); and examples of Klunchuen's solo works are *The Sacrifice of Phya Chattan* (Phya Chattan, 2004) and *I Am a Demon* (Phom pen yak, 2005). Not only do these works attract audiences who usually attend either only traditional or modern performances, but they also draw expatriates and tourists. While they frequently receive negative **criticism** from traditional Thai artists, they actually serve as a means for preservation of the traditions.

Appealing to Western artists and scholars, some are invited as Thai representatives at dance and theatre **festivals** overseas.

Pawit Mahasarinand

Experimental Theatre: Vietnam

Experiments modernize traditional **Vietnamese** theatre or localize international influences. In *tuong* Ngo Xuan Huyen (1942–) effectively adapted Shakespeare's *Othello* in 2000. Vietnamese-American Theatre Exchange's *A Midsummer Night's Dream* toured the United States in 2004. Today's potpourri of classical scenes with supertitles reintroduces the genre to contemporary audiences.

Cheo innovations include Doan Hoan Giang's (1936–) *Princess Sita* (Nang Sita, 1988). **Critics** panned its modern language, but audiences flocked. A 2005 **festival** showed *Beautiful Girls Gambling* (Ma hong trong cuoc do den) by a provincial troupe, but traditionalists preferred work based on Ho Chi Minh's (1890–1969) 1940s *Prison Diary* (Nhat ky trong tu).

Kich noi experiments center in Ho Chi Minh City. In the 1980s, students of Nguyen Tuong Tran formed the Directors' Club (Cau lac bo dao dien). By 1997, it evolved into the Small Stage Drama Theatre (Nha hat Kich San khau Nho). Another experimental company is the Youth Theatre (Nha hat Tuoi Tre). Theatre festivals held every five years since 1989 have allowed national and international groups to share ideas, thereby encouraging innovation. Contemporary experiments may use controversial material or involve international collaborations, including nonrealistic performances. Controversial subjects include sexuality and drugs. Ho Chi Minh Stage and Film Institute students toured work discussing HIV/AIDS, while Nguyen Thi Hong Ngat's (1948?–) *Flying to Paradise* (Len tien, 1994) dealt with heroin addiction. International collaborations often go against prevailing realism. The stylized *Tartuffe* (Cau Dong, 2004) of the French Cultural Exchange Institute showed French influences in **scenography** and movement.

Lorelle Browning and Kathy Foley

FESTIVALS AND THEATRE

Festivals and Theatre: Cambodia

Cambodian festivals that take place on local and national levels honoring spiritual and natural events and cycles often include performance. Bon Kathin, for example, marking the end of the monks' rainy season retreat with the presentation of new robes and other necessities, usually in November, is celebrated with *lakhon bassac*, *yiké*, and *ayai* (improvised, flirtatious repartee singing) on temple grounds. The local community (or one wealthy benefactor) sponsors the performances, which sometimes require the construction or bringing in of a wooden or bamboo **stage**.

Before the war of the 1970s, the Siem Reap *lakhon sbaek* (see Puppet Theatre) troupe would perform at a temple or local field during Pchum Ben, the annual celebration of the dead in September or October, and at the cremation of notable **religious** figures. The annual reversal of the Mekong River's flow continues to be recognized in Phnom Penh during the Bon Om Tuk in November. Races of decorated boats take place while thousands of onlookers cheer from the riverbank in front of the Royal Palace. The grounds adjacent to the palace host performances of *ayai* and of singing **storytellers** who accompany themselves on long-necked lutes (*chapey dong veng*).

Since the late 1990s, National Cultural Day has been held every April in Phnom Penh, with a focus on **robam kbach boran** in an indoor setting, and **lakhon khol**, *lakhon bassac*, or *lakhon sbaek* to huge outdoor crowds. There are also festivals at the temple of Angkor in Siem Reap every year or two that may feature **folk** and/or classical **dances** and even troupes from abroad.

Toni Shapiro-Phim

Festivals and Theatre: China

Festivals have played an important role in the survival and development of modern **Chinese** theatre. The festivals, mostly government organized and subsidized after 1949, have encouraged the production of "spoken drama" (*huaju*; see Playwrights and Playwriting) and other genres, facilitated the circulation of new **theories**, technologies, and works of distinction, and nurtured public attention and interest in the performing arts.

The Chongqing Fog Season Public Performances between 1941 and 1945 was an early festival that caught public attention. The outbreak of the Second Sino-**Japanese**

War (1937–1945) forced many practitioners to move to Chongqing, a southwestern city where the Nationalist government was relocated. The festival was named after the heavy fog that shrouds the area from October to May each year, thereby protecting the city from air strikes. Over four years, more than 150 productions, mostly *huaju*, were staged.

In 1952, the People's Liberation Army of China held its own Performing Arts Festival in Beijing. In 1956, the Ministry of Culture organized the first National Spoken Drama Showcase, which gathered theatre artists from all over China and from twelve foreign countries. The festival honored almost all the participating **theatre companies** in order to encourage *huaju*'s growth. The event inspired many provinces and major cities to initiate similar activities of their own.

From January 1979 through February 1980, the Ministry of Culture held a Performing Arts Festival to mark the thirtieth anniversary of the founding of the People's Republic of China. It consisted of 137 shows and 931 individual performances by 128 participating companies from throughout China, including *huaju*, **geju**, **wuju**, **xiqu,** and **puppet theatre**. Numerous awards were distributed.

Organizing theatre festivals has become a major enterprise for almost every province and major city. To some companies, festival awards have become a significant resource for financial survival.

Besides performance showcases, festivals also have been organized to celebrate individual, especially foreign, playwrights, such as the Shakespeare Festivals (1986, Beijing, Shanghai; 1994, Shanghai), the O'Neill Centennial Festivals (1988, Nanjing, Shanghai), and the Chekhov Festival (2004, Beijing).

Current noteworthy festivals include the National Theatre Festival of China, founded by the All-China Dramatists Association; the National Art Festival of China, held every four years by the Ministry of Culture; the International Little Theatre Drama Festival, run by the Shanghai Theatre Academy (Shanghai Xiju Xueyuan); the Beijing International Drama Season; and the National College Theatre Festival, overseen by the All-China Dramatists Association and the Beijing Dramatists Association.

Nan Zhang

Festivals and Theatre: Hong Kong

Hong Kong is a city of year-round festivals, except for May and June, when school examinations take place. Not only do these festivals provide ample opportunities for theatre appreciation, they comprise important income sources for many **theatre companies** because what they receive from the Arts Development Council covers only part of their operation and production costs. Apart from the prestigious "big" festivals, there are also smaller ones with thematic platforms highlighting the specialties of the participating groups.

Run by the Hong Kong Arts Festival Society, Ltd., since 1973, with blessings from the colonial government, which was urgently trying to put behind it the traumatic leftist riots of 1967, it has become the most prestigious international festival, taking place in February and March over four weeks. It was not until 1980 that a local group, the Hong Kong Repertory Theatre (Xianggang Huaju Tuan), was given exposure in the festival. However, since 1996, the festival has included work from **experimental** groups. It thus has been able to foster a younger image, and programs of this type have been sponsored by Exxon Mobil Vision from 2001.

The City Fringe Festival, which evolved from the Hong Kong Festival Fringe (1983–1998), was modeled after the Edinburgh Fringe Festival. It focuses on urban culture and offers an open, uncensored platform for independent arts programs. It believes it has a role to play in Hong Kong's transformation from a colony to a modern **Chinese** city.

Corresponding to the Hong Kong Arts Festival was the Asian Arts Festival, organized by the Urban Council, which ran from 1976 to 1998. It was replaced by the Legends of China and New Vision Festivals in alternate years. Both are run by the Leisure and Cultural Services Department.

When the Hong Kong Repertory Theatre Company was inaugurated in 1977, it ran the Urban Council Drama Festival for amateur groups, who made it a popular venue for exposure and recognition. With the abolition of the Urban Council in 2000 (see Politics in Theatre), the festival gained a new lease on life under its next organizer, the Hong Kong Federation of Drama Societies.

Since 1994, the Hong Kong Arts Centre has organized small-scale theatre festivals with specific themes, such as Climactic Shorts (1994–1996), Wave Festival (1998–2001), and Little Asia (2002–). The latter was part of a regional arts exchange network with programs not confined to theatre.

Hardy Tsoi

Festivals and Theatre: India

Festivals are the major meeting points of several streams of many **Indian**-language theatres. These festivals are organized by government-supported institutions, government departments, universities, and independent theatre organizations. Indian festivals can be clustered into different categories. Just as India has heterogeneous cultural practices the festivals are heterogeneous in character, incorporating diverse forms and genres, from the traditional to the avant-garde. They include **folk theatre** festivals, festivals of classical theatre, campus theatre festivals, university and interuniversity theatre festivals, school youth festivals, festivals ranging from those organized by local bodies to those on increasingly higher hierarchical levels all the way to the national, children's theatre festivals, street theatre festivals, international, national, and regional theatre festivals, and festivals based on themes and categories, like those focused on **women**'s theatre, marginalized peoples' theatre, and so on. Some festivals are annual fixtures, some are occasional, some are competition-based, and some are noncompetitive.

Apart from the occasional national festivals organized by the National Academy of **Music**, **Dance**, and Drama (Sangeet Natak Akademi), that organization, in 1984, began the All-India Theatre Festival, designed to promote young **directors** doing **experimental** productions using traditional forms. It was organized on a two-tier level divided into zonal levels and culminating in a national level at New Delhi. Plays in the first and second zonal festivals were invited to the national level, which showcased the best productions in nearly all Indian languages performed by young artists with new ideas. The academy abandoned this scheme in 1992 and did not replace it. The academy supports other national theatre festivals in many states, but infrequently.

In 1999, New Delhi's National School of Drama (NSD) started a festival called Bharat Rang Mahotsav, featuring productions of national level **theatre companies** from various states, and usually presenting more than fifty plays—sometimes as many as one hundred. Occasionally, foreign productions are invited to participate. At present, it is one of India's most prominent government-sponsored national theatre festivals. Every year the NSD organizes a national children's theatre festival. Also, the NSD Repertory Company frequently goes to many parts of the country to organize festivals of its own Hindi productions. In addition, the NSD occasionally organizes national and international festivals with themes focusing on women's theatre and the like.

Different zonal cultural centers operated directly by the national government's Department of Culture often coordinate folk and modern theatre festivals in their respective areas, although these are not part of the centers' regular policy. Many state theatre academies organize annual amateur and professional festivals on the zonal level within the state as well on the state level, where selected plays from the zones are presented. Kerala's National Academy of Music, Dance, and Drama does this regularly on a competitive basis with prizes. Such festivals are seen also in many other states. Rangayana, the government repertory company of Karnataka, and the Kerala Academy began organizing national theatre festivals in 1995 and 2001, respectively, but had to stop because of financial reasons.

People's Theatre Platform (Jana Natya Manch) and **Safdar Hashmi** Memorial Trust, cultural organizations associated with the Communist Party, offered support to all-India street theatre festivals from 1989 onward, creating a place for street theatre in many languages to perform on a national level. Inspired by this, cultural groups affiliated with the Communist Party started organizing regional festivals under Safdar Hashmi's name in many states.

Prominent festivals organized by independent organizations include the Prithvi Theatre Festival in Mumbai (Bombay), the Attakkalari Festival of Movement Arts in Bangalore, and the Nandikar Festival in Kolkata (Calcutta). The first two festivals feature productions from abroad, the Prithvi being annual and the Attakkalari biannual. Many other festivals, like the Theatre Olympiad in Cuttak, Orissa; the Kalidasa Natya Samaroh in Ujjain, Uttar Pradesh; the **Bhasa** Theatre Festival in Trivandrum (Thiruvananthapuram), Kerala, and so forth, foster the enhancement of Indian theatre culture in an organized manner.

B. Ananthakrishnan

Festivals and Theatre: Indonesia

With the development of a modern theatrical culture in the late 1940s, festivals served as significant venues for new productions, as well as catalysts for exchange between **Indonesian** artists. Festivals first proliferated with the emergence of new troupes and **training** institutions in the mid-1950s. In 1956, troupes from throughout the country met in Menado, Medan, Yogyakarta, and Surabaya. In the late 1950s and early 1960s, one-time arts festivals provided venues for modern theatre in most of the regional capitals, though they did little to promote the development of local theatre.

Since the majority of troupes were formed as student "study groups," it is not surprising that the most influential festivals of the Sukarno years (1945–1966) were the four Student Arts Festivals conducted in Yogyakarta (1958), Jakarta (1960), Denpasar

(1962), and Bandung (1964). Many of the most innovative, contemporary young artists showed their most **experimental** new work at these festivals, inspiring each other to expand their theatrical vocabularies.

After 1967, the construction of major arts centers, such as Taman Ismail Marzuki, provided more continuous forums for theatrical activity, relegating festivals to a less prominent role. A series of theatre "meetings" served more as commemorations of aging luminaries than as forums for experimental work. In the 1990s, Indonesia joined the international festival circuit with such venues as Art Summit Indonesia (conducted annually in Jakarta). However, these festivals feature guest artists from abroad, and provide limited opportunities for less established troupes.

Evan Winet

Festivals and Theatre: Philippines

Theatre in the **Philippines** has long been part of **religious** festivals and, in recent decades, **theatre companies** and institutions have initiated festivals showcasing plays.

Christmas and Lent have been occasions for plays on such subjects as "the way of the Cross" (*via crucis*); the "Moriones" (literally, "helmets") playlet on the beheading of Longinus; the meeting of Mary and Christ (*salubong*); the "seven words" (*siete palabras*) dramatization of the agony on the cross; the "kings' parade" (*tatlong hari*) on horses following a star; and the "search for an inn" (*panunuluyan*), reenacting Joseph and Mary's journey. Similarly, when festivals (*fiestas*) were held celebrating a town's patron saint, a **sarsuwela** troupe was invited and/or a long poem of praise (*loa*) declaimed or dramatized. Mimetic jousts (the Maranao *bayok* and the Cebuano *balitao*) were also performed at harvest celebrations, weddings, and feasts.

In 1983 and 1984, the Philippine Educational Theatre Association (PETA) organized two National Theater Festivals featuring performances, workshops, and symposia. Among plays performed in 1983 and later anthologized were the improvisational *Farm Worker* (Sakada) by Negros Theatre League; *People's Oratorio: A Nationalist Declaration of Human Rights* by PETA; the **puppet** play *The Trial* (Ang paghuhukom), written and **directed** by Amelia Lapeña-Bonifacio (1930–); the **bodabil** play *Ilocula* by Peryante; and Barasoain Kalinangan's *Massacre* (Masaker), which draws from poetic traditions in articulating militarization experiences.

The Cultural Center of the Philippines has organized five theatre festivals: First Scene/Meeting (1992); Second Scene/Meeting (1996); the Philippine International Theatre Festival to celebrate the Philippine Independence Centennial (1998); the Asian Children's Arts Festival (2001); and the Third Scene/Meeting (2004) focusing on Philippine **music** theatre.

Joi Barrios

Festivals and Theatre: Singapore

Created in 1977 and occurring annually since 2000, the **Singapore** Arts Festival is the country's pre-eminent festival for theatre, **dance**, and **music**. Since Singapore's government, in an influential 1988 report on the arts, articulated a detailed strategy to "create a culturally vibrant society by 1999," this festival has become one of the primary tools to help raise the standards of Singaporean audiences by exposing them to world-class performance work. Before becoming an annual event, it alternated with the Festival of Asian Performing Arts.

Under the leadership of Goh Ching Lee since 2000, the festival now seeks to forge an identity as both "cutting edge" and strongly Asian. Nearly half the total number of performances hail from Asian countries, including an increasing number of collaborations linking Singaporeans with other Asian artists. Singapore's National Arts Council commissions most of the new Singaporean work and has been known to make suggestions that have shaped the final artistic product. The main program also features a number of costly but crowd-pleasing performances by well-established companies that return large revenues. Programming companies such as the Royal Ballet or the Philadelphia Orchestra attract mainstream audiences, providing a counter to the work of avant-garde **Western** • **directors** such as Robert LePage or Robert Wilson, both of whom have staged work at past festivals. In addition to major performance events, the festival presents a range of free and outdoor performances around the island, creating a highly visible presence for the performing arts every year in late May and June.

FURTHER READING

Peterson, William. *Theater and the Politics of Culture in Contemporary Singapore.*

William Peterson

Festivals and Theatre: Sri Lanka

During the second half of the twentieth century, **Sri Lankan** theatre's development owed much to its sponsorship by the state-sponsored Annual State Drama Festival, established in Colombo and run at first by the newly created National Theatre Trust, established by the Ministry of Cultural Affairs. The National Theatre Trust found itself stymied by the problem of rivalries from competing groups, and it was disbanded, being replaced by a Drama Advisory Board, appointed by but semi-independent of the government.

From its inception in 1959, the typical festival procedure was to present ten or so plays chosen as the best Sri Lankan works already given their first showing that year in Colombo, and presented over a week or ten-day period. The festivals were a great success, providing an outlet for numerous plays of all sorts. The country's top artists took part. Nine plays were submitted in 1959; by 1982, the number had grown to two hundred. A couple of years later, only those **playwrights** who had not previously submitted were permitted to do so. The events were much publicized and critically discussed—often with much controversy regarding the relative quality of the selections—for months afterward. Theatre business was greatly increased as a result.

The government expanded the festival to the provinces in 1978, with the best examples to be shown in Colombo. The state attempted to suggest themes for the writers, but widespread dissatisfaction with this practice led to its abandonment after two years.

Other state drama festivals eventually sprang up, the most notable being the Youth Drama Festival, designed to stimulate young playwrights and **directors**, often still in their teens, who frequently provided highly innovative writing and productions.

FURTHER READING

Obeyesekere, Ranjini. *Sri Lankan Theatre in a Time of Terror: Political Satire in a Permitted Space.*

Samuel L. Leiter

Festivals and Theatre: Thailand

Most theatre festivals in **Thailand** are organized by private organizations. Although they receive some financial support from governmental agencies, none are fully funded, like the Bangkok International Film Festival. In general, these festivals are restricted to certain venues and specific target audiences. It is noteworthy, however, that there are no traditional theatre festivals, perhaps because such performances are already an integral part of other festivals, ceremonies, and celebrations year round.

Since 1999, the Bangkok Fringe Festival has been held every December at the Patravadi **Theatre**. Because the company's main direction is *lakon khanob niyom mhai* ("new traditional dance-drama"), a modern dance-drama using some speaking, local and foreign traditional and modern artists share the **stage**. With support from foreign cultural agencies, intercultural and cross-disciplinary **music**, **dance,** and theatre programs, as well as documentary films on dance and theatre, are presented in the various spaces of this riverside complex.

Each November since 2002, the Bangkok Theatre Festival has hosted more than fifty traditional and modern productions, workshops, and discussions. Organized by the Bangkok Theatre Network, comprising professional and student **theatre companies**, the productions are limited to small-scale and local works offered free or for low admission prices.

The latest festival addition is Hoon Town, an international showcase of **puppet theatre** organized as a community fair. Both new works developed during pre-festival workshops and collaborative works by foreign and Thai professional puppeteers are staged.

The country's priciest annual performing arts festival is Bangkok's International Festival of Music and Dance, held every September since 1999 and no longer showcasing local works.

Pawit Mahasarinand

FOLK THEATRE

Folk Theatre: Cambodia

Rural performance traditions in **Cambodia** are rich and varied, and often associated with the agricultural cycle or Buddhist **religious** celebrations. Temple fairs may feature theatrical entertainment, such as *lakhon bassac* or shadow **puppets**. Itinerant or local **storytellers** who sing epic tales while accompanying themselves on long-necked lutes (*chapey dong veng*) are extremely popular at **festivals** and other celebrations where they can command attention for hours. They may be heard at a marketplace or other site as well, with passersby stopping for just a while to hear an episode of a popular legend or a lament about contemporary events.

Trot. *Trot*, a ceremonial folk **dance**-drama found in various places, had its origins in Siem Reap. In that region, *trot* ensembles sing and dance from house to house and village to village over the course of days or weeks at New Year's time, at ceremonies marking the monks' rainy season retreat, or at cremations of religious personages, enacting an ancient tale about a deer hunt, and collecting funds for their local monastery. **Actors** portray hunters, deer, and buffalo, and dancers don peacock feathers. **Musicians** play goblet drums, upright fiddles, and a bamboo flute, while singers ask for permission to perform, refer to the arrival of the rains, or seek gifts for the temple and then bless those who have given through improvised lyrics. Though the origins of this tradition and story are obscured in myth, by killing the deer the hunters are believed to quash a threat to traditional order.

Toni Shapiro-Phim

Folk Theatre: China

Small in scale and based on folk songs and **dances**, folk theatre is ancient and regionalized in **China**. Almost all of China's approximately 330 regional styles began as folk theatre, many remaining so to this day.

Folk song was a major source of theatrical **music** from *nanxi* on. From about the seventeenth century, various song and dance styles, performed as part of a **festival**, harvest-reaping, or other social or economic activity, developed into short dramas with simple stories. Types include "tea-picking plays" (*caicha xi*), which developed from songs sung while picking tea leaves in early summer, "flower drum plays" (*huagu xi*), and "flower lantern plays" (*huadeng xi*), all popular in central and south China.

Folk plays typically have two characters, usually a flirting or quarreling couple, sometimes with one or two subsidiary characters. The themes are comic, frequently bawdy, and very simple. Performers are amateur or semiprofessional. This pattern has remained largely unchanged for many centuries.

The Chinese Communist Party (CCP) always placed emphasis on folk mass theatre. During the war with **Japan** (1937–1945), CCP artists developed simple plays from ancient folk songs and dances of north China called "seedling songs" (*yangge*). They kept the simplicity and comedy of folk theatre, but replaced traditional themes with **politically** revolutionary ones. Instead of flirting or fighting, the couple engages in revolution and resistance against the Japanese.

After 1949, the CCP continued to favor revolutionized folk theatre, giving special preference to amateur troupes during the Cultural Revolution (1966–1976). The reform period has seen the revival of traditional patterns and themes. In many villages, peasants still perform simple plays for their peers at festival time or other social occasions. However, folk theatre has suffered from competition with other forms of entertainment, especially television.

FURTHER READING

Mackerras, Colin. *Chinese Drama, A Historical Survey*.

Colin Mackerras

Folk Theatre: India

There are few nations as richly blessed with numerous varieties of folk theatre as **India**. This country, in which, English aside, nearly a dozen and a half official languages associated with specific geographical regions are multiplied by over seven hundred dialects, contains a remarkable range of folk theatres (not to mention **dance** forms, the more dramatic of which—like, *chhau*—are sometimes considered folk dance-dramas); some are highly sophisticated, some crude; some are flourishing, some nearly extinct. They are found in every state, from Assam, Bengal, Orissa, Manipur, and Bihar, to Maharashtra, Kashmir, Andhra Pradesh, Uttar Pradesh, Rajasthan, Tamilnadu, Gujarat, Karnataka, Punjab, Himachal Pradesh, and Kerala. Half a dozen or more distinct genres can be found in certain states. There is such an abundance that, while the most familiar are thoroughly documented, little has been written about many.

On the other hand, there are a number of elements that join large numbers of these forms together; they generally are rural in nature, associated with village life, and shared in by the entire community, cutting across castes; often have **religious** aspects or associations, including trance possession; and are performed for celebratory or ritualistic purposes, generally at specific **festival** times or other occasions tied to the agrarian calendar. They frequently begin and end with ritual activities (*purvaranga* and *mangalam*); depend on oral transmission, not texts; commonly are experienced in all-night performances (sometimes requiring multiple performances lasting a week or even more); and are overseen or even narrated by a **director-actor** figure, often called, as in ancient **Sanskrit theatre**, the *sutradhara*, although other names—such as *bhagavatar*, *ranga*, kattiyankaram, and *vyasa*—exist. Many are given out of doors, in open spaces—of varying shapes and sizes, and sometimes using raised platform **stages**—surrounded by spectators seated on the ground; and present tales from national or local myths, legends, and epics—such as the *Ramayana* and *Mahabharata*, as well as the Puranas—or from the lives of famous heroes. For the most part noncommercial, these forms often favor all-male ensembles with **women**'s roles played by men; employ indecent sexual comedy (in forms using female impersonators as well as those with actresses); have satirically humorous characters—especially some version of the Sanskrit clown (*vidushaka*)—who, using colloquial language, like to poke fun at social and **political** issues; and allow for banter with audience members.

The majority employ highly stylized **costumes** as well as **masks** or flamboyant **makeup**, but only a minimum of **properties**; allow for asides, monologues, and soliloquies; combine choral singing with solos and duets; depend strongly on **musical** accompaniment, keeping their musicians visible throughout; and encompass multiple performance elements, including song, dance, poetry, and prose in a "total theatre" style. Folk theatre embodies the joys, sorrows, ideals, history, philosophy, wit, beliefs, and morality of the people.

Of course, not all genres contain all these features; some depend on texts, for example, others, like *tamasha* and (of late) *jatra*—although in the minority—use female performers, or may be performed only for three or four hours instead of through the night. In some cases, dialogue (as in *jatra* and ***bhavai***) is primary, in others it is song (as in ***khyal***, ***nautanki***, ***maanch***, and ***swang***) or dance (as in ***kathakali*** and ***krishnattam***). Some, like *nautanki*, *jatra*, and *tamasha*, are primarily secular, despite vestigial ritual touches; in fact, folk theatre in general has been divided into the religious (as in **terukkutu**, ***ramlila***, and ***raslila***) and secular. Actors may remain visible throughout in some genres, awaiting their entrances, while in others they may appear by walking through the audience or entering from behind a specially manipulated half-**curtain**. Locales typically switch instantaneously, through verbal or physical conventions established by the form.

The players commonly are born into the art and are trained by their parents from childhood in its mysteries. Occasionally, an actor is chosen for a role because of some external factor, like the prepubescent boys who play Rama and Krishna in *ramlila* and *raslila*, respectively, so as to keep these roles in the hands of the purest vessels, the boys themselves being revered as incarnations of the gods they portray.

There are genres that are hundreds of years old, dating perhaps to the fifteenth or sixteenth centuries, when folk theatre is said to have emerged in full force following the decline of Sanskrit and the rise of vernacular languages, and those that are relatively recent in origin, ***burrakatha*** having been born as recently as 1942. The more polished and sophisticated genres, like the venerable *kathakali* and ***kutiyattam***, are at the end of the spectrum that brings them closer to classical than to folk theatre, from which they presumably evolved, while forms at the other end, like ***nacha***, have little of the classical about them. Other highly developed forms, like *jatra*, *nautanki*, *bhavai*, *ramlila* and *raslila*, *tamasha*, ***yakshagana***, and *terukkuttu*, move away from the classical into the more vivid atmosphere of village entertainment, although, like *jatra*, they may have evolved into large-scale, commercial events attracting thousands. Moreover, there is a substantial group of **puppet theatres**, including glove, rod, shadow, and string puppet genres, and these too fall within the realm of folk theatre. They share many conventions with the live actors, including music, stories, and costumes.

In the nineteenth century, Hindi **playwright • Bharatendu Harishchandra** explored the possibilities of using folk theatre to invigorate his dramaturgy. When a number of outstanding mid-twentieth-century directors and playwrights, influenced by nationalist tendencies, began to do likewise on what turned out to be a rather wide-ranging scale, there arose the "theatre of roots," creating what some have called urban folk theatre. Practitioners such as **Habib Tanvir**, **K. V. Panikkar**, and **Ratan Thiyam** built their careers on works that drew inspiration from native forms. The movement has had its share of controversy, but it remains prevalent in the work of many contemporary artists.

FURTHER READING

Chopra, P. N., ed. *Folk Entertainment in India*; Gargi, Balwant. *Folk Theater of India*; Vatsyayan, Kapila. *Traditional Indian Theatre: Multiple Streams*.

Samuel L. Leiter

Folk Theatre: Indonesia

Rural and urban folk theatres performed in regional languages and various dialects of Malay can be found today or in the recent past in most of western **Indonesia**, particularly the islands of Java, Sumatra, Bali, Kalimantan, Madura, Sulawesi, and Lombok. These are known generically as "people's theatre" (*teater rakyat*), which is also used to refer to popular theatres such as ***sandiwara***, or "regional theatre" (*teater daerah*), which is also applied to forms associated with the royal courts, such as ***langen driya***. The lack of an exact Indonesian equivalent of the English category is indicative of the dynamics of theatrical circulation.

Many forms recognized today as "classical" and associated with the courts are in fact polished versions of folk forms that were once the sole purview of amateur **actors**, **dancers**, and **musicians** who performed for the amusement of local audiences and the appeasement of local spirits. Other former folk forms, such as ***ludruk***, ***kethoprak***, ***abdul muluk***, ***lenong***, and ***kecak***, have been elevated over the last century to proscenium **stages** and performed by professionals in public **theatres** for ticket-purchasing spectators. ***Randai***, the signatory folk theatre of West Sumatra, traces its origins in the opposite direction—it is descended from the itinerant professional theatres of ***bangsawan*** and ***komedi stambul***. Increasingly, *randai* troupes are turning semiprofessional, performing for money. It seems that no folk form stays purely folk for long.

A huge variety of ***barong*** and ***reog*** • **masked** theatres, and related forms of folk masquerade such as *sang hyang* (in Bali) and *kuda kepang* ("hobbyhorse dancing") and *jaran dor* in Java and Sumatra, were performed until 1942 in western Indonesia to ward off harmful influences and ensure a village's fertility and prosperity. Troupes were assembled ad hoc from villagers, with little if any rehearsal. Animal masks were (and in some areas still are) sacred and stored year round in village halls, cemeteries, or temples. Possession and the circumambulation of villages were common. These ritualistic forms are increasingly rare due to a combination of economic and **religious** factors—troupes that survive are largely dependent on extra-village patronage.

Secular folk theatres were also common in the past. Village youths performed their own versions of itinerant professional theatres, acting out well-known tales and legends to the accompaniment of *gamelan* **music**. Sometimes makeshift backdrops were painted on burlap cloth, but usually these forms were given in the round, illuminated by one or more torches. **Costume** items were borrowed from friends and neighbors. Many troupes were all-male, and involved cross-dressing. Sometimes donations were solicited. This sort of theatre was known by a variety of names, depending on the locale. For example, in Cirebon, West Java, such activity was called "porous theatre" (*jeblosan*) in the 1930s, as, unlike ***tonil,*** one could watch from all sides.

Even *wayang* (see Puppet Theatre), normally associated with highly skilled itinerant professionals, has its folk variants. Children often perform with handmade or prefabricated cardboard puppets with bang-on-a-can *gamelan* instruments, and sometimes work up enough skill to perform publicly. Another folk variant of *wayang* is *jemblung* (also known as *dhalang jemblung* or *wayang jemblung*) of western Central Java, in which no puppets or instruments are used—all music is "played" by vocal imitation, described by one source as "an irreverent, low-rent view of the classical tradition."

FURTHER READING

Arps, Bernard, ed. *Performance in Java and Bali: Studies of Narrative, Theatre, Music, and Dance*; Emigh, John. *Masked Performance: The Play of Self and Other in Ritual and Theatre.*

Matthew Isaac Cohen

Folk Theatre: Japan

Japanese folk theatre (*minzoku geinô*) comprises a wide variety of dramatic, **dance**, narrative, and **musical** presentations featured at events ranging from long-established shrine and temple **festivals** to newly created folk culture and tourist programs. Almost every village, town, and city has its own version of one or more types of folk performance—adding up to some twenty thousand separate presentations found throughout Japan today. Scholar Honda Yasuji divided these arts into five main categories: *kagura*, *dengaku*, *furyû* (large-scale events such as *bon* festival dances), "benedictory arts/narrative pieces" (*shukufukugei/katarimono*, including *manzai* comedies and *kôwakamai*), and "stage arts" (*butaigei*, including folk versions of *nô* and *kabuki*).

Almost all performers are community volunteers, many of them members of the preservation societies (*hozonkai*) that locally administer the folk performing arts. Although most performers are adults—both men and women—whose **acting**, dance, and music skills may equal those of professionals, one of the most striking aspects of *minzoku geinô* is the frequent participation of children. The Nagahama City Float Festival (Ishikawa Prefecture), for example, features children's *kabuki*.

In recent decades, rural depopulation and the pressures of contemporary life have greatly reduced the number of volunteer performers. At the same time, folk performance has become officially regarded as an essential element of Japan's cultural heritage and identity, giving rise to efforts at all levels of government to recognize and sustain it. The Cultural Properties Protection Law (1950; revised, 1975) includes a category called "folk cultural properties." To date, approximately two hundred such arts have received the highest designation of nationally "important intangible folk cultural property." Designation brings little more tangible reward than a small stipend to cover the cost of **costumes** and such, though the Festival Law (1992) was enacted to help local economies develop festivals and their folk performances as tourist attractions for visitors seeking a taste of traditional culture.

The festival held each December 17th at Nara's Kasuga Wakamiya Shrine provides an excellent opportunity to see, sequentially within about seven hours, dances and dramas that include *kagura*, *azuma asobi*, *dengaku*, *sarugaku*, and **bugaku**. A few examples of well-known arts associated with other locales are *hayachine kagura* (Iwate Prefecture), *kurokawa nô* (Yamagata Prefecture), **mibu kyôgen** (Kyoto Prefecture), and *ayako mai* (Niigata Prefecture). *Awaji ningyô-jôruri* (Hyôgo Prefecture), a precursor of *bunraku* (see Puppet Theatre), is one of several such arts that have toured overseas. One of the most prominent showcases for folk performance is Tokyo's National **Theatre** (Kokuritsu Gekijô), where groups are invited to perform on two or three weekends each year.

FURTHER READING

Thornbury, Barbara E. *The Folk Performing Arts: Traditional Culture in Contemporary Japan.*

Barbara E. Thornbury

Folk Theatre: Korea

Korean folk theatre is informal, being performed by local people reflecting the lives and beliefs of their particular region. Performed as part of local **festivals** or ceremonies, or associated with **religious** practices of exorcism or prayers for abundant agriculture and fishing, these collective works by anonymous **playwrights** are transmitted orally, the stories often based on regional legends. Performances center on **dance**, **music**, singing, and **acting**, with less emphasis on language; decor consists of **costumes**, banners, and **properties**. Some require many participants, sometimes in the hundreds or even thousands. Competitions often are involved. Performed outdoors, no conventional **scenographic** devices or **theatres** are needed; performers and audiences often mingle freely.

There are approximately two hundred folk plays, although changing demographics and lifestyles have reduced the number performed recently. Today, folk plays are often presented to appreciative audiences at regional festivals.

"The Chariot Battle" (*Ch'ajŏ nnori*, or *Dongchaessaum* in the Andong area) is traditionally performed on the fifteenth day of the first lunar month to promote a cooperative spirit among the townspeople, but a nineteenth-century book of customs suggests it was presented to predict which district would be blessed with abundant crops.

It demands many participants and for each performance. Andong is divided into two districts that are pit against each other in battle. After solemn rituals, chariots are made with two long, clean logs roped together in an A-frame. A platform with a straw mat is fastened near the top of the A, on which the captain of the team, urging on his team of hundreds of strong young men, rides as a battle rages. The winner is determined by downing the opposing team's chariot and capturing its banners.

"The Pyokgolje Dragon Play" (*Pyokgolje ssangyongnori*) in Kimje depicts squabbling between two dragons, the blue representing storm, and the white representing serenity. The first scene is about repairing a storm-damaged dam, while the next two are about the battle between the two dragons, moved by a few dozen people inside each. The blue dragon wins, causing a storm. Seeing danger to the village, a beautiful young lady charms the dragon to keep the storm away, ensuring the village's safety. The grand finale incorporates ecstatic dancing, singing, and music by performers and audiences.

"The Tug of War" (*Juldarigi*) and many variations have been widely performed in Korea, but are more popular in the agricultural southwestern region. Performed to pray for a good harvest and health, the performances pit teams of **women** against men. Unmarried men, interestingly, battle on the women's side. If the contest happens to be between two villages, each side still battles as either male or female.

"The Palanquin Battle" (*Kamassaum*) of the Uisŏng district is said to have been started by village students. Each contending group usually contains several dozen children pulling a palanquin on four wheels. A **puppet** made from a pumpkin representing the mayor is placed inside the palanquin. Students pulling their palanquin battle opponents as their teammates push from the rear. Seizure of the opponent's palanquin and banners determines victory. After the battle, the victors march to music through their village. In earlier days, the parents of the winning team's students believed a victory meant a higher number of their children would pass civil service examinations. The contest also offered the children a chance to improve their physical fitness after exhausting their minds in school.

"The Old Man's Play" (*Yonggamnori*), a shaman's play from Cheju Island, was initially presented to heal sick people. Music, dance, singing, and pantomime with improvised dialogue provide the spectacle. The performance uses a sacrificial table with a steamed pig head, sorghum cake, and a small straw boat. Various tales are performed, the most popular depicting the ridiculous behavior and cure of a lovesick old man. In the beginning, a young shaman in an old man's **mask** appears. The old man is enamored with a young woman, and the scene depicts the inner workings of the sickly man's mind. Humorous dialogue discloses why he likes beautiful women. After a while, the old man dances to music with a straw boat in his hand, pantomiming loading various cargos, suggesting he is shipping away his immoral lovesickness. In the final scene, his family members and the audience join him.

FURTHER READING

Cho, Oh-Kon, trans. *Traditional Korean Theatre*; Cultural Properties Administration. *Korean Intangible Cultural Properties: Folk Dramas, Games and Rites.*

Oh-Kon Cho

Folk Theatre: Sri Lanka

Playwright, **director**, and scholar E. R. Sarachchandra (1914–1996) suggested that the lack of traditional literary drama in **Sri Lanka** may be attributed to most literate men having been Buddhist monks for whom drama was taboo; although **Sanskrit theatre** was known to Sinhalese writers, they attempted every other form except drama. This absence of classical Sinhalese drama is reiterated by Christopher Reynolds (1987), who argues that native drama flourished as a folk theatre derived from and integrated with rituals. Some dramatic pieces had **masked • dancers** and were based on South **Indian** or Roman Catholic origins (introduced by Portuguese colonizers).

Despite the possibility that Buddhism may have held back the development of formal dramaturgy, the **religion**'s practices are highly theatrical, as demonstrated by many still enacted Sri Lankan rituals. Among exorcistic healing rituals related to the native folk tradition are those involving the numerous gods and demons doing battle on behalf of good or evil. The demons must be ritually mollified before they will desist from afflicting someone. The rituals typically employ verse narration, **dance**, dialogue, **makeup**, **costumes**, **properties** and decorative accessories, improvisation, dramatic episodes based on stories associated with the participating gods or demons, and a circular "performance space" (*ranga mandala*). One group of rituals is for an entire village (at harvest time or in the case of epidemics); another is for an afflicted individual. Only in a couple of types is there a physical structure built for the event, although even these are out-of-doors, where audiences move about freely. Torches supply the illumination, and may even be manipulated as properties by acrobatic dancers. Dancers, "amateur" though they may be, are highly **trained**.

The *kohomba kankariya* (literally, "rite of God Kohomba") of Kandy is a five-episode (each has its name), open-air ritual performed under a roofed structure. Its disconnected elements—in which elaborate Kandyan dancing (with the dancers wearing beautiful headdresses) accompanied by drumming—include a fairly dramatic episode in which the hunting for and killing (with bow and arrow) of a wild boar is mimed, as is the distribution of its meat to participants. The sequence includes a dancer who mimes a buffalo being used as a decoy to attract the boar (represented by a bamboo property). The "meat" distribution scene has a socially satirical touch in that the worst parts go to the upper social echelons, the best to the most in need.

The widely revered goddess Pattini—associated with contagious diseases—is the focus of a number of important rituals, such as the *gammaduva* (literally, "village hall"), which involves the entire village and is performed at night in a specially erected pavilion or shed (*maduva*). The entire village believes that a *gammaduva* will bring blessings for agricultural success. The shed is generally around sixty feet long by twenty feet wide and decorated with coconut leaves. Its construction begins at an auspicious time when a vow is made to the gods promising to hold the ritual on a specific date. During the nightlong ceremony verses invoking the blessings mentioning these gods are sung, and numerous traditional dances are performed to drum accompaniment.

Another important group of ritual performances is *bali-tovil*. *Bali* refers to rites devoted to the planetary deities (represented by large, clay effigies), while *tovil* (or *thovil*) are highly dramatic, exorcistic "devil dances" in which masked performers portray illness-causing demons, and in which the patient may go into trance before the demons leave. Different types of *tovil* are "destruction of the sorcery" (*suniyam kapilla*), "seven barren queens" (*rata yakuma*), and "demon Yakuma" (*sanni yakuma*), which differ in the nature of the illnesses (or, as in *rata yakuma*, the dangers of childbirth and/or the problem of infertility) being addressed, each illness represented by a different mask. There are eighteen in *sanni yakuma*.

The beginnings of Sinhalese drama, in both style and content, are found in such rituals for the invocation and propitiation of supernatural beings. Since ceremonies are enacted through the night, when audiences are restless and tired, a dramatic interlude is performed that may only be loosely connected to the ceremony.

More theatrically developed is **kolam**, which has survived especially in the coastal regions. It is performed all night long, with an array of masked dancers representing characters from various sources, not always connected to any story. The performance ends with the enactment of a dramatic scene or two presented with songs and impromptu dialogue.

Sokari, another folk theatre, was traditionally confined to the up-country (*uda rata*), and presents a story in sophisticated mime, with its clown in a mask. The story, about the seduction or elopement of an Indian woman named Sokari, varies from one part of Sri Lanka to the others.

The best-known folk theatre is **nadagam** (or *nadagama*), which came to prominence around the beginning of the nineteenth century. Its works are termed folk operas and are enacted mostly through song accompanied by suitable gestures, poses, movement, and dance. *Nadagam* appears to have emerged from South Indian folk forms, namely, Tamilnadu's **terukkuttu** and Andhra Pradesh's "street theatre" (*viti nataka*).

Three other folk forms are *kamakootham*, **puppet theatre**, and the Roman Catholic passion play (**pasku**). The first is a Hindu **festival** drama performed every spring by the Tamil tea and rubber plantation workers of central Sri Lanka for anywhere from eleven to thirty days. It is performed in honor of the Hindu god of love and passion, Kama, with professionals mingling with local people whose involvement is connected with the fulfillment of some sort of vow. It stems from a belief that Lord Shiva reduced Lord Kama to ashes when the latter disturbed his prayers. Kama's wife convinced Shiva to bring her husband back to life, which he did but only in invisible form. The participants debate whether Shiva actually did incinerate Kama, while street theatre episodes depict scenes from the Hindu myths, with performances—including song, **music**, and dance—springing up all over the village.

Puppet plays, probably derived from India, are more recent and are believed to have been born around a century ago. The puppets, who appear on a raised **stage**, are three to four feet tall, and are manipulated by strings tied to a plain horizontal bar or two bars fixed crosswise and held in the hands.

Pasku originated (like *nadagam*) in the Catholic areas of Jaffna and migrated to the Sinhalese-speaking parts along the west coast.

FURTHER READING

Reynolds, Christopher. *An Anthology of Sinhalese Literature of the Twentieth Century*; Sarach-chandra, E. R. *The Folk Drama of Ceylon*.

Neluka Silva

Folk Theatre: Vietnam

Folk performances, including temple ceremonies, courting songs, and small-scale theatricals, are ancient in **Vietnam**.

Cheo. The main folk theatre form, *cheo*, shows the integration of **music**, poetry, song, and **dance**. Stories come from popular tales, usually showing the good side of the masses, like the poor fisherman Truong Chi, who wins a princess's heart. A major character is the clown (*he*), noted for improvisation; female characters are pre-eminent, with dance, including gestures and hand movements, full of feminine grace. Singing comes from folk songs, using peasant language, often witty and earthy, with many popular sayings.

Until recently, there were no written scripts, with plays handed down orally. Though mainly entertainment, *cheo* could be part of **religious • festivals** outside of temples. Other sites included village community halls or any open space. **Properties**, musical accompaniment, **makeup**, and **costumes** were very simple. Performers were ordinary peasants, but there were also professionals, very low in status, and **acting** often ran in families.

Mua roi nuoc. A unique and important form of Vietnamese folk theatre is water **puppetry** (*mua roi nuoc*), which dates at least from the early twelfth century. This involves brief comic or fighting scenes staged on ponds, the hidden puppeteers using long rods to manipulate the puppets, which are thirty to forty centimeters high. There are still active water puppet companies, especially in the Red River delta, while in Hanoi, a professional company performs for tourists.

Colin Mackerras

FUKUDA TSUNEARI (1912–1994). Japanese • *shingeki* • **playwright**, critic, **director**, translator, and novelist. Although a published dramatist at twenty-two, Fukuda inclined more toward **criticism**. His Tokyo University graduate thesis (1936) was on D. H. Lawrence, whose influence underlies Fukuda's subsequent writing. He published studies of **Western** plays, such as *On Macbeth* (Makubesu ron, 1947), and on Japanese writers.

After the war, he resumed playwriting, concerning himself mostly with issues of modernization. His best-known plays are *Typhoon Kitty* (Kitii taifû, 1950), satirizing Japanese intellectuals with a quasi-parody of Chekhov's *The Cherry Orchard*, and *The Man Who Stroked the Dragon* (Ryû o nadeta otoko, 1952), exploring true love in a godless country, with evocations of Eliot's *The Cocktail Party*. His later plays include *Akechi Hidemitsu* (1957) and *I am Damned if I Know It* (Wakatte tamaruka, 1968).

Among his lasting contributions is his translation of Shakespeare's major plays into vital and natural modern Japanese, as compared against **Tsubouchi Shôyô**'s solemn classical translations. Fukuda's staging of *Hamlet* in 1955, using his translation, remains legendary.

A member since 1952 of the Literary **Theatre** (Bungaku-za), which staged many of his plays, Fukuda resigned in 1963 to found the **theatre company** Cloud (Kumo), with Akutagawa Hiroshi (1920–1981); it later split into Akutagawa's Circle (En) and Fukuda's the Pleiades (Subaru). A social conservative activist, Fukuda also wrote on issues ranging from the revision of Japan's constitution to language reform.

Guohe Zheng

FUKUDA YOSHIYUKI (1931–). Japanese • *shingeki* • **playwright** who graduated from Tokyo University, where he was active in theatre. Fukuda wrote plays reflecting his strong socialist commitment. In early plays, like the well-received, historically grounded *A Long Row of Gravestones* (Nagai bohyô no retsu, 1957), detailing the **censorship** of liberal martyr Kawai Eijirô (1891–1944) and his forced resignation from Tokyo Imperial University, he exhibited the socialist realist influences that were a *shingeki* staple.

Fukuda was at his most **politically** influential as a founding member of the Youth Arts Theatre (Seinen Geijutsu Gekijô, 1959). Known as Seigei, this **theatre company** was born from the fervor of student demonstrations against the 1960 renewal of the U.S.-Japan Mutual Security Treaty and was a significant force in the post-*shingeki* movement (see *Angura*). Fukuda's first play for Seigei, *Document Number 1* (Kiroku numbaa wan, 1960), illustrates a critical shift in his dramaturgical and ideological orientation. Created from interviews with **actors** involved in the demonstrations, the play departs from conventional socialist realism, combining invented scenes with documentary techniques to portray the struggle in Brechtian style.

Fukuda's most celebrated Seigei work, *Find Hakamadare!* (Hakamadare wa doko da, 1964), furthers his stylistic and political exploration with an episodic **dramatic structure** that follows a group of villagers acting in the name of the Robin Hood–like title character. When the real Hakamadare proves to be a ruthless opportunist, the villagers kill him and resume their activities in the name of the Hakamadare of their dreams.

Michael W. Cassidy

FURUHASHI TEIJI (1960–1995). Japanese • **director** and media/performance artist, the inspiration behind dumb type (1984), an **experimental theatre** collective of Kyoto University of Arts graduates. Sometimes with dumb type, sometimes solo, Furuhashi distinguished himself for daring multimedia collaborations tackling race, gender, and sexuality, issues shunned by other contemporary artists.

An early video work, "Conversational Styles" (1985), was shown at New York's Museum of Modern Art. Furuhashi's first major dumb type production was *PLEASURE LIFE* (1988), a performance-art installation, featuring **actors** rushing repeatedly through a matrix wired with sensors, reflecting life's tedium in a wired world. *pH* (1990), a work highlighting humanity's subjection to technology, had performers dodging a sliding mechanism resembling a bar code scanner. These works were harbingers of a salient thematic strain of 1990s Japanese drama. Both also played internationally to great acclaim. "Lovers," a solo video installation, premiered in 1994.

The same year, Furuhashi addressed homosexuality and AIDS in his last collaboration with dumb type, *S/N* (1994), "S" meaning signal and "N" noise. Its cast included gays, foreigners, sex workers, and people with disabilities, all marginalized minorities in Japan. Combining video and computer-generated images, text, **music**, ambient noise, and live performance, it was among the first works to problematize race, gender, and sexuality in Japanese theatre.

Despite Furuhashi's untimely death, dumb type continues to perform, featuring a video of him in performances of *S/N*.

M. Cody Poulton

GAGAKU. *See Bugaku.*

GAMBHIRA. Ancient **Bangladeshi** and **Indian** form in which earthy **folk** characters, typically a grandfather and a grandson, sing about social ills through wisecracking repartee. *Gambhira* emerged out of an earlier tradition performed as **religious** ritual preliminary (*puja*) to popular Hindu deities, such as Dharma Thakur, and only later became uniquely associated with Shiva worship.

The word *gambhira* relates to the inner sanctum of a Shiva temple and also is similar to one of Shiva's names, Gambhir. Two different *gambhira* originally flourished: one was narrative, dramatically enacting a social problem; the other related the joys and sorrows of the common people. Both types were performed before an image of Shiva, housed in a small hut behind the playing area. At the performance's beginning, four chorus members chanted praise songs to Shiva. Following this **musical** invocation, an **actor** portraying Shiva would enter dressed in a tiger skin loincloth and matted hair, and would remain for the rest of the performance.

The distinctive **musical** style found in *gambhira* has continued to evolve and now reflects the tastes of moviegoing audiences. Several prominent performers recently have emerged in the region of Nawabganj, northwest of Rajshahi. *Gambhira* is also performed in Bengal, where it is part of the Gambhira **Festival** in Shiva's honor held every year in the Maldah District from April to June.

Robert Petersen

GAMBUH. Balinese (see Indonesia) classical **dance**-drama, usually performed in conjunction with **religious** ceremonies or **festivals** in the middle courtyard of a temple compound. **Stages** are often thatch-roofed platforms fitted with an upstage **curtain** for entrances. The very complex **music** is provided by a unique ensemble, the *gamelan penggambuhan*, which features extra-large flutes and a range of special percussion instruments.

Much of the performance's duration (formerly given over three or four days from late morning to afternoon) is taken up with the detailed opening scenes (*peposon*) sung in Old Javanese, introducing each of a series of key characters (called by feudal titles, not names), divided between refined (*alus*) and coarse (*kasar*) **role types**. Comedy is provided by clownish servants. This is followed by a relatively short narrative section derived from an episode of the *Malat* (Bali's version of the **Panji** cycle).

Although *gambuh* is considered Bali's oldest performing art, with roots beginning in tenth-century Java, most historians of *gambuh* suggest that it first emerged during the sixteenth century, when classical Javanese influences from Majapahit were prominent in Bali. In the precolonial period, *gambuh* was patronized by royalty, but after the dissolution of these traditional power bases, with the arrival of the Dutch in 1906, *gambuh* declined in favor. The genre has, however, undergone something of a revival—supported by local initiatives, the government, and outside funding—since the late twentieth century. The troupe of Denpasar's Arti Foundation has also developed *gambuh* with a twist in their *Gambuh Macbeth*, performed since 1998.

FURTHER READING

Dibia, I Wayan, and Rucina Ballinger. *Balinese Dance, Drama and Music: A Guide to the Performing Arts of Bali*; Yousof, Ghulam Sarwar. *Dictionary of Traditional South-East Asian Theatre*.

Laura Noszlopy

GANDHI, SHANTA (1917–2002). Indian • **playwright**, **director**, **dancer**, **actress**, philosopher, and singer. Born in Nasik, Maharashtra, she dedicated herself to exploring a theatre idiom rooted in her native culture. In 1936, while studying medicine in England, she came in contact with Indian freedom fighters, and ended up dancing to raise funds for the Spanish Civil War. After returning, she joined Uday Shankar's (1900–1977) Cultural Centre and was trained in dance by Sankaran Namboodiri. A dedicated communist, she became one of the founding members of the Little Ballet Troupe attached to the Indian People's Theatre Association and performed across the country to raise socio-**political** consciousness.

After accidentally encountering the ancient *Treatise on Drama* (Natyashastra; see Theory), she translated it into English. She produced and directed **Sanskrit** plays like *Vyayoga of the Middle One* (Madhyam Vyayoga) and *Vikram Won by Valor* (Vikramorvasiya) in an ancient style called *natyadharmi*. She also directed Gujarati and Hindi plays. She taught classical Indian drama at the National School of Drama (NSD). During her tenure as the director of Bal Bhavan, children's activities in drama, dance, **music**, and painting received special impetus. She produced *Jasma Odan* and *Amar Singh Rathor*, attempts at revitalizing **folk** forms. Gandhi was the first to reinterpret the classical and the folk for a contemporary sensibility. She also served as the chairperson of the NSD and received the National Academy of Music, Dance, and Drama (Sangeet Natak Akademi) award in 2001, among other honors.

Debjani Ray Moulik

GANGULI, USHA (1945–). Indian Hindi-language **director**, auteur, and **actress**, born in Jodhpur, Rajasthan, but based in Calcutta (Kolkata), a Bengali-majority city where since 1970 she has contributed to the effort to establish significant theatre in Hindi. After working for some years with Hindi **theatre companies** that were patronized by the wealthy expatriate community of North Indian industrialists and businessmen, Ganguli founded the group Rangakarmee in 1976 to create a socially

Usha Ganguly's production of *The Mourner*, based on the original Bengali story by Mahasweta Devi, for Rangakarmee, Calcutta (Kolkata), India, December 1992. (Photo: Courtesy of Natya Shodh Sansthan)

conscious, **politically** responsible theatre, and to expand the playgoing audience by drawing in hitherto marginalized groups. Her activist approach to issues of gender and class has galvanized audiences, with open-air performances being attended by up to two thousand.

Ganguli's eclectic repertoire includes Hindi productions of major contemporary plays, such as Ratnakar Matkari's (1938–) *Folktale* (Lok-katha, 1987) and **Mahesh Elkunchwar**'s *Fire Ritual* (Holi, 1989), as well as canonical **Western** plays, such as Wesker's *Roots* (1978), Ibsen's *A Doll's House* (1981), and Brecht's *Mother Courage* (1998). Her breakthrough productions, however, were adaptations of two stories by Bengali author Mahasweta Devi (1926–), *The Mourner* (Rudali, 1993), in which Ganguli played a professional mourner, and *Liberation* (Mukti, 1999), which she directed. Ganguli also acted the lead in a Hindi version of Kroetz's *Request Concert* (1986). In 2002, she won acclaim for *The Journey Within* (Antar-yatra), a solo piece that interweaves autobiography with the voices of **women** from various plays, and a commentary on women's role in theatre.

Aparna Dharwadker

GAO XINGJIAN (1940–). Chinese • **playwright**, novelist, **stage** and film **director**, **critic**, **theorist**, translator, essayist, and painter, awarded the Nobel Prize in Literature in 2000. Born in Ganzhou, Jiangxi Province, he received a degree in French language and literature in 1962. His theatrical debut, *Signal Alarm* (Juedui xinhao, 1982), was produced by the Beijing People's Art **Theatre** (Beijing Renmin Yishu Juyuan). Its modernist style and departure from the convention of praising communist leaders energized the burgeoning **experimental theatre** movement but resulted in Communist Party censure. *Bus Stop* (Chezhan, 1983), an absurdist play about passengers waiting indefinitely for a bus that fails to arrive, was performed only thirteen times before being **censored** for its antisocialist message. *Wild Man* (Yeren, 1985), an epic drama about ecology and civilization, fuses the modernist influences of Beckett, Ionesco, Artaud, and Brecht with indigenous techniques.

After *The Other Shore* (Bi'an, 1986), a despairing view of collectivism and salvation, was suspended on **political** grounds, Gao left China and, in 1987, immigrated to Paris. Gao's party membership was revoked and his works banned after he wrote *Exile* (Taowang, 1989), about three characters fleeing arrest during the Tiananmen Square crackdown.

While Gao's pre-exile plays focus primarily on collectivism, his post-exile plays offer a poetic and self-conscious contemplation of the self while developing original techniques that blend Chinese and **Western** traditions. *Between Life and Death* (Shengsijie, 1991) examines the complex psychological landscape of a woman tormented by her sinful past and fears of death and unattainable salvation. *Dialogue and Rebuttal* (Duihua yu fanjie, 1992) expresses the futility of language and communication between man and **woman**, and *Nocturnal Wanderer* (Yeyoushen, 1993) explores morality, multiple levels of consciousness, and the blurring between reality and dream worlds.

A fundamental aspect of his theory and practice is the tripartition of **acting**, in which the actor embodies the self, the neutral actor, and the character. The neutral actor functions to observe the performance of the self as the character and infuses the actor's performance with a dimension of self-consciousness. His plays also experiment with shifting narrative modes. Characters speak in the conventional first person but also refer to themselves in the second and third persons, allowing them to simultaneously embody three different perspectives and psychological states.

FURTHER READING

Quah, Sy Ren. *Gao Xingjian and Transcultural Chinese Theater*; Tam, Kwok-kan, ed.. *Soul of Chaos: Critical Perspectives on Gao Xingjian.*

Jonathan Noble

GEJU. **Chinese** genre inspired by the introduction of **Western** opera during the New Culture Movement (1916–1920s). Its **musical** composition typically follows Western structure and harmonic principles while the melodies are strongly influenced by traditional theatre and **folk** music. *Geju* can also refer to Western opera.

Geju began with Li Jinhui (1891–1967), who composed children's song-and-**dance** dramas in the 1920s, such as *Sparrows and Children* (Maque yu xiaohai). He synthesized Western harmonic techniques with melodies from *xiqu*, folk songs, and children's rhymes.

In 1935, **Tian Han** and Nie Er (1912–1935) wrote *Storm on the Yangtze River* (Yangzijiang baofengyu), a "spoken drama" (*huaju*) (see Playwrights and Playwriting) with songs. From the mid-1930s into the 1940s, many *geju* followed the conventions of grand opera, among them *Akiko* (Qiu zi, 1942) by Huang Yuanluo.

In 1942, at the Yan'an Forum, Mao Zedong (1893–1976) emphasized that art and literature should serve the masses and that artists should find inspiration from the life of common people. The talks gave rise to the birth of *yangge ju* (literally, "rice-seedling song drama"), combining indigenous theatrical techniques, folk songs, **dance**, and percussion, usually with a simple plot. The best known *yangge ju* included *Brother and Younger Sister Cultivate Wasteland* (Xiongmei kaihuang).

Inspired by the idea of integrating folk culture such as *yangge* into a high artistic form, the Lun Xun Fine Arts Institute produced *The White-haired Girl* (Baimaonü, 1945) in Yan'an. In it, a peasant girl, after being raped by a landlord, escapes to a mountain cave where her hair turns white because of her privations. Rescued by communist soldiers, she reunites with her family, and the landlord is punished. Composed with melodies from folk songs and regional theatre, *The White-haired Girl* achieved exceptional popularity and is considered a milestone. It also inspired other *geju* that portray communist heroism, such as *Red Guards on Honghu Lake* (Honghu chiweidui, 1959), *Jiang Jie* (1964), and *The East Is Red* (Dongfang hong, 1964).

After the Cultural Revolution (1966–1976), new *geju* emerged, but few have drawn much attention. Major **theatre companies** today include the China National Opera and Dance Drama Ensemble (Zhongguo Geju Wuju Yuan), focusing mainly on Chinese *geju*, and the Central Opera (Zhongyang Geju Yuan), Liaoning Opera (Liaoning Geju Yuan), and Shanghai Opera (Shanghai Geju Yuan), which produce both Western and Chinese *geju*.

FURTHER READING

Mackerras, Colin. *Chinese Theatre from Its Origins to the Present Day.*

Nan Zhang

GENDHON HUMARDANI (1923–1983). Indonesian arts administrator, **critic**, choreographer, and dancer, a reformer of traditional Javanese arts in the postcolonial period. Gendhon studied Javanese **dance**, in both the Surakarta and Yogyakarta classical styles, along with martial arts (*pencak silat*), from age eleven. He choreographed his first dance for the Jakarta branch of the Dance and Music **Training** Center in 1944, and, as a medical student and teaching assistant at Gadjah Mada University in Yogyakarta, he founded and was president of the Students of Culture Association from 1952 until 1960. Through it, Gendhon produced condensed versions of *wayang* (see Puppet Theatre), wordless dance-dramas that were precursors of *sendratari* and the radical dance-dramas of **Sardono W. Kusomo**, traditional dances in new **costumes**, and dances and dance-dramas that crossed regional styles, including Javanese dance accompanied by Balinese *gamelan* **music**. These **experiments** were controversial, but Gendhon was vociferous that tradition had to adapt to modern life to be meaningful.

After studying medicine and dance in Britain and the United States in the early 1960s, Gendhon returned to Indonesia and oversaw the establishment of the College of Traditional Indonesian Arts (ASKI) in Surakarta, Indonesia's first tertiary institution for traditional performance. In 1970, Gendhon was appointed director of the newly established Central Java Arts Center (PKJT) and in 1975 was formally named head of ASKI-Surakarta. Gendhon transformed ASKI from conservator to center for experimentation in tradition, and PKJT became its public outreach arm. Under Gendhon's leadership, ASKI and PKJT revived nearly extinct royal court and **folk** genres, crossed regional traditions, produced experimental *wayang* forms (*pakeliran padat, wayang* *sandosa, wayang buddha*), and modernized music, dance, dance-drama, and **puppetry**. Gendhon also facilitated the tertiary education of ASKI lecturers, and produced foreign tours featuring ASKI staff and students.

Matthew Isaac Cohen

GEZAIXI. *See* Taiwan.

GHOSH, GIRISH CHANDRA (1844–1912). **Indian** Bengali-language **playwright**, **actor**, **director**, **scenographer**, manager, poet, composer, and teacher, born in Calcutta (Kolkata). Ghosh worked as a bookkeeper for a British company, but his literary and philosophical interests led him to begin writing. He began his theatrical career composing songs for **Michael Madhusudan Dutt**'s *Sharmishtha* (1867) for Calcutta's Baghbazar Amateur Jatra Party. In 1871, some members of the Baghbazar Amateur Jatra Party formed the National Theatre, where Ghosh was active until leaving because he objected to the commercial practice of selling tickets. In 1880, Ghosh, eventually associated with all the major Calcutta **theatres** of his day, became manager of the Great National Theatre (1873), where his first play, *The Homecoming of the Goddess* (Agamani), had been performed in 1877. **Binodini Dasi**, indebted to Ghosh for her **training**, acted in *Chaitanya's Play* (Chaitanya lila) at the Star Theatre in 1884. Soon after Ramakrishna (1836–1886), the Hindu religious reformer, visited the play, Ghosh fell under his spell and abandoned his immoral ways for a life of rectitude. Many of his plays also assumed a **religious** perspective.

Ghosh wrote approximately eighty plays, including serious historical works as well as myth-based works. He also wrote plays derived from the ***Ramayana***, dramatized well-known Bengali novels, and created **musicals**, farces, and burlesques. Some plays expressed his nationalistic, anti-imperialist **political** positions, others dealt with various social issues. His work is considered a blend of traditional (as in ***jatra***) form and **Western** dramaturgy.

Among his significant plays are *Killing of Ravana* (Raban badh, 1881), *Sita's Forest Exile* (Sitar banabas, 1881), *Abducting Sita* (Sitar haran, 1882), *Hiding of Pandaber* (Pandaber ajnatavas, 1882), *Prahlad's Life* (Prahlad charitra, 1884), *Praphulla* (1889), and *Siraj the Minister* (Siraj addaula, 1905). His adaptation of *Macbeth* (1893) flopped, for which he blamed the debased tastes of Bengali audiences, whom he claimed preferred trivial themes and musical numbers to meaningful drama. One of his innovations was the development of "Girish's meter" (*gairish metre*), an influential poetic line based on the verse of Michael Mahusudan Dutt.

Ghosh's productions were appreciated for their spectacular scenography, lavish **costumes**, and remarkable effects using magnesium wire, lighting, and chemicals. He was ahead of his time, and even founded a **dance** school in Calcutta to train prostitutes for the **stage**. Known as the "Garrick of Bengal" after his 1877 performance as Meghnad in his *Killing of Meghnad* (Meghnad badh), he was considered Bengal's finest actor. Ghosh's all-around contributions earned him the title of "father of Bengali theatre."

Sreenath K. Nair

GIGAKU. Ancient **Japanese** performing art, now extinct. According to the eighth-century *Chronicle of Japan* (Nihon shoki), it arrived in 612, brought by an immigrant from a **Korean** kingdom who had studied the art in **China**. Under court patronage *gigaku* reached its peak during the Nara period (710–794) when it was overshadowed by *bugaku*. *Gigaku* continued to be enacted in provincial areas until dying out in the fourteenth century.

Historical descriptions are rare, and the main source for understanding *gigaku* is a rather opaque program in the 1223 text *Selections for Instruction and Admonition* (Kyôkunshô) by Komachi Kazane (?–1241). Komachi describes a procession of **masked** dancers and **musicians** leading to a site where **dances** and pantomimes occurred accompanied by flute and percussion. Komachi lists a "lion dance" (*shishi mai*), the dance of the Chinese Prince Kuregimi (Gokô), and the dances of several Buddhist divinities followed by more dances and pantomimes, including a phallus dance involving the symbolic impregnation of one or more females. It is uncertain if these performances were solemn or comical or both, and if this program was indicative of *gigaku* at its earlier peak.

Scholars detect continental influence in the masks, which are of painted wood and fit over the entire head. Approximately 250 dating from the sixth to early eighth century survive in repositories in Nara, offering a glimpse at what this lost art may have looked like.

FURTHER READING

Leiter, Samuel L, ed. *Japanese Theatre in the World.*

Eric C. Rath

GOMBEYATA. *See* Puppet Theatre: India.

GUAN HANQING (CA. 1220–CA. 1300). Chinese • **playwright**, author of over sixty *zaju*, of which up to eighteen are still extant. In addition, he also wrote a good number of *sanqu* art songs, a song form **musically** and aesthetically closely related to *zaju*. His works encompass renderings of standard motifs from the official histories, lesser known tales from historical sources, stories featured in the **storytelling** tradition, and plots probably of his own invention. Credited as the originator of mature *zaju*, his extant plays' thematic range covers almost all the well-known topics. At the same time, his plays often exhibit an idiosyncratic twist when compared with treatments of these motifs in other vernacular works. This is particularly true with regard to his representation of heroines.

Among the early extant *zaju* printed in the Yuan dynasty (1280–1368), we find four probably written by Guan Hanqing, even if the extant texts themselves do not actually name him as author. *Lord Guan Goes to the Feast Alone* (Dandao hui) and *The Dream of Western Shu* (Xishu meng) both relate to the story cycle of the military conflicts of the Three Kingdoms period (220–265), a popular topic in official historiography, private histories, storytelling, and the emergent novelistic tradition. While the first song-drama depicts one of the principal heroes, Guan Yu (160–219), at the height of his power, the second focuses on the period after his death. Each is riveting in its lyricism of glory and of defeat, respectively.

Guan's other two Yuan-printed plays, *The Moon Gazing Pavilion* (Baiyue ting) and *Arranging a Match* (Diao fengyue), are romantic family dramas. The former showcases a young **woman** of a respectable family who, when circumstances pit filial piety against romantic fidelity, not only opts for the latter, but ultimately succeeds in being vindicated. *Arranging a Match* develops a theme frequently treated in Yuan-printed art song, that is, the faithless male lover. However, rather than simply lamenting the acts of faithlessness, the maidservant, having given in to a dalliance with a Jurchen noble on account of his vows of fidelity, does not quietly resign herself to being pushed aside by his marriage to an aristocrat. Instead, she delivers a spirited diatribe at the wedding, which appears to result in her being chosen as a concubine.

Extant only in revised Ming (1368–1644) versions, Guan's outright romances nevertheless are typically quite inventive, either greatly expanding upon their source materials or featuring altogether apocryphal figures. Among the scholar-courtesan dramas, a play like *Xie Tianxiang*, rather than focusing on the male figure of Liu Yong (980–1053), a well-known *ci* poet with many liaisons in the demimonde, centers on an otherwise unknown courtesan, the eponymous Xie Tianxiang. She earns the respect of the official establishment not on account of her devotion, but by virtue of her ability to compose a virtuoso lyric impromptu, an aesthetic value that resonates with exceptional language play in *zaju* and *sanqu* songs.

However, Guan's corpus features romantic stories set in gentry circles as well. In a reworking of an anecdote from a compendium of historical anecdotes, Guan's *The Jade Mirror Stand* (Yujing tai) portrays an older scholar-official, who resorts to various subterfuges in order to convince his young and reluctant gentry wife of the sincerity of his devotion to her. The portrayals of both the main male and female character depart from the usual cast of young love-struck scholar-officials and the coy, but willing, figure of the gentry heroine. In this play, impromptu composition, this time by the main male character, also saves the day, turning a nominal marriage into affectionate companionship.

Guan's plays dealing with social manners, particularly *Rescuing a Coquette* (Jiu fengchen) and *Injustice to Dou E* (Dou E yuan), feature ingenious female protagonists, whose actions invoke and exceed the norms of female virtue. In the former, a courtesan ingeniously dupes an abusive merchant into divorcing his ex-courtesan wife, so that the latter can be married instead to a poor but respectable and kind scholar-official. In reworking the scholar-merchant-courtesan triangle in this fashion, the play assigns the principal role of rescuer to an older courtesan, a remarkable departure from the standard story where older courtesans-cum-madams invariably opt for the rich merchant as most desirable. In *Injustice to Dou E*, the title character, a young and poor gentry woman railroaded into execution for a murder she did not commit, posthumously has her name cleared, thanks to a defiant display of widow chastity and filial piety.

Given the large number of works attributed to Guan, it is likely that he wrote professionally. However, while some of the prominent scholar-officials of his day remarked on the merit of his *sanqu* art songs, and Ming aristocrats commented on his role as *zaju*'s originator, individual authorship was not an organizing principle for Yuan or Ming *sanqu* or *zaju* anthologies, which did not group his plays as a unit, but interspersed them throughout.

Guan's reputation as an individual author did not really begin until the early twentieth century, when Republican-era **critics** sought to establish counterparts to the masters of **Western** drama. The focus on Guan's authorial persona intensified after 1949, when scholarly works not only invented him as a literary revolutionary who sympathized with ordinary people, but contemporary dramatists used his persona to reflect upon their own delicate position in the turmoil of party **politics** and mass campaigns.

FURTHER READING

Shih, Chung-wen. *Injustice to Tou O* (Tou O Yüan): *A Study and Translation*; Sieber, Patricia. *Theaters of Desire. Authors, Readers, and the Reproduction of Early Chinese Song-Drama, 1300–2000*.

Patricia Sieber

HAHOE PYŎLSHIN-GUT. East-central **Korean** • **festival** play from the Hahoe **Folk** Village (Hahoe Minsok Maŭl). Its exact origin is unknown, but it may have evolved from fishing village exorcisms or heaven-worshipping rites. Performed as an exorcism of subterranean deities to ensure prosperity in the village and prevent evil spirits from entering households, it took place on the fifteenth day of the first month, the last day of the festival.

Because it was a **religious** exorcism, *pyŏlshin-gut* participants strictly observed purification rites. All performers, led by the officiant, took sanctifying baths and boarded together for the duration of the festival. Sacred straw ropes prevented outsiders from tainting the space with impurities.

Performances required twelve types of wooden **masks**, believed to be products of the Koryŏ dynasty (918–1392); only nine types have survived, notable for their expressiveness and rich humanity. When not in use, the sacrosanct masks were enshrined. Even today, *pyŏlshin-gut* performers treat their masks reverentially.

The script, with its episodic **dramatic structure** and inconsequential plotting, was transmitted orally until the twentieth century. Comprised of **dance**, dialogue, improvised comedy, pantomime, and **music**, performances satirized transgressed Buddhist monks, corrupt officials, and the educated upper-class. Authentic performances of *hahoe pyŏlshin-gut* are occasionally presented today, but, more commonly, abbreviated versions laced with topical allusions are staged for tourists in Hahoe nearly every weekend from May to October.

FURTHER READING

Cho, Oh-Kon, trans. *Traditional Korean Theatre*.

Oh-Kon Cho

HAKSAR, ANAMIKA (1959–). Indian • **director**. After majoring in history, she acted in a 1976 street play by **Badal Sircar**. She graduated from New Delhi's National School of Drama in 1982, and then studied directing at Moscow's State Institute of Theatrical Arts. Each of her productions is an **experiment** "where the play is the space on which **actors** and audiences alike discover the potency that lurks deep within all of us."

In 1988, Haksar founded Nirakar, a **theatre company** that aimed to explore a new theatre language. In 1989, she directed **Rabindranath Tagore**'s "Post Office" (Dakghar), *Viy*, and *Story of the Planets, Statements of the Planets* (Grahon ki kahani, grahon ki zabani). Other stagings of the time include *Dream of Reason* (Vivek ka toota awapna, 1990) and *The Great Coat* (1991).

The Inner Journey (Antaryatra, 1993) was an exciting production whose direction was lauded because it took a highly fanciful plot—about a doctor who has been given the power over life and death by the goddess of death—and somehow made it completely believable. *Mirror of the Raj* (Raj darpan, 1994), a masterpiece of theatricality, depicted both theatre history and the effect of British imperialism on the Indian psyche. In *Hooriya* (1997), she protested against the influxes and influences of colonialism, which are as powerful today as a century ago. Synge's "Riders to the Sea" (2000), Haksar's landmark production, explored theatre as a channel for interpreting history. *The Mad* (Baawla, 2003), based on Dostoevsky's *The Idiot*, revealed the transience of human life and the courage needed to face recognition of it. Haksar, winner of the Sanskriti Award, uses a painterly approach that transforms even the most mundane images into a magical experience.

Debjani Ray Moulik

HANG TUN HAK (1926–1975). Cambodian • playwright, educator, administrator, and **political** figure. Following advanced theatre studies in France in the 1950s, Hang returned to Cambodia, where he was instrumental in the development of "national drama" (*lakhon chiet*), later called **lakhon niyeay**. He began by **training** public school teachers in its performance, and later cofounded the National Conservatory of Performing Arts. **Actors** under his tutelage toured Cambodia for months at a time, performing both **Western** plays (often French) translated into Khmer, and plays written by Hang and other local playwrights for a paying audience.

His best-known works, including *The Sun Is Rising* (Preah arthit reah haey) and *Our Elders* (Ream chbong yeung), both written in the late 1950s, all deal with then-contemporary societal tensions, many of which remain relevant: attitudes and power relations between rich and poor, and between family members of different generations; life choices for those without access to resources; and cultural stigmas.

Hang served as rector of the Royal University of Fine Arts during the 1960s. During the same period he was a close colleague of Queen **Sisowath Kossamak** in the oversight of the country's royal **dance** troupe, and wrote about the court dance in *La revue Française de l'elite Européene*. He was also briefly Cambodia's prime minister in the early 1970s. Dubbed "the Cambodian Molière" both because of his focus on the audacity of those with power and because he was celebrated and comfortable among royalty and everyday people, Hang maintains a contemporary presence through the staging of his plays and their use in acting, playwriting, and production classes.

Toni Shapiro-Phim

HAN T'AE-SUK (1950–). Korean • director and **playwright** whose productions in the 1970s, especially her rendition of Baraka's *Dutchman*, earned critical attention. However, she quickly left the theatre to work in television and other media. After a ten-year hiatus, she worked as a freelance director before founding the Mulli **Theatre Company** (Kŭkdan Mulli, 1988). She staged one historical drama after another: *Na*

Unkyu, about the eponymous first Korean movie director (1999), *Poor King Gwanghae* (Gwanghaeyugam, 2002), about a king denied a posthumous title, and *I, Gim Su-im* (Na, Kim Su-im, 1997), about an accused spy. She also produced the psycho-drama *Whatever Happened to Baby Jane?* (Kŭ chamae ege musŭn il i ilŏnanna?, 1994) and the remake of an old folktale, *Baejanghwa Baehongryŏn* (2001).

Characters in Han's works must face either the brutality of history or an insurmountable obstacle leading to their fall, disclosing the hidden interrelation between power, sexuality, and **politics**. This psycho-dramatic focus was most obvious in her production of *Lady Macbeth* (Reidi Maekbesu, 1999), a re-interpretation of *Macbeth* through the eyes of Lady Macbeth, utilizing the style of "objet de drama," the incorporation of installation art on **stage** to obtain different symbolic allusions. Never one to shy away from controversial issues, Han wrote and directed *China Express* (Sŏanhwacha, 2003), Korea's first drama dealing with homosexuality. Meticulous, analytical, and visual, Han prompts her audience to become not mere viewers but collaborators in the dilemma and demise of her misguided and misunderstood characters.

Alyssa S. Kim

HARISHCHANDRA, BHARATENDU (1850–1885). Indian Hindi-language **actor, director, playwright**, manager, and poet. Born to an aristocratic merchant family of Varanasi (Benares), this "father of modern Hindi theatre" was fluent in Persian, **Sanskrit**, and Bengali. He became a journalist at sixteen, editing a newspaper and writing socially and **politically** motivated essays. In 1867, he founded the Chaukhamba School,

Vedic Violence Is Not Violence by Bharatendu Harishchandra, produced by Bharatendu Natak Mandali for Anamika Festival, Calcutta, India, 1974. (Photo: Courtesy of Natya Shodh Sansthan)

hoping to raise India's educational standards. In 1874, he started a magazine, *Harish-chandra Chandrika*, which serialized dramas, besides publishing scholarly articles.

Harishchandra, hoping to use theatre as a transformative weapon and to demonstrate to his Euro-centered countrymen that India could produce quality drama, formed his own Hindi **theatre company**. As a playwright, he made many structural and linguistic advances, including the use of Hindi, with its unique poetic qualities, as a **stage** language. His theatre stood out for its nationalistic socio-political slant, although his work is laced with humor. His wide-ranging sensibility borrowed from Sanskrit, **folk**, and **Parsi theatre**, while Bengali theatre influenced his modernist sensibility.

Works include *India's Plight* (Bharat durdasha, 1875), *Truthful Harishchandra* (Satya Harishchandra, 1876), *City of Darkness* (Andher nagari, 1881), and *Nildevi* (1881). Among Harishchandra's works are outstanding translations of Sanskrit, Bengali, and English plays, including Shakespeare. Harishchandra was dubbed the "Moon of India" (Bharatendu).

Debjani Ray Moulik

HASEGAWA SHIN (1884–1963).

Japanese • **playwright** and popular novelist. A tough childhood inculcated in Hasegawa a keen sympathy for the common people. As a young man, he worked as a laborer on the Yokohama docks and at other odd jobs, then served in the army. Mostly self-taught, he was hired by scholar-**critic** Ihara Seiseien (1870–1941) to work for a newspaper, the *Capital News* (Miyako Shinbun), in 1911, a post he kept until 1925, when he devoted himself full-time to writing.

Kutsukake Tokijirô (1928) marked his debut as a popular playwright specializing in works about righteous outlaws and pure-hearted drifters of the Edo period's (1603–1868) waning days. His plays are full of sentiment and sword fighting, and his typical characters are gangsters, thieves, pickpockets, pimps, and prostitutes. His most famous works, like *Mother of Dreams* (Mabuta no haha, 1931), feature orphans. (The play foreshadowed Hasegawa's own reunion with his estranged mother in 1933.) Likewise, Komagata Mohei, the hero of *A Lone Sword Enters the Ring* (Ippon-gatana dohyô-iri, 1933), is a failed sumo wrestler who has lost both parents and is forced to eke out a living as a bodyguard and enforcer. Hasegawa's plays were immensely popular in the 1930s, performed as ***shinkokugeki*** and ***kabuki*** (by **theatre companies** such as Progressive **Theatre** [Zenshin-za]) and adapted for film; many are still performed.

M. Cody Poulton

HASHMI, SAFDAR (1954–1989).

Indian Hindi-language **playwright**, **actor**, **director**, **political** activist, and founder of People's Theatre Platform (Jana Natya Manch, or Janam, literally "Birth"), an agitprop, primarily street **theatre company** begun in 1973, supported by the Communist Party, and seen throughout India during its heyday.

Hashmi, who joined the Communist Party in 1983, saw theatre as a pedagogical tool for generating political awareness and action on immediate as well as long-range issues. He abandoned the proscenium **stage** for outdoor found venues, such as parks, factory yards, lawns, and stadiums, because his politics led him to believe in the communicative power of street theatre. His efforts resulted in the creation of a new street theatre language—including **music** he wrote himself—devoid of the stereotypical conventions generally used in propaganda. Rejecting the "theatre of roots" (*tanatu natakavedi*) approach whereby indigenous forms were appropriated for modern expression, he sought an individualistic style and cultural spirit for the oppressed working class struggling under capitalism.

His first play was *Machine* (1978), a widely produced drama about worker exploitation, followed by nearly twenty others, including *Killers* (Hatyare, 1978), *From the Village to the City* (Gaon se shahir tak, 1978), *Woman* (Aurat, 1979), *Raja's Music* (Raja ka baja, 1980), *Attack!* (Halla bol, 1988), and an adaptation of Gorky's *Enemies* (1983) for the National School of Drama. Their problem-based themes included migrant farm workers, oppressive fare hikes, **women**'s issues like dowries and wife beating, and unemployment. His adaptation of Hindi writer Munshi Premchand's (1880–1936) short story *Moteram's Hunger Strike* (Moteram ka satyagraha, 1988) was directed by **Habib Tanvir** as a proscenium production presented, respectively, by the People's Theatre Platform and the National School of Drama. By 1989, Janam had given over four thousand performances, mainly of Hashmi's plays.

Hashmi was beaten to death by a rival politician and a band of hoodlums during a performance of *Attack!*, about the need for wage increases in the face of government repression. It happened in Sahibabad (near Delhi), and is remembered annually by a street play at the site.

B. Ananthakrishnan

HAT BOI. *See Tuong.*

HIJIKATA TATSUMI (1928–1986). **Japanese** dancer, choreographer, and *butô* pioneer. Hijikata studied modern German **dance** in his native Tôhoku. In 1952, he entered Tokyo's Andô Mitsuko Dance Research Institute, where his first performance was *Birds* (Tori, 1954), danced with **Ôno Kazuo**. *Forbidden Colors* (Kinjiki, 1959), its title taken from **Mishima Yukio**'s novel, its content from Genet, inaugurated *butô*. His distinctiveness lay in exploring humanity's dark side by using the body to crystallize inchoate speech and words to enliven the body.

Subsequent noteworthy performances include *Masseurs* (Anma, 1963), *Rose-Colored Dance* (Bara-iro dansu, 1965), and *Tomato* (1966). Soon after, he turned to Tôhoku themes, creating *Hijikata Tatsumi and the Japanese: Rebellion of the Body* (Hijikata Tatsumi to nihonjin—nikutai no hanran, 1968), *Sickle Weasel* (Kamaitachi, 1970) with photographer Hosoe Eikô, and *Gibasa* (1970, best known by its Japanese title, meaning "seaweed"). His 1972 series, *Twenty-seven Nights for Four Seasons* (Shiki no tame no nijûshichiban), was famously branded "Tôhoku *kabuki*" by **critic** Gunji Masakatsu for its womb-like interiority in contrast to the grand exteriority of traditional *kabuki*. From 1974 until his death, Hijikata focused on choreographing and **training** young dancers. His legacy remains vibrant in the work of, among others, Ôno Kazuo, Ashikawa Yôko and her group, White Peach Room (Hakutôbô), and Tanaka Min. Hijikata's last work was *Tôhoku Kabuki Project 4* (Tôhoku kabuki keikaku 4, 1985).

Yoshiko Fukushima

HIJIKATA YOSHI (1898–1959). Japanese • *shingeki* • **director**. An aristocrat by birth, Hijikata shocked the Imperial Household Ministry when he entered the theatre world. In 1920, he met **Osanai Kaoru**, who took him to a performance by the Labor Troupe (Rôdô Gekidan), where he was overwhelmed by the intense rapport between **stage** and audience. After working briefly for Osanai in *shinpa*, Hijikata traveled to Europe in 1922 to observe contemporary theatre and was excited by Meyerhold's work at the Revolutionary Theatre in Moscow. Returning to Japan in 1923, he founded, with Osanai and others, the Tsukiji Little Theatre (Tsukiji Shôgekijô). He personally financed the theatre's construction—*shingeki*'s first purpose-built venue—and operating expenses. While Hijikata and Osanai were the resident company's main directors, Hijikata's play choices were noticeably more progressive and contemporary than Osanai's.

The Tsukiji Little Theatre disbanded soon after Osanai's death in 1928, and Hijikata founded the New Tsukiji Company (Shin Tsukiji Gekidan), one of the two principal 1930s leftwing **theatre companies**. Committed to proletarian drama, Hijikata represented this movement at the 1933 International Drama Olympiad in Moscow, remaining there to work in Meyerhold's theatre until he was expelled from the USSR in 1937. Back in Japan in 1941, his **politics** led to his imprisonment throughout the war. He subsequently led a varied life, organizing May Day cultural events, directing, and teaching theatre. He was a demanding director whose productions were known for fast-paced, compelling dialogue.

Brian Powell

HIRATA ORIZA (1962–). Japanese • **playwright**, **director**, and **theorist**. Standard-bearer for the "quiet theatre" (*shizuka na engeki*) movement, including **Iwamatsu Ryô**,

Tokyo Notes, written and directed by Hirata Oriza, Agora Theatre, Tokyo, Japan, 2004. (Photo: Courtesy of Seinendan Theatre Company)

Matsuda Masataka, **Miyazawa Akio**, and **Suzue Toshirô**, Hirata founded the Youth Group (Seinendan) **theatre company** in 1986 and has toured worldwide. With tightly crafted language and plots, Hirata's plays verge on the antitheatrical; set in confined "semi-public" spaces with typically large casts speaking overlapping dialogue in resolutely normal, sometimes barely audible speech.

Hirata won the **Kishida [Kunio]** Prize for *Tokyo Notes* (Tôkyô nôto, 1995), paying homage to film director Ozu Yasujirô's *Tokyo Story* (Tôkyô monogatari, 1953). A European war touches the lives of people passing through a Tokyo museum lobby. The constant comings and goings interrupt and diffuse the climactic trajectory of individual sensitivities and confrontations, with only hints of resolutions. War consciousness also informs *The Balkan Zoo* (Barukan dôbutusen, 1997) and *A Journal of South Sea Island P.O.W.s* (Nantô furyoki, 2003). The latter, featuring Japanese P.O.W.s, who express scant hope for victory or cultural survival, reflects Hirata's view that Japanese culture, under pressure of **Western influence**, is being diminished.

A year in **Korea** inspired *Citizens of Seoul* (Sôru shimin, 1989), about a Japanese family in occupied Korea in 1909. Portraying typical Japanese attitudes toward Koreans, Hirata is neither didactic nor polemical, leaving audiences to draw their own conclusions. This approach characterizes other plays, including *From S Plateau* (S kôgen kara, 1991), *Afflictions of the Flesh, or Carnage?* (Kataku ka, shura ka?, 1995), and *Confessions of a Feeble Mind* (Angu shôden, 1996).

John D. Swain

HÔJÔ HIDEJI (1902–1996). Japanese • **playwright** and **director**. Born in Osaka, he was the commercial theatre's leading postwar dramatist, completing 216 works for *kabuki*, *shinkokugeki*, *shinpa*, and Japanese **dance**. His work is noted for its structural originality, elaborate technique, and rich lyricism. His wrote his first play, *Columbus's Expedition* (Koronbusu no ensei, 1917), in high school, winning first prize in the **Takarazuka** Opera Contest.

After college, Hôjô was working in an electric company when he joined **Okamoto Kidô**'s Young Group (Futaba-kai) in 1933 and began writing plays for the journal *Stage* (Butai). His first success was a *shinkokugeki* play, *Before and after the Award Ceremony* (Hyôshôshiki zengo, 1937). After Okamoto's death in 1939, he quit his job and devoted himself to playwriting. His popularity increased with a *shinpa* play, *Your Excellency* (Kakka, 1940), awarded the Shinchôsha prize. His best work was a trilogy about the life of famous chess player Sakata Sankichi, *The King* (Ôshô, 1947–1950), which he also directed. Major plays include *A Fox and a Piper* (Kitsune to fuefuki, 1952) and *Court Lady Kasuga* (Kasuga no tsubone, 1974) for *kabuki*; and *The Sound of the Fog* (Kiri no ne, 1951), *Kyoto-style Dance* (Kyômai, 1950), and *Grand Courtesan* (Kottai-san, 1955) for *shinpa*. His last play, *Issa in Shinano* (Shinano no Issa, 1993), reunited two *shinkokugeki* actors, Shimada Shôgo (1905–2004) and Ôgata Ken (1937–).

In 1993, the then ninety-one-year-old Hôjô received a PhD from Kansai University for his dissertation on the history of Japanese commercial theatre.

Yoshiko Fukushima

HŎ KYU (1934–2000). Korean • director, playwright, and innovator, whose influence and contributions are among the most significant in modern Korean theatre. Although he directed **Western** plays early in his career, he soon focused solely on the creation and development of an independent tradition not based on the influence of Western or **Japanese** theatre. Hŏ's theatre would have a spirit and methodology emanating exclusively from Korean traditions and culture. He turned to traditional arts, such as **folk** songs, *p'ansori*, *t'alch'um*, **puppet theatre**, and shamanistic rituals, and undertook a variety of projects wherein the modern theatre could emerge from an amalgam of such elements.

In 1960, he cofounded the influential Shilhŏm **Experimental Theatre** Company (Shilhŏm Kŭkdan). Throughout the 1970s, he was a leading figure in *madanggŭk* (literally, "open-air drama"), a form that blended folk culture and social protest. In 1973, he founded the Minye **Theatre Company** (Minye Kŭkdan), requiring **actors** to be **trained** in traditional **music** and **dance**. In 1977, he directed the first play he wrote, *The Curve of Water* (Muldoridong), a story of Hahoe **mask** makers during the Koryŏ dynasty (918–1392). This dramatization of folklore set the tone for later works in which traditional music, dance, and shamanistic rituals constituted not complementary but central dramatic roles. Coming to *ch'anggŭk* in the 1980s, he became a leading director, working to traditionalize the genre by bringing it back to its roots in *p'ansori* and other folk arts.

Alyssa S. Kim

HONG KONG. Developed from a collection of fishing villages when claimed as a crown colony by Britain in 1841, Hong Kong is a cosmopolitan city on **China**'s southeastern coast, spreading over 1,100 sq. km. Ninety-five percent of its 7 million people are Chinese. English and Mandarin are official languages, but Cantonese is spoken most widely. On July 1, 1997, Hong Kong was re-unified with China and became a Special Administrative Region under the so-called "One Country, Two Systems" arrangement. The city's unique fusion of Eastern and **Western** cultures, with old and new living side by side, is reflected in its theatre.

***Traditional Theatre: Cantonese* Yueju.** *Xiqu* remains Hong Kong's most popular performing art. The earliest performance of Cantonese *yueju* in Hong Kong dates back at least to 1786, when plays were staged at a temple in Yuen Long to celebrate a lawsuit victory. The troupe probably came from the Pearl River Delta area, where local troupes (*bendi ban*) were evolving to replace visiting troupes (*waijiang ban*) from provinces outside Guangdong. The formation of *bendi ban* during the late eighteenth and early nineteenth centuries marked *yueju*'s flowering. Although, initially, **stage** dialect was "official speech" or Mandarin (*guanhua*), Cantonese dialect was gradually introduced in the 1920s. The early twentieth century also saw *yueju* plays written as **political** propaganda to spread ideas like democracy, revolution, modernization, and the abolition of the absolute monarchy; performances were in Cantonese for the general public.

Hong Kong's earliest commercial theatre dates from 1890. Up to the 1920s there were at least five *yueju* **theatres**. Pioneer **theatre companies** were either entirely male or entirely female: it was not until 1933 that the Hong Kong government allowed mixed troupes.

Cantonese *yueju* is still the major form, and the only one staged by full-size professional troupes with local artists. Styles like *chaoju*, *fulaoju*, Shaoxing *yueju*, **jingju**, and **kunqu** are frequently staged by troupes from mainland China, and occasionally jointly performed by professional mainland and Hong Kong artists, sometimes featuring local amateurs.

From the 1960s to the mid-1990s, two local *fulaoju* and five *chaoju* troupes were active in Hong Kong. Nowadays, it is almost exclusively mainland artists that present these two styles to highlight traditional **religious** rituals. Such performances are held in temporary theatres built of bamboo scaffolding, wooden plates, and tin sheets.

Since the 1990s, the influx of Shanghainese-speaking immigrants has bought many Shaoxing *yueju* enthusiasts and some professional artists to Hong Kong. In 2005, there were three companies performing this form, comprising both professionals and amateurs.

There are some thirty professional Cantonese *yueju* troupes performing an average of one thousand plays annually, among which 40 percent are part of rituals, while the rest are commercial performances charging admission. Major ritual occasions include the birthdays of deities and purification **festivals**.

Founded by the artist Tang Yuen Ha (1956–) in 1986, the Jingkun Theatre (formerly known as Hong Kong Jing Kun Arts Association) is the only local group staging *jingju* and *kunqu*; such presentations often feature mainland professionals.

Post-1949 Developments. The founding of the People's Republic of China in 1949 brought the imposition of strict **censorship** on traditional mainland theatre. Taking advantage of Hong Kong's freedom of expression, Tang Disheng (1917–1959) created numerous masterworks from 1950 to his death, including *The Floral Princess* (Dinü hua, 1957), *The Purple Hairpin* (Zichai ji, 1957), and *The Twin Immortals at the Moon Pavilion* (Shuangxian baiyue ting, 1958). Probably the most prolific **playwright** in Chinese history, Tang wrote more than 440 Cantonese *yueju* plays, many becoming classics. Star **actors** who frequently collaborated with Tang in the 1950s include Fang Yanfen (1929–), Bai Xuexian (1928–), Ren Jianhui (1913–1989), He Feifan (1919–1980), and Wu Junli (1930–).

The Hong Kong Arts Development Council (founded 1995, formerly known as the Council for Performing Arts) and the Leisure and Cultural Services Department, both official bodies under the government of the Hong Kong Special Administrative Region, have been actively financing and commissioning the creation of new Cantonese *yueju* works. Preliminary statistics record the premiere of about 150 plays from 1995 to 2003.

The Hong Kong Academy for Performing Arts (Xianggang Yanyi Xueyuan) is the only higher institution that offers diploma and advanced diploma **training** programs for Cantonese *yueju* actors, while research courses on *yueju* **music** are offered by the Chinese University of Hong Kong's Music Department. Supported by grants from the Hong Kong Arts Development Council, the latter also runs the Chinese Opera Information Centre, which serves the local and international public.

FURTHER READING

Ingham, Mike, and Xu Xi, eds. *City Stage: Hong Kong Playwriting in English*; Law, Kar, and Frank Bren. *From Artform to Platform: Hong Kong Plays and Performances 1900–1941*; Liley, Rozanna. *Staging Hong Kong: Gender and Performance in Transition*.

Sau Yan Chan

Development of Modern Theatre. Hong Kong's first nonindigenous theatre activities started soon after its colonization in 1841, when British troops and European merchants needed entertainment. Modern theatre, however, did not appear until the early 1900s; the first recorded production was Ching Ping Lok's (Qingpingle) *Zhuangzi Testing His Wife* (Zhuangzi shiqi, 1911). Productions tended to be illusionist; one play, for example, *Leung Tin Lois Royal Plea* (Liang Tianlai gao yu zhuang, 1928), used real fire.

The Second Sino-**Japanese** War (1937–1945) turned Hong Kong overnight into a cultural haven, with artists and cultural notables fleeing there to avoid the war. Agitprop anti-Japanese productions proliferated, and Hong Kong became a destination for touring mainland troupes. Such activities halted when the colony was occupied by the Japanese in 1941. After the war, the first groups to revive were the English-speaking Garrison Players and Hong Kong Stage Club. In the Cold War era of the 1950s, the mainland link was severed. While English-language drama continued to stress entertainment, the handful of new Chinese productions adopted nonconfrontational themes based on traditional values. Hong Kong was considered a cultural desert.

The Watershed of the 1960s and 1970s. The true **Western** influence on Hong Kong's theatre did not start until the mid-1960s, when student societies started organizing the annual Federation of Students Drama Festival (1966–1985), a vital force in local drama development. In addition, an increasing number of people with theatre degrees returned from overseas institutions. The local cultural void made it natural for Hong Kong's Chinese theatre to seek inspiration from the West. Until the 1980s, Hong Kong's stage was dominated by translations of the West's major modern dramatists. The best of the few original Chinese works was Yale graduate Yao Ke's *Back Alley* (Lou xiang, 1968), on which several groups collaborated.

China's Cultural Revolution (1966–1976) and pressing socioeconomic problems led to two large-scale riots, in 1966 and 1967; the latter, using terrorist tactics, was organized by leftists. In response, the government and society at large united to quash the riots and open the door to reform. The Urban Council embarked on a ten-year arts development plan, including planning new venues, arts programming, and, in particular, formation of the colony's first professional companies, beginning with the Hong Kong Repertory Theatre (Xianggang Huaju Tuan) in 1977. Two years later, the second troupe, the Sino-English (Chung Ying) Theatre Company (Zhongying Jutuan) was inaugurated under the aegis of the British Council. Although English activities continued, the Chinese theatre had become by far the major stakeholder. In substance, it reflected an East meets West hybridization, with a Western outlook but traditional Chinese spirit. In addition, free government-sponsored entertainments were organized in parks and squares for ordinary citizens.

The Booming 1980s. Local theatre experienced many developments in the 1980s. Until the advent of professional companies in 1977, amateurs had dominated theatricals. Joining their ranks in 1985 was Hong Kong's first community theatre, which emphasized topical issues and educational activities. Ultimately, around 150 new productions of all sorts—amateur and professional—were being produced annually, although the so-called "short run" syndrome makes this figure somewhat deceptive. Plays in translation began to be superseded by indigenous works, and certain political developments began to play a part in drama during the decade, notably the signing of the Sino-British Joint Declaration (1984) and the Tiananmen Square Incident (1989), each having both positive and negative effects on theatre work.

In 1982, the Council for the Performing Arts was established. That same year, Danny Yung (Rong Nianzeng) founded Zuni Icosahedron (Jinnian Ershi mian ti), an anti-establishment **experimental theatre**. In 1985, the Hong Kong Academy for the Performing Arts was inaugurated. The same year saw the inception of the first community theatre program in Sha Tin (a populous district in the New Territories), emphasizing drama education and indigenous subjects. Soon, community theatre spread to many other areas in the territory and assumed a crucial role in Hong Kong. In mid-1985, the Sino-English Theatre Company staged *I Am Hong Kong* (Wo hai Xianggang ren), remembered, among other things, for its bold recognition of identity, adept use of bilingual text, and the longest run for an original play (114 performances over two years, including tours). Moreover, the Federation of Drama Societies was established this year. Its functions include organizing the annual Hong Kong Theatre Awards.

Diversified Theatre since the 1990s. Although China's political problems disturbed the local theatres' sense of direction at the end of the 1980s, activity picked up quickly and reached unprecedented volume in the early 1990s. According to a three-year (1989–1991) survey, 1991 was the most active year, with eighty-two groups producing 173 shows, which ran for 800 performances seen by 250,000 spectators. A 1998 survey revealed that audience totals rose to 300,000, while troupe numbers also increased. Still, the total number of theatregoers is comparatively small for a metropolis of over 7 million.

Hong Kong theatre is imbued with the spirit of eclecticism and interdisciplinary experimentation. Mainstream activity—exemplified by the Hong Kong Repertory Theatre Company and Sino-English—together with many small-scale companies of all sorts offer a large and diverse program: Western and Chinese masterpieces run alongside original plays by local playwrights; expensive, sophisticated productions are juxtaposed with low-budget presentations. Beginning in the late 1980s, experimentation for its own sake began to lose ground to work more relevant to Hong Kong society. Hong Kong's colonial background long kept its theatre largely apolitical and devoid of social commentary. Sino-English's *Yes, Chief Executive* (Haige, teshou, 2004), for example, was organized around a tottering residential building symbolic of today's Hong Kong. It handled the sense of loss and frustration following the 1997 takeover through "laughter and cursing." Nevertheless, such thematic commitment has made barely a dent, since commercial interests trump political ideology.

The Hong Kong Academy for the Performing Arts, a multidisciplinary institution that includes schools of drama, **dance**, music, and technical arts has also made great contributions since its first graduates emerged in 1990.

The changes in the socio-political environment and the depletion of expatriates greatly influenced English-speaking groups. The Garrison Players and the Hong Kong Stage Club merged into the Hong Kong Players in the early 1990s, a demonstration of the continued blurring of boundaries between the English and Cantonese theatres.

The theatre's rapid development has required critical support. The Hong Kong Drama Symposium in 1991, organized by Sir Run Run Shaw Hall at the Chinese University of Hong Kong, was the first initiative, and was followed by additional conferences and festivals. In 1997, the Hong Kong Drama Program was established at the Chinese University, forming a link between academia and local theatre. Its *Hong Kong Drama Review* is the only journal of its kind in Hong Kong.

The *Guardian Angels of Hong Kong: A Fantastic Temple Rendezvous*, a touring, open-air performance with religious and legendary content, presented as part of the Community Cultural Ambassador Scheme 2005. (Photo: Fung Wai Sun; Courtesy of Prospects Theatre)

Hong Kong is famous for its world-class facilities, and troupes visit from all over the world, giving local audiences access to a great variety of performances, and offering practitioners artistic inspiration. Considering its brief history, Hong Kong theatre has made noteworthy achievements, but theatre remains a marginalized concern with little social impact. Theatre **criticism** and research remains weak, and few plays or productions make a lasting impression. To make true progress, society as a whole has to come to grips with its new political paradigm, which, in theory, should call for proper education and civic values that treasure theatre and the arts.

Hardy Tsoi

HONG SHEN (1894–1955). Chinese • director, playwright, and critic. He was active in dramatic activities as a university student in Beijing before entering The Ohio State University as an engineering major in 1916 and transferring to Harvard three years later to study playwriting under George Pierce Baker, making him the first Chinese to study theatre abroad. In addition, he took courses in **acting** and **dance** at Boston's School of Expression and worked at the Copley Theatre. After receiving his master's, he worked in touring **theatre companies**.

In 1922, Hong returned to Shanghai hoping to become China's Ibsen. However, his first play, *Yama Zhao* (Zhao Yanwang), an expressionist piece modeled after O'Neill's

Emperor Jones, confused the audience. In 1923, **Ouyang Yuqian** introduced Hong to the Shanghai Drama Society (Shanghai Xiju Xieshe), where his 1924 *The Young Lady's Fan* (Shao nainai de shanzi), adapted from Wilde's *Lady Windermere's Fan*, became the first successful "spoken drama" (*huaju*) production of a **Western** play. In this and other Drama Society productions, Hong's emphasis on such modern principles as the director's centrality, the rehearsal process, mixed-gender casting, and three-dimensional **scenography** marked *huaju*'s break away from its predecessor, "civilized drama" (*wenming xi*). He also joined forces with other Shanghai theatre companies, in particular **Tian Han**'s Southern China Society (Nanguo She). In 1928, inspired by Tian's objection to the dichotomy of new (*xin*), that is, Western-style, versus old (*jiu*), that is, traditional theatre, Hong proposed *huaju* to replace *xinju* ("new drama"); it has become the standard term for modern theatre.

Hong wrote over thirty plays, including the well-known *Rural Trilogy* (Nongcun sanbuqu, 1930–1932). Starting in 1922, he also worked in films. His *The Woman Shentu* (Shentu shi, 1922) was China's first full-length silent film script and his *Red Peony, the Singing Girl* (Genü Hong Mudan, 1931) the first sound movie. Hong also taught theatre at several universities. Through his extensive writing and translation, Hong systematically introduced to China contemporary Western theatre and film **theories** on acting, directing, and playwriting.

During the Second Sino-**Japanese** War (1937–1945), in addition to playwriting and directing, Hong oversaw wartime motivation efforts using theatre. After 1949, he was in charge of international cultural exchange programs for the People's Republic of China.

Siyuan Liu

HONG SHENG (1645–1704).

HONG SHENG (1645–1704). Chinese • *chuanqi* • **playwright** often paired with **Kong Shangren** ("South Hong, North Kong") as major Qing dynasty (1644–1911) dramatists. Both wrote historical romances in the long shadow of **Tang Xianzu**'s *Peony Pavilion* (Mudan ting, 1598), responding to his depiction of love with reference to the **politically** fraught circumstances of their lifetimes. Each man's depiction of love's role in human life was distinct, reflecting differences in temperament and life situations.

Like Kong, Hong was from a prominent lineage (in Hangzhou), but unlike Kong his family's relationship to the new dynasty was uneasy. Hong's father was impeached and exiled in 1679, a decline in fortunes made worse by domestic strife that poisoned relations with his adult sons. But Hong's childhood was happy, spent among teachers who nurtured poetic and **musical** talents and friends who would also become playwrights. Hong's self-image was that of heroic poet; poems written at his wedding (1664) made local celebrities of him and his wife.

High expectations soured after he went to Beijing in 1668, despite promising prospects as a student. In 1669, he returned to Hangzhou and for several years neglected efforts to pass the imperial examinations, preferring instead to travel. Although he returned to Beijing in 1674, his career as an official made no headway. Poverty-stricken, Hong supported himself by writing. He married a cousin who shared his talent for poetry and music, and his plays sometimes celebrated companionate relationships between men and **women**.

Of his twelve plays whose titles are known, only two remain. *Four Fair Ladies* (Si chanjuan) was modeled on *Four Cries of the Gibbon* (Sisheng yuan) by **Xu Wei**, and consists of four one-acts in *zaju* style. Each depicts a famous female talent (two poets, a calligrapher, and a painter) matched to an equally talented husband. At least four other lost plays also featured outstanding women, reflecting a preoccupation with female talent that found fullest expression in *Palace of Lasting Life* (Changsheng dian, 1688), a fifty-scene *chuanqi* (ca. 1679–1688).

It retells the story of the Tang dynasty (618–907) Emperor Xuanzong (a.k.a. Minghuang) and Precious Consort Yang (Yang Guifei), a "nation toppler" whose hold on the aging emperor's affections nearly destroyed the dynasty. Unlike most preceding dramatizations, Hong purifies Yang's character without suppressing her sensuality, and departs from typical *chuanqi* romances by exploring how the lovers negotiate their relationship after they are married. Part One (Scenes 1–25), set in the Tianbao era (742–756), portrays the love between emperor and favored consort as passionate but flawed. Xuanzong's infidelities and Yang's jealousy cause a series of quarrels and reconciliations that distract the emperor and enable a scheming courtier, An Lushan, to foment rebellion. In Scene 25, Yang is forced by soldiers to commit suicide as the couple flees the capital. This sets the **stage** for Part Two (Scenes 26–50), in which the lovers appear in alternating scenes, earthly and celestial, to repent the self-indulgence that brought them and the nation misery, experience grief and longing, and realize that their devotion has deepened with death and separation. Only in Scene 50 are they reunited in heaven by sympathetic deities.

Palace of Lasting Life, like Kong's *The Peach Blossom Fan* (Taohua shan), combines romance and history to reveal private lives and loves crushed by a national catastrophe. Hong's friends and teachers had suffered from Manchu repression, although the play's references to the recent past had to be oblique. Hong's play differs from Kong's in its resolution of the problem of excessive commitment to private feelings. It ends on a triumphantly lyrical note, as celestial maids-in-waiting to the goddess Chang'e perform "Rainbow Skirts, Feather Robes"—traditionally associated with Yang Guifei—for the blissfully reunited couple. Kong would also incorporate theatrical performance into the conclusion of his masterpiece, but that play's performers, rooted in worldly realities, give a more clear-eyed and detached commentary on events they witness, denying that love can endure in a politically compromised world.

Hong took pains to make his plays singable, including detailed directions in the printed edition and authorizing a twenty-eight scene abridgement that could comfortably be performed over two days, as was standard. Until modern times it usually has been performed as excerpts.

A private performance of Hong's play in 1689 during a period of national mourning attracted a **censor**'s attention, who reported the event to the Kangxi Emperor (r. 1662–1722). Hong was briefly imprisoned, then expelled from the Imperial Academy, after Kangxi found the play offensive. Ten years later, Kong Shangren suffered a similar fate after Kangxi read *Peach Blossom Fan*. Subsequently, the number of scholar-officials who wrote plays declined sharply.

Catherine Swatek

HÔSHÔ KURÔ. Japanese • *nô* • actors' name, often taken by the head of the Hôshô school family, who perform as *shite* (see Role Types). Not every Hôshô has adopted this name, perhaps because of its prestigious legacy. The last to do so was Hôshô Kurô Shigefusa XVII (1900–1974), only the eighth to have taken the name.

Hôshô Kurô Tomoharu XVI (1837–1917) is renowned for helping to preserve *nô* during the Meiji period (1868–1912) following its loss of patrons with the shogunate's downfall. In 1848, at twelve, he participated in Edo's (Tokyo) last great benefit (*kanjin*) *nô* by performing one lead a day for fifteen days.

Financial difficulties in early Meiji forced him to try his hand at business, but he soon won support from aristocrats seeking to use *nô* as entertainment for foreign dignitaries. At Prince Iwakura Tomomi's residence in 1879, Kurô performed for ex-President Grant. He gained popular recognition with **Umewaka Minoru I** and **Sakurama Banma** as one of Meiji's three *nô* luminaries. An authority on all aspects of performance, he was noted for his **stage** "dignity" (*kurai*) and his "chanting" (*utai*). He abandoned acting in 1906 to focus on *utai* and teaching (both professionals and amateurs). At his death, his son, Shigefusa, succeeded to the Hôshô leadership, but postponed taking the Kurô name for two decades. Shigefusa worked to sustain *nô* after World War II, becoming the first chairman of the Nô Professionals Association in 1954.

Eric C. Rath

HOTTA KIYOMI (1922–). Japanese • *shingeki* • **playwright**, known for his plays' realistic portrayal of the working class and deep concern for the disenfranchised. Born in Hiroshima, he worked in a Hitachi factory after World War II, joined the company's drama group, and, while there, wrote his first play, *The Son of a Driver* (Untenko no musuko, 1947). He belonged to the Self-Reliant Theatre Movement (Jiritsu Engeki Undô), which promoted postwar workers' theatre. In 1950, Hotta's leftist **politics** led to his losing his job during the "Red Purge." In 1955, he joined the People's Art Theatre (Mingei).

He worked as an assistant **director** for several People's Theatre productions and wrote his signature play, *The Island* (Shima), winning the **Kishida [Kunio]** Prize in 1958. Among the first to address the Hiroshima bombing, Hotta focuses on the trials of Kurihara Manabu, a teacher exposed to radioactive fallout, struggling to resume his life after this catastrophe. The play also links Manabu's plight to the suffering and death of Taira Kiyomori in the medieval epic *The Tale of the Heike* (Heike monogatari), thus connecting events of the bombing with elements of history, **religion**, and tradition.

Despite Hotta's successes with the People's Art Theatre, he stopped writing plays on leaving the company in the early 1960s.

David Jortner

HUAJI XI. **Chinese** comic theatre of the Southern Yangtze River area, which covers Shanghai and parts of Jiangsu and Zhejiang Provinces. *Huaji xi* did not emerge as a genre until the 1940s, but its development can be traced back to the turn of the twentieth century—a time of military defeats suffered by the Manchus and of growing **political** consciousness—when a local form of "speaking and singing" was created by a group of sweets vendors. Du Baolin introduced into his sales pitch daily news items, making topical jokes, and mocking the locals' bad habits. Others soon emulated him, and Du's students became professionals touring the locality. They told jokes, imitated dialects, and performed sales pitches, **folk** songs, and local *xiqu*. The Chinese call this "solo performance" (*dujiao xi*), although sometimes it involved two entertainers.

Huaji xi's other source was the "funny drama" (*quju*) in "civilized drama" (*wenming xi*), the predecessor of "spoken drama" (*huaju*; see Playwrights and Playwriting). Like England's sixteenth-century interludes, *quju* was short, treated miscellaneous comic and satirical themes, and was performed with songs and mime. Unlike the first piece on a *jingju* program, *quju* was often performed by stars, which popularized it further.

Weekly Troupe (Libai Tuan), the first *quju* **theatre company**, was founded in 1923, separating itself from *wenming xi*. Many *quju* actors also started performing *dujiao xi*, introducing into it additional theatrical elements. By the early 1940s, full-length *huaji xi* plays began appearing, performed mainly as spoken drama in different dialects but including miming, folk songs, pop **music**, and local *xiqu* arias. Shanghai Huaji xi Company is one of the major **theatre companies**.

Ruru Li

HUAJU. *See* China; Playwrights and Playwriting.

HUANG ZUOLIN (1906–1994). Chinese • **director** and **theorist** of "spoken drama" (*huaju*; see Playwrights and Playwriting). His advocacy of *xieyi* theory, which infuses techniques of traditional theatre into *huaju*, has helped to end the dominance of illusionism in Chinese modern theatre. As an undergraduate studying social science at

The Great Circus, directed by Huang Zuolin and adapted by Shi Tuo from Andreyev's *He Who Gets Slapped* for the Shanghai Art Drama Company, 1942. Actors include Shi Hui (second from left), Dan Ni (far right), and Zhang Fa (far left). (Photo: Huang Shuqin)

the University of Birmingham (1925–1929), Huang's involvement in community theatre led to his making contact with George Bernard Shaw. Encouraged by Shaw, Huang, after various business experiences, put his focus on theatre, studying Shakespeare at Cambridge (1935–1937). Meanwhile he and his wife, Dan Ni (1912–1995), studied directing and **acting**, respectively, at Michel St. Denis's London Theatre Studio.

Huang returned to China in 1937 at the outbreak of the Second Sino-**Japanese** War (1937–1945) and established himself as a major director, equally successful at drama, comedy, and satire. He also taught drama and worked in films.

After the establishment of the People's Republic of China (1949), Huang became deputy president and, subsequently, president and artistic director of Shanghai People's Art Theatre (Shanghai Renmin Yishu Juyuan). Over the years, he made a concerted effort to end Stanislavski's dominance over *huaju* by adopting the techniques of traditional theatre and those of Brecht's epic theatre. His bold production of *Mother Courage* (1959) confused theatregoers because it shook their rigid opinion of what *huaju* should be. In a landmark speech (1962), Huang proposed adopting Brecht and *xieyi* (the nonrealistic style of *xiqu*) as alternatives to illusionist realism.

Severely attacked during the Cultural Revolution (1966–1976), his theory eventually helped *huaju* dislodge itself from Ibsenian-Stanislavskian realism. Two years after the Cultural Revolution ended, he and Chen Rong (1929–2004) successfully directed Brecht's *The Life of Galileo*; the protagonist's tragic life in the Renaissance reminded audiences of their own recent experiences. In 1986, he directed *The Blood-Stained Hands* (Xie shou ji), an adaptation of *Macbeth*, in traditional style. The following year, he staged *China Dream* (Zhongguo meng), an exemplar of his *xieyi* concept, using a combination of *xiqu* and **Western** styles and a flexible mise-en-scéne. These last two productions won him world acclaim as a master of intercultural theatre.

Siyuan Liu

HUN. *See* Puppet Theatre: Thailand.

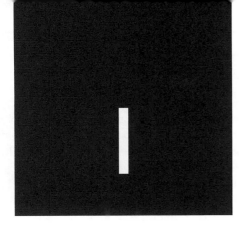

ICHIKAWA DANJÛRÔ. Twelve generations of **Japanese** • *kabuki* • **actors**, representative of the flamboyant, superheroic Edo (Tokyo) "rough style" (*aragoto*). The family's "house name" (*yagô*) is Naritaya, derived from its close association with a temple in Narita. The greatest in this consistently superior line were Danjûrô I, II, IV, V, VII, VIII, IX, XI, and XII. Danjûrô III (1721–1742) and VI (1778–1799), both promising, died young, and Danjûrô X, son-in-law of Danjûrô IX and not originally an actor, gained the name posthumously because of his efforts on the line's behalf.

Danjûrô I (1660–1704) began acting at thirteen as Ichikawa Ebizô I, playing Sakata Kintoki, a violent young superman popular in contemporary *kinpira jôruri* **puppet** performances (see *Ko-jôruri*). Danjûrô I made fierce poses and faces (*mie*) while acting. His wild looks, resembling Buddhist statuary, were exaggerated with stylized red and black **makeup** (*kumadori*) and heightened by a robust, swaggering exit style (*roppô*). This combination of movement, poses, and guttural speech gave birth to *aragoto*; scholars differ as to whether this was in 1673 (at Danjûrô's debut) or later, in 1684/1685. Danjûrô was also a **playwright** (as Mimasuya Hyôgo), and created the first versions of such iconic works as *Wait a Moment!* (Shibaraku, 1694). The object of petty jealousies, he was murdered onstage by a fellow actor.

Danjûrô II (1688–1758), son of Danjûrô I, premiered many of the family's "Kabuki's Eighteen Favorites" (*kabuki jûhachiban*) collection, including *Sukeroku: Flower of Edo* (Sukeroku yukari no Edo zakura, 1713), in which the hero combined both *aragoto* and the "gentle style" (*wagoto*) associated with Kyoto/Osaka *kabuki*. His other *jûhachiban* plays included *The Arrow Maker* (Yanone, 1725) and *The Whisker Tweezers* (Kenuki, 1742). He also perfected *kumadori* by softening its lines (*bokashi*). He passed his name to a pupil, retiring as Ichikawa Ebizô II.

Danjûrô IV (1711–1778) was, as **Matsumoto Kôshirô** II, adopted by Ebizô II after Danjûrô III's death. Danjûrô IV was a "villain" (*katakiyaku*) **role type** specialist. He carefully observed human nature and approached his characters with a studied realism. His versatility was displayed in both "leading male" (*tachiyaku*) and "female impersonator" (*onnagata*) roles; he was one of the rare Danjûrô actors—famed for their strong, male roles—to be good at such parts. A progressive who ran an actors' study group at his house, he retired as Ebizô III.

Danjûrô V (1741–1806), son of Danjûrô IV, was also versatile enough to play female roles; he emerged from a dissolute youth to become Edo's foremost actor. Somewhat eccentric, he retired several times—preferring a hermit-like life—finally ending his career in 1802.

Danjûrô VII (1791–1859), remarkably versatile, became Ebizô IV at five, and Danjûrô VII at nine. He excelled at quick-change plays and "raw domestic plays" (*kizewa mono*). Danjûrô VII was responsible for compiling the "Kabuki's Eighteen Favorites" collection, which he established with his performance as Benkei in *The Subscription List* (Kanjinchô, 1840). It originated the "pine-board play" (*matsubame mono*) genre adapted directly from *nô*. A wealthy (but debt-laden) star who flaunted the period's sumptuary laws, he was exiled from Edo in 1840 for seven years for wearing real armor on **stage**. He gave his name to Danjûrô VIII in 1832 and played out his career as Ebizô VI.

Danjûrô VIII (1823–1854), eldest son of Danjûrô VII, took the name at nine and excelled as handsome heroes. Renowned for his charm and beauty, which made him the sex symbol of his times, he committed suicide at thirty-one, leading to a remarkable outpouring of "death pictures" (*shini-e*) in his honor.

Danjûrô IX (1838–1903), fifth son of Danjûrô VII, was adopted by the Kawarasaki acting family and became Kawarasaki Gonnosuke VII. At thirty-six, he became Danjûrô IX. A pioneering artist intent on moving *kabuki* into the modern world, he supported the Society for Theatre Reform and created a realistic, psychologically accurate method called "gut acting" (*haragei*). He sponsored the historically authentic new genre of "living history plays" (*katsureki mono*); most proved dull, and the genre was abandoned. A versatile actor of males and females, he was best known in the former role. In his last years, fearing a loss of traditions, he revived *aragoto*. Danjûrô IX's progressiveness was visible in his **training** his two daughters to become *kabuki*'s first modern actresses, a venture that ultimately failed.

Danjûrô XI (1909–1965) was the eldest son of Kôshirô VII, a former student of Danjûrô IX. In the postwar period, he took *kabuki* by storm in plays like *Sukeroku* and became the leading star, creating a "Mr. Ebi" (Ebi-sama) boom in the 1950s, when he was Ebizô X. In 1962, he became the first living Danjûrô in half a century, but he died only three years later.

Danjûrô XII (1946–), eldest son of Danjûrô XI, became Danjûrô in an auspicious ceremony in 1985, celebrated in Japan and on tour in the United States, a highly unusual event. In his youth, when known as Ichikawa Shinnosuke, he was popular as one of the "Three Sukes" because of his friendly rivalry with Onoe Kikunosuke (later **Onoe Kikugorô VII**) and Onoe Tatsunosuke (1946–1987). He is often paired with *onnagata* **Bandô Tamasaburô V**. He is an *aragoto* specialist but plays many other leading male roles as well. After forced to leave the stage for several years because of leukemia, he returned triumphantly in 2006. His only son became Ebizô XI (1977–) in 2004 and is a popular young star.

FURTHER READING

Kominz, Laurence R. *The Stars Who Created Kabuki: Their Lives, Loves and Legacy.*

Holly A. Blumner

ICHIKAWA ENNOSUKE. Japanese • *kabuki* • **actor** line known for its innovative spirit. Ennosuke I (1855–1922), son of choreographer Bandô Santarô, was famed for his **stage** stunts (*keren*) and battle to end discrimination against actors at minor **theatres** (*koshibai*). He became a disciple of **Ichikawa Danjûrô IX** in 1870, but was expelled from the Ichikawa family in 1873 for appearing at a *koshibai* without Danjûrô's permission. He toured, appearing mostly in *koshibai*, gaining popularity, until forgiven in 1890, when he became Ennosuke. In 1910, he became Ichikawa Danshirô II.

Ennosuke II (1886–1963), his son, was noted for his influence in the New **Dance** (*shin buyô*) movement and considered by many a revolutionary like his father. After debuting as Ichikawa Danko II, he became Ennosuke II in 1910. In 1909, he joined **Ichikawa Sadanji** II's *shingeki* • **experiments** at the Free Theatre (Jiyû Gekijô). After his influential 1919 travels to Europe and the United States to study theatre and dance, he premiered many innovative new dance-dramas. In 1963, he became Ichikawa En'o I, passing the Ennosuke name on to his grandson.

Ennosuke III (1939–), famous for quick changes (*hayagawari*), flying (*chûnori*), and action-packed scenes in traditional *kabuki* and newly commissioned "super" (*supaa*) *kabuki*, forged his own path since losing his father (Ichikawa Danshirô III, 1908–1963) and grandfather at a young age. Assigned only minor roles in his twenties in *kabuki*'s conservative world, he began producing his own small-scale productions, becoming a sensation by the 1970s. He produces, **directs**, and costars with brother Danshirô IV (1946–) in his own **theatre company**, which has toured internationally. He has also directed abroad. Devoted to creating a *kabuki* for the twenty-first century, he is both the target of criticism and a leading star. In the early 2000s, illness forced him from the stage.

FURTHER READING

Bach, Faith. "The Contributions of the *Omodakaya to Kabuki*"; Kominz, Laurence R. *The Stars Who Created Kabuki: Their Lives, Loves and Legacy.*

Julie A. Iezzi

ICHIKAWA SADANJI. Line of four **Japanese** • *kabuki* • **actors**. The family "house name" (*yagô*) is Takinoya. Sadanji I (1842–1904), adopted son of Ichikawa Kodanji IV (1812–1866), was one of the Meiji (1868–1912) triumvirate comprising himself, **Ichikawa Danjûrô** IX, and **Onoe Kikugorô** V (known collectively as Dan-Kiku-Sa). His earlier names were Ichikawa Tatsuzô, Ichikawa Koyone II, and Ichikawa Shojaku. He became Sadanji I in 1862 and moved from his native Osaka to Edo, where he was supported by **playwright** • **Kawatake Mokuami**, under whose guidance he became skilled at the "rough style" (*aragoto*). He was one of the privileged actors involved when the imperial family made its historic first viewing of *kabuki*, in 1887. Sadanji managed the Shintomi **Theatre** (Shintomi-za) in the 1890s, followed by the Meiji Theatre (Meiji-za).

Sadanji II (1880–1940), son of Sadanji I, took the name in 1906, his earlier names having been Ichikawa Botan, Ichikawa Koyone III, and Ichikawa Enshô. In 1906, he became the first important Japanese actor to travel to Europe, where he studied **Western** theatre, bringing his learning back to Japan in 1907 and, in 1909, cofounding Japan's first modern **theatre company**, the Free Theatre (Jiyû Gekijô), which pioneered *shingeki*. He produced and starred in many *shin kabuki* plays as well, and revived several long-unproduced plays from the Ichikawa family's collection, "Kabuki's Eighteen Favorites" (*kabuki jûhachiban*). In 1928, he headed the first *kabuki* foreign tour when he led a troupe to the USSR, where *kabuki* influenced the work of **directors** like Meyerhold and Eisenstein.

Sadanji III (1898–1964), son of Ichikawa Monnosuke VI (1862–1914), held the names Ichikawa Otora IV and Ichikawa Omezô IV before becoming Sadanji in 1952. He headed Onoe Kikugorô VI's troupe after that actor died in 1949. He specialized in the handsome young lover **role type** (*nimaime*) but also excelled as a "female impersonator" (*onnagata*) and in old men's roles.

Sadanji IV (1940–) is a popular supporting actor known for his *aragoto* characters. He became Sadanji IV in 1972.

Samuel L. Leiter

ICHIMURA UZAEMON. Seventeen generations of **Japanese** • *kabuki* • **actors**, the first fourteen of whom were "actor-managers" (*zamoto*) of Edo's (Tokyo) Ichimura **Theatre** (Ichimura-za). The line's "house name" (*yagô*) is Tachibanaya. There is confusion regarding the attribution of ordinal numbers to members of the line, which can be done by more than one method, and of the seventeen actors to whom the name has been attributed, only twelve officially received it. Several did not accept the name because of inherited debts amassed by predecessors. The most significant were Uzaemon VIII, IX, XII, XIV, XV, XVI, and XVII. Uzaemon XIII was better known as **Onoe Kikugurô V.**

Uzaemon VIII (1698–1762), younger brother of Uzaemon VII, became the manager of the Ichimura Theatre at five. His father actually managed the **theatre**, and the license was held by Uzaemon V's wife. As an adult, Uzaemon VIII excelled at "young male" (*wakashugata*), "young female" (*wakaonnagata*), "leading male" (*tachiyaku*), and "villain" (*katakimono*) **role types**.

Uzaemon IX (1725–1785), eldest son of Uzaemon III, took the name in 1762. Because of his father's debts and a fire that destroyed the theatre in 1784, Uzaemon IX temporarily delegated his producing license to the Kiri Theatre (Kiri-za). Uzaemon IX acted both in Edo and the Kyoto-Osaka area as an actor-manager. His specialties were Soga brother plays, *aragoto*, and "transformation pieces" (*henge mono*).

Uzaemon XII (1812–1851), second son of Uzaemon X, commonly known as Ichimura Takenojô V, reestablished the Ichimura Theatre and succeeded to Uzaemon in 1821, but in 1841 the theatre burned down. In 1842, it was forced by the Tenpô Reforms of 1841–1843 to rebuild in Saruwaka-cho, Asakusa, on the city's outer edge. In 1851, Uzaemon XII became Takenojô and awarded Uzaemon XIII to his son, the later Kikugorô V.

Uzaemon XIV (1847–1893), third son of Uzaemon XII, sold the rights to the Ichimura Theatre because of hereditary debts. He was the last manager in the line and changed his name from Uzaemon to Bandô Kakitsu. A versatile actor, he excelled at "gentle style" (*wagoto*) acting.

Uzaemon XV (1874–1945), adopted son of Uzaemon XIV, was extremely popular. He specialized as young romantic males and in "raw domestic plays" (*kizewa mono*). Often paired with **Onoe Baikô** VI, he placed his family's most successful plays into the "Kakô's Ten Choices" (*Kakô jisshû*) collection; Kakô was his poet-name (*haimyô*).

Uzaemon XVI (1905–1952), adopted son of Uzaemon XV, debuted in 1910 and succeeded to the Uzaemon name in 1947. He excelled as "young females" (*wakaonnagata*) and "young lovers" (*nimaime*), but died at the height of his career.

Uzaemon XVII (1916–2001), grandson of Kikugorô V, took the name in 1955. Prolific in "history plays" (*jidai mono*), he was a member of the Onoe Kikugorô Acting

Company (Kikugorô Gekidan), a master teacher, National Living Treasure, and a great source of theatrical expertise.

Holly A. Blumner

IKRANEGARA (1943–). Balinese-born **Indonesian** poet, novelist, **playwright**, **director**, and **actor**. The first of ten children, his parents wanted him to become a medical doctor. As a child, he was exposed both to traditional Balinese **dance**-theatre and productions of modern theatre. He wrote his first play, *The Girl at That Coffee Stand* (Perempuan di warung itu, 1963), while in high school (where he was a class-mate of playwright-director **Putu Wijaya**), inspired by a village incident.

While studying medicine in Yogyakarta, Ikranegara became increasingly busy as an actor, as well as joining the student movement to overthrow the government. After two years in Yogyakarta, he was called home to Bali because of the unstable **political** sit-uation, which resulted in a coup and the overthrow of President Sukarno (1901–1970). While helping his father run the family business during these years, he still was able to write and produce a play in Denpasar.

After the founding of the Jakarta Arts Center (1968), Ikranegara moved to Jakarta, where he worked with both **Rendra** and **Arifin C. Noer**, and was influenced by their desire to blend modern and traditional forms. In 1975, he founded his own **theatre company**, Just **Theatre** (Teater Saja), producing his own plays as well as directing and acting. His *The Great Anger of the Forest* (Rimba tiwikrama, 1978) included per-formers from his group and a Balinese traditional group, and incorporated techniques, **masks**, and **puppets** from traditional Balinese theatre.

Ikranegara's *The Lords* (Agung, 1976) and *Shhh!!!* (Ssst!!!, 1978), both at Jakarta Arts Center, were inspired by events of the Sukarno years and incorporated elements of tradi-tional theatre. He also acted in Noer's Little Theatre (Teater Kecil) from 1968 to 1997.

Ikranegara's later works include plays inspired by social and political incidents, such as *How Dare You Want to See Godot?* (Kok berani-beraninya mau ketemu Godo, 1993), *How Could You Set the Forest on Fire?* (Kok bisa-bisanya sih kaubakar hutan Itu?, 1997), *The Voice* (2002), inspired by the story of a dancer who decided to stop dancing for pay, and *The Temple of Sacred Masks* (2003), a solo performance piece.

Ikranegara's numerous grants and awards include Fulbrights in 1979 and 1989 and a Ford Foundation grant to research and write about contemporary Indonesian theatre (1991). He lives in Washington, D.C., and writes, performs, and teaches at American universities.

Craig Latrell

INDIA

A Complex Background. India geographically is a subcontinent that extends south-ward from the Himalayan mountains in the north to Kanya Kumari, the tip of India in the very south. While its **religions** and cultures are predominantly Hindu, there are very influential and important Muslim, Sikh, and Christian populations. In 2006, the nation's enormous population was estimated at over 1 billion, 95 million.

India presents students, scholars, visitors, and interested observers with an ancient, colorful, complex, sometimes baffling, but always fascinating tapestry of peoples, languages, cultures, climates, culinary traditions, regions, and religious traditions. Its genres of traditional theatre are derived from and recreate this remarkable tapestry. Found in all regions and employing most of the nation's important languages, these genres do not conveniently fit into the typical **Western** categories used to classify performance, such as drama or **dance**, religious or secular, but straddle or envelop them. In a sense, traditional genres so powerfully manifest and recreate the nation's various cultures, religions, and languages that Western categories cannot contain them. The study of traditional theatre, therefore, takes us not just on a profound exploration of India's theatrical conceptualizations and genres but of our own.

To look at India's traditional theatres within its complex cultural-linguistic-religious tapestry we must divide the country into regions: South India, North India, East India, and West India. We must bear in mind, however, that such a division is just an analytical tool and that all of these regions, while different, in many ways will also be similar, and that their traditional genres will also share in this unity in diversity.

The Epics. The great font of dramatic themes, narratives, and episodes for traditional forms are the two great Hindu epics, the *Mahabharata* and the *Ramayana*. It may be said that the traditional genres of the various regions are in actuality cultural filters that take this vital material that is at the heart of the Hindu tradition and recreate and revitalize it in each cultural and linguistic region through the media of traditional theatre. Even if the figures from each of these epics are not explicitly named or identified, the vast majority of the **role types** in these genres is modeled on them, whether king/prince/hero, queen/princess/heroine, clown/jester, and so on.

The *Mahabharata* focuses on the five heroic Pandava princes and their queen, Draupadi, and its epic universe inspires episodes focusing on heroism, chastity, morality, philosophy, and warfare. The *Ramayana* concerns the exile of Rama and his wife Sita from his kingdom, creating circumstances that provide episodes, themes, and dramatic models that are transmuted into theatre throughout India.

Artistic Syntheses. Most traditional genres represent a synthesis of drama, dance, and **music**. Each genre, however, manifests this synthesis in its own distinctive and characteristic way. For example, in *terukkuttu*, of Tamil-speaking Tamilnadu, South India, the performance is basically operatic, with each **actor**/performer enacting his role by singing, chanting, delivering both scripted and improvised prose dialogue, and dancing. In Kannada-speaking Karnataka, South India, *yakshagana* uses a different synthesis of drama, dance, and music. A background vocalist with a small traditional orchestra, in an area adjacent to the performance space, sings and performs all the narrations and songs constituting an episode, while the actor/performers on **stage** speak only scripted or improvised dialogue. Thus, while most traditional South Asian genres use a drama, music, and dance synthesis, the synthesis will be unique and distinctive to each.

Such theatrical syntheses have been recognized by commentators from ancient times. In the Sanskrit analytical and critical tradition, mention is made of three basic conceptualizations of performance: (1) *nrtta*, pure dance, abstract and ornamental; (2) *nrtya*, facial or physical mime (*abhinaya*), and conventionalized hand gestures (*mudra*) used to perform a narrative or story; and (3), most important, *natya*, the synthesis of *nrtta*, *nrtya*, and elements of song, poetry, and prose, that is, theatre.

Natyashastra. Only a brief look at origins can be offered here. Given such an ancient and complex culture, it is important to offer a basic idea of the major influences in the development of these forms. One of the most vital influences was the classical **Sanskrit theatre** tradition, which developed around **theoretical** concepts that have had a powerful impact on the development of most genres.

While limited evidence makes it impossible to know how and where it developed, the Sanskrit tradition appears to date from the first century BC. The earliest play fragments have a well-developed **dramatic structure** that shows a primary influence from the *Treatise on Drama* (Natyashastra), India's remarkable ancient theatre manual. In addition to its influence on Sanskrit theatre, it probably was an important element, along with localized elements, in the development of most major genres. Each such genre synthesizes *Natyashastra* and more regional elements and, in more extended terms, classical, **folk**, pan-Indian, and local. Each regional genre, therefore, truly represents a synthesis of cultural diversity.

The *Natyashastra*'s theoretical discussion of theatre's origin places it firmly in ancient India's mythology and religion. Thus two vital areas must be kept in mind in studying India's traditional genres. First, most, if not all, genres reenact episodes or stories based in classical or local mythology, or a synthesis of both; second, presentation of these episodes will have a religious or ritual function. In many cases, as with *terukkuttu*, the performance will be a powerful expression of a regional Hindu tradition, with mythic episodes during which performers and audience members will lapse into a form of entrancement/possession.

Ritual/Religion to Theatre/Entertainment. The discussion above indicates that traditional theatre is embedded in a complex nexus of religion, ritual, mythology, and local and pan-Indian tradition and history. In some cases, as with *terukkuttu*, this nexus is explicitly acknowledged and identified; in other cases, it is obscured under layers of modernistic innovations, as with northeast India's Bengali-language *jatra*. One constant thread is a spectrum of traditional performance that ranges from dramatic ritual to ritual/religious drama, that is, from ritual/religion to theatre/entertainment. Each traditional genre can be found along this spectrum, some closer to the ritual pole and some closer to the dramatic pole, but still firmly embedded in the religious/mythological/historical nexus.

The traditional forms of the various linguistic and cultural areas of South India are close to the ritual pole of the spectrum in several crucial ways. First, they are direct manifestations of powerful Hindu traditions; most performances are put on in the ritual contexts of temples or religious **festivals** or ceremonies. Second, and very importantly, they draw on and re-enact episodes from the epics. *Terukkuttu*, with its performances that re-enact the *Mahabharata* in a cycle of ten all-night episodes, is a direct expression and manifestation of a tradition where Draupadi and Dharmaraja, major female and male figures, are worshipped as deities. The complex **makeup** and **costuming** of *terukkuttu* is also ritually based.

The traditional forms of Kerala, the Malayalam-speaking region of the southwestern-most Indian coast, share these *terukkuttu* characteristics. *Kathakali* re-enacts significant episodes from both epics. More important, many of these performances are put on in the ritual contexts of temples. *Kathakali*'s makeup and costuming is also ritually based.

Another major Keralese form is *kutiyattam*, one of the last Sanskrit theatre traditions. Its episodes, too, are primarily derived from the epics and it is a direct expression and manifestation of South Indian Hindu practices.

These characteristics of Hindu mythology-based episodes expressing the traditions of the specific linguistic and cultural region continue as we move northward through South India. The *yakshagana* of Karnataka takes its most important episodes from the epics and is directly related to traditions and rituals of this area. Similarly, **kuchipudi** in the eastern part of central South India has a directly analogous approach.

Farther north, some of the traditional forms become less ritually charged in performance and orientation, despite their ritual/religious origins. While the Marathi-language *tamasha* of Maharashtra can be traced back to devotional song forms, today it is much closer to the entertainment pole of the spectrum, strongly emphasizing historical themes relating to social injustice. In East India's Bengal, *jatra* has moved similarly away from its ritual origins toward the entertainment pole with a focus on contemporary, nondevotional themes. Moreover, *jatra*'s thematic modernization has been accompanied by a shift to prose dialogue in a form once primarily characterized by beautiful singing. One central characteristic of traditional forms, no matter where they are located on the spectrum, is an origin in devotional ritual performance, usually related to Hindu tradition.

A fascinating concomitant to the ritual aspect is humor. It appears as a vital thematic and performative element in all forms discussed above and, in the vast majority of traditional genres, acts almost as a counterbalance to their ritual/religious elements. Many of these forms have vital clowns, such as the *kattiyankaran* of the *terukkuttu* and the *vidushaka* of *kutiyattam*, central elements that propel and punctuate performances with their comedy. **Bhavai** of Gujarat in West India and *tamasha* are characterized by strong comedic elements; "*tamash*" actually means "funny" or "joke."

The ritual, religious, and epic roots of traditional Indian genres counterbalanced by humor and humanity gives these forms a performative power that transcends the veneer of the modern world to engender dramatic performances with personal and spiritual relevance and truth for their audiences.

FURTHER READING

Gargi, Balwant. *Theatre in India*; Richmond, Farley, Darius L. Swann, and Phillip B. Zarrilli, eds. *Indian Theatre: Traditions of Performance*; Varadpande, M. L. *History of Indian Theatre: Loka Ranga; Panorama of Indian Folk Theatre*; Vatsyayan, Kapila. *Traditional Indian Theatre: Multiple Streams*.

Richard A. Frasca

A Pluralistic Modern Theatre. "Indian theatre" is too broad a concept to refer to this country's national theatre, because—given India's many states, languages, dialects, and cultures, each complete and unique in and of itself—there are many Indian theatres. **Politically** and geographically, India denotes a country, but in terms of theatre it represents many types manifested in at least sixteen officially recognized languages (and eight script systems) across twenty-five states and six union territories, populated by well over a billion people. The pluralism thus exhibited is often the cause of political and cultural strain.

Though India has a long history of theatre practice, dramatic literature, dramaturgy, and scholarship, going back to the ancient Sanskrit theatre and including many still practiced folk theatre and theatrically important ritual traditions, modern theatre's roots lie in **Western** traditions implanted during the colonial period. The initial inspiration for India's modern theatre, then, regardless of the language involved, was imitation of Western practices, which began in the late eighteenth century and flourished in the nineteenth, when British influences were strongest. This process began when a Russian named Herasim Lebedeff produced a Bengali version of a British play in Calcutta (Kolkata) in 1795, for which the proscenium **stage** was introduced to an Indian audience (although present locally since the 1753 construction of the Calcutta Playhouse, built for English audiences). Calcutta was the heart of the British *raj*, and long remained a chief site for visiting British troupes and amateur theatricals focusing on stock repertory items. Bengalis, even the upper classes, were mostly restricted from attending these performances.

Each of India's regional-language theatres maintains its own history; these show different evolutionary developments and varying practical applications in the way they express the relationship between text and performance, actors and audience, and art and society. Lal's *Oxford Companion to Indian Theatre* provides—in addition to English-language theatre—separate essays on theatres in Assamese, Bengali, Dogri, Gujarati, Hindi, Kannada, Kashmiri, Konkani, Maithili, Malayalam, Manipuri, Marathi, Nepali (in the Nepali-speaking areas), Oriya, Punjabi, Rajasthani, Sindhi, Tamil, Telugu, and Urdu. Some are primarily rural, others rural and urban, and others mainly urban in nature. According to Aparna Dharwadker, there is a "four-tier hierarchy" of theatre languages in contemporary urban theatre: in tier one are Bengali and Marathi, the principal languages spoken in Kolkata and Mumbai (Bombay), formerly the centers of the most active colonial theatre cultures, and still dominant today. Tier two includes Hindi, Kannada, Gujarati, Tamil, and Malayalam, found in such cities as New Delhi, Jaipur, Lucknow, Bangalore, Mysore, Mumbai, Ahmedabad, Chennai (Madras), and Thiruvananthapuram (Trivandrum). Tier three covers English, Punjabi, Urdu, Manipuri, and Telugu, while tier four comprises languages such as Kashmiri, Sindhi, Oriya, and Assamese.

Since the 1950s, each language has been associated with a regional state, Kannada with Karnataka, for instance, or Tamil with Tamilnadu. The disputed "national language" is Hindi. English is, with Hindi, an official bureaucratic language although fewer than 5 percent speak it.

Western-Inspired Beginnings. The earliest period of modern Indian playwriting was inspired by Shakespeare and other British dramatists as well as by the adaptation and translation of Sanskrit texts into the regional languages. This took place in three port cities founded by the British: Calcutta, Bombay, and Madras, located in the east, west, and south, respectively; the first two, plus Delhi, are today's principal theatre centers. The standard was English plays acted in English by touring Englishmen in proscenium **theatre**s for English-educated middle-class spectators. The proscenium theatre and its accoutrements became universal for urban production, which performed the same plays in Indian languages in imitation of British methods.

Native drama acted by native actors began as romantic spectacles staged in private residences and at court with lots of music and dance. The most renowned early example was *The Court of Lord Indra* (Indar sabha, 1855) by Urdu playwright Amanat Lakhnawi (1815–1859). Subjects were largely conventional, based on myths and epics, as when Vishnudas Bhave (1819/24–1901) wrote the first Marathi play in 1843, *The Wedding of Sita* (Sita Swayamvar), based on the *Ramayana*; however, in 1866, Bengali playwright Ram Narayan Tarkaratna (1822–1886) wrote *New Play* (Naba natak), a satire on the Brahman practice of polygamy, making it the first Indian play on a socially provocative theme; it, too, was staged at someone's home. Political awareness was notable in the plays of Hindi dramatist **Bharatendu Harishchandra**, whose early death seriously hampered Hindi theatre's development, especially as he was the first modern playwright to attempt plays based on indigenous forms like *raslila*. But rising anger against British rule saw the trend of socially and politically concerned drama continued by Bengali playwrights **Michael Madhusudan Dutt** (in works like *Is This Civilization?* [Ekei ki bale sabhyata, 1860]) and **Dinabandhu Mitra** in his notorious *The Indigo Mirror* (Nildarpan, publ. 1860; first prod. 1872), whose 1875 Lucknow revival was shut down by an angry British mob. This letter led to **censorship** through the imposition of the Dramatic Performances Control Act of 1876, which, though infrequently called on, caused producers concern throughout the twentieth century. *The Indigo Mirror*'s first production (1872) was by Calcutta's nationalistic new National Theatre, which a bit later divided into the Hindi National Company and the Bengali National Company.

A commercial outlet arose in **Parsi theatre**, an entertainment-for-entertainment's sake theatre influenced by British melodrama and pantomime, produced in proscenium houses, performed in Hindi and Urdu, using epic subjects, and filled with music, color, dance, melodrama, farce, and spectacle. Originally centered in Bombay, it was created and backed by the Parsis (a Zoroastrian business community) of Maharashtra and Gujarat, and spread throughout South and Southeast Asia, being performed in multiple languages. Its success led to the construction of playhouses in the manner of London's Covent Garden and Drury Lane. One of the Indian musical theatres developed under its influence was the *sangeet natak* of Maharashtra, which brought female impersonator **Bal Gandharva** to fame.

Other important late nineteenth-century developments included the use of Karnataka's musical form *sannata* to present contemporary sensationalistic incidents, while, shortly after the turn of the century, Bengal's **Girish Chandra Ghosh** and Marathi playwright Krishnaji Prabhakar Khadilkar (1872–1948) upset the authorities with politically sensitive plays like *Sirajuddaula* (1905) and *Killing of Kichaka* (Kichak vadh, 1907). Both were banned.

In the 1930s, as Parsi theatre was overwhelmed by sound films, playwrights began to realize that the Western tradition is not primarily English but is equally indebted to other European traditions. Dramatists started to examine the powerful contributions of, for instance, the French, Norwegians, and Germans. Bengali playwrights like **Sisir Kumar Bhaduri**, Naresh Mitra, and Adeendra Chaudhuri; Marathi playwrights like Mama Varerkar and P. K. Atre (1898–1969); Telugu playwrights like P. V. Rajamannar and Bellary Raghava (1880–1946); Malayalam playwrights like K. Damodaran, Pulimana Parameswaran Pillai, E. V. Krishna Pillai (1894–1938), and N. Krishna Pillai (1916–1988); and Hindi playwrights like **Ram Kumar Varma** and Upendra Nath Ashok tried to transform their own theatres based on their understanding of these other traditions. Some wrote on socially relevant issues in order to create a realistic theatre in the Ibsenian vein, while others explored theatricalist modes like expressionism.

The explorations of Bengali **Rabindranath Tagore** are of importance here because of his aversion to Western traditions as models for imitation. His dissatisfaction with contemporary practices and awareness of the latest developments in foreign theatre, as well as his deep commitment to his native culture—including Sanskrit drama—and the clarity of his own means of expression, led him to **experiment** with the creation of a new form of Indian theatre. In it, he synthesized artistic practices from elsewhere with the spiritual warmth of his poetic genius.

Indian People's Theatre Association. From the late 1930s through the freedom struggle of the 1940s, nationalist consciousness and anti-imperialist feelings spread, from the Hindi and Bengali theatres to the many regional theatres, which began to pursue social relevance. In 1943, the catastrophic Bengal famine led to awareness-raising street performances across India. This was epitomized in the formation in Bombay, in 1942–1943, of the Indian People's Theatre Association (IPTA), founded by the Communist Party, with branches in each state. Marxist-leaning nationalist sentiment attracted artists across the language spectrum, tying people together beyond linguistic and cultural boundaries. IPTA provided a nationwide outlook for modern theatre. It tried to reduce the distance between the dramatic text and its presentation, between folk traditions (which began to include political messages) and modern theatre (as in **Bijon Bhattacharya**'s landmark *New Harvest* [Nabanna, 1944], about the famine), and between performance and society. It sought to create awareness of theatre's artistic seriousness and its social relevance. It raised production standards and established the profession of the stage actress, **women** having made their first such appearance in the Marathi-language *School for the Blind* (Andhalayachi, 1933), but not yet having gained acceptance. As such, it represented a transformational phase.

Among IPTA's founders were **Shombhu Mitra**, Balraj Sahni (1913–1973), **Utpal Dutt**, **Habib Tanvir**, Sheila Bhatia (1916–), and many other important artists, who believed that theatre should have an indigenous channel through which to address its own issues rather than via borrowed formulae from the West. Toward this end they concentrated on folk traditions and native mythologies—the so-called "theatre of roots" (*tanatu natakavedi*), discussed below—to invent new forms. As dance is a central component of traditional expression, IPTA did not divorce it from modern theatre and created the Central Ballet Troupe in 1945. But IPTA was unable to sustain its potential contributions because of the interference of political dogmatism, leading to the defection of many. In 1950, when the nation was suffering the agonies of post-independence (Partition in 1947 and Gandhi's assassination in 1948 caused major disruptions), the organization splintered. During the 1950s, although the Communist Party showed a growing inclination to cooperate with the new national government, and IPTA's formal party affiliation had become tenuous, IPTA nevertheless found its work subject to censorship and its productions subject to the entertainment tax despite its being a nonprofit organization, thereby bringing economic hardship. Its influence on modern theatre has been great. Many independent groups emerged as IPTA offshoots, and IPTA's centralized activities were diffused throughout the regional theatres, where meaningful work proceeded.

Indian National Theatre. Another noteworthy development was the 1944 founding in Bombay of the Indian National Theatre (INT). A counter-organization to IPTA, this Gujarati organization was nationalist in nature, and was created by socialist artists and activists in the Indian National Congress. They shared some of IPTA's beliefs in modern theatre's goals but not its revolutionary agenda. They began by working with folk artists and the documentation of folk theatre. Playwright-director

Chandravadan Chimanlal Mehta (1901–1991), **Adi Marzban**, and husband and wife acting team Pravin (1936–1980) and Sarita Joshi (1941–) were prominent cofounders. The dance-dramas *Discovery of India*, *Look at Your Bombay* (Dekh teri Bambai), and *Pearls Scattered in the Yard* (Moti veranan chokman) were among major contributions. Both IPTA and INT are still functioning but their original motivations have faded.

Prithviraj Kapoor, founder of Bombay's Prithvi Theatres, was another major modern theatre visionary, shifting to theatre after becoming established in films. He produced many plays on the burning issue of Partition. His endeavors helped elevate Indian theatre and its artists to a respectable level.

Advances of the 1950s. After independence arrived in 1947, an effort to inject an indigenous flavor of "Indianness" in form and content spread to all types of artistic activity. Indirectly, this stemmed from Prime Minister Jawaharlal Nehru's (1889–1964) concept of reconstruction. Nehru's government established the National Academy of Music, Dance, and Drama (Sangeet Natak Akademi) in 1953, inspiring many state governments to start their own drama academies. Following the ascension of theatre in the post-independence years, activity in all regional-language theatres became a part of a new sensibility and national affirmation; **theatre companies** of different types and philosophies were created nationwide.

Playwriting was influenced heavily, as well. **Dharamvir Bharati**'s antiwar *Blind Age* (Andha yug, 1962), whose action—set on the last day of the great war in the *Mahabharata*—alluded to Partition and other national wounds, caused widespread ripples. In 1949, the Indian Theatre Guild (Bharatiya Natya Sangh) was founded in New Delhi as the Indian branch of the International Theatre Institute; regional centers came into being to help coordinate the nation's theatrical activities.

In the 1950s and 1960s, many amateur regional groups sprang into being with workshops and productions. These groups, which produced the plays of European dramatists, from Brecht to Pirandello, as well as modern Indian playwrights, included Prasadhana Little Theatre, founded by **G. Sankara Pillai**; Telugu Little Theatre, founded by Kopparapu Subba Rao (1890–1950); Andhra Pradesh Natya Sangh, founded by A. R. Krishna; Hindustani Theatre Company, founded by Qudsia Zaidi and Habib Tanvir; Suguna Vilasa Sabha, founded by **Pammal V. S. Mudaliar**; Little Theatre (later, People's Little Theatre) founded by Utpal Dutt; New (Naya) Theatre, founded by Habib Tanvir; Rangayan, founded by **Veejay Mehta** and others; Nandikar, founded by Ajitesh Bandopadhyay (1933–1983), and so on.

During the 1950s, many seminal theatre ideas were disseminated. The National Academy of Music, Dance, and Drama organized an Indian theatre seminar in 1956, during which it recommended the founding of a National School of Drama (NSD). This was realized with the NSD's 1959 establishment in New Delhi; over the next half century it produced hundreds of well-**trained** graduates from all over India. During his directorship (1962–1976), **Ebrahim Alkazi** stabilized the NSD by introducing specializations in acting, directing, and stagecraft. A repertory company began in 1964. During these years, there was an emphasis on Western models, Alkazi being a product of London's Royal Academy of Dramatic Arts. He concentrated on perfecting all aspects of production, with deep research and preparation during preproduction. His stagings became benchmarks of Indian theatre. Although many graduates ended up making their living in films and television, the NSD's influence remains visible on the national scene through the companies it inspired and the work of alumni, such as directors **B. V. Karanth**, **Ratan Thiyam**, **Mohan Maharishi** (1940–), Bansi Kaul (1949–), **Prasanna**, **S. Ramanujam**, and many others.

New Initiatives of the 1960s. Indian theatre in the 1960s showed a different picture on the basis of initiatives developed in the previous decade. By now, many regional-language theatres, like the Bengali, Hindi, and Marathi, were able to stand on their own with their own artistic identity in response to nationalist developments and the ability to react to political concerns. Bengali theatre had artists on the level of Shombhu Mitra and Utpal Dutt, but many theatres outside the mainstream began to progress toward meaningful work in their regional languages. Malayalam, Tamil, Kannada, Telugu, Oriya, Gujarati, and other dialect theatres were striving for a new sense of theatre appropriate to local needs. They conducted workshops on all areas of theatre from acting to theory to trends developing nationally and internationally. Often, these workshops were held in association with the NSD, Indian Theatre Guild, stage academies, and so forth. Such workshops examined directing as a process of collaboration with other artists in relation to textual interpretation. They fostered an understanding of theatre as a complete art form. The director's vision was recognized through the work of Alkazi, Tanvir, Dutt, and Mitra.

The "theatre workshop" (*nata kalari*) movement in Malayalam led by G. Sankara Pillai, C. N. Srikanthan Nair (1928–1976), S. Ramanujam, and **Kavalam Narayana Panikkar**; the efforts made by **N. Muthuswamy** and S. Ramanujam in Tamil; the initiatives of **K. V. Subbanna**, B. V. Karanth, and V. Ramamurthy (1935–) in Kannada; the activities of the Navrang Dramatic Club and Rangmanch in Kashmir; and the work of A. R. Krishna and Abburi Ramakrishna Rao in Telugu completely changed practices in their respective regions.

Postcolonial Playwriting and the "Theatre of Roots." The postcolonial period saw impressive playwriting advances. There was a clear departure from Ibsen-based methods and a deeper penetration into Indian realities. **Vijay Tendulkar**, **Mahesh Elkunchwar**, Satish Alekar (1949–), and **G. P. Deshpande** in Marathi; Manoj Mitra (1938–), Bijon Bhattacharya, Utpal Dutt, and **Badal Sircar** in Bengali; Sriranga (a.k.a. Adya Rangacharya, 1904–1984), **Chandrasekhar Kambar**, Chandrashekhar Patil (1939–), Patre Lankesh (1935–2000), **Girish Karnad**, and H. S. Shiva Prakash in Kannada; Komal Swaminathan (1935–1995), N. Muthuswamy, and Indira Parthasarathy (1930–) in Tamil; Arun Sarma (1931–) and Phani Sarma (1910–1970) in Assamese; S. M. Mehndi and Habib Tanvir in Urdu; Geet Chandra Tongra (1913–1996) and Arambam Somorendra (1935–2000) in Manipuri; Manoranjan Das (1921–), Bijay Mishra (1936–), Harihar Mishra, and Subodh Pattanaik in Oriya; Radhakrishna Bhamidipati, Rachakonda Viswanatha Sastry, Gollapudi Maruthi Rao, N. R. Nandi, Attili Krishna Rao, Tanikella Bharani, and Yandamuri Veerendranath in Telugu; N. Krishna Pillai (1916–1988), G. Sankara Pillai, C. N. Srikanthan Nair, C. J. Thomas (1918–1960), and Kavalam Narayana Panikkar in Malayalam; **Mohan Rakesh**, Jagdish Chandra Mathur (1917–1978), and **Ram Kumar Varma** in Hindi; Labhshankar Jadavji Thaker (1935–), Adil Mansoori, and Hasmukh Baradi in Gujarati; Pritosh Gargi (1923–1978), Gurucharan Singh Jasuja (1925–), Ajaib Kamal (1932–), Ravindra Ravi (1938–), and C. D. Sidhu (1938–) in Punjabi; and many other playwrights enriched playwriting and production after 1947.

Many also directed their own works. Some sparked important movements, like Badal Sircar, who was responsible for the "Third Theatre" (Anganmancha, literally, "open-air theatre") concept, in which production elements were stripped away and performances were given gratis in open-air venues, and which gave rise in the 1970s to numerous politically engaged street theatre troupes. Sircar and Delhi's **Safdar Hashmi** were prime movers in this movement, which performed activist plays to the underprivileged in free performances in urban and village environments; Hashmi paid the ultimate price when he was beaten to death during a factory performance, sparking a national protest. Later artists in this movement include Tripurari Sharma (1956–), leader of the Alarippu group, whose plays—produced in conventional venues as well as the streets—deal with subjects ranging from the ostracism of lepers to women's issues. And, since 1967, Aloke Roy and his Awakening (Jagran) troupe—known for its **mask**-like white makeup—have produced plays on topics like alcoholism and malnutrition in out-of-doors locales for people in the lowest socioeconomic strata.

Postcolonial nationalist reconstruction inspired artists to turn toward indigenous theatres in their search for a new means of expression. As noted above, this "theatre of roots" (*tanatu natakavedi*) movement began in IPTA's early days. Different regions produced new forms of presentation from this encounter between tradition as a quest for identity and the search for roots as a way of creating an organic interface between traditional and modern theatre. Official institutions such as the NSD, National Academy of Music, Dance, and Drama, and the various state academies provided funding to propagate the movement. Reflected in playwriting as well as in all areas from **training** on, it examined traditional martial arts, costumes, makeup, rituals, numerous physical and vocal techniques that privileged body and voice over verbal performance, and all those expressive conventions whose appropriation could provide viable methods for contemporary theatre. Thus parable narrative structures became familiar in the work of Tanvir, Panikkar, Kambar, and others. Music became essential as an underpinning for bodily movements. Some, like Thiyam, Tanvir, and Karanth sought to escape the proscenium, searching for a more intimate actor-audience relationship, even using "found" sites in places like ruins.

Directors who investigated indigenous forms to advance modern theatre included Karanth, Utpal Dutt, **Heisnam Kanhailal**, Thiyam, Veejay Mehta, Arun Mukherji, S. Ramanujam, Bhanu Bharti (1947–), Jose Chiramel, Bansi Kaul, Waman Kendre, **Ram Gopal Bajaj**, C. Basavalingaiah, Dina Gandhi, Chandradasan, R. Raju, Vadivel Arumugham (1955–), Mangai, Jabbar Razak Patel (1942–), N. Muthuswamy, M. Ramaswamy, Probir Guha, and Sheila Bhatia. But some, like Mahesh Elkunchwar and Safdir Hashmi, rejected the "theatre of roots" as redolent of "revivalism," complaining of its lack of social relevance, or pointing to its serving the director's interests over those of the actors or play. "Theatre of roots" eventually lost momentum although it remains vibrant in a small number of companies.

A Heterogeneous Theatre Culture. Contemporary Indian theatre presents a heterogeneous picture on both a cultural and stylistic level. It represents different schools of production in many contemporary Indian dialects as well as Sanskrit and English, although translations of plays from one regional language to another are limited. Acting and design include appropriated versions of traditional performance culture as well as modern multimedia technology employed to create effective productions dependent on a director's interpretation; this can range from the intimate to the spectacular, and can be realized in conventional **theatres** or in a variety of outdoor venues, including the streets. Relative to its size and the richness of its theatrical culture, theatre **festivals** in India are not abundant, and there is no major international example.

The heterogeneity of Indian theatre includes multiple streams addressing the cardinal issues of the nation's diversity. Its evolved and appropriated forms of theatrical expression are visible under the broad rubrics of protest, community, propaganda, Dalit ("untouchables"), feminist, street, and developmental theatre. Present alongside Indian plays are numerous Western dramas, from the Greeks to Broadway. Much use has been made of adaptations of Indian and foreign novels and other narrative forms.

Although there is a robust number of respected directors at work, the actors and companies they work with are largely amateur, commercial theatre being severely restricted. It is difficult for theatre artists to earn a living in a field that requires grants and subsidies to survive. Most practitioners hold other employment to pay their bills; films and television, crucial economic supports for many, are also responsible for dwindling theatregoing, despite the low ticket costs, which are usually higher than movie tickets.

FURTHER READING

Dalmia, Vasudha. *Politics, Plays, and Performances: The Politics of Modern Indian Theatre;* Dharwadker, Aparna Bhargava. *Theatres of Independence: Drama, Theory, and Urban Performance in India since 1947;* Lal, Ananda, ed. *The Oxford Companion to Indian Theatre.*

B. Ananthakrishnan

INDONESIA

Background. Indonesia is a Southeast Asian nation of six thousand inhabited islands, with an estimated population of 240 million, stretching between Australia and **Singapore**. More than seven hundred ethnic languages are spoken. Over half the archipelago's population lives on the island of Java, which is also the center of business, government, education, and media. Indonesia's national language, Indonesian (Bahasa Indonesia), is spoken by over 90 percent of the population. Approximately 85 percent are Muslims; there are also smaller numbers of Christians, Hindus, Buddhists, and practitioners of indigenous faiths.

In the following, Indonesia's traditional theatre is examined under the geographical subheadings of Bali, Java, and the Outer Islands.

Bali. Bali is a small tropical island, with a land mass of 5,632 sq. km., located due east of Java. It has a population of just over 3 million, 95 percent of whom are adherents of the Balinese version of Hinduism (Agama Hindu Bali) and are considered "ethnic Balinese." The **religious** beliefs of the remaining population are Muslim, Christian, or Buddhist. Although agriculture remains an important part of the rural economy, Bali—particularly its south—is heavily developed and relies on tourism and handicrafts export for its income.

The influence of Hindu Java entered during the reign of King Airlangga in the first half of the eleventh century, but it was not until the legendary leader Gajah Mada of the Majapahit dynasty defeated the Balinese rulers that the power center was moved to

Gelgel (near present-day Klungkung) in the late fourteenth century. As Majapahit collapsed in Java under pressure from Muslim sultanates, there was an exodus of the courts—including the priest Niratha, as well as many artists and scribes—to Bali, which culminated around 1478. Most Balinese, except for the Bali Aga ("original Balinese"), trace their ancestry to Majapahit, and many of Bali's performing arts share the roots of this Javanese tradition, in terms of language, aesthetics, and **music**.

Hinduism is a very important part of everyday life, and an intricate calendric system determines when, and what kind of, offerings must be prepared and presented to a wealth of deities, and to the supreme god, Sang Hyang Widhi. Much traditional music and **dance** is performed on this "island of a thousand temples" for ceremonies in a temple setting. As a rule, every Balinese village has three main temples, and each has an "anniversary" (*odalan*) that is celebrated every 210 days. There are also individual temples in each ancestral home, as well as special temples for clans, castes, and other descent groups. When the gods descend for *odalan*, the temple is beautifully adorned with ornate offerings of food and flowers, and the villagers gather to pray together. *Gamelan* music, dance, drama and *wayang kulit* (see Puppet Theatre) are integral features of the temple **festival**, although they have officially been divided into three basic, if sometimes arbitrary, groups. Those performed in the inner sanctum are offerings for the gods; those in the courtyard are considered to be "ritual" performances; and those performed outside these confines are for human entertainment.

Historically, Bali has long taken on foreign influences and adapted and incorporated them into the indigenous traditions. Early on, these were mostly Javanese and **Chinese**, but since the twentieth century, both Dutch colonialism and international tourism have had major impacts on culture and performance. Javanese language (Old Javanese or Kawi) and aesthetics (both in **costume** and gesture) are visible in the more courtly of traditional Balinese dance-dramas—*gambuh, arja, topeng*, and *legong*. They are also still visible in *sang hyang* and *jauk*, although these owe more to indigenous tradition. In some instances, genres—such as *kecak*—were even initiated by foreign visitors before being adopted into the "traditional" corpus. Other popular, nonritual genres, such as *jangger* and *drama gong*, have clear **Western influences**.

Tourism is the mainstay of the economy, and performing arts have been a key commodity in Bali's unique "brand" of cultural tourism. Thousands of tourists daily watch commercialized dances and dance-dramas in dozens of specially designated sites around the island. Foreign touring has been a priority since a group predominantly from Peliatan performed at the 1931 Exposition Coloniale Internationale de Paris, famously witnessed by Artaud. Innumerable foreign students have studied dance and music for months or years in Bali, and many Balinese regularly teach abroad. Since the 1970s, there has been much debate over which kinds of performance are appropriate for tourist and secular consumption and which are too sacred for performance outside of the temple.

The influence of government, particularly under President Suharto's (1921–) New Order regime (1966–1998), was felt strongly in the performing arts scene. Art schools were established to "conserve and develop" traditional arts, which were viewed as "peaks" of Indonesian national culture. In addition, the annual Bali Arts Festival was established in 1979 to showcase the best traditional arts. It takes place annually during the school holidays and draws crowds from across Indonesia to witness performances and competitions, as well as to go shopping and people-watching. The hegemony of these institutions has led to the standardization of styles across the island, as local groups are increasingly led by alumni of the schools, and compete for funding and prestige on the **stages** of the festival. Nonetheless, the combination of institutional backing and the traditionalist ethos of Balinese religion has kept the performing arts very much alive.

FURTHER READING

Arps, Bernard, ed. *Performance in Java and Bali: Studies of Narrative, Theatre, Music, and Dance*; Dibia, I Wayan, and Rucina Ballinger. *Balinese Dance, Drama and Music*; Kartomi-Thomas, Karen Sri. "Tradition and Modern Indonesian Theatre"; Mohamad, Goenawan. *Modern Drama of Indonesia*.

Java. Although Java has been inhabited for at least 1.7 million years, little remains of its early history. Buddhism and Hinduism arrived in the first half of the first millennium in the wake of Indian Ocean trade and mapped over a substrate of animistic spirit beliefs. Along with religion came technologies, such as writing and irrigated, terraced rice fields. Local big men and women were elevated as monarchs and worshipped as incarnated deities. Monasteries and religious orders were founded to prop up theocratic regimes and inculcate religious beliefs. The **Ramayana** was adapted into Old Javanese between 900 and 1200, as were books of the **Mahabharata**; both remain important theatrical sources. Inscriptions and manuscripts from Java composed between 840 and 1500 describe theatrical performances of *wayang kulit*, dance, clowning, and *raket*, a form of **masked** performance with clowning that is a likely predecessor of *gambuh* and *topeng*. Pageants were a preoccupation of nobility. Ancient Javanese theatre was occasioned by religious festivals, royal rituals, and rites of passage. Performances were linked to religion and governance; as royalty was identified with Hindu deities, the enactment of Indic epics authorized regimes.

Following the establishment of Islamic sultanates on Java's north coast in the early fifteenth century, the old beliefs of Hindu-Buddhism receded, and practitioners retreated to inaccessible mountainous areas and neighboring Bali. Islam brought with it Arabic, frame drumming, and new theatrical sources, such as the tales of Mohammad's uncle, Amir Hamzah. The old expressive forms and Indic tales did not disappear with Islam, however, but continued to be performed in royal courts and the rural countryside in conjunction with rites of passage and communal celebrations. The arts were reinterpreted according to Islamic tenets. *Suluk*, a form of mystical poetry believed to originate in the Cirebon region before the sixteenth century, interpreted *wayang kulit*, **barong**, *topeng*, and *ronggeng* (a form of social dance) as symbols for progress on the path to divine union. Shadow puppet morphology became more abstract, arguably a concession to Islamic tastes; the influence of Islamic design is apparent in Java's leaf-shaped, so-called tree of life (*gunungan* or *kayon*) puppet. Chinese mercantile communities emerged and sponsored their own arts. They hosted touring Chinese theatre troupes and built their own **theatre companies** with Javanese **actors** and actresses. Glove puppetry and lion dancing were also sponsored by Chinese, as were Javanese arts.

European explorers and traders arrived in the early sixteenth century to take control over the archipelago's lucrative spices. The Dutch established Batavia (Jakarta) in western Java as a trading post in 1619, and through conquest and alliance colonized Java and much of the rest of the archipelago during the next two centuries. European military thespians occasionally gave performances in eighteenth-century Java. In 1821, a purpose-built **theatre** with a proscenium stage was opened in Batavia. Similar theatres were later constructed in the port cities of Surabaya and Semarang. These theatres, as well as clubs in towns and cities, were receiving houses for itinerant opera, drama, and variety companies from Western nations. Local amateur societies also performed. Audiences were limited to Europeans and a sprinkling of Javanese and Chinese elites. As cities grew in the nineteenth century, public theatres catering to non-Europeans were constructed by Chinese entrepreneurs, initially housing itinerant Chinese and *topeng* companies.

Colonial rule drained the central Javanese royal courts of Surakarta and Yogyakarta of much of their power; energies once devoted to warfare and governance shifted to creating spectacles such as **wayang wong**, **langen driya**, and *langen mandra wanara* (a *Ramayana* dance-drama). Week-long performances in high-ceilinged pavilions (*pendhapa*) could involve a full year of rehearsal. **Scenography** was minimal but costumes were sumptuous, and performances were attended by both Javanese and Dutch elites. Court dancers, musicians, and puppeteers went on payroll; elaborate sets of *gamelan* instruments and shadow puppets were constructed and raised to the status of "potent heirlooms" (*pusaka*); performance manuals, scripts, and story compilations, such as Ronggawarsita's (1802–1873) *Book of Kings* (Pustakaraja) were authored; village puppeteers and dancers were summoned to the courts for advanced **training**, and court etiquette thereby infused village performances. Court dance masters were hired by producers to fashion commercial versions of *wayang wong* and *langen driya* that played in public theatres.

The late colonial period saw a flowering of popular theatres on public stages. **Komedi stambul** (a.k.a. "Malay opera") originated in Surabaya in 1891 as a Malay-language response to European opera and Indian **Parsi theatre** (which arrived in 1883 or possibly earlier). Itinerant troupes played public theatres to wild acclaim. (In 1893, Javanese performers of *gamelan* and *wayang* were a popular feature of the "Java Village" at the Chicago Columbian Exposition, becoming the first Indonesian performers to tour the West.) *Komedi stambul*'s influence resulted in the elevation of **folk** forms, such as **ludrug** and **kethoprak**, to proscenium stages; its scenography also infused *wayang wong* and Chinese theatre. The popular, Malay-language **tonil** emerged in 1925 from *komedi stambul* and **bangsawan** (which reached Java from **Malaysia** starting in 1893). Jazz-age troupes such as **Miss Riboet**'s ORION and Dardanella, starring **Devi Dja**, performed six-act Hollywood-style melodramas interspersed with song-and-dance routines.

The recording industry and radio tapped into Java's traditional performance culture. Performers altered routines to suit media requirements. Radio emphasized comic forms of *wayang* over more somber varieties; "modern" instruments such as guitar and ukulele were added to traditional ensembles; and new genres such as **dagelan** *mataram* were created. Night fairs (*pasar malam*) likewise demanded abbreviated performances, and elevated folk forms previously enacted at ground level to raised stages.

Starting with the founding of the Javanese nationalist movement High Endeavor (Budi Utomo) in 1908, Javanese classical arts including dance, *gamelan* music, and *wayang* were cultivated as markers of distinction and national identity. The Dance and Music Training Center, founded in Yogyakarta in 1918, offered classical music and dance training to the public, including foreigners. Practical study of Javanese dance and music and knowledge of *wayang* and other arts were highlighted in the Montessori-influenced curriculum of Garden of Students (Taman Siswa) nationalist schools starting in 1922. Three part-time courses in shadow puppetry opened in Surakarta and Yogyakarta between 1923 and 1931, allowing dedicated amateurs to study *wayang kulit*.

Java's Dutch colonizers had minimal direct impact on indigenous production. Taxes were sometimes levied on performances, subversive performers could be caned or imprisoned, and **abdul muluk**, *wayang wong*, Chinese theatre, and other forms were banned for periods in parts of Java, typically in response to licentious audience behavior. The Java Institute (founded 1919) was an important arts patron; the Sundanese classical opera *gending karesmen*, for example, originated in a commissioned performance for the Institute's 1921 Bandung conference. Members of the Java Institute wrote scholarly articles and monographs on performance, sometimes influenced by theosophy. The state publisher Balai Pustaka (founded 1917) issued performance texts, including a thirty-seven-volume edition of *wayang kulit* summaries (1927–1932), providing an authoritative definition of the canon. International tours of Javanese dance-drama under colonial auspices and exhibitions of masks and puppets entranced generations of Western modernists.

Japan invaded in 1942 and remained until 1945. The Japanese, unlike the Dutch, promoted theatre and related arts as propaganda media. *Tonil* was replaced by **sandiwara** due to an occupation ban on Dutch. A theatre school for training *sandiwara* performers and a Javanese Sandiwara Union under **Armijn Pané** were formed. The Central Office for Cultural Affairs in Jakarta mandated performances of propagandistic scripts and synopses by *sandiwara*, *dagelan*, and *wayang* troupes to rally the masses to Japan's side. Most European **playwrights** were banned; because of Norway's neutrality, Ibsen remained acceptable.

The Ministry of Information continued to use traditional theatre for propaganda after independence was declared in 1945, even creating new *wayang kulit* genres to instill patriotism. In the 1950s and early 1960s, **political** parties courted puppeteers such as **Abyor Dayagung** and *ludrug*, *kethoprak*, and **lenong** companies to serve as their conduits. Amplification and electricity were common in rural theatre by the 1960s, and traditional troupes could play to audiences in the thousands.

Indonesia's first president, Sukarno (1901–1970), an amateur painter and playwright in his youth, used *wayang kulit* symbology in his public addresses and sponsored *wayang kulit* performances with covert messages that forewarned of future policies. Sukarno disliked Western popular culture and encouraged the purification of Javanese tradition. Secondary-level schools for the arts were established, beginning in 1950 with Surakarta's Music Conservatory. Tertiary-level arts conservatories were founded in Surakarta, Yogyakarta, and Bandung in 1963, 1964, and 1967. These standardized theatre, dance, music, and puppetry, flattening regional variations and discouraging populist gestures. A new form of dance-drama, **sendratari**, was created in 1961 to perform *Ramayana* stories against the backdrop of the national archaeological park Prambanan in a bid to attract tourists and glorify tradition.

The brutal establishment of Suharto's (1921–) "New Order" military regime in 1966 led to the killing or banning of many traditional performers with links to socialist and communist politics. Under Suharto, traditional artists were policed by "cultural inspectors" and shied away from politics, although performances regularly presented social criticism. The New Order created competitions among troupes, issuing prizes for décor, etiquette, and costumes, thereby encouraging standardization. Puppeteers and actors were encouraged to quote government policies on family planning and recommended rice strains.

Thousands of audiocassettes of traditional plays were released starting around 1970. These were avidly consumed through the 1990s, contributing to further standardization and the establishment of certain companies and the elevation to superstar status of performers like puppeteers Nartosabdho (1925–1985) and **Asep Sunandar Sunarya**.

The end of Sukarno's anti-Westernism and the 1968 founding of Jakarta's Taman Ismail Marzuki Arts Center catalyzed new syncretic hybrids of traditional and modern art. **Directors** and choreographers like **Rendra** and **Sardono W. Kusumo** created exciting work yoking European frameworks such as absurdism and "poor theatre" to traditional processes and forms. Foreign arts students returned to Indonesia in the early 1970s and studied in conservatories and villages. Traditional actors, dancers, and puppeteers taught and studied abroad in increasing numbers and performed in global works by Robert Wilson and Peter Sellars.

Traditional theatre is cheaply recorded and is a mainstay of late-night television programming. Since 1999, video compact disc versions of traditional theatre, mostly pirated, have superseded audiocassettes as the preferred medium.

Since Suharto's fall in 1998, some traditional artists have become politically active and use performances to lambaste corruption and abuses of power, but most remain wary of politics.

Outer Islands. Lombok, Madura, and the Banjarese cultural area of southern Kalimantan bear the imprint of cultural contact with Java predating European imperialism. Theatrical forms such as *wayang kulit* and *topeng* are practiced in regional variants, and Javanese story sources such as **Panji** are well known. Bali's colonization of Lombok brought Balinese arts to this island, as well. Malay influences date to the late nineteenth and early twentieth centuries: Banjarese *mamanda* shows the influence of *bangsawan*, while Lombok's nearly extinct *kemidi rudat* appears to be derived from *komedi stambul*. Traditional theatre on Indonesia's so-called outer islands lacks the level of official support found in Java and Bali, and has generally declined in recent years. Cultural preservation and development projects launched by the government since the 1970s and the interest of foreign scholars and tourists have brought limited relief.

Traditional theatre in Sumatra is in healthier condition. *Bangsawan* troupes from Penang, Johore, and Singapore toured Sumatra by the 1880s. Local companies were established in imitation, and hybrid genres emerged. Hundreds of *randai* troupes, a folk theatre of the Minangkabau that arose in the 1930s and that was dramaturgically influenced by *bangsawan*, are active in West Sumatra, and *randai* has been exported abroad. *Opera batak*, a *bangsawan*-influenced musical spectacle from North Sumatra originating in the 1920s, has lost popularity recently, but its songs survive as music videos. Local authorities in South Sumatra have taken an interest in *abdul muluk*, though audiences are in decline. North Sumatra's *bangsawan* and Riau's *bangsawan* and *mendu* (closely related to Kalimantan's *mamanda*) are failing to compete against modern media.

Traditional forms of **storytelling**, ritual, and dance from other islands are sometimes typed as theatre in government publications, but with the exception of a small number of *bangsawan*, *tonil*, and *sandiwara* troupes active in Sulawesi and the Maluku islands, there was very little theatre in Eastern Indonesia before 1950.

FURTHER READING

Brandon, James R. *Theatre in Southeast Asia*; Holt, Claire. *Art in Indonesia*; Sedyawati, Edi, ed. *Performing Arts*.

Matthew Isaac Cohen

Modern Indonesian Theatre. Distinctions between "traditional" and "modern" theatres are as unstable in Indonesia as anywhere else. Many genres universally taken as "traditional" in Bali, for example, have long been animated by competitions between villages and provinces, fueling a "modern" spirit of frequent innovation. Conversely, some genres that are "modern" insofar as they emerged recently (for example, *kethoprak* in the 1880s) may be classified as "traditional" insofar as they have developed in relation to traditional cultural structures and processes. **Putu Wijaya** has called the modern theatre a "new tradition" (*tradisi baru*). Likewise, there is no traditional genre that has not undergone profound transformations in response to modernity.

Colonial Models. However, modern theatre is commonly understood as spoken (not sung) performances from Western models. In this sense, Indonesia can trace modern theatre to the 1620s, when the Portuguese gave puppet performances in colonial Batavia, or to the first known performance of a European play, in 1629. The Dutch colonial period saw various developments, including the construction of theatres. The brief British takeover from 1812 to 1816 saw additional activities, as was true of the Dutch after they resumed control, performing standard plays from the canon, and, in 1830, Ten Kate van Loo, an Indo-European actor, wrote two original Western-style plays in Dutch. Visiting French troupes were increasingly active after 1837.

This European tradition left an unclear legacy on the development of modern theatre. Neither theatre companies, nor repertories, nor individual artists passed from one to the other, and only one of the European theatre's venues survives. Significantly clearer is the legacy of "Malay opera" (*bangsawan* or *komedi stambul*), offered from the mid-nineteenth century by Chinese-Indonesian producers in public theatres, for non-European elites. Malaysian *bangsawan* (imported in the 1880s) and *komedi stambul* provided exciting new material for theatres in Surabaya, Batavia, and elsewhere.

Native Literary Drama. These forms incorporated traditional and modern traditions from Eurasia into popular variety shows similar to vaudeville and music hall fare. They used proscenium stages and kept up-to-date with new fashions reflected in mass media. In the early twentieth century, some troupes began to incorporate more aspects of Western literary dramaturgy. The amateur Opera Derma troupe was founded in Batavia's Weltewreden district in 1908. Like earlier amateur theatres, it produced scripted plays whose texts were sold to spectators. This literary emphasis paved the way for the amateur nationalist theatre of the 1920s. Willy Klimanoff established Dardanella in 1926, and led efforts to make Malay opera rely more on scripted drama. Though Dardanella lasted until 1952, the number of Malay opera performances dwindled through the 1940s and disappeared in the 1950s.

Most critics cite Roestam Effendi's (1903–1979) *Essential Freedom* (Bebasari, 1926) as the first Indonesian play, and the beginning of modern theatre history, although this is arguable. The first play written in Indonesia, and the first modern drama in Malay/Indonesian, was actually F. Wiggers's *The Story of Lady Soerio Retno* (Lelakon raden reij Soerio Retno, 1901). And numerous modern plays were written for the Malay opera. Nevertheless, *Essential Freedom* was the first play by a native Indonesian to take the idea of a unified nation as its frame of reference.

Effendi and other major playwrights of the 1920s and 1930s (Mohammed Yamin, Sanoesi Pané, **Armijn Pané**) were not professionals of the *stambul* tradition, but radicalized students, committed to anticolonial and nationalist agendas. Their plays were published in *Modern Poet* (Poedjangga baroe) and performed, if at all, in "study groups." *Modern Poet* dramatists viewed drama as an intellectual forum for raising political consciousness through radical treatments of narrative traditions (for example, *Essential Freedom* reimagines the *Ramayana*) or history (as when great leaders from Indonesia's past are shown as protonationalists). They thus distanced themselves from the Malay opera traditions.

The Dutch regime ended in 1942 with the Japanese invasion. The occupiers (1942–1945) did much (sometimes unintentionally) to promote nationalism. For example, its **censorship** board promoted literary drama at the expense of improvisatory theatre by requiring all scripts to be reviewed. The military government promoted a variety of arts initiatives for propaganda purposes, including a theatre school and an arts center in Jakarta. In 1944, Usmar Ismail (1921–1972) and D. Djajakusuma established the Illusionist's Theatre (Sandiwara Penggemar Maya), and **Andjar Asmara** established Eastern Light (Tjahaja Timoer), the first professional, modern, nationalist troupes. Although the war's end and the ensuing revolutionary struggle prompted both to disband prematurely, they set a precedent for post-independence theatre.

Postwar Developments. The Generation of '45 brought a fervent enthusiasm for creating a national culture to the Sukarno years (1950–1965). Jakarta, Yogyakarta, and Bandung emerged as postcolonial theatre centers. In Jakarta, the Indonesian National Theatre Academy was established in 1955. It instructed students in "Method acting," and promoted the performance of Western plays, many of which were translated into Indonesian. Teguh Karya (1937–2001) and Soekarno M. Noor (1931–) were among its graduates. Meanwhile, in Bandung and Yogyakarta, student groups predominated. In 1958, Jim Lim (1936–) and Suyatna Anirun (1936–2002) established the Bandung Theatre Study Club (Studiklub Teater Bandung), which produced an avant-garde Western repertoire and **experimented** with incorporating traditional theatre into modern staging. In Yogyakarta, the Indonesian Academy of Drama and Film (founded 1948) served, along with Gadjah Mada University, as an academic infrastructure for the activities of many student troupes. Rendra and **Arifin C. Noer** first began working in Yogyakarta during this time.

From 1950 to 1965, artists looked predominantly to Western theatre, but also began finding ways to "Indonesianize" theatre by incorporating traditional elements. Meanwhile, the ascendance of the Communist Party exerted influence and censorship on the arts. Many sympathized with the communists, but since 1965, much of their legacy has been forgotten.

The theatre culture of the Suharto years (1966–1998) was shaped most profoundly by the establishment of state arts centers and by Rendra's singular influence. Suharto initially built legitimacy among youth by not interfering with freedom of expression. State centers served as significant artistic havens after 1967, although many later viewed them as conservatories run by a cadre of established artists. Nevertheless, following the communist ideological regulation of the early 1960s, these institutions offered significant protection.

Rendra began his activities in the 1950s, but made his most profound impact upon returning from study in New York in 1968 when he founded the Workshop Theatre (Teater Bengkel), combining ensemble techniques of American avant-garde theatre with Javanese village culture. Rendra inspired Arifin C. Noer, Putu Wijaya, and subsequent generations of practitioners to move beyond Western dramaturgy and create original plays using techniques and company structures with closer links to Indonesian cultures.

Rendra viewed theatre as a form of cultural resistance through which clowns spoke truth to the authorities. This put him in conflict with the government, and, in 1978, he was banned from performance for seven years. After 1978, artists practiced self-censorship, and generally avoided direct criticism of the government. Many continued to experiment with interculturalism, but adopted abstract or absurdist idioms to soften their themes. During the 1980s, economic prosperity brought a rise in middle-class audiences. **Nano Riantiarno** developed a new comic "opera" style, suggestive of Malay opera, but also influenced by Brecht. Riantiarno's comedies about contemporary social issues were popular and (usually) avoided censorship. In Yogyakarta, Lightning Theatre (Teater Gandrik) began performing in Javanese, challenging the equation of modernity with national culture.

With the end of the Cold War, Indonesians began pressing for greater freedoms. The banning of Riantiarno's *Succession* (Suksesi) in 1991, along with the persecution of **Ratna Sarumpaet** for *Marsinah: Song from the Underworld* (Marsinah: nyanyian dari bawah tanah, 1993), prompted dissatisfaction. At the same time, leading artists of the 1970s and 1980s became ensconced as celebrities, and younger artists despaired of their apparent monopoly over limited venues. Suharto's resignation in 1998 brought dissidents such as Sarumpaet and Rendra to renewed prominence, while fresh venues, such as Galeri Utan Kayu in Jakarta, presented new groups. Younger troupes still engage in the intercultural experiments of the previous generation, but also incorporate foreign styles such as Japan's *butô*. Such troupes now perform in international festivals and promote themselves through the Internet. As elsewhere, Indonesian theatre is moving rapidly from postcolonial nationalism to participation in the cultures of globalization.

Evan Winet

INOUE HISASHI (1934–).

Japanese • playwright, director, and novelist. Born in Yamagata, Inoue worked his way through Sophia University as a French major by writing skits for the French Theatre (Furansu-za), a burlesque **theatre** in Tokyo's Asa-kusa section. His theatrical debut occurred in 1969 with *The Japanese Belly Button* (Nihonjin no heso), a **musical** comedy about a stuttering stripper.

Inoue's plays generally portray weighty issues through multilayered plots with unexpected twists, rhythmic wordplay, puns, nonsense jokes, Brechtian alienation effects, musicality, and Beckettian absurdism. He is at once witty, grotesque, mordant, and mocking. He keeps his distance from commercial theatre, *shingeki*, and *angura*, in depicting common people's reality and, with satire and parody, directing **criticism** against officialdom. His biographical dramas on great people in Japanese history and literature brim with humanism and crystallize a distinctively Japanese spiritual sensitivity.

Inoue's first real success was the **Kishida [Kunio]** Prize–winning *The Adventures of Dôgen* (Dôgen no bôken, 1971), a satirical song-and-dance comedy, portraying the eponymous Kamakura-period (1192–1333) Zen monk. Inoue's comedic style shifted from light to dark in *The Great Doctor Yabuhara* (Yabuhara kengyô, 1974), the first play of his Edo (Tokyo) trilogy and his initial collaboration with director Kimura Kôichi (1931–). Yabuhara is an evildoer who, through blackmail, theft, rape, and murder, advances to the highest ranks of the blind but in the end is sentenced to death by trisection. In 1979, with Kimura, Inoue produced the Yomiuri Prize–winning masterpieces, *Deeply, Madly Japan: General Nogi* (Shimijimi nihon Nogi taishô), a surreal parody of the Meiji emperor's loyal servant Nogi's life from the perspective of his four horses' forelegs and hindlegs, and *Kobayashi Issa*, about the revered *haiku* poet suspected of stealing money.

After forming the **theatre company** Komatsu Theatre (Komatsu-za) in 1984, Inoue produced the magnificent comic trilogy, *History of the Common People of the Shôwa Era* (Shôwa shomin den, 1988), including *Twinkling Constellation* (Kirameku seiza, 1985), depicting a record shop in Asakusa, soon to be put out of business by the war; *Flowers in the Dark* (Yami ni saku hana, 1987), provocatively questioning Shintoism and its war responsibility; and *Snowed In* (Yuki ya kon kon, 1988), describing the lives of two women—a theatre owner in a hot-spring town who focuses on staging itinerant popular theatre (*taishû engeki*) and the head of an itinerant troupe suffering from declining popularity.

Indeed, after Emperor Hirohito's (1901–1989) death, war issues became principal motifs in Inoue's playwriting. *Manzanar, My Town* (Manzana waga machi, 1993) concerns a Japanese-American internment camp in California; *The Face of Jizô* (Chichi to kuraseba, 1994) depicts the guilt of a daughter, who has survived the Hiroshima bomb, living with the ghost of her father killed by it; and *Kamiyachô Cherry Hotel* (Kamiyachô sakura hoteru, 1997), written to inaugurate Tokyo's New National Theatre (Shin Kokuritsu Gekijô), portrays the vastly different lives of a secret imperial envoy, a Special Higher Police detective, and a traveling theatre troupe's members—all soon to be killed by the bomb.

Yoshiko Fukushima

IWAMATSU RYÔ (1952–). Japanese • **playwright**, **actor**, and **director**. Born in Nagasaki, Iwamatsu studied Russian at university but dropped out on becoming involved in student drama. He worked as an actor and director in the early 1970s, then joined the Tokyo Electric Battery Theatre (Tôkyô Kandenchi) in 1976 where he developed improvisational scenarios with actors and began writing plays. He wrote two trilogies for this company: *Plays about the Neighborhood* (Chônai-geki shiriizu), including *Tea and a Lecture* (Ocha to sekkyô, 1986), *Kitchen Lights* (Daidokoro no hi, 1987), and *Romance Is Banned* (Ren'ai gohatto, 1987); and *Plays about Fathers* (Otôsan shiriizu), including *Futon and Daruma* (Futon to Daruma), awarded the 1988 **Kishida** [**Kunio**] Prize, *Dad's Bathing* (Otôsan no kaisuiyoku, 1989), and *Dad's Dad* (Otôsan no otôsan, 1990). He created another trilogy, *Plays about Men* (Otoko no shiriizu), for the Takenaka Naoto Company (Takenaka Naoto Kai), including *The Man Next Door* (Tonari no otoko, 1990), *The Man Holding a Potted Plant* (Uekibachi o motsu otoko, 1993), and *The Man Breaking Down* (Kowareyuku otoko, 1993).

Identified with **Hirata Oriza**, **Miyazawa Akio**, and **Matsuda Masataka** as part of the 1990s "quiet theatre" (*shizuka na engeki*) movement, Iwamatsu's signature style is everyday language that renders compelling representations of crises and subtle psychological portrayals of ordinary life within families and social groups. In addition, his television and film work is reflected in plays like *TV Days* (Terebi deizu, 1996), while his more unusual projects include adapting and directing *Wuthering Heights* (2004).

Kevin J. Wetmore, Jr.

IYER, SAMI VENKATADRI. *See* Samsa.

IZUMI KYÔKA (1873–1939). Japanese • *shinpa* • **playwright** and novelist. A disciple of popular novelist Ozaki Kôyô (1868–1903), Izumi debuted in the 1890s with fiction noted for its biting social critique and melodramatic plots. One story, *Loyal Blood, Valiant Blood* (Giketsu kyôketsu), was quickly adapted by **Kawakami Otojirô** in 1894 as *Taki no shiraito* and sparked a trend in popular fiction dramatizations. Other successful adaptations included *A Vigil's Tale* (Tsûya monogatari, 1909), *A Woman's Pedigree* (Onna keizu, 1908), *The White Heron* (Shirasagi, 1910), and *Japan Bridge* (Nihonbashi, 1913). These works typically featured handsome young students or professional men in love with beautiful, tragic entertainers: actresses, prostitutes, and geisha. Thanks to the skills of such **actors** as Ii Yôhô (1871–1932) and the "female impersonators" (*onnagata*) Kitamura Rokurô (1871–1961) and Hanayagi Shôtarô (1894–1965), these works have become standard *shinpa* repertoire.

Dissatisfied with the liberties that people like Kawakami took with his work, Izumi began writing his own plays after 1900. Increasingly, both his fiction and drama strayed from *shinpa*'s melodramatic formulae into the stranger territory of myth and the occult. Maeterlinck's plays and Hauptmann's *The Sunken Bell*, which Izumi helped translate in 1907, were likely models for a symbolist turn to his drama, but traditional narrative and drama (many relatives were *nô* actors and **musicians**) were also strong influences. He wrote more than a dozen original plays and several adaptations of his own fiction. His best work, including *Demon Pond* (Yashagaike, 1913), *The Ruby* (Kôgyoku, 1913), *The Sea God's Villa* (Kaijin bessô, 1913), *The Castle Tower* (Tenshu monogatari, 1917), and *Kerria Japonica* (Yamabuki, 1923), was written in the Taishô era (1912–1926).

Izumi Kyôka's *The Castle Tower*, 1974. (Photo: Courtesy of Waseda University Theatre Museum)

Izumi's romanticism and poetic language appealed to younger writers like **Tanizaki Jun'ichirô** and **Mishima Yukio**, but his decadent, wildly surrealistic, absurdist style and subject matter deterred staging most of these plays until the 1950s, when works like *The Castle Tower* premiered in combined *shinpa* and *kabuki* productions. The post-1960s generation of *angura* directors, like **Terayama Shûji** and **Ninagawa Yukio**, and **theatre companies** like **Miyagi Satoshi**'s Ku Na'uka and the neo-*kabuki* Hanagumi Shibai, have resurrected Izumi as a counterculture standard-bearer.

FURTHER READING

Poulton, Cody. *Spirits of Another Sort: The Plays of Izumi Kyôka.*

M. Cody Poulton

IZUMI SCHOOL. One of two extant schools (*ryû*) of **actors** from **Japan**'s *kyôgen*, the other being the **Ôkura school**. The Izumi now comprises the Izumi, Nomura, and Miyake family lines, active mainly in Tokyo, Nagoya, and Kanazawa.

The Izumi school, as with the Ôkura, is said to have been founded by *sarugaku* actors from Tanba, Yoshino, and Ômi. Scholars reliably trace the founding to Izumi Motonobu, seventh head (1659–), who in 1614 became vassal to the Tokugawa shogun. The Izumi school, split between serving the shogunate in Owari (Nagoya) and the imperial court of Kyoto, comprised three independent families, each with its own scripts and styles: the Yamawaki-Izumi, Miyake Tôkurô, and Nomura Matasaburô clans. Powerful lords sponsored favored performers and families at their own feudal lands. Under such imposing sponsors, the tenth headmaster moved to Nagoya, some of the Miyake family to Osaka and Kanazawa, and the Nomuras to Kumamoto. Until the dissolution of the shogunate in 1868, the Izumi "headmaster" (*iemoto*) was in service to the imperial court in Kyoto, but gradually moved with the shifting **political** and economic tides following the Meiji Restoration (1868) to Tokyo, where most families are now based.

Along with the dissolution of central control under the shogunate, *kyôgen* became more family-centered and individually flavored, making the headmaster a mere figurehead. Consequently, there have been many upheavals and even lawsuits among families and even among family members. Izumi Motohide (1937–1995) served as the nineteenth head from 1943 until his untimely death, causing great strain within the school by promoting his daughters and young son. He **trained** the first two modern *kyôgen* actresses, Izumi Junko (1969–) and Miyake Tôkurô (1972–), yet they have not been accepted by the rest of the *nô-kyôgen* world. Their brother Izumi Motoya (1974–) assumed the headship while still in his twenties, yet his claims were rejected by other Izumi members.

The Nomura Matasaburô branch returned to Nagoya with the twelfth generation, joining the Izumi-based Kyôgen Association, semiprofessionals who do not follow the normal family-head system. The Miyake family continues in Tokyo, although diminished since the death of Miyake Tôkuro IX (1901–1990), a Living National Treasure (1979); in addition to being a powerful and detailed performer, he revived and wrote many *kyôgen*.

The Nomura Manzô clan, originally disciples of the Miyake family in Kanazawa, came into prominence after World War II as Japan's most dynamic *kyôgen* family.

Nomura Manzô VI (1898–1978) was designated a Living National Treasure (1967), and was famed as a performer, **mask** carver, and author of invaluable texts. His acting balanced technique with psychological realism, while his treatises plotted the actor's lifetime training through challenging roles.

His two sons, Nomura Mannojô VII (now Nomura Yorozu, 1930–) and Nomura Mansaku (1931–), appeared in **Takechi Tetsuji**'s (1912–1988) *kabuki* performances with the Shigeyamas of the Ôkura school; in adaptations of **Mishima Yukio**'s modern *nô* plays; in *The Hawk Princess* (Taka-hime), an adaptation of Yeats's *At the Hawk's Well*; in **folk** plays by **Kinoshita Junji**; and in **experiments** by **Suzuki Tadashi**. Mansaku teaches and tours abroad frequently, and has trained English-language exponents such as Yuriko Doi and Don Kenny. These rival brothers were each designated Living National Treasures in 1997.

Mansaku's eldest son Mannojô (posthumously Manzô VII, 1959–2004) presented *kyôgen* at Eugenio Barba's ISTA seminars, and directed adaptations of Japanese horror stories and imaginative children's tales such as *Snow White* and *Little Red Riding Hood*. Drawing on Asian mask traditions from **Tibet**, Bali (see Indonesia), and **India**, he revived the lost art of *dengaku*.

Perhaps today's brightest star is Mansaku's son, Nomura Mansai (1966–), who studied in London in 1994, returning with a new perspective on *kyôgen*'s place on the world **stage**. His tremendous popularity extends beyond *kyôgen*, having made a name for himself in films and television. He has shown an affinity for Shakespeare, directing adaptations of *The Comedy of Errors* (2001) as well as starring in an all-male, British-**directed** *Hamlet*. He has staged adaptations of *Rashomon* both on and off *nô* stages, and starred in **Ninagawa Yukio**'s well-received *Oedipus* (2002). Mansai was named artistic director of the Setagaya Public **Theatre** (2002), tours the country frequently, and is a popular public television language instructor.

Jonah Salz

IZUMO NO OKUNI (?–1613?). Dancer-**actress**, credited with creating **Japan**'s •
kabuki theatre. Believed to have been a temple priestess from the major temple in Izumo, Okuni assembled a troupe of performers and entertained spectators with **folk** • **dances** called *yayako odori* and *kaka odori* in the mid-1580s. She later performed *nenbutsu odori*, a tenth-century joyful song and dance to Buddha. Often her *nenbutsu* performances were set to contemporary, secular **music**. By 1603, she was performing on the dry bed of Kyoto's Kamo River.

Okuni gained a following by imitating the *kabuki mono*, a group of contemporary anti-establishment samurai who challenged feudal conventions and the early Edo-period (1603–1868) government. They displayed their rebellious attitudes through flamboyant dress, extreme hairstyles, oversized swords, and violent behavior. Their name, like the theatrical form they influenced, was a corruption of *katamuku* ("to tilt"), suggesting their offbeat characteristics.

Okuni's riverbed performances included a farcical prostitute-buying scene in which she played a swaggering samurai who approached the madam of the teahouse-brothel to procure a prostitute. Sometimes these scenes featured an actor portraying the ghost of Nagoya Sanzaburô, Okuni's *kabuki mono* lover. These short skits were influenced by "dream" (*mugen*) *nô*.

Okuni dressed outrageously in Portuguese pants, often wore a Catholic rosary around her neck, and carried a long sword. Prostitutes throughout Japan quickly imitated her troupe's performances, and their style became known as "**women**'s" (*onna*) *kabuki* or "prostitutes'" (*yûjo*) *kabuki*.

FURTHER READING

Ariyoshi, Sawako. *Kabuki Dancer: A Novel of the Woman Who Founded Kabuki.*

Holly A. Blumner

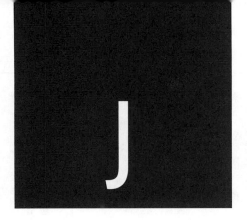

JALAN, SHYAMANAND (1934–). Indian Hindi- and, occasionally, Bengali-language **director** and **actor** based in Kolkata (Calcutta), a Bengali-majority city where since the 1950s he has played a pioneering role in the establishment of serious Hindi theatre. Jalan was a cofounder and principal director for the Anamika group from 1955 to 1972; in 1972, he founded Padatik, which he has managed for more than three decades. He also has had a long and important association with Kala Mandir, an arts organization patronized by Calcutta's North Indian industrialists and businessmen.

Like **Satyadev Dubey** and **Rajinder Nath**, Jalan is a leading metropolitan director whose principal commitment is to contemporary and translated plays in Hindi. In 1960, he was the first to stage **Mohan Rakesh**'s landmark *A Day in Early Autumn* (Ashadh ka ek din; publ. 1958); during the 1960s, he became one of Rakesh's premier directors, with productions of *The Royal Swans on the Waves* (Lahron ke rajhans) in 1966, and *The Unfinished* (Adhe adhure) in 1970. Jalan's intensive collaborations with Rakesh, which often led to changes in a play's text, were distinctive features of these productions. His other directing ranges from Ibsen's *An Enemy of the People* (1959), Brecht's *The Good Person of Setzuan* (1977), and Shakespeare's *King Lear* (with Fritz Bennewitz, 1988), to multiple plays by **Girish Karnad**, **Badal Sircar**, and **Vijay Tendulkar**. Jalan revived **Kalidasa**'s *The Recognition of Shakuntala* (Abhijnana Shakuntalam) in 1980, and between 1978 and 1987, also successfully produced individual plays by **G. P. Deshpande, Mahesh Elkunchwar,** and Mahasweta Devi. His important **stage** roles include leads in *The Unfinished*, *An Enemy of the People*, and *King Lear*.

Aparna Dharwadker

JANGGER. Balinese (see Indonesia) choral **dance**-drama that developed in the early twentieth century from the choral accompaniment to trance rituals (*sang hyang*). The earliest examples were performed only by men (often made up of harvest-time, palm wine–drinking groups), but female choruses based on *sang hyang* were soon added. The songs and movement of the two choruses are distinct, with men and **women** alternating in a "call-and-response" manner. Women demurely kneel and sway with lyrical gestures, singing songs of flirtation and love. Men sit cross-legged, moving arms and shoulders to a rhythmic chant of nonsense syllables similar to the *kecak* chorus.

In the 1920s, *jangger* (also *janger*) groups were often led by a now rare male dancer-singer (*daag*) who functioned as **storyteller**. In the 1930s, particularly in North Bali, *jangger* became conflated with *komedi stambul* and was sometimes further

Balinese *jangger* performance at Bali Arts Festival, 2002. (Photo: Margaret Coldiron)

combined with episodes of Balinese **arja**, creating a bizarre mix of traditional and non-traditional styles despised by foreign purists but popular with Balinese.

Performances begin with elaborate entrances for each of the choruses as they take their places in the large, square performing area serving as a **stage**. Songs may be interspersed with dramatic episodes drawn from the Hindu epics or *arja* romances, performed either by chorus members or an additional cast of **actor**-dancers. The distinctive headdress (*petitis*) of the women's chorus is based on the traditional bride's crown of flowers, and, although there is a great deal of regional variation, **costumes** are usually based on formal temple dress.

Jangger has flourished during periods of social and **political** upheaval. In the revolutionary period of the 1940s and 1950s, its malleability made it a useful tool for propaganda and demonstrations of patriotism. This "dual function" came to the fore again in the early 1960s (prior to the 1965–1966 violent regime change) and more recently in the post-Suharto (1921–) period.

Jangger is also the name of a genre closely related to Central Javanese **kethoprak** performed in the East Hook region of East Java, an area with close historical ties to Bali.

FURTHER READING

Spies, Walter, and Beryl de Zoete. *Dance and Drama in Bali.*

Margaret Coldiron

JAPAN. Japan is a chain of islands in the north Pacific Ocean, east of Korea, with a population of nearly 127.5 million (2006) living in a nation roughly the size of California. Possessed of one of the world's highest literacy rates, its population is 99 percent Japanese, the three largest minorities being **Korean**, **Chinese**, and Brazilian. Eighty-four percent of the people observe both Shintoism and Buddhism; of the remaining 16 percent, 0.07 percent is Christian. Most of Japan's forty-seven prefectures are spread out over the four large islands of Honshû, Hokkaidô, Kyûshû, and Shikoku. Tokyo, formerly Edo, has been the capital since 1868. The country is a constitutional monarchy with a parliamentary government. The imperial family rarely had power since medieval times, the premodern government having been controlled principally by a succession of military dictators (shoguns); the last shogunate (or *bakufu*), headed by the Tokugawa family, lasted from 1603 to 1868, known as the Tokugawa or Edo era (after the city of the shogun's residence). With the Meiji Restoration (1868), the shogunate ended, and the emperor was restored to power. Since the end of World War II, the emperor has been a ceremonial figure.

Japan was closed to the West, except for a tiny port at Nagasaki, from the 1630s to 1854, when the Americans forced the country to open its doors. Subsequently, Japan rapidly **Westernized** and became a major world power. It remains a leader in the global economy, and its people enjoy the highest standard of living in Asia. Following its military defeat of China (1894–1895) and Russia (1904), Japan became an increasingly imperialistic nation with militaristic ambitions that eventually led to aggressive acts resulting in its embroilment as a member of the Axis Powers in World War II, which it lost in 1945 after being subjected to the atom bombing of Hiroshima and Nagasaki. The postwar constitution forbade the country from having a standing army or navy, and its military is instead called a "self-defense force."

Traditional Theatre. Japan's four best-known traditional theatre arts are ***nô***, ***kyôgen***, *bunraku* (see Puppet Theatre), and ***kabuki***. The first two are closely linked, as are the latter two. In addition, there are a number of earlier forms, all of which continue to exist, some vestigially, others more reflective of their premodern practices, although even the most conservative have undergone important developments. For all the emphasis on tradition in premodern Japanese theatre, there actually was continual change and evolution. Chief early exemplars are ***gigaku***, ***bugaku*** (or *gagaku*), ***kagura***, ***dengaku***, and ***kôwakamai***. Innovation in *nô*, *kyôgen*, *bunraku*, and *kabuki* continues today, sometimes very subtly, and sometimes dramatically. Essentially, however, these genres still clearly purvey a powerful sense of what audiences viewed before the mid-nineteenth century.

Early Forms. Japanese theatre's legendary origins are part of an eclipse myth about the sun goddess, Amaterasu, who shut herself up in a cave in a fit of pique. To lure her out, another goddess, Ame no Uzume, **danced** on an overturned tub outside the cave before the assembled gods, who laughed so loud when she exposed her privates that the sun goddess could not resist peeking to see why everyone was having so much fun; light thereby returned to the world. The close relationship between **religion** and performance was thus established, and is still maintained in the multifarious Shinto ritual performances known as *kagura*—some versions of which have been associated with shamanism—performed at shrines throughout Japan, in both rural (mainly) and urban areas.

More formal entertainments were introduced in the early seventh century by a **Korean** named Mimasu who presented dancing called *gigaku*, now known mainly by a number of carefully preserved ancient **masks** and by the ubiquitous "lion dances" (*shishi mai*) common to Japan and mainland Asia, and that are part of various *kagura* performances. Masks remained a significant part of later Japanese performances. Both Korea and Tang dynasty (618–907) China played a crucial role in providing an even more sophisticated form, *bugaku*, which evolved into the highly formalized dance and **musical** art associated with imperial court ceremonies since the Heian period (782–1184). Also from China came the variety show called *sangaku*, which displayed acrobatics and sword dancing among its specialties; it arrived during the Heian period, and gave rise to humorous sketches **acted** in an imitative style (*monomane*), leading to the birth of *sarugaku* (literally, "monkey music"), which eventually became *nô* and *kyôgen*.

Sarugaku came to be associated with Buddhist temples, and produced the medieval song and dance art of *ennen* (a.k.a. *ennen no nô*), performed chiefly after memorial services; it was a principal precursor of *nô*. Another medieval form, now known only as a rural **folk** performing art (*minzoku geinô*), is *dengaku* (literally, "field music"), originally performed with *sangaku* acrobatics at rice-planting ceremonies. In its early days, it was a powerful rival of *nô*, which gradually eclipsed it in popularity. Early *nô* (a.k.a. *sarugaku no nô*) and *dengaku* (a.k.a. *dengaku no nô*) had close similarities, except that the former emphasized chant, dancing, and acting over *dengaku*'s predilection for acrobatics and comedy.

Nô *and* Kyôgen. The great period of rivalry between *dengaku* and *nô* extended from the fourteenth into the fifteenth century, with each form benefiting or suffering from the degree of official patronage afforded them by the Ashikaga shoguns. These art forms competed for official favor, especially during the Muromachi period (1333–1568) when *nô*'s foundational artists—**Kan'ami** and **Zeami**—appeared, with the latter, at twelve, gaining the support and affection of the teenage shogun, Ashikaga Yoshimitsu (1358–1408), after performing for him in 1374 or 1375.

Nô, originally a popular form, gradually grew into a highly formalized art patronized not only by the shogunate but by various powerful feudal lords (*daimyô*). Its plays, architecture, **costumes**, masks, music, dance, and performance conventions became highly codified and, one might say, even ritualized during the Edo period, during which it assumed the position of the samurai class's "ceremonial music" (*shikigaku*). Beginning with Zeami, its aesthetic and literary principles had been discussed in secret **theoretical** treatises, ranging from the practical to the highly esoteric. The five major *nô* schools of the Edo period—the Kanze, Hôshô, Kongô, Konparu, and Kita—continue to dominate *nô*. During these years, it was seen by the general public only on special occasions, principally for the purpose of raising funds for the presumed purpose of building or renovating religious sites. On the other hand, many cultured commoners diligently studied *nô* chanting (*utai*) with specialists. When the Meiji emperor's forces overthrew the shogunate and restored the emperor to power, *nô*, associated with the now discredited samurai class, was practically abandoned, being saved only by the relentless efforts of a small number of persistent artists and patrons.

Nô, highly serious and austere, employs a strikingly spare, brilliantly polished wooden **stage**, with four thick pillars supporting a gabled roof, decorated with a painted pine tree on the rear wall, and equipped with a long bridgeway (*hashigakari*)

for entrances and exits. Its plays, respected for their literary values, have themes ranging from Buddhist and Shinto spiritual issues, including the treatment of ghosts (such
as those of dead warriors) and nature spirits, as well as those concerned with dramatic
conflicts among living humans. It is performed in a strictly controlled, often extremely
slow style redolent of ceremony, with exquisite masks worn by certain characters, and
with music (played by onstage musicians) and chanting (including a seated chorus)
combined with theatrically heightened speech. In modern times, **women** have entered
nô's ranks, but it traditionally has been all male.

Kyôgen, which also emerged from *sangaku* and has a similar tradition of all-male
performance, shares the same stage with and is sandwiched between *nô* plays on a traditional program, offering a comic or sentimental take on human experience. There are
also characters written into many *nô* plays that can be played only by *kyôgen* actors,
although their function in *nô* is not to provide comedy. *Kyôgen*, like *nô*, uses masks,
but much less commonly, and with a far more down-to-earth sensibility. Deities are
laughed at, priests are parodied, servants befuddle their masters, and nature is turned
topsy-turvy. There are records of *kyôgen*-like sketches dating from the eleventh century, but *kyôgen* seems to have come into its own in the fourteenth, when it emerged
as an improvised comical entertainment dependent more on dialogue than song and
dance, although those play their role as well. Only in the seventeenth century, it seems,
were attempts begun to set down *kyôgen* plays in writing, and even then it was chiefly
scenarios—as in *commedia dell'arte*—rather than scripts that were recorded. The plays
reflected contemporary conditions, and their acting style, although polished and highly
stylized, was quite realistic when contrasted with the hieratic manner of *nô*. Two
schools of *kyôgen*—the **Izumi** and the **Ôkura**—remain predominant.

Bunraku *and* Kabuki. The sixteenth century witnessed a series of wars that tore
Japan apart, but by the end of the century, peace was imminent; it was established at
the start of the next century chiefly through the ascendance of the Tokugawa shogunate.
This brought great prosperity to the nation's cities, especially the young city of Edo, in
the east, where the shogun resided, and the older, more tradition-bound cities of Osaka
and Kyoto, in the west, an area known by various names, such as Kamigata; the imperial family lived in Kyoto. Japan's two other major genres now were born, both in
Kamigata, one being the puppet theatre known then as *ningyô jôruri* (*ningyô* meaning
puppet, and *jôruri*, a fictional princess whose story gave rise to the narrative-musical
style that influenced the puppet theatre) and from the late nineteenth century as *bunraku*. The other form was *kabuki*.

Puppetry had been present in Japan for centuries, its earliest versions apparently
having arrived with itinerant Koreans who played at shrines and temples, using the
puppets for a variety of ceremonial purposes. A later form, *ebisu kaki*, associated with
the Ebisu Shrine in Nishinomiya, near Osaka, offered versions of *nô* and *kyôgen* plays
using one-man puppets in boxes hung from the performers' necks. Sometime late in
the sixteenth century these wooden figures were combined with the narrative-musical
art of *jôruri* (itself influenced by an earlier art in which the war chronicle *Tale of the
Heike* [Heike monogatari] was recited by a **storyteller** playing the lute-like *biwa*) and
the playing of the three-stringed *shamisen*. This vital instrument originated in China
and was imported through the Ryûkyû Islands (Okinawa) several decades before. The
new form developed into a sophisticated and very popular form in Kamigata and Edo
during the seventeenth century, but achieved true greatness as a dramatic genre only

after the confluence in the mid-1680s of chanter (*tayû*) **Takemoto Gidayû** and **playwright** • **Chikamatsu Monzaemon** at the former's Takemoto Theatre (Takemoto-za) in Osaka's Dôtonbori entertainment district. Their artistry was so revolutionary that the pre-Gidayû-Chikamatsu puppet theatre came to be known as *ko-jôruri* ("old *jôruri*").

The eighteenth century saw remarkable advances in the art of *ningyô jôruri* as Osaka's Takemoto and Toyotake Theatres competed for dominance, as major playwrights, chanters, puppeteers, and *shamisen* musicians continued to advance the art. Moreover, the rival form of *kabuki* fought hard to attract audiences by ravenously borrowing and adapting the most successful puppet plays and even performance methods. Depending not on private patronage, like *nô* and *kyôgen*, but on the ticket-purchasing urban masses, the **theatres** of the Edo period were large-scale commercial enterprises, using advertising and programs to attract their customers, and constantly seeking artistic innovation to gain their market share. The puppets morphed from simple one-man dolls to technologically advanced wooden actors manipulated by three-man teams who made the puppets—with their movable facial features and articulated fingers—seem almost as lifelike as their *kabuki* competitors. Although primarily an Osaka phenomenon, *ningyô jôruri* also experienced considerable success in Edo in the late eighteenth and early nineteenth centuries. But this was after Osaka's puppets had lost the battle for supremacy to *kabuki*, and were reduced to performing mainly at shrine-ground theatres. It was not until the 1870s that the puppets re-emerged as a significant theatrical force, when the Bunraku Theater (Bunraku-za, named for a man who, along with his descendants, had helped *ningyô jôruri* survive until then) opened. Since then, *bunraku* has been the term of choice for this important art form.

Kabuki appeared when various popular and semireligious performance streams converged in the activity of a female dancer named **Izumo no Okuni**, said once to have been a priestess (*miko*) at the Grand Shrine of Izumo, who headed an itinerant troupe of mainly women dancers that performed in the dry bed of Kyoto's Kamo River in 1603, the year the Tokugawa shogunate was born. *Kabuki* caught on rapidly and soon spread to Edo, where, over time, significant differences emerged between Edo and Kamigata methods. From what began in Okuni's time as popular dances and sexually charged sketches set in the brothel quarters, with cross-dressed casts, and the influence of itinerant *kyôgen* actors, *kabuki* went through many phases over the next three centuries. Its early years were filled with change and turmoil as one type of troupe succeeded the other, with identifying terms like "prostitutes'" (*yûjo*) *kabuki*, "boys'" (*wakashu*) *kabuki*, and "men's" (*yarô*) *kabuki*, the latter arriving in the 1650s only after the types centered on women and pretty boys had been outlawed; in fact, from 1629, women no longer performed in *kabuki*, their place being taken by "female impersonators" (*onnagata*), which remains the convention today.

Although *kabuki* was performed in many cities, the chief venues were located in Kyoto, Osaka, and Edo. The former two (in Kamigata) specialized in plays whose dramaturgy emphasized rationality and psychological realism, while the plays of Edo, with its aggressive samurai population, favored exaggerated theatricality and lots of violence. Thus arose the "gentle style" (*wagoto*) of Kamigata acting, associated with **Sakata Tôjûrô** I, and the "rough style" (*aragoto*) of Edo acting, associated with the **Ichikawa Danjûrô** acting line, although these terms are extremes, and both styles could be found to some degree in either region. Numerous dramatic genres, many shared with the puppets, emerged, and *kabuki*'s repertoire was increasingly enriched during the eighteenth century by adaptations of the finest puppet dramas; these included the "three masterpieces" of *Sugawara and the Secrets of Calligraphy* (Sugawara denju tenarai kagami, 1746), *Yoshitsune and the Thousand Cherry Trees* (Yoshitsune senbon zakura, 1747), and *The Treasury of Loyal Retainers* (Kanadehon chûshingura, 1748). *Kabuki* also borrowed plays from *nô* and *kyôgen*, and, eventually, some of these became *bunraku* pieces as well. The plays, often lasting all day, catered to the townsmen class, emphasizing Confucian values, and often creating heartrending situations testing one's mettle when forced to choose between social duty (*giri*) and personal inclination (*ninjô*). *Kabuki* acting, costumes, **makeup**, wigs, **scenography**, and **properties** reflected the broad range of styles, from the flamboyantly theatrical to the grittily naturalistic. Dance was fundamental to all *kabuki* movement, whether in dance plays or straight plays, where beauty of form remained paramount, even in seemingly realistic contexts. As with all forms of traditional Japanese theatre, all the arts combined to create a total theatrical experience.

Kabuki performances began in outdoor venues using *nô*-style stages to indoor **theatres** with many special features, including stage traps (*seri*), two auditorium runways (*hanamichi*) for entrances and exits, a large revolving stage (*mawari butai*), and spectacular devices for shifting scenery or creating special effects. Actors—who either specialized in specific **role types** or capitalized on their versatility—were idolized like today's pop stars or athletes and memorialized in cheap but brilliant woodblock prints, and acting traditions were handed down in family lines many of whose names, with different ordinal numbers, remain active today. Resident playwrights, among the most brilliant of whom were **Tsuruya Nanboku** IV and **Kawatake Mokuami**, are now revered as classical artists.

The coming of **Western influence** in Meiji would threaten all these forms, but somehow they managed to survive and eventually to gain the admiration of theatregoers worldwide. *Nô* and *kyôgen*, while available at numerous *nô* theatres throughout Japan, may be seen at the National Nô Theatre (Kokuritsu Nôgakudô) in Tokyo, while *kabuki*—produced at multiple theatres around Japan—is officially preserved at Tokyo's National Theatre (Kokuritsu Gekijô), and *bunraku* has its principal venue at the National Bunraku Theatre (Kokuritsu Bunraku Gekijô) in Osaka.

FURTHER READING

Brazell, Karen, ed. *Traditional Japanese Theatre: An Anthology of Plays*; Inoura, Yoshinobu, and Toshio Kawatake. *The Traditional Theater of Japan;* Leiter, Samuel L., ed. *Japanese Theater in the World*; Leiter, Samuel L. *Historical Dictionary of Japanese Traditional Theatre*.

Samuel L. Leiter

Modern Japanese Theatre: Meiji Period. Suddenly thrust into the modern world by the overtures of American Commodore Matthew C. Perry in 1853–1854, Japan abruptly confronted the challenges of building a new nation. Could Japanese be citizens of both Japan and the world? Confusion and ambivalence abounded, as in the late Edo-period cry, "revere the emperor, expel the barbarian" (*sonnô-jôi*), hardly conducive to amicable diplomacy. Yet Japan's leading modernizer, Fukuzawa Yukichi (1835–1901), advocated "leaving" Asia to learn from the West. Confusion and ambivalence continued under the Meiji-era rubric "civilization and enlightenment" (*bunmei kaika*): the utter novelty of things **Western** catalyzed ludicrous cultural developments, including disdain for things Japanese—countless woodblock prints and traditional art objects left Japan with Western collectors—while some intellectuals indiscriminately urged replacing Japanese with English and intermarriage with Westerners to improve the Japanese race.

Although a nationalistic backlash in the 1880s tempered such extremes, confusion over personal and national identity persisted as Japanese struggled to find a modern voice to express modern realities. Many intellectuals who had visited Western countries were ambivalent about what they learned; though recognizing Western achievement in social and **political** organization, they nonetheless rejected slavish imitation, striving instead to maintain their perceived Japanese identity and form a modern Japan, including a modern theatre, on its own terms.

It was not smooth sailing. Early Meiji-era attempts to modernize theatre focused on reforming *kabuki* by, for example, eliminating such perceived anachronisms as sex-and-violence-filled scenes and even its signature role, the *onnagata*, and resulted less in reform than reducing *kabuki*'s charm. *Kabuki* offshoots emerged, attempting a more modern voice. By the 1890s, *shinpa*, under impresario **Kawakami Otojirô**, gained traction with mixed-gender casts (women were officially allowed on stage from 1891), showcasing his wife **Kawakami Sadayakko**'s undeniable star power as Japan's first marquee actress, and with plots reflecting contemporary life and politics. Kawakami augmented *shinpa*'s appeal by **staging** translated Western plays and building Japan's first venue for modern theatre, the Kawakami Theatre (Kawakami-za, 1896). In addition, the growing dissatisfaction with *kabuki* among key modernizing figures like playwright-scholar **Tsubouchi Shôyô**, founder of the groundbreaking **theatre company** Literary Arts Society (Bungei Kyôkai, 1906), and the increasing influence of Western drama stimulated the development of *shin kabuki*, distinguished from *kabuki* by greater realism, psychological ingredients, and lack of certain traditional conventions, like theatrical poses (*mie*). Tsubouchi's *A Paulownia Leaf* (Kiri hitoha, 1894), generally considered the first *shin kabuki*, inspired other playwrights, like **Okamoto Kidô**, to try the new form. By the 1920s, another genre, *shinkokugeki,* fashioned by the swashbuckling actor **Sawada Shôjirô**, became extremely popular, regularly filling Tokyo's largest theatres with realistic swordfights and Robin Hood–like heroes. But these were superficial changes, all three forms clearly *kabuki* derivatives anchored in the past. Following their initial glory days, *shinpa* and *shinkokugeki* gradually lost appeal and after the 1950s were infrequently performed.

Beyond *kabuki*'s strong grasp, such tentativeness at forging a new kind of theatre—especially with Western elements—is hardly surprising. The prevailing sense that Western countries had taken advantage of Japan—particularly with the "unequal treaties" signed prior to the Meiji Restoration (1868), giving Western countries advantageous rights—incubated the lurking fear that Japan could be overwhelmed, even annihilated by the West. In response, government officials launched the slogan "rich country, strong military" (*fukoku kyôhei*), and Japan experienced periodic nationalistic outbursts. Kawakami leveraged this atmosphere, staging hugely popular *shinpa* plays extolling Japan's victory in the Sino-Japanese War (1894–1895).

Japanese resentment over perceived Western arrogance and the accompanying confusion about Japan's role in the world—that is, about identity—persisted. Was a new theatre based on reforming the old even possible or must the old be scrapped in favor of a modern—Western—model? The latter notion, in the form of *shingeki,* gradually took hold. Japan's first substantially Western-style theatre, the Yûraku Theatre (Yûraku-za), opened in Tokyo to sell-out crowds in 1908, and **Osanai Kaoru**'s 1909 staging of Ibsen's *John Gabriel Borkman* at the Free Theatre (Jiyû Gekijô) is considered Japan's first *shingeki* production. Tsubouchi and Osanai became the prime movers in mounting productions of translated plays, mainly by Ibsen, Chekhov, and Shakespeare.

Taishô and Early Shôwa Periods. The first widely popular modern theatre, however, was the all-girl **Takarazuka** song-and-dance revue, begun in 1913, early in the Taishô era (1912–1926), as a purely commercial venture to lure customers onto the newly completed Hankyû Railway in western Japan to Takarazuka, a resort town. The revue evolved into full-blown, melodramatic, French-style musicals; popularity soared, especially following the landmark success of *Mon Paris* in 1927. Accommodating demand, two Broadway-style theatres were built, one in Takarazuka (1924), the other in Tokyo (1934). Shows continue to sell out.

Meanwhile, Osanai and **Hijikata Yoshi** oversaw Japan's first European-style "little theatre," the Tsukiji Little Theatre (Tsukiji Shôgekijô) in 1924, *shingeki*'s only purpose-built space until after the war. Osanai's initial policy to stage only translated Western plays successfully presented an idea of modern theatre to the Japanese public, though it limited Japanese playwrights' opportunities. Even when Osanai consented, in 1926, to stage Tsubouchi's *En the Ascetic* (En no gyôja, 1916), the production, despite Western-tinged psychological elements, had the look and feel of *kabuki* and was hardly compelling theatre.

Japanese acting and declamation, despite earnest intentions, remained in *kabuki*'s grip. Three developments helped loosen it. First was the emergence of the **director**, as against actor-centered traditional theatre. Tsubouchi protégé **Shimamura Hôgetsu**, especially after forming his own company, Art Theatre (Geijutsu-za), in 1913, was the key pioneer. To pry acting and declamation from *kabuki*'s grip, Shimamura, who had studied in Europe, demanded that his actors stick to the text, exactly memorizing their lines with prescribed movements and gestures. The second development occurred as proletarian theatre, gathering force in the 1920s, demanded realism in its tendentious stage action and created a context for departures from traditional, stylized practices. Third, **Kishida Kunio**, after observing theatre in Europe in the 1920s, returned to Japan, three years before the onset of the Shôwa period (1926–1989), with contemporary European ideas of stagecraft. In 1937, Kishida established the Literary Theatre (Bungaku-za), the most influential *shingeki* company, to inculcate his vision for modern Japanese theatre— realistic, nonpolitical portrayals of contemporary Japanese society. Enhancing this realism was the emergence of accomplished actresses. Once Sadayakko broke the taboo, others followed. **Matsui Sumako**, nurtured by Shimamura, showed that actresses could outdo *onnagata* in femininity and became Japan's first *shingeki* superstar. Major female stars ultimately included **Yamamoto Yasue**, who carved an enduring legacy playing Tsû in **Kinoshita Junji**'s iconic *Twilight Crane* (Yûzuru, 1949) over one thousand times; **Mizutani Yaeko**, *shinpa*'s greatest actress; and **Sugimura Haruko**, Japan's best-known modern actress, whose achievements included playing the heroine in **Morimoto Kaoru**'s *A Woman's Life* (Onna no isshô, 1945) for fifty-one years.

Shingeki also produced excellent actors, **Takizawa Osamu** foremost among them. Steeped in Stanislavski's psychological realism, Takizawa relied on close textual reading to crystallize his characters' personalities, motivations, and social situations. He starred in **Murayama Tomoyoshi**'s plays and in **Kubo Sakae**'s *Land of Volcanic Ash* (Kazanbaichi, 1937–1938), perhaps the best proletarian play.

Rampant in the 1930s, proletarian proclivities inevitably clashed with Japan's increasingly militarist government. In 1940, Takizawa, Murayama, and Kubo, among many others, were detained for "thought crimes," most proletarian companies were disbanded for the duration of the war, and important theatre artists were arrested. The marked tendency away from the divinities and stylized forms of traditional theatre established *shingeki* by the 1930s as Japan's modern theatre, unremittingly realistic.

Morimoto, Kishida's protégé, mastered this approach with *A Woman's Life*, rendering the tragic experience of a woman unreservedly sacrificing herself for family, effectively crystallizing the spectators' war-induced sense of futility and despair. A smash hit, the production revealed that whether their theatre is new or old Japanese prefer characters whose inner strength is emphasized—by enduring the unendurable, not, as with self-assertive Western heroes, by rebelling against it.

Postwar Shôwa and Early Heisei Periods. This incipiently modern voice gained timbre after the war as proletarian troupes resumed activities, Kishida's Literary Theatre continued, and other *shingeki* companies emerged, including the vibrant Actors' Theatre (Haiyû-za), founded by **Senda Koreya** in 1944; its influence spread, especially with its new building in 1954, the first constructed specifically for *shingeki* since Osanai's Tsukiji Little Theatre. However, Japanese elements began to penetrate *shingeki*'s unrelenting realism. Kinoshita's *Twilight Crane*, for example, though performed realistically, features a Japanese folktale's mythic celestial being, decidedly nonrealistic, to lament Japan's loss of innocence and disconnect with traditional values. Gradually, realism, so foreign to Japanese performance traditions, ran its course; as the 1950s unfolded, **Hijikata Tatsumi** and **Ôno Kazuo**, developing the dance form *butô* to counter pervasive Western-influenced realism and reconnect with traditional Japanese myths and values, completely abandoned it.

This trend culminated in the cultural ferment sparked by the nationwide demonstrations in 1960 over renewing the U.S.-Japan Mutual Security Treaty (Anpo). Ensuing public discourse, largely predicated on the traumatic experience of war, bombing, and defeat, and the consequent impact on the Japanese sense of identity, was cogently dramatized in alternative, nonrealistic ways by the burgeoning *angura* and *shôgekijô* movements. Abandoning staid *shingeki* realism, directors like **Suzuki Tadashi** and **Ninagawa Yukio** defined the *angura/shôgekijô* ethos in rejecting Western-style acting and syncretistically adapting aspects from multiple genres, Japanese and Western. Eventually moving from cramped, makeshift *angura* spaces to larger stages, these two directors, initially influenced by Western theatre, then reacting against it, attained international renown and now are influencing Western theatre artists. Suzuki developed *On the Dramatic Passions* (Gekiteki naru mono o megutte, 1967–1970), a performance series with searing images of war's ravages, to showcase the remarkable histrionic abilities of **Shiraishi Kayoko**, Japan's foremost contemporary actress. Deftly embodying Suzuki's distinctive theories of physical movement and with inimitable vocal power, she was crucial to his success.

New plays, like **Akimoto Matsuyo**'s emblematic *Kaison the Priest of Hitachi* (Hitachibô kaison, 1965), often evoked mythic divinities to transcend Western influence and revivify Japan's primal past. Playwrights and directors began to question the very idea of theatre, performances often occurring, as if spontaneously, in vacant lots or on makeshift stages in warehouses, abolishing the actor-spectator distinction. **Terayama Shûji**'s iconoclastic *Throw Away Your Books, Go Out into the Streets* (Sho o suteyo machi e deyô, 1967) crystallizes the zeitgeist: nothing is set, everything, including proscenium and identity, is up for grabs. **Kara Jûrô** concurs, privileging physicality over words in his zany, nonlinear, often allegorical plots. **Tsuka Kôhei**'s satirical *For My Father, Who Failed to Die in the War* (Sensô de shinenakatta otôsan no tame ni, 1972), among many plays limning Japanese war attitudes, features a man unable to deploy because his draft card has been stolen; feeling deprived, he resolves to find another war to realize his "opportunity" to fight—action calculated to affirm his identity.

Indeed, during its headlong pursuit of postwar economic prowess, Japan often has subsumed, as though wearing blinders, the critical issues of war and identity—as in the 1980s ludic conspiracy of figures like **Noda Hideki** or **Kôkami Shôji**, showcasing rapid-fire, nonstop, comic book (*manga*)–like hilarity. Once Japan's economic "bubble" burst in 1991, followed by years of economic doldrums, many playwrights took a more serious tack, partly to counter 1980s frenzy, mainly to reflect their times. **Hirata Oriza**, with his milestone *Tokyo Notes* (Tôkyô nôto, 1995), stimulated development of "quiet theatre" (*shizuka na engeki*). Another trend, historically grounded plays like **Kaneshita Tatsuo**'s *Ice Blossoms* (Kanka, 1997), about political leader Itô Hirobumi's (1841–1909) **Korean** assassin, draw concrete connections with the past to encourage engagement with contemporary socio-political realities. There is also an increasing concern with meta-theatre, as in **Miyazawa Akio**'s haunting memory play, *Hinemi* (1993), or **Furuhashi Teiji**'s mesmerizing tour de force, *S/N* (1994); woven with socio-political overtones reflecting the era, both plays are ultimately self-reflective, probing not only identity but the very phenomenon of theatre. Finally, **Miyagi Satoshi** has gleaned inspiration from *shinpa*, now considered a relic, combining it with structural aspects of *bunraku* into award-winning fusion, as in his adaptation of **Izumi Kyôka**'s *The Castle Tower* (Tenshu monogatari, 1996).

This wide-open approach now accommodates all forms, traditional and modern, Japanese and Western. Indeed, *nô, bunraku*, and *kabuki* survive and even flourish—*kabuki* tickets can be hard to get—in their own national theatres. Broadway musicals, Shakespeare, *shingeki*, and the avant-garde all have appropriate venues throughout Japan. Rife with **experimentation** and no longer simply derivative of Western forms, Japanese theatre today ranks with the world's most vibrant.

The critical modern issue of identity—personal and national—still without consensus, often underlies these multifaceted, creative efforts, continuing to fuel public discourse and theatrical expression. Given its blindingly rapid, tortuous itinerary since the 1850s, often through the same socioeconomic changes and aesthetic movements shaping Western countries over the half millennium since the Renaissance, Japan perhaps has yet to thoroughly sift and internalize this onslaught of the new and different. Abruptly unmoored from traditional verities, Japanese in the modern era have often felt a personal and national sense of anomie, as though adrift in an uncharted sea. Many modern Japanese plays—*shingeki, angura*, or otherwise experimental—attempt to reflect that experience and stimulate creative means to make sense of it.

FURTHER READING

Eckersall, Peter. *Theorizing the Angura Space Avant-garde Performance and Politics in Japan, 1960–2000;* Powell, Brian. *Japan's Modern Theatre: A Century of Continuity and Change;* Rimer, J. Thomas. *Toward a Modern Japanese Theatre: Kishida Kunio;* Rolf, Robert T., and John K. Gillespie, eds. *Alternative Japanese Drama: Ten Plays.*

John K. Gillespie

JATRA

Origins and Development. **Indian • folk theatre** that flourishes in rural Bengali-speaking areas and **Bangladesh**. The neighboring states of Assam and Orissa also have thriving *jatra* activity. *Jatra*, which means "procession" or "journey," is an itinerant, year-round, professional theatre. A similar form can be found in Puri, Orissa, which employs the Oriya language and is named *yatra* (pronounced *jatra*). There is no evidence that *jatra* had any connection with ancient **Sanskrit theatre**, though, as a popular folk genre, its origins remain obscure. Perhaps as early as the twelfth to fifteenth centuries, *jatra* was formed from the prevailing Vaishnavist (a branch of Hinduism) **religious** processions honoring Krishna. The predecessor of contemporary *jatra*, *krishna jatra*, is first mentioned in a passage in *Lord Chaitanya* (Chaitanyabhagavad, 1548), which mentions a performance by the Hindu Saint Sri Chaitanya Deb (1485–1533) in the role of Rukmini, Krishna's wife. Due to Sri Chaitanya's popularity as a religious leader, after his death, a rival form of *krishna jatra* called *chaitanya jatra* featured stories from his life.

Early performances of *krishna jatra* in the seventeenth century were most likely performed in connection with religious rites as ecstatic devotional songs, performed outdoors with the audience gathered all around. The **music** was a congregational singing style (*pala* and *kirtan*) accompanied with instruments such as the *mandira* and *karatal* (metal percussion instruments) and drums (*khol* and *dholak*). By the eighteenth century, the dramatic source material had expanded to include numerous episodes from the **Mahabharata** and **Ramayana**, as well as other legends and myths. *Jatra* began to assume a form similar to that of today, with a slightly raised **stage** and a four-foot-wide pathway leading off stage. The pathway doubles as an **acting** space and, not unlike **kabuki**'s runway (*hanamichi*), allows for dramatic entrances and exits.

Principal Features. Some of *jatra*'s long-standing features include the *adhikari*, who functions as the **theatre company**'s **director** and sometimes **playwright**. He also introduces the play, comments on the songs, and narrates the action as it unfolds. Actors do not come from any particular caste, but up until the 1940s, when actresses began performing, only men were permitted, and female impersonators performed **women**'s roles. Prior to the twentieth century, actors improvised formulaic verse interspersed with numerous songs. Only the *adhikari* used prose to interject his commentary.

Music. Music remains central, as audiences often say they have come to hear a *jatra*. The number of songs has been dramatically reduced from over fifty to about eight. Audiences eagerly await these numbers, whose popularity can rival movie tunes. Today, actors sing their own music, though for a time in the mid-nineteenth century a double (*juri*) sang for them. In that system, four singers would station themselves on each of the stage corners and take turns singing for the performer. Following British colonial expansion, troupes began introducing **Western** instrumentation, such as the violin, harmonium, and clarinet.

Toward Secularism and Social Consciousness. In the later half of the nineteenth century, plays by Krishna Kamal Goswami (1810–1888) and Gobinda Adhikari were written and published. Though no copy of these has been preserved, surviving excerpts indicate these playwrights were determined to make the art more refined and cultured so as to appeal to Western-educated Indian audiences. Madanmohan Chattopadhyay was an influential *adhikari* who worked toward strengthening *jatra* by de-emphasizing music and **dance** and giving greater attention to prose dialogue. Despite such efforts *jatra* was not widely accepted by Calcutta's (Kolkata) rising urban middle class. However, *jatra* became increasingly secular as a popular entertainment. By the 1930s, *jatra* was a major force in the rising "Swadeshi" (Home Rule) nationalist movement. Works by Mukunda Das (1878–1934) and Bholaath Shastri appealed to anti-British senti-ments, but Brajendra Kumar Dey's play *Debtar Gras* (1936) is actually credited with ushering in socially oriented themes.

In the 1940s, women entered the *jatra* stage along with a rising social consciousness in the ongoing struggle for independence. A physical manifestation of *jatra*'s social awareness was represented in the new character of the "conscience" (*vivek*). The *vivek* was introduced by musical director Bhootnath Das in 1911 as a way to check the excesses of the *juri* singers. The *vivek* could appear at any time or place in the guise of a madman and sing about the characters' inner turmoil.

The 1947 partition of Bengal into the Indian state of West Bengal and the Pakistani state of East **Pakistan** (now Bangladesh) was a deep blow to many *jatra* artists; it di-vided them politically and devastated them economically. The division would eventu-ally lead to two culturally distinct *jatra* traditions across the India/Bangladesh border. Following World War II, the movie industry's meteoric rise likewise adversely affected audiences, but it also provided impetus for changes in style and content. Rural forms, such as *gunai jatra* and *bhasan jatra*, remained popular despite the urban decline.

It was only in the 1960s, with renewed interest in folk forms sparked by the "theatre of roots" movement, that *jatra* began recovering from its steep descent. Artists such as **Utpal Dutt** began writing and directing in *jatra* style, infusing the tradition with a Brechtian class consciousness. Dutt produced a number of plays on international revo-lutionary topics, such as Lenin, Mao Zedong, and the **Vietnam** War. Other major urban theatre artists who have contributed include lighting designer Tapas Sen (1924–) and actor-director Tarun Roy (1928–1988).

Jatra *Today*. *Jatra* has recovered some from its competition with film and television to become a vibrant and unique popular entertainment, sometimes attracting anywhere between five thousand to ten thousand spectators to a single show. Greatly enjoyed by the middle classes, it flourishes all year round, and has perhaps one hundred troupes just in Kolkata. *Jatra* is now an estimated $21 million a year, highly competetive industry. A record of recent play titles includes *Wife Missing at Nine P.M.*, *Rama during Day, Ravana at Night*, *Who Is this Girl at OMP Cross Road?*, and *Every Girl Is Not Sita and Savitri*, which demonstrate *jatra*'s preoccupation with female relations and religious themes confronting modernity. Other plays reflect contemporary **political** realities, with subjects such as the 9/11 attack, the London mass transit bombings, and the war in Iraq. Sensationalism has become so prevalent that many fear for *jatra*'s future.

FURTHER READING

Gargi, Balwant. *Folk Theater of India*; Sarkar, Sushanta, and Nazmul Ahsan, eds. *Origin and Development of Jatra*.

Robert Petersen

JAUK. Balinese (see Indonesia) **masked-dance** genre, distinct from the *topeng* reper-toire, particularly associated with the magic play of *barong*. *Jauk* also appears as a spiritually powerful or demonic central character in dance-dramas drawn from the **Ramayana** and **Mahabharata**. Currently, the favorite story is the tale of Sunda and

Upasunda, two giant brothers whose arduous meditation is rewarded with power to rule the universe. However, when they plan to attack the heavens, the gods send a beautiful nymph to seduce them, thereby distracting them from their mission and leading them to fight for the nymph's affections. Both protagonists wear *jauk* masks; the "nymph" is unmasked.

Jauk masks are of two types: "strong" (*keras* or *jauk durga*)—powerfully red in color, vividly demonic, with fang-like canines and wild, bulging eyes—and "sweet" (*manis*), a white mask of slightly gentler character. The latter is particularly popular for solo dance featuring virtuosic improvisation with the flute or drum **music** of the *gamelan* orchestra.

Movement resembles that of *baris melampahan* (a Balinese military dance-drama) but with more exaggerated suddenness and violence. The **costume** is the same as that for *baris*, consisting of long, fringe-like, decorated panels, but featuring a distinctive conical headdress (*gelung*) and gloves decorated with goat hair and long buffalo-horn "nails," like those worn by the *barong*'s antagonist Rangda in *Calon Arang* ritual drama. *Jauk* is frequently performed as a solo item in tourist performances or as a prelude to *Calon Arang* in temple ceremonies.

FURTHER READING

Dibia, I Wayan, and Rucina Ballinger. *Balinese Dance, Drama and Music: A Guide to the Performing Arts of Bali.*

Margaret Coldiron

JIAO JUYIN (1905–1975). Chinese • **director, theorist**, and translator, who played a crucial role in staging "spoken drama" (*huaju*; see Playwrights and Playwriting) in the 1950s and 1960s. Together with **Cao Yu**, he founded the Beijing People's Art Theatre (BPAT; Beijing Renmin Yishu Juyuan) in 1952. The plays he directed and the **actors** he **trained** through his directing established this **theatre company**'s house style, which has received domestic and international acclaim.

Born in Tianjin, he was a well-educated son of a poor teacher, and won a scholarship to study **politics** at a Christian college. He took an interest in drama and started writing about theatre and translating foreign plays. In 1930, he organized the first co-educational *jingju* school to train actors and **musicians**, aiming to reform *jingju* through providing a more rounded education. This school gave Jiao hands-on experience in *xiqu* and laid the foundation for his research and practice.

In 1938, Jiao completed a doctorate at the University of Paris; his thesis, an analysis of traditional and modern theatres, was published in France. That year he returned home to participate in the anti-**Japanese** resistance. Although he directed a few important plays, he remained an "amateur" and mainly taught **Western** literature at universities and at the National Drama School until 1952, when he was appointed general director of the BPAT.

During the 1940s, he did research on *xiqu* and the Stanislavski System; he also wrote prolifically on theatre. His translations include Nemirovich-Danchenko's *My Life in the Russian Theatre*. Jiao developed a number of new ideas, including his "theory of mental images" and "Sinicization of *huaju*." The former emphasized the imagery in the actor's mind before using Stanislavski's "magic if" and helped actors create characters with specific personalities rather than merely presenting the performers themselves. Jiao believed that there was no "fourth wall" and that theatrical creation was jointly made with the audience's participation. For everything on **stage**, from sound effects to **scenography** to **properties**, Jiao paid close attention to minute details. His ultimate guideline was for "creating poetry on the stage through the deep foundation of real life. Never reveal too much. Instead, we should leave enough for the audience's own imagination."

Ruru Li

JIKEY. **Malaysian** hybrid **folk theatre** of the states of Kedah and Perlis, combining humorous song, **dance**, and dialogue, featuring an all-male cast, and accompanied by a **musical** ensemble of eight to ten featuring drums, a bamboo flute, bamboo clappers (*cerek*), tambourines, and bells; the musicians also sing. *Jikey* amalgamates various **Thai** and Malay forms, including *bangsawan, mak yong, manohra*, and *liké*. Performances are spontaneous and uninhibited. No attempt is made at suspending disbelief: musicians function as **actors'** interlocutors, and "backstage" chatter—such as why an actor's entrance has been delayed—is clearly audible. **Costumes** are simple but colorful elaborations of everyday dress. A **curtain** separating audience from performers is shaken vigorously for entrances and exits.

Performances begin with a ritual of preparing, cleansing, and "opening" the **stage**. Musicians then play loudly to signal the performance to villagers. Plays are introduced by the signatory "Indian Market" (Makit keling), a comic sketch unconnected to the main story. An **Indian** merchant and his wife arrive at a Malay village and request permission to trade and buy animals. The merchant meets a Malay local, a buffoon called Awang, who reports the incident to the village headman. The headman instructs Awang to locate Pek Seng (a **Chinese** man), who can help in the transaction. After the trader has collected enough cows and other animals, he and his wife depart. The Indian wears bright clothing, his wife does not wear a sari but a blouse and long skirt, reminiscent of how Malay **women** dress. Awang is dressed comically, with tattered shirt and pant legs of uneven lengths. At the conclusion of this multiracial introductory scene, an emcee announces the main story.

Jikey titles include *The Tale of Two Princes, The Fiery Dragon, The Poor One, Mahsuri, The Gaping and Closing Cave*, and *The Scarred Awang*. Common themes include how a poor man becomes rich or how filial impiety is punished; a number of plays are based on legends and folktales. *Jikey* is fading despite attempts to preserve it.

FURTHER READING

Chua Soo Pong, ed. *Traditional Theatre in Southeast Asia*.

Solehah Ishak

JINGJU. A style of "**Chinese**," "Peking," or "Beijing opera" (*xiqu*) originating in Beijing and often regarded as the most representative national theatre form. It is a complex art integrating song, **dance**, **acting**, mime, acrobatics, **music**, and dialogue with elaborate **costumes** and performance techniques. Its music integrates various styles, the most important being *erhuang* and *xipi*. The essence of *jingju* is the combination of these two styles in Beijing.

Historical Background: Eighteenth Century. An important landmark in Beijing's theatre was the arrival of Sichuanese female **role type** (*dan*) actor **Wei Changsheng** in 1779. He made Beijing a main theatre center for the first time in centuries. His artistry was absorbed into the developing *jingju*.

The combination of *erhuang* and *xipi* first appeared in Beijing in 1790, which is sometimes taken as *jingju*'s main "birthday"; 1990 saw its second centenary celebrated. Specifically, in 1790, the Three Celebrations (Sanqing) troupe traveled from Anhui to Beijing to take part in celebrations for the Qianlong emperor's (r. 1736–1796) eightieth birthday. By 1793, the leader was *dan* actor Gao Langting (ca. 1774–ca. 1830), whose guidance gave Three Celebrations a long life. It and three other Beijing troupes created the "four great Anhui **theatre companies**" (*sida mingban*), which ruled the theatre world. Two lasted until 1900, when fire destroyed many theatres following the Boxer Uprising and eight-power invasion.

Nineteenth Century. Records suggest it was *dan* actors recruited from the south who dominated *jingju* until at least the late 1820s. At that time another group of actors, this time from Hubei Province and including some "male role" (*sheng*) performers, came to Beijing, also combining *erhuang* and *xipi*, and joining existing troupes. Although the *dan* persisted, the emphasis shifted to mature actors performing "older males" (*laosheng*). The top actors were **Cheng Changgeng** (called "the father of *jingju*"), **Yu Sansheng**, and **Zhang Erkui**, all *laosheng*.

From 1860, *jingju* spread, initially to Tianjin, Hebei, Shandong, in the northeast, and then to Anhui and Hubei. In 1867, *jingju* came to Shanghai, eventually a major center. By the early twentieth century, *jingju* was present in far south provinces like Guangdong, Fujian, and Yunnan, and later appeared virtually throughout the country. This is why, apart from Beijing's significance as the capital, *jingju* is generally regarded as China's traditional national theatre.

In the late Qing dynasty (1644–1911), *jingju* enjoyed imperial patronage. The avid *jingju* enthusiast Manchu Empress Dowager Cixi (1835–1908) had special **stages** built, two large ones at her Summer Palace and a small one in the Imperial Palace. The Rising Peace Office, set up in 1827 to supervise *kunqu* performed at court by eunuchs, turned some attention to *jingju*. From 1884, Cixi regularly invited city actors to perform for her. Because security was so tight and the idea of allowing mere actors into the palaces outrageous, special passes were issued to allow them entry.

By the late nineteenth century, great actors were appearing in all role types. They included *laosheng* Sun Juxian (1841–1931) and Cixi's favorite, **Tan Xinpei**, and *dan* specialists Mei Qiaoling (1842–1882), grandfather of **Mei Lanfang**, and Chen Delin (1862–1930).

Traditional Repertory. All nineteenth-century items were set in China's past. The repertoire consisted of "civilian plays" (*wenxi*) and "military plays" (*wuxi*). Items dominated by *dan* and civil *sheng* actors were *wenxi*, which dealt with domestic matters, morality tales, and marital hardships, usually in an indefinite period. On the other hand, many were *wuxi*, with "martial male" (*wusheng*) roles dominant. These featured war stories, with thrilling acrobatic displays representing battles. They were based on traditional novels and set in specific periods. Many derived from the civil wars around the time of the collapse of the Han dynasty (206 BC–220 AD), as told in the novel *The Romance of the Three Kingdoms* (Sanguo zhi yanyi). A number combine both civil and martial elements.

Twentieth Century. Although the Boxer Uprising ended the great nineteenth-century companies, famous actors continued to found troupes. Stars who would dominate the twentieth century included the "four great *dan*," Mei Lanfang, **Chang Yanqiu**, **Xun Huisheng**, and **Shang Xiaoyun**; *laosheng* **Zhou Xinfang** and **Ma Lianliang**; "older female" (*laodan*) Li Duokui (1898–1974); and "painted face" (*jing*) Qiu Shengrong (1915–1971). Each developed a distinctive style assiduously studied by others, thereby being recognized as having founded a performance "school/style" (*liupai*). Meanwhile, the early twentieth century also saw both the beginnings of a highly influential **training** system, and far-reaching reforms, with implications for content and style.

Two distinctly different styles developed. "Beijing style" (*jingpai* or *beipai*) valued traditional purity and was more conservative; "Shanghai style" (*haipai*), more daring and **experimental**, saw more reforms, including new plays concerned with social issues, and elaborate "machine-operated **scenographic** techniques" (*jiguan bujing*) for audience appeal. Many actors achieved pre-eminence partly because they successfully worked in both cities.

The Cultural Revolution and After. *Jingju* has been of paramount importance to the Chinese Communist Party since Mao Zedong's (1893–1976) 1942 advocacy of traditional arts as **political** vehicles and his explicit praise for the play created in response, *Driven up Mount Liang* (Bishang Liang Shan). In 1949, the party called for the revision of many traditional plays and the creation of "new historical plays" (***xinbian lishi ju***) and "contemporary plays" (*xiandai xi*), focusing particularly on *jingju*, and initiating several decades of close concern with the training, organization, and creative process and output of artists. Leftist **criticism** of *Hai Rui Dismissed from Office* (Hai Rui baguan, 1961) is viewed as the "spark that ignited the Cultural Revolution [1966–1976]," during which ultimately more than fifteen "revolutionary contemporary model works" (*geming xiandai **yangban xi***) were created, while traditional and *xinbian lishi ju* performances were **censored**.

After the Cultural Revolution the bans were reversed, and traditional and *xinbian lishi ju* performed by older stars drew large audiences. With growing competition from other media, however, audiences dwindled as the average age rose. Moreover, new priorities led to steadily decreasing government funding. Reform efforts have attempted to stabilize the situation, but the problem has been particularly acute for *jingju*, at least partly because of its long-standing political importance. Experimentation has been closely monitored by a government concerned with the health of the national theatre form, making independent efforts difficult, while audiences have mistrusted idealistic expressions, especially in *jingju*.

The most far-reaching efforts have therefore been economic and organizational. To reduce costs and concentrate investment, many troupes have been disbanded. Records show 248 *jingju* troupes in 1978 but only 126 in 1990; more have been disbanded since then, and most also have been reduced in size. Incentive-based salary structures, "extra-income enterprises" such as restaurants and hotels, corporate sponsorship, and outreach efforts aimed at developing new student audiences are among major avenues being explored. Cultural tourism, with high-priced performances for (generally) foreign tourists, is another. **Festivals** and contests are being organized to build indigenous interest. For instance, the Festival of Jingju Arts, initiated in 1995, is held every third year in a different city and features competitive performances of new and traditional plays with carefully crafted national television coverage. Such festivals are a principal means of encouraging both the preservation of traditional standards and new developments in practice.

Musical Practices. The most fundamental practices are associated with vocal music, as these styles in essence define the form. *Jingju* follows beat-tune musical structure (*banqiang ti*) and is characterized by music from the *pihuang* system, named for its two principal mode or tune types (*shengqiang*), *xipi* and *erhuang*. Distinctive patterns of musical structure give each a characteristic atmosphere; *xipi* is experienced as bright, energetic, and purposeful, while *erhuang* is relatively dark and profound.

Numerous instrumental and vocal conventions exist so that actors fluent in them instinctively combine the patterns of a chosen mode and metrical type with the word tones in a lyric passage to create specific, nuanced melodies expressing a character's thoughts and feelings. Lyrics written in couplets facilitate this process, with seven written characters per line for faster metrical types, and ten for slower. Actors' voices are classified as male or female. Male voices characterize *laosheng*, *wusheng*, *laodan*, *jing*, and "comic male" (*chou*); all employ the "natural" voice, though each has its own distinctive timbre. Of the female voices, the various young *dan* all use falsetto, and "young male roles" (*xiaosheng*) use a combination of natural and falsetto. For every type, the same vocal quality is maintained in both song and speech.

A two-string spike fiddle (*jinghu*) usually leads the civil (*wen*) melodic section of the orchestra. For *gaobozi*, however, the double-reed *suona* may be substituted, and for *chuiqiang*, the horizontal bamboo flute (*qudi*). The conductor playing the clapper (*ban*) and drum (*danpigu*) leads the martial (*wu*) percussion section. In the 1970s, **Western** instruments joined traditional orchestras for some *yangban xi*; they are still prevalent, and contemporary efforts to draw new audiences have included using musical influences from other *xiqu* forms and Chinese as well as Western performing arts, such as elements from Western concert music and more recent musical styles.

Repertory. Today, approximately two hundred traditional plays are considered "outstanding repertory pieces." Many are in twentieth-century revisions. For example, **Tian Han**'s *The White Snake* (Baishe zhuan), tighter than earlier anonymous versions, is the contemporary standard, and the Monkey King triumphs over his divine opponents in contemporary versions of *Havoc in Heaven* (Nao tiangong). **Playwrights**, included in most troupes since the 1950s, have made substantial contributions. For instance, Fan Junhong (1916–1986) revised many traditional plays and wrote both kinds of new ones, including (with Lü Ruiming) the historical play *Women Generals of the Yang Family* (Yang men nü jiang) and the contemporary play *The White-haired Girl* (Bai mao nü). In some cases, new plays are created for targeted audiences; the Shanghai Drama Society's (Shanghai Xiju Xieshe) award-winning *Cao Cao and Yang Xiu* by Chen Yaxian was designed for urban intellectuals.

FURTHER READING

Mackerras, Colin. *The Rise of the Peking Opera, Social Aspects of the Theatre in Manchu China*; Mackerras, Colin. *Peking Opera*; Pan, Xiafeng. *The Stagecraft of Peking Opera*; Wichmann, Elizabeth. *Listening to Theatre: The Aural Dimension of Beijing Opera*.

Colin Mackerras and Elizabeth Wichmann-Walczak

JIT, KRISHEN (1939–2005). Malaysian • actor, theatre activist, **theorist**, educator, **critic**, scholar, **director**, and producer. He devoted more than four decades to developing both Malay- and English-language theatre. Jit developed historical perspectives about drama, encouraged new theatrical visions, and identified new trends. His own productions were **experimental**; he sought to push boundaries and break new ground. In 2003, he received the Lifetime Achievement Award at the first BOH Cameronian Arts Awards ceremony.

Jit had been active in the expatriate-led Malayan (later, Malaysian) Arts Theatre Group and was the first local actor to play a leading role in one of the group's productions: in 1959 he starred in *Julius Caesar*. Eventually, this group, under local rather than expatriate leadership, initiated locally scripted English-language drama.

In 1960, while an undergraduate at the University of Malaya, Jit, together with Tan Jin Chor, cofounded the university's Literary and Dramatic Society. After receiving an honors degree in history, he received a Fulbright scholarship to continue graduate studies at the University of California at Berkeley. In 1967, after earning his master's, he taught history at the University of Malaya and continued his involvement in English-language theatre. However, after the ethnic riots of May 13, 1969, Jit and other artists, such as **Syed Alwi**, Faridah Merican (1939–), and Rahim Razali (1949–), decided it

Leow Puay Tin's *Family,* 1998, codirected by Krishen Jit and Wong Hoy Cheong at the Five Arts Centre, Kuala Lumpur, Malaysia. (Photo: Courtesy of Five Arts Centre)

was more appropriate to work in Malay theatre to connect more directly with society at large. In particular, he lent considerable support to the emerging **experimental** Malay theatre.

In 1972, Jit began publishing a weekly commentary, "Talking Drama with Utih," in the *New Straits Times*. The column, which ran through 1994, documents the development of the Malaysian theatre scene within a broad historical framework; he also discusses the future of Malaysian theatre. His writing articulates stimulating perspectives on the country's diverse art world; his insights were not limited by linguistic or ethnic boundaries.

By the 1980s, Islamic revivalism began to affect Malay theatre. The experimental, absurdist nature of the preceding decade's theatre was critiqued by **religious** points of view. In addition, the plays had become increasingly difficult to understand, and audience interest waned. The renewed focus on Islamic identity and decreasing enthusiasm for experimentalism led Jit return to English-language drama.

First, however, he received a grant to study performance theory at New York University. Back in Malaysia, his involvement with Malay-language theatre was less than before. In 1983, he, his spouse (**dancer**-choreographer Marion D'Cruz), and others cofounded the Five Arts Centre to promote innovative expression. Jit was especially interested in developing English works depicting the various dimensions of Malaysian life. Initially, he directed communal plays: K. S. Maniam's (1942–) *The Cord* (1984) and *The Sandpit* (1988) reflect issues faced in Malaysia's **Indian** community while Leow Puay Tin's (1957–) *Three Children* (1987) and *Two Grandmothers* (1988) portray the complexities of **Chinese**-Malaysian life. Later, Jit worked in multiethnic and multilingual theatre, directing company-devised plays, such as *Work* and *Us*. He also directed a multiart production of Maniam's *Skin Trilogy*.

Upon retiring from the university (1994), Jit founded the theatre program at Kuala Lumpur's National Arts Academy. Throughout his career, Jit directed, among others, works by **Usman Awang**, Syed Alwi, Dinsman (1949–), K. S. Maniam, Kee Thuan Chye (1954–), Leow Puay Tin, David Hwang, Dick Lee, **Kuo Pao Kun**, Lloyd Fernando (1926–), Jit Murad, Huzir Sulaiman (1973–), and Stella Kon (1944–), gaining fame even in **Singapore**, where he worked cooperatively with TheatreWorks and Practice Performing Arts.

FURTHER READING

Jit, Krishen. *Krishen Jit, an Uncommon Position: Selected Writings.*

Nancy Nanney

KABUKI. **Japanese** theatre that, with *nô*, *kyôgen*, and *bunraku* (see Puppet Theatre), forms one of Japan's quartet of classical genres. It was born simultaneously with the Edo period (1603–1868) as a commercial, urban theatre that developed in new directions over the centuries, and, indeed, even now is subject to innovation.

Kabuki has been likened to a chimera, a mythical beast each of whose component parts belong to another animal: here, dialogue drama was the head, **musical** narrative (*jôruri*) the body, and **dance**-drama the tail. This creature was born during the "early modern" (*kinsei*) period when, except for trade with a tiny Dutch settlement in Nagasaki, Japan was closed off from the **West**. Osaka and Kyoto in western Japan (Kamigata) and Edo (Tokyo) in the east were the nation's cultural centers, and *kabuki* was the theatre that mirrored their townspeople's lives and dreams. *Kabuki* developed from the beginning of the seventeenth through the end of the twentieth centuries, creating numerous styles and features that give it a kaleidoscopic (or chimerical) appearance.

Birth and Development: Seventeenth Century. Chaos reigned in Japan during the late sixteenth century, a time of conflict among various warlords. When the dust cleared, people who had fled the carnage to live in the big cities expressed their relief and joy by dressing in boldly colored clothing and flowered hats and cavorting in mass street dances called *furyû odori*, keeping time to drumbeats. These townsmen were said to be "*furyû*" in the sense of the older word *fuga* ("elegant, tasteful"). Unlike the repression of feelings in earlier forms, like *bugaku* and *nô*, where the face was masked or **mask**-like, the new dancing allowed for individual expression, later a distinct *kabuki* quality.

In 1603, **Izumo no Okuni**, a wandering shrine priestess (*aruki miko*) from the grand shrine at Izumo, arrived in Kyoto and, with a troupe of supporting players, began performing in the river bed of the Kamo River. Her shows combined elements of *furyû odori* with comical sketches (*sungeki*), as well as a popularized version of a "Buddhist prayer dance" (*nenbutsu odori*) performed while striking a brass bell, that was called "*kabuki* dance" (*kabuki odori*). The noun *kabuki* derives from the verb *katamuku* ("to tilt"), and was used to refer to rebellious young samurai—*kabuki mono*—who dressed and behaved flamboyantly. Chief among Okuni's dance-sketches was one in which a young rake flirted with a teahouse proprietress. These performances, in which Okuni cross-dressed as the youth, were accompanied by *nô* musical instruments. The female troupes that soon competed with *okuni kabuki* and were called "women's" (*onna*) *kabuki* added the three-stringed *shamisen*, and it became the central component of *kabuki* music, helping the form gain immense popularity.

The shogunate (*bakufu*), run by the Tokugawa family, considered *kabuki*'s overt expressiveness a dangerous incitement to public disorder, and frequently interfered in its affairs. This meant the abolition of *onna kabuki* in 1629 and the squashing of its replacement, the homoerotic "boys'" (*wakashu*) *kabuki* in 1652; *kabuki* could return only if its **actors** shaved their pretty forelocks as per the style of adult men (*yarô*). Thus, in 1653, *yarô kabuki* was born, although the official name was *monomane zukushi kyôgen*, a term implying that performances would emphasize imitative acting (*monomane*) rather than song and dance. Needing to hide their shaved pates, the "female impersonators" (*onnagata*) covered them with purple silk caps (wigs came later) to play opposite "male role" (*tachiyaku*) actors in pieces showing incipient signs of dramatic development. Various **role types** arose under the chief rubrics of *onnagata*, *tachiyaku*, and "villain" (*katakiyaku*) in multi-act plays (*tsuzuki kyôgen*) that replaced the outmoded one-acts (*hanare kyôgen*).

The century ended in a blaze of "renaissance-like" glory during the Genroku period (1688–1704), a time of cultural efflorescence in which the townsman class had the funds and leisure to consume various pleasures. Kamigata audiences had different theatrical tastes from those of Edo. The former preferred relatively realistic plays about contemporary young men from well-off merchant families who ruined themselves by affairs with expensive courtesans from the flourishing brothel quarters, with whom they usually committed double suicide. The **acting** of such young men was in the "gentle style" (*wagoto*) associated with **Sakata Tôjûrô** I, while Edo's bombastic, exaggerated "rough style" (*aragoto*) was connected with the superheroic samurai played by **Ichikawa Danjûrô** I for an audience familiar with the swaggering warriors filling the streets of Edo. Characters like Soga Gorô were manifestations of powerful minor deities (*goryô*) who used martial prowess to aid innocent victims. Other great actors of the time were *onnagata* genius **Yoshizawa Ayame** I and Edo *wagoto* specialist Nakamura Shichisaburô I, while leading **playwrights** were Tominaga Heibei, Mimasuya Hyôgo (a.k.a. Danjûrô I), and **Chikamatsu Monzaemon**, the first professional playwright. With the arrival of playwriting specialists, actors abandoned their reliance on scenario-supported "improvisation" (*kuchidate*).

The Eighteenth Century. Post-Genroku *kabuki* saw the establishment of important musical and dance styles. *Kabuki* and the puppet theatre (*ningyô jôruri*, a.k.a. *bunraku*) engaged in a dynamic rivalry, with the puppets—experiencing their golden age— generally in the ascendancy because of their plays' superior literary quality, their brilliant chanters (*tayû*), and their advanced techniques, including the 1734 invention of the three-man puppet system. The dramaturgic apogee was reached in 1746, 1747, and 1748, when the "three masterpieces," *Sugawara's Secrets of Calligraphy* (Sugawara denju tenarai kagami), *The Treasury of Loyal Retainers* (Kanadehon chûshingura), and *Yoshitsune and the Thousand Cherry Trees* (Yoshitsune senbon zakura), appeared. *Kabuki* had been borrowing *bunraku* plays since 1717, when it adapted Chikamatsu's *Battles of Coxinga* (Kokusenya kassen), so each of these works also soon became a *kabuki* classic.

At the same time, *onnagata* like Segawa Kikunojô I (1693?–1749) and Nakamura Tomijûrô I (1721–1786) were making important advances in the art of dance-plays (*shosagoto*), reaching a high point during the Tenmei period (1781–1789), known for its lighthearted humor, when Nakamura Nakazô I (1735–1790) reversed the trend of *onnagata* dominance by creating dances centered on *tachiyaku*. While earlier dance had employed *nagauta* music, with its verbal lyricism, more narrative-based music now began to accompany dance in the form of *tokiwazu*, *tomimoto*, and, a little later, *kiyomoto*.

The eighteenth century had seen the evolution of **theatre** architecture, including the roofing over of the originally out-of-doors space, the establishment of the "flower path" (*hanamichi*) runway and its secondary version, the "revolving **stage**" (*mawari butai*), elevator traps (*seri*) for lifting actors as well as sets, and so forth. *Kabuki*'s stage, which had resembled *nô*'s from its inception, abandoned the gabled roof and its pillars by the end of the century, standing forth as a unique architectural entity in its own right. Taking advantage of its new arrangements, *kabuki* introduced its memorable "outside the curtain exits" (*maku soto no hikkomi*), by which actors stood before the closed draw **curtain** (*hiki maku*) with no **scenographic** distraction behind them and made spectacularly dramatic exits through the auditorium.

Nakamura Utaemon VI on the runway (*hanamichi*) in the *kabuki* play, *Mt. Imo and Mt. Se: An Exemplary Tale of Womanly Virtue*, Kabuki Theatre (Kabuki-za), Tokyo. A secondary runway is located at the other side of the auditorium in this scene. (Photo: Courtesy of Waseda University Theatre Museum)

Late Eighteenth and Early Nineteenth Centuries. The years from 1789–1830, covering the Kansei (1789–1801), Kyôwa (1801–1804), Bunka (1804–1818), and Bunsei (1818–1830) periods (Bunka and Bunsei usually being conflated as Kasei), were alive with important developments. There was a shift from the comic perspective of the Tenmei years to more realistic, logically constructed plays of **Namiki Gohei** I, with their respect for character depiction. When Gohei moved from Osaka to Edo in 1794, bringing with him Osaka's playwriting methods, he essentially revolutionized Edo dramaturgy, writing plays like *Five Great Powers that Secure Love* (Godairiki koi no fûjime, 1794) in which there began to be seen a breakdown in the depiction of the traditional master-retainer, husband-wife morality in which duty was expected to trump personal feelings. Realistic actors like Sawamura Sôjûrô III (1753–1801) helped make such works succeed.

Realism reached its apex in the Kasei-era plays of **Tsuruya Nanboku** IV, whose dark depiction of the lowest echelons of society—thieves, murderers, adulterers, and streetwalkers—established the new genre of "pure" or "raw domestic plays" (*kizewa mono*). Nanboku's plays captured the period's overripe decadence, although his realism was tempered with mystery and spectacle. He was already in his fifties when his career blossomed, especially with his pioneering "ghost plays" (*kaidan mono*), a type of *kizewa mono*, in which the gritty everyday reality of the surroundings made the introduction of vengeful ghosts that much more believable. He was greatly aided by the inventive methods used to depict the ghosts by Onoe Matsusuke II (1744–1815) and **Onoe Kikugorô** III. Plays like *The Ghost Stories at Yotsuya on the Tôkaidô* (Tôkaidô Yotsuya kaidan) still frighten audiences.

Gohei had brought to Edo the Osaka style of having a day's program divided into two separate plays, a "history play" (*jidai mono*) and a "domestic play" (*sewa mono*), but Nanboku preferred the old Edo style of a single long play in which the "world" (*sekai*) of the history portion that began the day was mingled (*naimaze*) with that of the domestic part. His plays made use of all of *kabuki*'s conventionalized scenes and conventions, including "murder scenes" (*koroshiba*), "combat scenes" (*tachimawari*), "love scenes" (*nureba*), "extortion scenes" (*yusuriba*), "quick changes" (*hayagawari*), and "special effects" (*keren*) such as "flying through the air" (*chûnori*). His use of background music was masterful, creating atmospheric effects unlike those in other playwrights' work.

Another sign of the times was public fascination with dance plays requiring multiple transformations. Actor-dancers like **Bandô Mitsugorô** III and IV specialized in these "transformation pieces" (*henge mono*) in which a solo dancer played up to a dozen strikingly different roles. An offshoot of this fascination with versatility was the performance of multiple characters by the same actor in a single well-known play, much as if an actor were to play Hamlet, Ophelia, Gertrude, Claudius, and Polonius in different scenes of *Hamlet*.

Late Edo Period. The last years of the shogunate, from around 1840, bustled with theatrical activity, despite social unrest, some of it connected to the forced opening of Japan to the West in 1853. Keeping the flame alive were playwrights Segawa Jokô III (1806–1881), Kawatake Shinshichi (later **Kawatake Mokuami**), and Sakurada Jisuke III (1802–1877); and actors Ichikawa Danjûrô VII and VIII, Sawamura Tanosuke III (1845–1878), Nakamura Shikan IV (1831–1899), and Ichikawa Kodanji IV (1812–1866). Especially popular were plays depicting society's bottom rungs, with characters such as romantic bandits pulled from the pages of cheap fiction, and with lots of sex, blackmail, violence, and torture thrown in. Many such plays were called "bandit plays" (*shiranami mono*). *Henge mono* remained a draw, but an important new type of dance-drama (*shosagoto* or *buyô geki*) appeared in 1840, when Danjûrô VII staged *The Subscription List* (Kanjinchô), based on the *nô* play *Ataka*. Unlike previous adaptations, *Kanjinchô* actually resembled *nô* with its pine-tree painted on the back wall, its authentic **costumes**, and its text a close approximation of the original, albeit adapted for *kabuki*. This new genre of "pine-board plays" (*matsubame mono*) became especially popular during Meiji.

Meiji and Beyond. Meiji was a time of renewal, when **Western** civilization was adopted en masse. During this period of "civilization and enlightenment" (*bunmei kaika*), *kabuki* tried to keep pace with Japan's rapidly changing social conditions, abandoning the dramatic liberty it had always taken with history, for example, to produce academically accurate "living history plays" (*katsureki geki*), or "cropped-hair plays" (*zangiri mono*) that mirrored the new hairdos, fashions, and artifacts of the day. Danjûrô IX led the way with the former, Kikugorô V with the latter. Both types were written by the prolific Kawatake Mokuami, whose death in 1893 marked the end of traditional *kabuki* **playwriting**.

With the unprecedented participation of businessmen, scholars, literary figures, and **politicians** in its affairs, *kabuki* witnessed a groundswell of interest in reforming it along the lines of Western theatrical art. The principal result of these efforts was to inspire new forms, such as **shinpa**, **shin kabuki**, and **shingeki**, in the creation of which *kabuki* actors took an active part. *Kabuki*, for three centuries the popular theatre of Japan, became in the twentieth century a classical, traditional art. Its artists, once deemed "riverbed beggars" (*kawara kojiki*), despite their enormous popularity, were now respected and often honored members of society. Still, despite its many twentieth-century vicissitudes, including its nearly being destroyed by the American Occupation **censorship** in the postwar years because its feudal themes were considered dangerous, it has managed to survive and continues to attract audiences to large theatres in Kamigata and Tokyo, as well as elsewhere. In fact, a National Theatre (Kokuritsu Gekijô) was opened in 1966 to help study and sustain its traditions. Troupes large and small tour the world regularly, and its influence on foreign theatre has been strong. Innovative actors, like **Ichikawa Ennosuke** III with his "super" (*supaa*) *kabuki* and **Nakamura Kanzaburô** XVIII with his Cocoon Kabuki, provide new and sometimes startling approaches to this four-hundred-year-old art, which shows no signs of abating.

FURTHER READING

Brandon, James R., William P. Malm, and Donald H. Shively, eds. *Studies in Kabuki: Its Acting, Music, and Historical Context;* Ernst, Earle. *The Kabuki Theatre.* Gunji, Masakatsu. *Kabuki;* Leiter, Samuel L. *New Kabuki Encyclopedia: A Revised Adaptation of Kabuki Jiten.*

Samuel L. Leiter

KAGURA. General term for **Japanese** traditional performing arts presented during Shinto shrine **festivals**, and for entertainments accompanying rituals carried out at the imperial court. Scholars generally agree that the word is derived from *kami* and *kura*—indicating a place where deities are believed to be present. In the definitive five-part division of Japan's **folk** performing arts developed by ethnologist Honda Yasuji (1908–2001), *kagura* is foremost.

Honda traveled to festivals all over Japan to study and analyze the thousands of different performances classified as *kagura*. He identified four subdivisions: "shrine maiden" (*miko*) *kagura*, "property" (*torimono*) *kagura*, "boiling water" (*yudate*) *kagura*, and "lion" (*shishi*) *kagura*. *Miko kagura* takes its name from **dances** performed by female shamans who serve as mediums through which a community's deity or deities communicate with the human population. The archetypal model is the mythic dance performed by goddess Ame no Uzume in front of the cave in which sun goddess Amaterasu hid herself. Curiosity about the dance brought Amaterasu out, thus restoring light and life to the world. *Torimono kagura* (a.k.a. *izumo kagura* after the city of Izumo) features performers holding objects—branches of *sakaki* (an evergreen used in Shinto rituals), fans, bells, swords, and so on—said to symbolize the presence of deities. In *yudate kagura* (a.k.a. *ise kagura* after the city of Ise), dancers perform near a cauldron of steaming water. Demonic-looking **masks** and **costumes** are said to please the deities who are drawn by the hot mists, which are offerings to them. In *shishi kagura* dancers wear "lion" masks regarded as manifestations of the deities.

Scholar Frank Hoff has suggestively defined *kagura* as "an environment for performance," thereby emphasizing the need to understand the patterns of belief that motivate the various presentations. Through festivals and their associated performances communities invoke assistance for successful harvests and help in averting or removing whatever might harm the populace. In court *kagura*, too, the desire to ensure the well-being of the imperial family and, by extension, that of the country as a whole underlies presentations. Hoff also underscores the complex historical relationship between the development of Japan's professional performing arts and ritual-related *kagura* entertainments. It is likely, for example, that *kagura* directly provided source material for *nô*. Over time, as different performance types, such as *kabuki*, developed and became popular, *kagura* presentations in turn were enriched by borrowing from them. *See also* Religion in Theatre.

FURTHER READING

Hoff, Frank. *Song, Dance, Storytelling: Aspects of the Performing Arts in Japan.*

Barbara E. Thornbury

KAHANI KA RANGAMANCH. **Indian** modern theatre in which works of fiction are dramatized using simple theatrical means. It came to attention in 1975, when Devendra Raj Ankur, later **director** of New Delhi's National School of Drama (NSD), produced three pieces based on short stories by Hindi writer Nirmal Verma (1929–) as *Three Situations of Loneliness* (Teen ekant). Subsequently, he produced twelve such programs at the NSD by 2001, using material in multiple languages and from varying cultures. Similar to the "story theatre" popularized in the United States by Paul Sills at around the same time, this "theatre of story" form allows for short stories and other forms of fiction, including novels, to be performed by having the **actors** behave as presenters of the story and its characters, rather than being completely immersed in their roles. Thus the narrative as well as the dialogue can be directly conveyed, with a minimum of movement, **scenography**, and **costumes**. The actors step in and out of their roles, as necessary, and use direct address where required. Stories thus performed are not dramatized on paper, but are presented in their original form, without alteration.

Ankur's productions typically combine multiple short works—by the same or different authors—under a single title. Although the form has been **criticized**, it has allowed a number of pieces of fiction to reveal interesting theatrical qualities that might otherwise have been ignored.

FURTHER READING

Dharwadker, Aparna Bhargava. *Theatres of Independence: Drama, Theory, and Urban Performance in India since 1947.*

Samuel L. Leiter

KAILASAM, TYAGARAJA PARAMASIVA (1884–1946). **Indian** Kannada- and English-language **actor**, **director**, **playwright**, poet, short story writer, and filmmaker, known as "the grand old man of farcical Kannada plays." He quit his government job as a geologist to work in theatre. Having studied in London, he was well acquainted with **Western** theatre as well as his own native dramaturgy. Kailasam emphasized social issues—from **religious** hypocrisy to child marriage—and revolutionized Kannada theatre, laying bare middle-class human weaknesses but using satire and humor to set things right.

Kailasam's plays lacked **music**, and their often witty dialogue was in the ordinary colloquial language heard in old Mysore, elements initially **criticized**. He opposed the then prominent "company theatre's" (*company nataka*; see Theatre Companies) obsession with mythology and excessive use of music and **dance**, traits he mocked in *Our Company* (Namkampani, 1944). In their place he brought to the **stage** a heavy dose of realism.

Kailasam descended on Kannada's stage with *Hollow-Solid* (Tollu-gatti, 1919), which brought instant fame. Among his produced plays are *Vulgar Kitti* (Poli Kitti, 1923), *Boycott* (Bahiskara, 1929), *Murder of Love* (Olavina kole, 1929), *Home Rule* (Hom rulu, 1930), and *Our Brahmanism* (Nam Brahmanike, 1945). Among his six English-language plays, all inspired by the *Mahabharata* and on a more rarified aesthetic plane than the social dramas, are *The Burden* (1933), *The Fulfillment* (1933), and *The Purpose* (1944). They remain unproduced.

Kailasam was sadly out of place in the suffocating milieu of his times. Misunderstood by his contemporaries, massacred by the critics, and rejected by his family, he became a social outcast with no moorings.

Debjani Ray Moulik

KAKUL, I NYOMAN (1905–1982). *Topeng* performer of Bali (see Indonesia), born in Batuan, Gianyar. **Trained** in the martial **dance** called *baris* and in **gambuh**'s refined style, he excelled as a teacher of Balinese and international students. Kakul was adept at both the older solo style of performance (*topeng pajegan*) required for rituals and the twentieth-century, multiperson *topeng panca* that served entertainment functions. He danced in international tours from 1953 until the 1970s.

Kakul's combination of expert dancing, innovative and **politically** biting comedy, and ability to teach the complex art in both its physical and spiritual dimensions was unsurpassed. His performance of *Jelantik Goes to Blambangan* (Jelantik Bogol) has been well documented. I Ketut Kantor (1938–), his son, carries on the family legacy of excellence in **mask** performance.

Kathy Foley

KALAPAM. South **Indian** • **dance**-drama, using song and **acting**, performed largely in Andhra Pradesh. *Kalapam*, suggesting a group or collection, is essentially an arrangement of songs with classical themes (such as Krishna's childhood tales) in differing meters. Of the four main texts, the two remaining are *The Resentment of Bhama* (Bhama-kalapam) and *The Milkmaid's Story* (Golla-kalapam). The stories are enacted in all-night performances by all-male troupes.

The chief character of *The Resentment of Bhama* is Satyabhama (Bhama), a wife of Krishna, and the supporting player is a clown-like (*vidushaka*) maidservant. Satyabhama does all the acting while the maidservant provides descriptions and narrative background. The performance expresses Satyabhama's character according to the classical **theoretical** concepts of *rasa*s and *bhava*s, as when she reveals her misery, brought on by jealousy, to her maid. The work's performance is associated with **kuchipudi**, but it also is presented by other groups, including one in which a **woman** performs Satyabhama.

In *The Milkmaid's Story*, the heroine is a Golla caste milkmaid, although—despite his association with the tale—Krishna plays no part. The other character is a male Brahman, and the subtext is the milkmaid's use of her superior wit and knowledge to destroy Brahmanic beliefs. Performances are limited to a small number of female temple dancers who perform it on the wedding night of well-off newlyweds. A strong knowledge of **Sanskrit** is required of the dancer-singers, who perform each song both in its original form and then in easy-to-understand translation.

Samuel L. Leiter

KALARIPPAYATTU. **Indian** martial arts system used in traditional **actor • training**, dating from at least the twelfth century, and important to various performance genres of Kerala. Many different styles or practice lineages exist. Intensive training traditionally takes place at least annually during the cool monsoon season (June–August) in specially constructed places (*kalari*)—traditionally an earthen walled pit dug out of the ground and covered by a thatched palm-leaf roof.

Kalari are considered sacred spaces. On entry one touches the floor, forehead, and chest, paying respects to the *kalari* deities. In Hindu *kalari* a variety of deities are understood to be present, most important a form of goddesses such as Bhagavati or Bhadrakali, or some combined form of Shiva-Sakti. In Muslim *kalari* Allah is present, while in Christian *kalari* the triune forms of Jesus are present (see Religion in Theatre).

Training begins with an initiation ritual. The training cycles are circumscribed by ritual practices intended to sanctify the space and ensure safe practice within. After initiation, students put gingely (sesame) oil on their bodies daily and learn a vast array of vigorous, deep "body exercises." It is said that a goal is to make the body as flexible as a rubber band. Animal poses, leg exercises, kicks, steps, circling of the body, and jumps are performed in increasingly complex and difficult gymnastic combinations. Most important is mastery of basic animal poses, such as the elephant, horse, lion, and serpent, comparable to yoga postures.

A full-body massage given with the feet and hands is traditional and lasts for fifteen days. This extremely deep massage requires approximately twenty to thirty minutes. The master holds onto ropes suspended from the rafters so that he can eventually apply maximum pressure to the body. He literally massages the forms of the basic training into the body. The massage does not relax the student, but is understood to "activate" him, because immediately after massage he engages in vigorous exercise.

Repeated practice of the exercises, combined with full-body massage, special breath-control exercises (practiced by some but not all masters/styles) renders the external body flexible and controlled, and "awakens" and raises the internal "serpent energy" (*kundalini sakti*) understood to lie dormant at the base of the spine. Ideally a master's body is understood to "become all eyes," that is, the practitioner develops an intuitive, animal-like ability to respond to his immediate environment and any dangers within it. Indeed, in the traditional sense of the term yoga—"to knot" or "tie"—*kalarippayattu* training is a yogic practice in that it activates the entire subtle body identified in the classical yoga of Patanjali.

Students are eventually introduced to combat through a variety of weapons—long staff, short stick, and curved stick (*otta*)—and then to combat weapons including dagger, sword and shield, spear, mace, and flexible sword. Empty-hand combat is learned initially as part of *otta* practice. Masters finally learn special therapies to treat a variety of injuries or conditions, such as bruises, muscular "catches," conditions affecting the "wind humor," or the setting of broken bones. These traditional therapies were the "hands-on" dimension of Kerala's renowned *ayurvedic* medical system.

Kalarippayattu influenced many indigenous performance traditions in content, techniques, and training, including **folk** dances, ritual performances where deified heroes or various gods are dramatically propitiated (**teyyam**), **kathakali**, and the Christian dance-drama **cavittu natakam**, which uses *kalarippayattu* to display the prowess of heroes like St. George and the emperor Charlemagne.

Kalarippayattu is used in training both inside and outside of India. Well-known Kerala **director • Kavalam Narayana Panikkar** began to use *kalarippayattu* along with a variety of other local genres, such as *kathakali*, to train members of his Sopanam Theatre. Choreographer-dancers, such as Chandralekha and Daksha Seth, also have trained their dancers in *kalarippayattu* as well as, respectively, **bharata natyam** or *kathak*. Both have created major new pieces of choreography in which *kalarippayattu* overtly plays a central role in the movement styles and aesthetics.

American Phillip Zarrilli has developed a psycho-physiological training system based on principles of *kalarippayattu*, *tai chi*, and yoga designed to heighten the actor's awareness.

FURTHER READING

Zarrilli, Phillip B. *When the Body Becomes All Eyes: Paradigms, Practices, and Discourses of Power in Kalarippayattu.*

Phillip B. Zarrilli

KALIDASA. Indian • playwright and poet. The greatest of **Sanskrit theatre** dramatists, he is known to later history almost exclusively from his works. Even within these there are almost no direct references to his time, place, or personal life. In addition to two epics and a pair of lyrical poems, he wrote three brilliant dramas: *The Recognition of Shakuntala* (Abhijnana Shakuntalam), the romantic comedy *Malavika and Agnimitra* (Malavikagnimitra), and the romantic drama *Urvashi Won by Valor* (Vikramorvashiya). The first is widely regarded as his masterwork, though the other two display similar poetic and dramatic skill. All three are dedicated to the god Shiva, and the playwright's name indicates that he was personally devoted to the goddess Kali.

Shakuntala, as it is best known, is based on a story from the **Mahabharata**. The narrative concerns a king, who is in need of an heir to sustain his dynasty, meeting in the forest a woman named Shakuntala. They conceive a child but are separated, only to meet again after the birth of the son who becomes the king's heir. Kalidasa's genius is evident in the way he restructures the epic tale to highlight its dramatic possibilities, including new features, such as the king and Shakuntala being subject to a curse that he forget her, and a lost ring on which his recognition of her is dependent. The drama's seven acts reveal careful attention to plot. Act I is paralleled by Act VII: the king in his chariot arrives at a hermitage, the sage in charge is absent, and he meets Shakuntala (Act I) or their son (Act VII). Acts II and VI are mirror images: in Act II, the lovers make the hermitage's grove (usually a place of ascetic practice) into a pleasure garden, while in Act VI the lovers' separation makes the palace's pleasure garden into a penance grove for the king, a place of solitary asceticism. In Act III the king goes to Shakuntala in love and is accepted, while in Act V Shakuntala goes to the king and is rejected. The conflicts in the drama (nature vs. culture, forest vs. city, and love vs. duty) are resolved through the son, who represents the union of all these opposites.

One of the few references in a drama that might enable us to place Kalidasa in an historical context is in the prologue to Act I of *Malavika and Agnimitra*, where the title and author's name are mentioned. The assistant to the **director** (*sutradhara*) asks, "Why ignore works of celebrated poets like **Bhasa**, Saumilla, and Kaviputra to bestow honor on a modern writer?" Unfortunately, of these three predecessors only the first is known to us at all from works attributed to him, and even these are much in dispute; the other two are unknown to us and to the Indian tradition of literary **criticism**. Although one school places him in the first century BC, others persuasively argue that he lived in North India's Gupta Empire about 400 AD, a time of **political** and economic stability.

His dramas and poetry have been highly influential, not only in India but outside as well. For example, Goethe borrowed the device of an apparently informal and conversational prologue (such as he found in *Shakuntala*) to introduce *Faust*. The Sanskrit verses recited by major characters, most often the hero, are consistently brilliant in their use of poetic imagery, the images densely packed with meanings to highlight the emotional state of the character at that moment, and to facilitate for the audience the experience of one or another of the drama's emotional moods (*rasa*; see Theory).

FURTHER READING

Stoler Miller, Barbara, ed. *Theater of Memory: The Plays of Kalidasa.*

Bruce M. Sullivan

KALSUTRI BAHULYA. *See* Puppet Theatre: India.

KAMBAR, CHANDRASEKHAR B. (1938–). **Indian** Kannada-language **playwright**, folklorist, poet, scholar, novelist, composer, and **stage** and film **actor** and **director**. As a theatre artist, he belongs to the "theatre of roots" movement whose work synthesizes traditional material, including myths, folktales, and earlier drama, with antirealistic production methods in which the body is as potent as words in communicating ideas.

His traditional plays, some of which have been performed in English, reinterpret **folk** myths, while his social plays satirize society's vices. His short plays include the absurdist *Narcissus* (1971) and *Man with Spectacles* (Chalesha, 1975). He uses folk influences in *Rishyashringa* (1973) and *Jokumaraswami* (1972), the latter—his most popular play—relating issues of fertility and sexual potency to ownership of the land in an agricultural community. The leading character in *Shirt over Shirt* (Animyalangi, 1975) is a man who learns to prize his wife's morality over her physical unattractiveness, while *Victory to Sidanayaka* (Jai Sidanayaka, 1975) suggests that more than dreaming is needed to change current conditions. His other plays, most of them employing allegorical situations, include *Sangya and Balya* (Sangya-Balya, 1975), an adaptation of a play by Nilakanthappa Pattar; the **political** satire *Sacrificial Sheep*

(Harakeya kuri, 1983); *The Shadow of the Tiger* (Huliya neralu, 1984), combining folk theatre elements with symbolism; *Siri Sampige* (1986), which employs **yakshagana** style; and *Mahamayi* (2004), which confronts the difficulty of accepting death.

In addition to his eighteen plays, Kambar has produced numerous literary works, feature films, documentaries, and film scores. His positions include being chairman of the National School of Drama. He is the winner of the National Academy of Music, Dance, and Drama (Sangeet Natak Akademi) award (1983) and the prestigious Kalidasa Award (2002–2003).

Debjani Ray Moulik

KAN'AMI KIYOTSUGU (1333–1384). Japanese • **playwright** and **actor**, considered, with his son, **Zeami**, a cofounder of *nô*. Kan'ami was also the first patriarch of the troupe that evolved into the Kanze school (*ryû*). According to legend, his parents saved him from a premature death by naming him after the Bodhisattva Kannon and commending him to a temple in Nara, where he began his career as a *sarugaku* actor of the Yûzaki troupe working for **religious** institutions in Yamato Province. Kan'ami and his son performed in Kyoto for Shogun Ashikaga Yoshimitsu (1358–1408) in 1374 (or 1375); their success secured Kan'ami's leadership of the troupe and the shogun's patronage.

Kan'ami's contribution can be understood through his son's **theoretical** treatises. Zeami credited Kan'ami for the instructions contained in *Style and the Flower* (Fûshikaden, 1418), and he explained how Kan'ami modified the Kanze troupe's style, which had focused on "role playing" (*monomane*), to incorporate the "grace" (*yûgen*) associated with *nô* troupes in Ômi Province. Kan'ami introduced new elements to *nô*, including the **music** of *kusemai* **dance**, influencing *nô*'s music and **dramatic structure**, as in the climatic *kuse* dance found in most plays. *Lay Priest Jinen* (Jinen Koji), *Komachi and the Hundred Nights* (Kayoi Komachi), and *Komachi at the Gravesite* (Sotoba Komachi) are considered his greatest works, albeit reworked by Zeami and others. In Zeami's *Talks on Sarugaku* (Sarugaku Dangi, ca. 1430), he is described as a consummate performer whose style appealed to the elite and general public.

Eric C. Rath

KANESHITA TATSUO (1964–). Japanese • **playwright** and **director**. Launching THE Gajira Theatre Production Group (Engeki Kikaku Shûdan THE Gajira) in 1987 with *Once Upon a Time in Kyoto* (the title is in English, like those of several of his plays), about Japan's pre–Meiji Restoration (1868) civil war, Kaneshita reveals a career-long structural device: opposing groups fervently believing in their respective causes. Often historically grounded and war-related, his plays examine contemporary Japanese socio-**political** attitudes through intensely probing his characters' emotional lives; they can be trenchantly critical of the Japanese denial of World War II atrocities.

Perhaps his best play is *Ice Blossoms* (Kanka, 1997), about **Korean** nationalist An Chung-gun, who assassinated Itô Hirobumi (resident-general in Korea following the Russo-Japanese War [1904–1905] and advocate of Korea's annexation) in 1909. It juxtaposes the virtuous, patriotic An, awaiting execution, and the corrupt, bigoted Japanese who regard him as a terrorist. Complexity is added with the Japanese prison authorities—political outsiders—ironically having greater affinity to An, whom they treat well, than to the assassinated insider Itô.

Kaneshita's attempt to stimulate historical consciousness and political awareness underlies, among other war-related plays, *Kasutori Elegy* (1994), influenced by Steinbeck's *Of Mice and Men*, on two repatriated soldiers' dashed dreams; *Vector* (1994), on World War II bacteriological weapons; *PW-Prisoner of War* (1997), contrasting the experiences of two repatriated POWs who defied the army's injunction to die rather than be captured; and the Japanese-Korean bilingual *The Sortie* (Shutsugeki, 2002), again addressing Japan's Korea colonization to emphasize the futility of war and ongoing disputes over cultural origins and superiority.

John D. Swain

KANHAILAL, HEISNAM (1941–). Indian Manipuri-language **director** and **playwright**, born to a poor family in Imphal, Manipur. Active from childhood in school theatricals, his inclinations were furthered at college, where one of his teachers was Manipuri playwright-director Geet Chandra Tongbra (1913–1996), for whose Society Theatre he worked for three years. Later he started his own Students Artists' Association.

In 1968, Kanhailal enrolled at the National School of Drama in New Delhi, but the language barrier and his resistance to its formal **training** system led to his departure after six months. He returned to Imphal to set up the Kalakshetra Manipur Theatre (1969), an **experimental • theatre company** whose performances often expressed Manipuri **folk** culture. In 1973, he worked with director **Badal Sircar**, whose "Third Theatre" (Anganmancha, literally, "open-air theatre") ideas influenced Kanhailal's development of a ritualistic, nontext-oriented style reliant on expressive movement, borrowing from Manipur's extensive body culture, including the *thang-ta* martial arts system. His **training** of **actors** involves considerable use of improvisation during the rehearsal period.

Among the thirty or so productions of Kalakshetra—typically driven by socially concerned Manipuri themes—were Kanhailal's *Haunting Spirits* (Tamnalai, 1972), *Half Man, Half Tiger* (Kabui keoiba, 1973), *Imphal 73* (1974), and *The Thieves' Song* (Huranbagi eshei, 1977).

He and his wife, actress Heisnam Sabitry (1946–), developed an intimate collaboration; she starred in works such as his *Pebet* (1975), *Memoirs of Africa* (1985), and *Draupadi* (2000). *Pebet*, based on a folktale about a bird who recovers her children from the cat that has abducted them, was an allegory about Manipur's **political** and cultural colonization, but—despite its artistry—it raised controversy when it was condemned as anti-Indian and anti-Hindu. Kanhailal's job at the Theatre and Dramatics Section of the Information Department was threatened before cooler heads prevailed.

Kanhailal sometimes takes his socially committed drama to the people themselves. He got one hundred **women** vendors to appear in one play, while in another, *Cowherds* (Sanjennaha, 1979), villagers played all the parts. He traveled all over the country with his productions, also presenting them at **festivals** abroad. He considers himself more deeply committed to Indian theatre than Manipuri director **Ratan Thiyam**, who he believes is more concerned with artistic consumerism than the problems of local people.

Among Kanhailal's honors were a Jawaharlal Nehru Fellowship (1981) and a Ford Foundation grant (1987) that allowed him to do research on acting methods. He was one of the first from his region to receive the National Academy of **Music**, **Dance**, and Drama (Sangeet Natak Akademi) award. He also received the Padmashree (2004).

FURTHER READING

Bharucha, Rustom. *Theatre of Kanhailal.*

Shashikant Barhanpurkar

KANZE HISAO (1925–1978). Japanese • *nô* • **actor** and theorist, one of the greatest of the twentieth century, whose achievements include bold **experiments** in **Western** drama, and the popularization of **Zeami**'s theories. Hisao reached maturity in the postwar period, when there were few opportunities to perform but there were unprecedented chances to study with actors of other schools. He extended his nonsectarian approach to the study of Western theatre, including Stanislavski and Grotowski, and he acted in Japanese versions of *Waiting for Godot* and *Medea*.

But Hisao also looked deeply at *nô*'s roots, studying **Zeami**'s writings with prominent academics and writing prolifically to explain the salience of these ideas to others. Hisao sought to deepen his performances and to revive *nô*, which, he felt, had become too elitist. With this aim, in the 1950s and early 1960s, Hisao participated in **theatre** **companies** such as the Renaissance Group (Renessansu no Kai), the Flower Group (Hana no Kai)—named after Zeami's concept for the apex of an actor's performance—and the Zeami Troupe (Zeami za), which toured Europe in the 1970s.

Hisao's principles brought him into conflict with the government—he rejected being honored as an "Intangible Cultural Asset" in 1965—and he frequently criticized the *nô* hierarchy for stifling individual expression.

Eric C. Rath

KANZE KOJIRÔ NOBUMITSU (1435–1516). Japanese • *nô* • **actor**, playwright, and musician, seventh son of the Kanze troupe leader **Kanze Motoshige** (a.k.a. On'ami), and father of Kanze Yajirô Nagatoshi. In contrast to the custom of modern performers who specialize in a single **musical instrument**, Nobumitsu followed the practice of his era of playing both the shoulder drum (*kotsuzumi*) and hip drum (*ôtsuzumi*). Nobumitsu wrote at least one treatise on music, *On Using the Voice* (Koe tsukau koto, 1511), but his enduring fame is as a dramatist of twenty-four extant works; sources indicate he wrote seven more.

Nobumitsu's plays include *Benkei aboard Ship* (Funa Benkei), *Viewing the Autumn Foliage* (Momijigari), *Jewel Well* (Tama no i), *Rashômon*, and *Spirit at Yoshino* (Yoshino tenjin). In contrast to **Zeami**'s preference for the **theoretical** concept of "grace" (*yûgen*), Nobumitsu favored exciting spectacle, which he created by using large casts, sizable **properties**, and action, a style continued by his son, Kanze Nagatoshi. In *Surrounded by a Bell* (Kane maki)—and the *nô* it later inspired called *Dôjô-ji Temple* (Dôjô-ji)—an actor disappears, usually by leaping, into a huge bell as it is lowered onto the **stage**. Given these qualities, many of Nobumitsu's works were later adopted for *kabuki*, among them *Ataka*, the inspiration for *The Subscription List* (Kanjinchô, 1840). Still, Nobumitsu's plays continue to excite audiences in their own right.

Eric C. Rath

KANZE MOTOMASA (CA. 1400?–1432). Japanese * *nô* * actor and playwright, son of **Zeami**, who succeeded to the leadership of the Kanze troupe when his father retired in 1422. Motomasa's career flourished until 1429, when his cousin, **Kanze Motoshige** (a.k.a. On'ami), who had earlier created a rival Kanze troupe, won the backing of the new shogun, Ashikaga Yoshinori (1394–1441). Under pressure from Yoshinori, Motomasa fled to the provinces, dying under mysterious circumstances in Ise. Motomasa's death caused Zeami to lament in *Flower of Returning* (Kyakuraika) that his art and troupe were destroyed. Some scholars conjecture that Motomasa and Zeami held **political** loyalties and perhaps familial connections rival to the Ashikaga shoguns, which may explain their persecution, but these **theories** are unproven.

As *Flower of Returning* further indicates, Zeami considered Motomasa his rightful heir and, up to Motomasa's death, Zeami probably wrote his theoretical works with him in mind. However, later apologists recognized Motomasa, whom they called Jûrô, as a minor playwright while omitting him from the genealogy of Kanze leaders. This affirmed On'ami's succession to Zeami's legacy, which was important because On'ami's descendants became the hereditary leaders of the Kanze school (*ryû*). According to tradition, Motomasa's descendants and followers formed the Ochi Kanze troupe, which preserved Motomasa's art and Zeami's treatises until these writings were rediscovered by the main Kanze line in the mid-1500s. The publication of Zeami's treatises in 1909, which referenced Motomasa, restored his place in *nô* history.

In *One Page on the Remains of a Dream* (Museki isshi), Zeami comments that Motomasa's playwriting skill exceeded Zeami's father, **Kan'ami**. Motomasa's plays include *Morihisa*, *Soothsayer* (Uta'ura), *Stumbling Priest* (Yoroboshi), and *Mount Yoshino* (Yoshinosan). His masterpiece, *Sumida River* (Sumidagawa), about the search of a mother for her kidnapped son, inspired later *kabuki* and *bunraku* (see Puppet Theatre) plays, as well as Britten's 1964 opera *Curlew River*. He is the likely author of other plays: the warrior (*shura*) plays *Tomonaga* and *Shigehira* are among strong candidates.

Eric C. Rath

KANZE MOTOSHIGE (ON'AMI) (1398–1467). Japanese * *nô* * actor, leader of the Kanze troupe from 1433 to his death. On'ami occupies a controversial place in *nô* history in view of his relationship with his uncle **Zeami**. Modern historical research has revealed that Zeami hoped to pass on the Kanze mantle to his son, **Kanze Motomasa**, although he may previously have adopted On'ami. Even before Motomasa's death, On'ami established a rival Kanze troupe that benefited from the patronage of the shogun, Ashikaga Yoshinori (1394–1441), at the expense of Motomasa and Zeami. The shogun's persecution ultimately drove Motomasa to flee into the provinces with the school's secret artistic writings and may have caused Zeami's exile to Sado Island. Yet, later Kanze school (*ryû*) apologists ignored Motomasa to recognize On'ami as the third Kanze troupe leader and Zeami's rightful heir.

On'ami established a close association with Yoshinori, laying a foundation for later shoguns to patronize the Kanze. He is also credited with gaining for his troupe the right to perform large benefit (*kanjin*) *nô* that charged admission for several days of performances, ostensibly for charity. On'ami organized two benefit performances at Tadasugawa in Kyoto in 1433 and 1464; they featured a circular *nô* **stage** surrounded by a covered viewing stand. At the 1464 performance, On'ami acted the primary role in twelve of the twenty-nine plays over three days, a remarkable feat considering his age. Although some apocryphal texts were ascribed to him, On'ami left behind neither plays nor **theoretical** writings.

Eric C. Rath

KAPOOR, PRITHVIRAJ (1906–1972). **Indian** Hindi-language film and **stage •** **actor**, **playwright**, **director**, and founder of a line of outstanding actors. Born in Lylall-pur, Peshawar, now in Pakistan, the son of a police officer, his theatrical aspirations bloomed while he was at Edward College; in 1928, after briefly studying law, and married with three children, he left to seek a film career in Bombay (Mumbai). His first starring role came in the silent film, *Cinema Girl* (1930), and he soon acted in talkies.

In 1932, he joined the Grant Anderson Theater company, which toured India performing Shakespeare in English. From 1933, he gradually became a popular Bollywood star. However, Kapoor remained theatrically involved and, in 1944, set up the renowned Prithvi **Theatres**, the first urban, professional Hindustani **theatre company**, which became the foundation of modern realistic Hindi theatre.

For sixteen years, Kapoor took this company exceeding 150 members all over India, staging eight plays under its banner, starring in all, and racking up 2,662 performances. His film earnings supported the troupe when profits sank. Major productions were *Shakuntala* (1945), *Wall* (Diwar, 1945), *Pathan* (1947), *Traitor* (Gaddar, 1948), *Artist* (Kalakar, 1952), and *Money* (Paisa, 1954). Many of his plays and films dealt with the wrenching issue of Partition (1947). *Wall* inspired death threats from opponents of his ideas.

Kapoor was very tall, powerfully built, gifted with a dominating, sonorous voice, strikingly handsome, and brilliantly able to cut to the heart of his characters. His work schedule took its toll, and, in 1960, his voice ruined, he had to give up theatre, although he worked in films until 1969.

Known for his humanitarianism and patriotism, Kapoor was awarded the first National Academy of **Music**, **Dance**, and Drama (Sangeet Natak Akademi) award (1956). Among other honors were the Padma Bhushan (1969), and the Dadasaheb Phalke award (1972), given posthumously.

Shashikant Barhanpurkar

KAPUR, ANURADHA (1951–). **Indian •** **director**, professor at the University of Delhi, and author of a major book on *ramlila*, who often employs video and film in her work, and who directs feminist-oriented street theatre. After completing her doctorate at Leeds University in England, she returned to India where she taught at the National School of Drama.

One of her primary directorial concerns is addressing the challenges of the modern world. Kapur collaborates with artists from different media—visual, literary, and musical—and, using bold visual and **scenographic** elements, voices socially and **politically** relevant themes.

A specialist in **Western** drama, her productions include works such as *Ala Afsur* (1989), *The Job* (1997), *Umrao* (1993), *Romeo and Juliet* (1995), an adaptation of Ibsen's *The Wild Duck* (1999), and *The Story Is Not for Telling* (1985). *Sundari* (1998), based on the autobiography of female impersonator **Jaishankar Sundari**, concerns his preparation for his final performance. Toured to London and Berlin, this work establishes a dialectical relationship between the format of a play-within-a-play and its thematic content. *The Antigone Project* (2003), a collaboration co-directed by Ein Lall (1948–), is based on Brecht's version of Sophocles' *Antigone*, and combined video and theatre. It focuses attention on the consequences of dogma and the genealogy of tyrants, the testimonies of survivors, and the questions that arise.

Kapur is a National Academy of Music, **Dance**, and Drama (Sangeet Natak Akademi) award winner.

Debjani Ray Moulik

KARA JŪRŌ (1940–). Japanese • *angura* • **playwright**, **director**, and **theorist**, a classic liminal figure, uncomfortable with established theatre forms. He rejected those aspects of traditional Japanese theatre that, he felt, perpetuated Japan's militaristic past and the standard practices of *shingeki*.

In 1963, Kara founded the Situation Group (Shichueishon no Kai), which became the Situation Theatre (Jôkyô Gekijô), and, in 1967, began using his signature Red Tent (Aka Tento) to escape the boundaries of conventional theatrical space. By placing the tent next to a body of water, for example, the wall could open onto a literal and theatrical "sea." His company's performances in public spaces, like the grounds of Shinto shrines or vacant lots, at once echoed Japanese **actors'** pre-modern **religious** functions and their earlier outcast status as "riverbed beggars" (*kawara kojiki*) and implied **criticism** of nationalistic Shinto and the emperor system as manifested in World War II. He appropriated *kabuki* elements, such as the runway (*hanamichi*) and cross-gender performance, to create audience intimacy and revive a sense of theatrical play, with the actor's body as the "privileged" theatrical tool.

The Situation Theatre, like many of Kara's characters, was nomadic, touring throughout Japan, and, in the 1970s, Europe and the Middle East. His characters, too, often wander in search of identity. In *The Virgin's Mask* (Shôjo kamen, 1969), which won the **Kishida [Kunio]** Prize (1970), characters are "beggars for a body." Set in an underground coffee shop named "The Body," the play confronts Japan's wartime actions and contemporary tendencies to bury historical memories. Former **Takarazuka** star Kasugano Yachiyo runs "The Body"; she attempts unsuccessfully to preserve her own diminished body by bathing in virgins' tears. Yet, she can no more escape, or cleanse, her body than can Japan its past. In *John Silver, the Beggar of Love* (Jon Shirubaa, ai no kojiki, 1970), the characters want physical love and meaningful social existence. They search for their past, a messianic replacement for the emperor, and lost wartime identities that seem to promise fulfillment. In *The Vampire Princess* (Kyûketsuki, 1971), aborted babies, and in *Matasaburô of the Winds: Kara Version* (Kara-ban kaze no Matasaburô, 1974), **puppet**-like fighter pilots represent the past. Blood features prominently in Kara's plays and generally represents an inescapable cultural and **political** heritage.

Kara articulated his theories in *The Privileged Body Theory* (Tokkenteki nikutairon, 1997). He "privileged" the body over words, convinced that logocentric theatre stifled full expression and, in *shingeki*, creation of a forthright theatrical form. Although his theatre centers on physicality, Kara's language has a rhythmic quality that reflects the cadences of *kabuki* chant, and ideas are articulated clearly.

Kara has also created plays for other troupes. In 1979, the **theatre company** Seventh Sick Ward (Dainana Byôtô) produced Kara's *Two Women* (Futari no onna), a play dealing with Japan's loss of traditional cultural anchors. The Situation Theatre disbanded in 1987, but Kara continued producing Red Tent performances with a new troupe, Kara Group (Karagumi).

John D. Swain

KARANTH, BABUKODI VENKATARAMANA (1928–2002).

Indian Kannada-language **director** of **stage** and screen, composer, choreographer, translator-adapter of plays, administrator, and **acting** teacher, born in Dakshin Kannad District, Karnataka. He debuted as an actor at seven, joined **Gubbi Veeranna**'s famous **theatre company** in 1944, and later received an MA in Hindi. He studied Hindustani **music** and subsequently entered the National School of Drama, New Delhi. Between 1969 and 1972, he was a schoolteacher.

Karanth became extremely active in Karnataka's theatre, gaining fame for the incorporation of different music traditions into his directorial ventures (he was the leading theatre composer of his time) and for inaugurating a nonverbal style in which a play could be interpreted through a language of music, rhythm, sound, and movement to create visual and aural feelings. To him, the actor's rhythmic movement was a principal imperative. His staging of a **festival** of plays in Bangalore in 1972 gained acclaim.

Karanth allowed his actors to enjoy their own performances, revealing the act of acting as they did so. He participated in the "theatre of roots" (*tanatu natakavedi*) movement, and—especially in his brilliant productions of **Girish Karnad**'s *Horse-Head* (Hayavadana, 1972, 1973)—**experimented** with a new idiom inspired by Karnataka's *yakshagana* with the goal of replacing **Western** conventions. He also used *yakshagana* in *Macbeth* (1979), but, whereas this genre's conventions had been introduced into Karnad's original text, they were imposed on Shakespeare by the director, a method (using other indigenous forms) also employed by certain other Indian directors.

Karanth's nearly one hundred productions, in both Hindi and Kannada, include *And Indrajit* (Evam Indrajit, 1969), *Jokumaraswami* (1972), *Samkranti* (1972), *Shadow of the Dead* (Sattavata neralu, 1975), *Birnam Wood* (Barnam ban, based on *Macbeth*, 1979), *Departure from Gokula* (Gokula nirgamana, 1993), and *The Little Clay Cart* (Mitti ki gadi, 2001). He had a very wide range and embraced plays from all periods of Indian and non-Indian drama; he was even devoted to children's plays.

Unlike many Indian directors, he avoided being identified with any specific group, and worked with many, in numerous Indian languages as well as English. He was the director of the National School of Drama (1977–1981), director of Rangamandal in Bhopal (1982–1986), and director of Rangayana, the state-run theatre in Mysore (1989–1995).

B. Ananthakrishnan

KARNAD, GIRISH RAGHUNATH (1938–). **Indian** Kannada-, Hindi-, and English-language **playwright**, **critic**, **actor**, translator, television and film **director**, and cultural administrator, born at Mathern, near Bombay (Mumbai), but based mainly in Karnataka. He studied at Oxford as a Rhodes scholar from 1960 to 1963. His love for theatre developed early in his life when he watched the **Parsi theatre**, *yakshagana*, and naturalistic **Western** plays. Though his childhood dream was to write English poetry, he found his vocation in theatre upon returning to India, becoming involved with the English-language Madras Players.

Karnad, greatly influenced by Camus, Beckett, Brecht, Pinter, Sartre, and Shakespeare, wrote his first play, *Yayati*, in 1961. Inspired by the ***Mahabharata***, it was a self-consciously existentialist drama on the theme of responsibility; Yayati's son, Puru, allows himself to take on the curse of old age aimed at Yayati by an angry sage. Karnad's best-loved play, *Tughlaq* (1964), is a compelling allegory on the era of Prime Minister Jawaharlal Nehru (1889–1964), inspired by Camus's *Caligula*; Tughlaq is a fourteenth-century Islamic ruler whose attempt to rule his Hindu people humanely leads to tragedy. *Horse-Head* (Hayavadana, 1972), deriving its plot from a twelfth-century **Sanskrit** folktale adapted by Thomas Mann as *The Transposed Heads*, poses the problem of human identity in a world of tangled relationships. When Padmini's husband and his friend each behead themselves, a goddess permits her to bring them back to life by rejoining their heads to their bodies. She accidentally attaches the wrong heads to the wrong bodies, creating tragic complications. His other plays include *Frightened Jasmine* (Anjumallige, 1977), reminiscent of Albee's *Who's Afraid of Virginia Woolf?*; *The Dough Rooster* (Hittina hunja, 1980); *Play with a Cobra* (Naga-mandala, 1988), a sexually charged tale about a woman's infatuation with a cobra passing itself off as her husband (it premiered in Chicago, and was also produced at Minneapolis's Guthrie Theatre in 1993); *Death by Beheading* (Talé-danda, 1989), about a twelfth-century poet and mystic and the elimination of an anticaste movement; and *The Fire and the Rain* (Agni mattu male, 1994), drawn from the *Mahabharata*.

Although he translates his plays into English, in 1997 Karnad wrote his first English play, *The Dreams of Tipu Sultan*, set in 1799 and treating themes of liberty and colonial oppression. He draws inspiration from folklore, mythology, and history, and seeks to fuse Western with **Sanskrit** and **folk** elements in his dramaturgy. His plays, many of them staged by **Babukodi Venkataramana Karanth**, typically allegorize themes of contemporary relevance.

Karnad was involved with many thoughtful Kannada films, and served as the director of the Film and Television Institute of India; he also chaired the National Academy of **Music**, **Dance**, and Drama (Sangeet Natak Akademi), and later directed the Nehru Centre in London. His numerous awards include the Jnanapith Award (1999), the Kalidasa Samman (1999), and the Padma Bhushan (1992).

Debjani Ray Moulik

KARYALA. **Indian** improvisatory **folk theatre** of the lower regions of Himachal Pradesh, performed around October, at the time of the Dussehra **festival**, and considered a form of thanksgiving. Also spelled *kariyala* and *karayila* (and known as *kadada*, *karala*, *karyara*, and so on), its origins (ca. eleventh through seventeenth centuries)—and the meaning of the term—are obscure.

Performance Circumstances. Most *karyala* performances, which are all-night affairs, take place around the time of important **religious** festivals, although performances can be given at any time; troupes move from village to village and are sponsored by people who are celebrating a wedding or have asked the gods for a wish and have promised the performance in return. The troupe receives cash, food, and lodging for its services. There may even be performances given just for their own sake, because it is believed the gods will be angry if *karyala* is ignored. The god most closely associated with *karyala* is Biju. The number of days given over to invited performances differs for each occasion, although traditionally it required sixteen consecutive nights.

The troupes of fifteen to twenty *karyalchis* contain only men of a specific caste. Reasons offered for the lack of **women** include their being exposed to immoral temptation, their being unsuited to speaking the vulgar language used to make evil spirits disappear, their lack of the stamina required to endure the vigorous, all-night shows, and their inability to project their voices to the far reaches of the crowd.

Performances used to be by torches on two sides of the acting space, but electric lights or petromax lanterns have taken their place. The venue is typically an open, outdoor space approximately 120 feet by 150 feet, with three and a half foot posts set up around the perimeter to demarcate the "sacred" enclosure (*khada* or *akhada*). A fire burns at the center. An old hut nearby may serve as a dressing room. Spectators sit around the perimeter, some on roofs and tree branches; they may also change places. Sometimes microphones are available.

Programs. The sequence of scenes may vary from troupe to troupe. A typical program begins with preliminary drumming followed by the "**Dance** of Chandravali" (Chandravali nritya), a ritualistic piece featuring a "female" dancer (Chandravali) who consecrates the space and **musical instruments**. Performed on behalf of goddess Saraswati, it is said to have been required ever since a beautiful princess named Chandresh Kumari got her princely abductor to vow that it would be performed before each *karyali* presentation. This is usually followed by "hermits" (Sadhu), in which comically dressed and bearded hermits—several saintly ones and a clown—engage in comic, often obscene, banter.

The rest of the performance brings on a series of witty, farcical, and satirical scenes (*swangs*), without a connected story, in which an assortment of rustics appear in a sequence of sketches derived from an orally transmitted repertory of fifteen traditional and several new pieces. Tragic stories, once included, have given way to comedy, which some bemoan. **Masks**, too, once were used, but have been abandoned. The show ends with ritual observances, among which may be the sacrifice of a goat by the sponsor.

Acting, Costumes, and Dance. The **actors** improvise (using rhyming couplets, double entendre, and local proverbs) and employ various comedic strategies, including physical buffoonery. The language—Pahari, Urdu, Hindi, or Punjabi, with some English thrown in—is crude and ungrammatical, but much loved. For example, a peasant takes advantage of his British employer's inadequate Hindi to pun on the meaning of *maila*, which can mean "festival" or "menstruation." Considerable interchange between audience and actors transpires, the topics being as diverse as religion, local customs, sex, education, and **politics**, always in a good-humored way. Still, *karyala* is considered a valid way of bringing complaints to the attention of officialdom. Some dance is used, but this is mainly a spoken genre, the funnier the speech the better.

Costumes are a mélange of traditional and modern, false beards and wigs are worn for some roles, and Englishmen (*sahib*)—a definite object of satire—appear in contemporary garments, the men with pith helmets, perhaps wielding canes, parasols, pipes, and cigarettes.

Dance and **music** are becoming more common, which some believe belies *karyala's* function as a dialogue genre. Song and dance are especially important in the interludes between scenes. Music is drawn from local folk songs, and played on drums (*dhol* and *nagara*), wind instruments (such as the S-shaped *ransinga*, the *karnal*, *nagara*, and double-reed *shehnai*), and the harmonium. Movie songs and dances have been introduced as well. *Karyala* is an endangered form needing internal rejuvenation and external support.

FURTHER READING

Ahluwalia, Kailash. *Karyala: An Impromptu Theatre of Himachal Pradesh.*

Samuel L. Leiter

KATAOKA NIZAEMON. Fifteen generations of **Japanese** • *kabuki* • **actors** famous for their Osaka-style artistry. The family "house name" (*yagô*) is Matsushimaya. The Nizaemon family began as "villain" (*katakiyaku*) **role type** specialists and later achieved recognition in acting the "gentle style" (*wagoto*) and "romantic young men" (*nimaime*). Nizaemon III, V, and VI never officially took the name and held it in trust only. The most significant members of the line are Nizaemon I, IV, VII, VIII, X, XI, XII, XIII, XIV, and XV.

Nizaemon I (1656–1715), originally a *shamisen* **musician**, studied under "leading man" (*tachiyaku*) Yamashita Hanzaemon (1650/52–1717), and became the most popular *katakiyaku* in Kamigata (Osaka-Kyoto area) during the Genroku (1688–1704) era. He was also the actor-manager of his own **theatre company**.

Nizaemon IV, son of an Osaka dry goods dealer, began by playing female roles (*onnagata*) and later became famous for villains. He stopped acting from 1740 to 1755 to work as a **playwright** under the pen name Katsukawa Sakiku.

Nizaemon VII (1755–1837) began in children's plays (*kodomo shibai*). In 1787, he revived the dormant Nizaemon name, being only the fourth to officially hold it. Known for his versatility, he became a high-ranking star in Osaka, Kyoto, Edo (Tokyo), and Nagoya.

Nizaemon VIII (1810–1863) was the adopted son of **Ichikawa Danjûrô** VII. After a dispute with Danjûrô VII, Nizaemon VII adopted him. Skilled in *wagoto*, *onnagata*, and *katakiyaku*, he was awarded the Nizaemon name in 1857.

Nizaemon X (1851–1895), son of Nizaemon VIII, gained fame in Tokyo as well as Osaka, and took the name in 1895. An expert at *wagoto*, *katakiyaku*, and *onnagata*, he went insane and died after his close relatives refused to participate in his name-taking ceremony.

Nizaemon XI (1857–1934), son of Nizaemon VIII, settled in Tokyo, although he became Nizaemon in Osaka in 1907. Like others in the line, he preserved Osaka *wagoto*, but also excelled at *onnagata*. He was especially admired as old men in classical *kabuki* and *shin kabuki*.

Nizaemon XII (1882–1946), son of Nizaemon X, was an *onnagata* and partnered with the romantic leading man **Ichimura Uzaemon** XV in Tokyo and Osaka. He established the family canon of acting roles, the "Kataoka Twelve Collection" (Kataoka Jûnishû).

Nizaemon XIII (1903–1994), son of Nizaemon XI, was a Living National Treasure. He worked to safeguard Osaka/Kyoto *kabuki* after World War II by founding two companies. Nizaemon XIII performed into his nineties. He wrote several books about his life and was the subject of a seven-hour documentary film.

Nizaemon XIV (1910–1993), a son of Nizaemon XII, was best known as Kataoka Gadô V. He received the name posthumously.

Nizaemon XV (1944–), a son of Nizaemon XIII, gained fame as a handsome leading man named Kataoka Takao; he succeeded to Nizaemon in 1997. In his thirties, he was memorably paired with *onnagata* **Bandô Tamasaburô** V. An outstanding *wagoto* specialist, Nizaemon XV is considered by some the most talented *tachiyaku* of his generation.

Holly A. Blumner

KATHAKALI. **Indian** • **dance**-drama that emerged in Kerala in the late sixteenth and early seventeenth centuries. Under the patronage of regional rulers, *kathakali* (literally, "story play") was created from a confluence of arts, including ***kalarippayattu***, the martial art whose Nayar practitioners provided the first **actor**-dancers, ***kutiyattam***, ***krishnattam***, and ritual performances, such as ***teyyam***.

Performance Circumstances. A highly physical dance-drama staging stories written in Sanskritized Malayalam and based on the ***Ramayana***, ***Mahabharata***, and the Puranas, *kathakali* is performed on a bare **stage**, with only stools and occasional **properties**, by three groups of performers: actor-dancers, percussionists, and vocalists. With a few exceptions, its all-male **theatre companies** use a highly physicalized performance style embodied through years of intensive **training** to play kings, heroines, demons, demonesses, gods, animals, priests, and some characters drawn from everyday life. Each character is easily identifiable as a particular **role type**. Roles are created by using a repertory of dance steps, choreography, a complex language of gestures (*hastas*) for "speaking" dialogue with the hands, and a pliable use of the face and eyes to express the internal states (*bhava*) of the character (see Theory).

Music is provided by a percussion orchestra including three drums, each with its own distinctive sounds, and brass cymbals, which keep the basic rhythmic cycles around which the dance-drama is structured. Two onstage vocalists keep the basic time patterns on cymbals and sing the text, including both third-person narration and first-person dialogue, in an elaborate, repetitious vocal style.

Kathakali, whose earliest presentations were outdoors within the compounds of family houses or just outside temple walls, takes place in a rectangular space measuring approximately twenty to thirty square feet, or about four to five feet in width and five to six feet in length. Poles are erected at each corner of the rectangle, and cloths are spread over and behind the poles to create a defined acting area. The audience gathers on three sides, with the largest concentration in front; **women** sit to the left, and men to the right, with a passageway separating them and allowing characters such as demons or demonesses to enter. Patrons, guests of honor, and connoisseurs sit closest to the stage. Around the outer perimeter vendors set up tea or food stalls.

City and town performances sponsored by cultural organizations are usually performed in multipurpose proscenium **theatres**, such as the Sri Kartika Tirunal Theatre, Thiruvananthapuram. The playing space is larger than the traditional outdoor one, but the raised stage and fixed seating eliminate *kathakali*'s time-honored audience-actor intimacy.

One venue especially designed to preserve such intimacy is the Kuttampalam Theatre at the Kerala State Arts School (Kerala Kalamandalam). This graceful and unique playhouse combines design instructions in the *Treatise on Drama* (Natyashastra) with elements of Kerala's unique temple architecture.

Before electricity was available, performances were held outdoors all night, lit by a very large oil lamp (*kalivilakku*) downstage center. With its multiple, flickering wicks, the lamp emits a yellow-hued light that dances across actors' faces and hands, casting shadows. In the past, the actor-dancers concentrated their acting and dancing near this lamp. The focus was on faces and hands, because little light fell on feet and legs. Today's performances are lit with neon tubes and/or large electric lights. The lamp remains at center for the ritual inauguration of the performance and to sanctify the space (see Religion in Theatre); however, the general illumination keeps both musicians and actor-dancers constantly lit.

Performances—announced by an opening drum call (*keli*)—traditionally begin at dusk with a series of preliminaries. Formerly, the preliminaries required two to three hours, and all-night performances would not begin until approximately 10:00 p.m. Performances end at dawn with a dance and singing of devotional verses.

Costumes, Makeup, and Role Types. *Kathakali*'s highly colorful **costumes** and **makeup** are part of the process that "transforms" the actor into a wide variety of idealized and archetypal role types, each individualized by the specific context, as well as the choices made by individual actors. Costumes and makeup have evolved from several sources, especially *kutiyattam*. From each actor's first entrance, knowledgeable audiences know what character type and behavior to expect. For example, "green" makeup (*pacca*) is used for divine figures like Krishna or Vishnu, kings such as Rugmamgada, or "good" epic heroes, such as Bhima, Rama, or Dharmaputra (Yudhisthira). They are the most refined male characters, being upright, moral, and ideally full of a calm inner poise—"royal sages" modeled on the heroes of **Sanskrit theatre** whose task as warrior caste (*kshatriya*) members is to uphold sacred law. For this type a white, beard-like outer-frame (*cutti*) sets off the green base, reflecting this type's inner refinement. The stylized mark of Vishnu is painted on the forehead with a yellow base and markings of red and black. The soft curving black of the eyebrows and black underlining of the lower lids extend to the side of the face, framing the eyes. The lips are brilliant coral red.

The most characteristic outer garment colors are the upper red and lower white shirt, with orange and black stripes. Two side panels accentuate the red motif for the lower body. Below the skirt the actor-dancer wears a set of bells strapped to each leg just below the knee, and heavily starched underskirts giving today's characters their "bulbous" shape. The majority of such characters wear the highly jeweled medium-size crown (*kiritam*).

A second, contrasting example is the "black" (*kari*) makeup used for demonesses, such as Simhika in *The Killing of Kirmira* (Kirmiravadham). Demonesses are dressed in black, wear a bucket-shaped headdress, and also have oversized comic false breasts. Their jet-black faces are offset by patches of red, outlined in white rice-paste, with the addition of dotted patterns of white rice-paste suggesting the makeup of the village

In the *kathakali* play, *The Killing of Kirmira* by Kottayam Tampuran (ca. 1645–1716), Sahadeva (right) intercepts the demoness Simhika (center) as she attempts to take away Panchali (on stool, left). (Photo: Phillip Zarrilli)

goddess, Bhagavati, traditionally associated with smallpox and its alleviation. The demonesses are shape-changers capable of transforming themselves into beautiful maidens in order to deceive and trick. They are often considered the most grotesque characters.

The makeup and costuming process is lengthy, and takes two to four hours depending on the complexity involved. Specialists apply the rice-paste patterns layer by layer, and the actors complete their own makeup by filling in the necessary colors. Assistants help the actors dress and wrap the yards of starched undercloth that give many of the characters their bulbous shape.

Actors and Training. Most agree that *kathakali* actors usually do not reach artistic maturity until about forty. The path to maturity is long and arduous, and used to begin at seven or eight. Today's students may begin training at ten or older, but formal instruction still lasts six to ten years, and the years immediately following are spent playing smaller roles as apprentices.

To become an actor in demand means undergoing a gradual, long-term process of (re)shaping the body-mind, perfecting basic techniques, growing and maturing personally, studying and reflecting, developing the imagination, and integrating these things into shaping and playing characters. The process begins with pre-performative training in which the body undergoes intensive psycho-physical training in yoga and martial-arts based exercises, complete full-body massage, and meticulous isolation exercises for eyes and facial muscles, rendering the entire body flexible, balanced, and controlled. For example, for control of the eyes, a series of exercises involves moving them up and down, side to side, diagonally, and in circles. These patterns are performed at three different speeds, with the forefinger and thumb holding the eyelids and eyelashes open. In addition, the student learns all the rhythmic and footwork patterns, as well as the "set" pieces of choreography. Eventually, he begins to learn simple roles where all his technical knowledge coalesces in performing the text. The subtleties of acting's "internal" side (*sattvika abhinaya*) take longest to develop as actors specialize in role types, each bearing the stamp of a particular actor's virtuosity.

Texts. *Kathakali* texts consist of third-person metrical verses (*slokas*), often in Sanskrit, that narrate what happens in the ensuing dialogue or soliloquy sections. Songs (*padams*) are composed in the first person in a mixture of Sanskrit and Malayalam, and interpreted onstage by the actor-dancers. *Slokas* and *padams* are also set in specific rhythmic patterns (*tala*) and tempos (*kala*). Successive generations have modified *kathakali* texts by handing down techniques and performance styles for specific plays.

In keeping with the theory of *rasa*, which encourages elaboration of all performative modes to enhance aesthetic pleasure, performative interpolations (*ilakiyattam*) are added. Lasting up to an hour, the best known are opportunities for senior performers to display one or more aspects of their virtuosic abilities, such as the choreographic *tour de force* of Arjuna's interpolation in *The Killing of Kalakeya* (Kalakeya vadham) in which he describes the sights of the heavenly abode, Devaloka, or the histrionic display of inner turmoil demanded of Nala in *King Nala's Law* (Nala caritam), when he enacts his decision to leave his beloved Damayanti to the wild forest's mercy.

One of the most popular emotional displays is that of King Rugmamgada in *King Rugmamgada's Law* (Rugmamgada caritam). As demanded by the enchantress, Mohini, in a divine "test" of his devotion to Vishnu, Rugmamgada must cut off his only son's head. At the highpoint of his dilemma, the actor psycho-physically embodies three emotional states in sequence—his "anger" at Mohini for requiring him to cut off his son's head, the "heroic" state represented by the sword with which he must cut off his son's head, and "pathos" over the impending death of his son and heir. What distinguishes such interpolations from the literary text is that they are not sung, but simply enacted without repetition, through action and hand gestures.

Modern Developments. Many plays still performed have been shortened to three- to four-hour performances. It is commonplace for an all-night performance to include three shortened plays focusing on scenes of most interest to connoisseurs. Since 1930, when the Malayali poet Mahakavi Vallathol Narayana Menon (1878–1958) founded the Kerala State Arts School, *kathakali* has been adapted both by practitioners from within the tradition and by artists and entrepreneurs from without. These **experiments** have included *kathakali* for tourists, writing and staging new plays based on epic and Puranic sources, transforming techniques into modern forms of stage dance and/or dance-drama, and writing and staging new plays based on nontraditional sources and/or current events. An example of the latter was the 1987 leftist production of *People's Victory* (Manavavijiyam), which pitted World Conscience against Imperialism. Non-Hindu myths or non-Indian plays have also been adapted for *kathakali*-style productions, such as the stories of Mary Magdalene, the Buddha, and Faust, as well as *The Iliad* and *King Lear*.

FURTHER READING

Iyer, K. Bharata. *Kathakali;* Pandeya, Avinash C. *Art of Kathakali*; Zarrilli, Phillip B. *Kathakali Dance-Drama: Where Gods and Demons Come to Play.*

Phillip B. Zarrilli

KATHPUTLI. See Puppet Theatre: India.

KATÔ MICHIO (1918–1953). Japanese • **playwright**. Deeply inspired by French theatre, especially the plays of Giraudoux and Anouilh, Katô joined **Kishida Kunio**'s Literary Theatre (Bungaku-za) in 1949. His major themes include the inability or failure to communicate in modern society, rendered through dichotomies between an idealized past and the postwar present and between dream and reality. He completed the one-act "Episode" (Sôwa) in 1948, followed by over a dozen plays, including his best, *Nayotake* (1951); his last, *The Man Who Sells Dreams* (Omoide o uru otoko, 1953), was completed several months before his suicide.

Katô's dramatic milieu spans the gamut from gritty realism to poetic fantasy. "Episode" presents a division commander's memories of killing several South Pacific islanders; mad with guilt, he remains on the island after the war to pray for forgiveness. It is among the first plays to deal with Japanese wartime atrocities.

Named after its otherworldly heroine, *Nayotake*, a popular folktale play (*minwa geki*) performed as *kabuki* (1951) and as *shingeki* (1955), is among the best early postwar dramas. Based on *The Tale of the Bamboo Cutter* (Taketori monogatari), the play concerns the love and longing of a young man for the unattainable Nayotake. Like his friend **Kinoshita Junji**, Katô sought to revitalize premodern Japanese culture by dramatizing folktales and classical stories for modern audiences. Their efforts were the forerunners of *angura*.

Katô's work and ideals inspired **Asari Keita** to found the Four Seasons Company (Gekidan Shiki) in 1953.

Kevin J. Wetmore, Jr.

KATTAIKKUTTU. See Terukkuttu.

KAVIGAN. See Bangladesh.

KAWAKAMI OTOJIRÔ (1864–1911). Japanese • **director, actor, playwright**, impresario, and politician. Failing at **politics**, Kawakami became known for performing the satirical song "Oppekepe" (a nonsense word) and acting in agitprop "hooligan plays" (*sôshi shibai*). With his **actress**-spouse **Kawakami Sadayakko** he spearheaded *shinpa* from 1891 to 1911. His documentary dramas of the Sino-Japanese War (1894–1895) were so successful that even *kabuki* imitated them. He opened his Kawakami **Theatre** (Kawakami-za) in 1896 but had to sell it six months later to settle debts, a characteristic of his flamboyant life. Subsequently, his became the first Japanese **theatre company** to travel to the West, touring Europe and America in 1899–1901, 1901–1902, and 1907–1908, and performing on Broadway and at the Paris Exposition. Returning to Japan, his troupe presented what Kawakami called "True Theatre" (*seigeki*), primarily adaptations of *Hamlet*, *Othello*, and *The Merchant of Venice*. He also opened Japan's first actresses's school and yet another playhouse, Osaka's **Western**-style Imperial Theatre (Teikoku-za, 1910).

A shrewd self-promoter lacking theatrical **training**, Kawakami shamelessly pandered to audiences' tastes for novelty. His contemporaries referred to him pejoratively as the "Osaka clown" (*ôsaka niwaka*). Recent scholarship, however, has reassessed Kawakami as an intercultural pioneer who made numerous positive contributions, including putting actresses on **stage** and initiating theatrical exchanges with the West. He popularized both *shinpa* and Shakespeare but was ultimately eclipsed by the auras of his more talented wife and *shingeki*.

Kevin J. Wetmore, Jr.

KAWAKAMI SADAYAKKO (1872–1946). **Japan**'s first modern **actress**. **Trained** as a high-class *geisha*, Sadayakko (her geisha name) married rising *shinpa* star and pioneer **Kawakami Otojirô** in 1893. Her **political** connections—Prime Minister Itô Hirobumi had been a patron—ensured backing for Otojirô's schemes in the 1890s, including visiting France in 1893 and building the state-of-the-art Kawakami **Theatre** (Kawakami-za) in 1896.

Propelled into the limelight accidentally (when another actor fell ill) on the Kawakami **theatre company**'s first **Western** tour (1899–1901)—subsequent tours were in 1901–1902 and 1907–1908—Sadayakko (known abroad as Sada Yakko or Sada Yacco) upstaged Otojirô and was hailed as a Japanese Sarah Bernhardt. She enthralled Americans and Europeans, including luminaries of *fin-de-siècle* culture such as Beerbohm, Gide, Picasso, Rodin, and Puccini. The Japanese couple shamelessly pandered to Westerners' superficial Orientalist tastes, providing sex-and-violence-laden pastiches of *kabuki* plays; this embarrassed many contemporary Japanese, who wanted to project a more civilized image of their modern nation.

On their triumphant return to Japan, however, Sadayakko and Otojirô pioneered Japanese productions of European plays, including adaptations of Shakespeare, Maeterlinck, Daudet, Dumas *fils*, and Sardou. They established the Imperial Actress School in 1908, headed by Sadayakko, to train actresses in both traditional and modern European theatre.

Sadayakko continued to perform after Otojirô's death but, increasingly disparaged for her age and melodramatic mannerisms, retired in 1917. Thereafter, she lived quietly as the mistress of financier Fukuzawa Momosuke, occasionally **directing** productions of children's theatre until the 1930s.

FURTHER READING

Downer, Lesley. *Madame Sadayakko: The Geisha Who Bewitched the West.*

M. Cody Poulton

KAWAMURA TAKESHI (1959–). **Japanese** • **playwright**, **director**, **actor**, filmmaker, and teacher. Kawamura founded the **experimental** • **theatre company** Third Erotica (Daisan Erotica) in 1980 with fellow Meiji University students. The company challenged theatrical convention with its energetic, apocalyptic vision and raw-edged **political** critique. Kawamura's major plays—most using English-based titles—include *Nippon Wars* (Nippon wôzu, 1984), *Last Frankenstein* (Rasuto Furankenshutain, 1986, filmed in 1990), *A Man Called Macbeth* (Macbeth to yû na otoko, 1990), *Tokyo Trauma* (Tokyo torauma, 1995), and *Hamletclone* (Hamurettokuron, 2000, 2003). At twenty-six, he received the prestigious **Kishida [Kunio]** Prize for *Eight Dogs of Shinjuku* (Shinjuku hakken-den, 1985).

Kawamura explores subcultures like criminal gangs and youth movements. Cyberpunk themes and images from horror movies inform his gothic sensibility, which doubles as a commentary on Japanese society. In *Nippon Wars*, android soldiers rebel against their leader only to learn that rebellion is part of their programming. *Hamletclone* explores Japan's violent modern history and nationalism. *A Man Called Macbeth* is set in the hyper-masculine world of the *yakuza*. Kawamura regularly cites films and popular **music**, and has a fascination for tabloid journalism and events from society's underbelly. Kawamura's directing emphasizes physicality and employs multimedia; his plays are metatheatrical and conceptual, mixed with irreverence and humor.

Since 2000, Kawamura has written for and directed plays with his new company, T-factory, gaining wider audiences. Daisan Erotica has become an experimental wing in a career that crosses into *shingeki* and international arenas.

Peter Eckersall

KAWATAKE MOKUAMI (1816–1893).

Japanese • *kabuki* • playwright, widely considered history's greatest, apart from **Chikamatsu Monzaemon**, who wrote mainly for *bunraku* (see Puppet Theatre). The son of an Edo (Tokyo) fishseller turned pawnbroker, Mokuami was turned out while still in his teens for keeping company with geishas. Drawn to the performing arts, Mokuami began studying **dance**, which introduced him to *kabuki*, where he eventually became the pupil of **Tsuruya Nanboku** V. Known as Kawatake Shinshichi II for most of his career, he became head playwright (*tate sakusha*) in 1843. Taking the name Mokuami in 1881, he retired from active playwriting eight years later, although he continued to write until his death. Many of the 360 works credited to him and his assistants, including his principal disciple, Kawatake Shinshichi III (1842–1901), are still in the active repertory, including "dance plays" (*shosagoto* and *buyō geki*), "domestic dramas" (*sewa mono*), and "historical dramas" (*jidai mono*).

Mokuami was a brilliant innovator and social **critic** associated with important work in several genres, including "bandit plays" (*shiranami mono*), "cropped-hair plays" (*zangiri mono*), "living history plays" (*katsureki geki*), and "pine-board plays" (*matsubame mono*) closely based on works from *nô*. He found inspiration from numerous sources, from contemporary novels and newspapers to earlier dramas and even **Western** literature. On a technical level, Mokuami's work is distinguished for its poetically rhythmic musicality. Following the lead of Nanboku IV, he made extensive use of dialogue written in the meter of alternating lines of seven and five syllables (*shichigochô*). Moreover, Mokuami creatively used the sound of plucked *shamisen* strings as background **music** (*aikata*) to heighten the emotional content of the words. In terms of content, Mokuami built on established Edo-era (1603–1868) playwriting practices while also taking *kabuki* into previously uncharted territory as a leader in the Meiji (1868–1912) theatrical reform movement.

As a *kabuki* playwright, Mokuami cannot be understood apart from the **actors** for whom he wrote. He developed bandit plays mainly for **Ichikawa Kodanji** IV, the last great Edo-period actor, achieving a masterpiece in *The Three Kichisas and the New Year's First Visit to the Pleasure Quarters* (Sannin Kichisa kuruwa no hatsugai, 1860). The eight-act, sixteen-scene work, with a double plot structure that suited the mid-nineteenth-century taste for complexity, focuses on three thieves who all share the same name. Mokuami's bandit plays, like this one, continue the often shocking onstage depiction of crime and passion—a style primarily developed by Nanboku IV in his "raw domestic plays" (*kizewa mono*)—but they also introduce the Buddhist concept of inevitable justice (*inga*) as an overarching thematic element. As attractively as Mokuami portrayed thieves and murderers, male and female, his audiences knew that cries of moral regret and scenes of punishment inevitably awaited. Such was the popularity of Mokuami's bandit plays that other actors wanted to star in them as well. **Onoe Kikugorô V**, for example, starred in Mokuami's *Benten Kozô* (1862).

Mokuami defined *kabuki* throughout the period of tremendous cultural shift following the Meiji Restoration (1868). Mokuami wrote the cropped-hair and living-history plays that brought the sights and sounds of city life to the **stage** and captured the sense of dislocation caused by contemporary social and **political** upheavals. Cropped-hair plays, written mainly for Kikugorô V, were a kind of domestic play that derived their name from the appearance of the newly short haircut men wore in place of their out-moded topknot. Mokuami inaugurated the genre with *The Tokyo Daily News* (Tôkyô nichinichi shinbun, 1873), a murder story. Although the genre's popularity faded by the early 1880s, a fascinating example is *The Woman Student* (Onna shosei Shigeru, 1877), about a young woman who disguises herself as a man to get the university education she desperately wants.

Living history plays were initiated in collaboration with **Ichikawa Danjûrô** IX, who was determined to make *kabuki* reform part of the modernization sweeping Japan. However, transforming *kabuki* plays into models of historical accuracy and proper behavior diluted their drama. In one case, the effort to reveal the historical truth produced unintended consequences: when *The Story of Kômon, a Lecture for Youth* (Kômon–ki osana kôshaku, 1877) opened, its veracity was angrily attacked as libelous half-truths by a fellow playwright who also happened to be a government official related to the Mito clan of the play. Only apologies and the closing of the play ended the matter. One of the few living history plays still performed is *Sakai's Drum* (Sakai no taiko, 1873).

About 140 Mokuami pieces were written as dance works. Of these, a number were *matsubame mono*, among them *Two Lions* (Ren jishi, 1872), *The Demon Ibaraki* (Ibaraki, 1883), and *Benkei aboard Ship* (Funa Benkei, 1885). Regardless of the genre, Mokuami infused his source material with an intensity befitting the large size of the stage, the enormous scope of its drama, and the demands of a culturally sophisticated audience.

FURTHER READING

Brandon, James R., and Samuel L. Leiter, eds. *Kabuki Plays on Stage: Darkness and Desire*; Brandon, James R., and Samuel L. Leiter, eds. *Kabuki Plays on Stage: Restoration and Reform*.

Barbara E. Thornbury

KECAK. Balinese (see Indonesia) **dance**-drama, a.k.a. *cak* and sometimes called "the Monkey Dance." Often performed for tourists, *kecak* is relatively new, first presented in the Gianyar village of Bedulu at the request of German expatriate artist Walter Spies during the 1930s. A local group, led by Limbak, a renowned performer of *baris*, a military dance, was commissioned to compose a new kind of **Ramayana** story, using the male chorus from the *sang hyang dedari* ritual trance-dance. *Kecak*, however, was primarily secular.

The all-male troupes, comprising up to one hundred performers, begin seated on the ground in concentric circles, five to seven deep. One acts as the chant leader, holding the rhythm and signaling changes in tempo and theme. The distinctive, complex, rhythmic chorus of "checka, chack, checka" gives *kecak* its name. Its interlocking patterns and colotomic form emulate *gamelan* **music**. Chanting is said to help sustain a trance-like state, although trance might not be achieved at tourist performances.

A smaller group, adjunct to the chorus, performs a dramatic episode from the *Ramayana*. A standard choice, based on the original Bedulu group's choreography, starts with the abduction of Sita and moves on to a battle scene between the monkey king Sugriwa and Rahwana's son, Meganada. In 1969, the choreography was changed, under pressure from tourism agents, and the episode was lengthened to about an hour to include an abbreviated narrative of the *Ramayana*. In recent years, various choreographers have introduced new versions. In 2004, an all-female *kecak* was introduced at the Bali Arts **Festival**.

FURTHER READING

Dibia, I Wayan, and Rucina Ballinger. *Balinese Dance, Drama and Music: A Guide to the Performing Arts of Bali.*

Laura Noszlopy

KETHOPRAK. **Indonesian** popular theatre from Java, patronized primarily by the lower classes and performed on proscenium **stages** with drop-and-wing **scenography**. Most dialogue is spoken, but lead characters also occasionally break into sung classical verse (*tembang*).

Kethoprak (also *ketoprak*) began around 1925 in Yogyakarta, central Java. Its name comes from an earlier semi-dramatic **folk • dance** form accompanied by the pounding *prak-prak* sound of the paddy pounder. This distinctive percussive sound remains essential, used to accompany dance. *Kethoprak* was initially sometimes called *stambul jawi* (Javanese *stambul*) as its dramaturgy was derived from **komedi stambul**. Plays were improvised in Javanese from the same mixture of toga dramas, European opera, fairy tales, and *Arabian Nights* tales. A small band of **Western • musical instruments** provided accompaniment. In 1927, however, troupes began to use *gamelan* music instead, and plays gradually shifted away from exogenous sources and toward Javanese legends and chronicles. As early as 1928, *kethoprak*'s popularity led to three hundred groups being active in the Yogyakarta region alone.

Until recently, *kethoprak* was a standard feature of night fairs and played to ticket-purchasing audiences for month-long stands in makeshift **theatres** throughout central and east Java; village **women** often idolized mustachioed leading men. *Kethoprak*'s **costume** dramas have been a prime source for displaying the customs of the nobility, inculcating traditional values, and defining norms of etiquette and politesse, offering a

Seniman Muda SKA, a semiprofessional *kethoprak* troupe, performing *Lutung Kasarung*, 1999. (Photo: Matthew Isaac Cohen)

romanticized window into the archaic ways of the court for the masses through drama, dance, and song. *Wayang*'s (see Puppet Theatre) influence is apparent on **role types**: lean, pale-faced male heroes are implacably "refined" (*alus*) nobles; stocky, red-faced villains are short-tempered embodiments of "roughness" (*kasar*).

During the 1950s and early 1960s, many **theatre companies** were associated with **political** parties. Messages about land redistribution or the dangers of separatism were woven into plays, and clowns in ***dagelan*** scenes articulated grievances of "the little man." After 1965, the repertoire shifted to nonpolitical subjects (horror plays were particularly popular), and *kethoprak* gradually lost ground. It was revitalized in the 1990s by Yogyakarta intellectuals, who used it to make oblique critiques of President Sukarno's (1901–1970) dictatorship, and on television as the satirical *Ketoprak Humor*, enacted in a mix of Javanese and Indonesian, and featuring a mix of seasoned *kethoprak* **actors** and guest celebrities.

FURTHER READING

Brandon, James R. *Theatre in Southeast Asia*; Susanto, Budi. *Ketoprak: The Politics of the Past in the Present-Day Java*.

Matthew Isaac Cohen

KHON. Thai ⁕ dance-drama in which most performers wear **masks** covering the entire head. The characters, stories, plots, and poetry of this refined, classical form come from the *Ramakien* (Thailand's version of the ***Ramayana***).

Masks and Music. Traditionally, all performers were male and all male roles wore masks. Today, performers playing nonhuman roles (mainly demons and monkeys) are played by men and wear masks, while those playing clowns, gods, and humans wear crowns. There are about 140 different demon and monkey masks and ten different crowns; each is standardized and a part of Thailand's decorative arts. The different styles and colors of masks and **costumes** provide character information.

Music, more than dance, structures *khon*. Since they wear masks and dance, *khon* performers cannot narrate the scenes they perform. They dance to the tunes called "special action for music" (*pleng naphat*), as male "narrators" (*kon park*) chant rhymed narratives (*tum-nong*) and dialogue (*cheracha*), accompanied by the classical ensemble, *piphat*. *Piphat* include one or two wooden xylophones (*ranad*), a Chinese oboe (*pi*), a double-faced drum (*taphon*), a circular set of gongs (*khong wong*), two drums (*klong*), and a pair of small cymbals (*ching*).

Subject Matter. Although eventually used to reinforce the sacred foundations and military might of royal power, *khon*'s precise origins remain unknown. Early evidence in the royal court of late fifteenth-century Ayudhaya ties it to *nang yai* **puppet theatre**, the royal inauguration ritual dance *Churning the Milk Ocean* (Chaknag dukdamban), and Thai martial arts (*krabi-krabong*). Performances center on "episodes" (*chut*) mostly from the "Battle Book" (Yudhakand) in the *Ramakien*, often to illustrate a Buddhist moral lesson. Typically, *khon* stresses the victories of the righteous Phra Ram (Rama) and his armies over the immoral giant Thosakand (Ravana), to show how Buddhist **religious** virtues defeat evils. Each battle ends with a massive still pose of its main characters, with Rama standing victoriously atop a defeated giant. This pose derives from traditional depictions seen in *nang yai* fighting poses, mural paintings, and old bas-reliefs.

Phra Chakra Avatar, a production combining *khon* and *nang yai* shadow puppetry, directed by Pairioj Tongkhamsuk, and produced by Pornrat Damrhung at the Royal Sala Chalermkrung Theatre, Bangkok, Thailand, 2006. (Photo: S. Riensrivlai; Courtesy of Pairioj Tongkhamsuk)

Twentieth-Century Developments. *Khon* honored the king at celebrations and other royal events, and embodied the might and glory of royal rule. Since the mid-nineteenth century, *khon* has been incorporated into performances of ***lakon nai.*** For a decade after the end of absolute monarchy in 1932, *khon* was seldom performed. In 1945, *khon* was revived at the School of Dance and Music of the Fine Arts Department, and **training** of boys commenced. At the time, **women** were finally allowed to play female roles. During the last half-century, *khon* has come to embody classical culture and the glory of the modern state.

Types. The oldest type, *khon klang plaeng*, is performed in an open field. *Khon rong nok* (or *khon nang rao*) uses a raised **stage** and a long bamboo bench for its male characters. *Khon na cho* is performed before a screen in the style of *nang yai*, with narration and dialogue by narrators. *Khon rong nai* is performed with choral singing and dancing similar to *lakon nai*. *Khon chark* is a modernized style created in the mid-nineteenth century, using a painted backdrop; *khon chakrok* is performed before a white screen—in fighting scenes, performers fly into the air to do battle. *Khon na fai*, enacted in front of the crematorium before wealthy persons' funerals, was originally much longer but has been shortened for presentation at cremations of less-wealthy people. Finally, *khon sod* performers put masks on the top of their heads, allowing their faces to be seen while they sing and speak.

FURTHER READING

Brandon, James R. *Theatre in Southeast Asia*; Rutnin, Mattani Mojdara. *Dance, Drama, and Theatre in Thailand: The Process of Development and Modernization.*

Pornrat Damrhung

KHYAL. **Indian** operatic **folk •** **dance**-drama performed in the villages of the northwestern states of Uttar Pradesh and, more important, Rajasthan. This secular form, dated to Agra in the early eighteenth century, and later influenced by **Parsi theatre**, is said to derive its name (also spelled *khyala*) from the Urdu for "imagination" or, more likely, from the Hindi word for "to play."

The subject matter comes from historical romances, mythology, folktales, love stories, and religio-heroic tales sung by regional singers expounding the virtues of their legendary leaders. Titles memorialize their names, as in *Laila and Majnu* (Laila-Majnu), *Pathan Shehzadi, Draupadi Swayamvara, Narsi Bhagat, Harishchandra*, and *Nala Damayanti*. The loosely assembled plots are accompanied by the **music** of percussion (*nagara* and *dholak*), bowed (*sarangi*), and wind instruments (*shehnai*), as well as cymbals (*manjira*) and harmonium. There is a great emphasis on the singing, and the audience shares the final verses with the **actors**.

The performance combines prose, verse, song, and dance. Melodramatics are in force, with an emphasis on strong emotional expression ranging from love to grief. With no **women** in the troupe, female impersonation is of a high artistic level. The troupe leader (*ustad*) sits onstage in a chair as he guides the action and prompts the actors from his script.

As with most other traditional theatres, rituals precede performances, on behalf of the elephant-headed god Ganesha and various other deities. Each style has its own rituals. One, for example, begins with a sweeper cleaning the **stage**, followed by some-one who sprinkles water to keep the dust down. Such personages will then also sing and dance and act comically prior to the appearance of the main actors, who will per-form other procedures before the commencement of the main piece. An improvising clown (*vidushaka*) is essential to poke fun at anything likely to get too serious.

There are many *khyal* styles often taking their names from a locale with which they are associated, as, for example, *mewari khyal*, *jaipuri khyal*, *kuchamani khyal*, *shekha-wati khyal*, and so on. Some are associated with composer-**playwrights** like Lac-chiram, Alibux, and Nainuram (1823–1905), while yet others are known by some special feature, such as their acting, as in *abhinaya khyal*. Music is one of the chief differentiating features among them, but so are their material, dialect, and the kind of stage used, although basic features are shared.

Stages—thought to reflect certain **Sanskrit theatre** practices—are raised, curtainless, wooden platforms, about four feet high, set in open village areas, with banana tree trunks adorning the corners, and the audience seated on three sides. Some productions are quite elaborate and include at the rear additional, raised, balcony-like platforms, called "palaces" (*mahal*) or "windows" (*jharokha*), twelve to twenty feet high, to rep-resent other places. Such structures, of which there may be two or more, are used for characters (especially queens) to come down to the main stage via ladders. Either a white sheet on the ground or a small, lower platform may be placed in front of the main stage. Torches provide the illumination. A pole is set near the main stage with the name of the company affixed to it. The dressing room is behind the main stage. After actors enter and finish their scene, they sit near the musicians, only to make their next entrance from where they have been sitting.

Costumes are based on historical models, and can be highly decorative but are gen-erally realistic, as are the **makeup** and wigs. *Khyal* is closely related to such folk thea-tres as *tamasha*, *nautanki*, *maanch*, and *swang*, among others.

FURTHER READING

Gargi, Balwant. *Folk Theater of India*; Vatsyayan, Kapila. *Traditional Indian Theatre: Multiple Streams*.

Samuel L. Leiter

KICH NOI. **Vietnamese** modern "spoken drama," initiated by the artists and intellec-tuals who founded the "new poetry" literary movement during the 1920s. In the early years, **playwrights** and **actors** **·** **experimented** with many approaches, frequently treat-ing issues such as resistance to French colonialism by combining *tuong* and *cheo* con-ventions. The first *kich noi* play, in Hanoi, was Vu Dinh Long's (1901–1960) *The Cup of Poison* (Chen thuoc doc, 1921), whose anti-French subtext was appreciated by the Vietnamese; the French thought it a breakthrough in the "civilizing" of traditional theatre.

In the 1930s, *kich noi* was further legitimized by a group of scholars and practi-tioners, who saw its potential in depicting Vietnamese stories and values, especially in light of French colonialism (1859–1954). A leader in this group was Nguyen The Lu, who cofounded (with Nguyen Xuan Khoa) the first *kich noi* **theatre company** (the Central Dramatic Company of Vietnam [Nha Hat Kich Viet Nam], 1952); Lu and his fellows were dedicated to developing *kich noi* into a form that reflected the fusion of **Western** conventions and Vietnamese language and values. Similar companies formed in Hanoi and the north; *kich noi* became popular, especially because of its focus on the dialogue of "the people," its depiction of contemporary problems—rather than Confucian morals—and its realistic **costumes** and **scenography**. Even before the French left, several companies mounted innovative productions of Molière and Shakespeare. Nguyen Dinh Nghi—The Lu's son—fused spoken dialogue with *cheo* conventions. Yet he was never satisfied that his many adaptations succeeded in making the combination work on the level of Western drama. One of his last productions was Luu Quang Vu's *Truong Ba's Soul [in] the Butcher's Skin* (Hon Truong Ba, da hang thit), which toured the United States in 1998.

The new companies were committed to assisting Vietnam achieve independence. In the 1950s, the troupes—especially the Central Dramatic Company, joined by the Saigon Dramatic Troupe (Nya Hat Kich Saigon) when it fled north after 1954—worked to prevent further occupation. *Kich noi*'s popularity, coupled with the Viet Minh goal of complete independence, created an opportunity to support the government's agenda. Spoken drama focused on agitprop until 1975.

In the late 1980s, as productions were mounted on relevant topics—the pains of rebuilding, grief over great personal loss, and social and **political** inequities—*kich noi* regained social influence. Although most northern **theatres** struggle for audiences, in an environment of new technology, explosive economic growth, and mass media, it is miraculous that live theatre companies still survive. Despite innovative marketing techniques and new artistic methods, the threat to live theatre remains daunting.

FURTHER READING

Brandon, James R. *Theatre in Southeast Asia*; Dinh Quang et al. *Vietnamese Theater*.

Lorelle Browning

KIKUCHI KAN (1888–1948). **Japanese** novelist and **playwright**. An avid reader of Irish drama while a college student in Tokyo and Kyoto, Kikuchi, with Akutagawa Ryûnosuke (1892–1927) and **Yamamoto Yûzô**, resurrected the literary magazine *New Tides of Thought* (Shinshichô) in 1914.

His early work—including the one-acts "Heroes of the Sea" (Umi no yûsha, 1916), inspired by Synge's "Riders to the Sea"; "Madman on the Roof" (Okujô no kyôjin, 1916); and "Father Returns" (Chichi kaeru, 1917), adapted from Hankin's *The Return of the Prodigal*—initially received little notice, but **Nakamura Ganjirô** I's performance as *kabuki* • actor • Sakata Tôjûrô in *The Loves of Tôjûrô* (Tôjûrô no koi, 1919) spawned numerous (chiefly *kabuki*) productions.

Ichikawa Ennosuke I's 1920 staging of "Father Returns" was a sensation. The play has been called a textbook for one-acts with its strong **dramatic structure**, economical dialogue, and psychological realism. Its theme of generational conflict caught the sentiment of the times and was typical of Kikuchi's plays in presenting a clearly identifiable problem with a possible resolution, often an attempt to reconcile traditional morality with modern liberal and humanistic values.

A vociferous critic of **Osanai Kaoru**'s decision initially not to stage any Japanese drama at his revolutionary **theatre company**, the Tsukiji Little Theatre (Tsukiji

Shôgekijô, 1924), Kikuchi was also an excellent editor and literary sponsor, founding *The Central Review* (Chûô kôron), a dominant magazine, and establishing two major literary awards, the Akutagawa and Naoki Prizes.

M. Cody Poulton

KIM KWANG-LIM (1952–). Korean * **playwright** and **director**, educator, and artistic director of the Yŏnu **Theatre** (Yŏnu Mudae). Currently, Kim is dean of drama and teaches dramaturgy at Korean National University of the Arts. He is known for unconventional dramaturgy in his search for a uniquely Korean style. Early examples are *A Changed Underworld* (Tallajn sesang, 1987), *Hong Tong-ji Is Alive* (Hong Tong-ji nŭn sarŏ itta, 1992), and *House* (Chip, 1994).

His realistic plays also have drawn critical acclaim. *In Search of Love* (Sarang ŭl ch'ajasŏ, 1990), a play-within-a-play, is the story of a claim investigation division's attempt to misrepresent a claimant's death as insurance fraud. The popular *Come and See Me* (Nal borŏ wayo, 1996) turns the story of an actual serial killer into a powerful "whodunit" that questions perceptions of truth. It claimed the Seoul Theatre **Festival** Grand Prize and Baek Sang Arts Award, and has been restaged often and adapted as a film. *Our Country Wuturi* (Uri nara Uturi, 2002), based on the legend of a giant baby, manifests the playwright's passion for cultural independence from the **West**, combining folkloric themes, **music**, and traditional forms such as *t'alch'um*, outdoor performance (*madangguk*), and martial arts. His other plays include *I Confess* (Na nŭn kobaek handa, 2000) and the well-received *A Butterfly's Dream* (Nabi ŭi kkum, 2000).

Hyung-jin Lee

KIM U-JIN (1897–1926). Korean * **playwright**, a pioneer of dramatic naturalism, realism, and expressionism. He began as a poet, but pursued playwriting following publication of his first play, *Noontime* (Chŏng-o, 1924). While a student of English literature at Tokyo's Waseda University, he cofounded the Dramatic Arts Society (Kŭkyesul Hyŏp-hoe) with student compatriots who aimed to study and introduce **Western**-style theatre, breaking away from the popular conventions of *shinp'agŭk* with its **Japanese** roots. He read philosophy, admiring Nietzsche and Strindberg. Of Western dramatists, he respected O'Neill and Shaw, translating the latter's *Mrs. Warren's Profession* and writing **criticism** of the former's dramas. His criticism of Korean works also is significant.

His *A Woman, Lee Yŏng-nyŏ* (Lee Yŏng-nyŏ, 1925), a groundbreaking naturalistic play, employed a prostitute, Lee Yŏng-nyŏ, as a central character to depict the deprivations of the lower classes. It was followed by *Disillusion of the Poet in Rags* (Dudŏgi siin ŭi hwanmyŏl, 1925) and *Shipwreck* (Nanp'a, 1926), which Kim subtitled in German an "Expressionist Story in Three Acts"; it depicts a mysterious love-hate relationship between a poet and his mother. Kim's last play and masterpiece, *Wild Boar* (San twaeji, 1926), portrayed an 1894 peasant uprising in Strindbergian dream-play style. In 1926, Kim committed suicide en route to Japan by throwing himself from a ferry into the sea with his mistress, Yun Shim-dŏk, a contemporary celebrity.

Hyung-jin Lee

KI NO KAION (1663–1742). Japanese • *bunraku* (see Puppet Theatre) • **playwright**, best known as the principal rival of **Chikamatsu Monzaemon**, whose work is said to have benefited from the competition. Born into a family active in literary pursuits, Ki no Kaion was a priest and a medical practitioner before turning to puppet play composition full time. In his mid-forties he became chief playwright of Osaka's Toyotake **Theatre** (Toyotake-za), the chief competitor of the Takemoto Theatre (Takemoto-za), where Chikamatsu was based. Although he suffers by comparison with Chikamatsu, Ki was a skillful technician with a sharp ear for language. He also had a knack for being the first to dramatize stories, like those of the lovers Osome and Hisamatsu, that captured the popular imagination and were later reworked by others.

During his fifteen years at the Toyotake Theatre, Ki no Kaion composed some fifty plays. The majority is "historical dramas" (*jidai mono*), including an early version of the forty-seven samurai story, but he is principally remembered for his "domestic plays" (*sewa mono*). Among his best-known works are *Wankyû and Matsuyama* (Wankyû sue no Matsuyama, ca. 1710) and *Love Suicides with Two Sashes* (Shinjû futatsu haraobi, 1722). Within days, Chikamatsu produced a play based on the same event as the latter.

In 1723, after inheriting his family's confectionary business, Ki retired from playwriting to pursue his interest in composing *haikai* and *kyôka* poetry.

Barbara E. Thornbury

KINOSHITA JUNJI (1914–). Japanese • *shingeki* • **playwright, theorist**, and **director**. Specializing in Elizabethan theatre at Tokyo University, Kinoshita by the 1970s produced a complete translation of Shakespeare's plays. He was a prolific dramatist, beginning with *Turbulent Waves* (Fûrô, 1939). His plays can be divided into two groups: **folk** plays (*minwa geki*), adapted from traditional Japanese stories, and historical plays (*gendai geki*), based on contemporary social and ideological conflicts.

The former, partly influenced by the writings of ethnographer Yanagita Kunio (1875–1962), began with *The Story of Hikoichi* (Hikoichi banashi, 1946), but *Twilight Crane* (Yûzuru, 1949) became his best-known play. The latter is partly influenced by Hegel because of his applicability to socialism and Christianity (though Kinoshita was an ambivalent Christian). Perhaps his most remarkable plays deal with the war: *A Japanese Called Otto* (Otto to yobareru Nihonjin, 1963), about the Japanese counterpart of Soviet spy Richard Sorge, and *Between God and Man* (Kami to hito to no aida, 1970), on the Japanese war crimes trials. In both groups, Kinoshita is didactic, seeking to transform the spectator into a socially responsible, active presence.

Kinoshita's influence was wide. He theorized provocatively that the key problem in *shingeki* realism was the insufficiency of modern Japanese as a **stage** language. With his longtime collaborator, **actress** • **Yamamoto Yasue**, he founded the **theatre company** Grapes Society (Budô no Kai), in 1947. He also promoted theatrical exchanges between Japan and **China**.

Kevin J. Wetmore, Jr.

KIRITAKE MONJÛRÔ. **Puppeteers** of **Japan**'s *bunraku.* Monjûrô I (1845–1910), the representative Meiji-era (1868–1912) puppeteer, was the son of a puppeteer whose name was pronounced the same but was spelled differently. He started his career as a disciple of Yoshida Tatsuzô III, using the name Yoshida Tatsusaburô, gaining experience while touring and playing in Edo (Tokyo). He became Monjûrô (old spelling) ca. 1865. In 1876, he joined Osaka's Bunraku **Theatre** (Bunraku-za), but because of a claim on his name held by someone else, he temporarily called himself Kiritake Kamematsu. In 1877, he returned to Monjûrô I (new spelling).

Known for a rather flashy style, he excelled at handling leading female puppets (*tateoyama*), and costarred opposite **Yoshida Tamazô** I (1829–1905) for years.

Monjûrô II (1900–1970) became a student of **Yoshida Bungorô III** in 1909 and performed as Yoshida Komon at the Horie Theatre (Horie-za). In 1915, he accepted Bungorô's request to join the Goryô Bunraku Theatre (Goryô Bunraku-za), and two years later, as Yoshida Bunshô, joined the Taketoyo Theatre (Taketoyo-za). At the Goryô Bunraku Theatre in 1918 he took the name Yoshida Minosuke II, and in 1927 became Monjûrô II.

In the postwar period, when *bunraku*'s artists split into two separate camps, the Chinami Kai and the Mitsuwa Kai, he joined the latter, which advocated for unionization. He was known for his exceptional skill handling female puppets. In 1965, he became a National Living Treasure.

Samuel L. Leiter

KIRLOSKAR, ANNASAHEB BALWANT PANDARUNG (1843–1885). **Indian** Kannada-language **playwright**, **actor**, **director**, and composer, born in Gurlhosar, North Karnataka, and educated at Pune. After failing his law exam, he began writing plays while teaching school in Belgaum. He was influenced by Vishnudas Bhave (1819/24–1901), father of Maharashtra's professional proscenium **theatre**. Bhave's plays, performed on a bare **stage** using only a few **properties**, employed a stage manager-director (*sutradhara*) who, together with a chorus and musicians, sat at the side and sang songs introducing each new character and providing expository background to the largely improvised dialogue.

This format developed into the popular "**musical** theatre" (*sangeet natak*) that dominated Marathi theatricals for half a century. The first true example of this form was *Shakuntala* (partial, 1874; complete, 1880), his Marathi adaptation of **Kalidasa**'s **Sanskrit** classic *The Recognition of Shakuntala* (Abhijnana Shakuntalam), produced by his new **theatre company**, Kirloskar Drama Company (Kirloskar Natak Mandali), which remained successful for many years after his death. The *sutradhara*'s participation was limited to the beginning of the performance, the chorus was removed, and the musical background came from a wide variety of classical and **folk** sources. There were over 180 songs in *Shakuntala*. The reliance on the actor-singers to move the story forward was a breakthrough. Both **Parsi theatre** and English romanticism influenced construction, characterization, and atmosphere.

Kirloskar's other plays were the still popular mythological romance *Musical of Saubhadra* (Sangeet Saubhadra, 1882) and the unfinished *Rama Giving up His Kingdom* (Ramarajya viyoga, 1882), three acts of which were staged by Kirloskar's company.

Samuel L. Leiter

KISARAGI KOHARU (1956–2000). Japanese • **playwright, director**, and cultural commentator. Born in Tokyo, Kisaragi began her career in 1976 at Tokyo Woman's Christian University, founding the student group Beautiful Freak (Kiko). She attracted attention in 1979 with *Romeo and Freesia at the Dining Table* (Romio to Furîjia no aru shokutaku), a metatheatrical parody of *Romeo and Juliet*. In 1983, she founded the **theatre company** NOISE.

Kisaragi's plays, antithetical to the *shôgekijô* movement—whose demise she declared in her book *Playhouses of City Folk* (Toshi minzoku no shibai goya, 1987)—are multimedia performances intentionally detracting attention from **actors**' bodies and emotions. She is often compared to **Noda Hideki** and **Watanabe Eriko**. The first NOISE production, *DOLL* (1983), inspired by a suicide involving female junior-high students, has become a staple of school drama clubs. *MORAL* (1984–1986), fragmented the script into small interchangeable elements, dispensing with narrative structure to present images nonrealistically. These and plays like *Era of Light* (Hikari no jidai, 1980) and *Factory Tales* (Kôjô monogatari, 1982) reflect the 1980s zeitgeist: burgeoning postmodern consumerism, the city as playground for humans and machines, and **women**'s changing social roles.

In later years, Kisaragi conducted workshops and frequently commented on culture in the mass media. Inspired by the International Women Playwrights Conferences (1988, 1991), she also chaired the first Conference for Asian Women and Theatre (1992). She was only forty-four when, while lecturing in December 2000, she died of a brain hemorrhage.

Ayako Kano

KISHIDA KUNIO (1890–1954). Japanese • *shingeki* • **director, playwright**, translator, and **critic**. Dedicated to drama as a form of literature, and a pioneer of dialogue-based psychological realism, Kishida was a significant, if controversial, figure, often viewed more positively by **Westerners** than by Japanese. He studied French at Tokyo University, then traveled to Paris in 1919 to work with Jacques Copeau. Kishida wrote his first play in French, "Old Toys" (Furui omocha, 1924). Returning to Japan in 1923, Kishida introduced the latest French developments. He sought to modernize Japanese theatre and became a model for younger playwrights.

Kishida's career has four distinct periods. From 1924 to 1929, he wrote one-acts, "Paper Balloon" (Kami fûsen, 1925) being the most successful. These plays generally feature two characters, often husbands and wives, as in "Autumn in the Tyrols" (Chiroru no aki, 1924), "The Swing" (Buranko, 1925), and "It Will Be Fine Tomorrow" (Ashita wa tenki, 1928). His principal themes include the disintegration of familial relationships, an absent or powerless father, and the sheer emotional complexity of everyday life. Copeau's influence is evident in Kishida's poetic language and blend of realism and symbolism.

From 1929 to 1936, he wrote multiact works, including his best, *The Two Daughters of Mr. Sawa* (Sawa-shi no futari musume, 1935). He founded *Playwriting Magazine* (Gekisaku) in 1932, which yielded the Playwriting School (Gekisaku-ha) of dramaturgy and stimulated the careers of playwrights like **Tanaka Chikao**. Kishida was also involved in founding the short-lived Tsukiji **Theatre** (Tsukiji-za) in the early 1930s, and he published articles advocating his brand of literary dramaturgy.

From 1936 to 1948, Kishida wrote less after becoming director of culture for the Imperial Rule Assistance Association, which led to postwar accusations of collaboration with the militarists. Yet, his theatre work was resolutely non**political**; recent **critics** have seen his wartime involvement as a form of resistance by providing balance. In 1937, he founded the Literary Theatre (Bungaku-za) with Iwata Toyô (1893–1969) and **Kubota Mantarô**, a **theatre company** dedicated to psychological, nonpolitical drama.

From 1948 to 1954, Kishida produced primarily satires on modern life. The period was problematic because of his wartime role and his having ignored social problems in his plays. From 1924 to 1935, he wrote fifty plays, but only five afterward.

Kishida's plays sought to evoke "emotional reality," with a focus on disintegration, paralysis, and dislocation as being characteristic of modern life. **Mishima Yukio** called them "chamber music for the theatre," and **Betsuyaku Minoru** has termed them "photographic realism." While Kishida's plays remain important, he looms larger because of his influence on younger playwrights and in every phase of modern theatre's development. The annual Kishida Prize for playwriting is named for him.

FURTHER READING

Rimer, J. Thomas. *Toward a Modern Japanese Theatre: Kishida Kunio.*

Kevin J. Wetmore, Jr.

KISHIDA RIO (1946–2003). Japanese • **playwright** and **director**. From 1974, as a member of **Terayama Shûji**'s Peanut Gallery (Tenjô Sajiki), Kishida coauthored several plays with Terayama, including *Knock* (Nokku, 1975) and *Shintokumaru: Poison Boy* (Shintokumaru, 1978). With his blessing, she founded With the Help of My Big Brother **Theatre** (Ka-i Gekijô) in 1978 to write about **women**. Later she established the Kishida Company (Kishida Jimusho), merging in 1983 with Wada Yoshio's company, forming Kishida Company + Optimists' Troupe (Kishida Jimusho + Rakuten-dan).

Around 1990, she began to explore international theatre, joining **Suzuki Tadashi** to organize the Heiner Müller Project. Her inclination toward Asia, however, and her long-standing interest in women's history soon led her to question **political** issues, such as Japan's patriarchy, the emperor system, and colonial policy. She created plays about Japanese sexual slavery of **Korean** "comfort women" during World War II, performing them in Korea, using a combination of Japanese, Korean, and sign language. Collaborations with **Singaporean** director **Ong Keng Sen** on the pan-Asian *Lear* (1997) and *Desdemona* (2000) resulted in intense controversies regarding style and content. When **Kisaragi Koharu** died in 2000, Kishida became acting director of the Fourth Asian Women's Theatre Conference.

Her signature play is *Thread Hell* (Ito jigoku), awarded the 1984 **Kishida [Kunio]** Prize. Characterized by classically styled, evocative poetry, surreal structure, allusions to traditional literature, and visually stunning theatricality, it considers the plight of Meiji era (1868–1912) female silk workers and attacks traditional patriarchy.

Carol Fisher Sorgenfrei

KITAMURA SÔ (1953–). Japanese • **playwright** and **director**. Guided by his motto, "risk your life for the sake of laughter," and influenced by avant-garde playwright-director **Kara Jûrô**, Kitamura infuses his plays with a light, dry humor. Working in Nagoya since 1973, he is among Japan's first playwright-directors successful outside Tokyo or Osaka.

Kitamura builds humor by drawing his characters' identities from literature, film, and drama. The Bible inspired *Ode to Joy* (Hogi uta, 1979), set during a ceaseless nuclear war. Two characters wandering the blasted landscape encounter a Christ figure; although his miracles provide food, they part ways, suggesting that salvation, if possible, is a personal struggle. The Marx Brothers' *Duck Soup* spawned *DUCK SOAP* (1987), a parody of Japanese commerce. *The Kenji Incident* (Kenji no jiken, 1992), concerns writer Miyazawa Kenji (1896–1933), universally respected for his Buddhist faith; selflessly developing agriculture in rural Iwate Prefecture, he undermined his health, dying at thirty-seven. The play irreverently re-interprets Miyazawa as a money-grubbing scoundrel who fakes his death to lead a profligate life. Unexpectedly, however, his escape to Tokyo inspires grudging admiration from those he helped most—a plot twist revealing Kitamura's characteristic optimism.

Kitamura also explores limits on theatrical space in plays like *Roof People* (Okujô no hito, 1990). In this humorous contemplation of contemporary sexuality, the characters interact on the delimited space of a rooftop. Finally, in a metatheatrical moment, one steps off and nothing happens, showing the constructed nature of **stage** space.

John D. Swain

KITA ROPPEITA NÔSHIN (1874–1971). Japanese • *nô* • actor, the four-teenth family head (*iemoto*) of the Kita school (*ryû*), specialists in the *shite* **role type.** Usually referred to as Kita Roppeita I, he oversaw the Kita school throughout much of the twentieth century. Although his father was a samurai working for the shogunate, his mother was the daughter of the twelfth Kita headmaster, and he was adopted into the Kita house in 1879, becoming headmaster at ten.

Roppeita consolidated the Kita school after a period of disorganization and worked to standardize its various regional acting styles. He won respect outside of his school, receiving a series of awards that culminated in his recognition as a National Living Treasure in 1955. In 1963 he retired, although he taught until his death.

He authored *Roppeita's Artistic Writings* (Roppeita Geidan, 1942), a collection of essays on practices such as **mask** use. The Kita Roppeita Memorial Nô Theatre (Kita Roppeita Kinen Nôgakudô), which opened in 1973 in Tokyo, bears his name. The Roppeita name has also been adopted by his grandson, Roppeita II (1924–), who became the school's sixteenth leader in 1986.

Eric C. Rath

KKOKTU KAKSHI. *See* Puppet Theatre: Korea.

KO-JÔRURI. *See* Puppet Theatre: Japan.

KÔKAMI SHÔJI (1958–). Japanese • playwright and **director.** Emerging from Waseda University's famous theatre culture, Kôkami founded Third Stage (Daisan Butai) in 1981. With his lighthearted, fast-paced, comedic style accurately capturing the effervescent 1980s *zeitgeist*, he soon became a megastar—on **stage**, screen, and

television. Although influenced by **Tsuka Kôhei**, Kôkami avoids *angura*'s earnestness and **political** fervor, humorously broaching individual **political** impotence, loss of cultural identity, and edginess from the threat of nuclear annihilation.

His best-known play, *With a Sunset like Morning* (Asahi no yô na yûhi wo tsurete, 1981), the first in his Nuclear War Trilogy, has toy-company employees developing a virtual-reality game. Amid malfunctions yielding nonstop gags, punctuated by cries of despair, an alternative reality emerges: are the employees mental patients awaiting their Godot, who must keep developing their game until Godot arrives? Which reality is real? Left alone, unable to shape meaningful existence, the employee/patients crystallize the 1980s' blithe nihilism. Kôkami, several of whose titles are in English, develops reality's unreliability further in *Trans* (1993), with self and other, reality and illusion, intermingling.

Similar themes inform Kôkami's science-fiction plays, including *Hush-a-bye* (1986), *Angels with Closed Eyes* (Tenshi wa hitomi wo tojite, 1991), and the **Kishida [Kunio]** Prize–winning *Snufkin's Letter* (Sunafukin no tegami, 1995). All feature Kôkami's pervasive walls, real or figurative—images of external control. Attempting to destroy the walls, his characters fail to realize their activities are merely being permitted within the walls' flexible boundaries. Vividly depicting this all-too-human plight is Kôkami's attempt to poke a hole, an escape hatch, in the wall.

John D. Swain

KOLAM. Sri Lankan • **folk theatre** found in the island's southern coastal areas. It is almost entirely secular, although scholars see some links with ritual in regard to its **masks** and presentation of characters. The full-face masks are considered similar to but more sculpturally detailed and comically realistic than those used in Sri Lankan "devil dance" (*tovil*). *Tovil* masks are of demons while *kolam* masks are of real people. *Kolam* means "comic impersonation" or "disguise."

The performances last all night, and are performed on an earthen circle **stage** surrounded by the villagers. After an invocation of song and **dance** to the gods (there is another at the conclusion), and before the play begins, any number (from about fifty possible examples) of masked and **costumed** stock village characters and authority figures appear, although unrelated to the play itself. Among them might be a headman, a washerman and his wife, the washerman's mistress, a soldier, a number of policemen, a king, a queen, a king's official, demons, beggars, a European woman, a teacher, a midwife, deities, and animals. Each character's entrance is introduced by verses delivered by the **musicians**. The character dances, mimes, and sings about himself or herself; sometimes multiple characters perform a satirical sketch; in one, the washerman's wife complains to an official about her husband's infidelity. Laughter is often provoked by off-color humor. When asked by a musician to state their purpose, they answer that they have come to announce the arrival of the king and queen to view *kolam*.

The characters' presentation is considered more entertaining than the main plays, none of which use masks, a hindrance to verbal expression. Of the dozen plays available, the principal ones—performed in tandem—are *Story of Sandakinduru* (Sandakinduru katava) and *Story of Maname* (Maname katava), drawn from Buddha's birth stories (*jataka*). The first concerns two mythical creatures (*kinduru*)—part bird, part human—whose love is shattered when the hunter-king falls in love with the female and shoots her lover. Spurned, he would slay her as well but is prevented by divine intervention, which also brings the lover back to life. In the second, Prince Maname and his wife are threatened in the forest by a hunter who seeks to take the wife. During the fight between the men, the wife, betraying her husband, hands a dagger to the hunter, who kills the prince and then departs, disgusted by the woman's infidelity. *See also Nadagam; Sokari.*

FURTHER READING

Sarachchandra, E. R. *The Folk Drama of Ceylon.*

Samuel L. Leiter

KOMATSU MIKIO (1941–). **Japanese • playwright.** Born in Kôchi Prefecture, Komatsu graduated from Waseda University and began his career writing and editing for *Teatro* magazine. He has created over eighty socially conscious plays of several types: ***shôgekijô***, children's theatre, **puppet theatre**, and even commercial theatre. He is particularly noted for turning novels into plays. His adaptation of Tatematsu Wahei's (1947–) novel *Distant Thunder* (Enrai, 1985) depicts farmers, beset by urbanization, caught between their land and greed. Through soliloquies, they reveal insecurities borne of their inability to communicate honestly. Komatsu's most noted adaptation, Minakami Tsutomu's (1926–2004) *Get Down From That Tree, Bunna* (Bunna yo ki kara orite koi, 1977), often revived, highlights Bunna's realization that only the fittest survive, to elucidate a Buddhist worldview.

Komatsu's first original play, *Death Match Renga* (Desu matchi renga, 1974), contrasts social disorder (postearthquake rioting) outside a police station with the apparently harmonious social consensus achieved inside by police and prisoners. This figurative, nonconfrontational "death match" by *renga* (group-composed poetry), a very Japanese scenario, elicited immediate response from young audiences for portraying Japanese life as negotiated interactions, lessening conflict through rules, and acknowledging blood ties and group identity.

Also commenting on indigenous society, *Mystery Tour* (Ame no wanmankâ, 1976) features a bus carrying, mostly, inhabitants of the same public housing complex (*danchi*). When the bus becomes lost, the "outsiders" (non-*danchi* passengers) are scapegoated and violently ejected. The *danchi*-dwelling group maintains harmony, evidenced by their final absurd laughter, but the bus is forever lost.

Hamilton Armstrong

KOMEDI STAMBUL. Malay-language **musical** theatre of late colonial **Indonesia**, a.k.a. Malay opera. *Komedi stambul* ("Istanbul theatre") initially referred to a single **theatre company**, the Komedie Stamboel, founded as a building-based company in Surabaya's Chinatown by **Chinese** impresario Yap Gwan Thay in 1891. **Actors** were of mixed European-Indonesian descent. A small band of European instrumentalists provided accompaniment.

The plays initially were based exclusively on *Arabian Nights* tales such as *Aladdin* and *Ali Baba*—thus the Istanbul designation. Comedy, spectacle, and song combined in equal measure. The style was similar to that of **Parsi theatre** and European opera and operetta companies, with proscenium **stages** and wing-and-drop **scenography**. Audiences were initially mostly Malay-speaking Chinese, but diversified over time. Plays lasted between three and four hours, and usually were followed by one or more tableaux vivants. Dialogue was not fixed, but relied on formulaic exchanges and the oral heritage of end-rhymed quatrains (*pantun*) and aphorisms.

Komedi stambul began to tour Java in late 1891 under the direction of **Auguste Mahieu** in a circus-like tent. Dozens of imitator companies were formed throughout western Indonesia, resulting in *komedi stambul* becoming a generic name. The repertoire quickly broadened, and, by 1900, the core repertoire of *Arabian Nights* stories was supplemented with Malay-language adaptations of European fairy tales (for example, *Snow White*), opera (*Aida*, *Norma*), true crime stories, **political** allegories, Persian and **Indian** romances, and even the occasional *wayang* (see Puppet Theatre) play and Southeast Asian chronicle. *Komedi stambul* was often associated with scandal. Audiences were rowdy, prostitutes lurked nearby, and the sexual mores of itinerant performers fell outside colonial norms.

Exchange of performers and dramaturgical conventions with *bangsawan* resulted in the effective merger of the two popular Malay genres by 1910. *Komedi stambul* was overshadowed by *tonil* and began declining after 1925. Such was its influence, however, that its dramaturgy, sets, **costumes**, acting, and other features are maintained in popular regional-language theatres like *ludrug*, *kethoprak*, *lenong*, *sandiwara*, and *drama gong*. A small revival took place in the Netherlands among "repatriated" Eurasians in the 1950s.

FURTHER READING

Cohen, Matthew Isaac. *The Komedie Stamboel: Popular Theater in Colonial Indonesia, 1891–1903.*

Matthew Isaac Cohen

KOMEDYA. **Philippines** verse play that usually dramatizes the epic narratives of love and hate between royal Christian and Muslim personages in historical or fictional medieval European and Middle Eastern kingdoms. Descended from the sixteenth-century Spanish *comedia*, this three-part play derived its stories (and even verses) from metrical romances called *awit* and *korido*, which circulated in popular pamphlet editions in the nineteenth and early twentieth centuries. *Komedya* stories found in Tagalog and other regional languages include *The Twelve Peers of France* (Doce pares de Francia), *Prince Roland* (Prinsipe Reynaldo), *The Seven Heirs of Lara* (Siete infantes de Lara), *Gonzalo de Cordoba*, and *Atamante and Minople* (Atamante at Minople).

By the late nineteenth century, *komedya* had established a convention of choreographed fighting (*moro-moro*), grand royal marches, stylized verse delivery punctuated by codified gestures and movements, and special effects (*magia*), such as flying giant birds, huge flowers unfolding to reveal a princess, princes turning to beggars, and vice versa. In the rural areas, *komedya*, sponsored by the local aristocracy, were given by local amateurs as a way of honoring the local patron saint on his feast day. In urban centers, *komedya* was produced by impresarios with professionals in **theatres** for paying audiences. In both settings, the epic drama unfolded in several parts on consecutive nights. The **stage** had a single set, the two- or three-level façade of a palace, with a balcony on the second floor and two passageways, stage left for Moors and stage right for Christians. Moors in red **costumes** were usually dark-skinned like the natives, while Christians in dark clothes were fairer and had European features.

During the Spanish colonial regime, *komedya* was the only dramatic entertainment acceptable to curates and colonial officials because its values helped to shape a colonial mentality among natives. With endings celebrating the triumph of Christians over the Moors, *komedya* affirmed European superiority of **religion**, **political** power, and race over the Moors of the Southern Philippines, as well as over the Christian Indios. By endorsing one supreme authority to be followed in all Christian and Muslim kingdoms, the play buttressed the rule of Spanish monarchs over the Philippines.

With the rise of ***sarsuwela*** in the early twentieth century, the spread of radio and film in the 1930s, and the introduction of a more secular education and culture under American influence, *komedya* slowly lost its audiences, from Manila to the provinces. Today's artists have tried to revitalize it by introducing more democratic and humane values while keeping its centuries-old conventions. But those that succeed in this endeavor are few and far between.

FURTHER READING

Chua Soo Pong, ed. *Traditional Theatre in Southeast Asia*; Tiongson, Nicanor G. *Komedya*.

Nicanor G. Tiongson

KONG SHANGREN (1648–1718). Chinese • *chuanqi* • **playwright** often paired with **Hong Sheng** ("North Kong, South Hong"), his contemporary. Born just after the Ming dynasty's (1368–1644) collapse, Kong experienced the ambiguous moral and **political** climate of his times from a unique vantage point and captured it in the forty-four-scene masterpiece *Peach Blossom Fan* (Taohua shan, 1699). A descendent of Confucius favored with an official appointment by the Kangxi Emperor (r. 1662–1722), Kong also enjoyed life at the margins of early Qing (1644–1911) society, befriending men who had refused to serve the new regime. A guardian of orthodoxy as a Confucian ritual expert, he wrote unofficial history as a playwright. Common to both pursuits was a fascination with performance; role-playing in both theatre and public life is central to *Peach Blossom Fan*'s dramatization of the Ming collapse.

In Qufu, Shandong Province, where he grew up, lineage elders cooperated with the new regime while socializing with men who were its resisters. As a boy, Kong learned of the resistance from family friends; as an official, he gained more first-hand knowledge when posted to the south from 1686 to 1689. He resided in Yangzhou, Jiangsu, a stronghold of Ming loyalism. Travel connected with official duties enabled him to visit Nanjing and other sites related to the resistance, and in Yangzhou he enjoyed southern cultural life, including *chuanqi*. He decided to recreate the lost world he kept encountering, and back in Beijing, began writing plays with the help of a *kunqu* expert.

Kong's forty-scene *Little Thunderclap* (Xiao hulei, 1694) was inspired by a prized antique instrument, around which emerged a historical romance set in the 800s. This little-remarked play anticipates *Peach Blossom Fan* by incorporating actual historical figures, relying on historical sources for scene construction, allowing public scenes (concerning **political** intrigue) to overshadow private ones (concerning love), and presenting morally ambiguous peripheral characters. Kong's scrupulous depiction of complex human motives was at odds with romantic *chuanqi*'s conventions, especially in *Peach Blossom Fan*.

In it, Kong dramatized still remembered events. As per *chuanqi*'s conventions, he interwove private scenes (centered on romance between scholar Hou Fangyu and courtesan Li Xiangjun) and public scenes (concerning the Chongzhen emperor's [r. 1628–1644] suicide and efforts to enthrone a successor in Nanjing and retake the north). Otherwise, his **dramatic structure** was unconventional, especially in its management of time. Forty scenes in two parts form a precisely dated sequence from early 1643 to mid-1645; additional scenes bracket each part. The bifurcation enables characters in the frame scenes to comment on the main sequence's events; moreover, in the two preludes (each dated 1684) that character is Kong Shangren as spectator of his own play. Efforts to underscore the play's theatricality extended also to many dramatized performances: by a **storyteller** (Scenes 1, 10, 13), by Li Xiangjun (2, 24, 25), and by various scholar-officials (at rituals staged in 3, 13, 32, 38, and 40). Performances are so pervasive that virtually every scene seems to feature one.

Peach Blossom Fan reflects ambivalence about the theatre, especially late Ming theatre. On the one hand, Kong saw *chuanqi*'s celebration of emotions (*qing*) as contributing to the Ming collapse. The characters of courtesan Li Xiangjun and official Ruan Dacheng are equally deluded in their belief that they can mold a reality that suits their desires. On the other hand, Kong, viewing theatre as a didactic medium, has an illiterate clown (*chou*) character play a clairvoyant artist who conveys judgments about events through his storytelling. Kong's ambivalence about romance is also evident in the unconventional ending, in which the lovers are reunited, only to be told that in a world turned upside down "happy endings prove unsound" and they must separate.

Peach Blossom Fan was enthusiastically received and widely performed, largely by private **theatre companies**; even the emperor requested a copy. In 1700, Kong was

"Military male" (*wusheng*) character in armor in "A Watery End" scene from *Peach Blossom Fan*. (Photo: Yuan Shuo; courtesy of Jiangsu Provincial Kunqu Troupe)

dismissed from office, his play perhaps contributing to Kangxi's growing coolness toward him. Despite its masterwork status, the play fared poorly on the Qing **stage**, no excerpts being included in *White Furcoat of Compositions* (Zhui baiqiu, 1763 and 1774).

FURTHER READING

Lu, Tina. *Persons, Roles, and Minds: Identity in Peony Pavilion and Peach Blossom Fan*; Strassberg, Richard E. *The World of K'ung Shang-jen, A Man of Letters in Early Ch'ing China.*

Catherine Swatek

KONPARU ZENCHIKU (1405–1470?). Japanese • *nô* • actor, playwright, and **theorist**, an early leader of the **Konparu** troupe, which took that name in his time. Formerly called the Enman'i (or Emai) and the Takeda troupe, the Konparu is said to be the oldest of the four Yamato *sarugaku* troupes that served **religious** institutions in medieval Nara. Yet, judging from Zenchiku's writings, **Zeami Motokiyo**, of the rival Kanze, had a larger impact on Zenchiku's ideas than his own family members, including his father, Konparu Yasaburô. Zeami developed a close personal relationship with Zenchiku, and transmitted to him several plays and treatises, including *Finding Gems, Gaining the Flower* (Shûgyoku tokka, 1428), written expressly for him.

Zenchiku reveals a profound fascination with metaphysics and poetics in his twenty-three treatises. His writings include *The Progression of the Five Modes* (Go'on no shidai), *Record of the Essentials of Song and Dance* (Kabu zuinô ki), and *Collection Illuminating Okina* (Meishukushû), which explores the nature of the divinities represented in the ceremonial *Okina* **dance**. His representative work is a cycle of eight texts on the "Six Circles and One Dew Drop" (Rokurin ichiro), which locate performance practices in a metaphysical context. Since his artistic writings were not widely disseminated until after World War II, Zenchiku was better known as a playwright who favored poetic imagery and "mysterious beauty" (*yûgen*) over dramatic action. Among the dozen plays attributed to him are *The Banana Plant* (Bashô), *Teika*, *Tamakazura*, and, perhaps, *Shrine in the Fields* (Nonomiya).

FURTHER READING

Atkins, Paul. *Revealed Identity: The Noh Plays of Komparu Zenchiku*; Thornhill, Arthur, III. *Six Circles, One Dewdrop: The Religio-Aesthetic World of Komparu Zenchiku.*

Eric C. Rath

KONPARU ZENPÔ (1454–1532?). Japanese • playwright, theorist, actor, and leader (*tayû*) of the Konparu *nô* troupe, Zenpô was the grandson of **Konparu Zenchiku**, and spent his formative years under the tutelage of his grandfather and father Motouji (?–1480), eventually becoming head of the Konparu troupe. Zenpô followed in Zenchiku's footsteps as both a theorist and playwright, but his ideas about performance were less abstract than grandfather's, as seen in his comparisons of *nô* with other arts, such as kickball (*kemari*) and tea ceremony. His references to these arts and to military studies indicate his broad interest in late medieval culture. These insights are preserved in *Zenpô's Conversations* (Zenpô zôtan), a record of his teachings by a disciple, and in his seven volumes of writings.

More familiar to later actors were Zenpô's **music** treatises, such as *On Musical Accompaniment* (Hayashi no koto) and *On the Five Modes* (Go'on no shidai), which were more widely disseminated and incorporated in other texts, including the late-sixteenth century *nô* encyclopedia now called *Eight Volume Treatise on the Flower* (Hachijô kadensho).

Six plays—*Mount Arashi* (Arashiyama), *Atsumori at Ikuta* (Ikuta Atsumori), *The Horned Hermit* (Ikkaku senjin), *Tung-fang So* (Tôbôsaku), *First Snow* (Hatsuyuki), and *Kurokawa*—are attributed to Zenpô, who probably wrote more.

Eric C. Rath

KOREA. A peninsular nation, bordering **China** and Russia, and situated west of **Japan**, Korea is inhabited by about 80 million people (48 million in the south and 22 million in the north) speaking a single language and sharing a similar culture. Since 1948, Korea has been separated into two **political** states: the Republic of Korea (ROK, a.k.a. South Korea) and the Democratic People's Republic of Korea (DPRK, a.k.a. **North Korea**). Today, traditional theatre is banned in the DPRK.

The genesis of Korean theatre is unknown, but may be traced to **religious** rites, **folk** observances, exorcisms, and wandering entertainers from the Asian continent. **Masked •** **dance-**drama, *kkoktu kakshi* **puppet theatre**, and *p'ansori* are the principal traditional forms. Loosely organized, without a highly codified **dramatic structure**, these dynamic forms remain rooted in the common people.

Early Religious Performances. Masked dance-drama antecedents, such as *much'ŏn* (literally, "dance to heaven"), were clannish rites combining songs, **music**, dance, and masks, presented as early as the second century BC to appease the heavens and various animistic deities in hopes of abundant crops, happiness, and safety. During the seventh century, *kiak*, a masked drama performed to proselytize Buddhism, was brought from China to the Paekche Kingdom (18 BC–660 AD). Though *kiak* did not long survive, it may have influenced the origins of today's masked dance, and most certainly was taken from Korea to Japan in 612 in the form of *gigaku* by someone named Mimaji.

During the Silla Kingdom era (57 BC–935 AD) "sword dancing" (*kom-mu*), *muae-mu* (court dance originating in Buddhist ceremonies), and *ch'ŏyong-mu* (celebrating Ch'ŏyong, the Dragon King's legendary son) were important performing arts combining dance and music. *Ch'ŏyong-mu*, the oldest surviving form of masked dance-drama, is known for its oversized, grotesque masks and vigorous movement.

During the Buddhist-dominated Koryŏ dynasty (918–1392), the court-sponsored Eight Vows **Festival** (*p'algwan-hoe*) and Lotus Lantern Festival (*yŏndŭng-hoe*) became important pastimes. The former was dedicated to various folk deities; the latter was a Buddhist commemoration of departed spirits. Both used colorful lanterns to adorn high **stages** on which somersaults, acrobatic dance, puppetry, and masked dance-drama were presented. In the tenth century, *narye*, a court exorcism using hideous masks, shed its shamanistic ritual characteristics, eventually to become a rudimentary masked drama.

Masked Dance-Drama. Steeped in Confucian ideals, the Chosŏn dynasty court (1392–1910) supported popular culture, including masked drama (*sandae-gŭk*). The

Master of the Revels (*sandae-togam*) arranged for masked dance-dramas to entertain foreign envoys, as well as for other purposes. The Revels Office was abolished in 1634; performers left the court, taking their art to the provinces. Though a few **actors** remained attached to the court, all actors during this period were social outcasts. Since that time, masked dance has remained in touch with the common people, performed by itinerant artists and local residents who continue to preserve today's regional forms.

Sandae-gŭk can be classified into two types: village festival plays (including **hahoe pyŏlshin-gut**, *kwanno*, and *pŏm-gut*) and court-originated plays (including **pyŏlsandae**, **t'alch'um**, **ogwangdae**, and **yaryu**).

Hahoe pyŏlshin-gut, presented every ten years to honor village deities (*sŏnang*), employs centuries-old, refined wooden masks. *Kwanno*, performed by male government servants in the Kangnung area, was purely an entertaining dance without dialogue or lampooning. The exorcism-derived *pŏm-gut* (literally, "tiger play") was performed as a village prayer for deliverance from attacks by ferocious animals.

Of the court-originated forms, the Yangju *pyŏlsandae* and the Pongsan *t'alch'um* are similar in many ways, but *pyŏlsandae* has refined dance patterns while *t'alch'um* is characterized by rugged masks. Among *yaryu*, the one preserved in Suyŏng is the oldest. Of **ogwangdae**, the T'ongyŏng and Gosŏng versions are representative with their five-act **dramatic structures**.

These forms emphasized dance and songs, supported by masks, music, and elocution. The language was an amalgam of patterns and dialects spoken by different classes, and physical characterization was often raw and lewd, satirizing corrupt officials, religious figures, and leading citizens, thus providing lower-class citizens a respite from their often difficult lives. Performances were held outdoors at night, with no stage or **scenographic** elements; grotesque masks made of wood, paper, or linen and **costumes**, their appearance intensified by torches, provided spectacle. Six musical instruments provided accompaniment; songs derived mostly from folk origins and shaman exorcisms.

Kkoktu kakshi. Puppets date back at least to the Koguryo kingdom (fourth to seventh centuries). Until the last half of the twentieth century, *kkoktu kakshi* puppeteers wandered from town to town, performing variations of the same play. These initially may have been related to Chinese and Japanese puppets, but a *kkoktu kakshi* rod-puppet performance was freer, less bound by convention and literature than Japan's *bunraku*, for example. Human as well as animal puppets enacted stories of jealousy and divorce, and the appearance of a naked puppet with oversize genitals established this as entertainment aimed at adults more than children.

P'ansori. *P'ansori*, a solo singer-actor performance of epic-style oral literature, emerged in Korea's southern provinces during the eighteenth century. Scholars variously suggest origins in early shamanism or comic performances. Only five pieces exist, although there once were up to twelve. The performer stood on a straw mat in front of a folding screen and, to the accompaniment of a single drummer, presented the story with songs, dialogue, and gestures. The singer-actor, holding a folding fan, began a performance with a short song (*t'anga*) followed by the long main work, consisting of shifting rhythms and tempo. Because the story was orally transmitted, performers often ad-libbed to make the scenes appealing. Performances could last several hours.

All forms of traditional theatre faced extinction under Japanese colonial rule (1910–1945), but these expressions of national identity endured, and today *p'ansori* and masked dance-dramas remain popular, a vibrant connection to Korea's past, frequently presented at the National Theatre (Kuknip Kŭkchang), in folk villages, and on television. Presentations of traditional *kkoktu kakshi* become rarer each year, though its influence continues in **experimental theatre** and theatre for young audiences.

FURTHER READING

Cho, Oh-Kon, trans. *Traditional Korean Theatre.*

Oh-Kon Cho

Japanese Colonialism. Korea, the Hermit Kingdom, was dragged out of isolation in the late nineteenth century by socio-political forces it could not control. Hyŏmnyulsa, the first indoor **theatre**, was built in 1902; the first **Western**-style theatre, Wŏn-gaksa, was built in 1908. A tumult-filled century later, South Korea actively participates in the global theatre community.

Japanese colonialism repressed traditional Korean theatre but introduced two modern forms: the short-lived *shimp'agŭk*, imitating Japanese *shinpa*, and *shingŭk*, based on Western realism, studied and promulgated by intellectual societies of Korean students in Japan (see Kim U-jin). *Shingŭk* **playwrights** such as **Yu Ch'i-jin** imitated works by Irish dramatists, such as Synge and O'Casey. Imitation of non-Korean models likely led to *shingŭk*'s later failure to capture wide interest, but it is also true that **censorship** limited *shingŭk*'s development as socio-political commentary.

Transition: 1945–1960. After World War II, ideological conflict previously held in check by colonial enforcement broke out between artists. Many leftist playwrights fled to North Korea after Korea was partitioned (1948). Some time after the Korean War (1950–1953), traditional forms there were sternly repressed, and North Korean theatre came to mirror proletarian models from Russia and China.

Though South Korea was impoverished, the National Theatre, with its own troupe, the New Association **Theatre Company** (Kukdan Shinhyŏp, 1950), was established, only to have the war intervene. Shakespeare performances in and around Pusan kept theatre alive during the war. Afterward, having returned to Seoul, about 50 percent of this company's productions were of translated Western dramas, but plays by Yu Ch'ijin also were significant.

Maturity: 1960–1988. During the 1960s, observers noted many obstacles facing their theatre: insufficient numbers and types of theatres; a scarcity of theatre-savvy playwrights; meager finances, and so on. Despite such problems, however, in the 1960s a Korean theatre speaking with its own "voice" emerged and matured. In the search for a theatre both modern and Korean, five trends stand out: great interest in absurdism (Beckett's *Waiting for Godot* is particularly popular); renewed respect for traditional forms as modern resources; intercultural experimental theatre; *shingŭk*'s demise; and the rise of the **director**. Small theatre groups (*tongin*) with a passion for meaningful art, not commerce, led the way.

In 1960, Korean-educated (as opposed to Japanese-educated) university graduates founded the Experimental Theatre Company (Shilhŏm Kŭkdan). Others followed. With few places to perform, they moved into basement spaces around universities, their visible legacy the numerous underground theatres in Seoul's University Street (Taehangno) theatre district.

During the 1970s, suffocating censorship forced artists to find inventive means of expressing dissent or criticism, paradoxically leading to a decade of intense creativity by artists such as Ch'oe In-hun (1936–), **Oh T'ae-sŏk**, Yu Dŏk-hyŏng (1938–), Kim Jŏng-ok (1932–), **Lee Kang-baek**, and many others. *Madangguk*, an outdoor form combining mask-dance drama, folk entertainments, and political content, became a weapon in student-led movements against military regimes for two generations, uniting students and common laborers, and challenging establishment concepts (see *Madangnori*).

The 1980s brought profound change: South Korea become a formidable economic power; the repressive Performance Law (1971) was revised; major theatres were built in Seoul; playwright/directors such as **Lee Yun-t'aek** and **Kim Kwang-lim** came to prominence; companies were free to travel, undertaking international exchanges and hosting international festivals; **women**'s issues were addressed; and, in 1988–1989, censorship restrictions were relaxed, permitting the premier of Pak Jo-yl's (1930–) *General Oh's Toenail* (O Changgun ŭi Palth'op, 1974), long banned as a symbol of the pent-up desire for Korean unification.

International Presence: 1989 Onward. Serious challenges from the 1960s remain (theatre spaces are still problematic, for example), and new challenges have emerged (defections to television). However, Seoul has become a major theatre center, hosting an international performing arts festival yearly. Koreans led the way in the establishment of the successful BeSeTo (Beijing-Seoul-Tokyo) Theatre Festival, and, globally, Korean theatre's ascent is symbolized by the honors given to *The Last Empress* (Myŏngsŏng hwanghu, 1995) during its international tour. Largely free of political constraints for the first time, Korean theatre now has a century of development on which to build and the self-confidence in native artistry with which to shape its destiny.

FURTHER READING

Kim, Yun-Cheol, and Miy-Ye Kim, eds. *Contemporary Korean Theatre: Playwrights, Directors, Stage-Designers.*

Richard Nichols

KOSSAMAK, SISOWATH (1904–1975). Cambodian princess (later queen mother, still later queen), full name Sisowath Kossamak Nearyrath, who arguably had the greatest influence on Cambodia's ***robam kbach boran*** of any twentieth-century royal. She not only championed and supported this royal **dance**-drama but also oversaw significant transformations of it.

When Kossamak's father, Sisowath Monivong (1875–1941), became king in 1927, French colonial authorities reconstituted Cambodia's primary *robam kbach boran* troupe as a state **theatre company** and moved it out of the royal harem. Kossamak and Khun Long Meak, Monivong's most influential consort, created a rival company within the harem, overshadowing the state company, which soon was disbanded. Thus this emblem of Cambodia's heritage was kept under royal and Khmer control. After Kossamak's son, Norodom Sihanouk (1922–), ascended the throne in 1941, Kossamak successfully fought another French attempt to supplant the troupe. Throughout Sihanouk's reign and that of Kossamak's husband (after Sihanouk abdicated in 1955 in favor of his father in order to pursue a more **political** role), Kossamak supported the dance and developed its use as a diplomatic tool. In addition, she raised her granddaughter, Sihanouk's daughter, Princess Bopha Devi (1943–), to become the country's premiere dance star.

As impresario of the royal dance troupe, Kossamak also modernized it. She brought boys into the formerly all-female troupe to play monkey (*sva*) roles, making those roles more acrobatic. She encouraged masters to create short versions of certain dances for use in programs for non-Khmer audiences. And she had masters create several works that emphasized the art's lyrical rather than dramatic dimensions. Among these are *Tep Monorom* and the *Apsara Dance*, the latter with movements and **costumes** based on bas-reliefs at Angkor Wat. Both remain among the most beautiful and popular in the repertory.

Kossamak went to **China** after Lon Nol's (1913–1985) 1970 coup. (She was allowed to leave the country partly through the intercession of **director • Hang Tun Hak**, who served in Lon Nol's administration.) She died there shortly after the Khmer Rouge overthrew Lon Nol.

Eileen Blumenthal

KÔWAKAMAI. **Japanese** song-**dance** performances by small troupes of mixed-gender performers that began to be popular among samurai in the mid-fifteenth century; it was brought to perfection as a narrative art in the sixteenth century, when professionals received samurai patronage. It was named for its fifteenth-century creator, whose childhood name was Kôwakamaru.

At first it borrowed both melodic and thematic material from early medieval **storytelling** and dance, especially narrations (*The Tale of the Heike* [Heike monogatari] or *The Tale of the Soga Brothers* [Soga monogatari], for example) accompanied by the lute-like *biwa*. The chanted texts at *kôwakamai*'s height focused on the samurai world of late medieval Japan. Early performances involved the chanting of short narratives, with rhythmic dancing accompanied by drums. **Costumes** were court headgear and robes, and a fan was used. From the end of the fifteenth century, when long narratives of heroic martial exploits were preferred, narration eclipsed dance. *Kôwakamai* narration eventually became a samurai amateur art, leading to its gradual disappearance as a professional genre. However, the narratives' dramatic nature led to their frequent incorporation into *bunraku* (see Puppet Theatre), and to a lesser degree, *kabuki*.

Around fifty texts remain. Scholarly conjectures regarding the nature of otherwise unverifiable aspects of *kôwakamai* in its heyday are based on practices of Ôe Kôwakamai, the sole remaining descendent of Kôwakamai, in Fukuoka Prefecture.

FURTHER READING

Araki, James. *The Ballad Drama of Medieval Japan.*

Katherine Saltzman-Li

KRAVEL, PICH TUM (1943–). Cambodian • playwright, actor, director, researcher, and teacher, well-known for playing Tum in his adaptation of the classical, epic Cambodian poem *Tum Teav* (1967) while an artist at Cambodia's National Conservatory of Performing Arts.

From 1966 to 1993, Kravel wrote more than twenty plays in various styles, including *yiké*, *lakhon bassac*, and *lakhon niyeay*. These plays, which tell historical, cultural, and social stories, include *The Development of the Nation of Kampuchea* (Dam noeu cheat Kampuchea, 1983), *The Blood of the Nation of Kampuchea* (Lohit cheat Kampuchea, 1984), *The Development of the Nation of Laos* (Dam noeu cheat Lao, 1989), and *The Life of the Nation of Cambodia* (Chivit cheat Kampuchea, 1993). They range in size from intimate productions to massive spectacles involving hundreds of performers.

Kravel has held many high positions in areas of cultural service and the preservation, promotion, and development of Khmer cultural heritage. He is adviser to the Royal Government of Cambodia on Cultural Affairs, and an emeritus professor at the Royal University of Fine Arts. In 1997–1998, he worked in Washington, D.C., for Radio Free Asia. He has received many high honors from Cambodian, Southeast Asian, and European bodies, including Officier dans l'Ordre des Palmes Académiques de France (2001) and Cambodia's first Southeast Asian Playwright Award (1999). Kravel has led Khmer delegations to international **festivals**, workshops, and conferences.

From 1975 to 1978, he was a slave farmer during the Khmer Rouge regime under Pol Pot. Kravel's documentation work has been vital in the resurgence of Khmer art forms after the Khmer Rouge's attempts to destroy Khmer culture. The Toyota Foundation, UNESCO/Japan Funds-in-Trust, the Cambodian Ministry of Culture, and the Southeast Asia Program of Cornell University published a number of his works, including his cowritten *Sbek Thom: Khmer Shadow Theatre* (1996).

Catherine Filloux

KRISHEN JIT. *See* Jit, Krishen.

KRISHNATTAM. Indian ritual theatre whose name is formed from Krishna, the deity, and *attam* ("play"). This **religious** genre is performed by one all-male troupe, which resides at the Maha Vishnu (Guruvayurappan) Temple, Guruvayur, Kerala, where most of its performances take place. Mesmerizing **music**, energetic and graceful **dance**, mime, stylized facial expression, and hand language together with ornate **costumes**, **makeup**, and **masks** convey the idea of action in another dimension, if not another world. *Krishnattam* is unique in portraying Krishna's life from birth to death and the return to his heavenly home, Vaikunta. The season, beginning around September, on Vijayadashimi Day (a Hindu holy day celebrating good's victory over evil), and concluding in May, opens with all eight plays followed by a repetition of the first one.

History and Development. Little is known about *krishnattam*'s history and development. *Krishnattam*'s text is from the *Songs about Krishna* (Krishnagiti), written in **Sanskrit** ca. 1654 by Manaveda, a member of the royal family of Kozhikode (Calcutta/Kolkata), who later became the ruler (*zamorin*) of that kingdom. *Krishnattam* remained secluded within the *zamorin*'s kingdom until 1958, when expropriation of revenue sources led to the Guruvayurappan Temple becoming permanent conservator of the troupe. This change allowed *krishnattam* to be performed outside the kingdom, in other areas of Kerala and India, and also abroad.

Makeup, Costumes, Masks. In the late afternoon, near the entrance to the temple compound, two drummers, accompanied by singers keeping the rhythm with small cymbals and a small gong, play an invitation to the night's performance. At dusk, in the dressing room within the temple compound, an oil-lamp is lit, and the intricate and time-consuming makeup begins. Each artist applies the colors for his character and, if appropriate, draws a character-distinguishing design on his forehead. Those playing most male characters and some playing females then lie on the floor for a makeup artist to begin the tedious task of building the *chutti*, a white three-inch-wide lamellar ridge extending along the chin, which helps concentrate the dim light toward the important and highly emphasized facial expressions. Beginning with a line of glue along the performer's jaw, successive layers of rice paste mixed with lime (made from river and seashells) are built up. Each layer must dry completely before another is applied, otherwise the *chutti* might crack or fall off during performance.

Basic makeup and mask colors consist of three mixed colors plus red, black, and white. The mixed colors are a red-orange, a yellow-orange, and a green with more yellow than blue. Females generally wear the more yellow-orange and males the redder. Krishna wears a basic green, adding degrees of blue to make it darker as he ages. The amount of both red and black suggests the degree of malevolence.

The basic male and female costumes are similar to those of **kathakali**. Some characters have unique costumes. Brahma, Bana, and Shiva attach extra wooden arms. Garuda has a wooden beak and painted wings. Devaki, birth mother of Krishna, wears a piece showing her pregnancy.

Krishnattam's larger-than-life masks depict such characters as the four-headed god Brahma, the fierce-looking demoness, monkeys, a demonic bird, mischievous spirits, the god of death, the demon-king, and his five-faced **political** minister.

Performance. After the last temple worship, about 10 p.m., the doors are closed, and drummers and singers rhythmically announce the performance. A handheld **curtain** of concentric colored rectangles conceals and later reveals female characters who dance in praise of Krishna. Following opening rituals, the singers chant the introduction to the night's story. All major characters enter behind the curtain, then reveal themselves and dance to the songs. Two singers alternate in singing the songs in the South Indian *sopana* style, simple, elegant, and meditative. They are accompanied by two barrel-shaped drums and an hour-glass-shaped drum.

There is no speech. The actor expresses song contents through dance, mime, and codified facial expressions and hand language. Dancing is stately, the steps wide, the movements undulating, swaying, and vigorous. The mime is easily understood. In the past, many spectators understood both the Sanskrit text and the hand language, but no longer. Now, a painted board explains the story in Malayalam.

Just before 3 a.m. there is the final dance and the closing poem, in which the author expresses his devotion to Krishna and hopes that his work will help devotees attain salvation. Performers exit, and the temple doors are opened to begin the new day's worship.

Krishnattam performance showing the characters of Satyabhama, sitting right, and Krishna (Arvindakshan Pisharodi), standing left. Towering above the curtain is Narakasura (Mannarathi Shankaranarayanan Nair). (Photo: Aditya Patankar; Courtesy of Martha Ashton-Sikora)

Performance Goal. Devotees pay to have certain plays performed for their specific desires, the first three of the eight being (1) Krishna's birth and childhood, for those desiring children; (2) Krishna's overpowering the serpent king, for the well-being of serpents and protection from them; (3) Krishna's youth spent with milkmaids, for the well-being of female family members and their marriage preparations, and so on.

Three beautiful tableaux vivants appear. Among them is the spectacular opening of the sixth play. When the handheld curtain is taken away Garuda appears with wings spread. Just behind and above Garuda is Krishna, and behind and above Krishna is Krishna's wife, Satyabhama. Garuda will fly them to Bana's kingdom and then on to Narakasura's kingdom, where Satyabhama takes up the bow and arrow and defends her seemingly fainted husband against Narakasura, whom Krishna eventually kills.

FURTHER READING

Ashton-Sikora, Martha B., and Robert P. Sikora. *Krishnattam*.

Martha Ashton-Sikora

KUBO SAKAE (1900–1958). Japanese • playwright, director, critic, translator, and novelist. Born in Sapporo, Hokkaidô, and raised there and in Tokyo, Kubo became interested in *kabuki* and *shinpa* at ten. His interest shifted in high school, when, amid the **Western influence** pervading Japanese theatre, he encountered *shingeki* and Western plays, even reading Schiller in German. This inspired him to major in German at Tokyo University and attracted him to German expressionism. Graduating in 1926, he joined the Tsukiji Little Theatre (Tsukiji Shôgekijô) and, by 1930, completed over half his nearly thirty German play translations.

The 1930s were his most productive period, beginning with *New Tale of the Battles of Coxinga* (Shinsetsu kokusenya kassen, publ. 1930), followed by *Hunan Province, China* (Chûgoku konanshô, 1932), *Writings in Blood at the Five-Cornered Fort* (Goryôkaku kessho, 1933), and his best-known piece, *Land of Volcanic Ash* (Kazan baichi, 1937–1938), set in Hokkaidô, which seeks to prove, scientifically and artistically, Marxist social theory.

Converted to Marxism after joining the Tsukiji Little Theatre, he became enamored with Soviet-style socialist realism yet insisted that any Japanese application of it be strictly faithful to local conditions. He was instrumental in founding the leftwing **theatre company** New Cooperative Troupe (Shinkyô Gekidan) in 1934. Inevitably running afoul of government authorities, it was forced to disband in 1940; troupe members, Kubo included, were arrested. Firm in his communist views, he was in and out of jail or under house arrest until the war ended. He spent this enforced leisure writing a biography of his Tsukiji mentor, **Osanai Kaoru**, and retranslating Goethe's *Faust*.

His postwar path was tragically bumpy on two **political** counts. First, communists disliked him for his **criticism** of their literary policies, which, to Kubo, were based on an illusion that the "freedom" bestowed by the Occupation was unconditional. Subsequent **censorship** and the Red Purge proved his criticism valid. Second, some *shingeki* figures looked askance at him because he questioned their war responsibilities. These difficulties led to Kubo's reduced productivity, negative reception, and isolation. He organized the short-lived Tokyo Art Theatre (Tokyô Geijutsu Gekijô), wrote *An Ascending Kiln* (Nobori kama, 1951), an incomplete novel, and published two plays, *Apple Orchard Diary* (Ringoen nikki, 1946) and *Weather Conditions in Japan* (Nihon no kishô, 1953). He committed suicide while hospitalized for manic depression.

Guohe Zheng

KUBOTA MANTARÔ (1889–1963).

KUBOTA MANTARÔ (1889–1963). Japanese • **playwright** and **director** whose career unusually spanned both commercial theatre (including *kabuki*) and noncommercial. In 1919, he directed **Izumi Kyôka**'s *A Genealogy of Women* (Onna keizu), which became a *shinpa* classic. This success spurred him to write more plays. He published *Ôdera School* (Ôdera gakkô, 1927), which became a great *shingeki* success at the Tsukiji Little Theatre (Tsukiji Shôgekijô) in 1928. It exemplifies Kubota's signature style, partly resulting from his tragic personal life: sympathetically rendered characters, frequently infused with a sense of loneliness and out of step with changing times.

In 1934, he enhanced his *shingeki* credentials with his sensational production of *Weasels* (Itachi) by **Mafune Yutaka**. Kubota had identified himself with *shingeki*'s non**political** wing, and in 1937 he became a cofounder of the Literary Theatre (Bungaku-za). Kubota was associated with yet another milestone in 1945, when he directed **Morimoto Kaoru**'s *A Woman's Life* (Onna no isshô), the play that defined the Literary Theatre into the 1950s.

When *kabuki*'s feudal content was under threat from the Occupation in the postwar years, Kubota advised on what plays might still be acceptable. More involvement with *kabuki* followed, and in 1951 he directed a landmark adaptation of *The Tale of Genji* (Genji monogatari).

Brian Powell

***KUCHIPUDI*.** South **Indian •** **dance**-drama originating in Kuchipudi Village, Andhra Pradesh. Its origins can be traced back to the devotion cult (*bhakti*) that engulfed India from the twelfth to sixteenth centuries. It gave rise to holy men (*yogis*), known as *bhagavatar* in Tamilnadu and *bhagavatalu* in Andhra Pradesh, who danced and sang God's praises (see Religion in Theatre).

Kuchipudi's genesis and growth as a separate form began in the sixteenth century, and it flourished in the seventeenth. Tirthanarayana Yogi, a devotee of the Hindu god Krishna, and considered the father of *kuchipudi*, firmly believed that "theatrical forms were vehicles" of devotion. He wrote *Poems on the Childhood Playing of Krishna* (Krishna lila tarangini), an opera in praise of Krishna, which he taught his students and presented in temples. His disciple Siddhendra Yogi wrote *The Stealing of the Flower Parijata* (Parijatapaharam), later known as *Satyabhama's Resentment* (Bhama kalapam), and taught Brahman boys near Kuchipudi to perform it. He also persuaded the village's Brahmans to take an oath that at least one male member of their families would play Satyabhama, the heroine, once in their life. These arrangements helped sustain the tradition.

Kuchipudi plays are written mainly in Telugu. Performance practice is based on the guiding principles laid down by the **Sanskrit theatre** manuals *Treatise on Drama* (Natyashastra), and the *Abhinaya Darpana* (see Theory). *Kuchipudi* consists of "pure dance" (*nritta*); "expressive dance" (*nritya*), comprising poetic compositions (*shabdam*); "love songs" (*padam*); and "**acting**" (*natya*), as manifested in "chants" (*sloka*) or solo acting pieces. *Kuchipudi* dance might seem similar to ***bharata natyam***, but there are significant differences between them. Kapila Vatsyayan observes that, in *kuchipudi*, the arms are used less tersely, with some curves and circular patterns. Another notable feature found in *kuchipudi* is characters introducing themselves (*daru*) before the play begins. Satyabhama in *Satyabhama's Resentment*, after singing the *daru*, throws the braided plait over the **curtain** toward the audience. This is perceived as a challenge to dispute the actor's artistry. If anyone accepts and defeats the actor, the braid is cut in two, and the play begins again with a new actor as Satyabhama. It also consists of an exquisite dance called *Poems on Child Krishna* (Balagopala tarangam) in which the dancer performs while standing on the edge of a brass plate and keeping a pot of water on his head.

Kuchipudi **makeup** is not elaborate, nor are the **costumes**. The **music** is of classical Carnatic style.

FURTHER READING

Naidu, M. A. *Kuchipudi Classical Dance*; Gargi, Balwant. *Folk Theater of India*; Vatsyayan, Kapila. *Traditional Indian Theatre: Multiple Streams*.

Arya Madhavan

***KUMI ODORI*.** Representative Okinawan **dance**-drama, using often spectacular **scenography**, **costumes**, **makeup**, and **acting** styles. It has led to Okinawa's traditional performing arts culture becoming better known in mainland **Japan** and around the world. In 2004, the National Theatre of Okinawa (Kokuritsu Gekijô Okinawa) opened in Urasoe to help sustain—and showcase to tourists and residents alike—*kumi odori* and the many other varieties of Okinawan performance.

Now a nationally protected art, *kumi odori* started as Okinawan court entertainment in the early eighteenth century. Although conquered by Japan in 1609, the Ryûkyû kingdom, the old name of Okinawa's islands, was permitted to retain its royal family and to keep up long-standing relations with **China**. A courtier named Tamagusuku Chôkun (1684–1734) inaugurated *kumi odori* in 1719 as entertainment to honor Chinese emissaries who came to the Ryûkyûs for the investiture of King Shô Kei. Chôkun is known to have traveled to Edo (Tokyo), and to have taken lessons in *nô* and *kabuki*—influences of which can be seen in *kumi odori*'s style and repertory. *Possessed by Love, She Takes Possession of the Temple Bell* (Shûshin kaneiri) is among the original pieces still popular today.

The **musical** accompaniment for *kumi odori* and Okinawan traditional song and dance in general is provided by an ensemble comprised of drum (*taiko*), flute, horizontal harp (*koto*), one-string fiddle (*kokyû*), and—foremost—the three-stringed *sanshin*, precursor to the *shamisen*.

FURTHER READING

Thornbury, Barbara. *The Folk Performing Arts: Traditional Culture in Contemporary Japan.*

Barbara E. Thornbury

KUNQU. **Chinese** genre meaning "*kun* songs," short for *kunshan qiang* or Kunshan **music**. It became an elegant (*ya*) style of southern *qu* (songs) when **Wei Liangfu** and associates reinvented it in the mid-sixteenth century. However, there have also been common (*su*) forms of *kunqu*, especially in and around its roots in the Suzhou hinterland. It absorbed influences from other regional *xiqu* styles as it spread nationwide and has influenced these styles in turn, such cross-fertilization being particularly productive with *jingju*, which supplanted *kunqu* in the eighteenth century. Today, some *kunqu* **training** is essential for *jingju* **actors** and also desirable for performers of other regional drama.

Emergence. In the early 1500s, *kunshan qiang* was a little-regarded style of southern *qu* sung by **folk** performers in Kunshan, Suzhou Prefecture, Jiangsu Province. By 1580, it was being embraced by the highest social echelons. *Kunqu*'s transformation from folk music to a national form came in two stages. First, its music, singing, and instrumentation were purged of coarse features and polished by Wei Liangfu, who codified his music and taught disciples how to sing it. By 1557, **Xu Wei** would write that the "flowing beauty and lingering mellifluousness" of *kunshan qiang* was captivating audiences throughout Wu (roughly, the lower Yangzi River region). Next, Liang Chenyu (1520–ca. 1593), Wei's disciple, adapted an old *nanxi* for performance to the new music. *Washing Silk* (Huanshā ji, 1579), a *chuanqi* about a woman whose beauty toppled the feudal state of Wu, proved an apt vehicle for music whose sinuous melodies epitomized the seductive femininity of Jiangnan ("south of the Yangzi River") culture. Conservative literati found *Washing Silk* vulgar and shallow, but as its popularity spread, *kunshan qiang* made the leap to the **stage** and became *kunqu*. *Nanxi* plays were adapted as *kunqu*, and **playwrights** began to write with its melodies in mind, but *kunqu* had not yet developed distinctive performance elements.

Drama miscellanies from the late sixteenth century reveal a kaleidoscope of musical styles for southern *qu*. Most catered to popular taste, but post-1600 miscellanies register *kunqu*'s growing prestige. Theatre lover Pan Zhiheng (1556–1622) noted that "correct" *kunqu* could be found only in Suzhou, Kunshan, and Taicang. One of China's wealthiest cities, Suzhou exported *kunqu* actors to other regions while her native sons published treatises on its prosody and collections of its model arias (*qupu*). *A Manual of Songs in the Nine Keys and Thirteen Modes* (Nan jiugong shisandiao cipu, 1610) by Shen Jing (1553–1610) marked *kunqu*'s elevation as the orthodox form of southern *qu*. Literati began using its songs in earnest when writing *chuanqi* and adapted the works of playwrights, such as **Tang Xianzu**, who preferred to use the music of their own locale. *Kunqu* in the meantime continued its spread throughout Jiangnan, albeit in hybrid forms.

This strong southern base enabled *kunqu* to reach Nanjing and Beijing, where theatricals were popular at court and official banquets, despite the disapproval of orthodox Confucians. In 1610, a diarist noted that he had attended a performance by "Wu actors" at a Suzhou "native-place association" (*huiguan*), evidence that plays were being performed as *kunqu* in Beijing. However, interest in *kunqu* outside official elites came only in the Qing dynasty (1644–1911).

Performance Styles and Elements. Though performed publicly, *kunqu* at this time was mostly household entertainment, performed by privately trained troupes of about twelve actors in well-to-do homes and gardens. Disaffected officials such as Qian Dai (1539–1620) took up theatre to "dispel lofty ambitions," while officeholders such as Zou Diguang (fl. 1573–1620) showcased their troupes before family members and guests; some even let them perform at temples or gatherings hosted by others. Many troupe owners purchased and trained children, whose careers peaked in early adolescence; some would have sexual relationships with them (Qian Dai took four actresses as concubines). Flawless singing was essential, and **dance** became an important element of some plays. Contemporary accounts reveal that dancing often stimulated spectators' sexual fantasies. But expressive acting was prized above beauty, with care taken that actors understood the script, grasped their character, and were able to create a "second self," with no improvisation permitted and the **director** having full control.

A square carpet sufficed as a stage, but platforms were sometimes used, as were lanterns to enhance the spectacle. Sound effects included offstage birdcalls, neighing, and thunder, while **properties** included real objects (sedan chairs, instruments of torture) as well as symbolic ones (a whip for a horse); they also reveal that mime (somersaulting from horseback, sailing in boats) was being used.

Romantic plays showcasing "male" (*sheng*) and "female" (*dan*) **role types** were favored by troupes, performed either piecemeal or complete over several days on special occasions. Extracts were favored at banquets, where guests selected scenes. Professionals performed at temples and in sheds, actress-prostitutes in wine houses, teahouses, and brothels; aesthetic standards for these professionals were lower than for household actors. Singing only remained popular at private gatherings and public competitions.

Transition from Ming to Qing. *Kunqu* rode a late Ming mania for theatre to its peak in the 1640s. Qi Biaojia (1602–1645), a busy official, wrote in his diary about eighty-six plays he saw between 1632 and 1639. On the one hand, maintaining a private troupe became a badge of status connoting true connoisseurship. On the other hand, amateurs performed with professionals as "guests" (*chuanke*) and sometimes joined their troupes. These interactions between amateurs and professionals fostered cross-fertilization between elegant and common styles. Public performances, mainly at temples, attracted crowds of men and **women** numbering in the thousands; even sedan chair carriers commented knowledgably on performances.

After the Ming collapse and devastation of the south, *kunqu* took new directions. Commoner literati began writing plays for a living, many of them circulating as manuscripts and designed to be performed complete. Scenes were fewer and **dramatic structure** tighter; arias were reduced in number to accommodate more dialogue. Speech in Ming *kunqu* had been declaimed stiffly; now Suzhou dialect appeared, especially in plays featuring "painted face" (*jing*) and "clown" (*chou*) roles, a departure from the *sheng/dan* pairings favored formerly. Journeymen playwrights tackled new subjects (labor unrest, peasant rebellions, anti-eunuch protests) and depicted ordinary townspeople in leading roles. Complete plays with vivid dialogue are indicators of popularized *kunqu*, and many became staples of *kunqu*'s repertoire, even though little remarked by connoisseurs. It is against this background that **Li Yu** wrote a widely influential treatise that encapsulated many of these trends.

The turn away from romance and intrusion of **politics** is also reflected in the works of **Kong Shangren** and **Hong Sheng**, among the last of the national elite to write elaborately long *chuanqi* in the late Ming style. Kong's *Peach Blossom Fan* (Taohua shan, 1699) explores, delicately, the causes of the Ming's collapse but proved too politically sensitive to be widely performed. Hong's *Palace of Eternal Life* (Changsheng dian, 1688) examines how love and politics became intertwined in the Tang dynasty (618–907), with veiled references to more recent events. When Hong was imprisoned for attending a private performance of it at a time of national mourning, scholar-officials took heed and ceased writing plays for public consumption.

Second Golden Age. In the next two centuries, few new *chuanqi* were written, and actors instead adapted scenes from the existing stock. Extracts, which had been popular at banquets, now became the chief vehicle, their texts collected in miscellanies. Extracts showcased ingenuity and skill as stars became identified with particular characters in well-known scenes. Performances featured acting in which every gesture (for example, brushing away tears) was minutely prescribed and matched to a line of text. A style of acting highly formalized and externalized in gestures replaced the interiorized acting favored in late Ming.

Meanwhile, literati mostly wrote for self-amusement and private performances. Many found actors' performances vulgar. "A good play is not performed; performance spoils a good play" became the motto of proponents of "pure singing" (*qingchang*), meaning either the old style of singing to instrumental accompaniment while seated at a table, or singing uncontaminated by contact with professionals. Despite these biases, interactions between amateurs and professionals eroded barriers between the two styles.

Kunqu's second highest tide came in the first half of the eighteenth century. Actors were brought from Suzhou to Beijing during the Kangxi reign (1662–1722) and housed at the Qing court in a part of the palace known as "Suzhou Alley." Touring the south in 1751, the Qianlong emperor (r. 1736–1796) was so impressed by a troupe assembled especially for him that extracts became the preferred entertainment at court banquets. When Jiaqing (r. 1796–1820) curtailed court theatricals, many of the Suzhou actors left to form troupes in Beijing. These preserved a southern style, but as other *xiqu* styles entered Beijing (especially *jingju*) the troupes could not compete. The last purely *kunqu* troupe disbanded in 1837. As Suzhou actors began performing in mixed-style troupes, a northern style (*beikun*) developed with singing and speaking using northern pronunciation.

Professionals from forty-three **theatre companies** are named on a stele erected in Suzhou in 1781; there were amateurs as well. The professionals were organized in a guild under the Imperial Silk Office, which vigilantly oversaw their activities at the height of Qianlong's literary inquisition (1780–1782). They performed in commercial theatres patronized largely by merchants. Yangzhou salt merchants assembled seven "great inner troupes" (*da neiban*) for Qianlong's southern tours. These were privately owned but performed at official functions and also on temple stages. Rivalry between Suzhou and Yangzhou troupes was fierce, leading to new heights of artistry. In other regions, especially Zhejiang and Jiangsu, *kunqu* shared the stage with plays performed in local dialect.

Decline and New Directions. On the eve of the Taiping rebellion (1850–1866), *kunqu* could no longer compete with *jingju* and other *xiqu* styles in Beijing, and, even in Suzhou, it came under pressure. Performances of too-familiar extracts seemed too formal and static. Suzhou's actors dwindled in number, and troupes moved to Shanghai, *kunqu*'s new base. But wages and working conditions were poor, and top actors defected to *jingju*. By the 1890s, performances were sporadic, and some desperate older actors even committed suicide. Faced with *kunqu*'s demise, concerned amateurs established a Suzhou training school (1921) and took steps such as teaching *kunqu* in the schools to revive interest. By the 1940s, however, *kunqu*'s fortunes again hung by a thread.

Since 1949, *kunqu* has struggled to redefine itself. In the 1950s, training schools were founded and troupes rebuilt in former urban strongholds. Nanjing and Suzhou are the most conservative; Beijing continues the northern style associated with *jing* actor Hou Yushan (1893–1996) and *dan* actor Han Shichang (1898–1976); and Shanghai is readier to **experiment**. Among successes of state-sponsored promotion was *Fifteen Strings of Cash* (Shiwu guan), adapted from an early complete Qing *chuanqi* in 1956 and hailed for "bringing *kunqu* back to life"; other complete plays followed. These efforts, cut short by the Cultural Revolution (1966–1976), resumed in the 1980s, but received little government support.

The situation changed for the better in 2001, when UNESCO added *kunqu* to its list of "Masterpieces of the Oral and Intangible Heritage of Humanity." The turnaround has been most striking in Suzhou, formerly in Shanghai's shadow. With government support, an Association for the Rescue, Protection, and Promotion of Suzhou Kunqu has been established. *Kunqu* in Beijing also has improved with government support, and the boundaries between northern and southern styles are blurring.

FURTHER READING

Birch, Cyril. *Scenes for Mandarins: The Elite Theater of the Ming*; Shen, Grant Guangren. *Elite Theatre in Ming China, 1368–1644*; Swatek, Catherine C. *Peony Pavilion Onstage: Four Centuries in the Career of a Chinese Drama*.

Catherine Swatek

Kuo Pao Kun's *Descendants of the Eunuch Admiral*, in the TheatreWorks production, 1999. (Photo: Alfie Lee; courtesy of TheatreWorks)

KUO PAO KUN (1939–2002). Singaporean • **playwright**, **director**, and teacher, regarded as "the father of Singaporean theatre." Born in Hebei Province, **China**, and raised in Singapore, he **trained** at Australia's National Institute of Dramatic Arts, returning to Singapore in 1965. The same year, Kuo founded the Practice Performing Arts School along with his wife, choreographer Goh Lay Kuan.

Kuo's earliest plays were imbued with a strong working-class consciousness, earning him four years of detention under the country's Internal Security Act (1976–1980; see Censorship). In the years immediately following his release, Kuo penned two significant one-acts, "The Coffin Is Too Big for the Hole" (1984) and "No Parking on Odd Days" (1986), which became among the country's most-produced dramas, both dealing with individuals facing an inflexible state bureaucracy.

In 1990, Kuo set up The Substation, providing a successful local model for an independent multiple-use arts facility. Kuo directed many of his own plays. His most important later works include *Lao Jiu* (1990) and *Descendents of the Eunuch Admiral* (1995), the latter using the story of Chinese explorer and eunuch Zheng He as a metaphor for modern Singapore.

Kuo was completely bilingual, writing, producing, and directing in both English and Mandarin, sometimes with his bilingual company, the Practice Theatre Ensemble (now The Theatre Practice), which he founded in 1986. With Kuo's passing, the voice of Singapore's older generation is largely absent in local theatre today.

William Peterson

KURAVANCI. **Indian** genre of dramatic Tamil poetic works that developed in Tamilnadu in the mid- to late-seventeenth century. Nowadays, these are most frequently presented as **dance**-dramas in the traditional genre of ***bharata natyam***. A traditional *kuravanci* was enacted by a cast of female temple-dancers (*devadasi*) and sponsored by local lords, landholders, and temple heads. The plot was set in the locality of a temple dedicated to an important regional deity, as seen in the celebrated work connected with Lord Shiva at the temple at Kurralam in southern Tamilnadu.

The involvement of temple-dancers with Hindu **religious** rituals was outlawed by the British colonialists in the early twentieth century. During the same period, the temple dance genre was transmuted into the classical dramatic dance form *bharata natyam* by important sponsor/dancers, such as Rukmini Devi Arundale (1904–1997).

Kuravanci pieces have a standard plot and characters that are recreated poetically in a different locality in each work. A young girl, playing with her girlfriend, happens to see the local ruler, or the image of the local deity in procession, and falls overwhelmingly in love with him. Lovesick, she invites a Kurava woman to read her future. (The Kuravas are a gypsy-like Tamil tribal group whose **women** are believed to have soothsaying powers.) The woman becomes inspired and tells the girl her lovesickness will end and she will be united with her love. The girl's friend takes a love message to the lord/god of her affection; he appears in disguise and attempts to sway her. She remains faithful to her first love. With her fidelity/chastity affirmed, the lord/god reveals himself and marries her. There is sometimes a humorous down-to-earth parallel subplot in which a handsome, lovesick Kurava man appears, searching for the soothsaying Kurava woman. She scolds him, asking him to control his emotions.

While the genre clearly draws on numerous **folk** elements, such as the Kuravas and fortune telling, performatively and literarily it lies within the realm of the classical. Its poetry is lyrical, sophisticated, and highly devotional, putting it into the category of classical devotional (*bhakti*) literature. *Kuravanci* works have always been presented as classical dance-dramas. In their current manifestation as a *bharata natyam* dance-drama form, a troupe of male and female dancers enacts the roles. A small group of background narrative singers and accompanying instrumentalists and percussionists sits to the side. The verses are sung in the Carnatic **musical** style as the dancers bring them to dramatic life in the rhythmic mimetic *bharata natyam* style.

Kuravanci manifests important themes and motifs deeply rooted in the religious traditions of South India and that are therefore found in other local traditional forms. These include the identity between god and king and between *bhakti* toward a god and faithful, chaste love toward a king.

FURTHER READING

Gargi, Balwant. *Folk Theater of India*; Vatsyayan, Kapila. *Traditional Indian Theatre: Multiple Streams.*

Richard A. Frasca

KUTIYATTAM. **Indian** genre of **Sanskrit theatre** that emerged around 900 in the southwest coastal region of Kerala. Originally known as *kuttu* ("drama"), *kutiyattam* (literally, "combined acting"; also spelled *kudiyattam*) came to be performed exclusively as a "visual sacrifice" to the primary deities of selected high-caste Hindu temples.

Kutiyattam first developed under the patronage of King Kulasekharavarman (ca. eleventh century), when Sanskrit drama was beginning to decline and becoming more the subject of commentators on the **theoretical** treatises than of actual practice.

Kulasekharavarman authored two dramas still staged, *Subhadra and Dhananjaya* (Subhadra–Dhananjaya) and *Tapati and Samvarana* (Tapati–Samvarana). Other traditional plays included **Kalidasa**'s *The Recognition of Shakuntala* (Abhijnana Shakuntalam), recently revived on the basis of staging manuals; one-act farces such as "The Hermit-Harlot" (Bhagavadajjuka), revived by Ram Cakyar in the 1980s; and plays attributed to **Bhasa**, such as *The Vision of Vasavadatta* (Svapna-Vasavadatta) and *The Broken Thighs* (Urubhanga).

Approach to Text. *Kutiyattam* is unusual in that it does not stage an entire text, but enacts only a single act of a particular drama on the final night at any given performance. The performance's remainder—lasting from one to three, five, or even forty-one nights—consists of an elaborate set of preliminary rituals (*purvaranga*) and solo performances enacting/telling the background story behind the actual drama. The "combined acting" of the text is followed by concluding rituals (*mutiyakitta*).

"The Hermit-Harlot" is one of the oldest plays. One traditional manual records how to stage a portion of it leading up to the "combined acting" over thirty-five nights. For seven of these nights, the clown-sidekick (*vidushaka*) to various heroes explains and comments in the local language on the play's philosophical issues.

Raman Cakyar plays the *vidushaka* role Shandilya in the *kutiyattam* version of "The Hermit-Harlot." (Photo: Phillip Zarrilli)

Only certain sections of the one-act are presented on specific nights. Indeed, when a portion of the scene between the two main characters—a teacher (Bhagavan) and his wayward pupil (Shandilya)—is enacted, rather than a farce, the evening becomes a rather serious allegory. The scene with the courtesan and her attendant in the garden before the exchange of souls is an opportunity for the two female performers (*nangyars*) to elaborate the erotic pleasures associated with the poetic images of the garden, emphasized through **dance** and facial expression.

Kulusekhara's Innovations. Assisted by a well-known, high-caste Brahman scholar, Tolan, King Kulasekharavarman is credited with innovations that gradually became the form's hallmarks: (1) the use of the local language, Malayalam, by the *vidushaka* to explain key passages (Sanskrit no longer being commonly understood); (2) the introduction of each character with brief narration of his past; (3) allowance for deviation from a script in its performance to provide elaboration on meaning and/or the state of mind/being of a character; and (4) the development of **stage** manuals recording details on how to present particular dramas, and acting manuals explaining how **actors** should elaborate particular passages. The performance score for a *kutiyattam* drama is exceedingly intricate and elaborate.

These conventions were originally controversial, as noted in an anonymous fifteenth-century text, *The Goad on the Actors* (Natankusa), which attacks actors for their "blasphemous" and "ill-logical" deviations from the precepts for staging Sanskrit dramas found in authoritative sources, including Bharata's ancient *Treatise on Drama* (Natyashastra). The author complains:

> Our only point is this—the sacred drama (*natya*), by the force of ill-fate, now stands defiled. The ambrosial moon and the sacred drama—both are sweet and great. A black spot mars the beauty of the former, unrestrained movements that of the latter. What should we do then [to correct these defilements]?

A Temple Art. Kutiyattam became associated with, and eventually exclusively performed within, particular high-caste Hindu temples as a "visual sacrifice" to their deities. Performances are held either in an inner hall or at temple **theatres** (*kuttampalam*). The design of these rectangular theatres is based on principles in the *Natyashastra* and traditional architecture texts. The audience seating area and the performance and backstage areas are approximately equal in size. **Religious** rituals ensure that purity is maintained so that the "sacrifice" of the performance pleases both the deity and the audience.

Kutiyattam is traditionally performed by three sets of temple-servants—*cakyars*, who play male roles; *nambiars*, who provide percussion accompaniment on large copper drums (*milavu*) upstage; and *nangyars*, who play the females. The *cakyars* and *nangyars* are learned performers able to perform both the combined acting of *kutiyattam* as well as solo performances (*kuttu*) used to elaborate stories from the Puranas.

For centuries, *kutiyattam* has been appreciated within its high-caste community of connoisseurs for such delights as the *vidushaka*'s lengthy set of humorous, philosophical elaborations on the audience's behavior. *Kutiyattam*'s sequestering within a limited temple context meant that it was unknown to a larger Indian or international public for centuries. As Kerala's socioeconomic conditions evolved under British rule, and again after independence (1947), the cultural context and audience base eroded.

Training. Acclaimed actor Ram Chakyar brought *kutiyattam* to wider attention when he made it a subject at the state arts school, Kerala Kalamandalam, and when performances began to be held outside temple confines. Today *kutiyattam* **training** is also given at Margi in Thiruvananthapuram and at the Ammannur Gurukulam in Irinjalakuda. It recently began to be taught at **Singapore**'s Theatre Training and Research Program. Recognizing *kutiyattam*'s place as what may be the world's oldest theatrical form with a continuous tradition, UNESCO places it among the world's "Masterpieces of the Oral and Intangible Heritage of Humanity."

FURTHER READING

Panchal, Goverdhan. *Kuttampalam and Kutiyattam*; Paulose, K. G., ed. *Kudiyattam: A Historical Study;* Raja, K. Kunjunni. *Kutiyattam: An Introduction.*

Phillip Zarrilli

KYÔGEN. Japanese traditional form consisting of stylized comedies linked with *nô* since the mid-fourteenth century. Plots range from fantastic parody to comedy of manners to farcical slapstick. *Kyôgen* has experienced a continuous surge in popularity since World War II, delighting audiences with verbal wit, evocative pantomime, dramatic verve, and spirited song and **dance**. Today, *kyôgen* by the **Okura** and **Izumi schools** are performed between *nô* plays as well as on independent all-*kyôgen* programs. **Actors** also appear as local villagers or priests in the "interval" (*ai-kyôgen*) sections between acts of many *nô* plays, narrating the backstory in colloquial language.

History. *Kyôgen* means "wild" or "nonsense" words, dangerous fictions said to lead Buddhists astray from the true path. **Chinese**-derived variety show (*sangaku*) skits and *dengaku* rice-planting songs and dances combined to form *sarugaku* (literally "monkey music"). This was later split into *kyôgen* comedy and *nô* drama, coupled on a single program since before the time of **playwright**-actor **Zeami**. In contrast to *nô*'s lyric abstraction, *kyôgen* employs straightforward language and relatively realistic pantomime to present dialogue plays of earthy **folk** humor. During the Muromachi period (1333–1573), *kyôgen* were *the* popular entertainments, performed by amateurs and professionals at weddings, **festivals**, and imperial parties. Once bitingly satiric and overtly salacious, *kyôgen*'s improvisatory spirit of the wily and rebellious underdog was diluted when absorbed with *nô* as the shogunate's "ceremonial **music**" (*shikigaku*) during the Edo period (1603–1868).

Kyôgen stories were passed down through acting troupes. Titles in the mid-eleventh-century *Records of New Sarugaku* (Shin sarugaku ki), such as "A Nun Searches for Swaddling Clothes" or "A Rustic's First Visit to the Capital," provided a loose frame for broad improvisation. Later compilations, such as the *Tenshô Kyôgen Book* (Tenshô kyôgen bon, 1578), include summaries of hundreds of plays. The first full scripts were submitted to the authorities only in the mid-seventeenth century, including **Tora'akira Ôkura**'s in 1642. Yet, many versions of the same plot were published, attesting to *kyôgen*'s popularity among townsmen, and diverse interpretations among rival troupes.

The Plays. *Kyôgen* humor taps deep veins of feudal era folly and knavery. Plays are generally twenty to thirty minutes long; place and time remain purposefully vague. Plots follow a simple **dramatic structure**. In the formal set-up, the lead character explains who he is, where he is going, and why. Soon his ignorance, laziness, curiosity, gullibility, or drunkenness causes uproarious consequences. Plays usually conclude in comeuppance, a rebuke, and a chase, but sometimes in laughter or celebratory dance.

There are currently 180 plays in the Ôkura school, 254 in the Izumi school, totaling, with overlap, 260 plays. Many began as true stories—the man who shed crocodile tears when leaving a mistress—or sharp satires about witless courtiers or clever Buddhist acolytes. Acute individual portraits were beveled over centuries into the familiar caricatures of universal comedy.

Kyôgen plots span slapstick, fantasy, situational comedy, and satire of the pompous and foolish. *Kyôgen* expresses a temporary rebellion against the status quo, before the rule of authority and reason reasserts itself, obviously appealing to townspersons educated in the arts yet wary of nouveau riche overreaching.

Plays are classified by leading character and atmosphere. The ritual dance-play *Okina* traditionally initiates a full program. Created earlier and considered separate from the *nô-kyôgen* repertoire, *Okina* contains two important dances by the *kyôgen* actor portraying the joyous old man Sanbasô: the vigorous ground stamping (*momi no dan*) followed by seed-planting bell-ringing (*suzu no dan*).

In celebratory plays (*waki mono*), such as the *God of Happiness* (Fukunokami) and *Ebisu Bishamon*, parishioners are blessed by the god's appearance. *Waki kyôgen* featuring humans have propitious themes culminating in a joyous song, such as *Fan of Felicity* (Suehirogari), or farmers assuring nationwide peace and fruitfulness.

In "feudal lord plays" (*daimyô mono*) a pompous yet ignorant feudal lord is shamed by a servant or host. He mispronounces words and cannot remember a simple poem at a garden-viewing party in *Bush-clover Lord* (Hagi daimyô). In *Two Lords* (Futari daimyô), a ridiculed passerby forces two swaggering lords at sword point to perform mock cockfights and silly songs.

Kyôgen's most representative character appears in "small lord plays" (*shômyô mono*) or "Tarô-kaja plays" (*tarô-kaja mono*) in which the devious servant Tarô-kaja manages to escape an unpleasant task. He pretends to have leg cramps in *Cramps* (Shibiri), cannot sing while standing in *Lap-singing* (Neongyoku), and even feigns his absence in *Called by a Song* (Yobikoe). Tarô-kaja is a glutton: eating sweets he should be guarding in *Poisoned Sugar* (Busu), gobbling the *Roasting Chestnuts* (Kuriyaki), swilling sake despite being *Tied to a Pole* (Bôshibari). The character is lazy yet clever, a cowardly braggart, a fun-loving Everyman ready for a laugh, a drink, or a song and dance.

"Son-in-law" or "bridegroom plays" (*muko mono*) feature auspicious first meetings of groom and father-in-law. Bad advice to the nervous groom make these auspicious first encounters go hilariously awry. He splits his divided trousers (*hakama*) in a struggle with his brother in *Two in One Pants* (Futari bakama). The son-in-law enlists his wife's help to defeat her father in *Adopted Son* (Morai muko).

The "**women** plays" (*onna mono*) feature females who wear a plump-cheeked **mask** if homely, or a white turban (*binan*) with dangling braids if shrewish. Feisty wives love too little or too much, ultimately giving in to their husband's demands. Unwilling to accept a divorce, a wife kidnaps her husband in *Fortune Bag* (Enmei bukuro); another scolds her spouse until he threatens to commit *Suicide by Sickle* (Kamabara). Yet the wife's affection is displayed when she agrees to share her hubby with his mistress in *Dontarô*.

Unlike the fierce ghosts and monsters of *nô*, the title characters in "demon plays" (*oni mono*) are forged in man's image: gullible, romantic, and fallible. Enma, King of Hell, often appears, but is far from frightening. He is voracious in *Bird-catcher in Hades* (Esashi jûô), losing a rope-pulling contest in *Tug-o'-war* (Kubihiki), and being bested by a powerful warrior in *Asahina*. Cute, wide-eyed demons are in love with maidens in *Equinox* (Setsubun). When the terrifying title character of *Thundergod* (Kaminari) falls from the sky, he winces as giant acupuncture needles cure his injured backside.

Mountain priests (*yamabushi*) descend from their ascetic ablutions with awesome powers in *nô*; in *kyôgen*'s "mountain priest plays" (*yamabushi mono*) they are vain, belligerent, and impotent. Their abracadabra spells invariably backfire: in *Mushrooms* (Kusabira) the mushrooms proliferate; in *Owls* (Fukuro), the owl spirit spreads; in *Dog Priest* (Inu-yamabushi), a pompous and belligerent priest loses a prayer contest with a Shinto priest.

"Blind men plays" (*zatô mono*), like their European morality play counterparts, mock the symbolic struggles of sightless unfortunates. In *Monkey Groom* (Saru muko) a monkey-trainer's wife runs off, leaving him the leashed monkey in her stead. In *Moon-viewing Blind Man* (Tsukimi zatô) a townsman enjoys drinking and singing with a blind man on a moonlit autumn evening, then returns to attack him just for the fun of it.

Holy men are mercilessly ridiculed for departing the ideals of wise, calm, nonattachment. The central figures in "priest plays" (*shukke mono*) are money-conscious (*The*

Dropped Robe [Suô otoshi]), argumentative (*A Religious Dispute* [Shûron]), or cowardly (*Bad Priest* [Akubô]). Acolytes are lecherous (*Drawing Water* [Mizu kumi]), or stupidly obedient (*Bones and Skin* [Honekawa]).

Miscellaneous *kyôgen* include plays not fitting into normal categories, including dance plays (*mai kyôgen*) parodying *nô*. Ghosts are not of fallen warriors, but of tea masters recalling their greatest tea parties in *Yûzen*. Spirits of birds and flowers are spoofed in *Cicada* (Semi) and *Octopus* (Tako). *The Fortified Beard* (Hige yagura) sends up *nô*'s samurai battles as an army of wives fights a pitched battle to shear a husband's beard.

Kyôgen comedies can appear almost Beckett-like in their dark irony. In *Buaku*, a servant is torn between loyalty to master or friend when ordered to kill his disobedient fellow. A couple divorcing because of the husband's poetry party extravagances is reconciled when the wife adds a link to her husband's farewell linked-poetry (*renga*) verse in *Winnowing-Basket Hat* (Mikazuki); delighted, he agrees to exchange poetry at home. Such sentimental and psychologically complex portraitures are perhaps precursors to the "domestic plays" (*sewa mono*) of *bunraku* (see Puppet Theatre) and **kabuki**.

Staging. Conventions demand austere minimalism. **Scenography** is absent and few **properties** are seen save ubiquitous fans and lacquered barrels (*kazuraoke*), used for various purposes, including sitting. Spectators immediately recognize **role types** through their codified **costuming**: a robe and lacquered hat (*eboshi*) and trailing *hakama* for the lord, and bright, broad-checked kimonos for townsmen. Masks are employed in only one-third of all plays, mostly for animals (fox, badger, crab, octopus, mosquito), old men, and plain women.

The master (Shigeyama Sensaku IV), frightened by the "ghost" of the servant Buaku (Sennojô Shigeyama), is comforted by Tarô-kaja (Kaoru Matsumoto) in the *kyôgen Buaku*. (Photo: Courtesy of the Shigeyama Kyôgen Association)

The actor is a consummate professional, indiscriminately portraying servants, masters, females, old persons, mountain priests, and demons. The stories leave ample room for interpretation. Without instrumental accompaniment for most plays, the actor creates his own rhythm with voice and song.

Vocalization is "as clear as a knife cutting green bamboo." Every syllable is enunciated, intoned according to family and school rhythm and intonation patterns, reaching the back of **theatres**. The actor manipulates the accumulated tension of wave-like patterns of single sentences over the course of a play for suspense and surprise. Although commonly thought of as dialogue-based situational comedy, over one-third of the repertoire contains songs and dance that create a festive atmosphere in even serious subjects. "Short dances" (*komai*) may be performed as independent drinking songs and party entertainments, paeans to beautiful maids at friendly inns, or the benevolence of the emperor.

Actors wear yellow toe-socks (*tabi*). The stance is low, knees bent, chin tucked, weight forward, poised for action. The face is frozen in a pleasant deadpan that subtly indicates reactions to events. Thousands of spectators once watched these outdoor performances, resulting in large, repetitive gestures and clear conventions. Acting is frontal: even during dialogue, actors face outward, toward the main audience, returning on cue at the end of a sentence. A diagonal stance is an aside; kneeling at upstage implies being temporarily "offstage." Gestures accompanied by onomatopoeic sounds convey a variety of actions: opening a door (*sara sara sara*), sawing through a bamboo fence (*zukazuka zukkari*), or sitting down (*eei eei yattona*).

Experiments. *Kyôgen* **experiment** since World War II has taken three forms: performing in new venues, plays, and genres. *Kyôgen* has forged a new identity as people's comedy, a repository of ancient customs and familiar values. Actors perform independently from the *nô* **stage** at civic halls, shrines, temples, and **Western**-style theatres in all-*kyôgen* shows. **Playwrights** or actors frequently rewrite plays using *kyôgen* conventions. Aristophanes, Shakespeare, and Molière have been adapted, while **Kinoshita Junji**'s *Tale of Hikoichi* (Hikoichi banashi) and the Grimm Brothers' fairy tale *Death-god* are frequently revived. When young members collaborated with *kabuki* and **shingeki** actors in the 1950s, they were nearly excommunicated. Yet this opened the door to experimentation in television, opera, modern theatre, and international collaborations. *See also Mibu kyôgen.*

FURTHER READING

Kenny, Don, trans. *The Kyôgen Book: An Anthology of Japanese Classical Comedies*; Morley, Carolyn Anne, trans. *Transformations, Miracles, and Mischief: The Mountain Priest Plays of Kyôgen*.

Jonah Salz

LAGOO, SHREERAM (1927–). Indian Marathi- and Hindi-language **stage**, film, and television **actor** and **director**. Lagoo began acting in 1946, while attending medical school (he became an ear, nose, and throat surgeon) in Pune, Maharashtra, and he later cofounded the Progressive Dramatic Association. His work in Marathi theatre parallels a successful film-acting career, which has made Mumbai (Bombay) his principal base.

As a director, Lagoo has been extremely selective, taking up important but controversial plays that others were unwilling to produce, or plays in which he wished to perform the lead. These impulses account for his outstanding ventures for his own theatre group, Roopwedh: **Vijay Tendulkar**'s *Vultures* (Gidhade, 1970), **G. P. Deshpande**'s *The Ruined Sanctuary* (a.k.a. *A Man in Dark Times* [Uddhwasta dharmashala, 1974]), and **Mahesh Elkunchwar**'s *Autobiography* (Atmakatha, 1988). Lagoo also has played notable leads in Vasant Kanetkar's (1922–2001) *The Madman's Home in the Heat* (Vedyache ghar unhat, 1957), V. V. Shirwadker's (1912–1999) *The Actor-King* (Natasamrat, 1972), Jaywant Dalvi's (1925–1994) *Evening Shadows* (Sandhya chhaya, 1973), and Anouilh's *Antigone* (1976). He describes himself as a realistic director-actor, and acknowledges Stanislavski's *An Actor Prepares* as a major influence.

Aparna Dharwadker

LAI SHENG-CHUAN [LAI SHENGCHUAN] (1954–). Taiwanese * **playwright**, **director**, and professor at the Taipei National University of Arts. Born in Washington, D.C., to a diplomatic family and brought up bilingually in the United States and Taiwan, Lai obtained a PhD from the University of California, Berkeley (1983). Lai's cross-cultural experience urged him to express the tensions between tradition and modernity. To date Lai has written and directed twenty-four plays that have been performed internationally and throughout the **Chinese**-speaking world.

In 1984, Lai founded the artistically innovative and financially successful Performance Workshop (Biaoyan Gongzuofang), whose well-received productions include *The Peach Blossom Land* (Anlian Taohuayuan, 1986; filmed 1992), which toured worldwide, and *That Night We Performed the Talk Show* (Na yiye women shuo xiangsheng, 1993), emphasizing that the theatre's appeal lies in its immediacy. *A Dream like a Dream* (Ru meng zhi meng, Taipei, 2000; Hong Kong, 2002; Taipei, 2005) was a seven-hour production inspired by Sogyal Rinpoche's *Tibetan Book of Living and Dying*. The play traces the life-stories of four characters through their temporal and spatial movements (dating from 2000 back to 1928 and from Taipei to Paris to

Shanghai). These stories unfold like a series of Russian dolls that contain, sustain, and question each other's existence in thirteen acts and ninety scenes. The production's most noticeable feature was its "circle" **stage**, which placed the audience in the center while the **acting** took place around them. This play received the 2003 Hong Kong Federation of Drama Societies Twelfth Hong Kong Drama Award.

Alexander C. Y. Huang

LAKHON BASSAC. **Cambodian** operatic drama. It developed in ethnic Khmer communities in the Bassac River region of southern **Vietnam** in the 1930s, with origins traced to **Chinese** *hi* (*xi*). **Costumes**, **makeup**, martial arts, acrobatics, and **musical** instrumentation recall its Chinese provenance. Stories, though sometimes adapted from Chinese, Vietnamese, or other sources, are most often distinctively Khmer.

Lakhon bassac was arguably the most popular Cambodian entertainment throughout the twentieth century. Before the war and revolution of the 1970s, **theatre companies** were firmly established in Phnom Penh, Battambang, and Siem Reap, and in other provincial capitals, performing in privately run **theatres**. Ticket sales kept troupes and venues in business. **Actors**, many in their teens and twenties, tended to come from the poorer urban sectors. In the countryside, *lakhon bassac* was a favorite at **festivals** connected with **religious** celebrations. In the courtyard of a Buddhist temple, or elsewhere in a village, a troupe would perform on a makeshift bamboo **stage** in the open air for hundreds of onlookers, with the actors paid by a patron. One story's enactment might take days, and a major festival could feature a month of shows, with pieces selected from oral legend and tales—always set in a mythico-historical past—inscribed on palm-leaf manuscripts. Urban troupes were sometimes brought in for these events, but amateur troupes using local farmers were also common.

Populated by certain **role types** (male and female giants, members of the royalty, prime ministers, generals, and always a clown or two), performances also include a variety of animals and supernatural beings. As each appears, he or she offers a sung introduction that might, in addition to identifying the character, help situate that character in the plot. Dialogue, sometimes improvised, is spoken or sung. Musicians accompany the singing and accentuate martial arts and other scenes with upright fiddles, hammered dulcimers, cymbals, woodblocks, large drums, and other musical instruments. Audiences judge a show by how well the actors sing in the highly stylized modes, enact specific character movements (walking, flying, battle, and so on), and convey emotions.

In the decade immediately following the overthrow of the Khmer Rouge (1979), *lakhon bassac* thrived again. Many of the old stories were performed, but with new, **politically** inspired interpretations. *Lakhon bassac* had been part of the curriculum at the Royal University of Fine Arts before the war, and was a popular subject afterward as well. Today, both the Department of Performing Arts and the Royal University of Fine Arts have troupes. Yet, as with so many of Cambodia's performing arts, the lack of venues and resources, and the affordability of videos as festival entertainment, have resulted in ever fewer actors and troupes.

Sang Saron (1922–1973), who performed to great acclaim from the 1930s until his death in the 1970s, is considered the finest actor ever. He remains the reference point against which accomplishment is judged, most especially in sung and spoken dialogue.

FURTHER READING

Brandon, James R. *Theatre in Southeast Asia*; Yousof, Ghulam Sarwar. *Dictionary of Traditional South-East Asian Theatre*.

Toni Shapiro-Phim

LAKHON KBACH BORAN. *See Robam kbach boran.*

LAKHON KHOL. **Cambodian dance**-drama with an all-male ensemble. Using a repertoire traditionally drawn from episodes of the *Reamker*, the Khmer version of the *Ramayana*, *lakhon khol* combines **dance**, mimed gesture, and chanted narration to the accompaniment of a *pin peat* **musical** accompaniment.

Evidence points to the existence of troupes in the nineteenth century, and most likely long before then. The governor of Battambang Province in the late nineteenth century had a troupe of about one hundred men that performed only the *Reamker*. It appeared at temple celebrations. During the same period, and into the twentieth century, an annual royal palace **festival**, Tang Tok, featured a range of theatrical events, including *lakhon khol* performances by a troupe from Svay Andet, a village across the river from Phnom Penh. Through performance of the Battle of Kumbhakar, the *Reamker* episode in which heavenly waters are eventually liberated and allowed to flow, the Svay Andet troupe helped call forth much needed rains for the village's planting season. Many people came from surrounding villages for the seven-day New Year performance that included elaborate **religious** rituals in honor of ancestral spirits, the Buddha, Brahmanic deities, and the spirits and teachers of the arts.

Few accomplished performers survived the war and revolution of the 1970s. Extreme poverty made rebuilding the troupe nearly impossible. Help came in the 1980s from the Ministry of Culture's Department of Arts, with support for musical instruments and elaborate **costumes**, resembling those worn by court dancers, and with special authorization to keep performers from the military draft. Today, the New Year performance lasts, at most, three nights. All performers, except those playing Neang Seda (Princess Sita) and her attendants (played by slightly built men), used to be **masked**, Preah Ream (Rama) with a green face and Preah Leak (Laksmana) with a yellow one. These days, Preah Ream and Preah Leak sometimes wear **makeup**. Monkeys and ogres wear masks akin to those worn by the same

The Battle at Night, a *lakhon khol* farce adapted by Chheng Phon from a traditional Chinese comedy, Phnom Penh, 1989. The white monkey general Hanuman (in front, performed by Soeur Soy) and his simian cohorts do battle with a group of giants. (Photo: Eileen Blumenthal)

characters in ***robam kbach boran*** (a.k.a. *kbach boran khmer* and *lakhon kbach boran*). Two or three men sit by the musicians, providing intoned recitation, interchanging types of poetic prose and verse. Dancers mime dialogue as it is recounted, moving upper body, hands, and arms, and sometimes shifting stances. They also dance during instrumental intervals.

Dancers have **trained** in *lakhon khol* as a professional art at the Royal University of Fine Arts since the 1960s. Today, Kompong Thom Province hosts a professional *lakhon khol* **theatre company**. The troupe based at the Department of Performing Arts in Phnom Penh is active in developing expanded episodes of the *Reamker* and tours internationally. Octogenarian Yith Sarin, originally from the Svay Andet troupe, was still teaching in 2006.

Toni Shapiro-Phim

LAKHON NIYEAY. Cambodian "spoken-word drama," a.k.a. *lakhon ciet* (literally, "national drama"). It developed in the 1950s initially under the guidance of **actor** and **director • Hang Tun Hak**, who had studied theatre in France. A National Conservatory of Performing Arts was established in the 1950s. The resident **theatre company** became so active that additional troupes arose from that original ensemble. **Training** emphasized the Stanislavski technique, and the troupes toured the countryside for months at a time. They performed **Western** plays in translation, and original works by Hang and other Cambodians. Some plays were controversial and **political**; most dealt with contemporary societal tensions.

During the 1950s and 1960s, a conscious effort grew on the part of cultural authorities to educate the populace and build a "national culture" through the performance of *lakhon niyeay*. This was a time when Norodom Sihanouk (r. 1941–1960; prince and head of state until 1970) emphasized nation-building, and many genres were enveloped in this process. In the mid-1960s, the Conservatory and Phnom Penh–based companies were incorporated into the newly established Royal University of Fine Arts. Well-known actors included **Pich Tum Kravel** and Pring Sokhon (1945–).

Peou Yuleng (1927–1981) was a director before the war and revolution of the 1970s, and the first director of the National Department of Arts immediately following the overthrow of the Khmer Rouge (1979). Once surviving artists regrouped after the genocide of the late 1970s, they quickly established *lakhon niyeay* troupes in the capital, at the School of Fine Arts (which became a university again in 1989), and at the Department of Arts, both under the Ministry of Information and Culture. There were also, throughout the 1980s and into the early 1990s, troupes in Kandal, Takeo, Prey Veng, and Svay Rieng Provinces. Radio broadcasts of original dramas were very popular.

The political messages infused in the plays of the 1980s (under the communist regime of the People's Republic of Kampuchea) made way for a return to explorations of society's concerns in the 1990s, especially after a peace accord and elections put an end to more than a decade of war. Today, *lakhon niyeay* has a much lower profile than it did in the 1980s and early 1990s, when troupes from Phnom Penh's cultural institutions toured regions torn by civil strife. Back then, through enactments of the horrors of the Khmer Rouge years, or of the evils of capitalism and Western imperialism, artists offered entertainment to a war-weary populace, while also attempting to build political loyalty and confidence. Nowadays, there is limited work for the troupes at the

Department of Performing Arts and the Royal University of Fine Arts, though training, including **playwriting** and production, continues.

Toni Shapiro-Phim and Catherine Filloux

LAKHON SBAEK. *See* Puppet Theatre: Cambodia.

LAKON CHATRI. Thai • **dance**-drama that emerged in the eighteenth century from an older form of southern dance-drama, *nora chatri* (see *Manohra*). Although King Rama III (r. 1824–1851) first brought male *nora chatri* dancers to Bangkok, the form came to both men and **women**, and finally became a women-only form, except for some minor clown and animal characters. *Lakon chatri* troupes are now centered in Petchaburi, Ayudhaya, Nakhonpathom, and Chacherngsau Provinces.

After **Rama IV**'s 1861 decree freed court dancers to teach and perform outside the court, the form incorporated elements of Central Thai **folk** dance-drama (*lakon nok*) into its basic southern form, and many of these new *lakon chatri* dancers settled around Bangkok, serving communities as ritual dancers for many occasions. Central Thai audiences liked and paid better for *lakon nok*–style dancers than for southern-style *nora chatri* dancers, so more troupes adopted elements of the former style. The new *lakon chatri* used *lakon nok* stories and the *piphat* **musical** ensemble, along with a mixed-gender cast who sang and danced. Today, *lakon chatri* dances are used as gifts of thanks to spirits credited with answering prayers, and so are also called *lakhon kaebon* (literally, "dance-dramas that end the plea").

All performances begin with a ritual dance to the spirit; the head of the troupe acts as the ritual facilitator and offers the dance-drama to the god (see Religion in Theatre). The dancers wear long, curved fingernails, tall, ornate headdresses, and use rapid hand and foot movements. Although all dances are accompanied by a *piphat* ensemble, the length and complexity of the thanksgiving dance relates directly to how much one pays. Each ranges from a short dance by a male-female couple to a day-long performance of a complex story by a full troupe of five to seven; troupes at temples list rates and types of dances available. Long performances start, like old *nora chatri* dances, by paying homage to the teacher.

FURTHER READING

Brandon, James R. *Theatre in Southeast Asia*; Rutnin, Mattani Mojdara. *Dance, Drama, and Theatre in Thailand: The Process of Development and Modernization.*

Pornrat Damrhung

LAKON DUKDAMBAN. Thai hybrid **dance**-drama-opera performed from 1899 to 1909. Many were staged by the multitalented Prince Narisaranuwattiwong (a.k.a. Prince Naris, 1863–1947), **playwright**, composer, **scenographer**, and **director**. He and his collaborator, Chao Phraya Thewetwongwiwat, chief of the Department of Royal Entertainment, produced these plays at his Ban Mo Palace's beautiful Dukdamban Theatre (Rong Lakon Dukdamban). This small proscenium **theatre** was open to a fee-paying public when performances were not commissioned for royal visitors. Although the plays combined elements from both *lakon nai* and *lakon nok*, they were revolutionary in their use of modern scenography and lighting, plots based on new excerpts from old stories, and new **music** that dancers sang as they spoke contemporary, often rather realistic, dialogue.

These efforts helped revitalize classical dance-drama, while adding elements from **Western** operas, operettas, and ballets. Although based on compressed versions of traditional stories, such as those from *lakon nai*, the *Ramakien* (Thailand's version of the **Ramayana**), *Inao* (the **Panji** cycle), and those from *lakon nok*, such as *Sang Thong*, and using traditional **costumes**, these performances abandoned traditional narration and choral singing in favor of having performers sing and dance their roles. **Folk** dances and songs were added, and the convention of introducing characters by formulaic expressions was discarded, as was the narration of actions already performed. The scripts concentrated on expressing passionate feelings and demonstrating character interactions. The use of the indoor proscenium **stage** provided a full three-dimensional space. Plays were divided into acts and scenes, and performances used colored lighting and set changes. The ensemble, *piphat dukdamban*, omitted noisy instruments and cushioned the percussive instruments, providing many new melodies.

FURTHER READING

Rutnin, Mattani Mojdara. *Dance, Drama, and Theatre in Thailand: The Process of Development and Modernization.*

Pornrat Damrhung

LAKON NAI. Thai • dance-drama, a.k.a. *lakon nang nai* ("**women**'s dance-drama of the inner court"), *lakon fai nai* (same meaning), and *lakon puying* ("female dance-drama"). Although *lakon nai* is performed today by female dancers in the inner court, historically it referred to a style of royal dancing of scenes from the *Ramakien* (the Thai version of the **Ramayana**), *Unarut* (stories of Krishna's grandson), and *Inao* (the **Panji** cycle), whether by women or men. More basically, it is distinguished from *lakon nok*, the **folk** dance-drama done outside the court. Using a restricted repertoire, *lakon nai* performances were limited to the royal palace and done for the pleasure and honor of the king, typically by women. They were central to royal ceremonies and used in many celebrations.

Lakon nai is tied to the divine king (*devaraja*) concept and derived from dances used in the early Ayudhaya period (1350–1767). Over time, these became more complicated and bound up with the complex story-cycles, which embodied great myths of kingship. These ensemble dances included performances of excerpts that focused on a solo performer and were accompanied by choral singing and *piphat* **musical** ensembles. Script-readers chanted refined verses from the three main cycles and had an all-female chorus sing them in a courtly style, while the main dancers repeated their verses in dialogue. Classical *naphat* music played by the *piphat* ensemble accompanied the dancers, who had mastered the refined and difficult, slow-moving choreography. Even today dancers' **costumes** are highly ornamented, resembling garments worn by royal court members centuries ago.

In 1861, King **Rama IV** issued a royal decree permitting these specially trained women to teach and perform outside the court, and permitting noblemen and aristocrats to found noncourt women's troupes if they did not perform pieces from the three major cycles. While used to raise taxes on entertainment, these decrees also helped to turn dance-drama from a royal patronage to commercial enterprise. Today, revived and standardized *lakon nai* forms are still performed by the National Theatre and the Fine Arts Department, and **khon**, the **masked** dance-drama, also has adopted *lakon nai*, since most of the important masters in the last century were court ladies. *See also Lakon ram.*

FURTHER READING

Brandon, James R. *Theatre in Southeast Asia*; Rutnin, Mattani Mojdara. *Dance, Drama, and Theatre in Thailand: The Process of Development and Modernization.*

Pornrat Damrhung

LAKON NOK. Thai • **folk** • **dance**-drama genre, also spelled *lakon nork*, originally performed outside the royal court (as opposed to **lakon nai**, performed inside the court) by companies of male dancers (*lakon puchai*); it probably emerged in Central Thailand by the seventeenth century. Along with **lakon chatri**, *lakon nai*, and **lakon phan thang**, it is one of Thailand's four major classical dance-drama genres (see *Lakon ram*).

Lakon nok's plots are based on Buddha's birth stories (*jataka*) and old folktales; five scripts are extant from the Ayudhaya period (1350–1767). *Lakon nok*, which reflects family life and its problems, is popular among ordinary people. It uses fast-paced action, and its plots focus on conflicts between lovers and jealousies among wives. Its stories are adventurous, with plenty of magic, giants, battles, and the winning of girls' hearts.

The pieces are often performed at Buddhist **festivals**; and the **costumes** are relatively simple when compared to *lakon nai*. A few characters wear **masks** for special

Scene from a *lakon nok* production of *The Horse-Face Lady* at the Fine Arts Department, Bangkok, Thailand, 2006. (Photo: Pairioj Tongkhamsuk)

scenes. The **music**, played by a *piphat* ensemble seated on stage right on the raised wooden **stage**, can be rapid with simple rhythms. Lyrics sung by offstage singers provide the basis for the dancing, and the dialogue—often comically off-color—is improvised by the dancers. Today's popular *liké* theatre emerged from *lakon nok*.

Under **Rama II** and many later princes there emerged more refined *lakon nok* scripts, dance patterns, and characters. Some forms of *lakon nok* involved a more elegant royal style; today, revived and standardized forms are still performed by the National Theatre and the Fine Arts Department of the Ministry of Culture.

FURTHER READING

Brandon, James R. *Theatre in Southeast Asia*; Rutnin, Mattani Mojdara. *Dance, Drama, and Theatre in Thailand: The Process of Development and Modernization.*

Pornrat Damrhung

LAKON PHAN THANG. Thai • dance-drama meaning, literally, "dance-drama of a thousand ways," but sometimes referred to as "drama in historical settings." It emerged in the nineteenth century from **lakon nok**, introducing many new stories from popular Thai and neighboring countries' dramatic literature and chronicles. This became controversial when its chief promoter, **Prince Narathip**, offended conservatives by using as characters actual Thai historical figures, who were considered too sacrosanct by the common people to be represented on **stage**.

Lakon phan thang debuted at Thailand's first public **theatre**, the Prince Theatre (1904), in Bangkok. Its hybrid style employed exotic **scenography** suggestive of foreign places, realistic versions of period **costumes**, **music** derived from various Asian (and even **Western**) backgrounds, and new dance methods to fit the many nationalities they represented.

Lakon phan thang dances are simpler than traditional Thai examples, with considerable dependence on interpretation. There is singing by the dancers and a chorus, but the melodies differ from traditional ones, expressing the nationalities and rhythms of the culturally diverse characters and their environments. The language sometimes uses both poetic prose dialogue and colloquial language, often including foreign words. A famous example is *Volunteer Mon Hero* (Saming phra ram asa), about fifteenth-century struggles between the **Burmese** and **Chinese**; it has a Chinese general dance in traditional Chinese costume. In *Phra Aphaimani*, Western manners and military behavior were introduced under the tutelage of Westerners.

FURTHER READING

Rutnin, Mattani Mojdara. *Dance, Drama, and Theatre in Thailand: The Process of Development and Modernization.*

Pornrat Damrhung

LAKON PHUT SAMAI MHAI. Thai modern "spoken theatre" genre, as opposed to *lakon ram* ("dance drama").

The term came into use in the late 1960s to refer to modern, *Western*-style plays, and soon replaced the earlier term, *lakon phut*, which is now rarely used. The longer term is also far wider in application, including not only "spoken drama," but Broadway-style **musicals**, Western physical theatre, and the recently developed *lakon khanob niyom mhai* ("new traditional dance-drama"), in which some speaking is incorporated in a dance-drama performance. Although King Chulalongkorn (Rama V, r. 1868–1910) earlier commanded the performance of spoken plays using scripts adapted from **lakon nai**, the first actual *lakon phut* is *Like Father, Like Son* (Som po som luk, 1904). It was written, designed, and **directed** by Prince Vajiravudh (later King Rama VI, r. 1910–1925), in connection with the opening celebration of his Club for Promotion of Intelligence (Dvipanya Samoson). Another historic *lakon phut* event was when Prince Vajiravudh performed in nobleman Bua Visetkul's *Acting Young* (Ploi kae, 1906), the first time ever that Thai royalty shared the **stage** with commoners. Moreover, the prince, on his official trips upcountry, took his troupe to perform *lakon phut* for government officials and the general public; they, in return, staged *lakon phut* for his pleasure. Even before he became king, *lakon phut* had been established in the Thai repertory. Hailed as the "father of modern Thai theatre," Vajiravudh/Rama penned more than fifty *lakon phut*— half of them translations and adaptations of English and French drama.

Under the leadership of university lecturers **Sodsai Pantoomkomol** and **Mattani Rutnin Mojdara**, modern Western plays were translated and adapted. From the late 1980s to the early 1990s, these plays enjoyed popularity when the commercial Montienthong Theatre was fully operating with a six-shows-per-week schedule, while Theatre 28 produced highbrow dramas annually.

Partly because it was first introduced in the royal palace and re-introduced in the university, *lakon phut samai mhai* has been considered an elite form whose target audience is mostly from the upper-middle class and university-educated urban population, who have increasingly eschewed traditional theatre.

FURTHER READING

Rutnin, Mattani Mojdara. *Dance, Drama, and Theatre in Thailand: The Process of Development and Modernization.*

Pawit Mahasarinand

LAKON RAM. General term for the multiple forms of **Thai** classical **dance**-drama in which dancers chant rhythmic prose and soloists and a chorus chant poetic narratives, most of them derived from Buddha's birth stories (*jataka*). *Lakon* (also spelled *lakhon* and *lakorn*) appears to be one of several variants of the Javanese word *lagon* ("dance-drama") used in mainland Southeast Asia for a wide variety of forms. *Lakon* is tied to various poetic stories, classical dance, and **music** for both singing and accompaniment.

There are three principal *lakon* divisions: *lakon ram* (comprising the classical and **folk** forms *lakon nai*, *lakon nok*, *lakon nora chatri*, *lakon chatri*, *liké*, *lakon dukdamban*, and *lakon phan thang*); *lakon rong*; and *lakon phut samai mhai*. The latter two are modern, **Western**-influenced forms. Many interesting historical and artistic connections exist among these forms.

Since the 1940s, a decade or so after Thailand's absolute monarchy ended in 1932, the Fine Arts Department of the Ministry of Culture and the National Theatre have remained the main guardians of Thailand's classical dance-drama forms. Audiences for *lakon ram* forms dwindled with the importation of foreign films in the mid-twentieth century, but the rise of television has revived interest in them, and popular *lakon*-influenced television dramas retain many classical features, including the use of traditional **role types**.

FURTHER READING

Rutnin, Mattani Mojdara. *Dance, Drama, and Theatre in Thailand: The Process of Development and Modernization.*

Pornrat Damrhung

LAKON RONG. Extinct **Thai** • **dance**-drama form that appeared in the 1890s. It imitated **Western** operettas or **Malaysia**'s *bangsawan*, and combined old and new Thai and foreign music—much of it highly emotional—with plotlines derived from Western plays; **scenography** and **costumes** were contemporary. Many credit its origins to **Prince Narathip**. Influenced by Western **musical** drama forms, it combined chorally sung Western romantic and adventurous narratives with spoken and sung dialogue using modern, colloquial language and written in prose and verse. Rama V (1868–1910) supported it handsomely at Narathip's private **theatres**.

All principal roles, male and female, were played by **women**, who sang, spoke, **acted**, and danced (mainly swaying movements and hand gestures) to songs performed by a female chorus; men usually played only comic roles. The scripts were often little more than translations or adaptations of colorful Western stories (like *The Arabian Nights*) or Thai contemporary works concerned with situations like love triangles; they were divided into acts and scenes like melodrama and vaudeville, although the acts had rhyming titles. Performances were on a proscenium **stage** and usually had four scenic changes.

Audiences were slow to accept the performances because they were unfamiliar with such plot- and situation-driven drama; they preferred to watch dancing as they chatted, rather than concentrating on story development. *Lakon rong* jumped in popularity with *The Story of Khrua Fa* (Sao Khrua Fa), an adaptation of *Madame Butterfly* in which the army officer is from Bangkok and the heroine from Chiengmai. Later plots dealt with contemporary incidents and situations. *Lakon rong* died out before World War II, and its only later revivals were for educational purposes.

FURTHER READING

Rutnin, Mattani Mojdara. *Dance, Drama, and Theatre in Thailand: The Process of Development and Modernization.*

Pornrat Damrhung

LAOS. Landlocked Southeast Asian country of slightly over 6 million, partly under the control of Siam (**Thailand**) for most of the nineteenth century and France for most of 1893–1953. Laos is today officially communist, although many espouse **religious** beliefs in Buddhism and animism.

Theatre in the Lao People's Democratic Republic (1975) remains a limited topic. Virtually all theatre known today originated in Thailand, though some Lao nationalists might dispute this. Two types are known, classical and popular. The former includes **masked** theatre or *khon*, formerly cultivated at the royal court and closely related to Thai *khon*, and **lakon •** dance-drama. Popular theatre includes two forms, **mawlam** (or *lam*) *luang* and *mawlam* (or *lam*) *ploen*, both imported from Thailand's Lao-speaking northeast.

Lao *khon*, like that of Thailand, performs only excerpts from the **Ramayana** (*Pha Lak Pha Lam* in Lao), accompanied by a classical *piphat* **musical** ensemble. *Lakon* was usually performed by females alone and was also accompanied by *piphat*. In the 1960s, some ninety performers and teachers were retained as members of the Royal Lao Ballet in

Performance of northeastern *lam luang* by the Baw Samaki troupe in Mahasarakham, Thailand, 1973. (Photo: Terry E. Miller)

Luang Phrabang, the royal capital; many had **trained** in Thailand. After the end of the monarchy in 1975, *khon* declined quickly as most performers fled the country, and the Natasin Fine Arts School in Vientiane, originally founded in the 1950s with American money, was renamed the National School of Music and Folkloric Dance. The school and Lao arts in general were then stripped of many Thai elements and restyled in a more Laotian form. Nonetheless, a partial restoration of classical arts began in 1976, and afterward the national troupe often performed *Ramayana* excerpts during international tours.

Remnants of the pre-1975 troupe, including teachers from the earlier Natasin, were resettled in Nashville, Tennessee, and Des Moines, Iowa. Although these groups attempted to keep performing, doing so became untenable, and today little more than miscellaneous dances are taught to community members. Some advocates, especially from the Nashville group, have made claims of a long and separate Lao history for the classical arts, or acknowledged a connection to the **Cambodian** court, but tend to refuse to acknowledge Thai influence. Such nationalistic readings of history stem from a long-standing rivalry between the Siamese and Laotians, last aggravated in 1828 when Siamese armies invaded and sacked Vientiane and carried off not only its treasures but a large segment of the population.

Both forms of popular theatre originated in Isan, in Thailand's Lao-speaking northeast. Though both *mawlam* and *lam ploen* originated sometime in the 1940s, they appeared in Laos only in the early 1960s, stemming from the efforts of an individual, Souphine Phathsoungneune, a *mawlam* artist from Nakhon Ratchasima, Thailand. During the later 1950s but especially in the 1960s, the United States Information Service (USIS) office in Bangkok began hiring both *lam klawn* repartee singers and *mawlam* **theatre companies** to perform anti-communist texts and stories. The Thai Luang Fair in Vientiane was a primary venue for such performances, which also included newly created "folkloric" dances (*fon*). The *lam klawn* singers, all from Isan, were considered to have been far more successful than the theatre troupes because USIS provided only scenarios rather than the scripts normally used by the troupes. Unlike Central Thai *liké* players, who can improvise, the *mawlam* performers lacked such skills. Around 1970, before the fall of the royal government, the revolutionary Pathet Lao established a pro-communist propaganda troupe in Hua Phan Province to communicate government plans and accomplishments to the people. This modified form of traditional *mawlam*, called *lakon lam*, included popular songs, among other things.

As Laos opened up during the 1990s, and especially after 2000, government control of theatre declined or ceased. Today, newly formed commercial *mawlam* troupes are thriving in areas where there is enough economic activity to support them. Several are concentrated in a village west of Pakse, near the border of Thailand's Ubon Province. These large, modernized troupes include sizable combos, female dancers, and pop singers, as well as **actors** and actresses, and are difficult to distinguish from *mawlam* troupes in nearby northeast Thailand.

FURTHER READING

Brandon, James R. *Theatre in Southeast Asia*; Miller, Terry E., and Sean Williams, eds. *Southeast Asia*. Vol. 4. *Garland Encyclopedia of World Music*.

Terry E. Miller

LAO SHE (1899–1966). Chinese • **playwright**, novelist, and poet, who played a major role in developing modern "spoken drama" (*huaju*) in the 1950s. His *The Teahouse* (Chaguan, 1957), one of the most frequently performed *huaju*, has also received popular attention abroad. Born in Beijing to a Manchu family, he enrolled in college at fourteen, graduating in 1918. In 1922, he taught Chinese literature in middle school, and in 1924 left for England, where he taught at the University of London and started writing novels. Back in China, he was a university professor while completing his most celebrated novel, *Camel Xiangzi* (Luotuo Xiangzi, 1936). During the Second Sino-**Japanese** War (1937–1945), he served as a director of the All-China Association of Literary Resistance. In 1946, he and **Cao Yu** were invited by the U.S. State Department to be visiting scholars.

After returning to China at the end of 1949, Lao She wrote twenty-six *huaju*, including the masterpieces *Dragon Beard Ditch* (Longxugou, 1950) and *The Teahouse*. The former depicts four families from the same neighborhood during the transitional period represented by the establishment of the People's Republic of China (PRC). The plot, typical of early PRC literature, emphasizes the oppression people experienced before the communist revolution in contrast to the post-1949 liberation. Despite the **politically** prescribed plot, the play promoted the development of Beijing-style *huaju* featuring colorful local language and vivid characters. Following its performance, the Beijing Municipal Government named Lao She a "People's Artist," a distinction reflecting his fondness for and devotion to the lives and aspirations of Beijing's commoners.

The Teahouse premiered at the Beijing People's Art **Theatre** (Beijing Renmin Yishu Juyuan) in 1958 and played a major role in establishing that **theatre company**'s style and reputation. Set in an old Beijing teahouse, *The Teahouse* stages the turmoil of the first half of twentieth-century China by following the lives of the teahouse's owner and customers from 1898 to 1945. The sixty characters represent all levels of society and present a microcosm of the social turmoil endured under the collapse of China's last

Dragon Beard Ditch by Lao She, directed by Jiao Juyin for the Beijing People's Art Theatre, 1953, with Yu Shizhi as Madman Cheng (center, standing). (Photo: Courtesy of Beijing People's Art Theatre)

imperial dynasty, warlord rule, and war. The play is acclaimed for its colorful, old Beijing language, masterful character verisimilitude, and inspired reflection of China's historical change.

Lao She also wrote for traditional forms, such as *jingju* and *geju*. After the founding of the PRC, he was an important member of many official organizations, including the National People's Congress and the Chinese Writers' Association.

FURTHER READING

Lao She. *Teahouse*.

Jonathan Noble

LEE BYŎNG-BOC (1927–). Korean • scenographic designer and, with Kim Jŏng-ok (1932–), cofounder of Seoul's Freedom (Jayu) **Theatre Company** (1966). The doyenne of contemporary designers, Lee is past president of the Korean Theatre Artists Association and past chairman of the Korean Center of the Organization of International Scenographers, Theatre Architects, and Technicians. She received an award at the 1991 Prague Quadrennial design competition and served as a panel judge in 1995. Lee has received all of the major Korean theatre design awards.

Lee studied sculpture and design in Paris in the late 1950s, later joining with Kim, whom she met there, to found the influential Freedom troupe. From its inception, Lee designed **costumes** for every Freedom Theatre production, later adding scene design to her responsibilities. After 1978, Lee and Kim focused on "group creation" and the development of productions with a Korean essence. They also transformed **Western** works, such as Lorca's *Blood Wedding* and Shakespeare's *Macbeth*, through the use of native elements, such as shaman rites, martial arts, **puppets**, and **masks**. Working in concert with the **acting** ensemble, Lee saw the **stage** as a blank paper for her imagination, which increasingly incorporated not only costumes and sets, but lighting and **properties** as well. Her minimalist designs established a high standard for creative use of color and materials. Especially noteworthy is her innovative use of paper in costumes.

Richard Nichols

LEE KANG-BAEK (1947–). Korean * playwright. His debut play, *Five* (Tasŏt, 1971), won first prize in a newspaper literary contest. He has written some forty plays, collected in seven volumes, and received every prestigious Korean playwriting award.

In 1998, the Lee Kang-Baek Theatre **Festival** in Seoul celebrated his devotion to playwriting and contributions to Korean theatre. Named Korea's best contemporary playwright in a 2003 poll taken by *Donga-Ilbo*, a leading newspaper, Lee has been translated and published in Germany, France, and Poland, and frequently performed at international **festivals**.

Perhaps because of his illness-induced isolation as a child, Lee writes in an objective, "distanced observer" style requiring active intellectual, rather than emotional, engagement from audience and reader. Known for his cunning use of metaphor and allegory, a technique developed to skirt authoritarian **censorship** in the 1970s and 1980s, his writings in those decades examine socio-**political** realities under South Korean military regimes. Later works feature existential and humanistic themes, such as sacrifice, redemption, and human compassion. Often borrowing themes from folktales and narratives, his writings manifest empathy for the isolated and powerless.

Major plays include: *Watchman* (P'asuggun, 1973), *Wedding* (Kyŏlhon, 1974), *Homo Separatus* (1983), *Spring Day* (Pomnal, 1984), *Chilsan-ri* (1989), *A Dried Pollack's Head* (Pukŏ daegari, 1993), *Travel Journal to Yŏngwol* (Yŏngwŏl haeng ilgi, 1995), *Feeling, Like Nirvana* (Nŭggim, kŭgnak kat'ŭn, 1998), and *Korea Fantasy* (Marŭgo daldorok, 2000).

Hyung-jin Lee

LEE KUO-HSIU [LI GUOXIU] (1955–). Taiwanese * playwright, director, and **actor**. Born in **Taiwan** in 1955, he became a founding member of the Performance Workshop (Biaoyan Gongzuo Fang) in 1984 (see Lai Sheng-chuan), and studied **experimental theatre** in **Japan** and the United States in 1985. Upon returning to Taiwan, Lee left the Performance Workshop to create his own group, the Pingfong Acting Company (Pingfong Biaoyan Ban), which became one of Taiwan's few nonsubsidized, commercially successful "spoken drama" (*wutai ju*, known in **China** as *huaju*) troupes.

Lee's plays are known for their witty style, wordplay, anagrams, mixed use of Mandarin and Taiwanese dialect, rehearsed "improvisation," and the devices of play-within-a-play and autobiographical performance. Lee's **theatre company** and plays are immensely popular. His productions often include metatheatrical comments on the contingency of performance.

Lee has written over thirty-five plays and nearly one hundred television dramas. Most of his plays are satires commenting on contemporary social and **political** issues ranging from the decaying of the traditional stylized theatre (*Beijing Opera Revelation* [Jingxi qishi lu], 1996) to the consumerist-driven media and corrupt politicians

Beijing Opera Revelation by Lee Kuo-hsiu, performed by the Pingfong Performance Workshop, in which a Taiwanese *jingju* troupe satirizes a mainland Chinese "revolutionary model opera" (*yangban xi*) production. (Photo: Courtesy of Pingfong Performance Workshop)

(*National Salvation Corporation Ltd.* [Zhushi jiuguo huishe], 1991) and Taiwan's need for a distinctive identity (*Shamlet* [Shamuleite], 1992). A number of his plays have toured abroad. Lee's honors include the playwriting award from the Taiwan National Endowment for Culture and Arts (1997) and Distinguished Artist of Asia (1999).

Alexander C. Y. Huang

LEE MAN-KUEI (LI MANGUI) (1907–1975). Taiwanese ⦁ **playwright**, **director**, educator, and Little Theatre Movement activist. Lee, born to a Christian family in **China**, wrote a number of plays in English while studying for her MA at the University of Michigan (1934–1936). After returning to China in 1940, she gained recognition for plays she wrote and journals she edited that reflected **women**'s concerns.

In 1949, when the People's Republic of China was established, Lee moved to Taiwan, hoping to escape the totalitarian cultural policy, only to find herself confined by equally suffocating ideologies and **censorship**. Her first play written in Taiwan, *Heaven and Earth* (Huangtian houtu, 1950), followed an anti-communist cultural policy and dramatized the agony of the Nationalists, who lost to the communists. However, as an artist, Lee was reluctant to let **politics** take precedence over artistic innovation. In 1956, she launched a series of Mandarin "spoken drama" (*huaju*) productions in Taipei's New World **Theatre** (Xin Shijie Juyuan). These nonpropaganda performances revived a theatre scene that had been dominated by rigid ideologies. Her *The Spring and Autumn of the Han Palace* (Hangong chunqiu, 1956), given forty-nine performances, was inspired by the *coup d'état* of Wang Mang (45 BC–23 AD) during the Han dynasty; it focused on Wang's characterization rather than the theme of legitimate rulership.

This pivotal figure introduced the "little theatre" (*xiao juchang*) performing style to Taiwan in 1960, when she founded the Little Theatre Promotion Committee. It defined *xiao juchang* as a noncommercial theatre that regularly performs **experimental** and nonpropaganda plays to loyal audiences.

Alexander C. Y. Huang

LEE YUN-T'AEK (1952–). Korean • **playwright**, screenwriter, **director**, Street Theatre Troupe (Yŏnhŭidan Kŏrip'ae) founder, National **Theatre Company** artistic director, and author of treatises on theatre and **actor • training**. One of South Korea's most visible and prolific theatre artists, Lee gained critical attention in 1989, directing his *Citizen K* (Shinmin K), a portrayal of *petite bourgeois* intellectual ambivalence during the South Korean military regimes of the 1980s. His trilogy, *O-Gu: Ceremony of Death* (O-Gu: chukŭm ŭi hyŏng-sik, 1990), *Mask of Fire: Ceremony of Power* (Pul ŭi kamyŏn: kwŏllyŏk ŭi hyŏng-sik, 1993), and *Dummy Bride: Ceremony of Love* (Pabo kakshi: sarang ŭi hŏng-sik, 1993), features Lee's characteristic blending of narration, **music**, **dance**, poetry, **masks**, and **puppets** to emphasize traditional values. His *A Learned Man, Jo Nam-Myŏng* (Shikol sonbi jo nam-myŏng, 2001) featured movement based on the Korean martial art *hapkido*. Lee deplores American influences and **Western** cause-effect realism in the Korean theatre, but he freely adapts foreign classics, among them *King Lear, Macbeth, Hamlet, The Tempest* (as a musical), *Oedipus Rex*, and *The Metamorphoses*.

In 1994, Lee founded the Uri Theatre Institute (Uri Kŭkyŏn Kuso) to support his vision of a Korean theatre, followed in 1999 by the Miryang Theatre Village (Miryang Yŏngŭk Ch'on), an **experimental theatre** community founded north of Pusan, Lee's hometown. An underground facility, the Guerilla Theatre (Gŏrilla Kŭkchang) in Seoul's Taehangno district was established in 2004, joining the Kamgol Theatre in Pusan as the second venue operated by Lee's Street Theatre Troupe.

Richard Nichols

LEGONG. Emblematic Balinese **dance** with stylized movement and a story. The exquisitely made-up face of a maiden wearing an elegant gilded headdress adorned with frangipani blossoms has come to personify Bali as an "island paradise" in tourist literature. *Legong* is used to teach the fundamentals of Balinese female dance (see also Indonesia).

Legend holds that *legong* originated in the eighteenth century, inspired by a dream of I Dewa Agung Madé Karna, king of Sukawati. An alternate version has it that *legong* derives from the dance of "celestial maidens" (*dedari*), who wore **masks** brought from Java by King Dalem Ketut many centuries before. The sacred *legong ratu dedari* (also known as *sang hyang legong*) is traditionally performed by prepubescent girls wearing these ancient masks at the anniversary of Payogan Agung Temple. Secular "palace *legong*" (*legong keraton*) is often based on the story of the prince of Lasem and his doomed courtship of princess Langkesari. Other versions include the extraordinary *legong prabangsa*, a confrontation between Prince Prabangsa and the powerful witch-goddess, Rangda, in which both dancers and spectators often fall into

ARTI Foundation performance of *legong* production, *Ritus Legong*, choreographed by I Kadek Suardana, a contemporary twist on classical *legong* and traditional anti-epidemic performances. (Photo: ISKANDAR)

trance, and *nandir*, now rarely performed, which features young boys rather than prepubescent girls. Other types include *jobog* ("monkey stories"), *legod bhawa* (the story of Brahma, Wisnu, and the Sivalinggam), and *semaradana* (the romance between the love gods Semara and Ratih). *Legong* has also become a general term referring to any number of so-called "repertoire" dances (*tari lepas*), performed outside a specific dramatic setting, as, for example, the dance-dramas **gambuh** or *Calon Arang* (see *Barong*).

FURTHER READING

Dibia, I Wayan, and Rucina Ballinger. *Balinese Dance, Drama and Music: A Guide to the Performing Arts of Bali.*

Margaret Coldiron

LENONG. **Indonesian** Malay-language theatre of the Betawi people of the environs of Jakarta in western Java. *Lenong* in the nineteenth century was a designation for a hybrid **folk • music** known as *gambang kromong*, a mixture of **Chinese** and Javanese instruments, traditional melodies, and jazz riffs. The theatrical form linking this ensemble to semi-professional **actors** performing scaled-down versions of **komedi stambul** and **bangsawan** emerged by the early 1930s. All-night performances took place on makeshift **stages** with minimal **scenographic** elements at Chinese New Year, ritual celebrations, and night fairs.

Lenong troupes traditionally divide the repertoire into two sorts of plays: "official stories" (*cerita dines*) set in ancient Indonesian, Hindustani, Arabian, and European kingdoms and "liberated stories" (*cerita preman*) set in colonial Java. Formerly, it was common for troupes to perform one each in a night, though today only the latter are recalled. Noble robbers, mistreated mistresses, and cruel landlords feature heavily.

Emphasis is on clowning and martial arts. The extemporized dialogue in *cerita preman* is largely colloquial Betawi Malay.

Shortened *lenong* was performed frequently at Jakarta's Taman Ismail Marzuki arts center, between 1968 and 1975, contributing to Betawi Malay becoming youth slang. Student versions (*lenong kampus*) appeared at universities in the 1970s. "Children's *lenong*" (*lenong bocah*) and "chatty *lenong*" (*lenong rumpi*) are televisual products of the 1980s and 1990s that share with traditional *lenong* only Betawi Malay. *Lenong* is rare today, but **actors** have found work doing television comedy.

FURTHER READING

Koesasi, B. *Lenong and si Pitung*.

Matthew Isaac Cohen

LI YU (CA. 1611–1680). Chinese essayist, *chuanqi* • playwright, theorist, fiction writer, garden designer, and inventor, known for his punditry and wit. Unable to pass the provincial examination, he lived from his talents and secured high official patronage during frequent tours, often accompanied by his female household troupe.

As **Xu Wei** did for *nanxi*, Li Yu wrote a treatise on *chuanqi*, *Casual Expressions of Idle Feeling* (Xianqing ouji, 1671), which comprises two parts (of eight) of his essay collection. There are fifty-four topics, arranged under eleven rubrics. Six—**dramatic structure** (*jiegou*), language (*cicai*), prosody (*yinlü*), dialogue (*binbai*), comedy (*kehun*), and form (*geju*)—concern play composition; five—repertoire (*xuanju*), revision (*biandiao*), singing instruction (*shouqu*), dialogue coaching (*jiaobai*), and imitation (*tuotao*)—relate to production. The only systematic treatment of drama in the pre-modern period, Li's treatise reflects practices that distinguish him from other *chuanqi* playwrights: an emphasis on invention (only one of ten extant plays draws on existing sources), economy (plots are organized around a single character and single event), dialogue (speech-like songs with much debate, dialogue, and soliloquy), and accessibility (plays must be intelligible without recourse to a script). Like Xu Wei, Li Yu disliked ornate and allusive language, but unlike Xu he wrote plays of ideas that progress logically according to neat symmetries.

A Li Yu play upsets *chuanqi* conventions either in its subject or treatment of that subject (or both). *Women in Love* (Lianxiang ban, ca. 1650) features love between **women** married to the same man; *You Can't Do Anything About Fate* (Naihe tian, ca. 1651–1655) features the "clown" (*chou*; see Role Types) playing an ugly man blessed with three beautiful wives; and *Woman in Pursuit of Man* (Huang qiu feng, 1666) has three courtesans, a widow, and a virgin pursuing a diffident hero. Li Yu's fondness for symmetry is exemplified by *The Mistake with the Kite* (Fengzheng wu, ca. 1650–1657), where two base characters—a "painted face" role (*jing*) and a *chou*—lust after the well-born hero (*sheng*) and heroine (*dan*), and *Ideal Love Matches* (Yizhong yuan, ca. 1648–1657), where two famous artists marry women who forge their paintings for a living.

Li's love of paradoxes is evident in *Sole Mates* (Bimuyu, 1661), where the simulated world of the **stage** enables true love to triumph, and *The Ingenious Finale* (Qiao tuanyuan, 1668), in which a son adopts his own parents. *Be Careful About Love* (Shen luanjiao, 1667) features a heroine who takes the initiative in love, a type found in several other plays as well. Only *The Illusory Tower* (Shengzhonglou, 1667) and *The Jade*

Clasp (Yu saotou, 1658) retell familiar stories, while four of the other eight extant plays are based on Li Yu's own vernacular fiction.

One measure of Li Yu's success is that eight of the above-mentioned plays have been adapted as *jingju*.

FURTHER READING

Hanan, Patrick. *The Invention of Li Yu*; Henry, Eric. *Chinese Amusement· The Lively Plays of Li Yü*.

Catherine Swatek

LI YURU (1923–). Chinese °*jingju*° actress of the female **role type** (*dan*). Born to a poor family descended from Manchu nobility, at nine she began **training** at the Beiping Private Advanced **Xiqu** School. She then became a disciple of the great female impersonators, **Mei Lanfang**, **Xun Huisheng**, **Chang Yanqiu**, and Zhao Tongshan (1901–1966), and acquired a profound knowledge of different acting and singing schools. A star at fourteen, Li enjoyed a seventy-year **stage** career that continued through wars, **political** campaigns, the Cultural Revolution (1966–1976), and China's current economic reforms. She formed her own repertoire and style. In 1979, Li married **Cao Yu**, the most important *huaju* ° **playwright**, which brought new directions to her career.

Li's best-known repertoire includes *The Red Plumblossom Pavilion* (Hongmei ge), *Marriage Associated with the Chest* (Gui zhong yuan), *Princess Baihua* (Baihua gongzhu), and *The Royal Concubine Mei* (Mei fei). In such works she not only combined different melodies and singing methods from various schools but also introduced ballet and **folk** ° **dance** movements. Li started writing in the 1980s and published the full-length *jingju Love and Hatred* (Qingsi hen, 1983), a novel, essays on *jingju*, and numerous newspaper columns. She is currently recording master classes of five plays through which she will explore *jingju* themes of tradition and innovation.

Ruru Li

Li Yuru, then sixty-two. as Yang Guifei, smelling a flower, in *The Drunk Imperial Concubine*, a *jingju* play from Mei Lanfang's repertoire, 1981. (Photo: Courtesy of Li Yuru)

LIKÉ. Thai ° **folk** opera (also spelled *likay*, *yiké*, or *yeekay*), a hybrid commercial genre that developed in the late nineteenth century, although its early history is unclear. Composed of elements derived from many other genres, such as improvisational singing, simple plots, simple *lakon nok*, and gaudy Malay-style **costumes**, it is

Thailand's most popular touring theatre for ordinary people. Its origins are southern and it retains, from **Malaysia**, some incantatory Muslim chanting (*dikir*) and ***bangsawan***-like **scenography**.

Liké from its beginnings has been a highly verbal performing art involving witty (and often bawdy) exchanges between men and **women**. Over the course of the last century, *liké* was reworked as it interacted with *lakon nok* and later with Central Thai folk **music**. Early in the twentieth century, *liké* adopted stories, **music**, and **dance** from *lakon nok* and added the Thai *piphat* orchestra to Malay drums. Although extremely popular during the 1930s and 1940s, it lost favor after World War II, but gained new interest when promoted by radio and television in the late 1950s. These interactions helped produce a distinctive musical concertlike style that remains *liké*'s most common feature.

Most of the more than one thousand *liké* **theatre companies** are in Central Thailand. Once regularly housed in indoor proscenium **theatres**, they are now just regular parts of outdoor temple **festivals** and amusement centers, using temporary thrust **stages** or permanent platforms at temples or in market squares. *Liké* scenography consists of gaudily painted backdrops and wings (which do not always match one another), and a bench and chairs that serve as the principal stage **properties**, the bench—as in **Chinese** theatre—able to represent various things. Settings include throne rooms, forests, gardens, and street and river scenes, although—depending on a troupe's resources—the same set can remain in use regardless of shifts in place. The **actors** enter and leave through passages in the backdrop at right and left. The stage contains three sections: the acting area proper, the backstage or dressing-room area (separated from the acting area by the backdrop), and the musicians' area at stage right.

Performers aim for the heartstrings and are frequently garlanded with strings of money by their devotees. Plays have conventional themes and stock melodramatic storylines, often borrowed from classical **khon** or *lakon* (see *Lakon ram*) originals; typically, this involves a host of love troubles and intrigues, children who are lost and found, and so on, usually employing surprising plot twists; comedy is essential and there is always a happy ending.

The story to be performed is told to the troupe by its **storyteller** (*khonruang*) after which the actors improvise it in song and dance. The performance, which may run from 8 p.m. to dawn, usually follows the three-part pattern of opening with a backstage invocatory musical prelude devoted to the god of music, continuing with a sung and danced introduction outlining the story and its moral, and concluding with the play proper. During the performance, linking narration is provided from backstage by the storyteller, who also cues the orchestra for entrances and exits and oversees the action, shortening scenes when necessary and inventing story elements to cover errors.

Performers wear heavy **makeup** (with an emphasis on the eyebrows), and beautiful, decorative costumes replete with sequins, brocades, costume jewelry, and plumed headdresses. (The form was originally all male, and female impersonation is still sometimes seen.) The eclectic costumes, which mix periods, and often use **Western** evening gowns for women, tend to have little relationship to characters or plot, and are mainly for spectacle. No one wears shoes, out of respect for the stage. Animals and demons wear **masks**. Characters belong to set **role types**, especially "male" (*phra*), "female" (*nang*), "father" (*pho*), male and female "villains" (*kong*), and male and female "clowns" (*chok*); each has its subdivisions. *Liké* performances retain a storyline, but because of their imitation of the popular concert format (including the use of a microphone), the use of pop

Liké production of *Prasanta Tor Nok*, produced by the Makhampom Touring Theatre Company, Bangkok, 2000. (Photo: Courtesy of Pradit Prasartthong)

love songs is designed to appeal to the fantasies of the mostly female audience. Melodies come from many sources, traditional and popular, country music and Indian songs. Improvisation is common.

FURTHER READING

Brandon, James R. *Theatre in Southeast Asia*; Chua Soo Pong, ed. *Traditional Theatre in Southeast Asia*; Rutnin, Mattani Mojdara. *Dance, Drama, and Theatre in Thailand: The Process of Development and Modernization.*

Pornrat Damrhung

LIM YOUNG-WOONG (1936–). Korean • director who began his professional career in the mid-1960s, gaining recognition with his 1969 landmark production of Beckett's *Waiting for Godot*. He became Korea's leading Beckett authority. In 1989, he and his troupe took a revival of *Godot* to the Avignon **Festival**, a first for any Korean **theatre company**; in 1990 the production performed in Dublin, where Lim was praised for conveying the essence of Beckett's play despite language barriers.

Known for his meticulous rehearsals and high standards, Lim pioneered the operation of a successful, privately owned and funded company, the Sanullim Theater Company (Kŭkdan Sanullim). To address the shortage of **theatres**, Lim opened the 150–seat Sanullim Theatre (Sanullim Kŭkchang, 1985). Its success lies partly in Lim's efforts to bring female audiences back to the theatre. In 1986, Simone de Beauvoir's *La Femme Rompue* enjoyed a record seven-month run of sold-out performances. It was the first in a series of Sanullim plays dealing with feminist issues. Besides *Waiting for Godot*, the Sanullim's permanent repertory includes Chekhov's *Three Sisters* and Arnold Wesker's

Letter to a Daughter, supplemented by other productions appealing to a largely female audience.

Alyssa S. Kim

LIN ZHAOHUA (1936–). Chinese • **director** of modern "spoken drama" (*huaju*; see Playwrights and Playwriting). After graduating from the Central Academy of Drama in 1961, Lin was assigned to the Beijing People's Art Theatre (Beijing Renmin Yishu Juyuan [BAPT]) as an **actor**. He began his directing career there in the late 1970s and was its vice-president from 1984 to 1998.

In 1982, Lin directed *Absolute Signal* (Juedui xinhao) by 2000 Nobel Laureate **Gao Xingjian**. The play was staged in a rehearsal room with suggestive **scenography**. It challenged both the theatre community and the general public, whose perception of *huaju* had been shaped predominantly by illusionism and Stanislavski's **theories**. The production ran for over one hundred performances and initiated China's **experimental theatre** movement. After this success, Lin directed several other plays by Gao, including *Bus Stop* (Chezhan, 1983) and *Wildman* (Yeren, 1985), both generating much **critical** debate. His innovative nonillusionist techniques were revelatory.

Since the early 1980s, Lin has directed over sixty productions of *huaju*, **geju**, and **xiqu** in a variety of styles. *Festivities of Marriage and Funeral* (Hongbai xishi, 1984) is considered an illusionist *huaju* classic of the 1980s, while *Wildman* and *Uncle Doggie's Nirvana* (Gouer Ye niepan, 1986) aimed at creating a theatrical stream of consciousness. These were the most avant-garde works of their time.

In 1989, Lin founded the Lin Zhaohua Drama Studio (Lin Zhaohua Xiju Gong-zuoshi, LZDS), the only private company with an official performance license since 2003. The studio provided Lin with great artistic freedom. Its productions—such as *Hamlet* (1990), *Romulus the Great* (1992), *Faust* (1994), *Chess Man* (Qi ren, 1995), *The Three Sisters-Waiting for Godot* (San jieme-dengdai Geduo, 1998), a fusion of Chekhov's *Three Sisters* and Beckett's *Waiting for Godot*, *A Parody 2000* (Gushixin-bian 2000), and *Richard III* (2001)—blurred the boundaries between different genres and integrated modern techniques with *xiqu* aesthetics. Besides *huaju*, Lin also has directed **jingju**, such as *The Minister Liu Luoguo I, II, III* (Zaixiang Liu Luoguo, 2000–2002), and *Farewell My Concubine* (Bawang bie ji, 2003).

In 2004, Lin initiated the Peking University Theatre Research Institute. Together with LZDS, it has invited internationally renowned artists to give lectures and conduct workshops.

FURTHER READING

Lin, Wei-yu. "Lin Zhaohua and the Sinicization of *Huaju*."

Nan Zhang

LIU CHING-MIN [LIU JINGMIN] (1956–). Taiwanese • **playwright**, **actress**, essayist, and founder and artistic **director** of U Theatre (You Juchang). Liu trained with a group of talented young **actors** under the tutelage of Wu Jingji, director of the Lanling Theatre Workshop (Lanling Ju Fang). After working on **stage** for four years, the pivotal point in her career came when she met Polish avant-garde director Jerzy Grotowski while studying acting at New York University. Grotowski's comment that Liu was a **Westernized • Chinese** (in performance) led Liu to reflect on the connections between her cultural identity and her physical **stage** presence.

Having grown up in the enclosed world of a military residential compound, Liu did not have the opportunity to interact with local traditions such as temple fairs and open-air performance. Grotowski's comments and **training** sent Liu in search of a new identity and homeland that, ironically, appeared foreign to her. Influenced by Grotowski's emphasis on body language rather than psychological realism, she founded the U Theatre (1988) to fuse local acting and folklore traditions with Western illusionism. The Chinese character for "U" in the name means "excellent" but also meant "actor" in ancient China. The **theatre company** is aptly named, as it seeks to redefine the craft of acting. U Theatre seeks to present its "Taiwanese bodies" through a wide variety of plays, ranging from *Underground Diary of Faust* (Dixiashi shouji Fushide, 1988) to *Listening to the Ocean with a Heart* (Ting hai zhi xin, 1997).

Many of these works have **religious** connotations and a ritualistic ambiance, successfully incorporating the ancient military deployment formation with "ceremonial striding" (*bajia jiang*), "drumming parade" (*chegu*), and Taiwanese "song opera" (*gezai xi*).

Alexander C. Y. Huang

LOK. *See* Pakistan.

LUU QUANG VU (1948–1988). Vietnamese • playwright, one of the most prolific, controversial, and gifted of the 1980s *doi moi* ("renovation") generation—when Vietnam resumed economic, **political**, and cultural contact with other countries. He wrote over thirty plays during a ten-year period before dying in an auto crash. After serving in the northern military (1965–1970), Vu began experimenting with poetry and playwriting, yet his plays were **censored** until 1984. His play *I and We* (Toi va chung ta, 1985) called for balancing the needs of the individual and society, while one of his last plays, *The Ninth Vow* (Loi the thu chin, 1987), contained thinly veiled references to officials who behaved like power-hungry mandarins or greedy thugs—unsubtle parallels to corruption in Vietnam's economic and political transformation. Besides criticizing abusive powers, his plays reflected the cynicism and despair of a society decimated by the "American War" and struggling in relative isolation for a decade, with little improvement in most people's lives.

He was married to one of Vietnam's most famous and outspoken reporter-poets, Xuan Quynh (1942–1988), who died with him and their son. Their deaths fueled rumors that the accident had not been "accidental"—a mystique that continues to haunt Vu's artistic legacy. Vu's most famous play, *Truong Ba's Soul [in] the Butcher's Skin* (Hon Truong Ba da hang thit, 1987), is about a gentle, virtuous gardener whose life is tragically cut short and whose soul is corrupted after being transported into the body of a brutal butcher. The play, directed by Nguyen Dinh Nghi, toured the United States as part of the Vietnam-America Theatre Exchange (1998).

Lorelle Browning and Kathy Foley

MAANCH. Indian • **folk theatre** of Malwa, Madhya Pradesh, whose name (also spelled *maach*, *mach*, and *manch*) means "**stage**." Probably originating in seventeenth century Rajasthan, and brought to Malwa by **playwright** Sri Gopalji Guru, this is a secular, **musical**, out-of-doors, village theatre, spoken and sung in Malwi or Hindi, and using minimal accessories. Stories derive from **religious**, social, historical, and romantic sources. Often seen at **festivals**, it bears similarities to *swang*, *nautanki*, *khyal*, and *bhavai*.

A ritual ceremony is performed by the company head (*guru*) a week or more before the performance when he erects the stage pole (*khamb*) on the site. The stage is high (as much as twelve feet) and around fifteen by twelve feet, backed by a scenic **curtain** and fronted by a low border hiding the performers' feet, and surrounded on all sides by the audience. Earlier stages had three stories, including one for the elite and another, rather high one, for musicians, who now sit at the other side. The old arrangement was abandoned because it forced the **actors** to look away from the audience to the musicians. Torches have been replaced by electric light.

The all-night show commences as late as 10:30 or 11 p.m. with ritual services. Verses are sung by the all-male company as it stands on stage, hands folded and eyes closed, in full **costume** and **makeup**. The "water carrier" (*bhisti*) sprinkles the ground in mime, and the "attendant" (*farrasan*) mimes spreading a carpet as they extol their jobs in song. Deities Ganesha and Bhairav are among those honored. These preliminaries require over an hour before the "herald" (*chodpar*) introduces the play and characters as the actors enter.

As the play proceeds, each dialogue section or couplet finishes with a refrain sung in chorus by the actors, grouped in a corner or standing near the musicians. Among the instruments, the drum (*dholak*) is crucial; it is struck to mark each ending refrain. Also important is the Indian fiddle (*sarangi*). This is a musical form, sometimes likened to operetta, and using around thirty different tunes derived from folk and classical melodies. The text is mostly sung but includes some spoken sections. Folk **dances** are sometimes added.

Performance is not highly codified, and actors have considerable freedom of movement, taking a seat on stage or even among the spectators if otherwise unoccupied. Entrances through the audience are common. A clown (*vidushak*), Shermarkhan or Sher Khan, serves as adviser to the leading character, commenting on the relation between the action and contemporary events. Female impersonators handle the **women**'s roles, even though some retain their mustaches. Women have begun to infiltrate the form, though.

FURTHER READING

Gargi, Balwant. *Folk Theater of India*; Varadpande, M. L. *History of Indian Theatre: Loka Ranga; Panorama of Indian Folk Theatre*.

Samuel L. Leiter

MACAO. Macao, located on the southeast coast of **China**, neighboring **Hong Kong**, is a small city of 27.3 kilometers square, equal to one twenty-third of **Singapore**. Its 2005 population was 449,198. Colonized by the Portuguese in the sixteenth century, it was the first European settlement in East Asia. Pursuant to an agreement signed by China and Portugal in 1987, it became the Macao Special Administrative Region (MSAR) of China in 1999. China has promised that, under its "one country, two systems" formula, China's socialist economic system will not be practiced in Macao, and that Macao will enjoy considerable autonomy in all matters except foreign and defense affairs for the next fifty years. Macao is known as "The Monte Carlo of the Orient" for its long history of gaming, the pillar of its economy.

Most theatre activities are amateur, performed by nongovernmental organizations. Genres include Cantonese *yueju*, modern "spoken drama" (*huaju*; see Playwrights and Playwriting), and **musical** and **dance** theatre. *Huaju* can be divided by language: Cantonese and Macanese. The former, spoken by the majority, is more popular.

Most drama is performed by amateur organizations, so government sponsorship is necessary, including assistance to cover production costs, providing **stages**, and **training**, including playwriting, **acting**, and **directing**.

Sponsorship has improved significantly since 1980. With the annual Macao Art **Festival**, Macao Fringe Festival, Macao Drama Festival, and Interschool Drama Competition, all organized by the government, and the numerous performances and small-scale competitions held by amateurs, local theatre became very popular. In 1999, the Macao Cultural Center, the first **theatre** with professional facilities, opened. Professional performances from Hong Kong and mainland China have been introduced more often, broadening horizons. In 2002, an amateur group organized the first nonprofit professional **theatre company**, Theatre Farmers (Xiju Nongzhuang); this marked the moment when Macao's theatre started transforming from amateur to professional.

Mainland influence made illusionist realism the most common style for Cantonese *huaju*. Alongside plays from the mainland and Hong Kong, translations and adaptations of **Western** classics are often presented.

As for local scripts, one-acts or short plays are most frequently seen because they are easy to produce. Most are serious, reflecting social issues and human relationships. Chau Si Lei (Zhou Shuli, 1938–) and Lei I Leong (Li Yuliang, 1955–) are leading playwrights. Their works are often revived, marking the maturity of the indigenous theatre. Chau and Lei enthusiastically advocate for Macao theatre, seeking to get its plays into the international arena. They are involved in numerous exchange programs with places from Hong Kong to Lisbon.

Chau, who sees education as theatre's main purpose, writes short plays with simple plots and stereotypical characters designed to bring out positive ethical themes. His plays are popular in schools. In 2005, the government awarded Chau the Medal of Cultural Merit for his contribution in popularizing theatrical arts.

Lei writes both one-acts and full-length plays. He portrays the real faces of Macao's common folk. Beneath his plays' superficially humorous language and comic scenes are the tragic and helpless lives of everyday people. Because of the honesty of his treatment of life's difficulties, his plays are favored by scholars and aficionados.

Macanese Drama is a unique community theatre. Its language is Patua, a dialect mixing Portuguese, Malay, and Cantonese that was nearly extinct by the 1970s. To save it for the next generation, the Macanese (mixed-blood Chinese and Portuguese born in Macao) used it in plays combining comedy and farce. Macanese theatre reflects the community's reality, exploring personal identity and cultural recognition in this former Portuguese colony.

Pak Tim Chan

MADANGNORI. **Korean** comic theatre, a new genre conceived in 1981, but with roots in *madanggŭk*, an outdoor performance played in a yard (*madang*). In contrast to *madanggŭk*, which focused on social problems in the 1970s and 1980s, *madangnori* emphasizes "playing" (*nori*). Like *madanggŭk*, the storylines reflect societal issues or conditions; however, by using satire and humor to re-interpret classical stories from the **storytelling** tradition, and ending happily, *madangnori* has established itself as family entertainment rather than an instrument for social change.

The performance includes traditional **folk** songlike **music** with an accompanying orchestra of traditional instruments, **costumes** mixing traditional clothing (*hanbok*) and Mardi Gras–style regalia, and **dance** choreography blending traditional elements with movements like those in a nightclub revue.

Productions suggest **Western** circus presentations. Because *madangnori* is usually played in an outdoor tent or gymnasium, with the audience surrounding the **stage**, modern **properties** and effects are used rather than **scenographic** elements to augment the theatrical (*nori*) aspect. It bears the stamp of the Beauty and Ugliness Company (Kŭkdan Michoo) and its **director**, **Sohn Jin-Chaek**, who staged the first performance; representative **actors** are Yun Mun-sik (1943–), Kim Sŭng-nyŏ (1950–), and Kim Jong-yŏp (1948–).

Alyssa S. Kim

Madangnori production by Korea's Beauty and Ugliness (Kŭkdan Michoo) Company, 2005. (Photo: Courtesy of Beauty and Ugliness Company; Michoo Theatre Company)

MAFUNE YUTAKA (1902–1977). Japanese • *shingeki* playwright. Reading Marx while studying English literature at Waseda University inspired Mafune to drop out and work on farms in Hokkaido and Shikoku. By 1926, he had published some plays, but it was not until the 1930s on returning to Tokyo that his career took off. He made a startling debut in 1934 with *Weasels* (Itachi), set in his native Fukushima, about an avaricious family squabbling over declining fortunes. While **director •** **Kubota Mantarô**'s skilled staging enhanced the play's success, Mafune's **dramatic structure**, characterization, and dialogue signaled a major talent.

His early plays portrayed village life as a microcosm of dog-eat-dog egoism and greed; subsequent works, like *Sun Child* (Taiyô no ko, 1936) and *Naked Town* (Hadaka no machi, 1936), had urban settings. **Senda Koreya** often directed Mafune's plays, including *Fugue* (Tonsôfu, 1937), *The Nakahashi Residence* (Nakahashi kôkan, 1946), *Yellow Room* (Kiiroi heya, 1948), and *Red Lamp* (Akai rampu, 1954).

Mafune spent much of World War II in **China**, and his later plays often feature Japanese residents in China or returnees. He modeled *Red Lamp*'s protagonist, a former secret policeman who has murdered a family following the Great Kantô Earthquake of 1923 and become cultural attaché in the puppet state Manchukuo, after Lieutenant Amakasu, murderer of the anarchists Osugi Sakae and Itô Noe. Mafune's work was typically apolitical, however; the cynicism of his earlier plays was leavened by touches of humor, and his later work tended toward more gentle satires of human foibles.

M. Cody Poulton

MAHABHARATA. One of **India**'s two great **Sanskrit** epics, and an important Hindu **religious** text. Many South and Southeast Asian dramas, where regional versions in local vernaculars flourish, are based on it. Written versions run to some 180,000 lines, making it the world's longest poem. It seems the product of a long **storytelling** tradition and elaboration over centuries, which continues today. Its reputed author, Vyasa, also known as Krishna Dvaipayana or Veda-Vyasa, figures prominently in the story, where he is depicted as a Brahman sage.

The title (*The Great* [*Story*] *about the Bharatas*), refers to the Bharata family, central characters in the narrative; but it can also mean "the great story of India," as Bharata is the subcontinent's ancient name. The story can be briefly summarized: the ruling family of north-central India, the Bharatas, split into two factions in a dispute over succession to the throne—the Pandavas (five brothers, sons of Pandu, who had ruled earlier), and their cousins the Kauravas (one hundred brothers, sons of Dhritarastra, the ruler at the time). The Pandavas had as their friend and ally Krishna Vasudeva, a prince who was also a god incarnate in human form (*avatara*) on earth to restore order. At a Vedic "royal consecration" (*rajasuya*) ritual, which would have declared the eldest Pandava, Yudhishthira, the emperor ruling over many kings, the Kauravas cheated at the dice match that was to have celebrated the rite's conclusion, and the Pandavas were exiled with their wife, Draupadi. After twelve years in the wilderness, followed by a thirteenth in disguise as they reentered society, the Pandavas returned to the kingdom to claim their share, but were rebuffed by their cousins. Both sides assembled their allies and met to fight a battle for sovereignty. After eighteen days of fierce fighting, the Pandavas won back the decimated kingdom, and ruled righteously for many years.

The characters and their situations have for centuries been regarded by Hindus as providing guidelines on how they should live their own lives, which remains true today. The *Mahabharata* also includes many passages that explicitly teach religious and philosophical doctrines, the most significant of which is the *Song of the Blessed One* (Bhagavad gita), the most widely known Hindu religious text. **Kalidasa**'s *The Recognition of Shakuntala* (Abhijnana Shakuntalam), Bhatta Narayana's *Venisamhara*, and about half the dramas sometimes attributed to **Bhasa** are among Sanskrit plays based on the *Mahabharata*. Revivals, especially by **Kavalam Narayam Panikkar**, have played an important role in modern production.

Although the story is essential to the corpus of numerous **folk** and pre-modern forms, most particularly *terukkuttu*, it has played a crucial part in the work of major **playwrights** and **directors**, including the colonial-period plays of **Michael Madhusudan Dutt, Rabindranath Tagore**, and Prabhakar Khadilkar (1872–1948): the latter's *Killing of Kichaka* (Kichaka vadh, 1907) used the story to express anticolonial feelings and was **censored**. The story's spectacular qualities were exploited by **Parsi theatre** troupes, and by southern India's **Gubbi Veeranna • Theatre Company**, which produced an open-air *Mahabharata* play using horses, elephants, and chariots. In the postcolonial period, the *Mahabharata* became a crucial site for dealing with contemporary **political** and social issues, both in urban literary dramas, such as those by **Dharamvir Bharati** and **Girish Karnad**, and those of **experimental**, performance-based directors, like Panikkar, **Ratan Thiyam**, and **Habib Tanvir**. These plays often interrogate postcolonialism from a **critical** position, one of the best examples being Bharati's *Blind Age* (Andha yug, 1962). The epic has been the subject of television serials and many movies. In 1989, in fact, a nine-hour play developed from the epic by British director Peter Brook, enacted internationally (but not in India), was made into a six-hour movie.

FURTHER READING

Varadpande, M. L. *The Mahabharata in Performance*; Vyasa. *The Mahabharata.*

Bruce M. Sullivan

MAHARISHI, MOHAN (1940–).

MAHARISHI, MOHAN (1940–). Indian Hindi-language **actor, director, playwright**, educator, **scenographic** designer, and poet, born in Ajmer, Rajasthan. At fifteen, he began acting in radio plays. He studied at New Delhi's National School of Drama (NSD), under **Ebrahim Alkazi** (1962–1965), and then performed with the NSD Repertory **Theatre**. Alkazi directed him in **Western** classics, ranging from Shakespeare to Beckett. Maharishi also directed **experimentalist** stagings of *Earth's Daughter* (Bhumija, 1963) and *Listen Janamejay* (Suno Janamejay, 1965).

Maharishi and others cofounded the **theatre company** Dishantar, which opened with **Badal Sircar**'s *And Indrajit* (Evam Indrajit, 1967); its altered ending created controversy. He moved to Jaipur, establishing a group called Sanket. The first production was *Ostrich* (Shuturmurg, 1968), by Gyandev Agnihotri, whose leftist **politics** led to further controversy and ended the production. Subsequent productions included plays adapted from Shaw, Ibsen, Brecht, and Dürenmatt.

In 1971, Maharishi became a television producer for India's national network, following which, in 1973, he was appointed a government cultural adviser in Mauritius, where he was instrumental in developing a youth theatre movement. In 1979, after a sojourn in Europe, he became a professor of drama at Punjab University, Chandigarh, where he staged outstanding productions, including one of Harcharan Singh's Punjabi play *Rani Jindan* (1981), which he also directed with foreign actors in the United States and Canada. His work was notable for its eclectic use of Indian and Western methods, and avoidance of being pigeonholed for any particular style.

Maharishi served as director of the NSD (1984–1986), but a managerial conflict forced him to return to Chandigarh, where he retired in 2004 before going back to Delhi. His NSD guest directing included his own *Einstein* (1994) and *The King's Kitchen* (Raja ki rasoi, 1998). *Einstein* was acclaimed for its introduction of a serious scientific theme within the context of excellent theatrical entertainment; the title figure was visualized in three contrasting images reflected in triangular mirrors that expressed his multidimensionality. Maharishi then undertook a sequel, *Einstein 2.*

He staged over one hundred plays, including his adaptation of Marsha Norman's *'Night Mother* (2004), in which his actress wife, Anjala Maharishi, returned to the **stage** after a twenty-year hiatus, and his own lauded translation of *Othello* (2005), which he also designed.

Shashikant Barhanpurkar

MAHIEU, AUGUSTE ("GUUS") KONSTANTIN PIERRE (1865–1903). Indonesian • actor-manager and composer of *komedi stambul*. Mahieu was the Eurasian son of a government clerk, born in Bangkalan, Madura. He attended secondary school in Surabaya and became an actor in the first *komedi stambul* **theatre company**, founded by Surabaya impresario Yap Gwan Thay (1891). Mahieu took over as **director** after the first one quit and achieved fame as an actor, singer, composer, and scenario writer.

Mahieu played guitar and violin, and had an expressive tenor voice and broad comic style. A spokesman for the rights of mixed-race European-Indonesians, Mahieu joined the Indies League in 1900 and presented allegorical plays and tableaux in support of impoverished Eurasians with his Light of the Indies (Sinar Stambul) troupe. In 1902, Mahieu acted in and **musically** directed Indra Zanibar, a **Malaysian** • *bangsawan* theatre company, thereby contributing to the merging of these two popular Malay genres. A composition attributed to Mahieu was adapted as Malaysia's national anthem in 1957.

Matthew Isaac Cohen

MAKEUP

Makeup: China

Xiqu makeup practices differ by **role type**. For "painted face" (*jing*) and "clown" (*chou*) types, graphic and colorful "face scores" (*lianpu*) convey information about personality and character through a complex system of conventional colors and designs. For "male" (*sheng*) and "female" (*dan*) characters, "handsome appearance" (*junban*) makeup idealizes the natural features.

Face Scores: **Lianpu.** The *lianpu* practice has roots in Tang-dynasty (618–907) *can-jun xi* and Song-dynasty (960–1279) *zaju* and *nanxi*, when comic and grotesque effects were created with black ink and colored powders for predecessors of the *chou*. In Yuan (1280–1368), full-face makeup signaling personality traits apparently was used for heroic *jing* characters. With the rise of **kunqu** in Ming (1368–1644), *lianpu* became fully established; its conventions were inherited and expanded for the rising **bangzi qiang** and *pihuang* forms of Qing (1644–1911).

Jingju offers a prime example. Most *lianpu* for *jing* characters are "drawn face" (*goulian*), with rich, opaque colors applied by brush to the entire front half of the head; some are "rubbed face" (*roulian*), translucent base colors being thinly applied with palm and fingers and only some brush delineation of features. Color significance includes red for loyalty and courage, matte white for cruelty and treachery, shiny white for obstinate bravery, black for integrity and straightforwardness, blue for fierce boldness, pink for loyalty in old age, yellow for cunning, green for impetuousness, light green for often-negative supernatural beings, silver for low-ranking deities and spirits, and gold for higher ranking deities, including Buddha.

For most *jing* in traditional plays, a general design is already established, and **actors** interpret character through the handling of details; one source lists twenty-two types of eyebrows, sixteen eye sockets, six mouths, and fifteen types of brows commonly used. To create *lianpu* for new *jing* in **xinbian lishi ju**, actors interpretively select colors and work with more than a dozen traditional styles.

The "whole/complete face" (*zhenglian*) is the simplest, used for extremely virtuous, positive characters; the entire face is one color, with eyebrows and sometimes expressive lines added in a second color. When matte white is used with thin black or gray eyebrows and lines, however, the character is extremely treacherous and negative. The "three pieces [of] tile face" (*sankuai wa lian*) is most fundamental; the three "tiles"—the forehead and two cheeks—are a single strong color characterizing the personality, while black and white exaggerate the eyebrows and eye sockets, and the upper lip and bilabial folds. For elderly characters, the eyebrows and eye sockets droop on the outer edges.

Most other major *lianpu* styles are derived from these two. To give one instance, the "fragmentary/shattered face" (*sui lian*) involves complex, detailed patterns and additional colors applied to the eye sockets and eyebrows, upper lip, and bilabial folds, nose, and three "tiles."

For male *chou*, the "piece of tofu" (*doufu kuai*) is used, involving a patch of white around the eye area and nose, with black and red delineation for eyes and mouth, and sometimes additional expressive lines. The patch is usually square or shaped like a kidney or a date stone, but many variations are possible.

Additionally, *lianpu* may be used by *sheng* playing monkeys. Certain bravura roles called "red *sheng*" (*hongsheng*) are portrayed with bright red faces, and even certain *dan* may wear painted faces.

Handsome Appearance: **Junban.** In Ming and Qing, *dan* actors wore light and *sheng* actors little or no makeup. *Junban* makeup, a.k.a. "spread/smeared color" (*mocai*) because it is primarily applied with palm and fingers, evolved rapidly in the late nineteenth and early twentieth centuries to accommodate social changes, including artificial lighting and modern beauty styles. Today, the basic design is the same for most *sheng* and *dan*: the face is pale with rouge around the eyes, the eyes and eyebrows are lined in black, and their outside corners are raised and tied up to enlarge the eye area and expression.

Young *dan* faces are almost white, "young males" (*xiaosheng*) a warmer cream, and "older males" (*laosheng*) a light flesh tone. Rouge for young *dan* and *xiaosheng* is deep rose, and for *laosheng* an orangish peach. *Sheng* actors also apply rouge between their eyebrows, extending onto their foreheads; it forms a spear point for martial *sheng*, a semicircle for civil *xiaosheng*, and is a soft indistinct patch for *laosheng*. Rouge and eye and eyebrow delineation is more concentrated and saturated for younger and stronger characters; very old characters may have no eye delineation and gray or white eyebrows. "Older women" (*laodan*) wear only a flesh-colored base, light rouge, and a little eye and eyebrow delineation. "Female clowns" (*choudan*) employ a gentle parody of the young *dan* makeup.

Change Face Technique: **Bianlian.** In some *xiqu* forms, both *junban* and *lianpu* practices include techniques known collectively as "change face" (*bianlian*), involving an instantaneous change to show a sudden alteration of state or emotion. The most famous *bianlian* are those of **chuanju**, but other forms had or now have such techniques. *Bianlian* can change all or part of the face; while some techniques utilize **masks,** two major ones involve makeup. In "spread sudden/violent eyes" (*mo baoyan*), the performer takes previously secreted color and applies it with a finger between the eyebrows, at the rim of the eyes, or to the bilabial folds to create a sudden appearance change. For "blow powder" (*chuifen*), performers blow on concealed colored powder, causing it to rise and adhere to oiled areas.

FURTHER READING

Yu Dexiang and Liao Pin (text); Zhou Daguang (design and ed.). *Peking Opera Facial Designs*; Wang-Ngai, Siu, and Peter Lovrick. *Chinese Opera: Images and Stories.*

Elizabeth Wichmann-Walczak

Makeup: India

The myriad forms of traditional theatre in South Asia utilize makeup conventions ranging from highly stylized to minimally stylized, semirealistic traditions. Genres like **nautanki**, **bhavai**, and **jatra** employ minimally stylized makeup that strives to create semirealistic images specific to and characteristic of time periods and dramatic contexts.

Ritual Entrancement. The conventions of several South **Indian** forms, on the other hand, are powerfully stylized and codified. These include Tamilnadu's **terukkuttu**, Kerala's **kathakali**, and Karnataka's **yakshagana**, and Kerala's **Sanskrit theatre** form, **kutiyattam**. Space allows a detailed look at only the first three. It is vital to understand that each is derivative of and performed in powerful Hindu **religious** contexts and that their makeup is rooted in and reflects these contexts, in which rituals of entrancement play powerful roles.

Terukkuttu developed in a region where **Mahabharata** cult rituals in temple settings are dominant, *kathakali* in a locale where entrancement rituals (**teyyam**) are central, and *yakshagana* where the "serpent worship" (*naga-mandala*) rite is important. While not drama per se, these rituals utilize **music**, song, and movement and, very importantly, makeup, characterized by facial and body painting that, along with these other elements, is believed to engender entrancement.

Terukuttu *Makeup*. We may use the ritually derived makeup tradition of *terukkuttu* as a paradigm with which to understand other traditional South Asian makeup styles. Each *terukkuttu* character has a basic color that puts him or her in a particular dramatic category. The three most important are red, green, and rose. Characters using red are malevolent or villainous, while characters with green are benevolent or heroic. Rose is used for a figure that is not clearly good or evil. The basic colors symbolize a dramatic and moral spectrum ranging from the poles of positive/benevolent green through a relatively ambiguous rose central range to negative/malevolent red. Over these basic colors will be drawn motifs and other designs that will more specifically identify and characterize particular characters.

Since performances most frequently occur in remote, rural settings, this complex, powerful makeup is applied by each performer himself sitting on the ground cross-legged holding a mirror in a simple palm-thatch greenroom. The makeup application can take several hours because the colors will be mixed on the spot on a ritually sacralized, small, flat makeup stone. Finely powdered colors are mixed with coconut oil on this stone into a smooth paste that is applied by hand. The other motifs and designs are developed by dipping thin sticks into the hand-mixed pastes. Performers refer to the makeup application as "writing" their characters. This system is believed to catalyze the onset of ritual entrancement that frequently occurs among spectators and performers.

Kathakali *Makeup*. *Kathakali*'s makeup traditions are homologous to the *terukkuttu* but display a distinctive spectrum and application of color. The three principal basic colors are green, "knife" (green with a red patch), and "polished" (flesh/rose color from a mixture of red and yellow). Green includes beneficent, virtuous and heroic characters; knife includes demoniac, evil, and aggressive characters; and polished includes characters showing restraint, gentleness, and poise. Upon these basic colors are painted patterns that bring individuality and specific dramatic and epic identity to the various figures. As with *terukkuttu*, finely powdered colors are mixed with coconut oil into a smooth paste that is applied by hand. The other motifs and designs are created by dipping thin sticks into the hand-mixed pastes. Like *terukkuttu*, *kathakali*'s makeup appears to have been influenced by rituals involving the sacralization of paintings utilizing similar colors and motifs.

Yakshagana *Makeup*. *Yakshagana* uses a makeup schema similar to *terukkuttu* and *kathakali* to create a **role type**. While utilizing color symbolism related to these other forms, it has its own characteristic approach. The face of an heroic, virtuous figure is covered with a pink-yellow on which are drawn lines in different colors, especially red, black, and white, creating clear dramatic identity. Demons, as with *kathakali*, will have a basic color combining red and green. The pastes are obtained by mixing colored powders with coconut oil and water.

These makeup systems are dependent on color symbolism derived from and reflective of the ritual contexts of traditional forms that provide a model and template from which to understand codified traditions in other South Asian regions. *See also Krishnattam.*

FURTHER READING

Ashton, Martha B., and Bruce Christie. *Yakshagana*; Ashton, Martha B., and Robert P. Sikora. *Krishnattam*; Zarrilli, Phillip B. *Kathakali Dance-Drama: Where Gods and Demons Come to Play.*

Richard A. Frasca

Makeup: Japan

Three of **Japan**'s four main traditional theatres, **kyôgen**, **nô**, and *bunraku* (see Puppet Theatre), do not use makeup, but **kabuki**'s highly developed methods are central to the expression of its characters.

Kabuki Makeup. *Kabuki* **actors** use the expression "create a face" (*kao o tsukuri*). As a general rule, makeup is rendered according to **role type**, and adjusted by each actor to fit his own physiognomy. Styles range from quite realistic in "domestic dramas" (*sewa mono*) at one end of the spectrum, to the bold lines of "shadow taking" (*kumadori*), mainly used for superheroes, spirits, and villains of stupendous proportion acted in the bombastic "rough style" (*aragoto*). White rice powder (*oshiroi*) mixed with water forms the basis of all makeup, with color adjusted to suit gender, age, and type. Young female and male lovers use white, signifying beautiful, fair skin, while many samurai, country people, and older females use darker base shades, which mix varying amounts of brown powder (*tonoko*) with *oshiroi*. Strong, young superheroes, and some evil characters and comic "red face" (*akattsura*) villains mix scarlet (*shudô*) for a red base. Greasepaints include light blue (*seitai*), used to indicate freshly shaven areas on male faces and heads; red (*beni*), for lips and red *kumadori* lines; and soft black (*sumi*), either as is or blended over red, for eye lines and brows. Various styles of eyebrows, eye lines, and lips, differing in size, angle, length, shape and thickness, are intended for specific types.

Before applying makeup, the actor applies a thin foundation of oil. The eyebrows are obliterated, either by being shaved, flattened with wax, or covered with a strip of skin-colored silk. A thin silk cloth (*habutae*) covers the hair and hairline.

Kumadori. *Kumadori* originated with **Ichikawa Danjûrô** I. Subsequent actors imitated and improved upon it, and it became common in "history plays" (*jidai mono*). Some fifty major varieties can be divided into two principal categories: (1) "red shadows" (*beni guma*), utilizing red lines indicative of righteousness and strength; and (2) "blue shadows" (*ai guma*), utilizing blue lines indicative of fear or evil. Patterns are specific to character, though a given character's *kumadori* may change in the course of a play, outwardly displaying an inner transformation, or indicating a character's changed relationship or function in a scene. Some characters use body *kumadori*, though today these muscle patterns are dyed on tights or padded body suits rather than painted on the flesh.

Wigs. Wigs are used to varying degrees in Japan's traditional forms. *Nô* wigs are of two basic types. Long, straight-haired wigs—black (*kurotare*) for younger characters, or white (*shirotare*) for older characters—may hang loosely or be gathered into a ponytail. Strands of hair hanging from the sides to the front of the shoulders signify disarray or turbulence. They are used mainly by females, deities, young males, or warrior ghosts. The second type, a larger, wildly flowing wig with shorter hair framing the face, comes in red (*akagashira*) for demons and ogres, white (*shirogashira*) for elderly characters, and black (*kurogashira*) for vengeful ghosts. Wigs similar to this second type are used in *kyōgen* for animals and supernatural beings. Female *kyōgen* characters do not wear an actual wig, but instead a highly conventionalized, white linen, turban-like headdress (*binan*) wrapped around the head, leaving long strips hanging from the ears at the sides.

Kabuki and *bunraku* wigs are highly developed and require two people to create. The wigmaker (*katsuraya*) cuts, shapes, and fashions a copper base (*daigane*), and fits it to individual actors' heads. He then attaches hair, sewn into a plain silk cloth that is pasted onto the base. Human hair is generally used, although materials such as yak tail, horse tail, bear fur, and silk are used for specific parts or styles of wigs. The stylist (*tokoyama*) coifs and maintains the wig and hair ornaments for the run of a play. Stylists usually specialize in male or female wigs, of which there are approximately four hundred and one hundred styles, respectively. Hair is styled according to role type, while accommodating actors' preferences and face shapes.

Wig classification is complex, with names that generally reflect a combination of the following elements: (1) shape of topknot (*mage*), side locks (*bin*), forelock (*maegami*), or nape hair (*tabo*); (2) type of base used; (3) role for which the style is used; (4) whether the hair is heavily pomaded or not. Like makeup, hairstyles range from real Edo-era (1603–1868) coifs to the highly pomaded imaginative male styles worn by *aragoto* characters.

Male wigs can generally be divided into highly pomaded hair (*aburatsuki*) and puffy back hair shaped like an inflated bag (*fukurotsuki*), used mostly in period plays and domestic plays respectively. An example of the former is an *aburatsuki honke bin no wakashu mage*, that is, a wig using only real hair (*honke*), with back hair pomaded and pressed to the base (*aburatsuki*), a young man's (*wakashu*) forelocks, and a topknot (*mage*). Its counterpart would be a *fukurotsuki honke bin no wakashu mage*, similar except for the treatment of the back hair. The length and positioning of the topknot, as well as the degree of back hair and side lock puffiness are indicative of station, age, and nature.

Most female wigs fall into one of three large categories, determined by the back hair shape: (1) *marutabo*, with short round tufts of hair in back, used in period plays; (2) *jitabo*, with a longer, more slender line of back hair forming a bag shape, used in domestic plays; and (3) *shiitake tabo*, with mushroom-shaped back hair highly pomaded and polished. The topknot shape, back hair, and ornament type are indicative of age, marital status, and position.

Bunraku follows many of the same conventions. The metal plates of the base are attached to the head with rivets, and hairstyles are modified to keep hair away from the neck line so as not to interfere with puppet manipulation.

FURTHER READING

Cavaye, Ronald, Paul Griffith, and Akiko Senda. *A Guide to the Japanese Stage: From Traditional to Cutting Edge*; Shaver, Ruth M. *Kabuki Costume*.

Julie A. Iezzi

MA LIANLIANG (1901–1966). Chinese • *jingju* • **actor**, a graduate of the Xiliancheng **Training** Company, who became famous for the "Ma style," noted for its "sweet," "fluent," and "natural" character. He started as a student of the "martial male" (*wusheng*) **role type** and later studied the "older male" (*laosheng*) with Jia Honglin (1874–1917) and **Yu Shuyan**, combining their art into a distinctive *laosheng* style of his own.

In the early 1930s, he was acknowledged as one of the four greatest Chinese actors of bearded roles. After 1949, he collaborated with Tan Fuying (1906–1977), Zhang Junqiu (1920–1997), and Qiu Shengrong (1915–1971) in adapting the **bangzi qiang** drama *Zhao Family Orphan* (Zhao guer) as *jingju*. He performed in the **xinbian lishi ju** *Hai Rui Dismissed from Office* (Hai Rui baguan, 1961), heavily **criticized** because of its supposed **political** implications, and the contemporary dramas *Azalea Mountain* (Dujuan shan; [final text: September 1973] later, one of the Cultural Revolution's "model works" [**yangban xi**]) and *More and More Every Year* (Niannian youyu).

In 1952, Ma established the Ma Lianliang Jingju Company (Ma Lianliang Jingju Tuan), which toured nationally. In 1955, it amalgamated with another **theatre company** to form the Beijing Jingju Company (Beijing Jingju Tuan), with Ma as head; another company joined in 1956, with Zhang Junqiu as head. Ma died early in the Cultural Revolution after being persecuted for his role in *Hai Rui Dismissed from Office*.

Trevor Hay and Ping Sun

MAKINO NOZOMI (1959–). Japanese • *shingeki* • **playwright**, **director**, and screenwriter. A gifted **storyteller** with comic sensibility, Makino utilizes the language of working-class Kyoto, where he joined the theatre while attending Dôshisha University. His plays usually feature strong females and well-known prewar Japanese artists or intellectuals committed to their respective goals, who speak out against their restricted freedoms.

Makino established his **theatre company**, M.O.P. (Makino Office Project), in 1981 and his early work featured multiple sets and quick changes. With *Pisuken* (1991), however, he began using a single set throughout, framing the central idea. The play concerns anarchist Ôsugi Sakae, fleeing the police (who murdered him in 1923), with Pisuken in an Osaka café run by Pisuken's lover, where they decry the corruption of democracy.

Summer Runners (Natsu no rannaa, 1998) uses baseball as a metaphor for life's struggles. The action pits a team of black-marketing gangsters in economically deprived postwar Osaka against American military police. Makino's characteristically strong **woman**, the "don's" daughter Ryûko, manifesting pride in Japan, urges the gangsters to sacrifice their meager profits to give their young pitching star a shot at professional baseball.

Tokyo Atomic Klub (Tôkyô genshikaku kurabu, 1997) is based on Nobel Prize winner Tomonaga Shinichirô's (1906–1979) research in nuclear physics. Humorously exploring a serious, often taboo subject, Makino, through Tomonaga's experience, gives Japan's race to develop its own atomic bomb a personal dimension, provocatively hinting at Japanese complicity in the tragedy of Hiroshima and Nagasaki.

John D. Swain

MAK YONG. Malaysian • **dance** theatre associated with Kelantan, and also found in Malay-speaking southern **Thailand**, where it originated. In conjunction with the shamanic trance ritual (*main puteri*), it can be used to heal the sick. Connected to the myth of the Javanese deity Semar, his sons, or the rice spirit, it is believed to originally have been a courtly art form performed by an all-female cast over four to eight nights. *Mak yong* (or *makyong*) is now commonly reduced to a two-hour production, generally beginning at 9 p.m. Plays, which have no written texts and employ improvised dialogue, feature four main characters/**role types**, all played by **women**: the eponymous Mak Yong (playing the queen, the king's mother, or mother-in-law), Pak Yong Muda (young prince), Pak Yong Tua (wise old prince, who can be the prince's father or his future father-in-law), and Puteri Mak Yong (young princess). Each is elaborately dressed in appropriate **costumes** and regalia. Other characters include a pair of male and female clowns (*peran*), who also function as retainers, attendants, gods, spirits, ogres, birds, and other animals. Hand **properties** are minimal, and **stage** props are nil. The **music** accompanying the **dance** and song consists of drums (*tawak-tawak*), a flute, gongs, and a spiked fiddle (*rebab*). All musicians are male.

Although *mak yong* is performed purely as entertainment, and even as urban commercial theatre, it is probably most closely associated with **religious** performance. Even the cardinal alignments of its performance space are dictated by ritual concerns. Performances begin with the rite of "opening the stage" (*buka panggung*) in which offerings are made to ancestral spirits and other invisible beings, who are invited to participate, help the performers perform better, and protect them and audience members from harm.

Vital sequences include the "dance before the *rebab*" (*tarian menghadap rebab*) and a "song before the *rebab*" (*lagu mengadap rebab*) and, finally, the play, interspersed with solo and group dances and music. There are about thirty *mak yong* pieces, those that are drummed and those that are sung. Their subjects address mythological themes. Titles include *The Young God* (Dewa muda), *The Triton-shell Princess* (Anak raja gadong), *The Spell of the Giantess* (Raja tangkai hati), and *The Identical Princess* (Raja dua serupa). **Acting** is stylized, including the use of *mudra*-like hand gestures. Performances end with the rite of "closing the stage" (*tutup panggung*), in which invisible beings are thanked for their assistance and sent off to their original abodes.

Mak yong benefits from state support, preservation, and rejuvenation, and while it is officially proscribed by Kelantan's Islamist government, is occasionally performed at the Palace of Culture (Istana Budaya), Malaysia's national theatre.

FURTHER READING

Yousof, Ghulam Sarwar. *Dictionary of Traditional South-East Asian Theatre.*

Solehah Ishak

MALAYSIA. Situated in Southeast Asia, Malaysia consists of two land areas separated by the South **China** Sea. West Malaysia, sharing its northern border with **Thailand**, comprises most of the Malay Peninsula, including Kuala Lumpur, the capital. East Malaysia occupies most of the northern part of the island of Borneo and contains the two states of Sabah and Sarawak, which border **Indonesia** and **Brunei**. Of Malaysia's approximately 24 million people, Malays account for about 51 percent of the population, Chinese 24 percent, indigenous peoples 10 percent, Indians 7 percent, and others 8 percent. Islam is the official state **religion**, and it is the religion of the Malay community; Buddhism, Confucianism, Taoism, Hinduism, Christianity, and Sikhism are also practiced. Malay is the official national language. English is also widely used. Mandarin is taught in Chinese schools, and several other Chinese dialects are commonly spoken, such as Cantonese, Hokkien, Hakka, Hainan, and Teochew. Many **Indians** speak Tamil, while other Indian languages are also spoken, such as Telugu, Malayalam, Bengali, and Punjabi. In the north, many speak Thai. In East Malaysia, Kadazan (in Sabah) and Iban (in Sarawak) are spoken by large segments of the population.

After ten centuries of Hindu cultural influence and the ascendancy of the Malaccan Sultanate by the beginning of the fifteenth century, the Malay peninsula, through contact with Indian Muslim traders, became in turn predominantly Muslim. With the fall of Malacca in 1511, the peninsula was successively controlled by various outside powers, including the Portuguese, the Achenese (from North Sumatra), the Dutch, the British, and the **Japanese**. The pre– and post–World War II period of British colonialism had a major impact until independence arrived (1957). In 1963, Sabah, Sarawak, and **Singapore** joined the union, from then onward to be called Malaysia; Singapore withdrew in 1965.

Today, Malaysia is a constitutional monarchy. There are eleven state sultans who, every five years, take turns as Supreme Head. **Political** power is held by a prime minister, who leads a bicameral parliament.

Traditional, Transitional, and Modern. Malaysian theatre reflects the country's multiethnic and multilingual heritage. Modern theatre includes plays written in all of the country's major languages. Malay-language theatre is usually divided into three categories: traditional, transitional (popular), and modern. Some traditional forms are *wayang kulit* (see Puppet Theatre); **dance**-dramas like ***mak yong, manohra,*** *mek mulong,* and ***randai***; trance performances, such as *kuda kepang* ("hobbyhorse dancing") and *main puteri*; poetic call and response (*dikir barat*); ***boria***; and traditional **storytelling** (*penglipur lara*).

Bangsawan, considered transitional/popular theatre, bridges the gap between traditional and modern drama. It was a commercial, improvisational theatre derived from **Parsi theatre** (*wayang parsi*), a style staged in Penang by Indian troupes in the late nineteenth century. *Bangsawan* was particularly popular in the 1920s and 1930s. **Actors** adapted tales from different sources—Arab, Persian, Indian, Malay, Chinese, and even Shakespeare—to attract large audiences. Its decline began during World War II and continued in the postwar period when rivaled by motion pictures, radio, and television.

Sandiwara, Realistic Drama, and Experimental Theatre. Modern Malay theatre has a historical development dating back to the 1930s and, since the 1950s, has actively kept pace with the nationalist movement and issues of nation-building. From the 1950s through the 1970s, a responsive modern theatre movement developed in three successive phases: ***sandiwara***, realistic drama, and **experimental theatre**.

During the 1950s, theatre was an established cultural activity at Malay teacher **training** colleges. The first generation of Malay **playwrights** (1950s–early 1960s), notably **Shaharom Husain**, Kalam Hamidi (1936–), Ali Aziz, and **Usman Awang**, wrote *sandiwara* scripts that drew upon history during the era of rising nationalism, before and after independence. *Sandiwara* historical dramas critiqued British colonialism as well as Malay feudalism and expressed support for democratic reform. *Sandiwara* plays also examine contemporary life, especially the moral dilemmas characters confront as they shift from rural to urban settings.

Realistic plays of the 1960s, often termed *drama moden* ("modern drama"), address the new nation's social problems. Playwrights attempted to ameliorate the ill effects of progress by a selective retention of traditional values. They found inspiration in the works of Indonesian and **Western** writers, especially Ibsen. In Malay realism, most plays feature plots with positive resolutions that lend support to the optimistic spirit of a recently independent nation. In general, these social dramas focus on Malay society, with the main action set in the sitting room of the primary characters' household. Here, both family and community members can meet to expose and resolve the issues of the day. Well-crafted works exemplifying *drama moden* are *For Wiping Away the Tears* (Buat menyapu si air mata, 1963) by Awang Had Salleh, *Tiled Roof, Thatched Roof* (Atap genting atap rembia, 1963) by **Mustapha Kamil Yassin**, and *The Unfortunate Is Lucky* (Sial bertuah, 1963) by Kalam Hamidi. A change in tone emerges in later realistic drama, such as A. Samad Said's *Where the Moon Always Cracks* (Di mana bulan selalu retak, 1965), **Syed Alwi**'s *Going North* (Menuju utara, ca. 1965), Usman Awang's *Visitors at Kenny Hill* (Tamu di Bukit Kenny, 1967), Aziz Jahpin's (1928–2005) *Household without a Name* (Warga tak bernama, 1970), and Kemala's (1941–) *Anna* (1972). These plays feature new settings, complex relationships among characters of diverse backgrounds, and/or somewhat ambiguous resolutions. Less optimistic and certain, these later plays also indicate forthcoming changes in style.

In the 1970s, Malay-language playwrights distanced themselves from realism. These experimental artists portrayed life's irrationality in the period following the ethnic riots of May 13, 1969, a tragic event that greatly shocked the nation. During this critical time, playwrights addressed increasingly sensitive social, political, and cultural concerns in a symbolic and discrete fashion. They rejected realism in favor of a distinctly Malay style; in their search for inventive **stage** images, they often combined surrealism and aspects of traditional forms.

Noordin Hassan inaugurated the experimental style with his groundbreaking **music-**drama *'Tis Not the Tall Grass Blown by the Wind* (Bukan lalang ditiup angin, 1970) an allegorical response to May 13th.

Prominent "third generation" playwrights of the 1970s, such as Dinsman (1949–), Johan Jaaffar (1953–), and Hatta Azad Khan (1952–), continued the exploration of a more abstract, avant-garde, Malay-language theatre. Dinsman's monodrama *It Is Not Suicide* (Bukan bunuh diri, 1974) focuses on a college student who casts aside standard secular and religious teachings to seek God and truth in a way that is personally meaningful. In *Dry Wind* (Angin kering, 1976) and *The One* (Dia, 1977), Jaaffar ironically captures a vision of the wealthy and poor trapped in futile illusionary and materialistic pursuits. In *Corpse* (Mayat, 1978), Khan presents a futuristic scenario in which a group of nameless characters confronts strangers who appear responsible for the suspicious disappearance of their deceased friend's body. As the experimental theatre became more obscure, however, audiences shrank.

Revival of English Drama. By the 1980s, there was a noticeable decline in Malay drama. Uncertain economic conditions and Islamic revivalism affected theatre participation. For some time, the government significantly decreased its support. Meanwhile, the English-language theatre, particularly in and around Kuala Lumpur, became rejuvenated.

Initially, English-language plays written by Malaysians were staged during the latter half of the 1960s through the beginning of the 1970s. Playwrights, such as Edward Dorall (1936–), Lee Joo For, Patrick Yeoh, and Syed Alwi, and other practitioners were engaged in developing an active English-language theatre. However, after May 13th, they felt disinclined to work in English. Some prominent artists such as Syed Alwi, **Krishen Jit**, Faridah Merican (1939–), and Rahim Razali (1949–) engaged instead with the Malay theatre world. The government, deciding that poverty, particularly in the Malay community, was an underlying cause of the riots, sought to remedy economic disparity by ensuring increased educational and economic opportunities for Malays. In addition, further emphasis was placed on the use of the national language (Malay), especially in the educational system, the media, firms, and government offices. A new national cultural policy acknowledged Malay culture as the foundation culture and Islam as the nation's basic spiritual source. While other ethnic groups could contribute to national culture, government funds were primarily allocated for the development of Malay culture.

By the mid-1980s, there were signs of a renewed English theatre, with the staging of *1984 Here and Now* (1985) by Kee Thuan Chye (1954–). The play demonstrates that relations between Malays and Chinese remain strained, but that theatre itself can be a means of promoting a more socially integrated country. Also, Shakespeare's plays began to reappear, with performances by English, Malay, Chinese, and Indian **theatre companies**.

Resurgence of Malaysian Theatre in the 1990s. In the 1990s, Malaysian theatre as a whole began to thrive again with increased numbers of local productions as well as visits by international companies. Renewed government support became available for English as well as Malay theatre. New groups in each language were organized. Also, new venues opened, including in 2000, the state-of-the-art Palace of Culture (a.k.a. Istana Budaya or National Theatre). To attract audiences, playwrights created new short pieces, often comical and realistic. Audiences could also attend large-scale productions of Malay plays and refashioned *bangsawan*. Chinese theatre enthusiasts could view traditional and modern plays as well as Mandarin productions of Western works. The Temple of Fine Arts, a performing arts association, stages large, impressive productions based on Indian stories as well as other traditions.

English-language theatre has continued to reinvigorate the Malaysian scene. Krishen Jit and the Five Arts Centre he cofounded in 1983 helped promote new work from a variety of writers. The group initially produced ethnic plays, such as K. S. Maniam's (1942–) *The Cord*, a depiction of Indian immigration to Malaysia, and *Three Children* by Leow Puay Tin (1957–), portraying the insights three young Chinese-Malaysians discover about their past. Subsequently, the Centre developed multilingual plays, such as *Work* and *Us*, which acknowledge Malaysia's diverse population. Their 1994 multi-art production of Maniam's *Skin Trilogy* sought to highlight the nation's common humanity.

Several companies, both established and new, promote socially relevant productions. Experimentation in presentation continues. Indeed, for the past several decades, Malaysian theatre has served as a means of rendering in diverse, imaginative ways the nation's past, the multifarious issues of the day, and the aspirations Malaysians hold for their future.

FURTHER READING

Brandon, James R. *Theatre in Southeast Asia*; Ghulam-Sarwar, Yousof. *Panggung Semar: Aspects of Traditional Malay Theatre*; Matusky, Patricia. *Malaysian Shadow Play and Music: Continuity of an Oral Tradition*; Nur Nina Zuhra (Nancy Nanney). *An Analysis of Modern Malay Drama*.

Nancy Nanney

MANI RIMDU. *See* Nepal.

MANOHAR, R. S. (1929–). **Indian** Tamil-language **actor**, **director**, and producer, born in Namakkal, Salem District, and known for the spectacular productions he produced and starred in. He became active in Tamil films (as a famous screen villain) and theatricals, establishing the National Theatre in 1954, where he began by producing patriotic plays inspired by the passions of post-independence India.

His production of *Lord of Lanka* (Ilankesvaran, 1956), a version of the **Ramayana** in which the hero was the traditional villain, Ravana, popularized the extravagant production style—using plays based on myths, legend, and history—for which he became known. These vehicles allowed him to perform characters best known as villains but, in his interpretations, transformed into super-valiant and noble heroes with sympathetic and heroic sides. His versions of familiar stories often used unusual variants, such as making Sita the daughter of Ravana. Manohar was so closely associated with *Lord of Lanka* that the title was used to refer to him.

He staged around thirty works during his career, the most popular including a series of popular plays starting with *Surapadman* (1968), *Indrajit, Duryodhanan, Sukracharyar, Chanakya's Vow* (Chanakya sapatam), and *Tiger-Chested* (Vengai marban). In 2003, aged seventy-four and recovering from a knee accident, he produced *Varaguna Pandiyan*, in which he brought great dignity to the titular role, an eighth-century Pandiya king who becomes enamored of Lord Shiva, and can thus produce miracles. His productions, reminiscent of **Parsi theatre**, were known for their visual splendor and theatrical effects, using the most advanced technology he could provide, including Tamil theatre's first stereo sound system.

Samuel L. Leiter

MANOHRA. Traditional **dance**-drama, also known as *menora, manora, nohra* (or *nora*) *chatri*, or *nohra*, encompassing a variety of related theatre genres practiced in southern **Thailand** and northern **Malaysia**. *Manohra* is the mythological half-bird princess who is a central figure in the traditional repertoire and credited with creating the genre, said to have originated in southern Thailand's Lake Songkala region more than five centuries ago. *Manohra* uses stories from story collections about previous lives of the Buddha (*jataka*), but better known are tales dealing with the tragic separations and occasional reunions of loving couples, particularly stories of the eponymous princess.

Nohra chatri. The theatrical form *nohra* originated as danced interludes within *nohra rong khru*, a three-day **religious** ceremony, still practiced in certain southern Thai provinces. It pays homage to ancestors, binds lineages to ancestors, expels bad spirits, heals illnesses, and blesses participants. Danced interludes were based on local tales and featured acrobatic postures, stylized movements, and rapid **music**. As communal interest in *nohra rong khru* declined, these episodes were excerpted and elaborated by troupes as touring theatre known as *nohra chatri*: while no longer directly linked to ritual, performers were still considered "powerful" (*chatri*), as the blessings of an ancestral god made them great artists.

Nohra chatri's earliest known forms used all-male casts without upper garments. The male lead (Nai Rong) wore the fullest **costume**, including a distinctive crown or headdress (*therd*), ornaments, and long fingernails. The female character (Tua Nang) and the clown (Tua Betaled) wore ordinary clothes and sometimes **masks** to depict different characters. The clown changed roles, playing a hunter, a hermit, or a horse, as the story progressed.

Traditionally, performers dance on the ground in a square marked out by four poles laid out in the cardinal directions and a bench placed in the performance space. At the center is a great pole (*mahachai*), which the artists believe houses their protector-deity, Phra Vissukarm. Dancers tie red cloths around it and attach a basket filled with the symbolic weaponry they use during dances. The accompanying music has a very rhythmic and fast-paced southern sound, and includes the Thai oboe for the melody along with drums, gongs, cymbals, and a wooden clapper.

Over the last century, *nohra chatri* has expanded to include a cast of fifteen to twenty dancers and musicians providing entertainment at **festivals** and temple events. This type of performance uses mixed casts, either by combining dancing with singing concerts for local audiences, or by showcasing acrobatic dances for tourists. In central Thailand, *nohra chatri* combined with local dramatic genres (**lakon nok** and *lakon puying*) to form the hybrid *lakon chatri*; elements of *nohra chatri* also entered into the court dances of Ayutthaya and Bangkok, especially during the reign of Rama III (1824–1851). Government officials and scholars have encouraged a revival of *nohra rong khru* in southern Thailand since around 1990.

Manohra. Traveling troupes brought the form as *manohra* (a.k.a. *manora* or *nora*) to the Malaysian states of Kedah, Kelantan, Terengganu, and Penang. Traditionally in Malaysia, three male performers played all the roles, including the royal figures, warriors, heroines, and clowns. Long-haired young boys dressed as **women** when playing the female roles. Women have been introduced recently, and troupes now have as many as seventeen members. The classical repertoire consisted of twelve tales, all featuring the half-bird princess, Manohra or Mesi Mala. Today's audiences prefer modern tales, especially the comic parts, and most troupes no longer know the full classical repertoire.

Originally, *manohra* was performed on level ground, covered with mats. Now troupes perform on a bamboo stage with a palm leaf overhang, open on all four sides. The eight to ten musicians play drums, gongs, cymbals, the oboe-like *serunai*, the stringed *rebab*, and wooden clappers. Music announces entrances and exits, accentuates dramatic moments, demarcates scene endings, and accompanies final songs. Dance enhances dramatic action, expresses emotional intensity, and demarcates scenes. In one sequence, handmaidens dance in a circle or in a figure-eight formation.

The lead dancer wears an ornate costume topped by a jeweled peaked headdress. Standard items include a beaded shirt or shawl, arm and wrist bangles, a wooden sword, bird-like wings tied around the waist, a colorful handkerchief and necktie, trousers with cloth hanging from the waist, ornate scarves, two strands of string, and long fingernails curling backwards. These features create a bird-like appearance, resembling the mythical birds (*kinnari*) that authorized sacred dances in the original Thai version. Female characters can wear a *sarung kebaya* (a long-sleeved blouse and a skirt wrapped around the waist). The two clown characters are attired in ordinary shirts and trousers and wear red half-masks.

Manohra can be performed for entertainment or fund-raising, and may be part of a wedding or Buddhist festival, staged in celebration of a company's success, included in a cultural show, or a community fair organized for a public holiday. Traditionally, however, *manohra* was originally performed to exorcise evil spirits, heal the sick, and supplicate spirits under the direction of a shaman (*bomoh*), sometimes the troupe leader. The performance area is consecrated with offerings laid out in front of the stage, such as smoked chicken, betel leaves, tobacco, rice, thread, joss sticks, a mat, a pillow, candles, and money. Invocations are offered to ancestors, teachers, and other spirits; sometimes performers go into a trance.

The decline of traditional beliefs among Muslim Malays and the difficulty of obtaining licenses for non-Islamic cultural performances have contributed to a major setback for *manohra*. *Manohra* is now usually sponsored by rural Thai farmers, fishers, and small landholders living in Malaysia, or by **Chinese** who speak in a mixture of southern Thai and local Malay dialects.

FURTHER READING

Rutnin, Mattani Mojdara. *Dance, Drama, and Theatre in Thailand: The Process of Development and Modernization*; Yousof, Ghulam Sarwar. *Dictionary of Traditional South-East Asian Theatre.*

Pornrat Damrhung and Nancy Nanney

MANSŎKJUNG-NORI. *See* Puppet Theatre: Korea.

MARZBAN, ADI (1914–1987). **Indian** Gujarati-language **playwright, director, actor, scenographic** and lighting designer, editor, and broadcaster, born in Bombay (Mumbai), who studied at the Pasadena Playhouse in California in the early 1950s. After returning to Bombay, he acted and directed for various institutions, including the Amateur Dramatic Circle, the Indian National Theatre, the Indian People's Theatre Association, and so forth. He staged popular **Western** plays (*Ah Norman* [1972], based on Ron Clark's *Norman, Is That You?* was a major hit) as well as his own very successful broad comedies, which included *The Head Is Lost* (Katariyun gap), *Knock at Midnight* (Ardhi rate ahat), *Uncle Behaves Funny* (Kaka thaya vanka), and *Behram's Mother-in-Law* (Behramni sasu). Their usual target was Parsi foibles.

Marzban and his manager, Pesi Khandalawala, were responsible for the so-called "new **Parsi theatre**." He initiated the then unheard of practice of paying his amateur actors and crew via a profit-sharing arrangement. Multitalented and expert at **dance**, ventriloquism, and magic, he was an excellent teacher to many student-actors who became important **stage** figures. His productions were known for their excellent integration of all performance elements, their use of dialogue developed from improvisations, their expert designs and realism, and their comical timing.

Samuel L. Leiter

MA SEN (1932–). Taiwanese * **playwright, director, critic, theorist**, and novelist, a major figure in Taiwan's **experimental** "little theatre" (*xiao juchang*) movement and founder of the Department of Drama, Taipei National University of the Arts (1983), where many modern "spoken drama" (*huaju*) **actors** are **trained**. Ma studied in Taiwan (1950–1957), at the Institut des Hautes Études Cinématographiques in Paris (1961), and received his PhD from the University of British Columbia (1977). He taught at the Centre of Oriental Studies at El Colegio de Mexico (1969) and Canadian and British universities (1977–1987).

Ma's cross-cultural experience within the **Chinese** diaspora is reflected in the dominant themes of alienation and troubled interpersonal relationships represented by his plays. *Flower and Sword* (Hua yu jian, 1977), for example, presents the tormented consciousness of a child who is struggling—like those in the Chinese diaspora—against his multiple origins and cultural roots.

Among Ma's many plays, the most thought-provoking can be found in the one-acts written during his Mexican sojourn, including "Flies and Mosquitoes" (Cangying yu wenzi, 1967), "Frogs' Play" (Wa xi, 1969; **musical**, 2002), and "Roles" (Jiaose, 1980). Ma appropriates **Western** absurdism and uses characters lacking distinct identities to address what he perceives as the most pressing and universal concerns of our time: the tensions between tradition and modernity and between different sets of values. Ma's contribution lies in both his plays and theoretical works, especially those on transcultural theatre and the formation of diasporic cultures.

Alexander C. Y. Huang

MASKS

Masks: Bhutan

In **Bhutan**, many Buddhist **religious** dramas rely on masked performers. The annual Thimpu Tshechu **festival**, honoring a ninth-century saint, includes masked **dances** that represent the triumph of Buddhism over various evil forces. Many masks, which are made to fit over **actors'** heads, resemble animals, such as deer and dogs. Fierce demon-deity masks also appear. These masks exhibit a distinctly **Tibetan** influence.

David V. Mason

Masks: Burma (Myanmar). *See* Masks: Southeast Asia

Masks: Cambodia. *See* Masks: Southeast Asia

Masks: China

Other than in certain forms of **Chinese** ethnic minority theatre, the mask is not nearly as common a method of symbolic expression in *xiqu* as the "painted face" (*hualian*) **makeup** worn by the *jing* **role type**. Masked **religious** ceremonial **dance** goes back to the earliest times. The most widespread kind of mask is made of wood, papier-mâché, or another firm substance, tied to the face or even held in front of it, or slipped over the head. However, cloth masks with colored patterns taut with the face and showing its shape are occasionally found.

In *jingju*, masks are rarely used, an exception being the good-luck spirits introducing highly traditional performances. In *chuanju*, painted full-face cloth masks are used for "face-changing" (*bianlian*) techniques. The **actor** pulls down different masks in such quick succession that his face changes instantaneously.

Masks in **Tibet**'s *ache lhamo* represent gods or demons or aspirations like long life or good luck. The introductory blessing includes hunters wearing black masks who purify the acting space.

A prominent mask use is in the ancient ritualistic *nuo*, still found in such southwestern provinces as Guizhou, Hunan, and Guangxi, and among several ethnic groups of the region, including the majority Han and minorities like the Zhuang, Dong, Miao, and Yi. The variety of *nuo* masks is wide, depending on the ethnic group using them and the figure wearing them, with color, pattern, and shape symbolizing character, status, age, and gender.

Sacred ritual in Tibetan Buddhism includes masked dance-dramas, with expressive and symbolic masks representing supernatural powers, often taking animal form. *See also* Mongolia.

Colin Mackerras

Masks: India

In spite of **India**'s numerous traditional theatres, **puppetry**, and **dance** forms and their great variety of ornamentation in **costumes** and **makeup**, the use of masks in mainstream forms is limited. Masks, mentioned even in the ancient **Sanskrit theatre**'s *Treatise on Drama* (Natyashastra; see Theory), are the central feature of *purulia* and *seraikella* **chhau**, and masks are sometimes employed in *ramlila*. Other forms, such as **kathakali** and **kutiyattam**, which seldom use full masks, employ mask-like makeup, headdresses, and devices to augment faces. Apart from these forms, India's use of masks occurs in predominantly ritualistic contexts. Often, masks so used develop their own sacred value and are treated with reverence. In South Asian countries like **Bhutan** and **Sri Lanka**, masks are common in **religious** ritual dramas.

Ritual practices surround all aspects of mask making and mask wearing. The mask's power must be brought to life through ritual, but that power also must be contained through other rituals. Mask makers must undergo special purification—including dietary and sexual—to prevent spiritual contamination from harming a mask during its creation. Masks become sanctified, revered by makers and users, and stored, in most cases, in sacred places, such as temples.

Masks are often associated with elaborate headdresses. **Actors** wearing combined headdress and mask arrangements—their size and appearance determined by **role type**—can look unusually impressive, as in **krishnattam**, *chhau*, *kathakali*, **teyyam**, *ramlila*, and so on.

Masked genres always are dance-oriented, as movement is closely tied to mask use. Mask makers always bear in mind the way their wearers will move. This pertains to the most aggressive, even frightening, masks, such as those of demons, and to those of beautiful young lovers.

South India. Among the few South Indian forms using masks are Kerala's *kathakali*, *krishnattam*, and *teyyam*. *Kathakali*'s mask use is infrequent and restricted to specific circumstances, especially to represent transformations (such as the change of a character's head into a goat's). Restricted to Kerala's Guruvayur Temple, *krishnattam* is indistinguishable from *kathakali*. In practice, *krishnattam* has a unique choreography and style, and its repertoire is exclusively dedicated to Krishna stories. Some of its characters, though, are represented through full-face, wooden masks for characters like Brahma (with its four faces), Yama (god of death), and demons, such as the five-headed Murasura, each head with its own color scheme. The masks are color-coded according to the same scheme as the elaborate *kathakali* makeup and are combined in one piece with intricate, peaked headdresses. Because of their ritual significance, the masks do not leave the temple precincts. Actors engage in ritual purification prior to donning the masks, regarded as a source of transcendent power.

Although *teyyam* relies more on brilliant makeup than on masks, one of its most striking traits is the enormous headdresses (*mudi*) some of its characters wear. *Mudi* are made of starched and painted cloth and paper affixed to wooden frames actors wear on their backs and heads. Round or peaked, some *mudi* extend to twenty-five feet high. The application of makeup and donning of the headdresses is done with ritual care, and often lead to the actors' being possessed by the supernatural characters they portray.

In Mellattur village, Tamilnadu, **bhagavata mela** employs masks, typically regarded as sacred and kept in the temple when not in use. The one for the elephant-headed deity Ganesha, painted red, is important to the preliminaries of this and other ritual-based **folk theatres**. The mask representing Vishnu's incarnation as Narasimha—half-man, half-lion—is worshipped during its annual appearance. A broad, red-painted mask combining lion and human features in slight relief, the Narasimha mask is tied to the actor's head. The reverence owed to this mask contributes to the state of possession into which the Narasimha actor enters. When the wearer of this mask in the *prahlad natak* form of Orissa goes into trance, he is removed from the playing area, and the performance continues with the mask placed on a stool to represent his presence.

North India. In North India, certain *ramlila* characters sometimes wear masks to represent **Ramayana** characters. These include Ravana, the principle antagonist, whose mask includes the representation of ten heads; Hanuman, the monkey god who acts as Rama's champion; Jatayu, the supernatural bird; and various demons. The masks vary from region to region. In some cases, half-masks are used, exposing the actors' mouths. In other cases, full masks are used as well as oversized masks that entirely cover the head. These are lifted or removed for speaking.

The *Ramayana* also inspired the masks used in two of the three *chhau* forms. *Chhau* masks are round and made to cover dancers' faces completely. *Seraikella chhau* masks tend to be larger and more fanciful than *purulia chhau* masks, which fit closely to dancers' faces and have a tendency toward the grotesque and fearful. *Seraikella chhau* masks tend to be uniform and idealistic, seeking an abstracted, dreamy representation of the human face. They have a smooth, uniform surface, and their faces are painted with graceful, oversized eyes, brows, and lips. *Purulia chhau* masks are less idealistic, including wrinkles, teeth, grimacing expressions, and natural angularity. Masks are made of muslin and papier-maché stretched over a clay model. The limited ventilation makes the dancers' work more difficult. Hair, crowns, peacock feathers, and other appropriate ornaments are often attached. Heroic characters in particular tend to wear elaborate headdresses. Colors are coded, so as to indicate characters and types clearly. Krishna's mask, for instance, is blue; Shiva's is white.

In addition to the more formalized theatrical uses of masks, India also has an extensive tradition of masks used in ritualistic tribal dances.

FURTHER READING

Awasthi, Suresh. *Performance Tradition in India*.

David V. Mason

Masks: Indonesia. *See* Masks: Southeast Asia; *See also Jauk*

Masks: Japan

Japan has several **dance** and dramatic traditions that use masks. The first masks linked to a performing art are those associated with *gigaku*, which arrived from the continent in the early seventh century. Some 250 examples survive in the storehouses of Shôsôin and Hôryû-ji Temple in Nara. *Gigaku* masks are large compared to those of *bugaku*, another continental form of dance and pantomime, which arrived in the eighth century. In contrast to *gigaku* masks that fit over the entire head, *bugaku* masks are smaller, sometimes have hair, and cover only the face and sometimes the sides of the head. Both *gigaku* and *bugaku* masks are carved from wood and then painted. *Bugaku* also uses masks called *zômen*, which consist of abstract designs painted in black on a rectangular piece of white silk. A few wooden masks dating from the twelfth and thirteenth centuries are inscribed with the maker's name, but little is known about these artists, who were likely carvers of **religious** statuary.

In **folk theatre**, such as *dengaku*, so-called hanging masks (*kakemen*) are used that are not worn on the face, but are instead attached to pillars or parade floats (*mikoshi*), or are worn on the top of the head. In the late fourteenth and early fifteenth centuries, *dengaku* professionals came into conflict with *nô* theatre **actors** over the authority to wear masks—a prerogative that *nô* performers succeeded in monopolizing. Masks are a defining feature of *nô* and, to a lesser extent, *kyôgen*.

Nô *and* Kyôgen *Masks*. *Kamen* is the generic Japanese word for mask, but *nô* and *kyôgen* performers prefer *omote* ("face"), in light of the potential of *nô* masks to express emotion. This happens when an actor moves a mask or the mask is seen in different lighting; in these instances the supposedly frozen expression on the mask appears to change, suggesting one or more emotions often simultaneously. Since *nô* masks sit rather high on the face when tied on—exposing the actor's chin—performers usually cannot see out of the small eyeholes, and must look instead out of the mouth or nose. Masks can be worn with a wig or headdress depending on the role. In *nô* plays that call for masks, only the main actor (*shite*) and sometimes the attendant (*tsure*) wear a mask, but never the *waki* or chorus (see Role Types).

There are five main *nô* mask categories: (1) Okina, (2) demon, (3) old men, (4) men, and (5) **women**. The masks of Okina and of demons are probably the oldest variety, dating from the early fourteenth century and harkening back to earlier *bugaku* masks. Masks of women, men, and old men appeared late in the 1300s. All such masks are made of carved cypress, which is then painted. Unlike *bugaku* masks, which are usually reserved for specific roles, most *nô* and *kyôgen* masks can be used in a number of plays.

The wizened, smiling features of Okina masks are distinctive by virtue of their circular eyebrows and detached lower jaw tied by cords to the bottom of the mask (there are also *bugaku* masks that share this feature). The white Okina and black Sanbasô masks in this category are restricted to performances of the "three rites" (*shiki sanban*), ceremonial dances by *nô* and *kyôgen* actors, who don their masks on **stage** before the audience. Modern interpretations hold that the actor donning the Okina mask becomes possessed by a divinity; this appears to be an invented tradition although performers treat the *shiki sanban* with great reverence.

There are three divisions of demon masks: open mouth, closed mouth, and miscellaneous. The "bulge" (*tôbide*) mask has an open mouth whereas the mouth of the "frowning" (*beshimi*) mask is closed, and the "divinity" (*tenjin*) mask falls into the third category. Old men (*jô*) masks are a cross between an old man and a demon; most, like the "frowning evil man" (*beshimi akujô*), are rather sinister looking, but this is not always the case, as shown by the "laughing old man" (*waraijô*) mask. There is a range of masks of men and women that differs according to the character's age: perhaps most famous are the "small face" (*ko-omote*) women masks, showing a young adolescent, and the mask of an older woman whose consuming jealousy has turned her into a horned snake-demon (*hannya*).

The names of early mask carvers survive and so do some works attributed to them, although exact dating remains elusive. One of the earliest lists of carvers appears in **Zeami**'s *Talks on Sarugaku* (Sarugaku dangi, 1430), which mentions famous carvers and their representative works, along with a few legends about famous masks.

There are approximately 450 different *nô* masks, but around the beginning of the Edo period (1603–1868) carvers largely stopped creating new masks and focused instead on copying older ones to the point of replicating scratches and concocting ancient-looking patina to give their masks an old look. Contributing to these changes was the codification of performance traditions, which standardized masks for given plays.

In contrast to the drama of demons, aristocrats, and deities of *nô*, *kyôgen* finds humor in daily life; consequently, it usually reserves masks for nonhumans. Indeed, part of the humor of plays featuring females is that the male actor performing the woman's role wears a streaming headdress of white cloth (*binan*) to signify long hair but does not—except in the role of a fat, homely woman—use a mask. *Kyôgen* masks, numbering only about twenty different varieties, are divided like *nô* masks into five main groupings—Okina (that is, Sanbasô), deities, mortals, ghosts, and demons. As a general rule, *kyôgen* masks, even for demons, have much more jovial and comedic features than their *nô* counterparts, as exemplified by the "god of happiness" mask (*fuku no kami*) and the ghost (*buaku*) mask. Animal masks, such as the monkey (*saru*) and fox (*kitsune*), are realistic in contrast to the stylized features typical of many *kyôgen* masks.

Kabuki Masks. *Kabuki* actors rely on elaborate makeup, but also make occasional use of masks in dances, such as *Three Shrine Festival* (Sanja matsuri) and the rarely seen *Seven Masks* (Nanatsu men). *Kabuki* masks are not intended to suggest that those wearing them are to be understood as the characters represented by the masks, but are simply accepted as theatrical **properties** donned in view of the audience to demonstrate the skill of dancing with a mask. The masks in *Three Shrine Festival* are worn only during one segment of the piece, and are interesting in that they represent no actual person but are abstractions consisting of circular props with flat surfaces; one has the ideograph for "good" and the other that for "evil" painted on it. And there is a special mask worn by an unnamed fighter in *The Suzugamori Execution Grounds* (Suzugamori), the *sogimen*, which is hinged so that when a sword blow passes by the mask, the face part falls forward revealing a comical version of what lies behind it. Finally, actors performing as animals (dogs, horses, rats, and so on) wear animal costumes with mask-like headpieces resembling the animal.

FURTHER READING

Leiter, Samuel L. *Historical Dictionary of Japanese Traditional Theatre*; Nishikawa, Kyôtarô. *Bugaku Masks*; Nogami, Toyoichiro. *Masks of Japan: The Gigaku, Bugaku and Noh Masks*.

Eric C. Rath and Samuel L. Leiter (kabuki section)

Masks: Korea

Large wooden masks depicting human faces with bulbous features were used in a Silla period (fourth through seventh centuries) court dance called *ch'oyŏngmu*. Descendants of these masks are still used, but the most highly developed examples belong to the **hahoe pyŏlshin-gut** (eleventh or twelfth century), perhaps linking earlier mainland Asia **dance** masks with those of **Japan**'s *nô*.

Pongsan *t'alch'um* masks are made of papier-maché, smaller than other masks, but ruggedly grotesque. *Pyŏlsandae* masks are made from dried gourd and additional materials, such as pine bark for a nose and dog fur for a beard. Color, painted spots, and details such as fur for eyebrows and the chin convey social status and character. Research suggests a link between masks and common skin diseases in villages: leprosy, smallpox, age spots, and the wrinkled, infected face of the village drunk are depicted in various mask-dance dramas. The most commonly represented animal mask is the oversized lion mask used in Pukch'ung, **North Korea**, and other masked-dances. A monkey mask is used in *t'alch'um* and a bird mask in Suyŏng *yaryu*.

In former times, when the dance-play satirized the upper class, government officials, and apostate monks, paper masks were burned or trampled on after a given performance, symbolically easing grievances with those satirized or believed to be bedeviled. Revered in the past, now stored in a sanctuary when not worn, dance-drama masks remain a respected symbol of Korean culture, often featured in **experimental theatre** productions.

FURTHER READING

Cho, Dong-il. *Korean Mask Dance.*

Oh-Kon Cho

Masks: Laos. *See* Masks: Southeast Asia

Masks: Malaysia. *See* Masks: Southeast Asia

Masks: Philippines. *See* Masks: Southeast Asia

Masks: Singapore. *See* Masks: Southeast Asia

Masks: Southeast Asia

Southeast Asian masks go back to prehistory and may link to use of artifacts representing ancestors or spirits. With the introduction of Hinduism and Buddhism around two thousand years ago and Islam after 1200 (see Religion in Theatre), animistic bases were elaborated into artistically developed masking. Contempory artists create masks that connect to the past but speak to the globalized present. Recurring categories are (1) chthonic/animal and (2) **role type** and character masks, which fall into four or five "types." Mask and **puppetry** share iconography, repertoire, and narrator (*dalang* [**Indonesia**], *nang nai* [**Thailand**]). Puppetry and masking are thought to precede and model unmasked drama.

Notable mask traditions are found in **Burma (Myanmar)**, **Cambodia**, **Indonesia**, **Laos**, **Malaysia**, and **Thailand**. Masks are not as significant in the theatres of the **Philippines**, **Singapore**, and **Vietnam**.

FURTHER READING

Chandavij, Natthapatra, and Promporn Pramualratana. *Thai Puppets and Khon Masks*; Emigh, John. *Masked Performance: The Play of Self and Other in Ritual and Theatre*; Slattum, Judy. *Masks of Bali: Spirits of an Ancient Drama*.

Burma (Myanmar). A 1649 inscription describes "bird" (*kinnari*) **dancers** on tightropes: avian forms are widespread in Southeast Asia. The best-known form is *zat gyi*. Papier-maché masks tell *Yama* (*Ramayana*) stories with role types divided into prince, princess, monkey, and ogre roles, following Thai models. When the Burmese conquered the Thai in 1767, artists were carried to Mandalay, introducing this form that continues today.

Cambodia. **Folk theatre** masking includes *trot* from Siem Reap Province: demons, a deer, and horned buffalo dance for rain. The court mask tradition, *lakhon khol*, linked to *lakhon sbaek* (a.k.a. *nang sbaek*) shadow puppetry, probably had its roots in the Angkor period (ninth to fifteenth centuries), but vanished when Khmer court dancers were seized by Thai conquerors at the fall of Angkor (1431). Current performance dates from the nineteenth century, when all-male groups, influenced by Thai models, presented the *Reamker* (*Ramayana*) for King Norodom using papier-maché masks. Role types are prince, princess, monkey, and ogre. Masking became part of the annual Tang Tok **Festival**, but unlike Thailand—where dancers were courtiers—performers were commoners. Current master Yith Sarin (1925–) descends from village artists of Svay Andet and was recruited by Queen **Sisowath Kossamak** in the 1950s as she sought to integrate men into the formerly all-female dance troupe in Phnom Penh.

Indonesia. Indonesia has a wealth of mask forms. These include animist *hudoq* of Kalimantan (where mask dances with links to hornbill birds, sun, and chthonic imagery are used to promote rice growth), Sumatran funeral dances representing the hornbill bird (*huda*), and elaborate dance-dramas of Java, Bali, and so on.

Chthonic figures abound and may link to Buddhism's lion dances and tantric imagery. Lion-like figures, demons, or large human body puppets are central to *barongsai* forms of north coast Java and *barong* parades of Bali. *Reog* and *kuda kepang* ("hobbyhorse dancing") of Java combine comedy, horse/animal dances, and trance performance to promote luck. Some forms like *reog ponorogo* are linked to stories of East Java's Prince **Panji**, transvestism, and, in times past, homosexuality. In *reog ponorogo*, peacock feathers wreathe a heavy wooden mask of ferocious image and a young child sits atop. The Balinese "widow witch" (Rangda) represents demonic forces that must be appeased, and the "lion" (*barong ket*), who in some versions represents the protector-god Wisnu (Vishnu), balances her and keeps her forces in check. Such masks are a way to trap chthonic power in performance structures that "tame" them.

Other mask theatres feature friendly animals. The *Ramayana*—where monkeys and birds become the faithful helpers of Rama—has spawned many forms. These helpful animals are the socialized side of the chthonic that by right choices promote enlightenment and good citizenship. Balinese **wayang wong** and Javanese *langen mandra wanara* present the *Ramayana*.

The "types" are used in *wayang topeng*—multiperson masked dance-dramas. *Mahabharata* tales dominate in the important *topeng dalang* of the island of Madura—where the mask of Baladewa, brother of Kresna (Krishna), is venerated. The *Ramayana*, *Mahabharata,* and local tales are presented in Java and Sunda. In East Java's "Malang *topeng*" (*topeng malang*), Panji tales are featured. In Balinese **topeng**, history chronicles dominate.

Older style masks are carved wood, held on by a bite-piece. Dialogue was secondary since a puppeteer-narrator often delivered dialogue while dancers mimed. Clown characters, by contrast, wore half-masks and their patter bridged the epic action with comic commentary. Old patterns of medium-dancer and shaman-narrator/clown may underlie this division.

Mask theatre (*wayang wong* [Java] and *topeng* [Bali]) is closely linked with *wayang* puppetry; hence some forms are called "human" (*wong*) puppetry. Iconography, repertoire, and **music** are shared between mask theatre and *wayang*. Unmasked theatre is based on puppet/mask models.

While there is variation, four or five basic role types predominate in most areas. In Cirebonese *topeng* (*topeng bakakan*), characters take names from the *Mahabharata* and Panji story of East Java. According to some, the five characters (Panji, Samba, Rumiang, Tumenggung, and Klana) are correlated with the five directions (north-east-center-south-west), the periods of life (birth, youth, perfection, maturity, death), and major aspects of the world (mountain, field, center, village, sea), as well as different colors, emotions, and so on. Though Cirebon's division into refined male, refined female, androgyne, strong male, and demon king is said to be the invention of fifteenth-century Islamic masters, related divisions are seen in Hindu Bali, and even Buddhist Thailand and Cambodia.

Mask genres such as *topeng babakan* or Balinese *topeng pajegan* feature solo dancers who have exorcistic/ritual functions. In Cirebon's *topeng*, the dancer begins with the refined male, moves to androgynous then dynamic male, and climaxes with the demon king. In Bali, *topeng* opens with the strong minister, progresses to a feeble old man, shares a story that includes a refined king and evil opponents, and ends with a rather demonic-looking yet exorcistic old man, Sidha Karya ("accomplishing the ritual"), who blesses the four directions and the center. A silent dancer using many masks and a talking clown/*dalang* may be the core pattern.

Indonesian mask/puppet theatre emphasizes human and cosmic changeability, showing a path beyond the microcosmic world of self to participate in the macrocosmic world of the demonic to the divine. Masks and puppets are tools to stretch beyond lived reality.

Laos. Village performance includes lions and the mythical Pu Nyeu and Pu Mai (old couple) paraded in the Pii Mai **festival** of Luang Prabang. Court mask performances were developed under Thai influence, and movement, mask, and repertory echo Thai **khon**. Short scenes rather than whole episodes are presented.

Malaysia. Malays in West Malaysia share many traditions with Indonesia and often trace their roots to the archipelago. They seem to have brought mask traditions with them. *Barongan* corresponds to Javanese *reog*. *Topeng* masks and dances relate to those of Java's coastal (Pasisir) region. Eastern Malaysian masks have similarity with the *hudoq* traditions of Indonesia's Kalimantan. Masks also feature in ritual dances of a number of aboriginal groups.

Thailand. Full-head papier-maché masks are used in **khon**. The repertoire and performance style are shared with the puppets of *nang yai*. In **lakon nok**, actors who play monkeys and demons wear small masks with the face of the character they portray on the top of their head. Before a *khon* or *lakon nok* performance, dancers honor teachers in front of the mask altar and each year remember gurus in an elaborate ritual.

Since the beginning of the twentieth century, unmasked **women** have played female roles (*nang*) and sometimes even prince roles (*phra*) in mask dramas of both the palace and popular traditions. Only the monkey (*ling*) and demon (*yak*) wear masks today. Mask dance is considered a national treasure, and hundreds of dancers trained in the academies continue to create impressive performances to honor King Rama IX (r. 1946).

Vietnam. Mask traditions corresponding to those of southern China are found among hill tribes. **Makeup** influenced by China was part of court performance and shares some conceptual links with masking. Other mask traditions of Vietnam include Buddhist lion and dragon dances.

Kathy Foley

Masks: Sri Lanka

We find in **Sri Lanka** many forms of masked **folk theatre** regarded as healing rites, but also as entertainment. There are two broad categories of masks: "devil **dance**" (*tovil* [or *thovil*] and *sanni*) and **kolam**. *Tovil* and *sanni* are exciting, exorcistic ritual performances conducted by a shaman or "witch doctor" (*kattandiya*). Ideally, eighteen different demons of illness appear, each wearing a presumably horrendous mask representing a specific ailment, such as paralysis, chest pains, and hearing loss. The goal is to rid someone of their physical problem. Cost or mask availability may mean that fewer than eighteen demons appear. Despite their fearsomeness, the humorous byplay of the shaman and drummer deflate the sense of fright. At the conclusion of all ceremonies, the benevolent *gara* demon mask, with its cobra appendages, appears.

Kolam is a secular form whose name means "mask" or "disguise." In it, a pageant of village types and authority figures (once as many as sixty) appears prior to the play proper, and each wears a heavy, satirically realistic mask. Characters include villagers, officials, royalty, demons, gods, and serpents; there is even a European couple.

Masks are carved from a special wood, *kaduru*. Once it is properly dried, the carver creates the facial features and supplementary features, after which the mask is painted and lacquered using a carefully considered symbolic color scheme. All features are based on prescriptive verses providing information on what each mask should look like, but the carver's imagination builds upon this to create original mask art. Demons tend to have bulging eyes, fierce fangs, wrinkled brows, flaring nostrils, and coiling cobras wherever space can be found. Facial hair is either carved onto the mask, or hemp or club-moss is used. Some masks are known to have been inspired by actual persons. A police inspector mask once worn was based on a photograph of the German kaiser. A number of masks worn by royalty are so large they are built in three tiers, and need two helpers to put on. Such masks are so heavy that the **actor** keeps them in place by means of a sword fixed to special holes in the crown.

Kolam masks are between five to six and a half inches wide, and eight to twelve inches high, while those for *tovil* and *sanni* are smaller. Among the most unusual *sanni* masks is the *maha kola sanniya*, symbolizing the chief demon, and containing multiple cobra heads and miniature versions of all the other demon masks. *Sanni* masks are mostly half-cut masks, while *kolam* cover the head.

Kolam characters are further distinguished by their elaborate headdresses, including crowns, fezes, turbans, caps, cobra-adorned headpieces, and so on. A character's stature and position can easily be determined by their headdress. Headdresses may be part of the mask or separate pieces attached after the mask is put on. Also aiding in identification are the various kinds of mustaches, beards, and sideburns.

FURTHER READING

Goonatilleka, M. H. *Masks of Sri Lanka.*

Samuel L. Leiter

Masks: Thailand. *See* Masks: Southeast Asia

Masks: Vietnam. *See* Masks: Southeast Asia

MATSUDA BUNKÔDÔ (FL. 1720–1740). Japanese ● *bunraku* (see Puppet Theatre) **playwright**, usually referred to simply as Bunkôdô, who followed in the footsteps of **Chikamatsu Monzaemon** by focusing on the literary merit of plays. Bunkôdô came to prominence during a period of great change in the puppet theatre. Audience numbers were swelling in response to the introduction of more technically intricate puppets and increasingly elaborate staging. Whereas **Takeda Izumo** I, his colleague and cohead playwright at Osaka's Takemoto **Theatre** (Takemoto-za), emphasized visual spectacle, Bunkôdô's approach remained more conservative and subtle. Chikamatsu occasionally added finishing touches to both Bunkôdô's and Izumo's work. Bunkôdô wrote primarily for **Takemoto Gidayû** II, the greatest chanter (*tayû*) of the day.

Among Bunkôdô's works are *Kiichi Hôgen's Secret Book of Tactics* (Kiichi Hôgen Sanryaku no Maki) and *War Story of the Dan Bay Helmet* (Dan no Ura Kabuto Gunki). A favorite plot device used by Bunkôdô is inclusion of an act of self-sacrifice on the part of a character who is emotionally overwhelmed by the extraordinarily loyal or dutiful behavior of an enemy.

Barbara E. Thornbury

MATSUDA MASATAKA (1962–). Japanese • **playwright** and **director**. Born in Nagasaki, Matsuda began writing plays while attending Kyoto's Ritsumeikan University. He formed his **theatre company**, Time-Space Theatrical Troupe (Jikû Gekidan), in Kyoto in 1990. There, he developed his distinctive style by plumbing Nagasaki's hard reality, the abiding impact of the bomb and floods, and with his "quiet-theatre" (*shizuka na engeki*) dialogue marked by the soft Nagasaki dialect.

Matsuda often focuses on death, as in his Nagasaki trilogy. His first play, *The Youth of Kamiya Etsuko* (Kamiya Etsuko no seishun, 1992), is based on his mother's experience, and treats daily life at the war's end. *The House up the Hill* (Saka no ue no ie, 1993), awarded the Ôgimachi Museum Square Prize (for Osaka/Kyoto-based playwrights), concerns three siblings whose parents died in a flood, and the **Kishida [Kunio]** Prize–winning *The Sea and the Parasol* (Umi to higasa, 1994) deals with a young husband and his terminally ill wife.

In 1997, after disbanding his troupe, Matsuda created his masterpiece, *Cape Moon* (Tsuki no misaki), directed by **Hirata Oriza**, about a sister and brother living together on a remote Nagasaki island. Their ordinary life is suddenly swept aside by calamitous incidents, the brother's marriage and affair with his student, his wife's miscarriage, the sister's old boyfriend stalking her, and her suicide. Characteristically, Matsuda enhances poignancy in contrasting upsetting events with quiet dialogue.

Collaboration with Hirata continues—as in *The Smoke of Heaven* (Ten no kemuri, 2004)—though Matsuda resumed directing in 2004 with his new troupe, Society of Strangers (Marebito no Kai).

Yoshiko Fukushima

MATSUI SUMAKO (1886–1919). Japanese • *shingeki* • **actress**. Born in Nagano Prefecture, she became interested in theatre at twenty-two, influenced by her second husband. In 1909, when **Tsubouchi Shôyô** expanded his Literary Arts Society (Bungei Kyôkai) with a theatrical **training** center, she joined immediately. In 1911, she debuted as Ophelia in *Hamlet*. Performing Nora in *A Doll's House* that year established her as *shingeki*'s first female star.

Around this time, her affair with **Shimamura Hôgetsu**, who taught at the training center and **directed** *A Doll's House*, led to her dismissal, followed by Hôgetsu's abandoning his professorship and family. In 1913, they launched a new **theatre company**, the Art Theatre (Geijutsu-za), and achieved considerable success. Her roles included Magda in Sudermann's *Heimat* (1912), the title role in Wilde's *Salomé* (1914), and Rautendelein in Hauptmann's *The Sunken Bell* (1918). Her performance of "Katusha's Song" in Tolstoy's *Resurrection* (1914) was a nationwide hit. However, soon after Hôgetsu's sudden death, she committed suicide while backstage during a production of *Carmen* in 1919.

Matsui was a pioneer. Acting as both feminist and femme fatale, she convinced skeptics that actresses were not inferior to *kabuki*'s "female impersonators" (*onnagata*).

A "new woman" in a new theatre, she challenged the status quo in both theatre and society—at a high price.

Guohe Zheng

MATSUO SUZUKI (1962–). Japanese **•** **playwright**, **director**, and **actor**. As a university graphic-design student, Fukuoka-born Matsuo formed his first **theatre company**, Dimple (Ekubo), then moved to Tokyo, establishing Adult Plan (Otona Keikaku, 1988) with actors gleaned from the arts-information magazine *Pia*. His early plays, satirical comedies with nonsense gags, were influenced by 1980s playwrights (especially **Miyazawa Akio**), as in his trilogy, *The Legend of Kindness* (Shinsetsuden, 1988–1989), and *The Master of the Game* (Gêmu no tatsujin, 1990).

Matsuo's characteristic style—absurdist black comedy, featuring grotesqueness, violence, eroticism, **political** fervor, and elaborate, Kurt Vonnegut–like plots—marks him also as heir to the avant-garde *angura* movement. *Fukusuke* (1991), treating adultery, incest, infanticide, and discrimination against disability, concerns a boy born deformed from his mother's drug use. Claimed by a cult as a child of God, he reunites with his mother after raping the cult enemy's leader (unaware it is his mother). Two mass murders conclude the play: a kamikaze attack against the cult and his father poisoning his mother's twelve lovers. The dreadful cruelty and lack of compassion constitute Matsuo's "critical punch" against the melodrama of 1980s theatre.

The deformity motif informs other plays, including the **Kishida** [**Kunio**] Prize–winning *Funky!* (1996), about incest between a father and his daughter born with cerebral palsy; *Heaven's Sign* (Hebunzu sain, 1998), a love story between a serial killer and a suicidal girl abused in her childhood; and *The End of Eros* (Erosu no hate, 2001), a science-fiction play about the sexual revolution.

Yoshiko Fukushima

MAWLAM. A term referring to both traditional singers and singing among the Lao-speaking people of both Isan and Laos, in northeast **Thailand** and **Laos** respectively, distinct as nations but closely related culturally. *Maw* is a skilled person, and *lam* is to sing in an improvised fashion.

Mawlam (*lam* for short) has long existed in narrative and repartee forms; the theatrical form developed only during the mid-twentieth century. Virtually all forms of *lam* are accompanied by one or more **musical** instruments; most typical is the *khaen* (also *kaen*, *khene*), a free-reed mouth organ. Toward the end of the twentieth century, modernized forms of *mawlam* theatre, sometimes mixed with Thai "country songs" (*phleng luk thung*), eroded traditional *lam*'s popularity.

Lam klawn. The most common *mawlam* type is the repartee form known as *lam klawn* (literally, "poetry singing"), in which males and females alternate in battles of wit or a feigned courtship. Narrative *mawlam* (*lam ruang* or *lam luang*; literally, "story singing") is probably the oldest *mawlam* form; its stories were the basis for theatrical *mawlam* (see Storytelling). One singer, male or female, accompanied by *khaen*, performs epic-length stories in *klawn* poetry: four-line stanzas with requirements for

Village performance of old-fashioned *lam klawn* at a New Year's celebration by veteran singers, accompanied by a *khaen* free-reed mouth organ, northeast Thailand, 1988. (Photo: Terry E. Miller)

lexical tones on certain syllables and internal rhyme. The stories are traditional tales of kings and princes, many considered to be Buddha's birth stories (*jataka*). By the early 1970s *lam luang* had become rare.

Lam mu. Theatrical *mawlam* includes two forms, *lam mu* (literally, "group singing") and *lam luang* (literally, "story singing"—the same term as for narrative singing), and *lam ploen* (literally, "spontaneous singing"). *Lam mu/lam luang* originated near Khon Kaen in 1952, but was created from two earlier forms: *likay lao*, the "Lao" or Isan form of Central Thai **liké**, and *maeng tap tao* (name of an insect), a highly localized form. *Likay lao* was a local adaptation with limited distribution and popularity during its heyday from the 1930s until the 1950s. *Lam mu* adopted many physical features from *liké*, including **stage** setup, painted **scenography**, and **costumes**, but its music was entirely Isan. *Maeng tap tao* was a somewhat short-lived semitheatre that flourished around Roi-et. The performance of *lam mu* consisted of **acting**, dancing, and *mawlam* singing accompanied by *khaen*. By the 1970s, troupes customarily added a drum kit and congas for some **dances**.

A *lam mu* troupe in the past consisted of eight **role types**: leading male and leading female, secondary male and female roles, a pair of older figures such as parents, the leading character's foil, a comedian, servants and soldiers, miscellaneous figures, and a hermit monk. Before the advent of electricity in Isan, all theatre was acoustic. Later, amplification made it possible for large audiences to hear, but singers and speakers were forced to stand at the single hanging microphone until the advent of wireless mikes.

Whereas *liké* troupes combine improvisation from a scenario with memorized material, *lam mu* troupes perform fully written scripts provided by a teacher, the sung portions being in standard *klawn* poetry. Because of the scripts, many troupes consist of local village youth with little or no acting experience. Virtually all stories are already known to audiences, having come from *jataka* or local, Central Thai, or Southern Thai literature. Two Central Thai classics, *Mr. Chang and Mr. Phaen* (Khun Chang Khun Phaen) and *Mr. Apai Mani* (Phra Apai Mani), are particularly prominent sources.

Lam ploen. *Lam ploen* came to resemble *lam mu* visually, but it originated far to the southeast in 1950 in Yasothon Province (then part of Ubon Province). Whereas *lam mu* was usually serious, *lam ploen* was more upbeat and often comic. Eventually it also copied the stage, costumes, and scenography of *liké*, making it visually difficult to distinguish from *lam mu*. Musically, however, it could be distinguished for its use of *khaen*, lute (*phin*), drum kit, and congas to accompany much of the singing, which had a strong, driving beat as opposed to *lam mu*'s speech-rhythm delivery. Typically, a character stood slightly off-stage and sang a speech-rhythm introduction using the words *buet pha gung* ("open the **curtain**") accompanied by *khaen* and *phin*, then entered singing to the metrical main part accompanied by all instruments.

A *lam ploen* troupe consists of most of the same stock characters as *lam mu* and plays many of the same stories, though it emphasizes certain favorite ones, such as *Horse-Faced Girl* (Kaeo na ma).

Competition from Popular Songs. Until about the mid-1980s, *lam mu*, *lam ploen*, and *lam klawn* were approximately equal in popularity, but all felt increasing competition from regionally derived popular songs (*phleng luk thung*). While such songs had been around since at least the 1950s, they now began to dominate the music scene. *Lam klawn* singers responded by creating *lam sing* (literally, "racing singing"), mixing traditional singing with conga, drum kit, amplified *phin*, and dancing. Being commercial and buffeted by popular taste, theatre as well felt it had to respond. Both *lam mu* and *lam ploen* expanded greatly, resulting in increased hiring costs. They soon required larger stages, with improved lighting and sound. Instrumental accompaniment expanded to include electrified instruments and even brass. Young **women** dancers were added to back up male and female soloists. The latter sang *luk thung* songs in the performance's opening phase, whose length grew to three hours. When the actual story finally began, much of the audience drifted away. Thus *lam mu* and *ploen* are now largely glorified *luk thung* shows emphasizing Las Vegas–style floorshows, outrageous costumes, and "crooners."

FURTHER READING

Brandon, James R. *Theatre in Southeast Asia*; Miller, Terry E. *Traditional Music of the Lao: Kaen Playing and Mawlum Singing in Northeast Thailand*.

Terry E. Miller

MAYAMA SEIKA (1878–1948). Japanese novelist, scholar, and **playwright** of

several genres. Born in Sendai, he showed early interest in literature; inspired by novelist Tokutomi Roka (1868–1927), he moved to Tokyo in 1903 to pursue a career writing naturalist novels. He also became a scholar of Edo-period (1603–1868) literature.

Mayama published his first plays in 1907–1908 and, by 1913, was invited to join Shôchiku (see Theatre Companies). Recognition as a major theatre figure began with the publication of *Genboku and Chôei* (Genboku to Chôei, 1924). Best known of his more than sixty plays are his historical pieces, covering a period from the tenth century, as in *Masakado of Taira* (Taira Masakado, 1925), to the twentieth, as in *General Nogi* (Nogi Shôgun, 1929–1932). His highest achievement is *Tsunatoyo at the Ohama Palace* (Ohama goten Tsunatoyo, 1940), part of his ten-play cycle *Genroku-Period Treasury of Loyal Retainers* (Genroku chûshingura, 1934–1941).

Conflict in his early plays was often based on the incompatibilities of characters, as in *Genboku and Chôei*, but status disparity emerged in his later pieces, as in *Tsunatoyo at the Ohama Palace*. Despite the claim of historical accuracy in his plays, their **political** intentions have been noted often as, for example, Marxism in *Sakamoto Ryôma* (1928) or nationalism in *Genroku-Period Treasury of Loyal Retainers*. Although Mayama wrote mainly for **shinpa** and, from 1928, **kabuki**, his plays also have received **shinkokugeki** and **shingeki** productions.

FURTHER READING

Powell, Brian. *Kabuki in Modern Japan: Mayama Seika and His Plays.*

Guohe Zheng

MEHTA, VIJAYA (1934–). **Indian** Marathi- and Hindi-language **stage**, film, and television **director** and **actress**, who has also staged plays in **Sanskrit** and German. Born in Baroda (Vadodara), Gujarat, Mehta launched her acting career while still attending college in Bombay (Mumbai), and trained with **Ebrahim Alkazi** as well as **Adi Marzban** in the early and mid-1950s. In 1960, she joined with **Vijay Tendulkar**, Madhav Watve, and Arvind (1932–1987) and Sulabha Deshpande (1937–) to launch the Rangayan **theatre company**, energizing the Marathi **experimental theatre** with her productions of Tendulkar's *The Python and the Celestial Being* (Ajagar ani gandharva, 1962) and *I Won, I Lost* (Mi jinkalo, mi haralo, 1963), Ionesco's *Chairs* (1962), and C. T. Khanolkar's (1930–1976) *Bajirao the Cipher* (Ek shunya Bajirao, 1966).

Subsequently, Mehta focused on important contemporary drama in Marathi and in translation, but also on Sanskrit revivals and intercultural experiments. For fifteen years she was the leading director of **Mahesh Elkunchwar**'s plays, including *Sultan*, *Fire Ritual* (Holi, 1970), *The Torture Chamber* (Yatnaghar, 1970), *Flowers of Blood* (Raktapushpa, 1981), and, most notably, *Old Stone Mansion* (Wada chirebandi, 1985; her role as the old mother is among her celebrated performances). During this period, Mehta undertook major productions of Vishakhadatta's *The Signet Ring of Rakshasa* (Mudrarakshasa, 1975), **Kalidasa**'s *The Recognition of Shakuntala* (Abhijnana Shakuntalam, 1979), and **Girish Karnad**'s *Horse-Head* (Hayavadana, 1973) and *Play with a Cobra* (Naga-mandala, 1991). All were also performed in German for various **festivals** in Weimar, Leipzig, and Berlin (1974–1992). Her productions of Brecht's *The Good Person of Setzuan* (1972) and *The Caucasian Chalk Circle* (with Fritz Bennewitz, 1974) are considered Brecht landmarks in India. Since 1997, Mehta has been director of Mumbai's National Centre for Performing Arts.

Aparna Dharwadker

MEI LANFANG (1894–1961). Chinese • actor, most renowned of the twentieth century. Mei created his own "school/style" (*liupai*) for the female **role type** (*dan*) and won acclaim as one of the "four great *dan*" of *jingju*. Throughout his career, he expanded the *dan* as a concept, creating new modes of expression and repertory, and was instrumental in facilitating the re-entry of **women** as actors. He was also first to bring serious international attention to *xiqu*, and established a remarkable image of the actor as a humble nontraditionalist, constantly learning, reinterpreting, and creating.

Son and grandson of *dan* specialists from Taizhou, Jiangsu Province, Mei was born in Beijing and began *jingju* **training** at five. He debuted in 1904, and entered a professional troupe five years later. In 1913, he performed in Shanghai, where his success catapulted him to national fame.

Mei began creating major new work in 1914 with a series of modern-dress *jingju* concerned with women's oppression. He decided that his abilities were best suited for innovation within tradition, and began creating "new ancient-**costume** plays" (*xin guzhuang xi*) for which he designed original costumes and hair arrangements to complement his choreography and **musical** composition. These attracted the attention of theatre scholar-**playwright**-impresario Qi Rushan, who collaborated with Mei, primarily as a script writer (1919–1931). Mei continued creating new plays featuring multifaceted females, combining and expanding traditional subcategories of the *dan* to do so. His favorites were *The Cosmic Blade* (Yu zhou feng, also translated as *Beauty Defies Tyranny*), and *The Favorite Concubine Becomes Intoxicated* (Gui fei zui jiu, also translated as *The Drunken Beauty*). His final new creation was *Mu Guiying Takes Command* (Mu Guiying gua shuai, 1959).

Between 1919 and 1956, Mei toured abroad, bringing Chinese theatrical performance its first international critical acclaim and inspiring **Western** theatre artists, including Brecht. In the 1920s, he was one of the first Chinese actors to begin professionally training women. He led theatrical resistance to Japanese expansion, and with the **Japanese** occupation left the **stage** entirely (1937–1945). After 1949, in addition to performing, he accepted positions of leadership in numerous national cultural and theatrical associations, and headed the China Jingju Company. He also taught both privately and at the China Xiqu Training Academy, where he was president. In 1955, major celebrations were held to honor Mei and **Zhou Xinfang** for their fifty-year careers. Mei's Beijing home has been turned into a museum in his honor.

FURTHER READING

Scott, A. C. *Mei Lan-fang: Leader of the Pear Garden*; Wu, Zuguang, Huang Zuolin, and Mei Shaowu. *Peking Opera and Mei Lanfang*.

Elizabeth Wichmann-Walczak

MEJUDHON, PATRAVADI (1948–). Thai • director, **actress, playwright,** producer, teacher, and television writer. She was **trained** in traditional Thai **music, dance,** and theatre since early childhood. She continued her education in **Western** dance and theatre in the United Kingdom, the United States, and Canada. Returning to Thailand, she introduced many modern techniques and won acting, writing, and directing awards for **stage**, television, and film work in the 1970s and 1980s.

Patravadi Mejudhon portrays Wilawan, the title character's first wife, in *Chalawan: The Likay Musical* at Theatre in the Garden, Patravadi Theatre, 2006. (Photo: Courtesy of Patravadi Theatre)

In 1992, she founded Patravadi Theatre, where she trained many young theatre artists. Mejudhon's productions in the *lakon khanob niyom mhai* ("new traditional dance-drama") genre—which includes some speaking in what is otherwise a dance play—have represented Thailand in many international **festivals**. Apart from hosting local, regional, and international dance and theatre workshops and performances, she has organized the Bangkok Fringe Festivals annually since 1999. Because of such lifelong contributions, her image appeared on the poster of Denmark's Images of Asia Festival 2003, where she represented Asian artists in delivering the opening speech.

Representative works include *Raai Phra Tri Pidok*, a series of plays begun in 1996 and derived from Buddha's teachings; they reflect her strong interest in Buddhism, and have attracted many nontheatregoers. Her most recent work is *Chalawan: The Likay [liké] Musical* (2006), on which she collaborated with National Artist Boonlert Najpinij in bringing the popular **folk theatre** of *liké* to a wider and more urban audience and bridging the gap between traditional and modern theatres.

Pawit Mahasarinand

MIBU KYÔGEN. Japanese • **folk theatre**, one of three Kyoto "great prayer dramas" (*dainenbutsu kyôgen*) performed annually by affiliated families at Mibu Temple, Senbon Enma-do Temple, and Saga Shaka-do Temple. In 1976, *mibu kyôgen* became the first folk art to be officially designated an Important Intangible Folk Cultural Property.

Engaku (1223–1311), a priest, introduced silent skits following his sermons to introduce Buddhism to the illiterate. These **religious** comic pantomimes combined invocatory dancing, Shinto exorcism and purification rites, and didactic Buddhist tales. Plays were absorbed from the ***dengaku***, ***nô***, and ***kyôgen*** repertoires.

The **actors**, all male, are **masked**, their heads covered with white cloths. Movement employs stylized and exaggerated rhythmic gestures to hypnotic, continuous accompaniment of flute, gong, and drum **music**. The **stage** resembles that of *nô* except that it is higher, has a railing facing the spectators, and an open space in front of the "bridgeway" (*hashigakari*) for dramatic leaps by demons and warriors. Spectators sit on benches in a separate building.

The repertoire consists primarily of farces and battles with monsters, although religious elements are common. Plays such as *Wrestling with Devils* (Gakizumo) and *Banks of Hell* (Sai no kawara) demonstrate the power of the Jizô bodhisattva to help humans overcome evil. Performances, held annually in April, begin with *Plate Smashing* (Horakuwari), in which pottery is destroyed, warding off bad luck. On the last night, *Pole Twirling* (Bôfuri), a ritual exorcism, is followed by *Water Boiling* (Yûdate), in which hot water is sprayed at parishioners while actors shout "Next year!" *See also Kagura.*

FURTHER READING

Leiter, Samuel L. *Historical Dictionary of Japanese Traditional Theatre.*

Jonah Salz

MISHIMA YUKIO (1925–1970). Japanese • playwright.

World famous for his fiction and notorious for his **politically** motivated ritual suicide, Mishima was Japan's leading dramatist of the 1950s and 1960s. His sixty-one **stage** and screen plays span many genres and styles. Most are in the modern, realistic *shingeki* style, but his six *kabuki* plays (he did not consider them *shin kabuki*), all in classical Japanese, earned Mishima recognition as *kabuki*'s finest postwar playwright. His fondness for the classical stages of *nô* and *kabuki* developed in him a love of formalism and native tradition. Mishima also admired classical European drama, adapting, for example, *Phaedra* for *kabuki* (1955), and *Britannicus* (1957), the *Oresteia* (1959), and *Heracles* (1967) for *shingeki*.

In 1950, Mishima's first "modern *nô*" play, "Kantan," received critical acclaim at the Literary Theatre (Bungaku-za). Mishima wrote nine modern *nô*, perhaps his best one-acts. Unlike traditional *nô*, they are contemporary psychological dramas of love and obsession, intended for *shingeki*.

Mishima's political and artistic ideals ran counter to the development of postwar Japanese drama. While other dramatists moved away from traditional constraints toward unfettered expression, he remained a dedicated formalist. Most others espoused leftist ideals, but Mishima championed rightwing, nationalist characters and themes; his plays often shocked, even outraged, audiences.

From 1957 to 1964, Mishima was staff playwright for the Literary Theatre. Later he founded New Literary Theatre (NLT), where he wrote *Madame de Sade* (Sado kôshaku fujin, 1965), often considered his finest play.

FURTHER READING

Kominz, Laurence R., ed. *Mishima on Stage: The Black Lizard and Other Plays*; Nathan, John. *Mishima: A Biography;* Scott-Stokes, Henry. *The Life and Death of Yukio Mishima.*

Laurence Richard Kominz

MITRA, DINABANDHU (1832–1873). **Indian** Bengali-language **playwright,** born at Chouberia, Nadiain, who attended the free missionary school run by Rev. James Long (1814–1887), and then Hindu College, Calcutta (Kolkata), where he began writing poems under the influence of Iswarchandra Gupta (1812–1859), the dominant Bengali poet. After abandoning college in 1855, and being appointed postmaster of Patna, his literary interests turned toward drama. He maintained a distinguished career in the postal service and the Indian railway system while engaged in writing plays.

Mitra's plays included *The Indigo Mirror* (Nildarpan, publ. 1860; prod. 1872); *The New Female Ascetic* (Nabin tapaswini [a.k.a. *Bijay and Kamini* (Bijay-Kamini)], 1863), inspired by Shakespeare's *The Merry Wives of Windsor*; *Lady on a Lotus* (Kamale kamini, 1873); and *Lilabati* (1872). His popular farces included *The Old Man Mad for Marriage* (Biye pagla budo, 1866), *The Widow's Fasting* (Sadhabar ekadashi, 1866), and *Barracks of Sons-in-Law* (Jamai barik, 1872).

The explosively controversial *The Indigo Mirror* was his most famous work; **Michael Madhusudan Dutt**'s English translation was edited and published by Reverand Long, an outspoken **critic** of the way his countrymen treated the indigo workers, the play's subject. Long was fined and imprisoned for so doing (making him a hero to the Bengalis). The play led to a series of other Bengali works intended to "mirror" contemporary abuses. The play's premiere coincided with the opening of Calcutta's National Theatre in 1872. It was frequently revived, and was a favorite of leftist groups following the establishment of the Indian People's Theatre Association in 1942–1943.

The play, focused on the plight of an old landowner and his family, concerns the oppression of the indigo workers by the white colonial planters in the 1850s. Its scenes of rape, torture, and murder reveal India's growing unrest under British rule with a remarkable mixture of realism and **political** propaganda. In 1875, when it was produced by a group of frustrated indigo workers in Lucknow, a rape scene in which a Muslim peasant humbled an English oppressor inflamed the audience, and several British soldiers entered the **stage** with swords drawn; the play was stopped, and the **actors** were returned to Calcutta by the magistrate. The ensuing controversy led to the creation of the Dramatic Performances Control Act of 1876. Such **censorship** forced political and social protests underground, and added fuel to the nationalist movement. The play has been compared to *Uncle Tom's Cabin* for its role in creating national political awareness. Despite his authorship of this contentious play, Mitra was awarded the prestigious Raisaheb title in 1871 for his service to the British empire.

Sreenath K. Nair

MITRA, SHOMBHU (1922–1997). **Indian** Bengali-language **actor-director.** Born in West Bengal, he started his career at seventeen and worked in the Calcutta (Kolkata) commercial theatre from 1939 to 1942, a disciple of **Sisir Kumar Bhaduri.** In 1943, dissatisfied with these theatres' stereotypical practices, he joined the just founded Marxist-oriented Indian People's Theatre Association (IPTA). He provided IPTA with a landmark production of **Bijon Bhattacharya**'s *New Harvest* (Nabanna, 1944), which he codirected and costarred in with the author. It was a **political** reaction to the disastrous man-made Bengal famine of 1943 responsible for the death of 3 million. *New Harvest* helped spark the politically engaged Bengali "new drama movement."

In 1945, he married actress **Tripti Mitra** and left IPTA because of ideological issues; his aesthetic approach was at odds with IPTA's message-oriented project. He organized Bohurupee (literally, "many, many forms"), India's first significant post-independence **experimental theatre** group, with Manoranjan Bhatacharjee (1889–1954). Bohurupee conducted its first **festival** in 1950–1951 with plays like *Traveler* (Pathik) and Tulsi Lahiri's (1857–1959) *Broken Strings* (Chhenra taar), the latter making a star of Mitra's wife. In 1951, he directed **Rabindranath Tagore**'s *Four Chapters* (Char adhyay) and demonstrated the **playwright**'s theatrical effectiveness. His staging of Tagore's *Red Oleanders* (Raktakarabi, 1954) was highly influential.

A perfectionist and disciplinarian, he attended to the smallest components of production. His assorted talents made him the leading Bengali actor-director, and drew national attention to Bengali theatre. His career was further elevated by adaptations of **Western** plays and plays by Indian playwrights like **Vijay Tendulkar** and **Badal Sircar**. At the end of the 1970s, he abandoned Bohurupee. The winner of many awards, and a writer of important theatre essays, Mitra's vision offered an original combination of classical and contemporary, Indian and Western plays, and established a strong foundation for modernity in Indian theatre.

B. Ananthakrishnan

MITRA, TRIPTI (1925–1989). Indian Bengali-language **actress**, **director**, and **playwright**, who debuted in 1943 in *Fire* (Agun), written by her cousin, **Bijon Bhattacharya**. After joining the leftwing Indian People's Theatre Association (IPTA), she acted in a number of its productions, leaving in 1947 to join her husband, **Sombhu Mitra**, in Bohurupee (literally, "many, many forms"), a **theatre company** he formed. She also began to make an impact in Hindi films.

In 1950, she was acclaimed for her performance as Phulnan in Tulsi Lahiri's (1857–1959) *Broken Strings* (Chhenra taar), which catapulted her to Bengali **stage** stardom. She went on to portray various roles with uncommon ability and intense sensibility: **Rabindranath Tagore**'s *Four Chapters* (Char adhyay, 1951), *Red Oleanders* (Raktakarabi, 1954), *Immersion* (Bisarjan, 1961), and *Raja* (1964); Ibsen's *A Doll's House* (1958); Sophocles' *King Oedipus* (1964); **Vijay Tendulkar**'s *Silence! The Court Is in Session* (Chop! adalat chalchhe, 1971); Nitish Sen's *Aparajita* (1971); and **Badal Sircar**'s *Remaining History* (Baki itihas, 1967). Productions she directed include *Aparajita* (1971), *Pterodactyl* (1972), Ionesco's *Rhinoceros* (1972), and Tagore's "Post Office" (Dakghar, 1957) and *Home and the World* (Ghare baire, 1974). In 1960, she wrote her first play, *Sacrifice* (Bali).

Mitra's unforgettable portrayals, her powerful presence, intense voice modulation, and penetrating understanding of character helped her to become the most important Bengali stage personality of her time. Along with Bohurupee's productions she also acted in various commercial plays. In 1979, she left Bohurupee to **train** and direct young actors.

She received the National Academy of **Music**, **Dance**, and Drama (Sangeet Natak Akademi) award (1962) and the prestigious civilian award Padmashree (1971).

Debjani Ray Moulik

MIYAGI SATOSHI (1959–). Japanese • actor and director. After founding a performance group while studying aesthetics at Tokyo University, Miyagi spent the 1980s acting and directing. In 1990, he founded the experimental Tokyo-based Ku Na'uka Theatre Company, from the Russian for "toward science." The name highlights both this group's use of technology and Miyagi's uneasiness over the effects of modernization. Dissatisfied with society's equation of modern with Western, Miyagi, like a number of his contemporaries, turned to traditional theatre in his search for a modern aesthetic.

Ku Na'uka's productions are marked by a strong visual style, site-specific staging, and a heavy reliance on both live and prerecorded music. Perhaps the most striking component of Miyagi's current work, and most reflective of his philosophical views, is his creation of a "logos and pathos" theatre. Finding inspiration in *bunraku* (see Puppet Theatre), Miyagi frequently separates the spoken text from the physical action, each role having a "speaking actor" (*kataru haiyû*)—"logos"—and a "moving actor" (*ugoku haiyû*)—"pathos." This separation stems from Miyagi's belief that an increasingly impersonal world, the result of modernization, has severed language from the body and created a profound sense of powerlessness. Miyagi has gained increasing acclaim for his work with Ku Na'uka, directing and adapting both Eastern and Western classics. His most frequently revived productions are versions of Wilde's *Salomé* (1993), Izumi Kyôka's *The Castle Tower* (Tenshu monogatari, 1996), and Euripides' *Medea* (1999).

Michael W. Cassidy

MIYAMASU (FL. 1429–1467). Japanese • *nô* • playwright. Little is known about his career and the troupe he led in the capital region. According to Edo-period (1603–1868) play lists, he wrote between ten and twenty-eight plays, nine still performed.

Miyamasu's plays are derived from folk stories and war tales; all but one are classified as "present-time" (*genzai*) *nô*, featuring a large cast of living characters in contrast to the "dream" (*mugen*) *nô* favored by Zeami and Konparu Zenchiku. His plays usually develop as a conflict between the main actor (*shite*) and the other characters (see Role Types), who receive almost equal dramatic focus. Due to these characteristics and the fact that Miyamasu's language is less poetic than that of his contemporaries, scholars conclude that he wrote for a more popular audience. Works attributed to him include the popular Soga brothers' revenge story: *The Soga Brother Comes of Age* (Genpuku Soga), *The Vengeance Ritual* (Chôbuku Soga), and *Soga Brothers' Night Attack* (Youchi Soga), considered influential in kabuki's development because of their exciting plots in which a character chooses between duty (*giri*) and emotions (*ninjô*).

Miyamasu was also a musician and his lineage produced several famous percussionists.

Eric C. Rath

MIYAMOTO KEN (1926–1988). Japanese • *shingeki* • playwright, director, and scenarist, born in Amakusa, in Kyûshû, and raised partly in Beijing. Repatriated in 1944, Miyamoto studied economics and worked for the government, but his disillusionment at Japan's bleak conditions moved him to organize a theatre company, Barley Group (Muginokai, 1951), to express concerns about the war and postwar injustices. While his first plays are left-leaning—spotlighting actual anarchists, feminists, or revolutionaries—later works, probing Japanese identity, have a more nationalist tone. His style appeals with trenchant dialogue and multilayered structures, often historically based, grounded in first-hand East Asian experience.

He won the 1962 **Kishida** [**Kunio**] Prize for *Republic of Japan* (Nihonjin minkyô wakoku) and *An Approach to **Musical** Drama* (Mekanizumu sakusen), the latter a jazz-infused, Brechtian-style critique of labor-movement difficulties. *The Meiji Coffin* (Meiji no hitsugi), awarded the 1963 Arts **Festival** Encouragement Award and the first play in Miyamoto's *Tetralogy of Revolutionary Legends* (Kakumei densetsu yonbusaku), portrays the Ashio Copper Mine pollution incident, the Meiji period's (1868–1912) salient catastrophe. *The Pilot* (Za pairotto, 1965) evenhandedly considers Japanese reactions to an A-bomb reconnaissance pilot.

Later plays include *Cherry-Blossom-Blizzard Love Suicide* (Sakura fubuki nihon no shinjû, 1972), featuring men's and **women**'s dashed hopes, and *China-bound Women* (Karayuki-san, 1977), about the "noble sacrifices" of post-1868 women sold into prostitution around Asia to support impoverished parents; also a popular television series, the action crystallizes Miyamoto's memories of *karayuki-san* and his sense of injustice at their plight. *See also* Politics in Theatre.

Hamilton Armstrong

MIYAZAWA AKIO (1955–). Japanese • **playwright** and **director**. Sometimes grouped with the 1990s "quiet theatre" (*shizuka na engeki*) movement, Miyazawa's plays are more overtly **political** and theatrical, confronting socio-political issues like Japan's collective (wartime) memory, cult **religions**, and school violence. He had early success as a comedian and in 1990 established the Amusement Park Renewal Operations Troupe (Yûenchi Saisei Jigyô Dan).

Miyazawa's *Hinemi* shared the **Kishida** [**Kunio**] Prize in 1993. A memory play where past, present, and future exist simultaneously, forcing confrontation with (mis)-remembered events, *Hinemi* features a man drawing a map of Hinemi, his now vanished childhood hometown. Disconnected from his past, the search for memories takes him forward to meet the grown daughter of a former resident and backward to his ·older brother's death. Such surreal time slips suggest the fragility of Japanese cultural memory and, therefore, the difficulty of cultural reproduction.

Similarly, in *The Pleasure Garden of Sand* (Suna no rakuen, 1996), the crew at a desert observation outpost has forgotten its objective. In a spare monochrome setting, seemingly unreal, one man tends a flower, but is he really dreaming of a **woman**? This could be Japan, but any conclusions, including about the crew's existential purpose, are left indeterminate.

This uncertainty, laced with fear, reflects 1990s Japan and propels Miyazawa's *Country of Fourteen-Year-Olds* (Jûyon-sai no kuni, 1998). Middle-school teachers, engaged in vaguely unsettled, apparently pointless conversation (echoing **Betsuyaku Minoru**), inspect a student-less classroom. Their growing angst foreshadows the play's violent ending.

John D. Swain

MIYOSHI JŪRŌ (1902–1958). Japanese • *shingeki* • **playwright**. A Waseda University graduate in English literature, Miyoshi gained prominence in the proletarian movement of the 1920s and early 1930s. During this time, he joined leftwing arts organizations, including the Japan Proletarian Literary Arts League (Puroren). Plays such as *The Much-Maimed Oaki* (Kizu darake no oaki, 1927) and *Coal Dust* (Tanjin, 1930) typify his early Marxist commitment; by the 1930s, leading proletarian organizations, including the Leftwing Theatre (Sayoku Gekijô) and the New Tsukiji Company (Shin Tsukiji Gekidan), were performing his works.

In the mid-1930s, Miyoshi broke with the Marxist theatre world over his growing dissatisfaction with its rigid dialectics and emphasis on **politics** over art. Although he continually favored the lower classes in dramas such as *The Stabbed Senta* (Kirare no Senta, 1934), Miyoshi felt that artists should depict all levels of society with equal detachment and without overt politicizing. *Buoy* (Bui, 1940), perhaps his most famous work, is a strong indicator of his personal and artistic struggles. It not only continues his commitment to capturing lower-class realities but also focuses on an artist, Kuga Gorô, who, like Miyoshi, was dealing with the death of his wife. Miyoshi, through Kuga's similar struggle, captures in vivid emotional detail his own ideological turn and renewed sense of self.

Miyoshi's withdrawal from the proletarian movement and overtly political theatre allowed him to be one of the few dramatists to remain active during World War II. While some of his works at this time were produced by nationalistic mobile theatre units (*idô-engeki*), he later anguished over his role as a collaborationist. This complex relationship to the war and its aftermath emerges as a dominant theme in his last plays, notably *The Ruins* (Haikyo, 1947), *Inside the Womb* (Tainai, 1949), and *Those Who Committed Crimes* (Okashita mono, 1952), which document characters struggling to bring meaning to their shattered lives and often to reach accommodation with their own wartime activities. In *I Know Not the Man* (Sono hito o shirazu, 1948), also from Miyoshi's mature period, a Christian protagonist watches his life and family become decimated for his traitorous refusal of military conscription, only to question society and his faith as the war ends and he is regarded as a hero.

Michael W. Cassidy

MIZUTANI YAEKO (1905–1979). Japanese • *shingeki*, *shinpa*, and film **actress**. Through family connections to **Tsubouchi Shôyô**'s Literary Arts Society (Bungei Kyôkai) and **Shimamura Hôgetsu**'s Art Theatre (Geijutsu-za), Mizutani debuted at eight, in a crowd scene in Maeterlinck's *Interior* (1913). Her official debut was in Tolstoy's *Anna Karenina* (1916), and her first leading role was Tyltyl in Maeterlinck's *The Blue Bird* (1920) at the People's Theatre (Minshû-za). In 1921, she made her film debut in *Winter Camellia* (Kantsubaki). Because she was still in school, her family made sure her billing was as "anonymous young lady" (*fukumen reijo*).

Subsequently, she appeared in *shinpa*, and, in 1928, was signed by Shôchiku (see Theatre Companies), thereby contributing to the late-1920s *shinpa* revival. In 1930, she first costarred in *shinpa* with Hanayagi Shôtarô (1894–1965), beginning a long and brilliant collaboration. When her brother-in-law, novelist and **critic** Mizutani Chikushi (1882–1935), revived the Art Theatre after the Great Kantô Earthquake (1923), she became its signature star, touring widely until the company disbanded in 1945 because of the war. Her major *shingeki* roles included plays by Chekhov, Ibsen (including Nora in *A Doll's House*), and Tolstoy; she even played Hamlet, being the first Japanese actress to act the Danish prince. She did this twice, first in 1933, at the Meiji Theatre (Meiji-za), costarring with movie idol Hayakawa Sesshû (1889–1973) and the *kabuki* actors later known as **Kataoka Nizaemon** XIII and **Morita Kanya** XIV, Mizutani's future husband. The second was in 1935, at the Tokyo **Takarazuka** Theatre.

Mizutani's marriage to Kanya lasted from 1937 to 1950; later, she often appeared in *shinpa* plays opposite leading *kabuki* actors. She and Hanayagi formed Theatre Shinpa (Gekidan Shinpa) in 1952; after his death, she was the premiere *shinpa* performer, taking on the great roles created for *shinpa*'s "female impersonators" (*onnagata*). Her stellar acting combined a *shingeki* actor's analytical understanding of scripts with a *shinpa* actor's glamorous stylization. Even her immense popularity, however, could not stem *shinpa*'s postwar decline. She is best known for *shinpa* plays like *The White Threads of the Waterfall* (Taki no shiraito); **Kawakami Otojirô**'s 1895 adaptation of **Izumi Kyôka**'s novel *Loyal Blood, Valiant Blood* (Giketsu kyôketsu, 1894); and *shingeki* plays like **Mishima Yukio**'s *Deer Cry Pavilion* (Rokumeikan, 1956), performed with *shinpa* actors in 1962. Her daughter Yoshie (1939–) inherited her name in 1995, a procedure common in *kabuki* but unprecedented in *shinpa*.

Ayako Kano

MONGOLIA. Situated between Russia and **China**, Mongolia has about 2,791,000 people (2005), around 94 percent being Mongolian. There are also 5,813,947 Mongolians in China (2000), especially Inner Mongolia, who are culturally very similar to those of Mongolia, despite very strong Chinese influence in the cities. The dominant **religion** is Tibetan Buddhism.

Under the Manchus, China conquered the Mongolian territories in 1691. Mongolia declared independence with the fall of the Manchus in 1911; in the north, events in 1921 and 1924 led to the establishment of the Mongolian People's Republic (which fell in 1991), but southern or Inner Mongolia has remained part of China. Under the Chinese, some Chinese theatre traditions spread to Mongolia, especially the south.

Tsam. Mongolians have a rich **dance** tradition, the most drama-like form being *tsam*. Introduced from **Tibet** along with Tibetan Buddhism in the sixteenth century, these dances represent the struggle between good and evil and mark ceremonies, such as Buddhist feast days. They feature complex **masks** that cover the whole head, and show spirits, some in the form of animals. Buddhist monks perform them in their monasteries. The **musical** accompaniment features long horns (*buree*) and cymbals.

Tsam dances and other traditional dramas were suppressed under the Mongolian People's Republic. With the fall of this state, *tsam* dances were revived. Monks still perform them annually on the birthday of the Future Buddha Maitreya (Mongolian: Maidar) at Mongolia's oldest Buddhist monastery, Erdene Zuu, located on the site of the thirteenth-century imperial capital, Karakorum. Professionals also regularly perform brief excerpts for tourists.

In China's Mongolian areas, Tibetan Buddhism, including the *tsam* dances, was suppressed during the Cultural Revolution (1966–1976). Although Tibetan Buddhism has revived, it remains much weaker among the Mongolians than the Tibetans. In the Mongolian areas, monks occasionally perform *tsam* in the monasteries, and brief excerpts survive as tourist attractions.

The Moon Cuckoo. The most important pre-modern drama is *The Moon Cuckoo* (Saran khökhöö, ca. 1831) by Danzanravjaa (1803–1856), considered a reincarnated Buddhist saint. It concerns an **Indian** prince, turned into a cuckoo, who defeats evil and continues to preach Buddhism to the birds. Lasting as long as a month, it was performed in many monasteries until the twentieth century, the roles being played

Mongolian *tsam* dance featuring masked dancers and representing the struggle between good and evil. Traditionally, *tsam* took place in Tibetan Buddhist monasteries, but this performance was in a special small theatre designed for tourists in Ulaan Baatar, April 2005. (Photo: Colin Mackerras)

increasingly less by monks than by laity, both male and female. Wandering **theatre companies**, containing both men and **women**, performed this and other plays. Grander venues included three-tiered **stages**, with **musicians** on the lowest, **actors** in the middle, and the **director** at the top. In 2002, *The Moon Cuckoo* was revived.

Colin Mackerras

Beginning of Modern Theatre: 1921–1945. Modern Mongolian theatre began in 1922, spreading revolutionary ideas to a largely illiterate audience. It was modeled on Soviet theatre and reflected the time's **political** values and policies. **Training**, techniques, and facilities improved after World War II. The ruling Mongolian People's Revolutionary Party (MPRP) imposed tight controls on **playwriting** and production until 1990, when the socialist system ended, and the Writers' Union, which had been in charge of the political tendency of plays, collapsed. Mongolian theatre is now free from **censorship** and ideological control. It responds to audience demand and is being integrated with world theatre as the country's isolation ends.

In 1922, the League of Revolutionary Youth formed an amateur drama group at the People's Leisure Centre in Ulaan Baatar. Early productions were loosely based on Chinese plays and incorporated songs and poetry. Characters were stylized, and princes, lamas, and Chinese officials and traders were portrayed as backward and evil, while poor commoners were honest and virtuous. Sonombaljiriin Buyannemekh (1901–1937) wrote and produced the first of many historical plays, *Viceroy Sando* (Sando amban, 1922), about the last Chinese viceroy of Urga. The young actors toured the countryside, often performing in the open air on felts spread out as a stage. Chinese traders were forced to fund the productions and were fined if they did not attend. The Green Dome (Bömbögör Nogoon), a circular building with a stage and orchestra pit, opened in 1921 and was home to the state **theatre** for many years.

A professional company was formed in 1931 with a Russian instructor, A. Efremov. The MPRP required drama depicting the struggle of the old and the new and the development of the modern man. Buyannemekh's *Dark Power* (Kharankhui zasag, 1933), Dashdorjiin Natsagdorj's (1906–1937) *Three Sad Hills* (Uchirtai gurvan tolgoi), and several works by Donrovyn Namdag (1911–1982) were produced in the early 1930s. Translations of plays by Chekhov, Gogol, and Ostrovsky enlarged the repertoire. Then the 1930s declined into state terrorism, and Buyannemekh and Natsagdorj perished as enemies of the people. Namdag survived and went on to write dramas promoting patriotism and Mongolia's support of the USSR against Nazism and **Japan** in World War II.

Postwar Period. After the war, the MPRP demanded drama that portrayed the socialist construction of Mongolia: collectivized herding, industry, arable farming, and urbanization. The national five-year plans included targets for cultural organizations. Theatre plans were monitored by the Ministry of Culture, the Writers' Union, and party cells in the theatres. More theatres opened, including the State **Puppet** Theatre (Ulsyn Khükheldein Teatr, 1948) and the State Children's Theatre (Ulsyn Khüükhdiin Teatr, 1950). In 1963, the State Theatre separated into a State Drama Theatre (Ulsyn Dramyn Teatr) and the Opera and Ballet Theatre (Duur' Büjgiin Teatr). There were also regional theatres and many amateur groups in schools and the workplace. Film (from 1938), radio (from 1934), and television (from 1967) were also drama outlets. Theatre workers were well educated and often trained in the USSR or Eastern Europe. Plays continued to reflect the political concerns of the period, and were censored and sometimes criticized for insufficient depth of character or inadequate portrayal of the conflict between self-interest and socialist morality. Mongol-Soviet friendship was a prominent theme, and nationalism was condemned. Namdag, Choijamtsyn Oidov (1917–1963), Choijilsürengiin Chimid (1927–1980), and Lamjavyn Vangan (1917–1980) were leading dramatists. However, in 1967, the MPRP complained that there were not enough Mongolian dramatists, and plays by Shakespeare, Schiller, and Lope de Vega were added to the repertoire.

Post-1990 Theatre. Mongolia adopted democracy and a market economy in 1990. The tyranny of political control and five-year plans ended but reduced state funding, and new responsibilities for policy and management were constraints for theatre. Today only the State Academic Drama Theatre (Ulsyn Dramyn Erdmiin Teatr), the Opera and Ballet Theatre, and the State Puppet Theatre receive state funding, although several alternative funding sources exist. Actors, musicians, and producers work on contracts. Local authorities and businesses support some provincial theatres, and private theatre companies and amateur troupes have emerged.

In the early years of transition there was a crisis of repertoire. Anti-capitalist plays that reflected socialist realism were instantly outdated although classical works by Shakespeare and Schiller remained valid. By the end of the twentieth century, younger dramatists had emerged, including Kh Narangerel, Ts Baldorj, and Bavuugiin Lkhagvasüren, sometimes as the result of competitions. New audiences are discovering spoken drama as management improves and performances are more widely publicized. The State Academic Drama Theatre stages three new plays each year.

Contemporary theatre is also invigorated by new contacts abroad. Theatre artists attend international workshops and **festivals**. Mongolia also hosts festivals such as the Third International Drama Festival of Mongolian-speaking Countries (2001). Foreign specialists run workshops and seminars to introduce new techniques.

Theatre audiences want plays that address the problems of contemporary society, such as the psychological shock of the transition, high levels of poverty and unemployment, and official corruption. Mongolia's prerevolutionary cultural traditions and values and modern issues such as AIDS and homosexuality, previously taboo, can also be staged. A new play, *Grey Street and Striptease Boys* (2005) by B Batregzedmaa, deals with conflicts between homosexuals and heterosexuals. The value of theatre for education has not been lost in the transition. "Street Law" is a radio drama project to raise awareness of legal reforms. Television drama has dealt with domestic violence and personal rights. Foreign aid projects are introducing drama as therapy for the disadvantaged.

FURTHER READING

Brown, William A., and Urgunge Onon, trans. and annot. *History of the Mongolian People's Republic*; Gerasimovich, Ludmilla. *History of Modern Mongolian Literature (1921–1964)*.

Judith Nordby

MORIMOTO KAORU (1912–1946). Japanese • *shingeki* • playwright. Born in Osaka, he exhibited playwriting talent in high school. Subsequently, plays such as *The Way of a Family* (Ikkafû, 1934) impressed Koyama Yûshi and **Tanaka Chikao**, who persuaded him to contribute to *Playwriting* (Gekisaku), a magazine for professional dramatists. His first contribution, *A Splendid Woman* (Migoto na onna, 1934), won enthusiastic praise from Iwata Toyoo (1893–1969) and established Morimoto's reputation. During the following three years, Morimoto produced several fine pieces, including *A Flamboyant Family* (Hanabanashiki ichizoku, 1935) and *So, It Is the New Year* (Kakute shinnen wa, 1936). He joined the Literary Theatre (Bungaku-za) in 1940 at Iwata's invitation and wrote numerous radio dramas, film scenarios, adaptations, and *Angry Waves* (Dotô, 1944) and *A Woman's Life* (Onna no isshô, 1945).

Morimoto's career falls into two periods, the first covering his college years until 1937; the second, from 1937 to his death from tuberculosis. While Morimoto was concerned with various family matters in the first period, his self-assertion in the second is often tinged with contemporary **political** overtones. Examples include *Bangued Highway* (Bengetto Dôro, 1943), a radio drama on the superiority of Japanese labor in constructing a highway in the **Philippines** after the Spanish-American War, and *A Woman's Life*. The latter, though commissioned by the military, contains subtle resistance. It not only survived the war but became one of the most staged postwar plays.

Guohe Zheng

MORI ÔGAI (1862–1922). Japanese **playwright**, translator, **critic**, and novelist. A giant in modern Japanese fiction, Ôgai was also important to *shingeki*'s development. Perhaps his most celebrated theatre accomplishments are his translations. The Free Theatre's (Jiyû Gekijô) 1909 staging of Ibsen's *John Gabriel Borkman* used

Ôgai's translation and was among the first *shingeki* performances. He also translated plays by Lessing, Strindberg, and Wedekind.

Although Ôgai considered himself an amateur, his output was varied and his contributions substantial. For example, his first play, *The Jeweled Casket and the Two Urashimas* (Tamakushige futari Urashima, 1902), was produced as *shinpa*. He is also considered a master of colloquial language, particularly highlighted in his celebrated *Masks* (Kamen, 1909). His linguistic style marked a break from traditional Japanese **stage** language, challenging both **actors** and audience. In addition, *Masks*, a dispassionate exploration of a young man's decision to carry on normally despite being diagnosed with tuberculosis, exemplifies Ôgai's preference for aesthetic distance and idea-centered drama.

His influence extended to discussions with **Tsubouchi Shôyô**, which were among the first on modern drama to garner public attention, and his critical writing fostered recognition of Japanese drama as literature. Indeed, Ôgai figured in the advent of plays published in literary magazines, as with his *Ikuta River* (Ikutagawa) in *Central Review* (Chûô Kôron) in 1910. This play also continued his relationship with **Osanai Kaoru**, who commissioned it for performance.

Michael W. Cassidy

MORITA KANYA. Fourteen generations of *kabuki* • **actors** and managers. The line was responsible for managing one of Edo's (Tokyo) three major **theatres**, the Morita Theatre (Morita-za), from the 1660s until it became the Shintomi Theatre (Shintomi-za) in the 1870s during the management of Kanya XII. He, Kanya XIII, and Kanya XIV were the most important members of the line.

Kanya XII (1846–1897) was one of the leading figures of the Meiji period (1868–1912). The son of a financial supporter of the Morita Theatre, he was adopted in 1863 by Kanya XI (1800–1863), better known as **Bandô Mitsugoro** IV, as Morita Kanjirô; when Kanya XI died that year, Kanjirô became Kanya XII and assumed the theatre's management in 1864. In 1872, he moved the Morita from its out-of-the-way location in Saruwaka-chô to Shintomi-chô, in central Tokyo. This revolutionary step led others to make similar moves. The theatre, which became the Shintomi Theatre in 1875, introduced many innovations, such as the introduction of **Western** architectural features and managerial methods, including gas lighting, some chair seating, matinees, plays adapted from Western sources, visits by distinguished foreign visitors, and so on. Kanya's close association with **Ichikawa Danjûrô** IX symbolized the reformist thinking in contemporary *kabuki*. As a result, the "Shintomi Theatre age" was born.

Kanya XII was also one of those responsible for having *kabuki* performed before the imperial family in 1887, an event that instantly raised *kabuki*'s social status from its traditional position in which its actors were considered "riverbed beggars" (*kawara kojiki*). Writing as Furukawa Shinsui, he wrote plays under the tutelage of **Kawatake Mokuami**. Despite great efforts, he was unable to keep the Shintomi Theatre out of debt. He was the line's last manager.

Kanya XIII (1885–1932), third son of Kanya XII, was known as Morita Mitahachi before becoming Kanya XIII in 1901. He played romantic leading roles, aided by his slender build and handsomeness. He actively produced new plays.

Kanya XIV (1907–1975) was Kanya XIII's adopted son. Although a specialist at handsome males, he had a wide range and played characters old and young, male and female. His resemblance to leading romantic actor **Ichimura Uzaemon** XV earned him the label "the sixteen-millimeter Uzaemon." He debuted as **Bandô Tamasaburô** IV in 1914, taking the name Bandô Shûka III in 1926, and becoming Kanya IV in 1935. During the 1930s, he belonged to the young acting group at the Shinjuku Number One Theatre (Shinjuku Dai-ichi Gekijô). He was married to the *shinpa* star **Mizutani Yaeko**, and his adopted son is today's leading "female impersonator" (*onnagata*), Bandô Tamasaburô V.

Samuel L. Leiter

MORO-MORO. *See Komedya.*

MUA ROI NUOC. *See* Puppet Theatre: Vietnam.

MUDALIAR, PAMMAL VIJAYARANGA SAMBANDHA (1873–1964).
Indian Tamil-language **playwright**, **director**, **actor**, producer, and theatre historian, born in Madras (Chennai). Originally a lawyer, Mudaliar (popularly known as Sambandha) was exposed to the urban commercial theatre, but disparaged what he viewed as the vulgar Tamil plays of his day. He altered his position in 1891 on seeing a high-quality production by a Madras **theatre company** made up of respectable government employees. Hoping to emulate the troupe's quality work, he founded the amateur Suguna Vilasa Sabha company in 1892, with actors from the legal and other professions, and produced his *Pushpavalli* (1893), as well as **Western** and **Sanskrit** plays, quickly gaining respect from the educated middle-class. Acting was raised to a respectable profession, and theatre became highly regarded. Mudaliar continued practicing law, eventually becoming a judge before retiring to focus on his company.

The company, which toured widely through India and Southeast Asia, emphasized nonmusical plays and realistic, Stanislavski System–based performance, using novel **scenography**. Mudaliar acted frequently, often in his own plays, among them being Tamil's first in prose dialogue: *Lilavati and Sulochana* (Lilavati-Sulochana, 1895), *Manohara* (publ. 1907), *Amaladitya* (a version of *Hamlet*, publ. 1908), *Ratnavali* (based on a Sanskrit classic, 1908), *Makapati* (based on *Macbeth*, publ. 1910), *Sabhapati* (publ. 1918), and *Chandra Hari* (1923). Unlike the eight-hour plays then common, his were only three-hours long. Some later became films.

Samuel L. Leiter

MURAYAMA TOMOYOSHI (1901–1977). Japanese playwright, director,
and **scenographer**. German expressionism influenced Murayama's early plays, and he achieved *shingeki* fame in 1924 with his constructivist set for the Tsukiji Little **Theatre** (Tsukiji Shôgekijô) production of Kaiser's *From Morn to Midnight*. Marxist ideology also influenced his work. Both tendencies are evident in plays like *Nero Wearing a Skirt* (Sukaato o haita Nero, 1927).

Murayama became a **political** activist, joining the Leftwing Theatre (Sayoku Gekijô) in 1927. Between 1929 and 1932, he wrote several major proletarian plays, including *Account of a Gang of Thugs* (Bôryokudanki, 1929), about a **Chinese** railway strike quelled by gangsters and soldiers. In 1934, with leftist theatre reeling under police pressure, Murayama published "Great Union of Shingeki Troupes" (Shingekidan no daidô danketsu), a program for establishing a single, large anti-commercial *shingeki* **theatre company** that would provide a new starting point for the fragmented *shingeki* movement. He partially realized his aim the same year by founding the New Cooperative Company (Shinkyô Gekidan), among the largest troupes of the time.

Arrested in 1940, when most *shingeki* companies were forced to disband, Murayama was released and fled to **Korea**, returning to Japan after the war. He re-established the New Cooperative Company in 1946, later merging with another company to form Tokyo Art Theatre (Tôkyô Geijutsu-za). Through much of the postwar period, Murayama directed both *shingeki* and commercial plays.

Brian Powell

MUSIC AND MUSICAL INSTRUMENTS

Music and Musical Instruments: Bangladesh. *See* Music and Musical Instruments: South Asia

Music and Musical Instruments: Bhutan. *See* Music and Musical Instruments: South Asia

Music and Muscial Instruments: Cambodia

Each of **Cambodia**'s numerous types of musical ensembles has unique instrumentation and a distinct repertoire. In performance, they may vary in number and variety of instruments.

The *pin peat* ensemble accompanies **lakhon kbach boran**, **lakhon khol**, *lakhon sbaek* (see Puppet Theatre), Buddhist temple ceremonies, and boxing matches. Instruments include a quadruple-reed hard wood or ivory oboe (*sralai*), high-pitched wooden or bamboo xylophone (*roneat ek*), low-pitched wooden or bamboo xylophone (*roneat thung*), xylophone with steel keys (*roneat dek*), low-pitched circle of gongs (*kong vong thom*), higher-pitched smaller gong circle (*kong vong touc*), double-headed barrel drum (*sampho*), large pair of barrel drums (*skor thom*), and handheld brass cymbals (*chheung*).

Operatic genres such as **yiké** and **lakhon bassac** are accompanied by combinations of instruments found nowhere else: *yiké* with large, flat, round frame drums (*skor yiké*), two-stringed upright fiddles (*tro ou* and *tro sau*), and a *sralai* or bamboo or wood flute (*khloy*); and *lakhon bassac* with a large and small hammered dulcimer (*khim*), large, handheld cymbals (*chhap*), flat gong (*khmuoh*), wooden slit drum (*pann*), two-stringed fiddle with the bow hairs placed between the strings (*tro chhe*), and *skor thom*. Regional, rural traditions include their specific groupings of instruments as well. Performers in the *trot* **folk theatre**, for example, play goblet drum (*skor areak*), bamboo flute with attached reed (*pey or*), and a pair of two-stringed upright fiddles (*tro ou* and *tro* *sau*). The long-necked lute (*chapey dong veng*) is a solo instrument played by itinerant **storyteller**/singers.

FURTHER READING

Miller, Terry E., and Sean Williams, eds. *Southeast Asia*. Vol. 4. *Garland Encyclopedia of World Music*.

Toni Shapiro-Phim

Music and Musical Instruments: China

Xiqu *Vocal Music*. Music is of central importance to **China**'s *xiqu*, as the name— "theatre [of] sung-verse"—suggests. Vocal music and instrumental accompaniment are the two main components, and the principal means for identifying individual *xiqu* forms. Vocal music is intimately related to the tones of spoken Chinese, which are different in each regional language and have melodic and rhythmic characteristics related to both listening comprehension and aesthetic value in song. Two main types of musical structure, each with its own distinctive relationship to the sung word, developed between the Tang (618–907) and the Ming (1368–1644) dynasties; both are employed today.

"Joined-song structure" (*lianquti*) is the older, having characterized Yuan (1280–1368) **zaju** and **nanxi**. *Qupai*, many of which originated as songs with nontheatrical lyrics, form the most fundamental compositional unit. Each *qupai* is named. New lyrics are "filled in" according to the patterns of each *qupai*, which specify such textual aspects as number of lines (usually of irregular length), number of written characters (each of one syllable) per line, placement of pauses, patterns of word tones, and rhyme. Each *qupai* also provides a melodic contour and/or melodic motifs that form the basis for the specific melody to which the new lyrics will be sung. Regardless of length or the use of meter, each is a complete musical unit. Every *xiqu* form that uses joined-song structure has its own extensive body of *qupai*.

"Beat-tune structure" (*banqiang ti*) is a newer structural type, having developed during Ming. The fundamental compositional units are the metrical type (*banshi*, literally, "beat style") and the "mode/tune type" (*qiangdiao shengqiang*). *Qiangdiao shengqiang* provide compositional patterns concerning aspects such as key, cadence, written-character placement within meter, length of musical line, and melodic contour and construction, which together produce a particular atmosphere. Metrical types provide patterns of meter, tempo, rhythm, and characteristic melodic tendencies, each appropriate for certain dramatic situations. As long as lyrics are written in the poetic form appropriate to the *xiqu* type in which they will be sung, **actors** and musicians can perform them, interpretively applying the patterns provided by *qiangdiao shengqiang* and metrical types.

As a given *xiqu* type became popular and its influence spread to other regions, its unique body of *qupai*, or of *qiangdiao shengqiang* and metrical types, was adapted to other already-existing forms, and in some cases was joined with regional language and **folk** music to create new forms. A family of *xiqu* forms with significant musical similarities—establishing a musical system—developed. The most influential systems from Ming through today are *yiyang qiang*, *kunshan qiang*, **bangzi qiang**, and *pihuang*. Joined-song structure is employed in the first two, and beat-tune structure in the latter two.

Yiyang qiang. *Yiyang qiang* arose during the Yuan dynasty (1271–1368) in the Yiyang region of Jiangxi Province. It featured solo singing with an offstage helping chorus (*bangqiang*, literally, "assist melodic passage") supporting the closing line(s) of songs, with only percussion accompaniment. During the Ming and early Qing (1644–1911) dynasties it spread to Nanjing, Beijing, Hunan, Guangdong, Fujian, Anhui, Sichuan, Yunnan, and Guizhou, forming *gaoqiang* (literally, "high melodic passages"). Although *yiyang qiang* itself has essentially disappeared, *gaoqiang*, with its solo singing and helping chorus, is still a feature of a number of *xiqu* styles, including **chuanju** (in Sichuan Province). It is known for its "loud and sonorous tone, and rich flavor of bright and clear declamation."

Kunshan qiang. *Kunshan qiang* originated in **kunqu**, from Kunshan in Jiangsu Province. It is generally accepted that **Wei Liangfu** and other mid-sixteenth-century artists in the Kunshan-Suzhou area devised *kunqu*'s music, drawing on a wide variety of sources, and creating a style noted as "delicate, exquisite, and sweet." *Kunqu* initially spread to Zhejiang, Jiangxi, Nanjing, Beijing, and Hunan, and in late Ming and early Qing to Sichuan, Guiyang, and Guangdong, developing various regional styles.

Bangzi qiang. *Bangzi qiang* arose from the folk songs of Shaanxi and Gansu Provinces, characterized as "loud and sonorous, intense and strong." From the sixteenth to eighteenth centuries its influence spread east and south, combining with local languages and musics, and in some cases northern *qu* singing. Styles created included Shanxi *bangzi* (*jinju*), Henan *bangzi* (*yuju*), Hebei *bangzi*, Shandong *bangzi*, Puzhou *bangzi* (*puju*), and *zhonglu* ("middle road") *bangzi*.

Pihuang. *Pihuang* takes its name from its two principal modes (*shengqiang*), *xipi* and *erhuang*, which arose separately in different *xiqu* forms; *xipi* is energetic and purposeful, *erhuang* darker and more lyrical; each has numerous independent metrical types. In late Ming and early Qing, each was primary in separate forms; with the creation of **jingju** they were joined in the same *xiqu* form. The resultant *pihuang* system spread throughout China, influencing many forms, especially in the south, and inspiring several new ones. Among other *xiqu* forms featuring *pihuang* are Cantonese *yueju* of Guangdong Province, and *chuanju*, where it is called *huqin qiang* after its leading melodic instrument.

Xiqu *Instrumental Music*. *Xiqu* instrumental accompaniment has two main types, melodic and percussive, the "civil section" (*wenchang*) and the "martial section" (*wuchang*) or "drums [and] gongs" (*luogu*). While many instruments are used in various forms, the leading melodic instrument is frequently a main characterizing feature. *Kunqu*'s is the *qudi*, a horizontal bamboo flute with six evenly spaced finger holes producing a mixture of whole and three-quarter step intervals. The *qudi* is relatively large and produces a rich, mellow sound; it is sometimes used in *jingju* as the leading accompaniment for *kunqu*-derived music. The *bangdi* is smaller and higher in pitch, with a melodious, clear sound; it is important in many *bangzi qiang* forms. Other primarily supporting wind instruments include the *xiao*, a vertical bamboo flute; the *guan*, a single or double reed instrument with a wooden body; the *suona*, a double reed instrument with a conical wooden body and a flared, movable metal bell; and the *sheng*, a multiple reed-pipe instrument with a single free reed on each pipe.

In *bangzi qiang* and *pihuang* forms, the leading melodic instrument is one of a number of two-string spike fiddles (*huqin*), most of which have a long thin neck and are played with a bow strung with horse hair running between the strings. For *bangzi* forms, it is the *banhu*, which has a half-hemisphere body about four inches in diameter made of bamboo, wood, or a half coconut shell, and a thin sheet of wooden board for a head; it produces a loud, sonorous sound. In *jingju* and many other *pihuang* forms, it is the *jinghu*, which has a two-inch diameter, a cylindrical bamboo body with a snakeskin head; it produces a high-pitch, piercing sound. The *erhu*, used in many *xiqu* forms, is somewhat larger, with a three to three and a half inch cylindrical body of wood or bamboo and a snakeskin head; its sound is lower and mellower. Several plucked string instruments also play important supporting roles, including the *yueqin*, a fretted lute with a short neck, a flat, round body, and two, three, or four strings played with a plectrum; the *sanxian*, an unfretted lute with three strings played with a plectrum; and the *pipa*, a fretted lute with a pear-shaped body and four strings plucked with the fingers.

The percussion section leader, who usually conducts the full orchestra as well, often plays two instruments in forms such as *kunqu* and *jingju*. The *ban* is a clapper consisting of two rectangular pieces of hardwood loosely strung together with a cord; one is held in the hand and swung to strike against the other. The *danpi gu*, a drum with a single, skin-covered head, is made from a solid piece of wood with a hole bored through the center, and is hit with one or two long thin sticks. In *bangzi qiang*, the principal percussion instrument is the eponymous *bangzi* clapper. It consists of two unconnected pieces of solid hardwood, one rectangular and one cylindrical; the former is held in the hand and struck with the latter. Other important percussion instruments include many different sizes of brass gongs (*luo*), some held in the hand and others by rope handles, some struck with padded sticks and others with flat, tapered pieces of wood; brass cymbals (*bo*); and many kinds of drums (*gu*), including *tanggu*, barrel-shaped drums with two ox-hide heads that come in a variety of sizes.

Xiqu instrumental accompaniment extends beyond song to other performance aspects. Both movement and speech are heightened and punctuated by music. The orchestra creates environment and atmosphere with sounds suggesting a boat on water, a battlefield, the night watch, wind and rain, thunder, and animals. Music of one sort or another pervades the entire performance.

FURTHER READING

Wichmann, Elizabeth. *Listening to Theatre: The Aural Dimension of Beijing Opera.*

Elizabeth Wichmann-Walczak

Music and Musical Instruments: India

Sanskrit Theatre. Music and **dance** are two vitally important ornamentations (*angahara*) of **Sanskrit theatre** as prescribed by the ancient *Treatise on Drama* (Natyashastra; see Theory), which devotes six chapters to theatre music. According to its rules, an ensemble consisting of at least seven performers enriches theatre's ceremonial prologues.

The *Natyashastra* says the human body itself is a musical instrument (*sareera veena*). It identifies four other kinds of instruments: stringed (*tata vadya*); covered (*avanaddha vadya*), including drums; solid (*ghana vadya*), such as bells or cymbals; and wind (*sushira vadya*), such as the flute. Two types of ensemble were considered appropriate for Sanskrit drama: *kutapa,* comprising a singer, his assistant, and players of melodic instruments, and *avanaddha varga*, providing rhythmic drum accompaniment.

Tamil literary works such as *The Story of the Anklet* (Silappadikaram) also classify instruments into five types: leather (*tole karuvi*); hollow (*tulai karuvi*); stringed (*narambu karuvi*); throat (*mitatru karuvi*), reminiscent of the *sareera veena* concept; and brass (*kancha karuvi*). It is difficult to say whether the *Natyashastra* influenced *The Story of the Anklet* or the other way round, since the antiquity of both texts can be traced back to almost the same period.

Hindustani and Carnatic Music. The Hindustani (North India) and the Carnatic (South India; the term derives from Karnataka) schools of music provide the two dominant styles prevalent in classical, **folk**, and ritualistic theatre and dance forms. The distinction between Hindustani and Carnatic music was first described in the fourteenth century. Unlike Hindustani music, which includes many styles and instruments, Carnatic is unified, and all its schools employ the same body of around three hundred classical modes (*raga*s), as well as the same instruments for melody, a string instrument (*veena*), flute, violin, double-sided drum (*mridangam*), and pot drum (*ghatam*). The best-known Hindustani instruments are those associated with classical music. These include the *sitar*, a string instrument, and the *tabla*, a percussion instrument; also common are the lute-like *sarod* and the *sarangi*, a bowed string instrument. Hindustani music uses about nine specific rhythms (*tala*s), while Carnatic music most often uses three, although it can utilize up to thirty-five.

Classical music is intimately tied to the lyrics of the poems it accompanies; expressive song is inseparable from theatre, and many methods of singing have developed. Carnatic lyrics usually emphasize devotional subjects, but romantic and socially oriented lyrics are known. ***Kutiyattam*** music, however, is not homogenous in either style or rendering with either of the schools mentioned above. It intends to evoke the dominant quality of a particular emotion (*rasa*) and closely resembles the Vedic chanting (*ottu chollal*) of Kerala. *Kutiyattam* music generally uses the pot drum (*mizhavu*), hour-glass-shaped drum (*idakka*), and a pair of cymbals (*talam*). The music of ritualistic Keralan folk forms like ***teyyam*** does not follow Carnatic rules, but that of Kerala's *sopana* tradition. ***Kathakali***, however, blends the Carnatic style with *sopana*, a slow-tempo, devotional style whose name refers to the temple's sacred space, and which developed out of local Vedic, folk, and tribal music.

Yakshagana, Karnataka's dance-drama, follows the Carnatic school and employs nearly 150 *raga*s, including rich blends of Carnatic, Hindustani, and pure Kannada music. Instrumentation uses the percussion instruments of *chende*, *mrdudanga*, and *maddale*, gong and finger cymbals, the flute-like *mukhaveena*, and the harmonium, although which instruments are used varies regionally. The singer (*bhagavatar*) also plays the finger cymbals and recites. Dance-dramas such as ***kuchipudi*** and ***bhagavata mela***, dance forms like ***bharata natyam***, and street theatre forms, like ***terukkuttu*** all follow Carnatic style. The *kuchipudi* and *bharata natyam* ensemble includes a conductor (*nattuvanar*), who also plays cymbals and recites rhythmic syllables (*jati*), a player of the horizontal drum (*mridangam*), a violinist, and a flautist.

The theatres of various northeastern states have exhibited a variety of musical traditions since the classical period by Hindu, Muslim, and Buddhist communities. *Lasya* styles, for instance, which appear in the Krishna theatre of Manipur, are characterized by a mellifluous flow that complements a sinuous and graceful dance style. The *tandava* music of **ankiya nat**, a theatre with both Hindu and Muslim branches, on the other hand, is driven by intense drumming and chanting.

Chhau, **nautanki**, **jatra**, **raslila**, and **ramlila** follow Hindustani style; instruments used include the drums called *nagara*, *dholak*, *dhamsa*, and *dhol*, and a wind instrument (*shehnai*). The dance and theatre of Himachal Pradesh shows the influence of Buddhism, whereas folk songs (*ruf*) are prevalent in Jammu and Kashmir. **Bhaand pather** is their folk theatre, and the musical instruments used in its performance are a wind instrument (*surni*), a frame drum, and a *dholak* drum. *See also* Music and Musical Instruments: South Asia.

FURTHER READING

Arnold, Alison, ed. *South Asia, the Indian Subcontinent*. Vol. 5. *Garland Encyclopedia of World Music*.

Arya Madhavan

Music and Musical Instruments: Indonesia

Music is essential to all traditional **Indonesian** theatre, and it is common for **actors**, **puppeteers**, and **dancers** to be expert vocalists and instrumentalists.

Gamelan. A variety of bells, drums, cymbals, lutes, trumpets, and shawms accompanied **dance** and other theatrical performances in ancient Java. The ubiquitous *gamelan* ensemble, found in many variants in Java, Bali, Madura, Lombok, Kalimantan, and elsewhere in Indonesia and **Malaysia**, developed after 1500. *Gamelan* (*gambelan* in Bali) refers both to a set of instruments as well as a form of music. *Gamelan* come in a variety of tunings, many of them using a pentatonic scale. Before the twentieth century, each *gamelan* had its own unique tuning, but standardization has crept in due to the mass media. Most *gamelan* instruments are percussion—gongs, kettle drums, and xylophones—made from bronze, brass, or iron, arrayed on wooden stands and casings that are sometimes elaborately decorated with carved and painted demon heads and dragons. One or two flutes, a fiddle, and other instruments can be added. Typically, a double-headed drum conducts and provides rhythmic sound effects to underline an **actor** or *wayang* **puppet**'s movement.

Many *gamelan* pieces have circular structures and can be repeated ad infinitum, facilitating accompaniment of dramatic scenes of flexible length. Music in puppet and related theatres is nearly continuous, played loudly during battle scenes, softly during dialogues. While a number of notation systems have been developed since the 1850s, in general, music is not written down, but learned by ear. Some instrumental parts are fixed, but others can improvise around a nuclear melody. Polyphony and complex interlocking patterns prevail over harmony.

In the past, each theatrical or dance genre was associated with one type of ensemble. For example, in Central Java, *wayang kulit purwa* was also played with *gamelan slendro* (with its five-tone scale), never with *gamelan pelog* (with its seven-tone scale), while Bali's *wayang kulit* was always accompanied by a pair or quartet of *gender wayang* (xylophone-like instruments played with two mallets). Such correspondence was always notional, never absolute. It is now the norm to see *wayang kulit* in Central Java accompanied by a so-called double *gamelan* made up of one *gamelan slendro* and one *gamelan pelog*, while Balinese puppeteers sometimes call upon a full-scale *gamelan* to accompany their performances. **Western** instruments, including drum kits and synthesizers, are commonly added to "traditional" *gamelan* and other ensembles.

Gamelan has inspired a host of non-Indonesian composers, including Claude Debussy, John Cage, Lou Harrison, and Steve Reich. Javanese and Balinese *gamelan* is now played in more than twenty countries, and integrated into music, dance, and theatre featuring both Indonesians and non-Indonesians. This is connected to the demand of ethnomusicologist Mantle Hood for academic students of foreign musics to study how to play instruments and aspire to bimusicality. Since the 1970s, many have traveled to Indonesia to study traditional music (and other arts), and Javanese and Balinese musicians (also often dancers or puppeteers) frequently teach in universities outside Indonesia.

Vocal Music. Vocal music also has a prominent place in theatre. Java, Bali, and other islands of the western part of the Indonesian archipelago under **India**'s influence possess **Sanskritic** poetic systems in which different verse types are associated with different melodies. Sung verse of this type is generally called *tembang*. *Tembang* is the primary expressive vehicle for pre-modern literature: nearly all knowledge traditionally deemed worthy of preservation, from eschatology to sexual positions, was cast in this form. *Tembang* are quoted and sung with or without accompaniment in many theatrical forms. Knowledge of *tembang* and a good singing voice are essential for Balinese **arja** and Javanese **ludruk** actors; all puppeteers are required not only to recite dialogue but also to sing *tembang* and archaic poetry (*kawi*).

Modern Music. Sumatran theatre derives many of its songs from oral literature and its accompaniment from **folk** and ceremonial music. ***Randai***, for example, combines musical features of *kaba*, a bardic form accompanied by spiked fiddle or a box of matches tapped on the floor, with *talempong*, a *gamelan*-like ensemble in which kettle drums are prominent.

Music from the Arabian peninsula, including frame drums, tambourines, shawms, spiked fiddles, and vocal styles associated with Quranic recitation, entered the archipelago with Islam and was incorporated into western Indonesian drama, dance, and **storytelling** by the seventeenth century. In areas of Java, Sumatra, and Kalimantan with many **Chinese**, traditional Chinese instruments not only accompanied *xiqu*, they also hybridized with *gamelan* instruments in **lenong** and related theatres during the late nineteenth and early twentieth centuries. This coincided in Sumatra with the spread of melodies and rhythms from South Asia, a reflex of the popularity of **Parsi theatre**, and its Malay offspring, ***bangsawan***. Popular theatre in the west coast of Sumatra ca. 1885 was accompanied by a hybrid ensemble of violins, zither (*kecapi*), tambourines (*rebana*), and drums playing a mélange of Malay, Parsi, and European melodies. Starting with ***komedi stambul***, guitar, piano, and other European instruments, along with Western harmonies and pop songs, have featured in much traditional and modern theatre.

The names of those who created music for the traditional theatre before the twentieth century are largely forgotten, and until today many compositions for *gamelan* and other traditional ensembles are anonymous. One of the first well-known theatre composers was *komedi stambul*'s **Auguste Mahieu**. In the 1940s, the famous *keroncong* musician and composer Gesang Martohartono (1917–) worked as musical director for the itinerant **sandiwara** troupe Surabaya Star (Bintang Surabaya), composing and adapting some of his best-known songs for it. Nartosabdho (1925–1985), Java's best-known puppeteer in the 1970s and early 1980s, began his career as a musician, and bequeathed hundreds of songs as his legacy. Composers who have integrated **experimental** and traditional music into their work for contemporary theatre include Rahayu Supanggah (1949–), Harry Roesli (1951–2004), Embi C. Noer (1955–), and Tony Prabowo (1956–).

FURTHER READING

Miller, Terry E., and Sean Williams, eds. *Southeast Asia.* Vol. 4. *Garland Encyclopedia of World Music.*

Matthew Isaac Cohen

Music and Musical Instruments: Japan

Traditional music in **Japan** shares several major characteristics with other Asian countries. Excepting court music (*gagaku*; see *Bugaku*), traditional music is monophonic, focusing on subtleties of tone, timbre, and rhythm rather than harmony. Further, since the range of traditional instruments is limited to plucked strings, bamboo wind instruments, and various-sized barrel and hour-glass drums, the range of timbre is narrow, resulting in instruments with highly refined subtleties. Melody is based upon the twelve-tone, unequal-tempered scale, within which are three types of scales: two five-tone scales, used in *koto*, *shamisen*, and various **folk** musics; a seven-tone scale, used in *gagaku*; and a tone system based on the tetrachord, used in Buddhist *shōmyō* chanting and *nō*.

Nō *and* Kyōgen Music. Beginning in the late twelfth century, the *biwa*, a four-stringed lute plucked with a large plectrum, began to be used by blind musicians to accompany ballads of the warriors of the Heike and Genji clans, marking the beginning of a musical **storytelling** tradition called *heikyoku*. This was important in *nō*'s development in the fourteenth century, and in *jōruri* (see *Bunraku*) in the fifteenth. *Nō* is a narrative musical **dance**-drama, with music made up of singing (*utai*) by one or more characters or a chorus of six to ten, and an instrumental ensemble (*hayashi*) consisting of a seven-holed transverse bamboo flute (*nōkan*), and three percussion instruments: a shoulder drum (*kotsuzumi*), hip drum (*ōtsuzumi* or *ōkawa*), and stick drum (*taiko*). The first two are used in all plays; the third in about half. The flute plays melodies independent of the vocal line, but fitting into the rhythmic patterns of the drums.

The tone system of *nō*, influenced by Buddhist *shōmyō* chanting, is constructed around three main nuclear tones: high, middle, and low, each separated by an interval of a perfect fourth, with additional important tones a perfect fifth above the high tone and another a perfect fourth below the low tone. In this highly structured music, based on an eight-beat rhythm, the chanted text is matched to the instrumental music in one of several rhythmic modes, and delivered in one of three basic vocal styles: a heightened stylized speech (*kotoba*), a strong pulsing dynamic style (*tsuyogin*), or a gentler melodic style (*yowagin*). Music may be purely instrumental, pure chant, or chant accompanied by the ensemble.

Costumed in black formal kimono (*montsuki*) and skirt-trousers (*hakama*), musicians enter via the "bridgeway" (*hashigakari*) and sit in a line upstage center, forming part of the *mise en scène*. Their prescribed order from **stage** left to right is: flute, shoulder drum, hip drum, and stick drum (when used). Like *nô* actors, musicians belong to one of several schools (*ryû*).

Kyôgen emphasizes the spoken word, although it incorporates a number of "short songs" (*kouta*) within plays. *Kouta* utilize either the gentle melodic or strong dynamic style of singing used in *nô*. Most are sung acapella, but when accompanied use the same instruments and musicians as the *nô* ensemble.

Bunraku *and* Kabuki *Music*. The *shamisen,* a percussive three-stringed banjo-like lute descended from **China**'s *sanxian,* arrived via the Ryûkyû Islands (Okinawa) around 1562, and was adopted by *biwa* balladeers. Throughout the Edo period (1603–1868), various *shamisen* genres arose, most originating with some charismatic artist after whom the genre was named. *Gidayû bushi,* used in *ningyô jôruri* (later, *bunraku*) and developed by chanter (*tayû*) **Takemoto Gidayû**, is a highly sophisticated narrative tradition using the thick-necked (*futozao*) bass *shamisen*. Music combines fixed melodic patterns for such things as act beginnings and endings, exits of major characters, expressing intense emotions, and various musical cadences, with longer nonpatterned melodies specific to a piece of text. Vocal delivery ranges from unaccompanied speech (*kotoba*), to more lyrical first- and third-person passages (*ji* or *jiai*), and highly melismatic phrases (*fushi*), both accompanied by *shamisen*.

A single chanter provides all character voices and descriptive passages, while the *shamisen* provides accents, musical decoration for the chant, and emotional punctuation; guides movement; and controls tension. Travel (*michiyuki*) and dance scenes (*keiji* or *keigoto*) use larger ensembles of four to eight. Except in minor scenes, musicians sit on a separate side stage (*yuka*) downstage left, in full audience view. When used in *kabuki* for plays adapted from *bunraku* or newly written plays and dances, *gidayû* is usually called *takemoto* and contains little *kotoba*, since actors deliver most dialogue.

Lyrical *nagauta* (literally, "long song") is a much lighter, melodious sound, played on a thin-necked *shamisen* (*hosozao*). Developed over several decades from existing *kouta* and *jiuta* (literally, "songs of the place") traditions, it is used in onstage ensembles (*debayashi*) to accompany dance, and offstage to provide an essential aural dimension. Offstage ensembles—performing in the stage right *geza* room, viewing the action through blinds—consist of an eclectic percussive ensemble (*hayashi*) of various drums, flutes, gongs, bells and whistles, along with *shamisen* and voice. Music is used to establish mood, place, and status; heighten tension; suspend time in emotional peaks; underscore dialogue; provide sound effects; and more. Onstage ensembles consist of *shamisen*, voice, flute, and the three drums of the *nô* ensemble.

Musical-Narrative Form. In contrast to lyrical *nagauta*, which emphasizes melody, rhythm, and poetic wordplay, narrative genres emphasize the chanted word, its rhythms, and story. Beginning in the mid-eighteenth century, several narrative genres developed from *bungo-bushi*, banned in 1739 by the shogunate for its eroticism and immorality. *Tokiwazu-bushi* (1747), with its strong clear sound, serious tone, and wide vocal range, features some of the classic dance-dramas, such as *The Barrier Gate* (Seki no To, 1784).

A later descendent of *tokiwazu* is *kiyomoto-bushi* (1818), more sensuous with its elaborately ornamented melodic lines and high tones. Both use a medium-necked (*chûzao*) *shamisen*. While numerous other genres developed, many died out or are heard only in concerts today. Each is distinguished by subtle differences in timbre achieved by varying physical aspects of the *shamisen*, such as body size, neck and string thickness, bridge height, or plectrum size and attack, and by stereotypical instrumental and vocal patterns.

FURTHER READING

Malm, William A. *Japanese Music and Musical Instruments*; Malm, William A. *Nagauta: The Heart of Kabuki Music.*

Julie A. Iezzi

Music and Musical Instruments: Korea

Most forms of **Korean** theatre involve music, and a particular form can be a genre's defining characteristic. **Western**-based theatres, such as classical opera and translated musicals, follow international practices, as does the background music in spoken theatre, but the indigenous genres often show distinctive forms and uses. Indeed, theatrical performance can sometimes appear as an accessory to music rather than the reverse.

Nongak. Such is the case with the farmers' percussion bands (*nongak* or *p'ungmul*), which use large and small gongs, two or three types of drum, and sometimes a strident double-reed instrument (*t'aep'yŏngso*). In entertainment contexts (as opposed to work or ritual), these bands were traditionally accompanied by a *chapsaek*, literally, a "motley crew" of **actors** costumed to represent **role types** such as the hunter, monk, shaman, maiden, and aristocrat. The *chapsaek* would **dance** and interact humorously with onlookers while the band played, and when it rested, they would improvise comic skits around familiar situations, sometimes incorporating songs and dances. More recently, rhythms derived from *nongak* have again been given a theatrical treatment in the popular nonverbal comedy production *Nant'a*, running continuously in Seoul since its international success at the Edinburgh Arts Festival in 1999.

T'alch'um. Some of the musical features of *nongak*, as well as the types impersonated by the *chapsaek*, recur in **t'alch'um**. Here, the music is extemporized by a flexible ensemble of instruments typically including the transverse flute (*taegŭm*), the cylindrical oboe (*p'iri*), and the two-string fiddle (*haegŭm*), as well as the drums and gongs of the farmers' bands. The actors both speak and sing, and the musical style used is essentially that of the local **folk** music. The athletic dance of *t'alch'um* is accompanied by an energetic rhythm used in much Korean music, a twelve-beat pattern with a syncopated accent on the ninth beat.

Kkoktu kakshi. Instruments derived from the farmers' bands also accompany **puppet** plays (*kkoktu kakshi*). The music for these is largely improvised from melodic and rhythmic materials shared with *t'alch'um* and the folk culture generally, and the dances and other puppet movements are often precisely coordinated with the instrumental sounds. In addition, the band provides overtures to each scene, changes of tempo and mood, and respite between bursts of action; one of the musicians often engages in commentary and conversations with the puppets.

P'ansori. More elaborate music has developed for the **storytelling** genre *p'ansori*, in which a distinctive husky singing voice is accompanied by a small barrel drum (*puk*). Sung passages are structured by a set of melodic modes (*cho*) and rhythmic cycles (*changdan*) which can be used in various combinations. Each melodic mode has certain emotional and symbolic connotations, associated with certain kinds of situations and characters, but these associations may vary depending on the rhythmic cycle. For instance, the most common mode, *kyemyŏnjo* (somewhat akin to a Western minor or "blues" scale), connotes extreme sadness when sung to the slow *chinyangjo* cycle, but can be lively and humorous when sung to the brisk *hwimori* cycle. As this example implies, each rhythmic cycle has an associated tempo range as well as a recurring pattern of beats (usually in groups of three beats, or two when the tempo is fast).

Ch'anggŭk *and* **Yŏsŏng kukkŭk.** *P'ansori*'s musical style is also used in the opera form *ch'anggŭk* and its all-female variant *yŏsŏng kukkŭk*. However, as these have expanded in scale, they have adopted other forms of traditional music and instruments as well, while their singing has often been regarded as a lighter and simpler form of *p'ansori*. Their accompaniments to recitative-like solo singing are still often extemporized, shadowing the vocal line, though more regularly structured passages may be memorized and played in unison or in a fixed arrangement. To varying degrees, *ch'anggŭk* and *yŏsŏng kukkŭk* productions since the 1970s have adopted Western practices such as staff notation, harmony and counterpoint, synthesizers, and the use of a conductor. This trend has been taken still further in the comedic *madangnori* form.

North Korea. In **North Korea**, socialist aesthetics has not favored traditional music in theatre, rejecting *p'ansori* and its derivatives for making the words difficult to understand. Instead, the preferred model has been "*Sea-of-Blood*-style opera" (*P'ibada-sik kagŭk*), a variant of revolutionary opera using simple strophic songs in the language of everyday speech.

FURTHER READING

Cultural Properties Administration. *Korean Intangible Cultural Properties: Traditional Music and Dance;* Howard, Keith. *Korean Musical Instruments*; Lee, Byong Won. *Styles and Esthetics in Korean Traditional Music.*

Andrew Killick

Music and Musical Instruments: Nepal. *See* Music: South Asia

Music and Musical Instruments: Pakistan. *See* Music: South Asia

Music and Musical Instruments: South Asia

Bangladesh, Bhutan, Pakistan, Nepal, and Sri Lanka. The theatre and music traditions of **Bangladesh** and **Pakistan** maintain an affinity with **Indian** traditions. Pakistan and

India shared the same cultural history until the recent past, and Bangladesh's theatre traditions borrow from West Bengal's culture. Pakistan's music tradition is closely related to the Hindustani style whereas *jatra* is a favorite entertainment of rural Bangladesh. **Nepalese** and **Bhutanese** forms confirm their strong allegiance to Buddhist musical traditions.

The musical tradition of **Sri Lanka** incorporates the traits found in Theravada Buddhist musical forms, the typical three-tone scale style of chanting of the Hindu Vedic music, and even the Afro-Iberian genre known in Sri Lanka as *baila*.

FURTHER READING

Arnold, Alison, ed. *South Asia, the Indian Subcontinent.* Vol. 5. *Garland Encyclopedia of World Music.*

Arya Madhavan

Music and Musical Instruments: Sri Lanka. *See* Music: South Asia

Music and Musical Instruments: Vietnam

Music is integral to **Vietnamese** traditional theatre. *Ca tru* sung poetry appeared in the ancient capital, Thang Long. Early instruments (mortar/pestle, bronze drums/gongs, copper bells, and *khen* [panpipes]) date to 1000 BC.

Sung courting poem competitions (*quan ho*) featured alternating male and female voices, and contributed to rural and royal drama. Blind minstrels sang epic songs. **Folk theatres** of the central coast (Khmer *bai choi*, *du ke*) and Cham opera influenced Hue's dynastic music. Courtesans with three-stringed lutes (*dan day*) entertained mandarins.

Cheo, inspired by folk music of Bac Ninh, dating to 100 AD, became a complex musical theatre. *Cheo* melodies connote particular characters or dramatic actions, utilizing sophisticated vocal combinations, including "metal" (*kim*), "earth" (*tho*), and "copper" (*dong*) voices. *Cheo* singers lead performances, accompanied by percussion (drums [*trong*], slit drum [*mo*], clackers [*phach*], and gong [*dong la*]); wind instruments (clay [*sao trung co*], gourd [*pan*], and bamboo flute [*sao*]); and string instruments (moon lute [*dan nguyet*], two-string fiddles [*dan nhi* and *dan gao*], and zither [*dan tam thap luc*]).

In *tuong*, the orchestra leads the action, using several drum types (*trong cau*, *trong com*, and *trong chien*), clackers, slit drum, two-string violin (*don co*), three-string lute (*dam tam*), flutes, reed instruments (*cay ken*), gong, and cymbals (*chap choa*). The *trong chau* drum—found also in *cheo*—is downstage, allowing audiences to critique the show by playing it during performances.

Cai luong, emerging in 1920 and known for the tune "Remembrances" (*Vong co*), combines **Western** and Vietnamese influences. Instruments include a zither (*don tranh*), violin (*don co*), moon lute, clackers, drums, cymbals, gongs, electric guitar, and other Western instruments.

FURTHER READING

Miller, Terry E., and Sean Williams, eds. *Southeast Asia.* Vol. 4. *Garland Encyclopedia of World Music.*

Kathy Foley and Lorelle Browning

MUSTAPHA KAMIL YASSIN (1925–). Malaysian [•] playwright and scholar, a.k.a. Kala Dewata, one of the first formally educated in the field of drama, who received his graduate degrees from Indiana University. As a scholar, Mustapha is credited for his work on *bangsawan*. But he is best known as a realistic playwright, having advocated realism over the theatricalism of *bangsawan* and *sandiwara*.

Scholars consider Mustapha's *Tiled Roof, Thatched Roof* (Atap genting, atap rembia, 1963) to have pioneered Malaysia's realistic theatre. This form, featuring a dichotomy between poor, rural and rich, urban characters, and set in a naturalistic environment (such as a living room), was much emulated by others until the **experimental** decade of the 1970s. Also noteworthy is *Two Three Cats A–running* (Dua tiga kuching berlari, 1966), which portrays a relationship between a **Chinese** man named Kuan and a Malay woman. To the woman's Malay family, all Chinese are communists; therefore, the relationship is doomed from the start. Kuan proves that he is not only a patriotic citizen of Malaya, but willing to convert to and embrace Islam, in spite of his family's disapproval. Kuan represents a nationalistic ideal, and dies defending his country. Among other works is *Behind the Curtain of Hope* (Di balik tabir harapan, 1960).

Solehah Ishak

MUTHUSWAMI, NATESAN (1936–). Indian Tamil-language **playwright** and **director**, born in Punjai, a village in Tamilnadu. He moved to Madras (Chennai) in the late 1950s and worked as a clerk. Urban life compelled him to write short stories about the relatively innocent and genuine nature of village life. He developed his own theatre style working closely with *terukkuttu* [•] **folk theatre**, incorporating its concepts and performance tools. His *Time after Time* (Kalam kalamaha, 1969) is considered the first modern Tamil play. In 1977, he founded Theatre Workshop (Koothu-P-Pattarai), a prominent Tamilnadu **experimental** [•] **theatre company** that produced all his subsequent works: *Chair Possessor* (Narkalikkarar, 1974), *Wall Posters* (Suvarottikal, 1986), *England* (Inkilantu, 1989), and *Tenali Raman* (1999), named for a court jester at the court of Krishna Devaraya of Andhra. He used *terukkuttu* to adapt plays from **Bhasa** and the *Mahabharata*, as well as to create plays on social issues such as AIDS.

His plays combine linear narrative and conversational logic to create a highly dramatic and poetic language dependent on visual expression derived from choreographic movement accompanied by stylized speech. Continuous and intensive practical work in creatively combining tradition and modernity helped him develop an approach rooted in traditional forms. His interest in tradition has encouraged him to establish a new visual culture for modern Tamil theatre. He also developed a new **actor** [•] **training** system and production method investigating the possibilities of a theatre language flavored by Tamil culture.

B. Ananthakrishnan

MYANMAR. *See* Burma.

NACHA. Indian • **folk theatre** of Chhattisgarh, also spelled *nachya*, in which **dance** (*nacha*) predominates. It gained recognition when it became a major stimulus for the "theatre of roots" work of **Habib Tanvir**. It is an all-night, all-male, improvisational affair, using **music** and acrobatics. **Costumes** are everyday wear, and the **stage** is any open space, with a place for the musicians; the audience surrounds the site. Torches have given way to electric lighting. Dramatic action is provided by sketches based on the experiences of the farm-worker performers, and often contains satirical commentary on socially sensitive themes like the untouchable caste, widowhood, and child marriage. The **actors** all possess music, acting, and dancing skills. Specialized **role types** are the beautiful, delicate, female fairy (*pari*), and the inventive clown (*jokkar*, from "joker").

Tanvir discovered the form during a 1972 workshop, while engaged in **experimenting** with various indigenous forms and employing the services of rural performers using their native tongue. During the workshop, Tanvir developed a performance based on three improvised sketches, to which songs were added, creating what was essentially an improvised musical play. The piece enjoyed success and led to Tanvir's continued exploration of *nacha*. However, his actors are professionals, and he uses full casts, not the two or three of authentic *nacha*. The plays he stages are far more sophisticated than *nacha* sketches, and the songs and dances, which are essentially decorative in *nacha*, play a more integral role in the dramatic action.

FURTHER READING

Varadpande, M. L. *History of Indian Theatre: Loka Ranga; Panorama of Indian Folk Theatre.*

Samuel L. Leiter

NADAGAM. Sri Lankan • **folk theatre** established around the end of the eighteenth century. While the two other principal folk theatres, ***kolam*** and ***sokari***, are of Sinhalese origins, *nadagam*'s roots are believed to have been Tamil; the term is from the Tamil *natakam* ("drama"), derived from the **Sanskrit** *nataka*. However, the form—also spelled *nadagama*—is often claimed to have been created by Roman Catholic missionaries who combined elements of South **India**'s Tamil ***terukkuttu*** (and Carnatic **music**) in order to spread their **religious** gospel among the Sinhalese. One scholar, though, links the origins to *terukkuttu* brought by South Indian migrant tradesmen of the twelfth to fifteenth centuries, while another argues for the origins to have been in poetic dramas dated to the thirteenth century.

Nadagam evolved on the western and southern coasts as an extremely popular secular musical form whose sung-through performance, using only bits of intoned spoken dialogue between songs, led to its being called "operatic." Despite its Christian background, it depends on fictional romantic stories free from standard myths and legends, a first in Sinhalese theatre.

Physically, it is more sophisticated than other local forms, using a temporary **theatre** structure consisting of a semicircular, raised, earthen **stage** roofed with palm leaves, but devoid of **curtains**; a painted backdrop separates the **acting** area from backstage. Audiences, once admitted free, pay a small fee and sit on the ground. On stage is the musical ensemble, a "presenter" (*pote gura*), and a two-man chorus. Like *kolam* and *sokari*, it is an all-night show (formerly given over five nights), lit by torches. It begins with an invocation to the deities, followed by the presenter narrating the evening's story, and explaining its time and place. Then, starting with the clown, he introduces a succession of stock **role types** described in sung verse by the presenter; each demonstrates their unique characteristics in dance and song, although they are not **masked**. They include a learned man and a pair of fortune tellers who discuss the ensuing story. Court drummers announce the king's arrival, criers prepare his way, court characters appear, and the long, complex play begins. **Costumes** are eye-catching, with reflective bits and pieces. All roles are played by men.

These are tales of love and intrigue—with printed scripts—peopled by colorful, romantic, royal characters, including foreigners, and spoken in Sinhalese sprinkled with Tamil (suggesting the presence of a Tamil audience) and esoteric words. Plays often contain violence, including murders and kidnappings; the action covers intrigues concerned with the overthrow of usurping tyrants, the demolishing of obstacles to true love, and so forth.

A presumed Catholic blacksmith of Colombo named Phillipu Singho (or Sinno, 1770–1840?) is claimed by many to have written the first *nadagam*, *The Sinhaley Nadagam* (Simhale nadagame, ca. 1824; publ. 1870), about the last Sinhalese king's surrender to the British in 1815; he wrote thirteen works and is called the "father" of the form. However, another theory holds that the first play was by M. S. Gabriel Fernando, and that it was *Raja Tunkattuwa* (1761), based on Christ's nativity; later versions became regular attractions at Christmas. If *nadagam* was actually a much earlier form, as some claim, such plays were merely their first written expression.

Affected by the popularity of movies, *nadagam* practically disappeared by the 1950s, but still can be found in certain rural areas. It influenced the burgeoning *nurti* and played an influential role in Sri Lankan **puppet** performances.

FURTHER READING

Sarachchandra, E. R. *The Folk Drama of Ceylon*.

Samuel L. Leiter

NADEEM, SHAHID (1947–).

Pakistani • playwright, journalist, television writer-**director**-producer, and social activist, born in Sopore, Kashmir. Nadeem's opposition to Pakistan's military government led to three imprisonments; from 1979 to 1988, he lived in London in self-imposed exile. He also worked for Amnesty International. In 1997, he was banned from Pakistani television production (see Censorship).

In 2001, he studied and wrote in the United States on a Villa Aurora Feuchtwanger Fellowship, presented to **politically** oppressed writers.

In London, Nadeem met **actress**-director Madeeha Gauhar (1956–), founder in 1980 of an alternative theatre in Lahore, Dawn of a New Day (Ajoka). They married and developed Dawn of a New Day into a highly professional, determinedly non-commercial, **theatre company**. In 1987, it presented his **women**'s rights drama *The Acquittal* (Barri). Nadeem returned to Pakistan in 1988. Like his television work, his over forty plays—written mainly in Punjabi—focus on provocative themes, such as the encouragement of Pakistani-**Indian** friendship, **religious** fundamentalism, over-population, and women's rights. They include *Bala King* (1986), adapted from Brecht's *The Resistible Rise of Arturo Ui*; *Toba Tek Singh*, adapted from Saadat Hassan Manto's tale of an exchange of mentally ill Pakistanis and Indians; *Aik Thi Naani* (1993), the true story of two famous actress-sisters separated by Partition; the bilingual *Dukhini*, about sex trafficking between **Bangladesh** and Pakistan; and *Bulha!*, which preaches antifundamentalism through its depiction of seventeenth-century Sufi poet Bulleh Shah.

In July 2001, *The Acquittal* was presented at the LA International Arts **Festival**. Shortly after 9/11, Nadeem staged *The Third Knock* with an all-Muslim cast in California, even though its fate had been doubtful because of the terrorist attack. Soon after, *Trapped*, inspired by 9/11, was given a staged reading in California.

Vibha Sharma

NAGAI AI (1951–). Japanese • **playwright, actress**, and **director**. Although she received a college degree in acting, Nagai was dissatisfied with the opportunities in her first troupe, so she and Ôishi Shizuka (1951–) formed the Two Rabbits Company (Nitosha) in 1981 to develop their own plays. Their first efforts, such as her *Kazuo* (1984), were hugely popular, two-actress, quick-change plays, with each actress playing multiple roles.

Nagai's plays, evincing the influence of Chekhov and Stanislavski, are often witty comedies of manners depicting postwar social issues—of customs, gender, and family—faced by common people in contemporary Japan, replete with psychological realism and her characteristically intriguing dialogue. She won the Agency for Cultural Affairs Grand Prize in Art, awarded for *Daddy's Democracy* (Papa no demokurashii, 1995). The second play in her trilogy on Japanese postwar life, it treats the confusion engendered by the sudden shift from militarism to democracy after World War II.

Major plays include *Time's Storeroom* (Toki no monooki, 1994), the first play in the trilogy, featuring lives unsettled during the early 1960s social ferment; the **Kishida [Kunio]** Prize–winning *Big Brother Returns* (Ani kaeru, 1999), a parody of **Kikuchi Kan**'s *Father Returns* (Chichi kaeru, 1917), comically depicting the dark side of Japanese family relations; *The Three Hagi Sisters* (Hagi-ke no san shimai, 2000), adapted from Chekhov's *Three Sisters*, casting new light on gender stereotypes in society; and *Hello, Mother* (Konnichiwa, kâsan, 2001), about corporate restructuring.

Yoshiko Fukushima

NAKAMURA GANJIRÔ. Line of **Japanese** • *kabuki* • **actors** known for excellence in the "gentle style" (*wagoto*) associated with Kyoto/Osaka (Kamigata) acting. The line's "house name" (*yagô*) is Narikomaya.

Ganjirô I (1860–1935), son of Nakamura Ganjaku III (1841–1881), was thought the handsomest actor of his time. His portrayals of romantic *wagoto* leads in the "gentle style" in **Chikamatsu Monzaemon**'s "domestic dramas" (*sewa mono*) were unsurpassed. His best roles included Kamiya Jihei in *The Love Suicides at Amijima* (Shinjû Ten no Amijima) and Chûbei in *The Courier for Hell* (Meido no hikyaku).

Ganjirô II (1902–1983), son of Ganjirô I, became Nakamura Senjaku I in 1941 and Ganjirô II in 1946. He played "female roles" (*onnagata*) opposite his father early in his career, also excelling at *wagoto*. He was one of the greatest Osaka actors of his time.

His son, Ganjirô III (1931–), debuted as Senjaku II in 1941, becoming Ganjirô III in 1990. Accomplished at *onnagata* as well as *wagoto* acting, he was designated a Living National Treasure (1994). In the early 1950s, his roles in "Takechi *kabuki*," produced by **director-critic** • **Takechi Tetsuji**, were pivotal in the revival of Kamigata *kabuki*. He is particularly noted for his interpretation of the courtesan Ohatsu in *Love Suicide at Sonezaki* (Sonezaki shinjû), which he has performed over one thousand times. In 1982, he formed the Chikamatsu Theatre (Chikamatsu-za), a **theatre company** specializing in revivals of Chikamatsu's plays written for **Sakata Tôjûrô** I. In December 2005, he became Tôjûrô IV, reviving the name after over 250 years.

Julie A. Iezzi

NAKAMURA KANZABURÔ. Line of eighteen generations of **Japanese** • *kabuki* • **actors** and actor-managers (*zamoto*), many of whom ran Edo's (Tokyo) Nakamura **Theatre** (Nakamura-za) from the seventeenth to the late nineteenth century. The family's current "house name" (*yagô*) is Nakamuraya. The name Kanzaburô was not officially given to any actors between 1850 and 1950, although actors who held other names were technically considered to be Kanzaburô XIV, XV, and XVI.

Kanzaburô I (1598–1658) began his career studying *kyôgen* acting, took the name Saruwaka (later Nakamura) Kanzaburô, and opened Edo's first permanent *kabuki* playhouse, the Saruwaka Theatre (Saruwaka-za), in 1624.

Kanzaburô II (1647–1674), son of Kanzaburô I, traveled around western Japan with his father after the Saruwaka Theatre burned in the Great Edo Fire of 1657. He acted and managed the family theatre—which he was the first to call the Nakamura Theatre—after his father's death.

Kanzaburô XVII (1909–1988)—the son of Nakamura Karoku III (1849–1919), brother of Nakamura Tokizô III (1895–1959) and **Nakamura Kichiemon** I (1886–1954), two of the era's top stars, and adopted son of **Onoe Kikugorô** VI—was first known as Nakamura Yonekichi III and Nakamura Moshiho IV; he became Kanzaburô in 1950. Famed for his ability to play both males and females, Kanzaburô XVII reportedly performed over eight hundred roles during his lifetime (placing him in *The Guinness Book of Records*), including *shin kabuki* plays and Shakespeare.

His son, Nakamura Kankurô V (1955–), became Kanzaburô XVIII in 2005. A charismatic and progressive performer, who sometimes produces *kabuki* in a tent that recreates the feeling of a nineteenth-century theatre, Kanzaburô XVIII has two sons,

Nakamura Kantarô II (1981–) and Nakamura Shichinosuke II (1983–), who often perform with him.

Holly A. Blumner

NAKAMURA KICHIEMON. Line of two **Japanese** • *kabuki* • **actors**. The line's "house name" (*yagô*) is Harimaya.

Kichiemon I (1886–1954) was the son of Nakamura Karoku III (1849–1919) and brother of two other greats, Nakamura Tokizô III (1895–1959) and **Nakamura Kanzaburô** XVII. Unusually, he retained the same **stage** name throughout his career. A star even as a child, he became actor-manager of a children's **theatre company** at fourteen. He and **Onoe Kikugorô** VI became popular rivals in the early twentieth century, especially after both were signed by the Ichimura **Theatre** (Ichimura-za) in 1908, where they created a "Kiku-Kichi golden age" lasting into the 1920s. He joined the Shôchiku Company, demonstrating his genius at playing heroes in "history plays" (*jidai mono*). In 1943 he created his own Kichiemon troupe. Although he was also outstanding in "domestic dramas" (*sewa mono*), he was not considered an outstanding **dancer**.

Kichiemon II (1944–), son of **Matsumoto Kôshirô** VIII and brother of Kôshirô IX, was the grandson of Kichiemon I. His earlier name was Matsumoto Mannosuke, and he became Kichiemon II in 1966. He was a teenage star, often acting with his brother. In 1960, he joined his father and brother in leaving Shôchiku for the rival Tôhô Company, considered a major act of rebellion, and often acted in commercial plays outside *kabuki*. Meanwhile, he and his brother headed a "study group" that produced *kabuki* and demonstrated their traditional acting talents. He is outstanding in manly heroic roles like those his grandfather and father played; he often performed in *shinpa* and *shin kabuki* as well. Like Kichiemon I, he is not known for his dancing. This tall, well-built actor, famed for his powerful voice, specializes in "male roles" (*tachiyaku*), but is excellent as the evil court lady Iwafuji in *Mirror Mountain: A Woman's Treasure of Loyalty* (Kagamiya kokyô no nishikie-e), in which he barely masks his masculinity. Kichiemon II's achievements include helping to revive performances at the nineteenth-century Kanamaru Theatre (Kanamaru-za) in Shikoku.

Samuel L. Leiter

NAKAMURA UTAEMON. Line of **Japanese** • *kabuki* • **actors** originating in Osaka. The family's "house names" (*yagô*) have included Kagaya, Yamatoya, and Narikomaya.

Utaemon I (1714–1791), son of a Kanazawa doctor, took his name at a provincial **theatre** in Ise, and moved to Kyoto in 1742. Going to Edo (Tokyo) in 1757 for four years, he attained great popularity before returning to Osaka. He was a "villain" (*kata-kiyaku*) **role type** specialist.

Utaemon III (1778–1838), was one of the first completely versatile actors (*kaneru yakusha*), able to portray both males and females, upright and evil characters. He excelled at quick-change **dances** (*henge mono*), portraying as many as nine roles in one piece. An Osaka native, he went to Edo in 1808, where he rivaled the local stars.

In 1831, the "actor critiques" (*yakusha hyôbanki;* see Criticism) gave him the unprecedented ranking "unequalled through all ages." He authored about twenty-five plays under the name Kanazawa Ryûgoku.

Utaemon IV (1796–1852), son of an Edo teahouse owner, was first adopted by dance master Fujima Kanjûrô I (?–1821) in 1807. In 1811, he apprenticed to Utaemon III, followed him to Osaka in 1812, and subsequently achieved popularity in both Osaka and Edo as a versatile master. He excelled as Kumagai in *Chronicle of the Battle of Ichinotani* (Ichinotani Futaba Gunki) and Ishikawa Goemon in *The Temple Gate and the Paulownia Crest* (Sanmon Gosan no Kiri).

Utaemon V (1865–1940) was the first "female impersonator" (*onnagata*) specialist in the line, though he continued performing important "male roles" (*tachiyaku*). Son of an Edo government official and adopted by Nakamura Shikan IV (1831–1899), he gained popularity as an *onnagata* while known as Nakamura Fukusuke IV. He became Shikan V in 1901 and Utaemon V in 1911. His most noted roles were Masaoka in *The Precious Incense and Autumn Flowers of Sendai* (Meiboku Senda Hagi) and Lady Yodo, featured in several *shin kabuki* plays.

Utaemon VI (1917–2001), son of Utaemon V, became Fukusuke VI in 1933, Shikan VI in 1941, and Utaemon VI in 1951. Internationally acclaimed, he was the most celebrated postwar *onnagata*. Designated a Living National Treasure in 1968, he performed more than five hundred roles before retiring in 1996. In addition to the roles of Masaoka and Lady Yodo, he was the only actor for nearly fifty years capable of portraying the courtesan Akoya in *Chronicle of the Defeat at Dan no Ura* (Dan no Ura Kabuto Gunki), a role requiring great **musical** prowess. His adopted sons are Nakamura Baigyoku IV (1946–) and Nakamura Kaishun II (1948–).

Julie A. Iezzi

NAMIKI SHÔZÔ (1730–1773). Japanese *bunraku* (see Puppet Theatre) and *kabuki* • **playwright** active in Osaka. First called Izumiya Shôzô, he became a disciple of playwright **Namiki Sôsuke** in 1750, and took the name Namiki Shôzô (possibly pronounced Shôza or Shôsa). After Sôsuke's death, he was the pre-eminent Osaka playwright, producing eighty to ninety plays.

He is credited for increasing *kabuki*'s dramatic qualities: his plays were famous for their grand and complicated plots, reflecting the influence of the puppet theatre. Many focused on "samurai family quarrels" (*oie sôdô*), while others treated "chivalrous townsmen" (*otokodate*) who championed the underdog in plays about commoners. Shôzô frequently teamed up with **actor** • **Nakamura Utaemon** I, for whom he created many large-scale "villains" (*katakiyaku*). His best-known play is *The Restoration of Vagabond Danshichi* (Yadonashi Danshichi shigure no karakasa, 1768).

While many of Shôzô's plays are no longer staged, he remains famous for his many contributions to **scenographic** techniques, including the revolving **stage** (*mawari butai*), trap-lifts (*seridashi*) for raising and lowering scenery, a wagon stage (*hiki dôgu*), and the *gandôgaeshi*, a device for turning over a large piece of scenery to reveal a new set. He also introduced real water as a stage **property**.

Katherine Saltzman-Li

NAMIKI SÔSUKE (1695–1751). Japanese *bunraku* (see Puppet Theatre) and *kabuki* • playwright. He took the name Namiki Sôsuke after early success at Osaka's Toyotake **Theatre** (Toyotake-za), where he apprenticed under Nishizawa Ippû (1665–1731), whom he succeeded. Although he began and ended his career at the Toyotake, he also wrote *kabuki* plays from late 1742 to 1745, and, for what may have been the most significant five years of his career (1745–1750), he wrote puppet plays for the Toyotake's rival, the Takemoto Theatre (Takemoto-za), writing as Namiki Senryû.

In collaboration with **Takeda Izumo** II and others, he produced *bunraku*'s three masterpieces, *Sugawara and the Secrets of Calligraphy* (Sugawara denju tenarai kagami, 1746), *Yoshitsune and the Thousand Cherry Trees* (Yoshitsune senbon zakura, 1747), and *The Treasury of Loyal Retainers* (Kanedehon chûshingura, 1748), among other classics. Returning to the Toyotake, Sôsuke (to which he reverted) produced his final masterpiece, the "Kumagai's Camp" (Kumagai Jinya) act of *Chronicle of the Battle of Ichinotani* (Ichinotani Futaba Gunki, 1751), incomplete at his death.

Katherine Saltzman-Li

NANG. *See* Puppet Theatre: Thailand.

NANG PRAMO THAI. *See* Puppet Theatre: Thailand.

NANG TALUNG. *See* Puppet Theatre: Thailand.

NANG YAI. *See* Puppet Theatre: Thailand.

NANXI. **Chinese** form, the earliest for which texts exist and also the first to have had a treatise devoted to it, **Xu Wei**'s *An Account of Southern Drama* (Nanci xulu, 1559). *Nanxi* ("southern play") is sometimes referred to as *xiwen* ("playtext"), *yongjia* **zaju** ("Yongjia variety show"), or *wenzhou zaju* ("Wenzhou variety show"). The origins of this forerunner of **chuanqi** and **kunqu** remain obscure because only around twenty texts (supplemented by fragments) have survived; what little was written about it during its heyday was soon forgotten. Its origins are placed in the southeastern city of Wenzhou; the earliest plays likely date from the late twelfth century.

Three pre-Ming dynasty (1368–1644) examples give some idea of *nanxi*'s amorphousness and lack of polish. *Prize Candidate Zhang Xie* (Zhang Xie zhuangyuan) is the longest, with fifty-three scenes (and about 170 arias); *Little Butcher Sun* (Xiao Sun tu) has twenty-one scenes and about 143 arias; and *Grandee's Son Takes the Wrong Career* (Huanmen zidi cuo lishen) has fourteen scenes and some fifty arias. Prologues range from one *ci* poem to more elaborate combinations of *ci* poetry and singing mixed with dialogue. Scenes lack discernible principles of organization, and their divisions are not clearly demarcated. **Musically**, **folk** songs mingle with *ci*, arias of different mode appear in the same scene, and there are no conventions as to who uses which song and when. Language tends toward the colloquial and even the vulgar. Plays begin with four lines giving the title and a synopsis. Of the seven **role types** (*sheng, dan, chou, jing, wai, tie,* and *mo*), the first four ("males," "females," "clowns," and "painted faces") could sing. *Nanxi* share many aria titles with Yuan *zaju,* but the music used to sing them was different as was the instrumental accompaniment, which consisted of percussion, woodwinds, and pear-shaped plucked lute (*pipa*).

Some early plots show an affinity with Northern Song (960–1126) *zaju,* which combined satire with humor and likely were a precursor of *nanxi.* Two lost works frequently mentioned in Ming sources (*Wang Kui* and *Zhao Chaste Maid* [Zhao Zhennü]) depicted men abandoning wives after passing the examinations and dying as a result; another (*Wang Huan*) tackled a **political** scandal and was **censored.** Two plays feature unsavory heroes (and, in *Little Butcher Sun,* an unsavory heroine as well). *Grandee's Son* has a love theme concerning an official's son who becomes infatuated with an **actress.** Thematically, the repertoire was diverse, reflecting influences from professional **storytelling.**

What distinguishes *nanxi* from *chuanqi* is the latter's formal sophistication, as exemplified by Gao Ming's (1305–1370) *The Lute* (Pipa ji), which marked a shift of *nanxi* style from simple colloquial to allusive literary, and of tone from crudely entertaining to morally earnest.

FURTHER READING

Żbikowski, Tadeusz. *Early Nan-hsi Plays of the Southern Sung Period.*

Catherine Swatek

NAQAL. North **Indian** • **folk theatre** found in villages in Punjab, Haranya, Uttar Pradesh, and Kashmir, and sometimes spelled *naqqal* or *nakkal,* Farsi for "to imitate." The primary aim of this all-male mixture of traditional speeches and improvisation, performed in Punjabi or Haranya Hindi and dating to the mid-nineteenth century, is to arouse laughter through repartee and clowning.

Troupes consist either of just two comic **actors** (known mainly as *bhaands* but also as *mirasis* [Muslim clowns] and *naqals*) or are larger **theatre companies** including **musicians,** singers, and **dancers.** During clown routines, laughs are garnered when one strikes the other's palm with a leather strap (*chomota*) at comic highpoints. The art of these sharp-tongued and often obscene clowns is passed on from father to son. They used to be like court jesters, employed in the halls of royalty, and were also hired by wealthy commoners, where they freely mocked their patrons. Such patronage has disappeared, and the form is therefore endangered.

The clowns mock the spectators through topical, often **politically** tinged, humor. A special skill is the ability to mimic animals and birds. For example, a performer could demonstrate how different dogs bark and how their behavior reflects who their masters—from singers to prostitutes—are. Skits are brief and deal with subjects like overbearing rich people, brides and fathers-in-law, thieves and policemen, soldiers and officers, and so on. Following the skits is a *swang* based on some legend or semi-historical tale whose words are sung, and which has comic sequences sprinkled through it.

Performances, which commence with a ritual invocation, are often seen at weddings and other celebrations, employing any available space, indoors or out, although most shows are out of doors. The small cast allows for actors to play multiple roles, with onstage **costume** changes visible to the audience. Males wear turbans and skirtlike lower garments (*tehemat*); females, who wear exaggerated feminine clothes and **makeup**, behave in outrageously bawdy ways.

FURTHER READING

Varadpande, M. L. *History of Indian Theatre: Loka Ranga; Panorama of Indian Folk Theatre.*

Samuel L. Leiter

NANGUAN. *See* Taiwan.

NARATHIP, PRINCE (1861–1931). Thai • playwright, director, nobleman, and popularizer of middle-class theatre. Also known as Krom Phra Narathip Prapanpong, he was half-brother of both King Chulalongkorn (Rama V, r. 1868–1910) and Prince Naris (1863–1947). Unlike Naris, who attempted to situate classical plays in realistic and naturalistic environments, Narathip emphasized romantic and exotic plots, scenes, and **costumes**. He helped to open up new possibilities by setting his productions in **Laos** (for *Phra Lao*), Chiangmai (for *Sao Kreur Fa*—adapted from *Madame Butterfly*), and Arabia (for *The Arabian Nights*). Filled with adventure and melodrama, his plays attracted the general public's interest.

Narathip's plays featured fresh choreography stemming from his mother, Chao Chommarnda Kien (consort to **Rama IV** and a leading **dancer** under Rama V), and new **musical** arrangements influenced by his wife, Mom Tuan (descended from a renowned musical family). Narathip initially wrote and staged patriotic historical plays and romances with Lakon Narumit, a private troupe he founded outside the court that eventually received royal patronage. This **theatre** at first received affluent and royal audiences, and performed for royals and dignitaries.

To revitalize flagging interest, Narathip **experimented** with plays having more adventurous characters and plots, especially those with highly emotional or tragic elements. These were performed not only at royal events but also for the public in **Western**-style venues.

Two innovative forms of *lakon* (see *Lakon ram*) sprang from Narathip's efforts. One is **lakon phan thang**, the other is **lakon rong,** which integrates features from operetta and Malay **bangsawan**, especially in its use of Western instrumentation and singing.

Pornrat Damrhung

NATH, RAJINDER (1934–). Indian Hindi-language **director**, born in Dalwal (now in **Pakistan**), but based in Delhi, where he received most of his education. Nath worked briefly at All India Radio in 1959, and was Lecturer or Reader in English at various Delhi University colleges (1961–1994), but his pioneering theatre work is associated with two groups, Abhiyan (1967), and the Shri Ram Centre Repertory Company, for which he was principal director during the 1980s.

Nath decided at the very beginning of his directing career (around 1968) that he would devote himself exclusively to new Indian plays, performed either in the original Hindi or in Hindi translation. He emerged as a leading interpreter not only of important Hindi **playwrights** such as **Mohan Rakesh** and **Dharamvir Bharati**, but of major playwrights in several other languages: Mohit Chattopadhyay (1934–), Debashish Majumdar, Manoj Mitra (1938–), and **Badal Sircar** (Bengali); **G. P. Deshpande**, C. T. Khanolkar (1930–1976), and **Vijay Tendulkar** (Marathi); **Chandrashekhar Kambar** and **Girish Karnad** (Kannada), and Madhu Rye (1942–) (Gujarati).

Nath's effort in making significant new plays available in a single target language has been crucial to the emergence of a post-independence canon. He has been recognized with a National Academy of Music, **Dance**, and Drama (Sangeet Natak Akademi) award for Best Director (1977), the Nandikar Award (1988), and travel fellowships from the Goethe Institute (Munich) and the JDR Third Fund (New York). From 1999–2003, Nath edited *Theatre India*, a major journal.

Aparna Dharwadker

NAUTANKI. North **Indian • folk theatre**, a relatively young form popular among rural audiences in Uttar Pradesh, Rajasthan, Punjab, and elsewhere. It is sometimes regarded as synonymous with folk theatres such as *bhagat, swang*, and *khyal*, with which it shares its history. In folk etymology, this name comes from a play about Princess Nautanki, romantically pursued by various suitors. *Nautanki* is particularly concerned with stories of romance and royalty. Although it has clear devotional elements, it is a secular theatre of popular entertainment dramatizing idealistic and conservative concepts of love, chivalry, heroism, and honor.

Historical Background. Nautanki may have its stylistic roots in the *ramlila* and *raslila* popular in northern India and with which it shares other features. If so, *nautanki*'s history reaches back into the sixteenth century. But today's form seems to have developed in the mid-nineteenth century alongside other distinctly popular entertainment, such as **Parsi theatre** and Urdu drama. Indeed, one of *nautanki*'s unique features is how it mixes Hindu and Muslim culture. Not only does it employ both Hindi and Urdu, but its subjects are drawn from Hindu and Islamic sources, and accompanying **music** combines styles drawn from different **religious** communities.

Two geographic regions produced important schools or affiliations (*akharas*). In the 1880s, a *khyal* poet named Indarman began composing dramas that became as popular in print as they were in performance. His successors, Chiranjilal and Natharam, organized a troupe famous throughout northern India by the turn of the century. After 1900, an affiliation developed in Kanpur, driven by social consciousness. By 1920, Sri Krishna Pahalvan (1891–1972) was the center of this *akhara*, producing plays critical of such things as child marriage and communal strife. Pahalvan participated in India's noncooperation movement by staging and publishing plays critical of the British colonialists, including *The Senseless Massacre* (Khune Nahak), about the killings of hundreds of Indians by British soldiers at Jallianwala Bagh in

1919. Besides his **political** activism, Pahalvan succeeded in introducing new **training** and performance methods.

Nautanki *Performance.* Troupes are nomadic, and performances typically take place in temporary circumstances, relying on spare theatrical trappings in favor of the **actors'** appeal. In the past, the space was in the round, with the performance itself occupying a slightly elevated **stage** playing to a large audience stretching out on all four sides. Performers required powerful voices, presence, and energy to project their words through the five- or six-hour productions. Recently, however, electronic amplification has become standard, and the space has followed the trend toward proscenium-style staging. Performances in locales such as village squares, in which architectural elements like balconies can be employed, are also known.

Scenographic pieces are uncommon, although proscenium staging employs painted backdrops. **Costumes** are uncomplicated, mixing modern and classical elements, and suggesting only a kind of ideal history; clowns enjoy considerable freedom to wear modern elements. *Nautanki* relies heavily on music and **dance**, which provide diversions from plots as much as mechanisms for playing them out.

Regional **festivals** are popular, since they provide ready-made audiences and circumstances amenable to *nautanki*'s happily bawdy and crass subject matter. In addition to stories of princes and princesses, noble bandits, and military heroes, plays involve prostitutes, beggars, drunks, and misers. In addition to reinforcing customary categories of nobility, servants, and villains, performances include a **director** figure (*ranga* or *kavi*), who interjects himself to provide narration. Plays also include a clown who interacts with the audience and provides humorous commentary on the action.

In the nineteenth century, all parts were played by males. Well into the 1940s, young **women** in love were played by boys. However, women have become accepted and even celebrated performers in *nautanki*. They first appeared in the 1920s, when *nautanki* was still a poorly regarded entertainment fit mostly for roguish audiences. After the 1940s, *nautanki*'s popularity increased as women began operating their own troupes. Audiences in the 1940s and 1950s could be upwards of ten thousand.

The music's signature tone comes from the *nagara*, a loud kettle-type drum, and the *shehnai*, a shrill, double-reed pipe; another feature contributing to *nautanki*'s popularity in the 1940s and 1950s was its folk adaptation of film-style music. Today, *nautanki* routinely borrows music, dance, and even plots from Mumbai (Bombay) film. Still, live performance and music have been significant in preserving *nautanki* against film's growing popularity.

FURTHER READING

Hansen, Kathryn. *Grounds for Play: The Nautankî Theatre of North India*; Richmond, Farley, Darius L. Swann, and Phillip B. Zarrilli, eds. *Indian Theatre: Traditions of Performance*.

David V. Mason

NEPAL. Landlocked between its giant neighbors, **India** and **China**, Nepal is small but diverse. In 1768, Prithvi Narayan Shah (1723–1775) united into one country many far-flung kingdoms and principalities. Today, as the world's only officially Hindu kingdom (although it has 2 million Buddhists), Nepal is one of the poorest and least developed of countries, with 28 million people belonging to over thirty-five language groups and numerous ethnic castes. The country's rugged terrain and fierce spirit—home to eight of the world's ten highest mountains, with Mt. Everest, at 8,848 meters, towering over the border with Tibetan China—kept colonizing powers at bay and, until recently, isolated it from modernity and international influence.

Rituals and Festivals. Nepal's theatre was traditionally associated with seasonal rituals and **festivals**; singers, **storytellers**, and **masked** dancers still provide the majority of theatrical entertainment. Ancient royalty enjoyed the artistry of beautiful young **women • trained** in sophisticated **music** and **dance**. Royally sponsored entertainments focused on stories from India's epics, the ***Ramayana*** and ***Mahabharata***.

Hinduism and Buddhism affect much of what happens in Nepal, including theatre. Ritual performances often exhibit a combination of Hinduism and Buddhism, and spectators interpret performances from their own **religious** viewpoints. Some of Nepal's early written dramas may be identified with **Tibet**'s ***ache lhamo*** Buddhist plays. These poetic dramas appeared as Buddhism's popularity increased in Tibet in the tenth century, and they dramatize legends in order to reinforce doctrine. *Lhamo* scripts, while studied in Nepal's Buddhist monasteries, are seldom staged.

Mani rimdu. Among the several religious festivals that include theatrical elements, the Buddhist *mani rimdu* takes place annually, though at different times of the year in various monasteries high in the Solu Khumbu region inhabited by peoples of Tibetan descent who adapted *mani rimdu* from Tibetan *'cham*. The best-known *mani rimdu* is performed in the late fall by Tengpoche monastery monks in the Khumbu region, when hundreds of foreign tourists are in the area. The most authentic *mani rimdu* is performed in early winter at Chiwong monastery, a few days' walk south in the Solu district and attended primarily by local villagers. The ritual lasts up to three weeks, including the meditation periods and the preparation of dough sculptures and sand *mandala*—sacred circular meditation diagrams—though public performances generally occur over two days. The second day includes a thirteen-act "play." Each act features different divine and demonic characters who work out a simple story through dance rather than dialogue. Monks wearing heavy masks and symbolic **costumes** play the characters. The day-long action is accompanied by music played on an eclectic assortment of instruments, both by the dancing monks and by other monks situated just to the action's side.

***Indra* jatra.** The Indra *jatra* (a.k.a. Indrayatra) festival takes place every fall in Kathmandu and, in lesser form, throughout the country. Although ostensibly a Hindu celebration, and prominently patronized by the ruling family, the event provides meaningful activity for Hindus and Buddhists alike. The Indra *jatra* is only one of several *jatra* festivals in Nepal, which are characterized by processions of decorated carts carrying **actors** costumed as deities and demons. The principal figure is the archaic Hindu deity Indra, whose mythical imprisonment and release provide the festival's premise, and link it to the agricultural cycle. The ritual focus is the *indradhaja*, a fifty-foot timber, ceremonially elevated and venerated, at the foot of which numerous Indra images and icons are symbolically imprisoned for the duration of the festivities. Lesser figures, such as the demon Bhairava, the living goddess Kumari, and the elephant-headed god Ganesha, maintain prominence, and are more actively engaged in the celebration.

Except for Kumari, these figures appear in the forms of actors in the processions, and engage in impromptu dances and mock battles wherever people have gathered. Rama-bhadra Sarman may have written the play *The Play of Harishchandra* (Harishchandra Nrityam) for performance during Indra *jatra* in 1651.

Barka naach. Every five years the Tharu people of southern Nepal's Dang Valley have traditionally performed the *Big Dance* (*Barka naach*). Stories drawn from the great war of the *Mahabharata* are told through dancing and choral singing of the traditional Tharu text. Fathers transmit orally to their sons the roles and the knowledge required to play them. This folk version of the *Mahabharata*, with colorful costumes and elaborate headdresses, begins and ends with complex worship (*puja*) and lasts an indefinite number of days, depending on how many villages request a portion of it be performed locally as a means of blessing.

FURTHER READING

Jerstad, Luther G. *Mani-Rimdu: Sherpa Dance-Drama*; Kohn, Richard J. *Lord of the Dance: The Mani-Rimdu Festival in Tibet and Nepal.*

Carol Davis and David V. Mason

Modern Developments

Eventually, dramatic entertainment moved out of the palace grounds and into the streets, where commoners enjoyed seeing comic skits and songs. Indian and Persian dance and theatre influenced Nepali style, which, save for the Newar Buddhist dances of the Kathmandu Valley, never achieved the codification that characterizes Indian dance.

Playwright, **director**, and actor Balakrisna Sama (1902–1981) ushered in the early modern theatre both with plays based on Shakespeare and those that demanded realistic acting. **Western** psychology and social theory showed up in the dramas of Gopal Prasad Rimal (1918–1973) and Vijaya Malla (1928–1999). Proscenium **theatre** at the Royal Nepal Academy and the National Theatre (Rastriya Naach Ghar) catered to nobles and the upper classes.

India's example influenced the explosion of street theatre during the pro-democracy movement of the 1980s in which university students lambasted corrupt politicians and a partyless **political** system with allegorical scenarios and agitprop skits acted out on streets, steps, and platforms around the Kathmandu Valley. With the coming of democracy in 1990, theatre became the tool of international aid organizations that found it an effective medium for educating a relatively illiterate populace.

The turn of the twenty-first century saw a return to the proscenium as contemporary artists led by director **Sunil Pokharel** and dramatist Abhi Subedi (1945–) attempted to reclaim aesthetic and indigenous elements. The newest plays wrestled with current problems, including the loss of democracy and democratic rights, the increasingly violent Maoist insurgency, women trafficking, AIDS, illiteracy, and police brutality.

The most important events are "enacted" by theatre artists, clergy and lay alike, completing essential rites of passage. The *katto* ritual, designed to help a deceased king find his way to the afterlife, performed in 2001 after King Birendra (1945–2001) was gunned down by his son, blurs the boundaries between theatre, religion, and personal life. In *katto*, a Brahman priest takes on the "role" of the king and, riding the king's own elephant, leaves his city, his home, and, in emulation of the deceased monarch, the life he has known, never to return.

Carol Davis

NIBHATKIN. Burmese Buddhist **religious** ritual theatre, now rare, likened to a mystery play. *Nibhat* means "the life of the Buddha" and *khin* is "to display." Although once performed by professionals, today it consists of tableaux from Buddha's life using townspeople amateurs. An image or cardboard cutout is used for Buddha. No **music** is needed. The improvised scenes are displayed on ox-drawn carriages or trucks at grand ceremonies of initiation for sons and ear-boring for daughters, with the town's youths participating voluntarily. In November, these rituals are seen at special ceremonies at which gifts are donated to monasteries. In October and November, tableaux by various neighborhoods are set up at the street fairs during the light **festivals** celebrated throughout the country.

The favorite scene is of Prince Siddhartha being shown the four omens—the old, the ill, the dead, and the monk. His father had protected him from experiencing life's pain, and only now does he learn the existence of suffering. That very night he leaves the palace to search for peace.

Sometimes scenes are taken from popular Buddha birth stories (*jataka*), such as the one about Prince Waythandaya, and show Buddha's wife, Madhi, gathering fruit in the forest, surrounded by wild animals. Another is of the beautiful Ohnmar Danni throwing flowers on King Thiwi, who once spurned her and gave her away to his general. The inclusion of comic material is thought to have inspired *zat pwe*.

FURTHER READING

Aung, Maung Htin. *Burmese Drama: A Study, with Translations, of Burmese Plays*; Singer, Noel. F. *Burmese Dance and Theatre*; Thanegi, Ma. *The Illusion of Life: Burmese Marionettes*.

Ma Thanegi

NINAGAWA YUKIO (1935–). Japanese • **director**. Starting out in 1955 as an **actor**, Ninagawa turned to directing by 1967, quickly becoming an *angura* and *shôgekijô* luminary. His breakthrough came with **Shimizu Kunio**'s *Hearty but Flippant* (Shinjô afururu keihakusa, 1969), initiating a still vibrant, post-*shingeki* director-**playwright** relationship.

Hired by the Tôhô **theatre company** to enliven their productions, his first effort was *Romeo and Juliet* (1974), which marked his shift from *angura*'s cramped venues and shoestring budgets to mainstream commercial theatre. This profoundly shocked his actors, many left-leaning, accustomed to his edgy productions of Shimizu's early plays, regarded as "struggle dramas" (*tôsô-geki*) for portraying implicit conflict with constricting social/**political** boundaries.

Romeo and Juliet's acclaim launched Ninagawa's commercial and, eventually, international success. Since 1983, when Ninagawa staged *Medea* in Greece and Italy, his

Ninagawa Company (Ninagawa Gekidan) has toured abroad annually. Key productions include three at the Edinburgh Festival: *Macbeth* (1985), *Medea* (1987), and *The Tempest* (1988). *Medea* was also the first production by a foreign company at London's Royal National **Theatre**, while *The Tempest* sold out its week's run at the three-thousand-seat Playhouse Theatre. There were also U.K. performances of *A Midsummer Night's Dream* (1996), *Hamlet* (1998), the Royal Shakespeare Company's *King Lear*, featuring Nigel Hawthorne (1999), **Mishima Yukio**'s *Modern Nô Plays* (Kindai nôgaku, 2001), and *Pericles* (2003). Several of these also toured to the United States. In 2004, he staged *Oedipus Rex* at Athens' Cultural Olympiad.

Ninagawa's distinctiveness emerges from startling visual imagery and elaborate stagings of many genres, Japanese and **Western**. *Hamlet* featured Muromachi–period (1333–1573) **costumes** and a tiered **stage** recalling the pedestal for displaying traditional Japanese dolls of the imperial family. *The Tempest* appropriated *nô* elements, while *NINAGAWA Twelfth Night* (2005) used *kabuki* and starred *kabuki*'s Onoe Kikunosuke. He transformed Mishima's word-centric, minimally dramatic *Modern Nô Plays* into riveting visual and aural environments, and he returned anew to his **experimental** origins with Shimizu's 1975 *By Illusion His Heart Pushed to Madness—Our Masakado* (Maboroshi ni kokoro mo sozoro kuruoshi no warera Masakado, 2005).

Ninagawa's many awards include the Asahi Performing Arts Award Grand Prix, Yomiuri Theatre Award, Kinokuniya Drama Award, and the Ministry of Education's Art Encouragement Award. The United Kingdom appointed him an artistic director of London's Globe Theatre and honored him as a Commander of the Order of the British Empire (2002). Currently, Ninagawa is artistic director at the Saitama Arts Theatre (Saitama Geijutsu Gekijô).

John K. Gillespie

NINGYÔ JÔRURI. *See* Puppet Theatre: Japan.

NÔ. **Japanese** genre incorporating **music**, **dance**, poetry, **acting**, sculpture (in its trademark **masks**), architecture (in its distinct **theatre** design), and beautiful **costumes**. These diverse elements well reflect the meaning of the word *nô*—"talent" or "ability"—since many such talents are in evidence in an art that has been performed continuously for over six centuries. *Nôgaku* can refer to both *nô* and **kyôgen**—the comedic art that developed alongside *nô* and is acted between *nô* plays, as in the case of the compound *nôgakudô*, the theatre in which both arts are performed today.

Early History. An earlier term for *nô* is *sarugaku*, dating from the Heian period (794–1185) and used through the Edo era (1603–1868). Performers felt some ambivalence about this word, since it could be written with the Chinese characters meaning "monkey music," which had derogatory implications. Accordingly, **Zeami**, who was instrumental in *nô*'s development from the turn of the fifteenth century, wrote *sarugaku* as "divine music" instead, writing *saru* with the Chinese character for the horary sign of the monkey rather than the character of the actual animal; he contended that *nô*'s origins came from ancient performances by Shinto deities as well as entertainments dating from the time of the historical Buddha.

Sarugaku is probably derivative of *sangaku* ("miscellaneous entertainments"), an acrobatic and pantomime art that came from Tang-dynasty **China** (618–907). In the Kamakura period (1185–1333), *sarugaku no nô* was used to designate that the art had become less focused on the tricks of the then departed *sangaku* and had become infused with dance, musical, and dramatic elements. **Religious** performing arts, such as ceremonies performed by temple functionaries (*shushi*), and another performing art, *dengaku*, which originally shared common elements with *sarugaku no nô*, provided the latter with sustenance and depth.

Nô crystallized in the late fourteenth century when its actors, associated with religious institutions in Kyoto, Nara, and other locations, created service "guilds" (*za*) that performed at religious **festivals** in return for patronage. Actors blended sacred performing arts with popular entertainments whose function was both to fete the deities and to entertain humans. The most prominent were the forerunners of the so-called four Yamato troupes (later known as Kanze, Konparu, Hôshô, and Kongô), named after the ancient province of Yamato (modern Nara Prefecture), and the troupes from Ômi Province (modern Shiga Prefecture). The Yamato troupes performed chiefly at Kôfuku-ji Temple, Kasuga Shrine, and the Tônomine complex in and around Nara, while their Ômi counterparts acted mainly at Hie Shrine, associated with powerful Enryaku-ji Temple on Mt. Hiei, which dominated Kyoto's geography (and **politics**).

Nô's ceremonial origin lingers in the ritual dance of *Okina*, which is part of the "three rites" (*shiki sanban*); it is still sometimes performed as the first piece on a program, especially at New Year's. Modern performers interpret *Okina* as a memory of *nô*'s supposed shamanistic origins, since the Okina dancer is said to become a deity when he dons his mask (a smiling old man) on **stage**; however, this is a modern invention. Various interpretations regarding the divine nature of *Okina*'s roles have existed since the late Kamakura era, when the dances probably originated.

Zeami. The Yamato troupes were noted for their ability at "imitation" (*monomane*) while their counterparts in Ômi won renown for "mysterious beauty" (*yûgen*). **Kan'ami**, a Yûzaki (forerunner of the Kanze) actor, and his son Zeami sought new elements to invigorate their performance. Kan'ami adapted the music and dance from *kusemai*, a narrative dance art, as evidenced in *Shirahige*. Zeami, while preserving a focus on *monomane*, emulated the *yûgen* of the Ômi; it became foundational in his **theoretical** writings. Both actors learned from *dengaku no nô*, whose actors were also **experimenting** with masked drama.

Zeami's writings provide the best sources for understanding *no*'s early development. *Talks on Sarugaku* (Sarugaku dangi, 1430), for instance, describes how Kan'ami took over the right to perform *Okina* at a performance in 1374 or 1375 at Imagumano, Kyoto. This performance is a watershed for three reasons: it marked a restructuring of the Yûzaki troupe and Kan'ami's rise to leadership at the expense of older actor-leaders who had customarily enacted Okina; the leader (*tayû*) would thereafter be associated with whoever acted the *shite* (see Role Types), indicating that such plays were now the troupe's mainstay rather than religious ceremonies; this was the first time that the teenage shogun, Ashikaga Yoshimitsu (1358–1408), witnessed *nô*.

Yoshimitsu became a Kanze patron and provided Zeami access to leading poets, such as Nijô Yoshimoto (1320–1388), and to aristocratic culture, which helped him transform *nô* into a high art. As a playwright, Zeami is mostly closely associated with "dream" (*mugen*) *nô*, plays that focus on supernatural beings who typically first appear in disguise and reveal their true form in the second half.

Zeami was the first actor to create "secret artistic writings" (*hidensho*), emulating a long-standing practice in the fields of poetry and esoteric religion. Zeami, who spent much of his last years in official disrepute (including exile to Sado Island), passed these writings on to his son, **Kanze Motomasa**, and to a few other performers, including **Konparu Zenchiku**. Zenchiku, who also composed secret writings, shared Zeami's fondness for poetry and elegance (see also Kanze Motoshige [On'ami]).

After Zeami. *Nô* endured in both the Yamato and Ômi traditions in the fifteenth century, and other groups also enacted it. Foremost was the troupe centered around **Miyamasu**, famous for his energetic plays derived from *The Tale of the Soga Brothers* (Soga monogatari). Other groups performed *nô*, including all-**women** troupes (*onna sarugaku*) who rivaled even Zeami at times, as well as ad hoc groups of commoners, children, and warriors, and performing artists who also enacted religious rites (*shômonji*). The sixteenth century also saw the rise of "skilled" *sarugaku* (*tesarugaku*)—often called "amateur" *sarugaku*—troupes unaffiliated with religious institutions but popularly acclaimed in Kyoto. This diversity supplemented *nô*'s dynamism.

Besides frequent smaller performances, periodic public benefit or subscription (*kanjin*) shows on a grander scale occurred, ostensibly to raise money for religious projects. An admission payment was required for shows featuring large outdoor stages surrounded by viewing stands. In 1464, On'ami led the Kanze in a three-day *kanjin* performance in Kyoto; the circular stage, with a bridgeway (*hashigakari*) at its rear, was still developing toward its classical form, not achieved until the late sixteenth century.

Nô survived the Ônin War (1467–1477), which laid waste to the capital, and the period of Warring States (1467–1573) that followed. The Yamato troupes fled Kyoto to seek the protection of regional warlords, while the Ômi, *tesarugaku*, and other troupes continued in the capital despite occasional skirmishes. The plays composed in the early to mid-1500s, such as *Horned Hermit* (Ikkaku sen'nin) by **Konparu Zenpô**, *Viewing the Autumn Foliage* (Momijigari) by **Kanze Nobumitsu**, and *Revolving Sutra Case* (Rinzô) by **Kanze Nagatoshi** reflect the bravado of the times. Breaking, but not completely severing, the attention to *yûgen* and *mugen nô*, sixteenth-century *nô* favored action, large casts, and spectacle, making it a precursor to **kabuki**.

Secret Treatises and Technical Writings in the 1500s. Actors continued to write secret treatises in greater numbers and in increased specialization, focusing on various instruments and on the finer points of performance. In place of the abstractions of writers like Zenchiku, sixteenth-century performers like Konparu Zenpô favored concrete advice on costumes, movements, and so on. By the end of the century, a new genre of "pattern-added" (*katazuke*) writings developed that described the exact movement "patterns" (*kata*) for every part of a play.

The proliferation of these writings reflects the gradual standardization of performance as well as the growing specialization of performers into specific roles, such as the different instruments of flute (*fue* or *nôkan*), shoulder-drum (*kotsuzumi*), hip-drum (*ôtsuzumi* or *ôkawa*), and stick-drum (*taiko*) in the early Edo period (1603–1868). Whereas, in the early sixteenth century, musicians might perform any instrument and even sometimes act or sing in the chorus (*jiutai*), a century later musicians specialized

Production of the *nô* play *Viewing the Autumn Foliage* at the National Nô Theatre, Tokyo, March 1992. The leading role (*shite*) is played by Kanze Kiyokaze. The photo shows the roofed, wooden stage, with the bridgeway (*hashigakari*) at the left. (Photo: Maejima Yoshihiro; courtesy of Kanze Kiyokaze)

in particular instruments undertaken as their family's art. Similarly, the secondary role of *waki* became distinguished from the chorus, and *waki* actors established their own familial lineages. Troupe leaders still dominated the *shite* role.

Edo through Meiji Periods. The Yamato troupe leaders, along with the new Kita school established by Kita Shichidayû (1585–1653), received stipends from the Tokugawa shogunate enabling them to become countrywide entities by incorporating previously independent lineages. Each troupe espoused its own style of performance, which they helped to define through the publication of play texts with musical notation for singing (*utaibon*). By the eighteenth century, the troupe leaders acted as "family heads" (*iemoto*) who determined the parameters of their school's (*ryû*) style and received revenues from publication fees and licenses sold to amateurs. This transformation was possible due to an interest by amateurs in performing unaccompanied chanting (*su'utai*), which they learned from professionals. Today's performers derive most of their income from teaching amateurs, and the schools profit from sales of licenses, texts, and other study aids. Thousands of plays were composed for *su'utai* chanting, but few are remembered today.

The shogunate's fall in 1868 meant that performers had to seek out new patrons. Members of the ruling elite, such as Iwakura Tomomi (1825–1883), recognized that *nô* could represent the best of traditional culture in an age when the country sought to modernize to achieve **Western** standards. Supported by the imperial household and business leaders, *nô* aimed to develop a popular audience without lowering its values. Actors, such as the three stars of Meiji-era (1868–1912) *nô*, **Sakurama Banma**, **Umewaka Minoru** I, and **Hôshô Kurô** XVI, demonstrated its continued vigor. Scholarly activities increased awareness of *nô*'s legacy, including Yoshida Tôgo's (1864–1918) publication in 1909 of a collection of Zeami's previously secret writings. In the early twentieth century, *nô* leaders succeeded in standardizing performance practices nationally and codified the canon of some 240 plays.

Twentieth Century. The late 1930s until the end of World War II were dark years. In the climate of ultra-nationalism, *nô*'s leaders excised plays thought to cast aspersions on the imperial line, such as *Semimaru* (about a blind prince), and performed new plays with militaristic themes. After the war, *nô* experienced additional disarray as it recovered from the loss of theatres and other war-created disruptions. Conversely, the lack of performance opportunities allowed actors to deepen their **training**, often with professionals outside of their own schools. For example, **Kanze Hisao** gained deep knowledge by studying with leading scholars in the 1950s; simultaneously, he struggled against *nô*'s past, especially the authority of its leaders and aspects of its rigid style. He was criticized for **experimenting** with Western techniques, but thereby pointed to new horizons while maintaining core traditions. Experimental plays, including several "Christian *nô*" performed by Kita Minoru (1900–1986) and *Well of Delusion* (Mumyô no i) by Tada Tomio (1934–), continue to be written while remaining outside the standard repertoire. Women, prohibited from performing in the Edo period, were allowed to become professionals, although *nô* remains male-dominated.

The classic five-play program (see Dramatic Structure) is rare today. Modern programs may last most of a day but there is not enough time to perform a play from each category, with one or more *kyôgen* sandwiched in between. Consequently, shortened dance pieces with or without music can replace a play, or an entire play can be chanted by a chorus in *su-utai* fashion without being acted. Performances occur regularly in the major cities and periodically on shrine stages or in outdoor torch-lit (*takigi nô*) shows in the summer.

FURTHER READING

Keene, Donald. *Nô: The Classical Theater of Japan*; Komparu, Kunio. *The Noh Theater: Principles and Perspectives;* O'Neill, P. G. *Early Nô Drama: Its Background, Character and Development 1300–1450*; Rath, Eric C. *The Ethos of Noh: Actors and Their Art.*

Eric C. Rath

NODA HIDEKI (1955–). Japanese • **playwright, director**, and **actor**. A Tokyo University dropout, Noda, influenced by **experimental** director-playwright **Kara Jûrô**, established his own **theatre company**, Dream Wanderers (Yume no Yûminsha, 1976), and created his signature style combining 1960s *angura* physicality with 1970s humorous wordplay. This style, referred to as "the body that won't stand still," was dismissed at first, but eventually became the 1980s avant-garde benchmark. Noda physicalized every aspect of the text, placing great demands on actors.

His first successes, like those of the *angura* generation, were in small theatres (*shogekijô*), but, his popularity burgeoning, he was soon selling out large arenas. In one day, over 26,000 people saw his trilogy, *Seven Variations on Stonehenge* (Sutônhenji nanahenge, 1986). One early success was *Young Boy Hunting: Groping in the Pitch Dark* (Shônen-gari: sue wa ayame mo shirenu yami, 1981), in which time ruptures, and the philosopher Nishida Kitarô (1870–1945) ends up in Kamakura ca. 1335 with Morinaga Shinnô (1308–1335), a deposed emperor's son. The fault lines of time and human relationships are explored in Noda's frenetic style. In 1989, he loosely adapted Shakespeare in *The Third Richard*, putting Richard on trial for his crimes, with Shylock as defense attorney. Noda combines clever wordplay with experimentation to explore theatre's illusions: Richard is always convicted even though jurors are selected randomly from the audience.

Noda disbanded his company in 1992 and spent a year in England. Returning in 1993, he established a new company, NODA MAP, and his work took on such socially conscious issues as xenophobia and intercultural communication. In *The Red Demon* (Akaoni, 1996), the main character, washed ashore in a small village and unable to communicate with the inhabitants, is treated as a monster. The play has been produced in different countries using vernacular languages. With *TABOO* (1996), Noda created an allegory critical of Japan's emperor system. A prince, raised thinking he is an idiot, becomes a *nô* performer. When he assumes the throne, the country is plunged into a war of succession, raising issues of class and the imperial family's mental capacity.

Noda's popularity continues through his penchant for grandiose, cinematic spectacle and vibrant language. He can call on the best available talent, gathering new actors (even non-Japanese) for every play, and has performed frequently abroad.

John D. Swain

NOER, ARIFIN C. (1941–1995). Indonesian • playwright, actor, screenwriter, and **stage** and film **director**, a major innovator of post-1968 theatre, especially playwriting. He described his work as a mishmash of styles influenced by his upbringing in Cirebon, a unique region combining West and Central Javanese traditions. Noer began his career in the 1960s in Yogyakarta, Central Java, as an actor in **Rendra**'s Workshop **Theatre** (Bengkel Teater), and as director of Muslim Theatre (Teater Muslim). In 1967, he moved to Jakarta and founded the Little Theatre (Teater Kecil), conceived as an **experimental** laboratory for actors.

Arifin's work was characterized by a blending of elements from indigenous **folk theatre** with an absurdist outlook that gave rise to rich performative possibilities. His first major production with the Little Theatre was *Clouds* (Mega-mega, 1969), a surrealistic, dreamlike play that became the foundation for his credo, "theatre without limits" (*teater tanpas batas*), which gave license for exploration into many different styles and methods. *Moths* (Kapai-kapai, 1970) continued this experimentation, and also added an element of veiled social critique. Other significant works include *The Bottomless Well* (Sumur tanpa dasar, 1964), *Madun Orchestra*, I–IV (Orkes Madun, 1974, 1976, 1979, 1989), and *Interrogation* (Interogasi) I and II (1984, 1990), as well as his adaptations of Camus's *Caligula*, Sartre's *The Flies*, and Ionesco's *Macbett*.

Cobina Gillitt

NOORDIN HASSAN (1929–2005). Malaysian • **playwright** and **director**, best known for having ushered in an era of **experimental** absurdist plays in the 1970s. He influenced a generation of playwrights, including Dinsman (1949–), Hatta Azad Khan (1952–), Aziz Jahpin (?–2005), and others. Noordin was originally trained in

1952 in England as a teacher, returning there in 1962 and 1977 to study English-language pedagogy. Between 1953 and 1967, he choreographed many **dances** and wrote several plays, but it was his *'Tis Not the Tall Grass Blown by the Wind* (Bukan lalang ditiup angin, 1970) that altered the form and content of modern Malay theatre.

Dubbed antirealistic, his notable subsequent plays include *The Five Upright Pillars* (Tiang seri tegak berlima, 1973) and *Door* (Pintu, 1995). *1400*, written in the eponymous Muslim *hijrah* (hegira) year (that is, 1979), ushered in a new philosophy of theatre-making he dubbed "theatre of faith" (*teater fitrah*). Noordin's other plays include *Children of This Land* (Anak tanjung, 1989), *Masks* (Peran, 1991), and *For Zaitun* (Demi Zaitun, 2004), which marked his return to theatre after a long absence due to ill health. In 1993, Noordin was awarded Malaysia's National Writer Laureate award, the Anugerah Sastera Negara, in recognition of his contributions to and innovations in playwriting and directing.

Solehah Ishak

NORTH KOREA. North **Korean** theatre history is uniquely linked to the socio-**political** history of the Democratic People's Republic of Korea, its founder, Kim Il-Sung (1912–1994), and his son and heir, Kim Chong-Il (1942–). Two dominant forms evolved under their influence: revolutionary plays (*hyŏngmyŏng yŏn-gŭk*) and revolutionary operas (*hyŏngmyŏng kagŭk*).

From 1910 to 1945, the Korean national struggle against **Japanese** colonization was a theatrical undercurrent, but in the face of strict colonial **censorship** much drama was staged purely for entertainment and emotional indulgence (see *Shinp'agŭk*). In the three years prior to Korea's division into North and South (1948), nationalist and communist ideologies contended in the theatre. Some leftist writers fled for North Korea, and, with the outbreak of the Korean War (1950–1953), others followed, in time creating a distinctive Korean literary tradition solely of and for proletarians. For a time, popular forms, such as *ch'anggŭk*, continued side by side with dramas espousing the Communist Party line. However, in 1970, the North Korean Communist Party adopted *chuch'e* (or *juche*, "self-reliance") as its official ideology. The 1978 landmark production of *The Shrine for a Tutelary Diety* (Sŏnghwangdang), under the supervision of Kim Chong-Il himself, signaled a particular focus on *chuch'e* and the people's revolution. Liberated from **religion** and superstition, the characters regain control of their own lives, an idea at *chuch'e*'s core. The play became the prototype for revolutionary drama, one of "five great revolutionary plays."

However, revolutionary operas of the 1970s are viewed as the summation of North Korean performing arts. Replacing *ch'anggŭk*, which fell from grace, and with similarities to **Chinese** revolutionary opera (*yangban xi*), North Korean *kagŭk* is divided into "revolutionary opera" (*hyŏngmyŏng kagŭk*) and "national opera" (*Minjokgŭk*), with its greatly simplified **music** and basis in **folk** songs rather than *p'ansori*. *Minjokgŭk* has remained popular, but its influence did not rival that of revolutionary opera until recently.

The "five great revolutionary operas" were written in the 1970s, ushered in by 1971's *Sea of Blood* (P'ibada), an opera satisfying party criteria by encouraging revolutionary thought through portrayal of the plight of peasants in the Japanese colonial era (1910–1945). Performed by the Sea of Blood Opera Company (P'ibada Kagŭkdan), it was the prototype for revolutionary operas to follow, such as *The True Daughter of the Party* (Tang ǔi ch'amdoen ttal, 1971) and *A Girl Who Sells Flowers* (Kkot p'anun ch'onyo, 1971).

The *P'ibada* production integrated **dance** scenes to highlight a character's thoughts and used **scenographic** innovations to visually express a character's perspective. In line with ideology placing higher value on collective work than individual artistry or achievement, more than two hundred performers usually participate in one production of *P'ibada* and others of its ilk. The chorus offstage sings *pangch'ang*, a multiverse song with rhymed lyrics, each stanza set to the same melody, its purpose being to convey character emotion or thought and to incite passion for the party and loyalty to the nation. Because a song often repeats the same melody, it is easy to remember; this fulfills the party's criterion that the play texts or opera tunes must be easy enough for everyone to understand and sing along with.

Since the 1970s, revolutionary opera has struggled because of North Korea's economic hardship. In addition, unlike *minjok kagǔk* companies invited to tour internationally, thus benefiting from contact with other artists, the Sea of Blood Opera Company has been restricted in travel largely because revolutionary opera, being limited to the expression of communist ideology and class consciousness, lacks universality.

While up-to-date, reliable information is not easily obtainable, there seem to be developments that provide indications of changes, however small. In 2000, the People's Opera Company (Minjok Kagǔkdan) performed in Seoul a version of Korea's traditional favorite, *The Story of Ch'unhyang* (Ch'unhyang-jŏn), a love story dating back to 1754. Along with "national opera," which may receive more future attention than "revolutionary opera," a form labeled "light comedy" (*kyŏnghǔigǔk*) also must be noted. Performed by movie, not theatre, **actors**, *kyŏnghǔigǔk* is still instructional and embodies the idealistic spirit of the revolutionary soldier. Considering that tragedy as a genre cannot exist under communist tenets, comedy seems to provide a new artistic outlet in North Korean theatre.

Yeon-Ho Suh and Alyssa S. Kim

NURTI. **Sri Lankan** form adapted from **Parsi theatre** after a Bombay (Mumbai) troupe played for a week in Colombo in 1877, presenting the **musical** spectacle *The Court of Lord Indra* (Indar sabah). This visit and many others over the years revolutionized Sri Lankan theatre, leading to a new, commercial, Sinhalese urban form called *nurti* (literally, "this new drama"; also *nurtiya* [from **Sanskrit** *nrtya*]) or *teeter* ("theatre"); it borrowed from Parsi conventions—a blend of European melodrama and **Indian** styles—and also mingled elements of the *nadagam* • **folk theatre**, which it supplanted. The episodic, operatic productions were lavish extravaganzas on indoor proscenium **stages**, with painted wing and drop **scenography**, spectacular effects, fanciful **costumes** on noble characters, fantastical stories, an act and scene **dramatic structure**, modern lighting (using kerosene-oil lamps), and an abundance of song and **dance** performed to popular North Indian Hindustani tunes (which replaced *nadagam* songs in popular favor) by male and female **actors**; indeed, *nurti* introduced actresses to Sri Lankan theatre.

The presence of **women** kept some middle-class spectators from attending, making working-class audiences more common. Respectable Sinhalese women were not expected to perform as singers and dancers, and those who did were disapproved of. The situation was less severe in smaller cities, since there were few other theatricals to vie for middle-class attention, and because performances were mainly by amateurs.

Shows lasted around three hours, not all night long, like folk theatre. *Nurti*'s popularity led to the erection of makeshift **theatres**—thatch-covered sheds, actually—throughout the country by the beginning of the twentieth century.

Nurti plays borrowed from Shakespeare and **Sanskrit** classics, used native historical and Buddhist **religious** themes, but also added contemporary issues, including nationalist ideas. The first major writer was C. Don Bastian Jayaweera Bandara (1852–1921), who began by adapting a *nadagam*, *Rolina* (1879), derived from an English source, to which he added new songs, including the nursery rhyme, "Jack and Jill." The play concerned Prince Harsor and Princess Rolina, who fall in love and then are parted by demons, forcing her to search for him until they reunite after her many adventures. Don Bastian then wrote a musical version of *Romeo and Juliet* (1884), considered the first true Sinhalese *nurti*. A man played Juliet.

The two other significant *nurti* **playwrights** were lawyers: Makalandage John de Silva (1857–1922), after whom Colombo's first state-built playhouse was named, and Charles Dias (1874–1944). De Silva's mission was to change *nurti* from a bastardized Anglo-Asian genre into one expressive of nationalist and religious ideas. He borrowed from native legends and history. One example was his *Sri Wickrema Rajasinghe*, intended to bring attention to the eponymous last Sinhala king, and the music, customs, clothing, manners, and language of the past. De Silva also revolutionized *nurti*'s musical structure by emphasizing the emotional appropriateness of the tunes via the system of dramatic sentiment (*rasa*; see Theory); in actuality, though, songs and plot often were unrelated. Moreover, he introduced Sanskrit dramatic structure—including the narrator (*sutradhara*) and clown (*vidushaka*)—into his later works.

Dias, son-in-law of the man who owned Tower Hall, opened that venue in 1911 with his play *Pandukabhaya*. His works were in the vein of de Silva, some of whose plays he adapted with new music. He also adapted plays by Shakespeare. Later playwrights included de Silva's son, Peter de Silva, and M. G. Perera.

By the 1930s, the form was dying in the face of competition from Indian movies that were themselves *nurti* descendents. *Nurti* plays, once read widely, now seem clumsy and disunified, but their importance in the Sri Lankan dramatic developments is profound. *Nurti*'s chief accomplishment was its creation of a body of popular music at a time when musical traditions were endangered. Today, *nurti* (if not referred to as such) lives on vestigially in amateur **festivals** with free performances on outdoor booth stages.

FURTHER READING

Sarachchandra, E. R. *The Folk Drama of Ceylon.*

Samuel L. Leiter